VIOLENT SANDS

SOME FREEDOMS ARE WORTH DYING FOR

By

SEAN YOUNG

Cover design by Jeremy Robinson

BREAKNECK BOOKS
PUBLISHING COMPANY

Published by Breakneck Books (USA)
www.breakneckbooks.com

First printing, November 2006

Printed in the United States of America.

Visit Sean Young on the World Wide Web at:
www.dreamcoatpublishing.com

For my wife, Carolyn

1

SIMEON GAZED from the ghostly shadows of the abandoned market place, fixing his eyes on Jerusalem's barracks across the street. The elusive moon appeared briefly from behind its thick blanket of cloud. Simeon tensed. He always felt more comfortable in the dark. The moon's milky luminescence fell on a lonely beggar in the street outside. He watched the man's aimless shuffle, broken by periodic stops, as he peered up the assorted alleys leading into the market.

Don't come here. He held his breath, willing the tramp to move on. He hooded his eyes to mask their reflection and his fingers curled instinctively around the ivory handle of the knife in his belt. The beggar continued on his way and the moon disappeared behind the clouds. Simeon relaxed once more.

Sound. He turned his head slightly. Roman Legionaries. The clatter of their hobnail boots was unmistakeable and their raucous, discordant singing told Simeon they'd already spent the bulk of their wages at Jerusalem's wine taverns. Just as he'd predicted.

"Shhh." One of the legionaries whispered as they approached the gates. "The centurion might still be hanging about."

The soldiers entered the barracks. Where was Barabbas? Simeon strained his eyes in the darkness. Still no sign of him. *Patience. He'll be here in good time.*

Once the legionaries had disappeared a hoarse voice whispered from the shadows behind him. "God smiles on us tonight, Simeon. He even hides the moon, to pave our way."

Simeon frowned in irritation, but made no reply. Yochanan was young but that was no excuse. Silence was imperative.

"Barabbas won't let us down." A second voice whispered. "He'll bring us victory single-handedly tonight."

"Quiet!" Simeon hissed. "By all that's holy, you screech like the mourners at a funeral."

He paused, silently daring his companions to utter another word. The moment passed and Simeon turned his attention back to the barracks across the street. Two Roman guards, he counted. All that lay between them and victory. Once his brother breached that barrier, the mayhem would begin.

The clink of metal on metal alerted him to a new presence. He glanced up the street, in the opposite direction and saw the lonely flicker of an oil lamp. The moon emerged for a moment and Simeon saw the man's silhouette behind the dim flame. He watched the soldier stagger, tripping over the uneven paving. The legionary cursed quietly, and Simeon smiled. *Finally.* Barabbas had taken his time, but he'd arrived.

Decimus sniffed. "Air's beginning to clear." Earlier, the acrid smoke from thousands of wood ovens had draped itself like a veil over the city of Jerusalem, but the cool, westerly breeze had driven the cloud eastwards. He was grateful. The fresh air would help keep him awake.

Beside him, Servius sighed and stretched. "Past curfew now. Do you think that's the lot of them?"

"Probably most. There's always a few stragglers on pay day, though."

Servius rubbed his hands, to ward off the slight evening chill. "What a waste! I should be out there with them, enjoying my money. Instead, they stick me with guard duty and on the second watch at that."

"Get used to it." Decimus was indifferent. He'd long since become accustomed to the tedium of night watch.

"You're telling me it doesn't bother you?"

"After fourteen and a half years, nothing bothers me any more."

Servius nodded. "So, only six months to go."

"Four, if I do night watch three times a week and every pay day."

The young man grinned. "You're eager to get home. What's her name?"

Decimus smiled. "Patricia. She lives in Brundisium, and you've never seen such beauty."

"Will she be of marriageable age by the time you leave?"

"She'll be eighteen this year."

Servius raised his eyebrows and Decimus felt the blood rush to his face. "We would have married years ago, but what with military duty and all —"

"And what do you plan to do when you get home?"

"Aside from getting married and starting a family?" Decimus was grateful for the change of subject. "I've always thought farming was the only noble occupation for a man. My father's already bought the land for me. The home's fantastic! Like a villa. A bit run down but, once I'm finished with it, it will be the envy of all Rome."

"Won't you miss military life?"

Decimus shrugged. "In a way." *The way I'd miss a toothache.* He would never dare verbalise his true feelings, for fear of being labelled a traitor to his emperor.

A foot scraped on the stone paving in the street outside. "Look out. Company." Decimus peered into the darkness, picking out the lonely flicker of an oil lamp weaving a path to the barracks.

The moon emerged for a moment and cast its light on the figure. He was tall and well built, but it was the legionary's uniform that arrested Decimus' attention. "That man is begging for a night in the dungeons."

He was astounded that a soldier would move about in such a state. The hard, metal helmet leaned to the left, with the feathers arching towards the ground. The man's belt had slipped so far around that the three copper studded straps hung down his left hip. It was clear that the belt had been loosened for the large quantities of wine the man had so obviously consumed.

The soldier tripped and lurched to his right. His short, straight sword flapped like an old, rusty weathercock from just behind his left hip, and the knife hung almost directly down his front.

"If that man needed to defend himself, he'd be dead before he could find the hilt of his sword." Servius muttered.

Normally Decimus would cut the stragglers some slack. They were comrades far from home and entitled to enjoy their earnings one night in the month, but this legionary had gone too far. The man staggered towards the gate. Decimus caught the pungent scent of stale wine. He must have got more on his uniform than he'd consumed.

"*Ave.*" The man grunted at Decimus and his companion.

"*Ave.*" Decimus found it difficult to hide his disdain. "Looks like it's been a busy night for the wine sellers."

"No more than every other pay day." The man hiccupped then groaned. "I'm going to regret this in the morning."

"No more than every other pay day, I'd wager. You're new here aren't you?"

The man shrugged and nodded. "Haven't been here long."

"A word to the wise, my friend. Jerusalem's a militant city, filled with insurgents. They see a lone soldier too drunk to defend himself, they might think he's worth sticking a knife into."

"I'll bear that in mind." The man turned to enter the barracks.

"Not so fast." Decimus placed a hand on the legionary's shoulder. The man tensed and slapped his hand away. Decimus' nerves prickled in warning. The stranger's reaction was too quick, the heat of his anger too intense.

He scrutinised the soldier more closely. "When did you say you arrived here?"

"Day before yesterday. With the maniple from the 34th legion in Caesarea."

Decimus' pulse began to race. It was a tiny error, but an error nonetheless. He smiled and shook his head sadly. "Your informants forgot to mention the switch. The maniple that arrived here came from Antipatris."

He glanced at Servius, who moved to the man's right, hand clamped around the hilt his sword.

Decimus took a deep breath. "Do you think we're stupid? We know all about your spies in Jerusalem."

The man said nothing, but held his gaze in sullen defiance.

"Who are you, and what do you want in the Roman barracks?" Decimus demanded.

It happened fast. The stranger lurched forward, spinning as he did so. Decimus sprang towards him, and brought his weapon up in a defensive gesture. The strike never came. Instead, the impostor turned on Servius. His sword swung out behind him, offering its hilt to beckoning fingers.

Servius thrust at the soldier's throat, but the man ducked under the swiping blade and continued his turn. He drew his weapon in a smooth arc, slicing a thin line across the young legionary's midriff. Servius gasped in shock and shrank from the strike. Decimus saw his opportunity and lunged at the man's exposed back. He was too late. The impostor changed his footing and eluded the blade. Then he drove his sword under Servius' protective breastplate. The blade sank deep – a lethal strike. No man could recover from that.

Rage engulfed Decimus. *Servius was a child!* He lashed out at the man again, but struck air. The action wrenched him off balance.

His antagonist's movements were little more than a blur. Leaving his sword embedded in the young legionary's torso, he spun to his left. Once again, he lashed out at the intruder. It was like trying to kill a ghost. The man ducked and rolled, coming to his feet in a fluid motion with his knife drawn. The lantern crashed to the ground, spilling oil and dousing its flame.

Decimus suddenly found himself overextended, with his foe well inside his strike line. He tried to bring his sword to bear, but the man moved with him. He thrust up with his blade, striking out at the soldier's kidneys. The man caught his arm at the crook of the elbow, rendering his fighting arm powerless. A moment later the iron blade penetrated his ribs. His chest erupted with vicious heat. A fist slammed like a pylon into his throat, stifling the scream which would have alerted the rest of the watch and awakened a sleeping army.

Decimus stumbled backwards and tripped. His head and shoulders struck concrete and the air was driven from his lungs. Apart from the jolt, he felt little else. He lay on the floor, gasping for breath, but air would not come. The searing pain in his chest slowly gave way to numbness and he felt his life begin to recede like an ebbing tide. He stared with horror into his antagonist's pale, golden eyes. There would be no retirement in four months, no farm and no family. Decimus' last thought was of Patricia's flowing, dark hair, wafting in the light breeze on the beach in Brundisium as she had waved farewell to him when he'd sailed to Palestine for the last time.

† † † † †

Barabbas glared at the body of the older legionary. *You just couldn't let it go, could you?* He shook his head. This changed everything. The entire plan had hinged on getting past the guards undetected. Now they lay dead at their post. How many minutes before they were discovered? Perhaps he should abort the mission. Never. He hadn't come this far, just to turn around at the barracks' gates. How many minutes? Five? Ten at the most. It was worth a shot.

He spun around and plucked his sword from the body of the first legionary. This he hid behind one of the thin, Ionic pillars flanking the barracks' entrance. Then he hauled the man's corpse across to the same pillar. Grunting, he propped the body up against the cold marble column. Like a sack of molten lead. It was a constant puzzle how dead men seemed to weigh so much more than live ones.

After returning for the second legionary, he took a moment to examine his work. A man would have to be blind to be fooled by this. But it might give him the precious seconds needed to accomplish his task.

He took a clean sword from the older legionary. A soldier moving about the barracks with a bloodied weapon would be definite cause for alarm. Barabbas took a moment to relight his oil lamp from one of the torches against the wall. Then he pressed on into the barracks.

The building's interior was a labyrinth of passages and doorways. Barabbas headed south. He didn't care which route he took, as long as it led away from the gates. He passed several doors and turned left, then right, making his way deeper into the barracks' bowels. Once he was well away from the entrance, he stopped to examine his surroundings. A dull glow emanated from four dying torches that hung against the walls. Barabbas strained his eyes in the dim light. The passage was narrow and musty. It had several doors fairly close together, possibly offices or private rooms for the higher ranks. He tried the first door on his right. It creaked as it opened, and he held his breath. Wasn't it possible to design a quiet door? Inside, he found an office with two stools and a desk. And drapes! It was unoccupied. Perfect.

The desktop was a mass of papyrus and stained inkwells. All good and dry. It only took a moment to light. He scraped more pieces together, forming a pyre, which began to billow with smoke. Once the flames strengthened, he ripped down the drapes and added them to the pile, fuelling the blaze with the fabric. Then he turned his attention to the stools. In a trice, he smashed and splintered the legs of the furniture. They would provide the heavier fuel to maintain the blaze.

Moments later, he emerged from the room and headed for the next office, further along and on the opposite side. At the end, Barabbas stopped to glance back down the passage. He could already hear the crackle and the stolen glance revealed thin wisps of smoke seeping from beneath several doors.

He needed to find his bearings. A random pattern would achieve little. If the strike was to be effective, he had to block off the exits. Flames would breed fear. If he could cause the sleeping army to panic, the soldiers would be enveloped by the inferno. He might even wipe out half the garrison in Jerusalem with a single stroke.

He prayed silently, begging God for a few more minutes so that the flames could be fanned into a rampant conflagration. *Minutes.* And the mayhem would be complete. Victory was almost in his grasp.

† † † † †

"Do you smell smoke, Marcus?" Gaius Claudius' voice echoed in the empty passage.

"No. It's probably just from the city outside."

"It seems closer than that, and thicker." Gaius tapped the vine staff he carried against his leg as he walked. He glanced across at Marcus' staff. It was pristine, with the bright colour of youth. He smiled. "So how does it feel, managing your first watch, centurion?"

Marcus' grip tightened on his staff and Gaius noticed the glow of pride in his aide's eyes. "It's a good feeling."

As they came in view of the guard gate, Gaius jerked to a halt. He stared dumbfounded at the sight. Then rage welled up in his heart.

"Asleep on the watch." He spoke with venom in his voice. "I never believed I'd see the day."

Marcus gaped at the scene. "Until tonight, I'd only heard the stories."

Gaius thought back to his days of training. He'd heard those same stories. The tales were all the same, and ended with gruesome punishments.

"What now, Gaius?" Marcus' voice quivered.

"Go and wake the sixth maniple. Tell them to relieve the eighth at once." He spoke in measured tones, his fury kept beneath the surface. "Then call the prison guard. Tell them to arrest the eighth and take them to the cells."

"But this has never happened before. Surely —"

"I have no choice, Marcus. The law is clear; they'll be sent to Caesarea for execution in the morning."

"Gaius, have a heart. The entire maniple —"

"No, Marcus! I follow my emperor's orders as do you. Now let me wake these idlers and write my report."

He strode forward and kicked the guard on the right, aiming for a spot just below the ribs, near the man's kidneys. The body slumped sideways revealing the stained tunic and fatal wound. Panic and relief struck simultaneously.

"Marcus!" He yelled after his aide. "These men have been killed. Raise the alarm."

Marcus wasted no time with stupid questions. The man snatched the trumpet hanging against the wall. The mournful call would carry to all parts of the barracks, signalling soldiers to their stations. He listened as the call was repeated. A moment later the building began to rumble and the sleeping army rose like a Phoenix from its ashes.

Gaius rushed to the centurion's post. He arrived running and saw a group of soldiers already lined up in the quad awaiting their orders. More streamed in with each passing second. He wasted no time catching his breath. The legionaries had to be mobilized.

"Take the second and fourth maniples. Search the entire barracks. I want the intruders found. Marcus, take the first maniple and increase the guard at the dungeons. They may be trying to rescue prisoners. Also send men to inform soldiers at all exits that we have intruders. Nobody is to leave the building. Make sure they're watching for possible attack from outside."

A second trumpet interrupted his train of thought. It signalled a new enemy in their midst.

"Fire." Marcus whispered, his eyes glazed with shock.

Gaius listened to the repeat of the trumpet call and began issuing new orders.

"Aulus, get your maniple to start taking care of that fire. I want it out and I want the culprits found. I'll have blood for tonight's insurgence."

The soldiers moved to obey their orders. Gaius felt a twinge of pride. This was the precision that made the Roman army great. There was no panic. Only efficiency as the machine moved to defend itself.

With everything being taken care of, he took some time to think. What had he not considered? Who was this daring foe and what would his - or their - next move be?

He prided himself on his ability to think like his enemies. *I will find you.* And I'll see to it that you bleed in agony on a crucifix, fighting for each miserable breath before you see another sunset.

Just keep control. That way, soldiers will be found at their posts and the intruders flushed out.

Marcus interrupted his thoughts. "You were right, Gaius. They were after the prisoners. By the time we got there, they'd already taken out the guards. One's still unconscious and the other looks like he'll be coughing up blood for a week."

Barabbas suddenly found himself facing a new set of problems. The passages were now swamped with legionaries. He put his head down and merged with the general flow of bodies, but he knew this ruse wouldn't hold for long.

Already, he could see soldiers lining up and taking positions. Every man seemed to know his place and Barabbas realised he'd soon stand out like a city on a hill.

Create a diversion. Quickly, he doubled back. He remembered passing the prison cells a few moments ago. There had only been two guards on duty.

He entered the cellblock and found the guards poised, ready for intruders. They relaxed when they saw a fellow legionary.

"What's happening out there?" one of the guards enquired.

Barabbas was curt and formal. "Intruders in the barracks. Centurion thinks they're after the prisoners. He's sent extra guards down. The rest will be here soon. They're still fighting the fires."

"Fires!" the second guard exclaimed. "What —" he got no further. Barabbas lunged, slamming his helmet into the guard's forehead. The man reeled under the blow and staggered into his companion. While the second legionary was still off balance Barabbas slammed his fist into the man's exposed throat. Both men collapsed in heap on the floor and he bent down to rifle through their belts for keys. He unlocked two of the cells, then flung the remaining keys at the escaped prisoners, allowing them to free their fellow inmates.

On leaving the cellblock, he found the barracks in an uproar. Soldiers ran to and fro with buckets of water dousing the raging flames. Others moved systematically from room to room, searching for the intruders. Two soldiers emerged from a smoke-infested room, carrying the inert body of one of their comrades. The man's face was badly burned and his neck was covered in what looked like a fine layer of dust that was his singed hair.

No time to gloat over your victory. Barabbas grabbed a bucket and headed for the stairs at the end of the passage. The enemy would have sealed all exits by now.

Consider everything your opponent can think of and then do something he could never have conceived. His trainer's words echoed in his head. He had to move fast. There was nowhere to hide, or run to, but he could fly. He turned and headed up the stairs. On the second floor he saw soldiers approaching - hunters seeking their prey. The floor was already nearly clear. Nobody remained behind the hunters. As they cleared rooms they sealed them off, systematically closing the net on their quarry. Soon all the legionaries would be congregated on the first floor, the fires doused and the intruder discovered.

He slipped around the corner, only to find more soldiers heading for the steps from that direction. At the far end was another group of hunters, herding legionaries down to the ground floor, closing the net.

He ducked into an empty room, side-stepping two legionaries who turned and headed down the stairs. It was another office with plenty of papyrus and inkwells for writing.

He began scraping the papyrus together and kindled another fire. The flames devoured the thin fabric. Barabbas dashed about searching for more fuel. He found several baskets woven from palm fronds, each large enough to carry a grown man. Minutes later the room was an inferno with scorching flames licking the walls and ceiling. Acrid smoke choked his breath, stinging his throat and eyes. He stumbled from the room, gasping for air.

"Quickly." He yelled at the passing soldiers. "We need more water."

The soldiers were well drilled in fire fighting. They soon formed a line, passing buckets down to drench the flames.

"As soon as this is out, proceed immediately to ground floor." a senior soldier instructed the fire-fighters.

Barabbas heaved his bucket over the pillars of flame, causing an explosion of sizzling steam and smoke. More buckets were passed. His eyes raked the room, seeking the moment to escape.

Suddenly water and fire exploded in a fit of steam and fury. One of the legionaries tumbled back under the searing blast. The man fell to the floor with a shriek, clutching his scorched face and gasping for breath. Buckets tumbled to the ground as his friends moved to save him. In the momentary distraction, Barabbas slipped from the room.

† † † † †

Gaius mulled over the legionary's information. "You have no idea who he was?"

"No, centurion. He wasn't part of our group. He was alone, fighting the fire when he called for our help."

"And nobody saw him slip away from the fire."

"We were too busy with the flames. Smoke was everywhere. It was impossible to see anything in that room. The first time we noticed he was gone was after the fire was out."

"Thank you legionary. You can return to your detail." Gaius gave the information some consideration and then called for Marcus.

"Spread the word among the barracks. The man we're looking for is in Roman uniform. Then take your maniple outside and check the perimeter of the building. Watch the windows on the upper floor. If he's still inside, that's where he intends to escape from."

"Yes, sir." Marcus called his men together.

Gaius turned to one of his remaining messengers. "I want you to go to the

Antonia. Take this order to them, and hurry." He handed the man a sealed letter.

The man raced from the quad, while Marcus gathered his troops together. Gaius watched them leave. Then he donned his helmet and followed them.

† † † † †

Slowly, cautiously, Barabbas inched his way around the north side of the building. The corridors were now deserted, and the reality of his victory began to sink in. His heart thumped with excitement.

He was black with soot and stank of smoke. The hair on his arms was powdery white, singed by the fire, and sweat drenched the inside of his tunic. But he'd won! He exulted in his triumph.

On the north side of the barracks, he found an unlocked door and slipped into the room. It was bare, apart from a desk and some chairs. The floor was decorated with an interesting mosaic, but it was too dark to make out the picture it portrayed. Dim light filtered through a single, tiny window.

It was narrow, but Barabbas was able to squeeze through. He was halfway out of the window when he heard approaching footsteps. He froze. A group of legionaries marched the length of the street, scrutinising the windows on the upper floor. Like a phantom, he retreated into the darkness of the room until the men had passed by. As the footsteps receded, he emerged again and crawled out onto the ledge. The second floor was not too high. If he hung from the ledge, he could get his feet within ten cubits of the ground.

It was quite a drop, but he was not likely to break a limb in the attempt. Carefully he turned, holding the window for support. He knelt down, gripping the walls inside to prevent himself from falling backwards as he lowered his legs over the edge. Slowly, he inched his body out until he hung from the ledge by his fingers.

Then he dropped. The thud sent shooting pains all the way up to his knees. Bending his legs, he rolled to absorb the impact. He scrambled to his feet. It was a perfect landing, but he could feel the numbness spreading through his ankles and shins.

Suddenly he heard a murderous scream. A body catapulted from the shadows. Out of the corner of his eye, Barabbas caught a glint of steel slicing through the blackness. He spun from its deadly path, drawing his own sword to defend himself. His fall had slowed his reflexes, however, and he felt the blade strike his breastplate.

Barabbas wavered in shock. He was exhausted from his exploits in the building and his feet still hurt from the impact of the fall.

Swordplay was all about footwork. This alone could win or lose a match and the soldier he faced was no ordinary swordsman. Already from their first encounter, he recognised a highly skilled warrior, one who knew his weapon, who was fast and competent.

"Who's there!" a voice called from the darkness. The group of legionaries who had passed earlier were already hurrying back to investigate the disturbance.

"It's me - Gaius. I've found the intruder."

With that, he lunged. Barabbas parried with his own sword and thrust at Gaius'

unprotected side. The soldier brought his sword up in a defensive move, blocking
the attack. He struck Barabbas' sword, flinging it aside, and thrust at the opening.
Barabbas moved as fast as he could, but his legs were sluggish. He deflected the
blow, but it was impossible to keep up the fight.

The other soldiers were only a few yards away. Soon he would be overpowered.
All his attention remained riveted on the centurion, Gaius. Even a moment's
distraction would cost him his life. Escape was impossible. He could never hope to
outrun ten or eleven men. All was lost and yet, in the burst of flame from the
windows of the ground floor, Barabbas resolved to fight. He might die, but he
would die fighting.

He locked his glare with that of his enemy. He could see the hatred in Gaius'
gaze. That hatred was reflected in his own eyes, he knew. Hatred for Rome, a cruel
oppressor and master. Hatred for an empire that had invaded his lands and imposed
harsh taxes on a defenseless Jewish nation. He hated the emperor who brought his
pagan armies to Judea, corrupting the people of Israel with idolatrous coins bearing
the faces of godless rulers. His hatred was more personal, however. And it went far
deeper than faces on coins.

In defiance, Barabbas thrust his sword inside the centurion's guard and struck.
The soldier spun away, but not before Barabbas' sword sliced a thin line across his
stomach, from which blood started to seep. The cut was minor, but it drove the man
into a frenzy. He rushed at Barabbas like a starved lion, released into the arena. All
caution was abandoned to an overwhelming desire to kill.

Then Marcus' men were upon them. They surrounded Barabbas, trying to
separate the two men bonded in their struggle. Barabbas' sword flashed in the dim
light. One soldier fell, but Barabbas knew he was losing. The Romans would soon
subdue and disarm him and then he would have to resign himself to whatever fate
the prefect decreed. Probably torture, certainly death.

As he waged his private war with Rome, he noticed a fleeting shadow across the
street. Quietly, ten men emerged from the marketplace and rushed the group of
soldiers. They moved silently and with deadly intent. Simeon, his brother, and their
small band of zealot warriors hit the soldiers' flank. Relief coursed through Barabbas.
The legionaries had neither seen nor heard the assault. They were caught completely
off guard. In the confusion he found an opportunity to escape. He lunged at Gaius
one last time, but his comrades were already pulling him away.

"Come Barabbas; let's live to fight again."

The zealots beat a hasty retreat and melted into the marketplace. Barabbas turned
reluctantly and followed his comrades into the shadows.

† † † † †

"Centurion, you're wounded." Marcus voiced his concern.

"It's a scratch. I'll live for many years yet." Gaius gazed into the market after the
fleeing men. He panted from the exertion of his battle and felt the sting of Barabbas'
cut. *Barabbas.* He'd remember that name. "You men go around the market to the
right. Marcus you go left. Make sure they don't double back. The rest of you can

come with me."

He turned and led his group into the market place. Already the other soldiers
were fanning out, blocking off the exits.

† † † † †

Barabbas raced through the market, leading his men north in a desperate attempt to
reach the exit to freedom ahead of their Roman pursuers. He rushed by the empty
counters, twisting through the labyrinth of narrow alleyways and streets.

"Do you think we'll make it?" Judas panted as he ran.

"We should. This is the most direct route." Barabbas replied. His eyes were fixed
on the street ahead.

"And if we don't?"

Silence. Barabbas had no wish to contemplate that train of thought. Behind him,
he could hear the dashing feet of pursuing soldiers following their trail through the
market place.

He ran blind, finding his way through the maze more by instinct than cunning.

"The exit!" Judas' voice was jubilant. "It's clear."

They surged forward, racing toward safety. Barabbas could sense the buoyant
spirit of his men. A moment later soldiers streamed in from both sides blocking their
path to freedom.

Barabbas' heart fell. How was this possible? Nobody could have gotten there so
quickly.

"Stop where you are!" a Roman voice boomed. "The market place is secure. All
the exits are blocked."

Barabbas gaped in despair at the entrance now swarming with soldiers. Anger
welled up like bile, flooding his soul and vision. He should have known. The market
was the obvious escape route. Gaius must have dispatched soldiers to block the exits
the moment he'd heard the trumpet's call.

2

"WHAT NOW?" Yochanan's voice quivered slightly as he gasped for breath.

"How many do you think are there?" Simeon asked.

Behind them, the alley echoed with the thud of Roman sandals.

Barabbas glanced over his shoulder, searching for the unseen soldiers to his rear. "I counted ten or twelve. The longer we wait the more time we give them to bring reinforcements."

Simeon nodded. "I say we take them."

Barabbas narrowed his eyes and glared at the legionaries ahead of them. "Strike and melt."

"Very well." Simeon rose from his hiding place.

Barabbas emerged with his brother and charged the group of soldiers blocking the exit. The rest of the men fell in behind him following his lead. The Roman soldiers didn't seem at all surprised by this turn of events. They shuffled into position, covering the aisle as they prepared for battle. Their rectangular shields formed a wall with which to repel their antagonists.

Barabbas stormed the wall undaunted. When he was almost upon them he shot a fleeting look at his brother. He caught Simeon's matching glance - a message exchanged. There was no room in the aisle blocked by Roman shields. He moved left and Simeon went right. Barabbas jumped onto the kiosk counter and rushed past the front row of soldiers, thrusting at the leading legionary as he did so. The confused soldiers spun to defend their flanks. Barabbas ran the gauntlet of slashing blades.

The soldiers at the rear moved to block his path and the inevitable holes in their front line appeared. His comrades made good use of these. Some followed him and Simeon over the counters, while others thrust through the gaps in the front wall, stabbing and slashing as they ran.

Barabbas struck out at his enemies. Thrusting between shields and blades, he cleared a path to freedom. Yoseph broke through first. Barabbas yelled in triumph and launched himself from the counter into the midst of the fray.

One by one his men emerged from the melee and fled gratefully into the welcoming darkness beyond. Finally, Barabbas found his way clear. He careened into the gap. Only one legionary moved to block his path.

Barabbas heaved his sword in an arc, letting it fly free. The soldier's eyes widened in shock and he threw up his shield in an awkward gesture of defence. The blade deflected harmlessly off the legionary's shield, but before the man recovered, Barabbas was upon him.

He smashed his shoulder into the shield, knocking the soldier off his feet. Ahead of him, Simeon broke free and raced for the shadows on the other side of the street. Barabbas rushed after him, closing the gap. Together they would reach the *Kainopolis* and freedom.

Gaius emerged from the web of alleys to find a battered contingent of soldiers holding two wounded prisoners.

"What happened here?" he asked quietly.

"They escaped, centurion." Marcus was out of breath. "We managed to capture these two, but the rest got away."

"Barabbas?" he turned to inspect the prisoners.

"I don't know, sir, but I don't think either of these men is the one you're looking for."

Gaius ignored the comment. He could see Barabbas was not among the prisoners.

"Which way were they headed?"

"North - to the housing district. We'll never find them now."

"You give up far too easily, my friend." Gaius admonished his aide. "I sent a message to the Antonia fortress, before leaving the barracks, to cordon off the north wall. Even as we speak, soldiers are searching the *Kainopolis* for any sign of them. Their orders are to arrest anyone moving about the streets."

Marcus was amazed. "How did you —"

"Think like your enemy, Marcus. Where would you want to be if you knew the entire Roman garrison in Jerusalem wanted your blood?"

"As far away from the city as possible."

"Exactly. They wouldn't be so foolish as to leave by the main gate in the morning. A posted legionary might recognise them. If it were me, I'd plan to leave by one of the windows in the city wall. The zealots are bound to have sympathisers who could let them down by a rope from one of the homes on the north wall."

Marcus grinned. "That limits the search to but a few homes."

Gaius nodded. "I want more soldiers for the search. We have to form a net, so that they don't turn south and disappear back into the city. We'll search every home between here and the city wall. There's no escape for them now."

Deborah sat on a hard, wooden bench, the only one in her humble lodgings. Her forehead furrowed in a deep frown and she absent-mindedly chewed the nail of her left forefinger. Her foot jiggled like a staccato drum beat on the flagstone floor. *Where is he?* She glanced up at the door, but it remained obstinately silent.

Opposite Deborah - seated on a large, wooden chest - sat Hephzibah. She was a portly woman in her early twenties, with a rotund, normally beaming face. She was not smiling now.

"Perhaps they've already achieved the victory they'd hoped for. Then there'd be no need to flee."

"Don't be ridiculous." Deborah snapped. "It was a suicide mission. The best they could have hoped for was survival." She stood up and paced the floor of the tiny apartment. "They should have been here already."

A lock of loose, auburn hair fell across her line of vision and she swatted it away in anger. It had been hours already.

Sounds emanated from the courtyard outside. "Wait." Deborah stopped her pacing and listened.

"Who is it?" Hephzibah's expression was intense.

Deborah quietly opened the door and peered into the darkness outside. She slammed it shut in disgust. "Just the old man across the courtyard."

Hephzibah wrinkled her nose. "Been drinking again?"

"Doesn't he always?" Deborah flopped back on the stool. "You'd think he could go and relieve himself out in the street, at least."

Unable to sit still for long, she rose and moved to the window. She peered into the courtyard once more. Outside, the old man raised a shaky head to look at the crescent moon. It emerged for an instant from behind the thick blanket of clouds that crept like demonic shadows across the blackened sky. He hiccupped, belched quietly and then, having completed his task, lurched back into his apartment, slamming the door behind him.

Deborah sighed. "I can't take any more of this. I must know what happened to them - what happened to him."

"I'm sure he's fine." Hephzibah comforted her.

"You don't know that, Hephzibah." Her glare was not directed at the stout young woman.

She closed her eyes and rested her head on a clenched fist. Her long nails dug painfully into her palms, but she barely noticed. Her eyes were moist, but tears would not come. Deborah was an unemotional woman, hardened by a world that had betrayed her.

She had cried a lifetime of tears when, at the age of seventeen, she had left her family in Jaffa - a family that had shunned and banished her. She had left a love who had defiled and then abandoned her, choosing to marry another who came from a wealthier, more socially acceptable background.

Weeping, she had headed for Jerusalem, far away from the painful memories. She'd sought a city where she could dissolve in a sea of people, where nobody would know her or her past and where she could start a new life. It had proved less promising than she'd hoped and the days had dragged into weeks as she searched for work, begging for scraps of food as her hunger drove her to the point of madness. That was when she had met the revolting, flabby merchant in the market place and discovered that the Holy City did not always live up to its name.

The sight of the man had turned her stomach, but hunger and a lack of self worth had driven her to accept his offer. She had cried the first time she'd given herself to the lustful brute, who was as ruthless in the ways of love as he was in business, but he had paid her well and taught her that beauty was a commodity like any other and a ready source of cash.

He had returned many times since the first, each time with the prescribed fee and, soon, others had found their way to her home. She had found a new life in Jerusalem and she had survived. Eventually the tears had stopped, leaving an empty, unemotional shell of the young girl who had once been.

Deborah was startled by a quiet knock on the door. She hadn't heard the men's approach over the steps and across the courtyard. Hephzibah leaped from her seat and rushed for the door, but Deborah beat her there. She opened it with a pounding heart, peeping hopefully into the courtyard beyond. The sight of the harried men outside brought both relief and disappointment. It must have showed in her expression.

"Could you be less happy to see us?" The larger of the two men greeted her. His eyes twinkled above a broad grin.

"Hello, Yoseph." Deborah forced a smile. "I'm sorry. I just hoped - well I thought you might not have made it."

"We made it." Yoseph's smile was reassuring.

He was tall, with broad shoulders and long, muscular arms. He had a flat round, face with a shock of dark, curly hair and a heavy beard.

"Did everyone make it?"

Yoseph hesitated. "No. Two were taken in a skirmish outside the market place. I don't think Barabbas was one of them." He entered the room with his companion.

Deborah was not comforted. "Are you sure?"

"I don't know. There were soldiers all over the place. I couldn't make out the figures in the darkness."

"Could you, Eleazor?" Deborah turned to the second man.

He had a morose look about him, with dark, penetrating eyes and jet black hair. His wispy beard had a slight ripple on the left cheek. The facial hair concealed a long scar down that side of his face, an injury from one of the battles in his youth.

He shook his head. "It was too dark to make out anything."

Yoseph flopped down on the bench against the wall. "Do you have food for some weary travellers, by any chance?"

Deborah went to a shelf in the corner and fetched two cakes of bread and some figs. She put them in a bag, woven of palm fronds, and gave it to Eleazor who was closest.

"Thanks." Yoseph jumped up from his seat. "We'd better be on our way. It would do you no good if the Romans found zealot rebels under your roof on a night like this."

Deborah waited by the door while Hephzibah escorted the men to the roof. Across the courtyard, three more men arrived, but they didn't come in. Instead, they joined Yoseph and Eleazor, heading for the roof.

She returned to her seat and fixed the open doorway with a morbid stare. After several minutes, Hephzibah reappeared and knelt at her feet.

"I thought I recognised Lazarus, but I couldn't see who the others were." Deborah's voice was a monotone.

"Joshua and Ya'aqob." The young woman clung to her waist. "Don't be afraid. He will come."

Deborah shook her head. She pushed her friend away and stood up.

Hephzibah rose and took her firmly by her shoulders. "Tell me, when has a Roman soldier ever got the better of him?"

Deborah tried to smile. She shrugged and dropped her gaze. "Yes, he'll come." she said with far more conviction than she felt.

✝ ✝ ✝ ✝ ✝

Simeon picked his way through the quiet streets of Jerusalem, past the rough stone buildings designed in the Hellenistic style that Herod the Great had loved so much. He could hear Barabbas' breathing to his right and a little to his rear and slowed down, allowing his brother to catch up.

On his right loomed the gigantic temple. The rough stones stood as high as Simeon's chest and the huge building seemed to dominate the dark skyline of the city.

"Better be careful we don't run into the night watch in the housing sector." He cautioned.

"I'm more worried about the guards from the Antonia." Barabbas replied. "They're bound to be on edge after tonight's attack and would probably arrest us just for walking the streets."

Simeon's gaze shifted to the giant fortress. It stood right up against the temple courts and was manned by some of the most vicious guards the Roman army had ever spawned. It was where all of the most dangerous criminals in southern Judea were housed and guarded.

"They won't be in the best of moods tonight," he agreed.

As he spoke, he saw a group of soldiers quietly emerge from the building. He ducked for cover. Barabbas evaporated in the darkness. Once again, Simeon stood in awe of the young man he'd raised since the death of their father in the Galilean uprising.

He listened, straining his ears for any sign of Barabbas, but could find none. Only the smell of smoke told him his brother was nearby. The soldiers trooped past quietly, chatting amongst themselves as they searched the shadows.

"They say he disguised himself as a legionary to get into the building."

"I don't believe it." argued another. "No single man could cause as much damage as they claim."

"Yesterday I'd have told you that no insurgent could even get inside the barracks," a third legionary countered.

"If my goods were destroyed in that fire, I'll make sure he never sees trial. I had a priceless collection of writings in the barracks for safekeeping."

The group was swallowed by the darkness. Their voices eventually trailed off.

"Barabbas, where are you?" Simeon called softly.

There was a stirring at his feet. His brother uncurled and stood up with a broad grin on his face.

"If I didn't know better I'd believe you were as blind as Bartemaeus of Jericho."

Barabbas' words conjured up an image of their contact in that city. Being blind and a beggar, he was considered harmless and was thus able to glean a wealth of information on Roman activities all over Judea, south of Jerusalem. This information was passed on to the zealots for a price.

Simeon smiled. "I'm not the one with the impairment. Didn't you hear when Zechariah told us Bartemaeus has received his sight?"

Barabbas shrugged. "I must have been bored with his ramblings. Tell me again."

They emerged from their hiding place and continued to the rendezvous. Twice more, they encountered soldiers and were delayed, hiding in the shadows, as they waited for the patrols to pass by. Each delay made travel more dangerous.

"We'll never make it if we have to stop and hide again." Barabbas whispered. His voice was tense as he glanced, first over his right, and then his left shoulder.

Simeon nodded. "Too many soldiers on the street and more arrive with each passing moment."

"Maybe we should hole up in the city for the night. We can hide here and try to make our escape tomorrow."

"With all this going on! You should know better." Simeon said hotly.

They made their way past the pools of Bethesda in the north eastern city district. The water shimmered and darkened in the fickle moonlight. In the morning the colonnades would be festooned with bodies as hopeful souls gathered, waiting for the waters to stir and release their healing powers to the lucky man or woman who was first to plunge into the therapeutic cisterns and wells dotted around the pools.

At this hour there were no more than a handful of faithful believers sleeping next to the water, having succumbed to exhaustion after many hours of vigil. One of the watchers jerked his head as if startled. The man awakened from a fitful sleep. He seemed angry with himself at his carelessness in dozing off. He stared with renewed vigour at the still waters. What ailed him, Simeon couldn't tell, but he could see that it wouldn't be long before exhaustion dragged her subject back into a troubled sleep, where he would undoubtedly dream of churning waters and a multitude of phantoms racing for the tiny, waterlogged caves in the vain hope of finding release from their torment.

"You're right." Barabbas agreed grudgingly. "Rome will search every house in Jerusalem to find the instigators of tonight's insurrection. No home would be safe."

"We might have been able to blend in with that sickly gathering at Bethesda, but in that uniform and looking the way you do, you'd call attention to yourself like a lamb at Passover."

"So we stick to the original plan. Deborah's home isn't far now."

"I only pray to God we make it. This place is crawling with soldiers."

"That centurion must have known we would head for the north wall. It's the only way he could get the soldiers here so quickly."

"He's not stupid and that's no lie. Would that you'd killed him when you had the chance."

"If I'd had the chance I would have killed him." Barabbas snapped.

Simeon realised he'd touched a nerve. "I'm not saying you didn't do all you could. I only wish he'd died in that skirmish. What was his name again?"

"Gaius. That's what his soldiers called him."

"I do believe," Simeon continued philosophically, "that the world would be a safer place for both of us if you had managed to kill Gaius outside the barracks."

Barabbas stared at the road, his face clouded in a dark frown. "It was impossible. I was in no condition to fight and he was good. If you hadn't arrived when you did, I don't know that I would have survived that encounter."

"I know. I only hope we don't regret that crossing of swords. He saw you and he heard your name. We made a dangerous enemy tonight."

Simeon's thoughts turned to another concern. They were now in the heart of the housing district called the *Kainopolis*, the New City. The rendezvous point was almost in sight, but already the streets were thronged with soldiers. Jerusalem had become a giant snare. Deborah's house might not prove to be the handy escape route he had hoped it would.

Barabbas interrupted his thoughts. "When the time comes, I'll deal with Gaius. For now, let's get out of the city. I don't want to die in Jerusalem tonight."

Simeon glanced at the young man by his side. As always, Barabbas was supremely confident in his own abilities. The Lord knew he had reason to be. He only hoped that his brother was not overconfident where the centurion was concerned. He'd seen the man fight. And he'd witnessed his strategies. Gaius was not to be underestimated. That was a mistake that even Barabbas might not survive.

Simeon was suddenly filled with an overwhelming sense of dread. A premonition of danger - even death - overcame him. He shook his head, as if to dislodge the thought, but it would not go away. Fear gripped his heart. He felt trapped in a vortex of terror from which there was no release. It was as if he'd seen a glimpse of their future and it terrified him.

✝ ✝ ✝ ✝ ✝

Gaius was still not satisfied.

"Tell me again, Marcus. I have to be sure everything is as secure as it can be."

"If it can be made more secure, I don't know how to do it."

He glanced north towards the housing district. "Are the homes along the wall secured?"

"Every home that stands against the wall, north and east of the temple, has Roman guards watching the entrances. Groups of legionaries are moving as we speak, searching homes between the market place and the north wall for any sign of the rebels, especially the spy in Roman uniform known as Barabbas."

Gaius sighed. "The Jews are going to be furious in the morning. The Roman army dragging half the city out of bed and searching their homes and belongings in the middle of the night will not please the local population."

Marcus fixed him with a grim smile. "We'll have a lot to answer for in the morning, centurion."

"I'll answer for it, but I want Barabbas found. He'll pay for the crimes he's committed tonight."

"We'll find him. No man could escape the snare we've constructed."

"What about the net of soldiers behind the search parties?"

"In place, centurion. Not even a rat could squeeze through that net. They are sealing off areas as the search parties finish. I predict we'll have Barabbas by dawn."

Another thought occurred to Gaius. "What about an external detail?"

"A what, centurion?" Marcus faltered.

"Have you considered the possibility that they may have already escaped the city walls?"

Marcus cursed violently, glancing wildly at his commander. The guilt was in his eyes. There was no reason to humiliate the man further by forcing him to verbalise his admission.

Gaius spoke gently. "Take a detail out of the Sheep Gate. Search the walls north of the temple. Look for any sign, a rope, a basket lowered down the wall. Move quietly. They may still be there. If we don't alert them, it's just possible that we could surprise and overcome them."

"Yes, sir." The embarrassed soldier turned to his task.

"You've done well tonight, Marcus." Gaius called after his aide.

The man looked back and nodded, forcing a smile. Gaius could see that the man did not agree.

† † † † †

After a harrowing journey through the streets of the *Kainopolis* Barabbas gazed in horror at Deborah's home from the shadows across the street. Soldiers stood at every corner along the north wall, each guarding their own block, alert for intruders trying to flee the mighty arm of Roman justice.

"I didn't believe they could mobilise themselves so quickly," he whispered. "Escape is impossible now. We'd better head back into the city."

Simeon grabbed his brother's arm. "Why don't you just slit your own throat and save Rome the trouble? If they could get men here so quickly, what do you suppose they have waiting back there?"

Barabbas spat a quiet oath in the darkness. "They've constructed a net that's impossible to escape from."

Simeon narrowed his eyes, examining the group of soldiers outside Deborah's block. "Difficult. Not impossible. If not cared for properly, nets can be torn; holes created, through which one or two fish might escape."

Barabbas grinned. "Always the strategist. What would I do without you?"

Simeon quickly outlined what he intended.

Barabbas nodded. "Good. You wait here. I'll do it."

"No, Barabbas." Simeon grabbed his sleeve. "It's my idea, I should carry it out."

"And leave me waiting here like a cub while the lion goes off to hunt? I don't think so."

Simeon refused to let go of his sleeve. "It's too risky, Barabbas."

"The plan's sound. How can it fail?"

"If they catch you they'll beat and torture you and who knows what else!"

Simeon pleaded.

"If." Barabbas jerked his sleeve loose from his brother's grip and disappeared down the street, leaving Simeon to seethe.

Two blocks east, he stepped from the shadows, approaching the group of legionaries across the street. At first wary, the soldiers relaxed when they saw their comrade's nonchalant attitude. Barabbas moved closer. *Only a matter of time.* He was covered in soot from the fire, his helmet was missing and his tunic was torn. Blood caked his left arm where a scab, broken through constant punishment, still wept.

No soldier in such a condition would have been permitted to leave the barracks. It showed the local population that the Roman army was vulnerable and would draw further aggression from an already militant people.

At last, the first soldiers realised that he was no legionary. With yells they stormed their prey. Barabbas fled in the direction of Deborah's block, drawing those soldiers into the chase as well. For Simeon's plan to work, he first had to engage them, and then lure them away. This was the most dangerous part of the plan. He found himself surrounded, front and back by ten to twelve men. Slipping between them, he evaded their blades. Barabbas lashed out at the guards with his unsheathed knife.

He feinted at one legionary and then ran left, back into the housing district. Behind him the soldiers panted in pursuit. He risked a glance over his shoulder and was pleased to see the road outside Deborah's home clear of all military presence. A shadow slipped quietly from a darkened corner under some stone steps and glided across the street.

Barabbas nodded in satisfaction. Simeon had made it. All that remained was to lose the aggravating pursuers and make his way back to Deborah's home before they worked out what he'd done.

The streets seemed to swell with troops as legionaries joined the chase from all quarters. Barabbas shot down one alleyway, then another, like a rabbit through a warren. By varying his pace, first running, then hiding, doubling back and pressing himself into small crevices he had learned to find in his youth, he managed to throw the soldiers into total confusion.

He could hear the yells and conflicting orders being barked behind him. The giant arch of an aqueduct loomed overhead bridging the narrow passage. A few more turns, and moments later Barabbas found himself back where he'd started.

He silently thanked the street urchins who had taught him to know the streets of Jerusalem as a child. They had fought and played with him, until he could run the alleys blind. He had needed that knowledge tonight.

He moved with caution through the shadows, reluctant to show himself for fear of other hunters lurking in the darkness. His concerns were far from paranoid. Under one of the stairwells, hidden from view, a lone soldier lay in wait. Obviously the man had doubled back, hoping to flush out a careless zealot from his cover.

Remaining in the shadows, Barabbas circled his hunter until he was behind him. He leaped like a panther from the darkness. The soldier never moved. He slipped his arm vicelike around the man's throat, cutting off the flow of air to his lungs. Then he drew his knife, stabbing up, under the sternum. The blade plunged under the soldier's breastplate, seeking out the lifeblood of the heart, cruelly severing the arteries and puncturing the very chambers of the sensitive organ.

He felt no remorse. Rome had taken more blood from him than he would ever take from her. Death was merely another part of life. He left the dying soldier on the pavement and headed for Deborah's courtyard.

He could already hear the yells of approaching soldiers rushing back to their posts in the hopes of pinning their prey at its final avenue of escape.

† † † † †

Barabbas slunk across the courtyard and knocked on Deborah's door. He heard the sound of rushing feet and a moment later the door flew open. Her eyes were wide with shock. Apprehension quickly turned to joy and she flung herself into his arms.

"Thanks be to the God of Abraham!"

Barabbas lifted her with one arm as he spun into the room, and closed the door behind him.

He laughed as he put her down. "You act as if you expected me to die." The exertion of lifting her had opened the wound on his arm again and blood flowed freely, matting the hair on his forearm as it dried.

"You're hurt."

"It's nothing." Barabbas dismissed the wound. "Did everyone make it out?"

"I'm still waiting for Levi, Yochanan and Judas. Yoseph said he saw two men taken at the market."

Barabbas snatched a bag from the shelf and packed a loaf of bread and some dried dates. "Did he say who?"

"No, it was too dark."

He nodded. "We'll have to rescue them tomorrow."

"Barabbas you can't!" Deborah cried. "You need to get away from Jerusalem as quickly as possible."

"We can't just leave them to their fate and I won't argue with you now. The soldiers will be here any minute. Get rid of any sign that we've been here tonight. You can throw the rope out of the window. I'll remove it."

Barabbas bent down to kiss her. Deborah pulled him to her and held him in a long and passionate embrace. He pulled away first, looked into her eyes and then he was gone. He ran up the stairs three at a time. Hephzibah was waiting for him on the roof. She nodded in greeting, but said nothing. Her eyes were drawn to the commotion outside Deborah's courtyard. Barabbas climbed through the window and slid recklessly down the rope, burning his palms on the rough hairs of the cord.

He touched ground and waited for several agonising moments before he saw the rope tumble from the window high up in the wall above him.

He was coiling it before the other end hit the ground. Dark thoughts clouded his mind. Had he been quick enough? The Romans were bound to check the homes along the wall where they'd been lured away. If they even found Hephzibah on that roof the conclusion would be obvious.

With the rope neatly coiled, he hoisted it onto his shoulder. *Nothing you can do about it now.* The women would have to look after themselves. He stared reminiscently up at the city exit he had used so many times. From where he stood, it looked like a thin, dark line in the stone wall that towered towards the sky. *Look after yourself, Deborah.*

The sound of stealthy footsteps brought him out of his reverie. He dropped to a crouch. People were moving about in the darkness, looking for someone - looking for him. Once again, the centurion called Gaius had thought ahead and outsmarted him. Was there no end to that man's cunning? Barabbas melted, like a wraith, disappearing into the shadows. He couldn't leave yet. There was more work to be done.

† † † † †

The courtyard against the north wall bustled like a market before the Sabbath. Gaius scrutinised the angry residents who stared back with sullen glares. He felt sorry for them, dragged from their beds while his soldiers ransacked their homes, upturning furniture and rifling through their meagre belongings.

Only one resident was not in the line. An old drunk lay in a heap over in the corner, having protested against the rough treatment by throwing up on one of the soldiers' tunics. It had lightened the moment, improving the collective mood of the residents and proving a great source of amusement to the unfortunate legionary's comrades.

His eyes raked the small group assembled in the courtyard. So far his questions had revealed little. Yes, some had seen the activities of the legionaries. No, nobody had seen anyone that fitted the description of the man he wanted. It was frustrating. He knew he would get no answers from these people. They were united in their contempt for Rome. The best he could hope for was to spot the lie. He examined each one's eyes as he probed their minds. If there was a hesitation, or if eyes strayed, searching for the truth, he would see it and pounce.

"Have you seen any strange men pass by here tonight?" He questioned the beautiful, young woman with dark, red hair.

"She sees strange men pass by every night." An old woman cackled amidst the guffaws of her companions.

The auburn haired beauty hung her head at the snide remark and mocking laughter of her neighbours. Gaius frowned.

"No, my lord." She shook her head. When she looked up, he felt a sudden wrenching in his chest. He gazed into the dark pools of her eyes and his sense of urgency seemed to melt.

Her moist lips parted slightly as she stared enquiringly at him. Her breathing was deep and measured and he had to forcibly drag his eyes away from the beckoning curve of her chest. A commotion at the steps broke their gaze. Two soldiers emerged dragging a stout, young woman between them.

"Who is this?" Gaius addressed the soldiers, but his eyes were drawn back by the sensual allure of the woman to his left.

"We found her on the roof, centurion."

"Who is this woman?" he asked the beautiful girl with auburn hair. Her body beckoned him, like a siren calling a sailor to her shore.

"She's my sister, my lord."

"Sister?"

"We are children of Abraham, daughters of Israel."

"What was she doing on the roof?" He wanted to tear his eyes away from her, but she would not permit it.

"Sleeping, my lord." The stout woman answered.

He glanced at her for a moment, then turned back to the first woman. "Are you in the habit of making your sister sleep on the roof?"

"I was waiting."

"For whom?" he demanded.

The woman hesitated. Was this the one? Was she the guilty one?

"I was waiting - for a customer. I work at night." She answered frankly. Gaius was struck by her vulnerability. He gazed into her eyes for a long moment.

"Alright. You can go." He didn't wish to humiliate her any further. "Let the other one go too," he instructed the legionaries.

The soldiers released her and both women fled gratefully into their apartment.

He waited until the auburn haired beauty had closed her door. "What was that woman doing up there?" He asked the legionaries quietly.

"She was asleep, just as she claimed."

"You found nothing up there, no sign of the rebels?"

"No, centurion. Just some sleeping mats and baskets with pottery jars in them."

"Nothing out of the ordinary." Gaius mused.

The soldier shook his head. "Just an ordinary harlot's home."

"Watch your mouth, legionary." Gaius snapped. His own anger surprised him. "You'd better learn to show these people some respect or, so help me, I'll have you sent to Gaul for the rest of your term of service."

The threat was unreasonable, but he couldn't help himself. He had to protect this treasure and felt compelled to fight for her honour.

The berated legionary held his tongue.

"Alright, let's move out." Gaius called his men. "There's no sign of them here. We'll check the next block."

The soldiers ascended the stairs, heading for the street. At the top, Gaius hesitated. He turned and glanced back down into the courtyard. The disgruntled residents were returning to their homes. He could hear their grumbling, but was unable to make out what they said. There was no sign of the auburn haired beauty. He gazed longingly at her door, but it remained shut. He felt robbed and yet relieved. Only a guilty person would open their door again to check whether they had covered their crime.

After a fruitless search along the north wall of the *Kainopolis*, Gaius dismissed the soldiers and sent them back to the barracks. Then he headed for the Antonia fortress. His mood was sombre. The zealots had struck a telling blow and the legionaries' morale was low.

The people of Jerusalem had not been happy at having their night disrupted and would voice their disapproval in the morning. With an insurrection and a smouldering barracks on his hands, all he had to show for his night-long search were a pair of convicts, an irate population and a demoralised army.

He realised that Pontius Pilate would have to be informed of the night's disaster. There was no other word to describe it. In a single evening, Rome's credibility had been all but destroyed in Jerusalem. By daybreak, hundreds of previously passive Jews would be flocking to join the zealot movement, buoyed by the victory of a man called Barabbas, the new champion of Israel.

Gaius considered what he would say to the prefect when he saw him. Pilate was a difficult man and he would want a scapegoat to blame for the night's fiasco. *It could well be the end of your military career.* He changed his train of thought. It was pointless to dwell on things he had no control over. At sunrise the following day he would head for Caesarea and face whatever consequences awaited him. But he intended to face Pilate armed with any information he could glean from his prisoners.

If he was lucky he might even extract information on Barabbas' whereabouts. He smiled at the thought. His expression changed abruptly. Such hopes were far too optimistic. Better to wait and see what information he could garner when he saw them face to face.

He crossed the drawbridge of the *Struthian*, the Swallow Pool, that guarded the entrance to the Antonia fortress. The structure was an impressive one, almost like a palace, but the immense temple against which it was built dwarfed it.

The fortress was constructed of the same giant masonry as the Holy Building, with large, chest high, rectangular stones. Large columns supported mammoth blocks of stone. The columns were crested with scroll motifs, typical of the Ionic style favoured by Greek architects.

Inside the court the soldiers stood to attention.

"Where are the prisoners we captured tonight?" He was in a hurry and had no time for niceties.

"In the dungeons, centurion. We've put them in stocks. Shall I show you?"

Gaius nodded curtly and strode across the large chamber, forcing the legionary to catch up with him. He glanced about, taking in the building's splendour. It was filled with great works of art and copies of sculptures done by the great masters of Greek legacy. The sculptures were offensive to the Jewish populace, as they could be construed as idols, but the Roman force didn't let that stop them from decorating the inside of their residence in Jerusalem.

The floor was covered by a huge red and black mosaic picturing a great battle. Gaius always found the nakedness of the protagonists in the scene vaguely offensive. His conservative, Roman nature baulked at the Greeks' macabre obsession with nudity.

He exited the court and followed a passage, turning the corner and heading down some steps toward the dungeons. The cells were particularly gloomy. Light emanated from a few oil lamps which burned day and night. Their smell and heat made the dungeons stuffy and oppressive.

The legionary stopped outside the fifth door. It was a studded, metal block, rusted with age, but still solid and impenetrable.

"In here, centurion. If you need me, I'll be at my post upstairs."

Gaius nodded, dismissing the man. He found the legionary's overly helpful attitude mildly annoying. A guard opened the door and Gaius entered the cell.

Inside, the prisoners were fettered in heavy, wooden stocks. The apparatus had been designed partly to limit the prisoner's movement, but mostly to enhance pain. Their feet were spread apart and locked in holes, while their hands were bound in front of their bodies. This put immense strain on the thighs and backs of the prisoners, who could never get comfortable in their awkward position. It also made breathing as difficult as possible. Cramps would set in within minutes, making the stocks an unbearable torture, as ligaments and tendons were pulled and sprained every time the prisoner tried to move.

The room housed several prisoners, but Gaius disregarded them. He was only interested in the two men captured that night. He marched up to the Jews who were seated in the stocks near the stone wall.

"What are your names, soldiers?" Gaius was polite, almost cordial. There might be a need for violence later, but he preferred the friendly approach to begin with.

The men stared sullenly at him but made no reply.

Gaius smiled. "Come now. Surely it can do you no harm to tell me who you are. It doesn't affect your fate one way or the other."

Carefully, he appraised the two rebels. As a commander of men, it was an essential tool of his profession to be able to assess character quickly and accurately.

"Your name, soldier." He addressed the weaker of the two men, his tone more commanding now than questioning.

"Yochanan." The man said reluctantly.

"And you?" He turned to the second man.

"Judas." The man glowered in the dim light of the oil lamp.

"Well, Judas, you seem to have done Rome some serious damage tonight." Gaius was pleased to see the man's almost imperceptible nod of satisfaction. "You're brave soldiers, men of Israel. I wish I commanded a hundred like you."

The men remained silent, still suspicious, but listening.

"I've commanded men all over the empire and I've never seen such daring and bravery anywhere in the Roman army. Where did you learn to fight like that?"

"We learned in the *Negev*. The desert was our teacher."

"Incredible." Gaius was pensive. "I should send the thirty fourth legion into the *Negev* for training. Maybe that would prevent mishaps like tonight from occurring."

"The only way you could prevent strikes like tonight is by withdrawing all military presence from Judea and giving Israel her freedom. We serve one God and we bow to no man."

"If I could." Gaius paused for effect. "But you must understand I'm a man under command with others over me. I have to follow the orders of my emperor and the prefect of Judea. They'll demand blood for tonight's raid."

The men fell silent again, dropping their gaze and staring at the floor. Gaius continued quickly.

"I believe, with your assistance we can avoid this."

"What sort of assistance?" Judas looked up nervously.

Gaius spotted the flicker of hope in the man's eyes.

"Confirmation."

The time had come to shock his subjects. By frightening them and then offering hope, he might learn the truth.

"Your contact in Jerusalem has given me information about your hideout."

"Our contact —" Judas was stunned.

"Yes. We took your contact and one other as he was trying to escape through the north wall." A gamble, but worth the risk. He still felt certain that was where the zealots had escaped from.

"Who?"

The fear was in Judas' eyes now. *Time for second shock. Demoralise them completely.*

"The man called Barabbas."

The men were visibly shaken. The fight in their eyes had been doused, just as the flames in the barracks had been smothered earlier that night.

Gaius spoke quickly, pressing his advantage and capitalising on their fear. "The information they gave me was to save your lives, not theirs. You can save them by confirming it. Of course if your information is different, well —"

"What information?" Judas asked nervously.

"Where is your hideout? Where do the zealots work from?"

Yochanan glanced at Judas. Each seemed to be waiting for the other to take the lead.

"Please." Gaius urged softly. "Help me save Barabbas." He watched carefully, allowing Judas to consider the possibilities. He could almost see the conflicting thoughts behind the man's confused and fearful eyes.

After much deliberation, Judas answered. His words were slow and measured. "Barabbas and I are like brothers, but he would watch me die slowly, in front of his eyes, before he told you the whereabouts of our hideout."

Gaius was surprised at the man's resolve. He would have to try a new ploy. He smiled. "You caught me. Barabbas told me nothing. However, you can still save him. Give me the information I want and Barabbas goes free. Who knows - you may even save yourself."

"If I told you, Barabbas would see me dead for the traitor I was. Better I die at your hands than his."

Gaius suddenly became harsh. "You won't be saying that when Pilate hangs you on the crucifix. Do you have any idea what that's like?"

He didn't care any more. The opportunity had passed. The resolve was in his prisoner's eyes; the man had turned to stone.

Gaius tried again to get his attention. "Have you heard the agonised screams as a seven inch spike is driven through wrists and ankles? Or the pain in men's eyes as they slowly expire for hours? They beg for someone to break their legs, just so that they can suffocate quickly and end the pain. Is that what you want, Judas? Do you want to die, begging me to break your legs?"

The fear in the Jew's eyes was apparent, but he would not bend. He merely gazed down at the floor in front of him and refused to utter a word.

Gaius turned to Yochanan. "Give me the information I want and you can walk free. I'll let you go right now, only tell me where your hideout is."

Yochanan looked away, gazing disinterestedly at the floor. It was plain that neither of them would be forthcoming with information.

Gaius snorted in disgust. "Tomorrow we leave for Caesarea. I assure you, Pilate will not be as lenient as I have been. Believe me, every word you've heard about him is true. In fact it's only the beginning of his cruelty. I've done all I can. Not even your God can save you now."

He turned and left the dungeons, heading back up the stairs. In the court he met the enthusiastic soldier who had shown him to the dungeons.

"See to it that those men are ready at first light to be taken to Caesarea. I want a guard of two hundred soldiers, seventy horsemen and two hundred spearmen ready to go with me. The prisoners will stand before Pilate and answer for their crimes."

"Yes, centurion. Consider it done. I'll be waiting outside the Antonia myself to accompany you."

Gaius held up his hand. "Please, I need you here to man the watch in Jerusalem. The people are going to be in a belligerent mood tomorrow and I need competent soldiers to keep peace in the city."

The soldier beamed at the compliment. "I understand, centurion. I'll have the guard waiting for you and I'll assemble another group to control the city. I'll oversee that myself."

"Thank you." Gaius was glad to be rid of this annoying buffoon, angling for promotion. "I'm going to check on the barracks now. I'll see you at dawn."

"*Ave*, centurion."

"*Ave*." Gaius had already turned his back on the man, but waved dismissively over his shoulder. He left the Antonia and walked back out into the dark, smoke filled city. Turning left, he headed west toward the barracks, through the now deserted streets.

The interrogation had proved fruitless. What else should he have expected? The Jews were a stubborn nation. It had been foolish of him to expect anything from them. Now his hope lay in Marcus and his detail outside the city. If Barabbas escaped, they would be waiting. With any luck they could capture him once he dropped from the city wall.

He could still smell traces of the smouldering barracks and hear the distant commotion of soldiers fixing and cleaning the destruction that Barabbas had left in his wake. As he trudged along the cobbled streets, thoughts of the night's disaster hung heavy upon him.

He stared wistfully at the district to the north. *Barabbas*. He would remember that name for the rest of his days. There would be no escape. He vowed to bring the man with the arrogant, golden bronze eyes before the mighty hand of Rome and see that justice was meted out for the crimes he had committed this evening.

3

OUTSIDE THE city wall, Barabbas hid quietly behind the twisted trunk of an ancient and deformed acacia tree, allowing its sinister shadows to enfold him. He crouched silently, holding his breath as he calculated his next move. What would he do if discovered; which way would he flee?

In the darkness he listened for the approach of his unseen foes. His ears told him that there were many. The intermittent cracking of twigs and the occasional furtive whisper told Barabbas they were trying to move in silence. He shook his head at the incompetence of the approaching rabble. *If my men moved with such carelessness, I would kill them myself.*

A sharp node bored painfully into his back, but he dared not move. The Roman soldiers - he could see now who they were - were too close. Any sound might alert them to his presence. With discipline born of a lifetime of struggle, he endured the discomfort, not even chancing to shift his weight for fear of alerting the legionaries to his presence.

They moved slowly, carefully inspecting each patch of soil in the darkness. Some searched the length and height of the city wall, looking for a rope or basket. The corners of his mouth curled into a slight smile at the comforting weight of the rope slung over his shoulder.

"Wait, look here!" the soldier's exclamation startled Barabbas and his smile vanished.

Others clustered around to see what had caught their comrade's attention.

"What is it?" A second voice called near the foot of the city wall.

"There seems to have been a lot of activity here. Look at all these prints."

"There's a window directly above us." The man pointed up at the thin slit in the city wall.

"It seems we've found our escape route." Barabbas recognised that voice. It was the man who had led the group of soldiers to block the exit at the market place. "Fan out and search the area. They may still be lurking about somewhere."

Barabbas tensed himself. It looked like he'd have to move after all. The legionaries quickly spread out in groups of two, searching amongst the rocks and dense foliage. Two of them approached the acacia tree. He reached for his knife. Inching his way around the thick trunk, he kept out of their line of sight. With each step, he felt the ground gingerly beneath him before resting his weight on it.

The soldiers drew closer, peering into the darkness. They stood no more than a few paces from him under the thick boughs of the ancient tree, scanning the lower branches. Barabbas could hear their breathing. After an agonising period the legionaries moved on, leaving him in the shadows.

Barabbas looked longingly at their unprotected backs. To kill them now would be foolish. The two men moved up the rise towards a group of round, bush laden boulders to continue their search.

He wasn't sure how long he'd waited, but it felt like an aeon. Finally the soldiers regrouped at the foot of the city walls.

"Alright." their leader called. "Let's get back to the barracks. We can come back here in the morning and show the centurion these marks. When he finds the person who lowered them down, he'll find Barabbas, even if he has to break them in half to get the information."

Barabbas remained hidden until the last sounds of the retreating footsteps had died away. Then he sprang into action. Deborah was a valuable asset to the zealots. He couldn't let her be discovered. It was more than mere concern for the cause, however.

He was fond of Deborah. She was a friend and companion in the struggle, a lover when he needed the tender touch of a woman, and a ready ear when he needed someone to talk to. They had a long history and he cared for her. Not that he believed they had any future together. Their relationship was one of convenience. Each shared moments when they could, never placing any demands on the other.

He scoured the rocky slope for a dead branch. His search didn't take long. He found a fallen date palm lying amongst the cluster of boulders, just above the acacia where he had hidden. He chose a small branch with lots of fine fronds. Back down at the city wall, he began sweeping the ground, eradicating all signs of the zealots' passing. He moved back and forth, covering tracks as he went. Every now and then he stopped to straighten a clump of grass, or remove a freshly broken branch, so that even his own drag marks were concealed. Finally he tossed the branch aside, satisfied that he had concealed the tracks as best he could. By morning, no trace would remain of the night's activity outside the north wall of the city.

Barabbas turned east, heading for the rendezvous on the Mount of Olives. Much time had passed and he hoped that the others would still be there. There was still much to be done and he needed their help. Cautiously, he made his way up the terraced slopes of the cultivated mountain at the opposite side of the Kidron valley. The trees were well tended, although old. About half way up, he found the rendezvous. The clearing was near a stone wall, between the beautiful trees with light bark which belied their roughness.

He approached silently, listening for any sign of his friends. The clearing was deserted and Barabbas swore under his breath. The men had obviously grown restless, wanting to put as much distance between themselves and Jerusalem as possible before sunrise.

This meant an arduous journey and slim chance of finding them in the dark. He tried not to think about it. He had to find them. His plan would need to be carried out before daybreak. He struck out along the road to Jericho. The weary group of men would almost certainly have followed that route. Then they would turn south towards the small town of Bethany. From there, they would make the rough descent into the Great Rift Valley and on to the Salt Sea beyond. If his plan was to work, he had to find them before they reached Bethany. A fleeting shadow to his left arrested his attention.

Barabbas froze in mid stride. Had he seen the movement, or had he merely sensed a presence lurking in the darkness? He searched the shadows, alert for the slightest sound, or any sign of movement.

Nothing stirred. He relaxed and began descending the Mount of Olives, heading north to intersect with the road to Jericho. It wasn't long before he saw the wide, paved track snaking its way eastwards through the hills towards the ancient city.

Twice more, Barabbas was convinced that he heard something, or someone, following him. First he sped up, trying to shake off the spectre. At one point, near a bend in the road, he doubled back, trying to flush out his pursuer.

Nothing. Maybe it was merely his imagination. He heard a shuffle to his right. Once again, Barabbas peered into the shadows. His pursuer was good. There was a flutter of wings as a panicked pigeon flew from its roost. What had disturbed it? He watched.

An owl glided noiselessly through the darkness, its keen eyesight seeking out the hapless dove that was its prey. Perhaps it was his imagination after all. He was tired and his mind was on edge. What he needed was a good night's sleep.

He proceeded towards Jericho, but remained plagued by thoughts of his pursuer. His senses revealed no sign of the hunter, but his instincts convinced him that someone was there. Suddenly he lurched forward, breaking into a sprint. Turning the corner, he left the road, cutting to his right. He moved silently through the undergrowth, seeking the road to Bethany. As soon as he felt sure that his stalker was no longer there, he slowed his pace, glancing through the sparse foliage at the rocky terrain. He always wondered at the stark contrasts in the flora. He was no more than a few miles east of Jerusalem and yet the dense plant life and green trees had already thinned, becoming arid steppe country, rocky and dry.

He hoped his last ruse had thrown off any would be pursuer, but he was still cautious and avoided using the road, preferring to travel in the relative cover of the rocks and sparse vegetation. He kept a close lookout until he was certain that whoever had been following him was gone. Finally he felt satisfied and returned to the road, where he could move more swiftly. He remained alert to the possible presence of a stalker as he searched the road for the zealots ahead.

After an eternity of hiking, he was rewarded with the soft murmur of voices ahead of him in the darkness. He turned his head, trying to locate the source. Presently he heard it again, off to his left. Quiet men sharing quiet thoughts as they rested for a moment on their journey. He recognised one of the voices and smiled.

"You'd better learn to keep your voice down, Yoseph. As the Lord lives, you screech like a desert crow."

There was an excited scrambling and exclamations as the men rose hurriedly to greet their comrade.

"Barabbas, we thought you must surely have been taken." Yoseph called. He emerged from the tree line and greeted his comrade and leader with a giant bear hug.

Simeon came next, thumping him on his back. "I thought it was the end of you, brother."

"There were times when I thought that myself." Barabbas replied. "Come let's sit for a moment. I can't remember the last time I tasted food."

He rejoined the group of men, greeting them with broad grins and friendly ribbing. Their mood was buoyant. They had struck a telling blow against Rome and were crowing at their victory.

Barabbas sagged in their midst, leaning against a smooth boulder, and opened his bag of food. His friends launched a barrage of questions about his evening's exploits, but he ignored them. He broke off large chunks of the soft, leavened bread and wolfed them down.

After he'd swallowed the last mouthful of bread, he became serious. "We lost three men tonight."

"I know." Simeon replied. "Yoseph and Eleazor saw two of them taken outside the market place."

"What of the third?" Barabbas enquired, looking around the group of men. Joshua and Ya'aqob shrugged and shook their heads.

"It's possible Levi made it." Lazarus ventured. "When I last saw him he'd torn himself free and was headed east, towards the temple. Several soldiers were after him and he was alone."

Yoseph snorted. "Since when would Levi be defeated by a group of mere legionaries. After what he's survived! How many men have lived through that?"

Ya'aqob shook his head. "I doubt he made it. There were mules all over the place."

He used the common term for Roman soldiers, a name they were known by throughout the empire. It stemmed from the great general, Marius, who had designed the Roman pack with weapons, bedding and building equipment, such as trowels and shovels. He had demanded that legionaries be able to march twenty miles a day in full kit, and the soldiers had become known as Marius' mules.

"After tonight's raid they'll be executed for sure." Yoseph voiced the concern they all felt.

"Maybe they still have a chance of escape." Joshua ventured. He was a young man, no more than eighteen, but a good fighter and strong.

"I believe they do." Barabbas announced.

"Impossible!" Yoseph was incredulous. "They'll almost certainly be in the Antonia by now and they'll be executed at first light."

"No they won't."

Yoseph snorted again. "You think Rome's going to wash their feet and release them in the morning?"

"They won't be executed because only the prefect can order their deaths."

"So?"

"So, the prefect is not in Jerusalem at the moment. He's in Caesarea."

"And what's stopping the soldiers from taking them to Caesarea in the morning?"

"Nothing at all. In fact, that's exactly what they'll do. It's what I'm counting on."

Yoseph held his gaze for a long moment. Finally he replied. "So, we're going back."

A hush fell over the group as they contemplated the prospect of returning to Jerusalem.

"It's impossible." Eleazor spoke for the first time. "The area's infested with soldiers. Search parties are probably being sent out in every direction as we speak. Only a madman would return to Jerusalem now."

"Call me mad, but we owe it to our comrades to return and try to save them."

"They're beyond saving, Barabbas. We can only fail."

"Then we fail, but we *will* try."

"You're insane!" Eleazor exclaimed. "Only a fool would try to attack a force that size without the cover of darkness to protect him."

Barabbas became very quiet. When he spoke his voice was like an icy wind. "Eleazor, we are going back to Jerusalem to free our comrades. This is not a Greek school of philosophy, where everyone gets to share an opinion. My word on the matter is final."

Eleazor rose. "Then you're a fool, Barabbas. What makes you think you can take on the might of Rome in full light of the sun and win?"

"As always, you're only concerned with your own well being. You're a disgrace to the zealots. Judas of Galilee would weep in is grave if he could see what poor, cowardly soldiers his memory had spawned."

"Judas of Galilee died because he underestimated the power of Rome. Make that mistake and you will meet the same end, Barabbas. They were fools that died in their folly, just like your father did."

Barabbas stood up slowly and faced Eleazor with murder in his heart. Simeon rose to restrain him, but Barabbas shook him off and advanced on the defiant figure. Several other men rose to stop Barabbas, but he ignored them. His fury went beyond reason and he drew his sword.

Eleazor remained where he was. He drew his own weapon and waited for Barabbas to come to him. His mocking smile only served to fuel Barabbas' rage. *I always knew it would come to this.*

A snapping twig from the tree line at the edge of the clearing caused the tense atmosphere to evaporate. Barabbas cursed and peered into the darkness. Simeon and Yoseph had heard it too. The soft crunch of soil underfoot. A stone dislodged, rattling against other stones until it rolled to a stop.

All the zealots were at once alert, swords drawn, eyes searching for the hidden enemy in the blackness beyond.

"Put away your swords. You look like a group of women at the well; it's embarrassing." A mocking voice called from the darkness.

Barabbas laughed with relief and sheathed his sword. He rushed across the clearing to greet his comrade who stepped from the darkness.

"Levi, we'd given you up for dead. What took you so long?"

"I was waylaid by some over anxious Romans and had to hide in the Bethesda pools until they'd moved on."

"More likely you stopped in one of the wine taverns." Barabbas grinned. "You're lucky you weren't killed, the way you loitered in the city while soldiers hunted every street."

"Ha! They couldn't kill me in the arena in Rome and they won't kill me in the streets of Jerusalem. If I told you of just half the battles I survived as a gladiator in Rome."

"Spare us. Come and eat rather. You may be immortal, but we're not. Our boredom might become terminal if we have to listen to any more of those stories."

Although Barabbas teased his friend, he had immense respect for the older man. Levi was one of the few among their number who had run with Judas of Galilee and fought in the uprising during the reign of Augustus.

When the rebellion had been quenched the zealots had believed Levi to be dead, along with the rest of the rebels who had followed Judas, the Galilean. An error had sent him to Rome, however, where he'd been forced to perform in the arena for the bloodthirsty Roman populace. There he became a legend and one of the few gladiators to survive a full four year term in the arena. He was pardoned by the emperor, as per Roman custom and, after another compulsory three years spent training new gladiators, he had returned to Judea, a hero.

He had cut covenant years previously with Barabbas' father, Cephas of Gamala, and had taken the brothers in when they had left their uncle's home to join the zealot cause. Barabbas had learned all he knew of warfare from Levi and was grateful to him for that knowledge.

"Already, I'm bored by the inactivity. I need to go back and fight. I need the smell of blood in my nostrils."

"You may have that chance, my friend. Eleazor was just telling me how we should return to Jerusalem and save our comrades, who were taken in the battle."

"That's funny. I thought Eleazor was a coward." Levi said with a mischievous smile.

The dark eyed, sallow man glowered at them from the edge of the group, but didn't reply.

"How do you suggest we return?" Yoseph asked. "Soldiers and horsemen will have been dispatched in every direction to look for us. We can't pass them without being seen."

"We don't have to." Simeon spoke softly.

"Are you suggesting we simply stroll by the search parties, waving our swords in the air?"

"What I mean is, it doesn't matter whether we're seen or not. What matters is what we *appear* to be when they see us."

Barabbas nodded. "Someone they're not looking for, heading in a direction they don't expect."

"I'm suggesting even more than that. What if we appear to be something they don't even want to approach?"

Barabbas considered his brother's words. "Of course! The rags."

Simeon nodded. "If they're still there."

Eleazor growled from the rock he sat on. "There's no question that will work, but what do we do when we get back to Jerusalem? The guard around them will be a hundred strong at least. How do you suggest we take on odds of ten to one, or more?"

"Did I say it would be easy? Barabbas glowered at the man. "I think we might be able to take them on one of the passes in the hills outside Jerusalem. Simeon, do you know of any rock fall already set up for ambushes?"

"There are always some set up between Jerusalem and Antipatris. We'd have to hunt for a suitable site, but I'm sure we'll find one."

"We'll need to route it in two directions, to cut off the soldiers on both sides of the prisoners. That way, if we drop them at just the right moment, we can isolate the prisoners from most of the Roman guard."

"That will be more difficult." Simeon frowned.

"I still think there are too many elements left to chance. If just one thing goes wrong, we'll all be taken and tonight's raid will have been in vain." Eleazor complained.

"If something goes wrong, we can pull back. We don't have to attack unless victory is certain, but we must at least try."

"I've got a bad feeling about this, Barabbas. You're going to get us all killed."

"So leave." Barabbas said.

"What?"

"If you don't have the stomach for this, you can go. The rest of us will handle it without you. We don't need people like you among our number. I'll just spread the word that you no longer believe in our cause and, like that traitor Simon, have chosen to leave the movement."

Perhaps this was the opportunity he'd been waiting for. Barabbas held Eleazor's gaze. The man glared back at him, hesitating in his response.

He'd never liked Eleazor. The man was a good swordsman, strong in battle, but he was also a drain on the other men's morale. It seemed to Barabbas that the man didn't truly believe in their cause. There was something sinister about his motives that Barabbas found impossible to read. However, every time Eleazor was faced with the prospect of leaving the movement, he chose to remain. It puzzled Barabbas, but he was certain of this much. He didn't trust Eleazor.

The man snorted and shook his head. "You're all mad." he said, but he stood up to join them.

Why? Even now, he can't bring himself to walk away. The man's motives remained an enigma. Unable to explain it, Barabbas realised he'd have to accept it. "Good man, Eleazor." He commended his compatriot.

"Know this, Barabbas. What you're doing is putting all our lives in jeopardy and I'm going to hold you responsible for every man that falls in this battle. If one life is lost, if one man is taken, I'll never forgive you. And I swear I will hunt you down until that man's blood is avenged."

"If you fight the Romans as bravely as you threaten me, there'll be no need for vengeance. Come sunrise, the battle will be ours."

For Barabbas it was a matter of honour. Their comrades had been taken and it was their duty to attempt a rescue. Had he known what his decision would cost him, perhaps he would have chosen a different path.

Marcus and a small group of horsemen raced east in the darkness, along the road towards Jericho. They were barely a mile away from Jerusalem, urgently hunting for the escaped insurgents that had instigated the attack on the barracks a few hours earlier. His eyes were crimson from smoke and lack of sleep.

He felt the power of the roan steed beneath him and urged the animal on to greater speed. The rhythmic sound of the horses' hooves pounded against the cobbled stones and the animals snorted as each one craned its neck, jostling for the coveted position out front.

He scanned the terrain, looking for any sign of the wanted men. Already, the horizon ahead of them was beginning to gleam, announcing the approach of dawn. Soon the dark purple hues would give way to the pastel pink and mauve shades of dawn and the sun would begin to cast its soft rays, like honey, over the undulating landscape.

In the early morning gloom, Marcus spotted a movement. The soldiers reined in their steeds and gazed upon the huddled figures trudging alongside the road towards Jerusalem.

"Good morning." Marcus greeted the motley band of travellers.

"Good day, my lord," some of the men replied.

They wore tattered clothes, more rags than garments and their faces were covered with torn pieces of cloth. The men also called a warning to announce their presence and warn off the unwary, or careless.

"You're moving about very early this morning." Marcus was amiable, but he was careful not to venture too close.

"Yes, my lord. We want to get to the Sheep Gate by dawn. Our hunger is great and we seek the food that the men of the city leave there for us."

"Have you seen a group of men - Israelites - travel along this road at all during the night?"

"No, my lord. We slept in the hills and rose not more than an hour ago. Since then the road has been deserted."

"Very well." Marcus bade them farewell and spurred his horse on towards Jericho.

The beautiful roan trotted ahead of the rest of the soldiers. Marcus bounced uncomfortably on the animal's bare back and urged it on to a more comfortable canter.

† † † † †

Gaius made his way towards the Antonia. He rubbed the dark mole on his cheek as he rode his bay mare up, past the temple on his right. The sky was lighter now and the huge bastion of the Jewish faith loomed in the darkness as the long shadows began to take shape. He arrived at the drawbridge that ran over the *Struthian* pool, to find a host of Roman soldiers guarding the two prisoners.

The soldiers were all clad in full kit for the journey. Each carried, aside from his weapons, a large backpack containing rations, bedding and a change of clothes.

Aside from this, the packs carried enough equipment to make their total weight equivalent to that of a twelve year old child.

Gaius nodded his approval. The soldiers were well trained and conditioned to march, with full kit, at a rate of five miles an hour. It was this form of self-sufficiency and rigid training that had made the Roman army the mighty fighting machine it was.

"Where are the prisoners?"

"Over here, centurion."

Gaius was pleased to see the two men trussed up in chains. They were mounted on two strong steeds, so that they would not slow the army down on their trip to Caesarea.

"Fine, let's go. I want to be in Antipatris by sundown."

The soldiers steeled themselves for a tough journey. It was a thirty mile march to Antipatris from Jerusalem. On average, a man might be expected to cover twenty miles a day. To do thirty in full kit was a fantastic feat. No soldier would query his leader, however. They merely shrugged on their packs and readied themselves for the task.

Gaius raised his vinewood staff and pointed towards the Sheep Gate, the city's eastern exit.

"Move out!" he yelled and the army of men lurched forward. An hour later they passed the fifth milestone and Gaius called a halt. The weary men gratefully sagged to the ground, removing their backpacks and reaching eagerly for water to quench throats, parched from the hard march. The milestone stood as high as a man's head, boldly proclaiming the distance to Rome.

† † † † †

A few hundred paces ahead of the soldiers, the road rose sharply, cutting a deep wedge between a pair of hills that jutted like giant domes on either side, supporting its passage through the pass. The hills consisted mostly of heavy boulders interspersed with dense patches of short stemmed trees, making them look like a camouflage patchwork of beige and green.

Hidden on the steep slopes, amongst rocky crags and dark foliage, Barabbas waited anxiously for his signal. His position had been carefully chosen to avoid the impending rock falls that nestled in malevolent silence in the hills above, heaving against the wedges that held them in place. Some of his men had left the sanctuary of their hiding places in order to better view the Roman detail, resting about a mile to the south.

It had not been Barabbas' first choice as a position from which to launch his attack. He felt it was too close to Jerusalem and wouldn't afford them enough time to prepare. However, his other options had proved unviable, as many of the rock-falls had already been sprung. This was unfortunate, but not unexpected. The traps comprised huge piles of stone, held in place by a single large boulder, which was in turn secured by a wedge at its base. The wedges were usually made of wood and more often than not, rotted and broke, springing the trap unexpectedly. With so little time at his disposal, he'd been forced to find a trap that was already set up.

"I can't stand this waiting." Levi spoke quietly, peering between two large, round boulders at the soldiers in the valley below. "They're in our sight, and we can't do a thing about it."

"Be glad they stopped, my friend. It's given us a chance to fortify our position and plot our escape route."

"I see you were not idle when you went off to scout the area earlier. How do you plan for our escape?"

"Directly below us." Barabbas pointed to his right, down the rocky, tree-lined slope. "There is a gully that runs through the trees and along the base of this hill. The bushes are thick. Even if we're observed, the soldiers will have a difficult time trying to reach us, but our way is clear."

"Lucky we have a gully there." Levi said with a thin smile.

"Lucky." Barabbas agreed.

Both men knew luck had nothing to do with it. Generations of warfare had led their predecessors to create escape routes exactly like the gully at the foot of the hill. It hadn't been difficult to find.

"It won't be long now." Yoseph murmured from his vantage point in the lower branches of an acacia, about ten paces to their left.

The tree leaned, as if it had fallen down the slope, and made an extremely comfortable watchtower from which an observer could monitor activities in the valley below while he remained unseen.

Yoseph called the alarm. "Quick, take positions. They're on the move."

"See the army rises like Goliath from his bed." Levi's voice took on a dreamlike quality as he gazed mesmerised in the direction of the approaching troops. "But we will strike like stones from David's sling."

"Quit your dreaming and get back against the rock face." Barabbas urged harshly.

Levi moved into position, but his eyes were glazed over. Barabbas couldn't be sure whether his friend had heard him or not.

From his vantage point, Barabbas watched his men. Quickly but stealthily they descended the hill, taking up positions where they would be sheltered from the impending rock slides. They moved like predators, hiding in the cover of the rocks and bushes, waiting for the moment to strike.

Only two men remained at the top of the hill. Simeon and Joshua had taken up positions to trigger the booby traps. All that remained was for the wedges to be dislodged and the rocks would cascade down the steep slopes, effectively blocking the road and cutting off the bulk of the Roman army from the action.

Barabbas could hear the approaching Roman troops from behind the rock, which now hid him, but he could not see them. He dared not move. They were extremely close now. Each moment that passed, he felt sure he would see them appear.

He could hear the crunch of hobnailed sandals as they struck a rhythmic beat on the cobbled stones. His tension burgeoned and time slowed to a trickle. Every moment became an agonised aeon of waiting.

Barabbas heard the sharp intake of breath as Levi tensed next to him. The first soldiers had stepped into view. He chanced a glance up the slope to where his brother waited, unseen, high above them, ready to spring the trap.

Another eternity of waiting. The soldiers were in full view now, but the hill remained silent. His mind turned to Joshua, who was positioned above him and to his left. Joshua's signal would be the first rock-fall. As soon as he saw Simeon's rubble hurtling down the slope, he would release the second wedge and lock the small complement of soldiers around the prisoners into the pass, leaving them vulnerable to attack.

"I see them." Levi pointed as Judas and Yochanan came into view. They were mounted on two horses. One was creamy beige with a beautiful, golden mane and tail, the other a chestnut. The prisoners were each manacled between two soldiers, who rode alongside them.

"It's time. Any moment now." Barabbas breathed deeply as he anticipated the impending avalanche.

He gazed down the slope and saw Gaius, riding just ahead of his captured comrades. Still the rock-fall remained in place.

"Come, Simeon. It's time." Barabbas whispered, willing his brother to pull the wedge.

Rank by rank, the soldiers marched through the pass. No rocks fell.

His agitation was beginning to tell. Barabbas searched the upper reaches of the steep rise, hunting for Simeon high above him. Nothing. No sound. The rocks remained stubbornly unmoved.

Levi was becoming restless. "Perhaps the rock-fall is stuck. If they're badly packed —"

Barabbas stared up the slope for what felt like the thousandth time. Silence.

Levi shook his head. "The prisoners are almost through."

"It's over. We'll have to call off the strike." Barabbas shook his head in resignation.

"At least Eleazor will be happy." Levi muttered dejectedly.

He had barely uttered the words when there was a sudden rumbling above them. The soldiers at the foot of the steep incline looked up to see what had caused it. Their cries of alarm reached Barabbas and his comrades who began to move with murderous intent.

The legionaries in front ran forward to get clear of the cascading, deadly earth that plunged towards them, gathering speed and debris as it did so. Further back, the soldiers around the prisoners were routed as the torrent of boulders fell directly in front of them.

Some were not lucky enough to get clear of the falling rubble and screams of agony penetrated the dull roar of the avalanche as men were crushed under the force of the giant boulders and pummelled by the smaller rocks that streamed like an unending waterfall from the slope above.

Barabbas glanced to his left. Already, the second rock-fall was raining down behind the guards immediately around the prisoners, cutting off their escape and any assistance from the soldiers bringing up the rear. With rocks falling on both sides, the zealots sprang from their positions and fell upon the unwitting soldiers.

They were outnumbered by three or four to one, but the soldiers were cumbersome under the weight of their packs, as well as stunned by the sheer shock of the avalanche and the unexpected attack. The zealots used their advantage well and, before the soldiers had even shed their packs, six lay dead on the ground.

Barabbas and Yoseph headed towards the two chained men, elbowing their way through the ranks of soldiers. As he approached Yochanan, he saw Gaius. The centurion had immediately taken action to protect his prisoners. He turned his horse and spurred it towards the manacled men, snatching a seven foot pike from one of the spearmen as he did so.

Barabbas forced his way through the mass of bodies that clustered around the prisoners, deflecting blows and thrusting with his sword in an effort to reach his friends. His eyes were fixed on Yochanan, who was the closer of his two captured comrades. With a quick glance, he checked that their escape route was clear and saw Eleazor beating a hasty retreat down the gully, fleeing the heat of battle.

"You'll die for your cowardice, Eleazor!" He yelled after the fleeing man. Then his eye caught the glint of a thrusting Roman blade. He spun to defend himself, ducking under the shining steel, and finally he was by Yochanan's side.

Barabbas reached for Yochanan's mount, slashing at the soldiers' hands that gripped the reins. One of the horsemen thrust his sword, stabbing at Barabbas' exposed throat. Barabbas fell to one knee, and the blade swept over his head. He rose immediately and plunged his blade into the horseman's midriff. The wound was not fatal, but the man toppled from his mount, clutching wide-eyed at the gaping wound, as if trying to hold the torn flesh together.

As he mounted the horse, sitting behind Yochanan, Barabbas saw Yoseph take Judas' steed by the bit, parrying a soldier's thrust as he did so. The two swords glinted in the sunlight as they clashed together. Yoseph smashed his foot into the man's groin and the soldier buckled in pain as the fight went out of him.

Barabbas spurred the horse on, dragging two wounded legionaries, still manacled to their prisoner, behind him like a scarlet wake churning frantically over the rough terrain. He guided the beautiful chestnut steed towards the gully, exhilarating in his victory. A guard of four hundred soldiers and seventy horsemen routed by a group of eight men was a feat that Judas Maccabeus himself would have been proud of.

Then he heard a sudden blast of air and felt the horse stumble beneath him. The magnificent beast sagged to its knees. Its beautiful white nostrils were stained red with bubbles of blood and the animal gasped for air, its eyes rolling, showing the whites in its pain.

Barabbas' heart sank. He didn't need to see the long pike sticking like a cruel barb through the animal's rib cage to know that a lung had been penetrated. He looked back for the source of the attack and saw Gaius bringing his mount around, lining his sights on Judas' beast of burden, with a second pike in his hand.

Barabbas watched helplessly as the pike drove cleanly into the golden-maned animal's chest, just below the withers. The beautiful horse arched its neck and reeled sideways, away from the vicious spike. Its knees, too, gave way and it stumbled and fell, pinning Judas under its weight, as its legs kicked spasmodically at the air.

The horse was dying and Barabbas' hopes of victory with it. Gaius turned and faced Barabbas, his stare devoid of expression. Barabbas glowered back at the centurion who had single-handedly robbed him of his victory.

The battle was over. The prisoners were pinned. All that remained was the hope of escape. Already the soldiers were making their way over the piles of stone and rubble to assist their fellow legionaries.

Barabbas turned and ran down the gully, following the footsteps of the men who had fought beside him, and their fathers who had fought before them. He wondered for a moment whether Judas Maccabeus and his *Hassidim*, or even his own father, had ever used this gully to escape an enemy. It struck him as odd that he should think of such a thing at a time like this.

The world seemed to condense itself about him, becoming a tiny bubble that had room only for him. Sounds became no more than a distant roar, like a raging gale heard from inside a room. He felt dizzy and colours seemed to take on a special hue, as if enhanced and blurred at the same time.

He remembered jumping over the fallen body of a man. The face was etched in his memory, eyes closed, mouth open. Blood trickled from the man's hairline and down a deep crease in his forehead. If Barabbas could have seen the future, he would have stopped and slain the unconscious man where he lay. There was no time, however and no way of knowing the loss that the fallen man would bring.

Barabbas ran. As he did so, he felt a dreamlike sensation come over him. He felt as if he were standing still as the ground moved beneath him. Later, these were the only things he could recall of the events that took place after the battle; the sensation he had felt, and the face of the man lying in the gully.

That and the expressionless gaze of the centurion who had destroyed his plans and robbed him of victory. His brother's words echoed in his ears. They had a frightening, prophetic ring about them.

I only hope we don't regret that crossing of swords. We made a dangerous enemy tonight.

4

GAIUS STOOD at the edge of the ravine and surveyed the damage wrought on his guard. He turned and gazed up the gully where the Jews had fled. His scouts would be back soon. Barabbas had chosen his ambush well. The ravine made pursuit on horseback impossible and with the two hills on that side, the only way out of the pass, other than the road, was the ravine.

"Shall I get a group of men ready to start clearing the road, centurion?" Gaius turned. He hadn't heard Marcus approach.

He sighed. "Yes. And have some of them attend to our wounded. I want a detail assembled to take those men back to Jerusalem."

"Centurion!" One of his scouts came racing down the ravine.

"What is it, soldier?"

"We found one, centurion."

"Found what, man!" Gaius was irritable. He had no time for cryptic messages.

"In the gully. We found a fallen zealot. He has a head wound."

"Is he alive?"

"Yes, centurion. He's unconscious, but he'll survive."

A slow smile spread across Gaius' face. "Bring him here as soon as you revive him. I want to see this man."

"Yes, centurion." The man shot back up the gully.

"Right." Gaius turned to the assembled group of men. "I want all these stones moved from the road at once. One hundred men will return to Jerusalem with our wounded as soon as they're fit to travel. The rest must be ready in one hour. Find more horses for the prisoners. We can't have them slowing us down."

The soldiers turned to their tasks. Gaius marched through the camp. He watched the medics dress the injured soldiers' wounds with olive oil and myrrh, while others removed the rubble from the road. A small group of men emerged from the gully.

Gaius turned and saw two legionaries dragging a bound prisoner between them. The man was wiry with dark hair and eyes. A kink in his beard marred the left side of his face and he had a surly look about him.

"I see they've dressed your wound." Gaius studied his new prisoner. The man held his gaze in defiance, but made no reply.

Gaius continued. "Did you truly believe a mere handful of men could take on a Roman guard of four hundred legionaries?"

"Don't insult my intelligence. Others made the decision to attack."

The man's insolence surprised him. "You sound discontent. Others made the decision - but you were taken."

The Jew said nothing, though Gaius could see the truth of his statement reflected in the man's eyes.

"What's your name?"

"Eleazor, son of Nahor."

"Your friends," Gaius nodded towards Yochanan and Judas, "were less than cooperative when I questioned them. They'll be executed, of course. I wonder if you would be more forthcoming with information in exchange for your own life?"

The man regarded him with suspicion. "What sort of information?"

"The whereabouts of Barabbas' hideout. I want to take him."

Eleazor chuckled bitterly. "You don't have the power to kill me, or to grant me a reprieve. If you can produce Barabbas, you might be able to save what's left of your ravaged career. I, on the other hand, will get little more than a crucifix for my troubles."

"Next to my honour, my career means very little. Barabbas destroyed the barracks on my shift. I intend to bring him to justice."

"So do I." Eleazor's eyes narrowed.

"Then help me. Tell me where he's headed, so that I can bring him before the prefect in Caesarea."

"When I see Pilate, I'll cut a deal with Rome. I'll deliver Barabbas in return for my freedom."

"Tell me now." Gaius insisted. He needed to approach Pilate with something concrete. Otherwise he might never be given the opportunity to bring Barabbas in.

"When we get to Caesarea. If you wish, you can tell Pilate that I insist on leading only you to the hideout. But, I'll reveal nothing if I don't have the prefect's guarantee that I walk as a free man once Barabbas is delivered."

Gaius was satisfied. He nodded. "Very well. We'll talk again in Caesarea."

He left Eleazor and went to check on the legionaries' progress with the road excavations.

† † † † †

For the second time in less than half a day, Barabbas and his group of weary men trudged along the road to Jericho. Simeon, Yoseph and Lazarus moved along the road ahead of him. They were dressed in the torn clothes of lepers, as before. Their hair was loose and their faces were covered from the top lip down, in keeping with Jewish customs. A small group of soldiers approached on horseback.

"Unclean! Unclean!" Barabbas yelled. Several of his companions joined in the chorus.

He checked his bag to ensure that his sword was properly hidden. The bag contained a change of clothes as well as his weapons. Most of the men with him carried similar baggage. The Romans were unlikely to search them. Though they didn't have the same concern for ritual cleanliness as the Jewish populace, they still exercised caution at the sound of the calls shouted by carriers of the dreaded disease.

There were numerous forms of leprosy, some contagious and some not. They ranged from mild skin disorders to horrific strains that caused painful scabs all over the body and eventually produced baldness in their victims.

Such strains ate away at their host's flesh, causing unsightly disfigurement. Fingers and toes began to curl and fall off as the nervous system succumbed to the disease. They slowly ate away the upper lips and palates of helpless victims as they progressed. These forms of leprosy were extremely contagious and always terminal.

Barabbas moved off the road and eyeballed the group of soldiers, allowing them to pass by. The legionaries stared back, but their gaze was more wary than searching. Once they had moved on, Barabbas' men hobbled back onto the road. They looked like a forlorn group of mummies, whose bandages had come loose, flapping wildly about them as they moved.

Levi turned to Barabbas. "The men are tired, but we'd better keep moving if we're to reach the *wadi Qumran* by nightfall."

Barabbas nodded. "There'll be time for rest later. For now, we should put as much distance as we can between ourselves and Jerusalem."

They continued in silence. Barabbas plodded forward, fighting his private battle with exhaustion but always scanning his surroundings, looking for any sign of the enemy. It seemed like an eternity, but he finally reached the turnoff to Bethany. Barabbas took a deep breath and sighed in relief. Bethphage was not far off. They could find water there and then proceed to Bethany.

He stopped and turned, gazing back across the Kidron valley, towards Jerusalem. The majestic city stood about a mile to the west. Its towering walls and splendid palaces reached towards the heavens, proclaiming their divine right to a place in the Holy City.

The temple dominated the metropolis, both physically and emotionally. He gazed at it in awe. Apart from covering approximately one eighth of the entire city area, it was the Israelites' very reason for being. It was God's abode on earth and the place where sacrificial atonement for the nation's sins was made.

It was also the one sacred place where Rome could not touch them, as non-Jews were forbidden beyond the court of the Gentiles. Their very presence beyond that court would bring a swift and merciless death. The Jews would not tolerate any unclean person profaning the house of their God.

"Have you ever seen anything so beautiful?" Yoseph breathed as he joined Barabbas, looking down on the city below.

"There is no city like it under the heavens." Barabbas murmured. "How I long to see Jerusalem standing in all its glory, free from Roman tyranny, dedicated once again to God alone."

"It will be a glorious day, my friend. May we both live to see it."

"So be it." Barabbas agreed. "We'd better keep moving. It's still a long way to the *wadi Qumran*."

They circumvented the small towns of Bethphage and Bethany. Lepers, as they appeared to be, were not allowed inside the villages for fear of contaminating fellow Israelites.

After Bethany, the road descended sharply and continuously, winding its way down the steep slopes into the Great Rift Valley that ran from northern Galilee, through the Holy Land and into the Negev desert and beyond.

Barabbas joined his brother, near the front of the group. Simeon was engrossed in thought with a deep furrow in his brow.

"What troubles you, brother?" Barabbas asked, offering him a handful of dates.

"I'm concerned for our fallen comrades." Simeon took the proffered food. "They have no chance of escape now. I fear for them."

"I love Judas and Yochanan like my own family." Barabbas hesitated. "I can't truthfully say I'll miss Eleazor."

Simeon nodded. "You were right to try and save them, Barabbas. At least they will die happy in the knowledge that their brothers did not abandon them."

"Still something bothers you. What is it?"

"I'm worried about Eleazor. He'll blame you for the fact that he was taken. That man bears a grudge."

Barabbas shrugged. "He's in Rome's hands now. The best he can expect is a fair trial followed by a spectacular crucifixion."

I'm less sure of that fact than you. He's a resourceful man and a dangerous one. He could still escape somehow."

"Too many thoughts give cause for too much worry. Believe me. We've seen the last of Eleazor."

✝ ✝ ✝ ✝ ✝

The soldiers covered just under thirty miles before sundown. At last Gaius called a halt and ordered the men to prepare a camp for the night, a few miles south of Antipatris.

Eleazor's mood was morose. It had been a gruelling day and the cool clouds that should have brought relief had instead brought the added aggravation of rain.

The light drizzle had drenched him, soaking through his clothes and chilling his very bones. The soldiers were tired, wet and hungry. Numerous fights had broken out among the legionaries, and some of them had taken their frustration out on him.

Inside the prisoners' tent he brooded over the day's events. The sound of hundreds of trowels echoed outside. The legionaries were digging ditches, fortifying their camp for the night. Gaius was certainly taking no chances.

His thoughts turned to Pontius Pilate and what awaited him in Caesarea. He had to face the inevitable now. Manacled between two legionaries who changed shifts every four hours, he had little hope of escape.

His only prospect lay with Pilate and that was a slim hope indeed. The prefect was not known for his compassion. Eleazor could only trust that Barabbas was worth enough to secure him his freedom.

Qumran. That was where his freedom lay. Barabbas would be found there and, by handing him over to Gaius, he could make good his threat of retribution. It was thanks to Barabbas' arrogance that he was now in the clutches of Rome. He would pay for that.

Eleazor's thoughts turned to the small community nestled in the foothills of the Great Rift Valley, just a couple of miles North West of the Salt Sea. It represented freedom in more ways than one. *Khirbet Qumran* was where his secret lay. He'd nurtured the dream since the age of fifteen. He could remember his father's conversation as if it had happened yesterday. It had been late one Sabbath when he had overheard the men in quiet, earnest chatter.

Their words had filled him with excitement, for they told of a secret that could ignite a multitude of passions in a young man's heart. Since that day it had consumed his every waking moment, for he knew he was one of the few who understood that the legend was true.

He'd spent his subsequent years following the trail, which had first led him to the zealots and then on to *Qumran*. The fact that he was betraying his father's secret meant little to him. Nahor had been an arrogant man, who belittled a son given to fear as a boy.

His taunting had caused a rift of resentment that had blossomed into hatred when Eleazor became a man. On his thirteenth birthday, he had vowed to kill his father when he grew strong enough, but the Romans had robbed him of his chance. When they had quenched the uprising led by Judas the Galilean, Nahor had been taken along with the other men who had led the movement.

That had given Eleazor a second reason for pursuing his goal. He could no longer hurt his father, but he could hurt the man's legacy by destroying what he had stood and worked for. This was an added bonus, however. His chief reason remained the incredible personal gain that this quest would bring to him.

A long trail still lay before him. First he had to bargain for his freedom. Then he could find the man who held the answers to the secret he had worked so long to uncover. Both paths lead to *Qumran*. That was where he would go.

† † † † †

The zealots continued their journey down the steep slopes of the valley, descending below sea level. The clouds above them evaporated, leaving the sky clear and blue. Behind them they could see the slanting grey streaks in the sky over Jerusalem, which now lay beyond the horizon.

"Looks like rain over the Holy City." Simeon murmured as they trudged along.

"Would that was happening here. This sun feels like a smelter's furnace." Barabbas complained. He wiped the stinging sweat from his eyes. Even though it was now low on the horizon, the sun's heat smothered him like an oppressive blanket.

The clouds, blocked by the Mount of Olives and the ridge in which it was situated, disappeared like dew, turning the area beyond into arid steppe lands with little vegetation or rainfall. They were no more than a few miles from Jerusalem, but the land had already become a semi desert with low, sparse scrub and very few trees.

Barabbas followed the path right and moved along the ridge, descending more gradually. To his left the ground fell away sharply, dropping into the flood plain and the lazy, snakelike coils of the Jordan River far below. The plain stood in sharp contrast to the barren hills above it. The area immediately around the river was filled with hardy evergreen shrubs. They grew thickly together, interspersed with patches of thorn scrub, creating an almost impenetrable thicket around the river inching its way southwards to the Sea of Salt.

"It'll be dark soon." Barabbas urged his men to greater speed. He increased his pace, struggling down the treacherous slope. The growing shadows alarmed him. They had to get off these cliffs before dark.

The thick scent of salt in the air told him that they were approaching their destination.

"*Khirbet Qumran* can't be far off now." Simeon said picking his way carefully along the rough, sandy road, deep in the great valley of the Jordan River.

The imposing cliffs of the rift valley towered above them like dark shadows watching their every move as they followed the narrow road to the small Essene community in the *wadi Qumran*.

Yoseph groaned as he walked. "Oh how I long for a dip in their pools and perhaps the comfort of one of the lovely daughters of the Essenes."

Levi chuckled. "We've got little enough welcome among the community without you antagonising them with your carnal appetites."

Yoseph feigned shock. "What? The Essenes love me."

"We love you, Yoseph," Simeon smiled, "but not a man among us would entrust a daughter of ours to your protection."

"Look at this face. It is the picture of innocence. No man could distrust a face such as this."

"Then I submit that you are a consummate actor and should seek employment among the many theatres in Greece or Rome. Only stay away from the Essene women. They're a pious community, even stricter than the Pharisees as regards the law, and far too good for the likes of you."

"We're there." Barabbas interrupted the friendly banter. He pointed to the dim lights of the commune up ahead.

Off to the left, about half a mile away and stretching to the south, the Salt Sea shimmered in the semi-darkness. The extensive buildings of the *Qumran* community lay directly ahead of them. The warm glow of oil lamps flickered through narrow windows. Barabbas could already make out the heavy wooden gates. There seemed to be little sign of movement inside.

An aqueduct flowed parallel to the track on which the men walked, carrying much needed water to the community. He turned off the road onto a narrower track that led to the main entrance. The footpath ran down a short slope, crossed the aqueduct, and hugged the walls of the community leading to the main entrance on the east wall of the dull, brown structure.

The commune stood on a narrow terrace with daunting cliffs towering above it to the west. The ground fell away to the east, where the Salt Sea claimed its position as the lowest place on earth.

"*Shalom*." Levi greeted the guards in the tower near the gate.

"*Shalom*, peace be with you." The men replied. "It's late to still be travelling."

"We've come from beyond Jerusalem. It's been a long journey."

The men remained silent, staring down at the motley band of travellers.

Levi asked. "Is Nathaniel here? We seek rest for the night - and food."

The guards were reluctant, but relaxed at the mention of Nathaniel's name.

One of them came to a decision. Barabbas heard the quiet instruction.

"Fetch Nathaniel. Ask him whether we should admit these men."

The second guard scurried off.

Yoseph tried to make conversation. "It's been a difficult day. The sun beats down heavy on the desert sands."

The guard was noncommittal in his reply. It seemed he was not in the mood for conversation. Presently the second guard returned, accompanied by an elderly scribe.

Nathaniel had a long, greying beard and his skin was thick and leathery, burnt bronze by the desert sun. His face bore the sadness of an extremely pious life, weighed down by the burdens of an Israelite nation that had turned away from its God.

He peered from the low tower in a feeble attempt to make out the features of his visitors.

"Who is that?" He enquired in a strained, hoarse voice.

"Levi and a group of zealots from Jerusalem."

The old man relaxed and smiled. "*Shalom*, Levi. It's good to see you again."

"*Shalom*, old friend. It's good to be back."

The elderly scribe turned to the aloof, young guard. "It's alright Mattithyahu. They're friends. We can let them in."

Mattithyahu dutifully came down from the tower and opened the gate for Barabbas and his companions. Nathaniel bustled down the steps after him.

"Come in, come in. You must be tired from your travels."

"We've not slept for two days."

"I'll get the women to prepare some food for you. In the meantime, I'll take you to the bath house, where you can wash."

"Thank you, my friend. The Lord knows we need it." Levi expressed the group's gratitude.

Nathaniel ushered them through the dimly lit passages and into the bath house, where they disrobed and sank gratefully into the water, still warm from the heat of the day.

He eyed the rough bandages covering their injuries. His expression was sad, although he never voiced his judgements.

"I'll send somebody to dress your wounds. When you're done, come through to the dining hall. I'll have your dinner ready for you."

Later that evening, Barabbas and his companions devoured a delicious meal that had been hastily prepared. There were small, dried fish all the way from Galilee and a delicious assortment of fruits to choose from. The meal ended with large chunks of freshly baked bread, dipped in honey. A tasty, sweet dish to round off their meal.

Simeon and Barabbas were among the last to retire. They finally excused themselves, leaving Levi and Nathaniel talking alone at the table. The rest had improved Simeon's mood.

"The blow you delivered on Rome was telling, Barabbas. We have to build on the victory of yesterday's battle."

Barabbas frowned. "Victory! We lost three men and the barracks in Jerusalem still stands unscathed."

"It stands, but it's not unscathed. Don't forget, this morning Jerusalem awoke with the smoke of a smouldering barracks still hanging thick in the air."

"Smoke is meaningless. They should have woken to the sight of a pile of rubble lying on the corpses of five hundred soldiers."

Simeon shook his head. "You think too much in absolutes, brother. Consider the morale of the population once word of the strike gets out. One man - you - attacked the Roman garrison and survived. You didn't destroy it, but, for a moment, you brought Rome to her knees in the Holy City."

"Three men."

"An entire Roman garrison buckled and four hundred men routed by eight zealot warriors. Can you imagine what a zealot army could accomplish? That's going to be the foremost thought in every man's mind in Jerusalem tonight - the main topic around every dinner table."

Barabbas was silent. He knew his brother was right, but he refused to gloat over the victory while three of his comrades faced execution.

Simeon continued. "Already, I'll wager, thousands of men are flocking like sheep to their shepherd, seeking to fight alongside the man called Barabbas. You've become the people's hero."

Barabbas shook his head, refusing to look his brother in the eye.

Simeon grabbed his arm. "Our three comrades gave their lives so that thousands would join the cry and take up arms against Rome. Don't you see it? This is what we've been waiting for. Israel has never been so ready for her freedom. It's going to happen."

Barabbas pondered his brother's words. "It's true. The people are ripe for an uprising."

"All they need is a leader who will take them to victory. You're that leader, Barabbas. Call for men now and they will come in their droves. Let them swear allegiance to you and we could raise an army that will overthrow Rome. Then we can finally lay our father's spirit to rest."

Barabbas grinned. "Let's talk again in the morning. I'm too tired to start an uprising now."

Simeon chuckled and then cursed. "I forgot the bag with my sword in the dining hall. I'll just go back and get it."

"That kind of stupidity could cost you your life one day. Wait, I'll come with you."

Barabbas quickly caught up with his brother. As they approached the dining hall, they could hear the animated voices of Levi and Nathaniel. The two men were in earnest conversation.

"I tell you, he knows something. Much more than he ought to."

"It's impossible." Barabbas recognised Levi's voice. "All of us were sworn to secrecy. I would trust every one of those men with my very life, God rest their souls. None would have breathed a word."

"Well somebody did. He asked some very pertinent questions. He even knew of the existence of the scroll."

"What did you tell him?"

"Nothing, of course. I was sworn to secrecy, just like the rest of you. Perhaps even more so."

"It's true. It was always in your care."

"Levi, I fear the cunning behind those dark eyes. He knew I was hiding the truth. It was as if he could read the very depths of my soul. Maybe the time has come to move it."

"Move what?" Barabbas asked casually.

The men whirled around. They looked horror-stricken at the realization of their predicament.

"How much did you hear?" Nathaniel choked out the words. His face was a mask of terror.

Simeon replied quietly. "Enough to know we shouldn't have heard any."

Levi quickly composed himself. "Swear to me that you will never repeat anything you've heard here tonight."

"How can we trust these men? They have no understanding of the matter, or its importance." Nathaniel blustered.

"It's alright, Nathaniel they can be trusted. These men are the sons of Cephas, of Gamala.

Nathaniel stared wide eyed at the two young men. First he examined Simeon, then Barabbas. There was a new respect in his eyes when he spoke again.

"I should have recognised the eyes." He murmured. "First gold, then bronze as the light changes. Barabbas, you truly are the son of your father."

Then he turned to Simeon. "The young boy I met so many years ago has become a man. You've followed in your father's footsteps, I see. Levi, I've seen these men before. Why did you not tell me who they were?"

Levi shrugged. "It wasn't important. I only told you now to set your mind at rest."

Nathaniel's features creased in a benign smile. "Your father was a good man, devout and righteous before the Lord in all his ways. I mourned his loss and wept for the family he left behind."

"Thank you." Simeon said quietly.

"Where did you bury him?" asked the old man.

"We didn't. He was taken in chains to Caesarea after the soldiers beat him senseless in front of my brother and me. We were forced to stand and watch, along with our mother, as they tortured him and plucked his beard. I followed them to Caesarea to ask for his body. They told me he had been burned, along with the others. Nobody would reveal where the bodies were buried."

"How old were you at the time?"

"I was twelve years old. My brother was five. I raised him in the way of the zealots. The way our father would have wanted it."

Nathaniel glanced across at Levi, then back at the two brothers. "You must swear to us that you will never repeat anything you heard here."

Levi rose from his seat. He glanced at the brothers and then looked down, deep in thought. It was several seconds before he spoke. "Maybe - maybe the time has come to share our secret."

The elderly scholar shook his head. "The fewer who know, the better it is for us."

"Please, Nathaniel. Neither of us is getting any younger. The others have all died. What if something was to happen to us?"

"There are two others besides us."

"One I know. He is a deserter, who left the zealots and walked away from his responsibilities. He can't be trusted. I know nothing of the other."

"I chose him from among the Essenes. He will be my replacement when I'm gone."

"Passive men, Nathaniel. Right now the scroll is in danger of being discovered. It needs warriors to protect it. These men are the finest fighters I know."

Nathaniel frowned and shook his head. "What is it with this penchant for violence?"

"Would you rather see the scroll discovered? Rather it fell into self seeking hands? These men are the sons of Cephas. He was one of us. A protector of the scroll."

"The secret is not an inheritance to be passed on from the father to the sons, you know that."

"Yes, I know. It's to be passed on to honourable men - men who will give their lives to protect it. These are such men. They already know of it. Don't you think it would be better if they at least understood it?"

Nathaniel glared at the table, tapping his finger on the rough surface as he considered Levi's words. It was a heavy decision that he was contemplating. Finally he looked up.

"Before I tell you anything, you will swear an oath, as your father did, to protect this secret with your very life. You will not breathe it to another living soul unless they first take a similar oath. Even then you must only choose honourable men who have proved that they are worthy of the secret."

Barabbas glanced at his brother. He saw the excitement he felt reflected in Simeon's eyes. Here was a memory of their father that they had never known. It was an opportunity to walk in his footsteps - to protect his legacy by guarding a secret that he had held dear.

He answered the scholar. "I swear it. I shall protect the secret with my very life. I'll show myself worthy, just as my father before me."

Simeon swore a similar oath and Nathaniel nodded, satisfied.

"Very well. I need a knife."

Simeon opened his palm frond bag and took out his sword. "Will this do?"

Nathaniel pulled up his right sleeve to show the siblings his forearm. "All the protectors are identified by a scar. If you'd looked, you would have seen one on the arm of Mattithyahu, at the gate."

Barabbas turned in shock to Levi. "You told me you received your scar in a battle during the Galilean uprising."

Levi scowled. "What part of your oath did you not understand?"

Nathaniel interrupted. "Give me your arm."

Barabbas held out his right arm for Nathaniel, who took the sword and cut a deep, semicircular scar half way along the upper side of Barabbas' forearm. Blood gushed from the wound. Barabbas winced slightly. Levi stepped forward with a hastily torn piece of cloth from his tunic and bandaged the wound tightly to stem the scarlet flow.

"Better keep that arm covered. You don't want to be forced to answer awkward questions from the rest of the men tomorrow."

Nathaniel turned to Simeon, who offered his arm for the covenant cut. When the ritual was over, Nathaniel turned to face both brothers. Levi walked to the door, where he made sure they would not be overheard.

The scholar began his story. "The secret dates back to the time of the Maccabees, long before Rome and the Caesars. In his war with Antiochus IV, Judas Maccabeus was assisted by the *Hassidim,* the righteous ones. These men were warrior priests who refused to bow to the foreign gods that were forced upon the Israelites."

"I know the story," Barabbas said. "The Seleucids even erected an idol to their god, Zeus, in the temple of Jerusalem."

Nathaniel nodded. "The *Hassidim* fought alongside Judas Maccabeus and won back much of Israel. Their greatest victory was when they took back the Holy City and destroyed the idol in the temple. They also took much treasure from the Seleucids, which was to be dedicated to the Temple and the Holy One of Israel. This never happened, however. Jonathan, the wicked priest, was made high priest of all Israel and many of the *Hassidim* withdrew. They took with them the secret of the Seleucid riches and then banded together to form the Essenes."

"Warrior priests, the fathers of the Essenes." Simeon exhaled audibly.

"Over the years we changed. Some were more militant, while others were more concerned with the scriptures. Eventually, the warriors and priests separated. The factions split, but one small core remained united in their shared secret."

Barabbas interrupted. "So the Essenes no longer know of the secret?"

Nathaniel shook his head. "Neither do the zealots. Only a small group of protectors remained. Your father was among the protectors in the last generation."

"Who were the others?"

"Judas, the man who led the uprising, Levi, Nahor, of Gamala —"

"Nahor?" Barabbas murmured. He knew the name, but was unable to place it.

"The father of Eleazor." Simeon reminded him.

The mention of Eleazor's name lit a fire in the old man's pale and weak eyes. "The son is not like the father."

"He certainly lacks his father's courage." Barabbas said bitterly.

Levi spoke quietly from his vantage point at the door. "It's his lack of honour that concerns us. He's consumed with greed. It's what Nathaniel and I were talking about when you walked in and overheard us."

Barabbas was puzzled. "What's the problem? He's not a protector, surely."

Nathaniel shook his head. The deep concern showed in his clouded expression. "Somehow he found out about the treasure. He confronted me and asked me about it. I told him nothing, but he knew I was hiding the truth. I could see it in his eyes."

"What did he want to know?"

"He was cunning. He masqueraded as a protector. Unfortunately for him, he lacked the telltale scar. His questions were indirect, carefully worded to sound innocent, but his motives were obvious."

"I have a question." Simeon spoke quietly.

"Ask." Nathaniel nodded.

"Why is this treasure so important? What is it being protected for?"

"We await the one who is to come - the Messiah of Israel. The treasure will be used to establish his kingdom."

"It must be a vast treasure indeed that will finance the establishment of a kingdom." Simeon murmured.

"You have no idea how vast. It contains more silver and gold than you can possibly imagine. However, its true power goes far beyond mere financial wealth."

"In what way?" Barabbas asked.

"You know enough. The less you are able to reveal, the safer our secret remains."

"Can you, at least, tell us where it's kept?"

Nathaniel sighed. "The scroll tells the secret. You are protectors of the scroll. It's hidden in the scriptorium. Only one man, besides me, knows where. If anything should happen to me, seek out Mattithyahu. He'll tell you where to find it."

"Besides us and Mattithyahu, who are the other protectors of the secret?"

Levi interrupted the scribe. "There is only one other still alive. Forget about him. He left the zealots and his responsibilities to the secret of the scroll. The last I heard, he'd become a follower of some new teacher - a man from Nazareth who travels all over Galilee proclaiming his message of peace."

Barabbas nodded thoughtfully. He knew the man Levi spoke of. There were not many, among the zealots, who had converted to this man's teachings. In fact, Barabbas could think of only one – a friend from his past that he had vowed to forget. Simon, the convert – had left the movement a few years earlier to follow the rabbi from Nazareth. Barabbas had taken his friend's conversion as a personal betrayal and their parting had been bitter. Like Levi, he preferred to think of their former comrade as dead.

Nathaniel interrupted his train of thought. "One more thing. Should you ever uncover the treasure, be careful what you do with it. It's to be presented to the Messiah, and his most trusted followers. The *Hassidim* proclaimed a curse on all those who would use the treasure for their own gain.

"Such men will be tormented in their souls until their own lusts destroy them. Their enemies shall rise up like an army about them. Their days will be consumed with agony and their nights with fear and weeping. They will end their years in suffering and none shall mourn their passing. That is the curse of the treasure and the scroll."

5

THE FOLLOWING morning, Barabbas awoke early. He listened carefully for the sound that had awakened him. There it was again. The quiet patter of feet on the cold, stone floor and the soft murmur of conversation.

The devout *Qumran* community was awake and moving about. Early morning prayers were an essential part of their ascetic way of life.

Barabbas was completely alert. To awaken slowly could mean death to a zealot. He could not afford the luxuries of heavy sleep. His thoughts turned to the previous night's conversation. Excitement welled up in him at the thought of his newfound purpose. *Protector of the Maccabee's treasure and the copper scroll.* How he longed for the day when he could retrieve the treasure and present it to Israel's Messiah. He smiled at the thought.

His meditation was interrupted as the men about him began to stir. All the zealots shared the same sleeping quarters and they were all light sleepers. Good men. He was honoured to have them fighting at his side. He glanced over at Simeon, who was lying on his back, staring vacantly at the ceiling.

Barabbas was the first to speak. "The Romans will be looking for us in the more remote places now."

Simeon nodded. "We'd do well to leave as soon as possible."

Just then Yoseph burst into the room. He was panting for breath and his complexion was pale.

"Romans!" he spluttered. "They're approaching from the north."

"Move!" Barabbas exclaimed. "Get your belongings and melt."

The men pounced from their sleeping mats, snatching for their *abeyahs,* shawl-like coats that doubled as blankets. They rolled up the mats and raced for the exit. Barabbas could already hear the approaching Roman Equites dismounting outside the main gate.

"Quickly." Levi urged. "There's another exit down at the other end of the bath house."

"But they can still see us from that side." Simeon's whisper sounded like a rasp on iron.

"Do you have a better idea?" Levi snapped.

Simeon stared at him for a moment, then turned and raced towards the bathhouse. All the men dashed frantically down the passage after him. Barabbas feared for more than their own lives. If they were discovered here, the Romans would not hesitate to destroy the entire Essene community.

They had to find a way out. Hundreds of innocent lives were at risk. Peaceful men and women who sought no harm, but merely offered hospitality to a group of men who had needed a place to rest for the night.

† † † † †

The rain had slowed to a light drizzle, though the blanket of cloud still hung ominously low in the sky. The weary soldiers trudged mile after interminable mile, their boots beating a sombre rhythm on the muddy road that led to Caesarea.

Gaius glanced back at his prisoners. Two were talking quietly together, while the third gazed disinterestedly at the contrasting landscape. The undulating hills reflected, and finally merged with the charcoal clouds at the horizon.

The smell of the Mediterranean began to permeate the air, growing stronger with each mile. The scent filled Gaius with mixed feelings. It signalled the end of his journey, but who knew what awaited him there?

He crested the last hill and set eyes on the majestic city of Caesarea for the first time. A murmur of relief rose from among the legionaries behind him.

The colossal *praetorium* overlooked the man-made harbour. It stood several stories higher than the surrounding buildings. The palatial structure was the prefect's residence in the province and represented Rome's supreme authority over the Jewish nation. It was also where he would hand the prisoners over for trial.

His gaze moved from the palace to the second feature for which the city was famous - the large harbour with its two monumental blocks of concrete that formed the breakwater. Its construction had been a fantastic feat, as the shore didn't form a natural port. Giant, ash grey swells foamed white as angry waves lashed out at the stone breakwaters blocking their path to the shore. Their turbulence reflected Gaius' mood.

His career hung in the balance. Jerusalem's barracks had been penetrated and Pilate would be looking for a scapegoat. There was a chance he'd be sent back to Rome in disgrace. What would he do? Gaius considered his future. His father owned a small plot near Pompeii, in the south of Italy. He could always rejoin his family and work the land. It was a respectable job and would give him some standing in the local community.

No. He was a soldier first and last. Perhaps one day he would retire to the farm, but he was still far too young. He loved the army. He was good at his job and he would not give up all his career prospects because of one man's treachery.

The Roman guard entered the city and made its way though the streets and up the path that led to the *praetorium*. The sun was nothing more than a dull white disk behind the oppressive wall of cloud that hung over the city and extended to the horizon. Darkness was premature. It felt like early evening, even though the sun had not yet set.

Still, work for the day was over. He would join his men in the *thermae*, baths, after handing the prisoners over and face Pilate in the morning. It was only when he arrived at the praetorium that he learned how wrong that assumption was.

† † † † †

Inside, the *praetorium* was even more majestic. The interior was a vision of marble and mosaic. Walls teemed with pictures - false windows - depicting life outside the palace. There were scenes of people bartering in the market place, inspecting goods as they decided upon their purchases. Huge marble pillars supported high ceilings and statues of Greek gods and Roman Emperors lined the walls of the court. It was the picture of splendour and opulence.

Exits led to exquisite gardens filled with ponds and fountains driven by water from the two large aqueducts that supplied the city. The gardens were filled with beautiful trees and a myriad of colourful plants with a variety of shapes and textures. Peacocks strutted between the lush foliage, decorating the beds with their spectacular plumage, as they pierced the serenity with their intermittent screeching.

A clerk appeared in the main hall to meet Gaius and his party. The man was short, slightly built and wore a small, pointed beard. "The prefect wishes to see you at once. He left strict orders to have you summoned immediately upon your arrival."

The man had an air of self importance about him that Gaius found instantly annoying. "Surely the prefect meant for me to report to him after securing the prisoners in their quarters."

The clerk shook his head. "He was very clear on the matter. You are to see him the moment you enter the palace."

Gaius was irritable. "Alright, I'll see him. But I warn you. These are dangerous men. They infiltrated and escaped from the Roman barracks in Jerusalem and they can do the same here. Would you like to explain to the prefect that they escaped under your charge, while I was seeing him in his quarters?"

The frail man shrank before Gaius' glare. No, he did not wish to explain. He didn't even want responsibility for the prisoners.

"I thought as much." Gaius' lips smiled, but his eyes were cold as the marble pillars that lined the giant hall. "Would you like to show me to the dungeons, so I can have these men secured?"

"Um, of course." The man led him through one of the gardens, across to a second block that housed the dungeons.

Later, having secured the prisoners in their stocks and freshened up with a quick wash and a change of clothes, Gaius followed the clerk, whose name was Quintus, to the prefect's quarters.

Quintus was agitated. "You said you were securing the prisoners, not washing and changing as well."

Gaius ignored the remark and strode on ahead, leaving the pompous man to catch up. He knew what Pilate was trying to do and he was damned if he would give him the advantage by appearing dishevelled, uncomfortable and unkempt before the prefect.

They arrived at the heavy, wooden door to the prefect's private chambers. Gaius pushed past Quintus and knocked, smiling at the scowl of disapproval it brought.

A dark haired slave answered and ushered him into the room. Quintus was not invited and Gaius was glad to be rid of him.

He was led into a large atrium that served as a reception hall. In the centre was a small, square pond with a rectangular table behind it, made of marble. Above the pond, the roof was open, forming a square skylight.

Several exits with purple drapes led off the atrium. The drapes spoke of the residence's opulence. They were coloured with an extremely rare and expensive dye that was valued more highly than gold. Only royalty or the extremely wealthy could afford to wear purple, let alone adorn their houses with large, purple drapes.

Beyond the atrium was a study with a round table and soft, comfortable chairs, covered with a thick, maroon material. The chairs were large, with high backs and arm rests. They were designed more for falling back and lying in than sitting.

Pontius Pilate lounged in one of the chairs on the far side of the table. He was a wiry man with a large, beak nose. His straight hair was cropped short and his eyes were thin slits - mere cracks above the sharply contoured nose. He didn't bother to rise.

"You weren't in any hurry to arrive, were you?" Pilate's voice seemed out of place in his thin, slightly feeble body. It was clear, deep and resonant. The voice of a born orator.

Gaius feigned misunderstanding. "It's a two day march from Jerusalem, prefect. Nobody could do it in less." He was being careful. The Roman political arena was as violent as any amphitheatre and the combatants more dangerous than even the most battle hardened gladiators.

"I meant after you arrived at the *praetorium*. You've been here over an hour already. Why did you not come to see me immediately, as I requested?"

"I was securing the prisoners, making sure there was no chance of their escape."

Pilate raised his eyebrows. "It took you an hour to secure prisoners in the stocks?"

"Perhaps if your staff weren't harassing me at every turn —"

"What staff!"

"Your clerk, Quintus, plain refused to leave me alone to do my job. He kept on at me about coming to see you."

"Then why didn't you listen to him and respect my wish to see you immediately?" Pilate's voice was harsh and now raised.

Gaius felt smug. He smiled. "I offered to. He refused to accept responsibility for the prisoners in my absence. I was left with no choice but to secure them myself. Then there was his constant whining and interrupting, not to mention getting in the way."

Pilate held Gaius' gaze, summing the centurion up. After a moment, he nodded, almost imperceptibly. Whatever judgement he came to, he kept to himself.

"Sit down." he said quietly, indicating the other chair at the marble table.

Gaius moved to the chair and sat down on the edge. He would not lean back into the seat. Pilate was not a man one could afford to be relaxed around.

The prefect continued. "Your letter was quite an interesting read. Insurgents in Jerusalem. Arson in the Roman barracks. And no trace of the perpetrator. One man nearly destroys the entire garrison in Jerusalem and then vanishes without a trace."

"It wasn't one man, prefect. He had help. We managed to capture three."

"Three? Your letter said two men were captured."

"There was a rescue attempt on the road between Jerusalem and Antipatris. It failed and we took another prisoner."

"The main perpetrator is still at large and unidentified, however."

"His name is Barabbas. I've seen him and I would recognise him again if given the opportunity." Gaius had deliberately withheld this information in his letter. He'd wanted to see its effect when delivered in person.

"How? It was pitch dark according to your letter."

"It was dark, but not as pitch. There was a large fire burning. His eyes were the most unusual I've ever seen. Golden or bronze, depending on the light."

"So you can recognise him. He's still at large. By now he could be half way to Egypt."

Gaius' confidence was growing. "I don't think so, prefect. He's a zealot, a freedom fighter. It's not in his nature to flee. He'll hide - bide his time - and when he thinks the moment's right, he'll strike again. As long as Rome rules Judea, Barabbas will work to overthrow her."

Pilate frowned in thought before replying. "That attitude, combined with his resourcefulness, makes him an extremely dangerous man." He paused for effect. "And you let him get away."

Gaius felt he was guilty on that count, but he refused to apologise or defend himself. Pilate was a bully; such a defence would merely invite further attack.

Pilate tapped his chin and stared at the fountain outside. "What should I say to Caesar in Rome? That I'm incapable of ruling my province because of the incompetence of my centurion in Jerusalem?"

Gaius made no reply. He merely maintained his gaze.

Pilate continued. "A centurion who allowed a Jewish national to march into the very heart of the Roman barracks and destroy it. And then to walk out and make good his escape! Do you think that was competent, centurion?"

"I can make up for it, if given the chance."

"How? You can't even guard the roof over your head." The irony dripped like bitter mead from Pilate's lips.

"One of the prisoners is willing to give us information in return for his freedom. He's willing to give us Barabbas."

Pilate gazed impassively at Gaius for a moment before replying. He raised his eyebrows. "It seems you forgot an incredible amount of detail in the letter you sent me."

"It's the prisoner we captured on the road to Antipatris. I didn't have the information in Jerusalem."

"Where is this Barabbas then?" Although the question was nonchalant, the hope glimmered in Pilate's eyes.

"He said he would lead me there, but only after he's received a pardon from you. He knew I didn't have the power to grant him a reprieve."

"Is he dangerous?"

Gaius leaned back in his chair. The battle was over. He'd won; his career was safe.

"Yes, but less so than Barabbas. He's not as proactive and extremely self-seeking. My guess is, once free, he'll flee Judea for fear of the zealots. When they find out he betrayed Barabbas his life will hold little value in the province."

"You make it sound certain they'll find out. Am I to assume that you would have a hand in that?"

"The thought had crossed my mind."

Pilate smiled. "That way we can legitimately grant him his freedom and then let the zealots take care of getting rid of the aggravation. What's this man's name?"

"Eleazor."

Pilate leaned forward, picking up a silver chalice of wine from the large marble table. He leaned back, taking a long sip from the cup. "Now, if this Eleazor's information proves correct and we can find Barabbas, you have an opportunity to redeem yourself. Bring me Barabbas and I'll leave out your indiscretion at the barracks in my next report to Rome."

"All I ask is the chance to catch him, prefect."

"See that you do." Pilate's voice bit like an arctic wind. "If you fail me again, I'll have you banished to Gaul, or worse. You'll spend the rest of your miserable life wishing you'd never met me. Do you understand, soldier?"

"Yes, prefect." Gaius smiled back at Pontius Pilate.

The prefect continued to glare at him through narrow eyes. Gaius was pleased to see that the man was irked by the grin and confident way in which he held his gaze.

"You can go now." Pilate said quietly. "Have the first two prisoners sent to my chambers for sentencing."

Gaius was suddenly confused. "Prefect, how can we try them at night? People are not available - there's no official court."

"Did I say something about a trial? They're insurgents involved in an uprising and they will pay for their crimes right now."

"Prefect, we can't do this. Our laws state —"

"I am the law in Judea!" Pilate shrieked, throwing his wine chalice against the wall. His face was suddenly flushed and his eyes blazed like a pillaged city. "Remember your place, soldier. Your career hangs in the balance and I have the power to save or destroy you. You're in no position to question my orders. Now go and fetch the two prisoners. When I'm done with them, you can bring me the third. Then I suggest you get a good night's sleep. I intend to dispatch you at dawn, with a force of men to capture the elusive Barabbas."

Gaius hesitated, and then nodded quietly. Pilate leaned back in his chair. A deep frown furrowed his brow as he looked at the spilled wine on the floor. He waved his hand dismissively at the door, refusing to acknowledge the centurion again. Gaius turned and strode from the room. Behind him, he felt Pontius Pilate's glowering eyes boring into his back.

† † † † †

When Gaius was gone, the prefect called for his clerk. Quintus entered, obsequious and fawning. He danced nervously before Pilate with a brittle smile on his face.

"You called for me, prefect?"

"Tell me, has Secundus, the slaver, sailed for Spain yet?"

"Not as far as I know, prefect. I heard he intends to leave in the morning, with the tide."

"Good. Invite him to my quarters for dinner, will you? There are two Jews - condemned men who won't be missed. I'd like to see whether he and I can come to an agreement on a price for their sale."

Quintus hurried away. Pilate's thoughts turned to the centurion. Although he knew the man by reputation, this was the first time he'd actually met him. The meeting had left him with a sour taste in his mouth. He loathed the man's self-confidence and fearlessness. It was the courage of a true soldier.

Pilate had, himself, served a compulsory tour of duty in the Roman army. Being born of the patrician upper class, he'd been commissioned by Caesar as a tribune in one of the Spanish legions. He'd been a terrible soldier, with no understanding of strategy or tactics and had never succeeded in the military. In fact, he'd detested every moment he had spent there.

When his tour of service had ended, he had decided to pursue a career in politics. It was there that Pontius Pilate had found his true vocation. He'd thrived in the devious nature of political life, supporting the right men at the right time and stepping on others as he climbed the treacherous rungs of the Roman political ladder.

The same dark haired slave that had met Gaius at the door, returned and began clearing away the mess of spilled wine on the floor. The prefect ignored him and rose to prepare for his meeting with Secundus. He had not seen the Jewish rebels yet, but had high hopes for his impending meeting. The men were warriors and obviously in good physical health. They would fetch a fine price in the markets of Rome and further west, in the many mines that littered Gaul and Western Europe.

✝ ✝ ✝ ✝ ✝

Later that evening Pontius Pilate reclined on a long chair around his dinner table. His purple braided toga was thrown carelessly at the foot of the chair as he weighed a large leather moneybag in his hand, with a satisfied grin.

"I always feel so much happier when a condemned man brings such unexpected financial reward." He purred as Quintus bustled about him.

"They certainly fetched a handsome price, prefect."

Pilate smiled with a satisfied nod. "And it's comforting to know they'll spend the last years of their lives rotting away in a tin mine in Spain."

"A fitting end to the upstarts who would try to overthrow a great empire such as Rome."

"Mmm." Pilate murmured. He stared lovingly at the moneybag. "You'll be sure there's no sign of their names on any of the official records."

"Absolutely, prefect. As far as Rome is concerned, they were never here."

"Good. Tell that centurion he can bring in the third prisoner. I'm ready for him now."

"Very well, prefect. I'll do it at once." He left the room in search of Gaius.

Pilate returned to the atrium and disappeared into the side chamber on the left, drawing aside the expensive purple curtain. A door was concealed behind it and he extracted a key from his belt to unlock it. The door creaked slightly as he opened it.

Once inside, he lit a lamp that hung against the thick stone wall. The room was filled with heavy, iron chests. They all stood about waist high and had intricate patterns adorning their sides. Pilate unlocked one of the safes with a disk like key. It was filled with turgid bags of coins. Silver and gold from the sale of condemned men, or excess tribute elicited from taxpayers. The safes also contained many gifts of cash given by businessmen in need of a favour, or a blind eye.

He glanced about the dimly lit room as he locked away his ill-gotten gain and then doused the lamp and left, locking the door behind him. He tucked the key away in his belt as he returned to the atrium.

At the dinner table he leaned back on one elbow. A bony knee protruded from his tunic as he swigged down more wine.

He waited. It wasn't long before there was a knock at the door. Gaius entered the room with Eleazor walking just ahead of him. The Jew's ankles were fettered in iron chains which effectively crippled him, making running impossible. His expression was surly, but Pilate noted the dark intelligence behind the eyes.

"Please sit down, centurion." Pilate motioned to a chair. Then he addressed Eleazor who stood at the other side of the table.

"I understand you have information that may interest me."

"It's information of great value. Not passing interest, prefect."

Pilate raised his eyebrows. "I think you should let me be the judge of that. Now tell me what you believe is so valuable."

"I'll give you the information in exchange for my freedom - nothing less."

"I'll give you whatever I feel it's worth. Now tell me. What is it you're selling?"

"The names of the zealot group that attacked the Roman barracks on the night before last and the whereabouts of their leader, Barabbas."

Pilate feigned disinterest. He had long since learned never to accept the first offer in a negotiation. By trivialising the value, more information would be forthcoming.

"What makes you think I have an interest in finding this Barabbas and his band of ruffians?"

The Jew's surprise showed in his expression. Pilate was pleased. The man had not expected this reaction.

Eleazor blurted. "Prefect, he's the most dangerous man among the zealots. Not only is he extremely efficient, but he draws others to follow him. It's like watching a sorcerer at work. He mesmerises and entrances men to the point that they'll do anything he says. Surely such a man is a great threat to Rome."

Pilate waved a dismissive hand. "Your mythical tales hold little interest for me. No single man is so powerful that he can overthrow the might of an empire. This – Barabbas – is nothing more than a common criminal. Furthermore, he's an embarrassment to me. By producing him I have to admit to Caesar that one man nearly caused the collapse of half the city garrison in Jerusalem. Do you think I'm going to risk my political career by displaying such weakness to Rome?"

"If you don't take him it will get worse. Even as we speak, men are rallying to the zealots' cause. They see in Barabbas the saviour of Israel. If you don't capture him and parade him before the Jewish nation you'll have a revolt on your hands that will pale this embarrassment into insignificance."

Pilate shook his head. "You don't understand me at all. Where politics is concerned, a crushed revolt looks far better than a single incident in which one man humiliated a Roman garrison."

He glanced at Gaius. Pilate knew this turn of events must come as a shock to the centurion. Gaius showed no surprise, however. He merely watched the proceedings with detached interest.

Eleazor's reaction was somewhat different. The man looked pale and his eyes betrayed the fear he felt. There was a slight quiver in the man's upper lip as he opened his mouth to speak. He stopped, thinking better of it.

Pilate smiled, baring his fangs like a coiled cobra as he continued. "Now what was it you really came to tell me?"

If he applied enough pressure, created enough fear, the man would break. Perhaps there was another useful piece of information the Jew was willing to part with.

Eleazor swallowed. "I can give you the names of our contacts in various cities, methods of communication."

Pilate winced and shook his head. "Just more of the same thing. An averted rebellion won't even be reported in Rome. Blood running in the streets, however - now that will get me the undivided attention of Caesar himself. Was this the information you prized so highly?"

Eleazor glanced wildly at Gaius and then back at the prefect.

Pontius Pilate waited a moment before calling. "Quintus."

The short, scholarly man entered the room. "Yes, prefect?"

Pilate waved towards Eleazor. "Take this human refuse back to the dungeons. He's an insurgent involved in a plot to overthrow Rome. Have him tortured and then crucified. I want him buried, along with his conspirators before sunrise."

"Yes, prefect." The clerk grinned broadly and took Eleazor's collar. He jerked him towards the door.

"You'd better go with them, centurion. We don't want our prisoner to escape.

Gaius rose and moved to open the door for Quintus.

Eleazor glanced wildly about him. Pilate watched with detached interest. The man looked like a bird in a cat's grasp. *Increase the fear.*

This was it. The Jew's last chance for freedom was slipping away. Any moment now, he would break. Then he'd reveal something of true worth.

He was already through the door. Pilate felt a twinge of doubt. Perhaps the man truly had no more to offer. With a sudden lurch, the prisoner grabbed the chain on his collar and wrenched it from Quintus' grasp. He dived back into the room. The centurion's movements were cat-like. In a trice, he knocked the prisoner down and pinned him to the floor. He held his drawn sword to the man's throat.

"Wait, prefect. Please listen to me. I have more information." Eleazor choked out the words.

Pilate looked up enquiringly. "Better hurry. Dawn approaches and your tomb is still empty."

"It concerns the Maccabee's treasure." He coughed as Gaius jerked him to his feet.

Pilate sighed and shook his head. "Another myth. I read the report written by the procurator, Coponius, during the Galilean uprising. He recorded the words of a dying Jew. The man spoke of a vast fortune, called the Maccabee's treasure, but never said where it was hidden. Coponius put it down to the ravings of a tortured man. He claimed it was little more than a legend."

"It's much more than that, prefect. It's real. My father knew of it first hand, before he died in that same uprising. There is a group of men who are still alive. They know where the treasure is hidden. I heard them discussing it one night, a long time ago."

Pilate leaned forward in his chair. The deadpan expression that had served him so well throughout his career was gone. His eyes were wide and his lip trembled with excitement. "What do you know of this treasure? Who are these men?"

"They're the protectors of a scroll. It's a copper scroll, penned by five men - the original protectors of the Maccabee's treasure. They wrote a detailed account of the treasure's inventory and where it is hidden. That scroll lies in their custody. It will lead you to the treasure."

"Where is it hidden! I want you to take me to it." Pilate demanded.

"In return for my life and my freedom." A measure of composure had returned to Eleazor.

"Where is this copper scroll?" Pilate pressed him. He was on his feet now, approaching Eleazor, consumed with his own greed.

"I don't know," he said, "But I can point you to the man who does."

"Then tell me. Who is he?"

Eleazor hesitated, but only for an instant, before replying. "The man you seek is the one I offered to give you. Barabbas. He'll be able to tell you where the scroll is hidden. Be forewarned, though. He's as stubborn as he is destructive. He won't give it up without a fight."

"Even a mule can be made to pull a plough. Tell me where he is."

"I have yet to see a letter guaranteeing my freedom."

"I can have someone transcribe one any time and sign it."

"Good. When you do, I'll lead you to Barabbas. Not before."

"Why can't you tell us now?" Pilate still did not trust the Jew.

"His hideout is too well hidden. Even if I told you where to look, you'd probably never find it. If you want him, we'll have to move quickly. There's no telling how long he'll stay there. After he leaves it could be months or even years before we trace him again."

Pilate made his decision quickly. "You'll leave at first light tomorrow. Quintus, I want you to draft a letter granting this man his freedom as soon as he delivers Barabbas to Gaius here. Take him back to the dungeons, but see to it that he's treated well."

Levi peered cautiously through the door and up the north side of the wall, to where a few soldiers milled about, watching the horses.

Barabbas whispered behind him. "Who are they?"

Levi shrugged. "Just a standard search party. Possibly the same one we saw on the road yesterday. They've been travelling for miles. You can see the dust caking their uniforms."

"Why can't we just borrow some clothes and join the community for prayer?" Joshua whispered behind him.

Levi shook his head. "That's the first place they'd look. Even with a change of clothes, we'd stand out like a city on a hill."

"There's no guarantee we'll be discovered."

"There's no guarantee we won't. Look at Barabbas' face. When was the last time you saw an Essene that was clean shaven?"

"What about the aqueduct?" Simeon suggested.

Levi groaned. "I wish you'd thought of that before we came all the way down here."

"It's impossible." Yoseph cut in. "There are Romans searching every passage in the commune by now. We'd never get past them without being seen."

"We might if we don't use the passages." Barabbas suggested.

"The roof is out. If we can reach it, so can they. They probably already have a patrol up there."

"I was thinking of going under the passages."

The unspoken glances among the men suggested that they thought Barabbas had finally and completely lost his mind.

Simeon came to his rescue. "Barabbas is right. There's a complex system of channels that links every cistern and water pool in the commune. They all lead back to the aqueduct. It'll be tight, but we should be able to move through the channels and escape."

Yoseph wasn't convinced. "What about the pools? Every time we pass through them we'll be exposed."

"I'll grant that, but it's a limited exposure. They can't see us in the piping system. If we find they're in a room, we can remain hidden in the channels until they move on."

"Then why bother moving at all? We can just hide in the pipes and wait for them to leave."

"And what if they do think to look for us in the water channels?" Barabbas answered. "If we assume our enemies are more intelligent than we think, they can never surprise us."

"Right. We can enter the system in the laundry. It's just behind the bath house." Simeon led the way.

The group slunk silently through the bathhouse and into the laundry beyond. Barabbas took the lead, dropping quietly into the dark water. He took a deep breath and sank beneath the surface. The water was icy, chilling his skin as it drenched his clothes. A moment later he surfaced and pointed out the inlet to the rest of the men, who were entering the water.

Then he plunged beneath the surface once more, pulling himself by his arms into the channel. He reached up with his head to find the thin pocket of air at the top of the inky black tunnel, breathing in the life-giving oxygen.

The tunnel was devoid of light. Not even a flicker reflected off the dark surface of the water. The air smelt damp and musty and the scent of wet stone hung heavy in the channel. The cold water was already beginning to numb all sense of feeling in his fingers. He clawed his way along the rough stone and concrete of the channel walls. Twice, Barabbas bumped his head against the flagstone ceiling where soldiers were possibly walking at that very moment.

The sound of water sloshing against the sides was magnified to terrifying volumes as the splashing echoed up and down the walls. Barabbas felt sure that the Romans must hear every scrape and bump.

Finally he saw the faint source of light emanating from the next pool. He felt for the edge of the tunnel and submerged once again. He broke the surface quietly and glanced to his left. Two soldiers wandered no more than three paces from the edge of the pool with their backs to him. He ducked under the water and back into the channel. Agonising moments passed as he waited to see whether he'd been discovered.

After several minutes it became apparent that the soldiers had not noticed the surreptitious form that had surfaced so close to their feet. Barabbas tried again. This time the room was empty. Quickly, he moved across the pool to the next channel. After one last look, he plunged beneath the water again, tapping the floor three times to indicate to the next man that the room was clear.

So they moved cautiously from pool to pool, while the Romans hunted the rooms above, marching on the floors that ran over the melanous channels. Each time he surfaced in a cistern, Barabbas glanced about to orientate himself. It was impossible, inside the dark pipes, to be sure which direction he was travelling.

After splashing about for what seemed like an aeon in the dark passages, Barabbas emerged into the court at the northern-most end of the complex. He reasoned that, since the Romans had started here, they would probably be on the other side by now. Still, he took no chances. He quickly moved along the open channel, towards the aqueduct outlet, passing the baptistery on his left.

When he reached the outlet, he found a stone grid blocking the exit. He disrobed and used his *abeyah* as a rope, looping it around one of the long stones. He waited for two more men to arrive. They applied their combined weight to the stone.

There was a wrenching sound as the coat began to tear and the men stopped. They hurriedly removed two more coats and wound them tightly together with the first, strengthening the cord. The second attempt was futile. Although the rope did not break this time, the stone remained unbudged.

Three more men arrived and applied their weight to the task before the stone finally began to give way. It only dislodged slightly, but it was all the encouragement the group needed. With a concerted effort, they heaved again and again until it finally came free with a splash and sank to the bottom of the channel.

Quickly they slipped through the newly made exit and emerged from the aqueduct outside the walls of the commune, fleeing into the rocky terrain beyond. From there they evaporated into the sparse vegetation like mists in the face of a rising sun.

Barabbas caught his brother's arm to get his attention. "You and Levi stay here. If anything happens, you can bring us news at the cave."

Simeon nodded and called softly for Levi. The two men headed east. They took up a position that offered decent cover, while still affording them a clear view of the commune's entrance.

Barabbas led the way west, following the narrow *wadi*, a valley with a dry river bed, as it cut its way deep into the mountainous slopes towering over the tiny community. It was several hours before they finally reached their destination - a cave way up on the northern slope of the *wadi*.

The grotto was large - about four metres high - and L-shaped, protecting its inhabitants from the elements. The front part of the cavern opened into two gaping holes with a thick pillar of rough, white rock between them. Loose bits of rubble and sand lay about the entrance, making it look like nothing more than a natural cavern from the outside.

It offered a fantastic view of the winding valley below. Barabbas turned and stared out over the gorge. Off to his left the rugged white cliffs slowly tapered away to darker, gentler slopes at the bottom. Further east and framed between the valley walls lay the Salt Sea, shimmering as white as the bright sky above it.

In the harsh, morning light, the cliffs of Moab beyond looked like nothing more than a thin stain on the pure, white sheet of sea and sky that formed the horizon.

Barabbas wiped the sweat from his forehead and turned to enter the cave. The inside was stark and bare, containing only a few sleeping mats and rocks that served as seats. There was a small fireplace and shelves hewn out of the stone walls for storing jars and food.

He hung his weapons on crude hooks against the wall and checked the lamps. They contained a healthy supply of olive oil. He nodded in satisfaction. Their predecessors had left the cave in good shape. It was an unspoken law among the zealots that these hideouts should be left well stocked. Thus men on the run always found a haven in the harsh desert climate, while their pursuers were forced to turn back.

It was late in the afternoon when Barabbas took over the watch. He propped himself up against a large boulder, sharpening his sword, and gazed out over the desolate valley. Simeon and Levi should have been here by now.

"I wish they'd get here." Barabbas was exasperated. "How long can it possibly take to see what happened and follow us here?"

"Maybe they got caught." Yoseph said with a wicked grin.

Barabbas laughed. "In Jerusalem, maybe, but not out here. No, they're probably back in the commune enjoying the Essenes' hospitality."

"It's obviously good news. If it had been bad they would have come straight here."

Barabbas ran his fingers across the sharpened blade. "You're probably right." He turned and yelled back into the cave. "Hey, Joshua, where's that food you were boasting about? We're starving out here."

Joshua looked up from his work over the fireplace. "Does the servant tell the master how to conduct his business? You can only cook quail so fast." He turned his attention back to the skewered birds roasting over the coals. Then he stoked the fire, adding a fresh log of wood to the edge, to keep new coals coming.

"Here they come." Lazarus alerted Barabbas from his position above the cave's entrance.

Barabbas sprang to his feet and marched around to get a better view. He glanced at Lazarus, who was staring intently into the valley below. "Where?"

"Down there." He pointed.

Barabbas searched the valley floor. He eventually spotted the two figures making their way up the dark incline near the foot of the gorge.

"They took long enough." He grunted and returned to his sharpening. He carefully ran the hard stone up the blade of the sword, one direction only. First one side, then the other. Every few strokes, he checked the sharpness with his fingers.

The scent of the plump, roasting birds wafted from the sizzling coals as fat dripped with each turn of Joshua's skewer. Barabbas sniffed the air longingly and his mouth watered.

"Your aim is straight and true, Joshua. That of a born hunter. Where did you find such treasures in this barren landscape?"

Joshua laughed. "If I told you that you'd have no more need for my services and where would that leave me?"

Outside, the figures in the valley grew larger as they approached the cave. Barabbas followed their journey up the slopes. They moved with a sense of urgency and as they drew closer, he noted the fear in their eyes. They climbed as quickly as their fatigued bodies would allow. His heart sank and he glanced once more at the fire inside the cave. He felt a strange premonition that the quails would never be eaten.

6

GAIUS JOINED the large group of horsemen in the dimly lit courtyard of the palace. He had just left Pilate's quarters and the man's humiliating barbs and threats still weighed heavy on his mind. All his anger was currently focused in the direction of his prey, Barabbas.

In his right hand he carried his centurion's staff, while his left held a rolled parchment, with Pilate's signature, guaranteeing Eleazor's pardon.

The courtyard was still dark and numerous oil lamps cast their dim light over the gloom. In the east, the first rays of the sun were beginning to grope at the horizon. First light had appeared, although dawn would not arrive for an hour yet.

He searched among the horsemen for Eleazor. It was difficult to make out features in the early morning darkness. Presently he saw the man, surrounded by a group of soldiers and trussed up in chains. Gaius approached the Jew, parchment in hand.

Eleazor was surly and complaining bitterly.

"This is an outrage, centurion. I am a free man, helping the empire on a mission and they fetter me like a dangerous criminal."

"You're not free yet. You still have to deliver Barabbas." Gaius handed Eleazor the parchment.

"This the letter?" Eleazor was a little mollified. He unrolled it gazing down with eager eyes.

"Take me to the light." He instructed the guards. "I want to read this."

One of the horsemen exchanged a glance with Gaius. He shook his head and held up a restraining hand. Then he motioned towards the light.

The anguished scowl on the horseman's face conveyed the legionary's feelings. He was not accustomed to being insulted and ordered about by prisoners, who were not even citizens of Rome . It was obviously taking all of the man's self control not to run his sword through Eleazor for his impertinence.

Gaius knew he could trust these men implicitly to do their job, but something had to be done to improve their morale. He followed the men to the light, where he waited for the next outburst.

"Get out of the way, you fool." Eleazor snapped at the frustrated soldier. "How am I supposed to read this with your fat form blocking the light!"

Gaius marched forward, changing his grip on the staff that signified his rank. With his left arm he reached up. Grabbing the surprised Eleazor by the cloth of his garment, he ripped him from his horse.

Eleazor struck the hard, stone paving, first with his forearm and then his cheek.

The whole courtyard reverberated with the jarring thud. Eleazor struggled up on his side. His eyes were wide with shock. Gaius struck him, with a vicious swing of the staff, on his exposed cheek and blood flowed from the corner of the Jew's mouth. Gaius leaned down and pulled Eleazor up by his hair to a standing position. Ironically, the stunned man still held the letter of reprieve in his left hand.

Gaius fixed him with a malevolent gaze, mere inches from his face. "Now you listen to me, Jew. My instructions are to keep you alive. That's a very broad term and it's a long way to Jerusalem. I suggest you show your captors a little respect, for your own good. That letter may save you from Rome's retribution, but it won't save you from mine. Do you understand?"

Eleazor glared at Gaius. His breathing was heavy and his eyes were filled with hatred. Gaius was pleased. Hatred was based in fear and, right now, Eleazor feared him immensely. He'd remember to watch his back, though.

Two soldiers moved to assist the subdued Eleazor back onto his horse. It was with satisfaction that Gaius noted the look of relief on their faces. A good morale was an essential part of any army. Battles had been won and lost on that facet alone.

He found his own horse and mounted it, raising his staff in the air and pointing it towards the gate. The group of Equites embarked on their quest for the man who had now become Judea's most wanted criminal.

"Something's wrong." Lazarus said.

Barabbas stared down at the pair of running figures in the valley below. Their cloaks were tucked up into their belts as they climbed the steep slopes towards the hideout's entrance.

He clenched his teeth. "What's happened, I wonder?"

"I don't know, but relaxed men don't tuck their cloaks in their belts and run for miles in the hills. See how they stumble? They've been running a long time."

"Look!" Ya'aqob cried the alarm from a second sentry post. He pointed further down the valley to the East.

A large force of Roman cavalry was making its way up the valley. It was still too far off to distinguish any features, but the white tunics and bronze helmets flashed in the sunlight, making the riders' identity unmistakeable.

Barabbas sheathed his sword and rushed back around to the cave's entrance.

"That's not the same group that came to *Qumran* yesterday." Lazarus murmured.

The stampeding cavalry kicked up a dust cloud in its wake. The men rode with purpose. They were not looking aimlessly about them. These soldiers knew where they were headed.

A chill ran through Barabbas as understanding dawned. Somehow the Romans had located the zealot hideout in the *wadi Qumran*.

Down in the valley, Eleazor spurred his horse on up the dry riverbed. He shaded his eyes against the late afternoon sun and stared anxiously up at the slopes ahead. It had been a hard ride from Caesarea, with several changes of horses, but their destination was in sight. He and Gaius led the group. A detail of fifty horsemen raced behind them, churning up a storm of fine white dust in their wake. Foot soldiers had been sacrificed for speed and the short time taken to reach the wilderness south of Jerusalem had been a fantastic feat.

His thoughts turned to his negotiation with Pontius Pilate the previous evening. He felt a grim sense of satisfaction over his performance. The Maccabee's treasure had been the essential bait to draw the prefect in, but he would never reveal its secret. *Lead them to your enemies. Barabbas - your freedom - but never point to Qumran. The treasure is for you alone.* To point them at Barabbas had been nothing short of brilliant. Pilate would torture and break him, searching for answers that Barabbas had no way of knowing. That would be his recompense.

"Wait." He cautioned the centurion ahead of him.

Gaius Claudius heard his call and reined his horse in.

Eleazor caught up. He'd long since managed to free himself from his Roman guards by leading the men along a series of paths too narrow for the soldiers to ride alongside him. They had released the chains that shackled him to them, but still kept him chained to his own horse.

Since his altercation with Gaius at the beginning of the journey, he had kept quiet and done as he was told. He'd also been a willing source of information, keeping only the essential facts hidden from his guards.

He stopped beside Gaius and pointed at the mountains towering above the valley bed. "We'll have to proceed on foot before long. It's up there. Do you see the cave off to the left with those white cliffs above?"

The centurion gazed up at the slopes. "You mean the two caves next to each other."

"It's actually one cave. It just has a double mouth at its entrance."

"It looks deserted. Are you sure they're there?"

"I'm sure. They're probably watching us right now."

Gaius narrowed his eyes. "How much further can we go on horseback?"

"About a mile. After that the path veers up at too steep an angle."

"Well let's keep moving." The centurion spurred his horse on up the sandy white river bed that reflected the glaring sun painfully into their eyes.

About half a mile further on Eleazor called again. "Up there, look." He shouted, pointing at two frantic figures silhouetted briefly against the mouth of the cave. The soldiers exulted at the thrill of battle and charged their mounts up the riverbed, their attention riveted on the cave's entrance.

In the excitement, Eleazor allowed his steed to drop back. He manoeuvred his mount to form a gap through which he could escape. The moment arrived and he reined his horse in, turning its head sharply. The beast slowed and the galloping soldiers overshot, passing him and leaving a clear line for his escape. He spurred his steed up a side gully that entered the river from the left.

There was consternation among the Roman ranks as their attention was suddenly divided between their enemies and their escaped prisoner.

"Forget about him. Go for the cave." Gaius barked. "You two follow the prisoner and bring him back. Just in case he's sent us on a fool's errand."

Eleazor glanced over his shoulder. Two soldiers had turned back and followed him up the gully. It wound and bent its way up the steep, rocky slopes.

Eleazor disappeared around one of the many bends in the steep ravine that had served as his escape route, trotting his horse around the large boulders in the riverbed. Just beyond the curve, he doubled back, heading up yet another ravine, hidden by rocks and vegetation in the bed. He spurred his horse up the second gully, which bent in a u-shape, placing him on a ledge higher up the ravine's side. Here he trotted along a path, screened by high rocks and dry vegetation.

The two pursuing Romans continued up the riverbed below, hunting for him along the winding path. Eleazor chuckled quietly. His escape was now complete. The Romans had no way of reaching him. He would be briefly exposed to the soldiers about half a mile further along, but this would only serve to show the men their error and the futility of giving further chase.

The only way they could reach him was by the gully he had used himself and then only if they could find it. Although he was merely a length or two above them, by the time they could double back and find the elusive gully he would have a lead of at least a mile on them. A minute or two spent covering his tracks would ensure that they could never hope to find him again.

It may have been an unnecessary precaution, but he knew the Roman mind too well to begin trusting their word now. Despite the letter granting him a reprieve, Pilate was not above leaving instructions to destroy the parchment once Barabbas and the others were safely in Gaius' custody. Escape was his only safeguard against such an event and Eleazor had left nothing to chance.

✝ ✝ ✝ ✝ ✝

Barabbas and his men stole quietly through the dark passage at the rear of the cave.

"Did they think we would be so stupid as to have no alternative escape?" Levi breathed heavily after his long run from the *Qumran* community. He and Simeon had seen the large force approaching from the north and rushed to warn the others.

Barabbas snorted. "They must think we're fools of note."

The passage led to a narrow shaft that angled sharply upwards, like a chimney, opening up much higher in the tall cliffs of the mountain range. It was dark and he found his way using a small pottery lamp. The ceiling dropped ahead of him and Barabbas sank to his belly, crawling under the low rock roof. Fifty paces further on, the narrow tunnel became too steep to crawl through.

He helped Levi and his brother, passing them weapons and lamps, taking turns as each man climbed the dangerous shaft to the next ledge. His hands were scratched and bleeding, scuffed by the sharp rocks that were their hand holds in the narrow tunnel.

Eventually, Barabbas saw the reflection of light that heralded the exit. He pulled himself up the last incline and crawled along the final stretch on his hands and knees, keeping his head low to avoid the rocks mere inches above him.

He crawled out first, and then turned to see that his comrades all exited safely behind him. One by one, the men emerged into the rocky terrain high above the cliff and valley below. The area formed a small basin with high rocks surrounding it on all sides. There was a low pass that served as an exit from the basin. The only other exit was the shaft, which led back down to the cave. It was convenient, as the high walls hid them from view in all directions. Once sure that all his men had made it through the tunnel safely, he proceeded towards the narrow pass out of the basin.

He was surprised to find his way blocked by two Roman sentries. They rushed at him from inside the escape route, followed by twenty more. The zealots drew their swords to fight, but it was futile. More Roman legionaries moved forward at the signal, lining the rim of the basin. A quick count revealed at least thirty legionaries around the perimeter, all armed with pikes and swords

Even if his men could kill the twenty legionaries blocking their exit, they would be cut down like wheat by the thirty spear bearers covering the ridge above them. Apart from that, there was no way of telling how many more soldiers lurked beyond the exit.

With an overwhelming sense of defeat, Barabbas called for his men to surrender. It was the most humiliating moment of his life to see his comrades' shock and fear as they pulled back and laid down their swords.

All but one responded. Ya'aqob rushed at the group of soldiers blocking the exit. It was an insane act, born out of helplessness and frustration. The futility of his attack became immediately apparent. Three soldiers stepped forward to counter his attack. The first parried his careening sword, while the two others attacked his flanks. Ya'aqob was quickly thrown on the defensive. He parried the blow of the soldier to his right, but the other legionary found his mark.

Barabbas and the others watched in despair as their comrade spun away from the slicing blade. There was a cry and Ya'aqob dropped his sword and fell, clutching the deep wound in his torso.

"Bandage him up." The first legionary instructed. "He'll make Jerusalem."

Two more soldiers ran to attend to the wounded man. They made a makeshift bandage by tearing strips off his tunic and wrapping them tightly over the cut. While they were busy, the rest of the soldiers turned their attention to the remaining prisoners.

"How could they know about this?" Yoseph stared dumbly about him. His shoulders sagged and his mouth hung open in morbid stupor.

Barabbas' features were clouded in rage. "Only a zealot who had stayed in the cave and knew of the exit could have revealed the information. That narrows it down to three men and I think I can guess who our betrayer was. When next I see him, he'll die."

The Roman soldiers began binding the zealots in fetters. They were brutal, beating the men as they chained them. Barabbas watched in fury as a soldier struck his brother repeatedly after he had tied him. Simeon fell before the sadistic legionary, blood seeping from numerous wounds on his face and neck. Once he had sunk to his knees, the soldier began kicking him.

The men watched silently as their comrade was brutalized. Levi, who was not yet fettered, took a step towards the man, but a second legionary levelled his sword menacingly. The first soldier looked up and then drew his sword. He kicked Simeon once more, flinging him onto his back. Then he drove the sword down at the exposed throat.

The point of the blade sunk harmlessly into the ground two inches left of Simeon's neck. The soldier turned to look at Levi's wide-eyed rage and laughed. He drove his boot into Simeon's kidney once more, before turning to Barabbas.

Barabbas watched impassively as the soldier approached him.

"Give me your hands." The man instructed.

Barabbas did so. His hands were fettered and the collar was placed around his neck. Once he was restrained, the soldier aimed his first blow.

Barabbas was ready for him. He ducked under the blow, moving in towards the source of attack. The soldier was caught off balance and Barabbas smashed his forehead onto the bridge of the legionary's nose. Before any of the soldiers could react, he reached down and drew the sword from the stunned soldier's own sheath, using both his tightly bound hands to clutch the handle.

The soldier reeled backwards and Barabbas lunged, driving the sword between the thick belt and the protective breastplate. Soldiers rushed to grab his arms, pulling him off their comrade. The sword slipped out of Barabbas' grasp and a torrent of blows rained down on him as he rolled, trying to protect himself.

A sharp order brought an end to the punishment. Barabbas rolled over, his bruised face covered with dirt, and saw Gaius standing at the cave's exit. The centurion gazed at the dying legionary. The man rolled about in agony. He gaped with horror at the short handle protruding from his abdomen.

The soldier clutched at the handle that had been driven up to the hilt. There was a choking sound and tiny red bubbles spewed from the man's mouth. Barabbas nodded with grim satisfaction. The bubbles signified a pierced lung which meant slow, but certain, death. It might be possible to delay the final reckoning by an hour or so, but there was no way to avert it.

Gaius looked back at Barabbas as the soldiers dragged him to his feet. "You murdered one of my legionaries." The tone had no inflexion. There was neither anger nor malice in his voice.

"He deserved to die."

Gaius gazed into Barabbas' golden eyes. When he spoke, it was with the same quiet tones as before. "Have you no respect for Rome?"

Barabbas spat on the ground. "Rome is a nation consumed with greed, living off land that is not her own. How can I respect a nation of thieves?"

"The man you killed was a Roman citizen. You would die for that crime alone."

"The son of a she wolf. He deserves to die as a dog."

Gaius was silent for a long time, looking intently into Barabbas' eyes. "If it were not for the copper scroll and Pilate's order, I would run you through with my own sword right now. Who knows? I may yet have the opportunity to do so."

The centurion's statement threw him for a moment. The words made no sense. How could the prefect even know of the scroll, let alone tie him to it? Slowly understanding began to dawn. He couldn't begin to fathom why Eleazor had mentioned the scroll to Pilate, but one truth was plain. In an effort to throw the prefect off the trail, Eleazor had unwittingly led him directly to the secret. Barabbas' heart burned with fury at the man's cowardice and folly.

As he stood in the violent sands of the Judean desert, Barabbas made himself a promise. If it took him the rest of his days, he would find Eleazor. And when he did, he would drive a sword through him, just as he'd done to the Roman soldier. Then he would sit on a rock and watch him die.

7

IN JERUSALEM the streets teemed with humanity. Leila pushed her way through the congested crowds, frustrated by her slow progress between cramped and shoving shoulders.

"Father, wait," she called. Ahead of her, her father turned, waiting for her to catch up.

The crowds were unbearable. All accommodation in the city was rented out at astronomical prices to thousands of pilgrims who had journeyed from the furthest reaches of the Roman Empire to attend *Pesah*, the Passover feast, held on the fifteenth day of the month *Nisan*.

The excitement was tangible in the heated scent of the shuffling horde and the thunderous volume of confused yelling in the streets. Many called out, attempting to locate lost loved ones in the mob, while others murmured their apologies as they tried to squeeze between tightly packed shoulders, bumping and pushing their way through the crushing mass like salmon trying to swim upstream.

Leila caught up to her father and sighed in relief.

Outside the temple, her attention was suddenly drawn to a disturbance further up the street. She craned her neck to see what was happening.

The crowd parted like water before the hull of a ship, making way for a party of Roman soldiers that had just entered by the Sheep Gate. The soldiers were on horseback and they paraded a group of prisoners, also on horses, each chained between two Roman guards.

Whispered questions echoed about her. *Who are these men and what have they done?* They're the zealots who attacked the Roman barracks the other night.

You mean the group led by Barabbas? That's right; the great zealot warrior who attacked the barracks single-handed. He nearly killed five hundred legionaries and brought the barracks crashing down about them.

Which one is he? Which one! Over there with the stubble.

Leila peered between congested shoulders to see the man they spoke of.

Where is his beard? Did they pluck it? No. They say he shaved it to disguise himself as a Roman.

She spotted him near the front of the group. He sat proudly and silently astride a giant bay mare, chained between two vigilant guards.

"What will happen to him, father?"

"I don't know, Leila. I doubt whether the Romans will let him live. He's too dangerous to them."

From his mount, the prisoner surveyed the throng of awe-struck people. Leila shuddered. The crowd's mixed feelings of fear and admiration were almost tangible. Or was it just her? Behind the soldiers, someone shouted.

"Behold the man who stands alone and slays legions! The one who will forever free Israel from Roman oppression."

The soldiers turned, but couldn't identify the culprit in the mob. Barabbas grinned and the crowd began to cheer him on.

The soldiers drew closer and the tightly packed shoulders parted, making way for the legionaries to pass. Leila suddenly found herself at the edge of the crowd, with a clear view of the prisoners. She peered up at the man called Barabbas and for a moment, their eyes locked.

Her heart quickened under the force of his piercing gaze. She would never forget those eyes. They seemed to bore into her very soul. Then he passed by and the moment was gone.

Incited by the boldness of the captives, the crowd began to cheer louder, chanting slogans of freedom as they yelled after the receding group. Some of the soldiers drew their swords for fear of a riot starting. They lashed out at bodies that pressed too close.

When the legionaries reached the gate at *Struthian* pool and entered the Antonia fortress, the crowd's yelling abated.

Leila's father took her arm. "Come, my child. It's already getting dark. Your uncle will be wondering where we are."

She continued to stare at the fortress, not heeding her father's words.

"Leila."

She snapped her head around and smiled to cover the guilt she felt. *Ridiculous. It's not as if he can read your thoughts.*

"Your mind travels far this evening. We must return to your uncle. He has a surprise for you."

"A surprise?" she smiled mysteriously.

"You'll see when you get there."

"I'd rather know it now." she said sweetly.

Her father grinned. "If I tell you now, it would ruin the surprise." He pushed through the thinning crowd in the indigo, evening light. They made their way to the wealthy district on the west side of the city.

Leila moved behind her father. "Why do you torture me like this? It would have been better if you hadn't said anything."

He laughed. "All will be revealed in time."

"Why can all not be revealed now?"

"It's not my place to reveal another's secret."

A wry smile crossed Leila's face. "Then why did you mention that he had a secret?"

He chuckled again. "You're right. I probably shouldn't have said anything."

"But now that you have, you might as well reveal all of it."

"Very well." He relented. "Your uncle and I believe we have found a husband for you."

Her smile suddenly became brittle. "A husband."

"Subject to your approval, of course."

She relaxed a little. She was the youngest of three daughters and had no brothers at all. Consequently, their father had doted on them, especially since their mother's death some ten years earlier.

She and her sisters had become his whole life and he had given them all he could. He'd even broken with the accepted tradition of arranged marriages, having long since decided that any suitor would have to meet with his daughter's approval, as well as his own, before any marriage could be arranged.

"What is he like?" She enquired, her interest only mildly piqued.

"He's wonderful." Her father sang the man's praises. "He's young, strong and extremely wealthy. He lives in Jericho, you know. He's a merchant who transports goods from the east."

"Yes, but what's he like?" Leila pressed her father. "Is he tender?"

"As a new-born lamb."

"I don't like soft men. I prefer them strong and ruthless."

"Well, perhaps tender is a little misleading. He's very strong - strong as an ox. And he has a fiery spirit. Ruthless, if you will."

She frowned and shook her head. "Not too ruthless, I hope. I could never marry a man I feared."

"No, no. Not too ruthless. More - passionate."

"Passionate is good." She encouraged him.

He nodded sagely. "Yes - passionate is perhaps a better word to describe him."

Leila laughed. "Father, I don't believe you know this man at all. Your talk is smooth, like a merchant trying to sell damaged goods."

"You make a mockery of an old man." He scolded.

"Not that old." She giggled.

"Leila, I only want to see you happy." He pleaded.

"I know, father. Why don't we wait until I meet him? Maybe he won't be that bad."

Her father groaned. "Not that bad! Can't you, at least, reserve judgement until you meet him?"

"You shouldn't have told me like this." She replied with a wicked grin. "You should rather have surprised me when we arrived home."

"But – but," he stammered.

Leila chuckled at his confused and outraged expression. She walked on ahead, leaving him to scrape together the last vestiges of his dignity.

Secretly, she wondered what this man was like. Could he be the man she was looking for? Perhaps he was everything she'd dreamed of. No, she told herself. Don't expect too much. That can only lead to disappointment.

Her thoughts turned to another. An arrogant and dangerous man, fettered between two soldiers on his way to the dungeons in the Antonia fortress. What was he doing now? She'd overheard two men discussing him as they had exited the temple, late that afternoon. One of them claimed that Barabbas had killed a Roman soldier with his own sword.

Stop it. The law strictly forbade killing. She had no business with a man of such violence. She must think of him no more. She turned her thoughts to the man awaiting her arrival at her uncle's luxurious home on the west side of Jerusalem.

† † † † †

In the dungeons of the Antonia, Barabbas struggled to find a comfortable position in the stocks. He'd only been there a few minutes and his limbs already ached. He raised his voice and spoke loudly, in Aramaic, making sure the guards could hear him.

"I hope those guards don't check our girdles. I have a pouch with twenty pieces of silver here."

He waited to see if the guards would respond. Twenty pieces of silver was a healthy sum and the word of a prisoner would never be believed over that of a legionary if the money was taken. There was no response. The iron door remained locked.

He glanced at his companions. "Well, either they're patently honest, or they don't understand a word."

Levi switched to Aramaic. "I opt for the latter. We'd sooner find a Pharisee bathing in pigswill than meet an honest Roman."

"Good. We can talk freely."

"What's there to speak of?" Simeon asked in a sullen monotone. "It's over. Only death awaits us now."

Barabbas was surprised by his brother's attitude. Simeon's spirits had sunk to an all-time low since their capture in the *wadi Qumran*. It was out of character for him to be so negative. "Keep talking like that and you can only be proved right."

"What other course is there?"

"There are many open to us if we remain alert. If we can break out of these stocks, we could surprise the guards and, perhaps, find a way out of the Antonia."

"That's insane." Yoseph protested. "There's no way we could get through all those soldiers out there. This is their headquarters."

"I'm not saying it's a likely option. We have to stay alert for every opportunity, that's all."

Levi shuffled in his stocks in the corner. "Well I hope your other opportunities are more viable. Otherwise we might as well give up now."

"I think they are. The way I see it, we have two likely moments for escape. First when we're taken for trial. That will either happen in the next few days, or directly after *Pesah*. They'll almost certainly hold the trial in the *Gabbatha*."

"And the second?"

"At our execution. We'll be led from the dungeons to be scourged, or crucified. The Romans will least expect an escape attempt then."

"You're forgetting we'll all be chained between two guards. Do you propose to drag them through the streets of Jerusalem in your escape?"

"If we can break the fetters on these chains and then wait for the right moment, we can be gone before they know what's happened."

"If you can do it." Levi was not convinced.

"I think I can."

"How?"

"Well. These clamps are a little rusty. If we can jam the bolts between the flagstones on the floor —" he grunted with the effort.

"It will take a lot of hours." Yoseph sounded dubious.

"I've got time." Barabbas replied and tried again.

The men soon joined him, trying to find a way out of their chains. They worked long into the night without success. Only Simeon did not participate. He sat quietly brooding in his stocks. Occasionally, he'd bury his head in his arms. He made no sound and Barabbas simply put it down to his brother's earlier display of hopelessness.

Later, long after the others had fallen asleep, exhausted by their efforts, Barabbas gave up. He turned and noticed his brother watching him in the darkness.

"You act as if you've seen your own grave." Barabbas said quietly.

Simeon stiffened, as if Barabbas had held a knife to his throat. It was a long time before he spoke.

"I've seen our future, brother. I see much sorrow. I also see suffering and death."

Barabbas shook his head. "It's not like you to give up so easily. Try to get some sleep. Things will seem better in the morning."

"No, Barabbas." There was an urgency in Simeon's voice. "I've seen it. Just as I saw it when we ran from the soldiers in the *Kainopolis*." He stared vacantly at the ground and then shook his head. "We each have a destiny to fulfil. There's no escape for us now."

Barabbas remained silent, staring at his brother's expressionless face in the dim light of the cell. Eventually he shook his head and applied himself once more to the task of breaking his fetters. Many hours later, before the rest of the men stirred, Barabbas stopped and fell back on the cold stone floor. His efforts had exhausted him and he let out a long, strained sigh.

He stared at his wrists for a long time. They were chaffed raw and covered with blood. He winced at the pain and shook his head. His arms couldn't take much more punishment. If he didn't break his fetters soon, all was lost. Best to rest now. He could always try again in the morning.

† † † † †

Two days later, all was in readiness for Pilate's journey to Jerusalem. The Jewish *Pesah* festival was now eight days away and he had duties to perform there. He entered the courtyard, accompanied by his wife, and marched across to the carriage.

Quintus was already there, awaiting his arrival. The carriage was drawn by eight horses, all fine specimens - dark with creamy white markings on their hocks and foreheads.

Quintus held the door for the couple and Pilate entered the luxurious vehicle. The interior was comfortably furnished with silk cushions on the seats. It was also well stocked with expensive foods and good wine, so that his every wish could be catered to during the journey. He settled in the soft, comfortable seat.

Quintus climbed in after him and motioned for a slave to follow. The slave was a handsome Spaniard with an olive complexion and long, curly hair that hung to his shoulders.

Pilate's wife reclined on the seat opposite him. "Comfortable, my dear?" He asked.

"I do so hate these journeys," she complained. "I wish you didn't have to attend all these annoying festivals throughout the year."

"It would be easier if we could govern all year round from Caesarea, but we must at least make a show of supporting local customs and beliefs."

"I don't see why. They don't acknowledge Rome's."

"Yes." Pilate mused. It was true that the Jewish people refused to acknowledge Roman gods, especially the imperial cults of Julius and Augustus Caesar. "But Augustus himself excused them from such practices and beliefs in the interests of peace. We have to honour his decree. Don't you agree, Quintus?"

"Most wholeheartedly, prefect. Didn't Augustus Caesar himself present an offering to the Jewish priesthood to be sacrificed on his behalf in order to acknowledge the God of Israel?"

"That was a long time before we came to Judea."

Pilate's wife was scornful. "They acknowledged nothing. It was a political show and nothing more; a token to appease the Jewish people."

"Perhaps you're right." Pilate regarded her thoughtfully.

She was young, compared to him, and beautiful. They had married when she was fifteen years old, just after Pilate had completed his tour of duty in the military and embarked on his political career. He smiled as he realised how much he had moulded her political ideas at that tender and impressionable age, in the early years of their marriage.

She was just as harsh and intolerant as he was of any beliefs opposed to Rome and the empire's political advance. She shared his lack of interest in local customs and resented having to bend to political pressure in favour of people she regarded as lesser mortals.

"Still," he continued, "we have rather more pressing reasons for attending the festival this year."

"What could Jerusalem possibly have that would interest us?"

"Prisoners, my dear. The upcoming trial and execution of the zealots that attacked the Roman barracks in that city. Unless they reveal the whereabouts of the copper scroll and the Maccabee's treasure."

"I don't understand the importance of this treasure. It's a vast sum, granted, but what do we need more wealth for? We lack for nothing as it is."

"The Maccabee's treasure is not wealth, my dear, it's power. That treasure has been hidden for hundreds of years. Tiberius would look very kindly on the man that could bring it to him as a gift. That man might receive a position in the senate or better yet, as a personal advisor to the emperor. The very empire could be within his grasp when Tiberius chooses his successor."

"Do you really believe that?"

"Coponius did, when he wrote about it. He spent years searching for it, before finally dismissing it as a piece of Jewish folklore."

"And now you think he was wrong?"

"The pieces fit. The Jewish informant had the time and place right. We'll know once I've interrogated the prisoners - one prisoner, in particular."

"How long do you think it will take to find it?"

He shrugged. "Who knows? It's been buried for centuries already. We'll know more once we arrive in Jerusalem."

"Hence your urgency to get there."

Pilate smiled and gazed wistfully out of the carriage window at the fleeting landscape. "I can already taste it. The sweet taste of power - and it's almost within my reach."

✝ ✝ ✝ ✝ ✝

Eleazor spurred his horse down, through the steep, rocky terrain that formed the wall of the Great Rift Valley. Off to his right, in the distance, lay the Sea of Salt. It shimmered like a powdery mirror in the scorching desert sun, reflecting pastel mauves and pinks off its glistening surface.

To the north-west, no more than fifteen miles away, hung the eternal bank of clouds, held at bay by the giant watershed, the mountains of Jerusalem. It was as if the clouds had struck an invisible obstacle that could never be crossed, leaving the land beyond barren and void of their life-giving moisture.

His horse faltered over some loose stones that had fallen into the path. Eleazor whipped the animal across its flanks with the reins. The beast flattened its ears and rolled its eyes to show its displeasure at the ill treatment. He ignored the show of aggression and dug his heels mercilessly into its ribs, trying to speed it up a little.

He had precious little time before his betrayal of Barabbas became accepted knowledge among the zealots. They would have no concrete proof, of course, but his freedom and Barabbas' capture were too much of a coincidence to go unnoticed.

With so little evidence, it was unlikely they'd seek to kill him, but he would not be welcome among them for much longer. He could not afford to be ostracised - not without the scroll in his possession.

This may well be your last chance. He thought about his conversation with the old Essene. That man had known something - hidden something. It was in his tone of voice, his eyes and his posture.

Eleazor knew the course that lay before him. *Qumran.* The answers to the secret lay there. The old man was a protector, he was sure of it. *Confront the Essene. Break him if you must. Learn the secret and find the scroll.*

First he had to infiltrate the community. That would be easy. Such devout men would be hard pressed to turn away an injured man, especially one who had escaped the Roman army, which all Jews despised. They would take him in and tend his wounds, ridding him of the hateful chains that bound him.

His thoughts turned to Barabbas and the men with him, captured and taken to Jerusalem. He'd never liked Barabbas - that was no secret. Perhaps it was because the man reminded him too much of his own father. Barabbas was out of the way now.

He could turn his attention to more important matters.

The stone walls of the Essene community jutted out of the landscape ahead of him. He felt buoyant, even victorious as he approached *Khirbet Qumran*.

† † † † †

In the dungeons, time became distorted. With no sunlight and the constant, dull glow of the oil lamps, there was no light or darkness to mark its passage.

Long periods of boredom were interspersed with irregular meals of bread, dipped in wine. The cheap alcohol was bitter on the palate.

Barabbas' ligaments were painfully stretched from the long period spent in the stocks. His ankles and wrists were swollen and rubbed raw by the constant friction of his rough bonds. He'd been forced to wage an unending war with the scavenging rodents, attracted by the filth and scraps of food strewn about the floor. The animals gnawed ravenously on anything that attracted their interest, including prisoners who had succumbed to sleep or pain.

Latrines were non-existent and, because of their immobility, he and his companions were forced to soil themselves where they lay. The stench suffocated them in their weakened state and the soldiers' visits had become fewer and further apart.

Fatigue, combined with the squalid conditions, had caused rampant sickness among the men. The dungeon echoed with constant, hacking coughs and Ya'aqob was already racked with fever. Sweat drenched his filthy clothes, and violent shivers rattled his chains with each new convulsion. He'd long since stopped complaining of the pain caused by his septic wound and the smell of pus and gangrenous flesh now mingled with all the other vileness of the cell, merely becoming part of a greater and more terrible whole.

Barabbas struck out at an over-adventurous rat with his chains. The chamber echoed violently. He coughed and glared in grim satisfaction at the tiny carcass of the animal. The door opened and the rodents scampered for cover, finding safety in the numerous shadowy cracks and holes to be found in the floor and walls.

"What's going on in here?" A soldier stood in the doorway, surveying the men. The stench caused him to gag and he brought his arm up to cover his face.

"That bread you gave us was a little crunchy, and Levi always was a noisy eater." Barabbas replied weakly.

The soldier regarded him with a cold glare, deciding whether or not to punish his impertinence. The foul smell of the chamber tipped fortune in Barabbas' favour, however, and the legionary scowled and hurriedly left the room. There was a clanging from outside as the iron bolt slid back into position.

"At least the soldiers give us some relief from the rats." Joshua wheezed through clogged sinuses.

"Sometimes I think I prefer the rats." Barabbas sighed, lying back on the floor, trying to relieve his muscles and ease his aching back.

He relaxed, allowing the vicious apparatus to stretch his limbs and tendons, trying not to fight against it. To wrestle with the instrument would only bring more agony.

The dungeon fell silent once more. The oppressive silence was broken by the delirious ramblings of Ya'aqob. He swatted a feeble hand at one of the more aggressive rats that circled ever closer. His limbs were already covered with festering sores inflicted by the tiny, but dangerous creatures. At first, he had filled the chamber with his hollow screams, but now, all he did was moan whenever the beasts gnawed ravenously at the decaying flesh and sodden bandages around his wound.

Barabbas and the rest of his companions could only watch helplessly as their friend died slowly before their eyes. They tried to keep the rodents at bay when they could, but it was impossible to reach him, bound as they were.

Joshua stared mournfully at Ya'aqob who lay more or less immobile on the floor. "Do you think he'll survive to the trial?

Levi shook his head sadly. When he spoke, his words were whispered, so that Ya'aqob wouldn't hear. "Death would be a mercy for him now."

"It would be a mercy for all of us." Simeon replied softly. "We face a death infinitely more painful than Ya'aqob, at the hands of Rome."

The prisoners fell silent. They knew all too well what their future held. The empire did not treat rebellions lightly, and their crimes demanded the harshest punishment that Rome could mete out.

As condemned men, they would probably be crucified, or sent to the mines as slaves to face a far slower, but equally certain death. Some had lived as long as twelve years in the mines, but these were few. None had survived the cruelty of the mines and the men that ran them.

Their gaping jaws were open graves that had claimed the lives of thousands in the pursuit of the hidden treasures lying deep within their shadowy bowels. Once sentenced to the mines, they might spend the rest of their lives imprisoned there, never to see the surface or sunlight again. Darkness would slowly give way to blindness and, finally, death. If faced with a choice, the crucifix was to be preferred.

The bolt on the door slid back again. Barabbas glanced up, startled. The heavy, iron barrier grated on the stone floor as it opened and Gaius entered the room. He wrinkled his nose at the stench in the chamber, but refused to cover his face.

"Get these men out of here." He ordered. "And wash them thoroughly before we take them to Pilate. Then clean this place up. It smells like pig's vomit in here."

He left in a hurry, fleeing the putrid smell of the chamber. The legionaries entered and began to free the prisoners from their stocks, starting with Barabbas. He was immediately chained between two soldiers.

"What about this one?" One of the legionaries asked, pointing at Ya'aqob.

"Leave him. There's no way he could make the journey to the *Gabbatha*."

Barabbas and the rest of the prisoners, now properly secured, were taken from the room. They looked back at their friend for the last time, certain that they would never see him again.

Outside, in the passage, Barabbas took a deep breath. The air was stale and warm. It was thick with the smell of burning olive oil from the lamps that hung against the walls, but to him, it smelled as sweet as the perfume on a maiden's skin.

The legionaries led him to a bathhouse. One of his guards shoved him towards the deep tub. "Here, clean yourself up and see that you do a good job."

He held his breath and plunged his head into the water. First, he drank gluttonous gulps of the sweet liquid, quenching his parched throat. Then he began scrubbing his head and shoulders, washing the foulness from his aching body.

The coolness of the water was refreshing and he began scrubbing the worst of the stains from his tunic as he washed his limbs and feet. If they ordered a change of clothes, all was lost.

"That's enough." The soldier said curtly and pulled him from the tub. Barabbas moved with the man, offering no resistance.

After this, they returned his *abeyah* to him. Then they marched him through the passages to the gate that led out, over the *Struthian* Pool.

† † † † †

Deborah watched the group emerge from the Antonia fortress. The pale and emaciated men shielded their eyes against the blinding light of the mid morning sun. The centurion, Gaius, strode ahead of the group, leading the way through the city towards the *Gabbatha*.

She followed with the crowd. The limp prisoners moved with tortured steps between their guards. She winced, feeling their pain. There was no cheering from the crowd today - only sympathy and fear for the broken men.

Barabbas stumbled to his knees between the two soldiers chained to him. Deborah gasped. The legionaries shoved him pitilessly and he reeled between them. One of the men grabbed him under his arm and lifted him to his feet, pushing him on. He stumbled again and the soldiers began to beat him.

She felt her heart wrench in two and tried to call, "Barabbas." No sound escaped her lips, however, and she merely mouthed the name.

He struggled to rise under the vicious blows of the soldiers. She was stricken by the sight of the once indomitable spirit of the man she knew, now broken before her.

Barabbas staggered to his feet. His guards jerked harshly at the chains. He held them between his hands to prevent them from chaffing his raw and bloodied wrists. Deborah bit her lip again and shook her head. The sight was appalling.

He'd barely moved ten paces when his legs gave out and he fell to the ground. The soldiers were jerked off balance and turned yet again to punish their prisoner's weakness. It happened too quickly for the guards to react.

Barabbas sprang to his feet like a cat. Gone was the weakness displayed earlier and the stumbling was replaced by the sure-footed confidence of a gladiator. The shackles snapped mystically from his wrists. The guards' expressions turned to mute horror at the sight.

As he rose, Barabbas drove his knuckles like a battering ram into the first soldier's throat. The man crumpled like ancient parchment, falling to the street. Then he spun around, smashing the second soldier on the bridge of his nose. Cartilage was crushed under the force of the blow.

Deborah exulted. This was the Barabbas she remembered. The parting crowd began to roar its approval, urging him on. Barabbas turned and ran.

The panicked soldiers quickly gave chase, taking their lead from Gaius. The centurion ran with furious speed, as if his very life depended on Barabbas' capture.

Barabbas moved with an alacrity Deborah barely believed possible for one who had been in the stocks for nearly two weeks. She felt awestruck by his power. Though Gaius ran like a gazelle, he was not gaining on his prey quickly enough. The crowd closed ahead of the centurion and Barabbas was making good his escape.

Then, fortunes turned. The mass of bodies pulsated about him. People jostled with one another, trying to get a better view, and closed Barabbas' escape route. A second path opened to his right and he darted down it, sprinting past waving arms urging him to take it. Deborah craned her neck and saw the corner beckoning ahead of him, like a beacon to freedom. His path was clear.

Suddenly a woman in a blue gown flew from the shoving mass, falling across his path. They collided and Barabbas fell on top of her crashing to the ground. Their eyes locked for a moment, but their gaze seemed to impart a lifetime of conversations. Deborah frowned. Had Barabbas met the woman before? Maybe it was just her imagination.

Then the soldiers were upon him. They jerked him to his feet, and dragged him back into his world of bondage. He tried to fight, but the legionaries struck him again and again until the fight was vanquished. Deborah's heart sank. *He'd come so close.*

Behind Barabbas, an older man ran to the woman's assistance. Her husband?

"Leila! Are you alright?"

The woman pushed herself to a seated position. The man took her arm and pulled her to her feet. She stared pensively after Barabbas, her moist lips parted and her chest heaving. Deborah recognised that expression and it filled her with loathing.

"Are you sure you're alright?" The man pressed her.

"I'm fine, father." The woman straightened her clothes.

Father! He took the woman by her arm and led her away. "Come. This is no place for a woman. And we still have plenty to do before *Pesah.*"

The woman followed her father into the crowd. Deborah's eyes bored like daggers into her back. *He would have escaped had it not been for you.* She glared at the receding form.

† † † † †

The sheer agony of the screams caused the blood in Barabbas' veins to curdle. The echoes filled the dingy cell. Once again, the obese Roman soldier glanced up at Barabbas, raising his eyebrows. Then he twisted the roller and Joshua's frenzied screams flooded the chamber once more.

This time there was a distinct crack as the joints in his arms gave way to the cruel wrenching apparatus and bones were ripped from their sockets. Joshua's screams died in a spluttering cough and a bitter, yellowish green liquid spewed from his mouth, running down his beard and neck.

Each turn of the rollers on the rack tore at Barabbas' soul. He had the information that could end his friend's suffering. One word and he could stop the agony and the screams.

But he was bound by an oath sworn on the grave of his father. Two others in the room shared his secret and yet they said nothing. They had taken similar oaths and would go to their graves protecting the secret that Pilate now asked him to reveal. No. He would never betray the secret.

"The rack is truly a marvellous invention, don't you think?" Pilate's tone was calm, almost conversational.

Barabbas spat in his face, gladly enduring the blows that followed.

When they had ended, he replied. "I told you. The Maccabee's treasure is a myth. Eleazor played you for a fool. Why don't you put me on the rack and establish the truth, you piece of Roman refuse?"

The legionary beside Pilate struck Barabbas in the gut again. He fell to the ground, gasping for air that would not come. While he lay, winded on the floor, several soldiers kicked him repeatedly. The pain receded and the vicious blows seemed to become mere bumps, as if being nudged by strangers in a crowd. Darkness began to cloud his vision.

"Stop." Pilate said quietly. The blows ended and the legionaries dragged Barabbas to his feet.

A slight smile touched the prefect's lips and he mournfully shook his head. "You'd love that, wouldn't you? That way you could take your secret to the grave. I need to keep you alive until you can tell me where the treasure is hidden."

"I can't tell you what I don't know."

"We'll see. There's some life in your comrade yet. Not to mention all your friends here."

One of the legionaries leaned across and whispered in Pilate' ear.

The prefect smiled, and turned to Simeon. "And brother! You can spare him and the rest of your comrades this humiliation now, by telling me where the scroll is kept."

"It exists only in the minds of a madman and the fool that believed him when he negotiated his freedom."

"You call me a fool?"

"The description fits." Barabbas remained sullen.

Pilate signalled the leviathan legionary, who smirked and turned the rolls another notch. Once more, volcanic screams erupted, heaping their ashes of guilt on Barabbas' head and filling him with shame. His mind screamed deafening confessions, begging for the pain to end but his expression remained impassive. He glared at Pilate and his heart burned with hatred.

The torture had been in progress for over six hours already. Barabbas had been surprised to learn earlier that they were not to appear in the *Gabbatha*. Instead, they had been taken past the open-air court and into Herod's Praetorium.

Once inside, they'd been thrown in the dungeons where the legionaries had introduced them to Publius, the resident Roman torturer. The man had a friendly smile, which wobbled between a squat nose and several chins. His expression was benign, which only served to prove how deceptive appearances could be.

"Where is it?" Pilate pressed Barabbas again.

He shook his head and remained stubbornly silent. The torment continued for several more hours. Publius was a master in his chosen art of cruelty, propagating the agony like a cancer throughout the body but never allowing his subject the luxury of oblivion, or death. Finally he stopped and shook his head. The session had come to an end. Joshua could take no more punishment.

Pilate nodded. "Call Gaius and have him take this man to the infirmary. The rest of them can be thrown in the dungeons downstairs. Perhaps they'll be more communicative tomorrow."

The prefect left the chamber, adjourning to his private quarters in search of a hearty dinner. Gaius entered the room and Joshua was taken from the rack. He was barely alive.

"Be careful with that man." The centurion ordered sharply. "He's suffered enough for one day."

The relief that Barabbas felt was soured by his expectation of the morrow and the anguish it would bring. Four legionaries carefully lifted the mutilated body from the rack and carried Joshua to the infirmary, where he would be given treatment and time to regain his strength. Then the torture would begin again.

Gaius eyed the torturer with a flint-like glare. The man toyed lovingly with his instruments of pain. Then he turned to the remaining prisoners.

"Come with me," he said quietly.

They trooped after Gaius, under the watchful gaze of several guards. When they arrived at the dungeons, Gaius spoke to the legionary in charge. "See that they're comfortable and make sure they get a decent meal. If I hear that they were maltreated in any way, I'll have the entire watch scourged."

"Yes, centurion," replied the dutiful legionary. He turned to the prisoners. "This way," he said, leading them to their new quarters.

Half an hour later, the prisoners were locked in a communal cell with ten guards outside their door. The rough lodgings felt like an inn, compared to their previous quarters in the Antonia. They were clean and, although the floor was cold, they had their cloaks to use as blankets for the night. Best of all, they were free of the agonising stocks and could find relative comfort against the walls of the cell, or stretch out and relax on the stone floor.

They'd eaten a hearty meal of bread and honey, with dried dates. Already, the men were dozing off, finding much needed sleep after the weeks of hardship, followed by hours of pent-up emotion under Pilate's evil power.

Barabbas lay on his back, staring up at the dimly lit ceiling. Conflicting thoughts tormented his ravaged mind. He had the power to end tomorrow's suffering and save Joshua from hours of pain. *Qumran.* That name alone would end the agony and bring a quick and merciful death.

Then his thoughts turned to Cephas of Gamala, the great man he had called father. He remembered the power of the man's arms as he flung his young son high into the air. The boy had squealed with delight as he fell back into the sure hands that would never let him fall.

He recalled the wrestling matches and the feigned pain as his father had recoiled from his tiny, pummelling fists, smiling his approval. His booming laugh had filled the universe as he had engulfed both his sons in a giant bear hug.

Barabbas' thoughts turned to loathing as he remembered a broken and bleeding father, being dragged away from his home by a group of Roman soldiers who laughed as they plucked his beard and smashed his body without mercy. That was the last time Barabbas had seen his father. Cephas had been taken along with Judas and many others to Caesarea, where they had stood trial for treason against Rome.

Levi was one of the few who had survived. Others had not been so lucky. Hundreds had been butchered and buried in mass graves outside Caesarea, Cephas of Gamala among them.

At the tender age of five, Barabbas had learned to hate. Urged on by his older brother, he had channelled that hatred by learning to fight. When he'd turned twelve, they had sought out the zealots.

There, they had been reunited with Levi, a close friend of their father's. He had taught them the ways of the desert and how to wage war against an enemy of superior force. The lessons had been drummed into Barabbas, feeding his hate as they created opportunities for revenge. And he had wreaked vengeance on Rome. He had destroyed mail posts and Roman patrols throughout Judea, robbing border posts of their taxes and leaving a trail of dead legionaries in his wake. Battles brought short-lived periods of relief. But the victories served only to remind him of his loss.

These thoughts served to harden his resolve. He was the guardian of a secret passed down through generations. That secret was to be protected, no matter what the cost. He would not betray his father's legacy by revealing a mystery that had remained hidden for hundreds of years.

† † † † †

Barabbas and his friends were roused at the usual hour. Days had passed and they had settled into a routine of horror. A small breakfast was always followed by a trip to the chamber. Joshua's now swollen and deformed body was brought into the room and laid out on the rack. His limbs were a twisted monument to pain. The joints bulged like grotesque rocks under distended skin and his breath came in shallow, sobbing gasps.

Publius waddled in like a mountain of lard and began to prepare his instruments, glancing up at Barabbas periodically with the ever-present smile on his bulbous face.

"We're going to have to kill that man one of these days." Levi whispered to Barabbas in Aramaic.

Barabbas nodded silently, never taking his eyes off the rotund legionary. They were interrupted by Pilate's arrival. His earlier, cordial manner had, by now, been replaced by an abrupt surliness.

"How long has he got?" He enquired of the torturer.

Publius shook his head. "Not long now, prefect. I've never managed to keep one as long as this."

Pilate sighed. "Well, let's get started. When we're done with him, we'll start on the next one."

The screams erupted and the day began. Joshua lasted far longer than anticipated, under Publius' expert touch. The hours dragged on into the afternoon and it was nearly sundown when he spluttered his last agonised breath.

The men were led back to their cell in the usual manner. Barabbas slumped down in a corner. He buried his head in his arms, with his eyes tightly shut, blocking out the sorrow, pain and hatred.

"Barabbas." He looked up as his name was called. Gaius stood at the door. "I implore you. Tell Pilate what he wants to know. He won't hesitate to kill every man here."

Barabbas shook his head. "I can't invent a treasure that exists in the mind of a fool."

"I hope for your sake that you're lying. Your brother goes on the rack tomorrow.

Barabbas' expression was blank. He simply held Gaius' gaze.

"What kind of man lets his family and friends die in front of him, without giving a single inch?" The centurion asked contemptuously.

"The kind that that doesn't have the answers." Barabbas replied in weary defiance.

The centurion stared at his subject for a long time, before turning to leave. The heavy iron door clanged shut behind him and the prisoners heard the bolt slide into position. Barabbas slowly turned and looked at his brother. There was a resolved sense of purpose in Simeon's gaze. There was no fear or malice in his eyes - only acceptance. He, too, had taken the oath and he knew the price that had to be paid to guard its secret.

Barabbas didn't eat that night. Nor did he sleep. His mind swelled with resentment at his own inability to affect a situation beyond his control. The passage of time was marked by sounds of the changing of the guard outside their cell. The third shift came just before dawn. It would not be long now and they would be called for the horror to begin once more.

It was the day before *Pesah*, the Feast of Unleavened Bread. Breakfast was served and the men ate in silence. Barabbas stared vacantly at his untouched bowl, punishing himself for deaths he could have prevented. After breakfast they waited. The soldiers would arrive any moment now. Time passed and still the soldiers did not come. Where were they? The men became anxious, pacing the floor of the cell. It was ironic that the routine, no matter what horrors it held, seemed preferable to the unknown.

Outside the praetorium, thousands of angry voices began yelling. The sound filled the streets, like a violent peal of thunder. It shook the palace and carried its cry to the prisoners deep within the dungeons. It was followed by long periods of silence and then more shouting. The dull roar of the mob outside the palace grew louder still, until it became a crescendo and Barabbas could finally make out the words that were being chanted. The others could hear it too, but none of them dared believe what they heard.

8

PONTIUS PILATE'S temper was violent. He hated having his breakfast interrupted and he resented having his routine broken to go and hear a trial at the insistence of the Jewish authorities. The fact that it was a religious dispute between the Sanhedrin and a young radical annoyed him even more.

He had no interest in their customs or beliefs and cared even less for their outlandish accusations of heresy. Even more aggravating than the religious accusations were the obviously trumped up political charges. The man had no political motivation. He wasn't a threat to Rome and he was wasting the prefect's time. Pilate counted every moment lost in this ridiculous trial as another obstacle in his quest for the Maccabee's treasure. Another day delaying his plan for political acclaim.

Then there was the crowd, incited by the Sanhedrin, screaming their fury. They wanted the evil perpetrator of heresy destroyed, lest he propagate his twisted lies further. It was this manipulation that Pilate detested most of all. He was the prefect - the supreme authority of Rome in Judea - and he would not be swayed. The man was innocent. His decision was final.

The frenzied crowd began to scream so much louder and Pilate was gripped with fear for the ensuing riot his verdict might cause. He'd told the Sanhedrin that he found no guilt in the man, but they could not be reasoned with. The prisoner had to die before *Pesah* and the Sabbath, which began at sunset.

He'd tried to reason with the unruly mob outside in the *Gabbatha*, but they'd only shouted all the more. Even his wife had come to him, begging him to have nothing to do with this prisoner's execution. She'd had a terrible dream the night before, of bad omen surrounding this trial. Pilate fidgeted with his toga, in an effort to conceal his fear. Omens were serious business and not to be treated lightly. As he considered his wife's words, he was reminded of stories from his youth. He had been raised on his parent's stories which taught him well to dread omens, and to respect the dire consequences that would follow if they were left unheeded. *But the crowd!*

He sat in the official seat at the edge of the *Gabbatha* and considered his options. His mood was morose and aggravated by the scorching breeze that gusted from the east. It marked the beginning of a *Khamsin*, a violent storm that blew in from the desert, invading the city with a fine, yellow powder that crept through every crevice and fold in one's clothing. Dark clouds would hide the sun, making Jerusalem a depressing twilight scene for most of the day. The people were always more moody when a *Khamsin* approached.

He yearned for the comfort of the praetorium where he could avoid the storm and the screaming mob. He also ached to get back to his interrogation deep within the dungeon chambers.

Finally he came to a decision. It was a last desperate attempt to save the helpless man. Pilate rose and made his announcement, reminding the crowd of a custom, forgotten in the mayhem. Every year, at *Pesah*, the prefect pardoned one prisoner, allowing him to walk free, regardless of his crimes against the empire. He glanced briefly at the young rabbi before him, and then offered to release the man, in keeping with tradition.

The reaction from the crowd made the blood turn cold in Pilate's veins. In his most terrifying nightmares, he'd never envisioned being forced to do what the people now requested of him. If he had thought for one instant of the possible consequences of his offer, he would have ordered the death of the young radical without hesitation and returned immediately to the dungeons in the praetorium.

As one, the crowd rose and called their prisoner forth. A single name rang out on the lips of every person in the mob. The innocent man had been rejected and one infinitely more guilty would walk free in his place.

✝ ✝ ✝ ✝ ✝

Back in the cell Barabbas heard the frenzied screams grow louder. The people were chanting something. It sounded - he couldn't quite make it out. The shouts receded and then returned, stronger than before.

From the cell it sounded like the distant crash of ocean waves on a stormy shore. Suddenly the roar grew in form and direction, pulsating in a new chant that carried clear to the dungeons deep in the of Herod's praetorium. Finally the men deep in the bowels of the praetorium could make it out.

They looked at one another, dumbfounded. "The crowd calls for you." Yoseph spoke in amazement.

"What could they want?" Barabbas was puzzled.

The shouting grew louder still and angrier as the frenzied pitch rose and fell to the rhythm of the chanted name. His companions glanced at one another with puzzled looks, nervous and yet intrigued by the unusual turn of events.

Where were the guards, where was Pilate? Why was the crowd calling for him? The angry roar continued, unabated.

"Perhaps they're demanding your freedom. Maybe they've started a riot." Levi ventured.

"With half a legion of soldiers in the city, I doubt it. Whatever is going on out there is an official gathering, probably at the *Gabbatha*."

The wave of noise receded and peace rested on the city once more. The men listened intently, but the storm had abated. Nothing from outside could be heard in the dungeons. Minutes passed. An ominous silence hung over the *Gabbatha* and the praetorium.

"Maybe it was a riot after all."

"Wait! Listen."

The roaring erupted again, like a violent and prolonged earthquake that shook the ground and walls of the castle. This time it brought with it a chilling message. The crowd no longer yelled Barabbas' name. The words pulsated as before, but with cruel and evil intensity, striking chords of fear in the men's hearts.

They all glanced furtively in Barabbas' direction, not wanting to look into his eyes. Barabbas leaned quietly against the wall, resigning himself to the inevitable fate of the horde's furious call. His face was impassive and a slight grin touched the corners of his mouth.

"Crucify him. Crucify him." The words rolled over and over off the tongues of the people in the crowd.

Barabbas sighed in calm acceptance of his lot. "Well," he said philosophically, "at least I'll be rid of Pilate's constant whining in my ear."

"You don't know what's happened out there." Lazarus tried to console him. "It might have nothing to do with you."

"They called my name. It has everything to do with me."

"But why? What have you done that the people of Jerusalem want your blood?"

"What does it matter? You heard the crowd. All that remains is for the guards to come."

Simeon spoke for the first time. "Regardless of the crowd, as long as Pilate believes this nonsense about the Maccabee's treasure, he won't let you die."

Barabbas shrugged. "Even Pilate is only so powerful in the face of such a violent people. He'll have no choice but to give in to their demands, no matter what he believes."

"Are you suggesting that a crowd like this can force Pilate to crucify a man, even if he doesn't want to?"

"A crowd that shakes the foundations of the praetorium with its bellow? I fear he'll be left with little choice."

Their discussion was interrupted by footsteps outside. The bolt of their door slid back. Gaius stood in the doorway with six soldiers behind him.

"Barabbas," he called.

"Over here." Barabbas sighed.

"The prefect wants to see you."

Barabbas stood up and strolled over to the door, holding his hands out for the fetters.

"Tie him up." Gaius signalled. "And see that you do it properly this time. Chasing prisoners through the streets is an excitement I can live without."

The guards obediently began fastening the fetters on Barabbas' wrists.

Gaius glanced about the room. "You two can come too." He said, pointing at Yoseph and Simeon.

"What makes us so special?" Yoseph remained seated against the wall.

Gaius affected a weary smile. "I'm always astounded at the boldness of the Jewish warrior. Do you people fear nothing at all?"

Yoseph smiled back. "We fear God. Not petty-minded Roman soldiers waving their sticks in the air."

Gaius clenched his teeth and the muscles on his forearm rippled with intensity as he clutched his centurion's staff. Barabbas scrutinised the soldier. There was far more violence beneath the surface than the centurion's controlled expression revealed. Still, his gaze burned holes in his antagonist's sockets.

Barabbas nodded. A dangerous enemy. Weaker men would have struck Yoseph on the floor where he sat, making the attack and, hence the man, predictable. Such men were easily defeated in battle, but Gaius had reacted differently. Barabbas made a mental note of the fact, in case one day he had the opportunity to face Gaius again in combat.

Then he realised the futility of such a thought. He was on his way to the crucifix. There would never be such an opportunity. He would be dead before sundown.

With infinite self-control, Gaius turned to the guards. "Take those two and bring them with Barabbas before Pilate. I'll wait for you outside." He turned and left the cell as the six legionaries moved into the room. Four stood guard over the rest of the prisoners, while the remaining two grabbed hold of Simeon and Yoseph. Barabbas' brother co-operated, but Yoseph refused to give up so easily. He rounded on his guard, smashing him to the floor with a roundhouse punch. Two more guards had to rush to the assistance of their comrade. They rammed Yoseph against the wall, striking him with the butt of their swords. Yoseph put up a brave fight. It took three soldiers to subdue him. Finally he was secured and joined Barabbas and Simeon outside the cell. The guards led them from the dungeons and through the plush passages of Herod's praetorium.

From there, they headed outside the palace walls, into the congested streets and across to the *Gabbatha*, where Pilate's court was held. It was a large, stone square, raised several feet above the level of the surrounding streets. It had no roof and was open to the horde of people that shoved and shouldered one another to get a better view of the proceedings.

The mob parted for the soldiers as they escorted their prisoners to Pilate. The prefect sat in the stone seat of judgement, surrounded by a cordon of soldiers at the far end of the court. Barabbas noticed a large, well built man with callused hands standing to one side. He was obviously not a mere observer. Barabbas pegged him as another prisoner on trial. The man already bore the marks of several beatings and a night of abuse.

"Who's that?" Yoseph asked, staring at their fellow prisoner.

"How should I know? I've never seen him before."

Pilate was questioning the man intensely, but the prisoner made no reply.

"Who is that man?" Yoseph asked his guards.

"The notorious religious leader from Galilee. The *Sanhedrin* has labelled him a heretic."

Barabbas studied the man with fresh interest. News of his teaching had spread throughout Judea. Many proclaimed that he was the *Messiah*, the one of whom the prophets had spoken that would free Israel from her oppression. Barabbas dismissed such nonsense. From what he'd heard, the man was too passive to be a redeemer.

Through such teachings, many supporters of the zealot cause would be lost to passivity. How could such a man save a nation from bondage? Still, he was impressed by the man's fearlessness. The prisoner remained stubbornly silent before his judge and accusers.

Pilate noticed the arrival of Barabbas and his companions and motioned for them to be brought forward. Barabbas' guards thrust him before Pilate. The prefect spoke quietly, so that the crowd wouldn't hear. His voice was low and menacing as he whispered in Barabbas' ear.

"The crowd has called for your release. Regretfully, as it's the Feast of Unleavened Bread, I'm forced to grant them their wish." Pilate paused. His face was drawn with the strain of what he had to do.

"Your brother and friends remain in custody, however. I may be forced to release you, but they will pay for crimes committed against Rome. They are thieves and robbers who steal taxes and harass Jews who are friendly to Rome. I could still prove lenient if you tell me where to find the copper scroll."

Barabbas shrugged. "Your deception breeds a madness in you. I suggest you forget about these myths before they destroy you."

The hope in Pilate's eyes smouldered and died. "Very well. You're free to leave with your secret, but I'll leave you with the pain of its price for the rest of your days. It will cost you the lives of all you hold dear."

Fury burned in Barabbas' eyes. He was powerless to prevent what was about to happen. If he saved his brother now, Simeon would despise him. He couldn't decide which alternative was more appalling. Silence made his decision for him.

"So be it." Pilate's voice was filled with contempt. He turned to Gaius who stood with the other guards. "These men are insurgents who have committed crimes against the empire. They are sentenced to death by crucifixion. Take them away. As for this other one, I have washed my hands of him. Let the Sanhedrin pass sentence as they see fit."

Barabbas looked again at the quiet man being led away by the Roman soldiers. He glanced about the crowd that had called for his crucifixion. Where were all his followers? Where was Simon, the zealot, in his leader's hour of need? Had he become so cowardly that he would desert the man he had chosen to follow at such a moment? He shook his head in disgust. It was as well that Simon had turned from his responsibilities to the cause. Neither the zealots nor the protectors needed such weak-willed individuals among their number.

Then his thoughts turned to his own troubles and the weight of his sadness overcame him. He sat down on the rough, flat stones of the *Gabbatha*. If only there was a way he could save Yoseph and Simeon. There was nothing he could do, however. They were bound to their fate, as tightly as he was to his oath. His only comfort was that, somehow, Simeon had known this would happen from the very beginning.

Although a free man in Jerusalem, Barabbas was trapped by his circumstances. Once again, the images bombarded his mind. Cephas of Gamala, with beads of scarlet covering his plucked jaw, being dragged away by soldiers who had broken his once solid frame. The image of his father's humiliated eyes haunted Barabbas' memory. The gaunt look had darted from one son to the other, conveying its last goodbyes and the vain hope that they would not remember their father like this.

But they had remembered and the memory had taught them to hate, while the hate continuously reminded them of the past. Where would it end? Memory bred hate and hate bred more memories, each growing stronger as it fed off the other.

† † † † †

Eleazor paced the room in the *Qumran* community, awaiting the hour of prayer. He considered the irony of his anxiety. He was not a religious man, but the hour of prayer was the only time that the scriptorium was empty.

He'd spent every opportunity there, searching diligently for the scroll, but to no avail. If it was hidden there, it was in a place he hadn't thought of. Yet it had to be there. He had to think. He considered all the possible hiding places. He'd examined every jar in the room, tapped every inch of the wall and floor, looking for a hollow chamber. He'd checked under shelves and desks, but found nothing.

Perhaps it was in Nathaniel's quarters? No. The living quarters were too public. People shared rooms and they moved too often. There was very little privacy in the community.

He heard movement in the passage outside. He quickly lay down on his mat, pulling his cloak over his body as a blanket. Two young men – a doctor and his apprentice - entered carrying fresh bandages and ointment for his wounds.

He was thankful for the wounds that Gaius had inflicted on him a few days earlier. They had given substance to his story of capture by Rome, followed by a daring escape. They had also helped him elicit sympathy from the closed community. Nobody was prepared to let a wounded man die in the desert and they had opened their doors to him. Even Nathaniel had grudgingly said he should stay. The old scholar did not trust him, but his decency would not permit him to turn an injured man away.

The doctors began to unwrap his bandages. He waited impatiently while they washed his wounds and gently rubbed in fresh ointment and myrrh. When they were done, they rebandaged the wounds, smiled kindly and left the room. Alone again, he resumed his pacing. Not much longer now. Every few minutes, he stopped and listened for the telltale sound of soft, pattering feet and quiet whispers as the community hastened to the gathering hall for prayer and devotions.

Presently he was rewarded. He risked a peek through the crack between the door and frame and saw the holy men making their way towards the hall.

He waited a few more minutes and then, once prayers had begun, slunk out into the passage, turning about and heading through the bathhouse. From there he turned left past the kitchen, carefully checking that nobody was around to see him.

Once he felt certain that he was safe, he entered the short, narrow passage with lightly coloured stone walls that led into the scriptorium. The room had a sacrosanct atmosphere about it that made Eleazor shudder. Several tables littered the floor, surrounded by hard wooden benches. There were a few oil lamps and inkwells on the desks, neatly arranged and ready for use.

The inkwells contained dry lumps of coloured granules, comprised mostly of vegetable matter, into which a wetted stylus could be dipped to liquefy the substance. The room's walls were a mass of shelves from ceiling to floor and the shelves, in turn, were filled with parchment, scrolls and a horde of pottery jars for storing manuscripts.

He gazed slowly about the room, deep in thought. Where he had not looked? He had checked every jar, on every shelf. He'd searched each of the scrolls in his quest, but had seen nothing resembling the one he was after. His eyes continued their roving until they rested on the tables.

The tables! Perhaps there was a hidden compartment he'd not seen. Slowly, he moved to examine each table. They all looked identical at a glance, but perhaps! He went to the first one, feeling underneath, checking the thickness of the wood. It seemed to be normal in every respect.

He began checking the second table. It appeared to be the same. After checking four tables, he began to get disheartened. Nothing appeared to be out of place in their design at all. What had he missed?

The old man would almost certainly keep it close, where he could guard it properly. The scriptorium was where Nathaniel spent most of his time, so it stood to reason that this was where he would hide it. When he reached the fifth table, his diligence paid off. The tabletop was far thicker than the wood appeared to be, indicating a double panel. *Finally*. He breathed his relief. He began feeling for a latch, or a handle - anything that would open the compartment. He found the lever on the inside of one of the side panels. It looked and felt like a knot in the wood and was probably just that.

Eleazor plunged his finger in and pulled first one way and then the other. He was rewarded with a click as the latch released. The panel slid back, revealing a hidden compartment.

A quiet shuffle of feet distracted him before he could examine the contents. In panic, he whirled away from the desk. He glanced about wildly, looking for any avenue of escape, or some place to hide. None were available, however, and he turned to confront his accuser.

He blushed as his guilty eyes confronted the inquisitive stare of a child. Her eyes were wide and her thumb glistened with saliva.

"*Shalom*, peace, little one." Eleazor regained his composure.

"Why are you not at prayer with the other men?" She asked boldly.

"I'm not allowed to pray with them. Are you allowed in here?" He smiled gently.

The girl hesitated, then shook her head. The shy eyes conveyed her guilt and she brought her hand back to her mouth and bit her thumb.

Eleazor winked at her. "Me neither." He whispered. The child's mouth opened wide in amazement at the revelation.

"Tell you what." Eleazor said in a conspirator's whisper. "I won't tell anyone if you don't, alright?"

The little girl nodded, smiling the shy smile of an accomplice in crime.

Eleazor grinned. "Good. Now run along, before someone catches you here."

The girl scampered off, delighted at the good fortune of her escape. Eleazor smiled indulgently and went back to the table.

He rummaged through all of the contents of the hidden drawer. They consisted of old parchments and valuable scrolls, but contained nothing resembling the copper scroll. He cursed and replaced all the parchments. Then he closed the panel.

The hour of prayer was almost over. He had to get back to his room. He couldn't risk being discovered before he had the scroll safely in his possession. He slipped quietly through the passages, filled with bitter disappointment. He'd felt so sure that he had found it. Already, he could hear the Essenes exiting the prayer room. He had no choice but to wait and resume his quest the following day.

Time was running out. The Essenes had believed his story of a daring escape and a hunt that had led a garrison of Roman soldiers across the desert, but it was only a matter of time before the zealots revealed suspicions of his treachery. Word travelled quickly in the desert. He lay down on his sleeping mat and thought once again about the layout of the room. Where would he search tomorrow?

† † † † †

The following day found Eleazor back in the scriptorium at the hour of prayer. He had already subjected the remaining tables to close inspection and found nothing. This had been followed by a search of the benches for any hidden compartments. That too, had proved fruitless.

Once again, he studied the room. What had he missed? He cursed Nathaniel's ingenuity. His eyes scanned the shelves, examining each scroll and parchment. He'd already searched all of them and found nothing.

Again, he allowed his eyes wander to the tables, with their sturdy, wooden legs. The limbs and edges were decorated with ornate patterns, curving gently as they followed the contour of the wood. The legs! His heart began to beat a little faster. The table legs were thick enough to conceal a scroll. He began to knock feverishly at the legs, listening for any hollow sound. He found it on the table with the hidden panel.

Bursting with excitement, he lifted the corner, twisting and pulling at the heavy limb. With a thrill, he discovered that, by twisting ninety degrees and pulling, the leg came clean off the table. The inside had been hollowed out, forming two long, cylindrical holes that could hold a scroll.

Eleazor flipped it over and, with the utmost care, let the scroll slide out, catching it in his left hand. He stared at the object for nearly thirty seconds without moving. Then he dropped the table leg and leaned forward, holding his head in his hand while he massaged his temples.

He stared again, in defeat, at the ancient papyrus scroll in his hand. It had faded Hebrew letters written on it - a passage from Isaiah, as far as he could tell. The words were unimportant. What mattered was the material. He gazed dumbly at the papyrus with its fraying, yellow edges. It glinted for a moment in the dim light of the scriptorium. A feeling of utter dejection crept over him as he slipped the scroll back into its recess.

As he considered the past few days, a deep depression began to eat away at him. Pent up frustration and failure had begun to take their toll. He considered his life. His entire existence revolved around failure. He'd never succeeded at anything. As a child, he'd failed his father's expectations. As an adult, he had never achieved a single goal. All that was left was the treasure and now he had failed in that. Foiled by an old man who was already half blind from years spent writing in dingy scriptoriums.

After a lifetime of searching, fate had brought him to this. A depressed and bedraggled figure forced to admit he'd accomplished nothing with his life. All his days had become meaningless. It would have been better if he had never lived.

His self-pity was interrupted by a noise in the passage outside. Quickly he replaced the scroll and reattached the leg to the table. He could hear voices and realised with horror that he had stayed too long. Prayer was over. There was no way out and discovery was now inevitable.

He held his breath and came to a decision. He walked boldly to the door. In the passage outside he was confronted by Nathaniel and Mattithyahu. The elderly scholar's expression turned livid.

"What are you doing in here!" He demanded. "This is an outrage. How dare you enter this place uninvited?" The rage was too hot and the words too harsh. It proved to Eleazor that his instincts had been right. What he saw was not rage, but fear, in the old man's eyes. Mattithyahu stood silently by Nathaniel's side and fixed Eleazor with an icy glare.

Eleazor tried to sound pleasant. "I was looking for you. I wanted to thank you for your hospitality."

"You knew we were at prayer. Why come here?" The old man's cry was hoarse.

"I thought prayer was over. I see I misjudged it by a few minutes."

Mattithyahu spoke for the first time. "I'm glad to see you're feeling better. I expect you'll be wanting to leave the community now that you're well."

Eleazor scowled. It wasn't a question, he realised.

"I'll just accompany you to fetch your belongings." Mattithyahu's voice was pleasant, but his gaze was guarded.

Eleazor had little option but to accompany the young Essene. No good could be achieved by resisting. Mattithyahu turned to Nathaniel and steadied his quivering arm. "You carry on here. I'll see to it that he leaves."

The old man nodded nervously and entered the room, while Mattithyahu accompanied Eleazor to his quarters.

Inside the scriptorium, Nathaniel rushed at the table with the hidden compartments. With trembling hands he removed the hollow leg and gingerly emptied the contents onto the floor. The scroll slid from its musty recess and Nathaniel sobbed with relief. He ran his hands over the old, papyrus scroll, gently fondling the antiquated material with frail, wrinkled fingers.

He spent a long time, deep in thought, weighing up his alternatives. After agonising over it until he felt twice his age, he came to a decision. He was too old to protect the scroll properly and *Qumran* was no longer the safe haven it had been for the past few years. Levi was right. The scroll was in danger and needed warriors to protect it.

With an air of resolve, he picked up the table leg and reattached it. He took the scroll in his hand, sat down and waited for Mattithyahu. He whiled away the time by reading the words penned by a younger, firmer hand so many years ago. It was a passage from Isaiah, his favourite among the prophets. His weak eyes could barely read the words on the paper, but he recited the passage verbatim. The words brought peace to his troubled mind, reminding him that God was sovereign and that no endeavours of man could ever change his truth.

Footsteps echoed outside and Mattithyahu entered the room. Nathaniel looked up from the scroll. "Is he gone?"

"Yes, old father. I made sure of it."

"He's an evil man, my son. He seeks the scroll we spoke of."

"The copper scroll?"

Nathaniel nodded. "We must remove it before it's discovered."

"He can't discover it now that he's gone. He'll never be welcome here again. We'll see to that."

"No, my son." Nathaniel shook his head vehemently. "You don't know these men. He's a zealot, a soldier of the desert. You're a peaceful man. You have no understanding of the violence he's capable of."

"But if he can't get in —"

Nathaniel held up a hand to interrupt him. "Don't you remember the zealots we sheltered?"

Mattithyahu inclined his head in a curt nod.

"They were here when the Roman soldiers arrived."

"I remember. We all feared their discovery."

Nathaniel nodded. "Romans blocking every exit, searching every room, and yet they found no sign of them."

Mattithyahu shrugged. "So they escaped somehow."

Nathaniel smiled. "Yes, they escaped. And yet we still have no idea how. They move without being seen and they strike without warning. How can you stop such a man from getting in, when an entire Roman garrison failed to see seven of them get out, and that in the bright light of the morning sun?"

"But there are four hundred men in the community."

"We are peaceful men. Scholars, not warriors. Eleazor could strike down ten of us at once in battle, even if we were armed. Would you risk the lives of our community for something they've never even heard of?" He frowned, shaking his head. "No, I've spent a long time thinking about it. The scroll is sought by a warrior. It should be protected by like minded men."

Mattithyahu glanced back at the scriptorium's entrance. "What would you have me do?"

Nathaniel gazed across at the young man. "I see you have perception beyond your years. I must make a journey. It will be my final act as a protector. You must go to Jerusalem. Find Levi and the siblings from Gamala. Tell them what has happened."

"Nathaniel, you know they were captured by the Romans. It's unlikely they're still alive."

"They are resourceful men. You place too little faith in their abilities."

"Still, you have to concede the possibility."

Nathaniel nodded sadly. "Yes, I know. Go to Jerusalem. There is a woman, called Deborah, who lives in the *Kainopolis*. She'll tell you how to find them."

"And if the worst has happened?"

Nathaniel hesitated. "Then you must find another. He's a former zealot, and now a follower of this new teacher from Nazareth. He no longer considers himself a protector, but he is honourable. If you go to him, he will help you."

Nathaniel discussed the details of his mission with Mattithyahu and finally they agreed. He would leave the following day and Mattithyahu would take the news to Jerusalem.

† † † † †

The following day as the sun rose, casting its rays over the pastel valley of the Dead Sea, Nathaniel packed his bags. He took with him a staff, food and money in his belt and set off south, heading for Masada - the Judean fortress built by Herod. Although it was still controlled by Rome, it had become a stronghold of the zealot underground in recent years.

As he left the community for the first time in many years, he glanced around, scanning the hills and valleys for hidden, searching eyes. Though he saw none, he felt sure that somewhere danger lurked. Eleazor knew where the scroll was and he would not be found far from it.

Nathaniel hurried off, glancing about him constantly. Every now and then he patted the scroll in his belt, as if for comfort. He kept his movements erratic, going first one way and then another, cutting new paths in the desert to make sure he was not being followed.

† † † † †

High above, on the ridge, Eleazor smiled laconically at the old man's pitiful attempts to shake off imagined pursuers. He moved quickly, keeping out of sight, but always in a position to observe Nathaniel's alluvial wanderings. Presently, the old scribe increased his pace and headed directly south.

Eleazor followed, flitting between boulders and ever-shortening shadows in the rising sun. He also didn't take any chances, doubling back twice to make sure that nobody else was following the old man. For two hours, he stalked his prey through the crevices and alcoves that the desert provided. Then he made his move. He quickly descended the slopes, falling on the old man as suddenly as an eagle swoops on an unsuspecting rabbit.

Nathaniel never saw him. Nor did he hear the movement. Suddenly Eleazor was upon him, with his weapon drawn. The scholar recoiled from the approaching apparition. Eleazor brandished his sword and forced the scribe back against the rock-face. Nathaniel's fearful expression turned to one of dismay. There was no escape.

"You left very early." Eleazor smiled. "You should be careful, journeying alone in the desert, old man. It's a dangerous place for solitary travellers."

"What do you want?" Nathaniel asked fearfully.

"I think you know. Your fear reveals your guilt and the secret you hide."

"You talk in circles, like a woman. How can anyone understand your ramblings?"

"Don't insult me, old man. Your life is worth little out here."

"Death holds no fear for me. At my age, it lurks in the corners of every room."

"I want the scroll."

"What scroll?" Nathaniel looked perplexed, but his hand touched his belt.

Eleazor smiled. "Give it to me. Then, perhaps, I'll let you live."

Nathaniel shrank from him, holding the scroll in his belt all the more tightly.

"I have no reason to kill you, old man. Don't give me one. The scroll in your belt. Let me have it."

The elderly Essene seemed to deflate before Eleazor. Resigned to defeat, he reached into his belt and pulled the scroll from its pocket.

Eleazor reached forward and snatched it from Nathaniel's hand, knocking the old man to the rocky earth. He dropped his sword and eagerly tore at the parchment, to see the scroll inside.

Once again, his world crumbled in disappointment. He stared blank faced at the same scripture he had seen in the hollow leg of the table in the scriptorium. It was a different scroll this time, but equally worthless.

"What is this?" His question was a dull monotone.

Nathaniel looked confused and scrambled to his feet. "It's the scroll you asked for."

"This is not the scroll I seek and you know it!" Eleazor's frenzied shriek echoed in the mountains around them.

The old man's face became calm.

"I want the copper scroll." Eleazor was on the verge of hysteria. He grabbed the old man's tunic and began tearing at his belt in search of the document.

"My son, you're not making sense."

"Why are you out here today? Where are you going?"

"I take news to brothers, fellow Essenes near Masada."

Eleazor slumped to the ground, wiping his sweating brow with the back of his hand. *All this for nothing.* Then a thought occurred to him.

He looked sharply at Nathaniel. "If that's true, then why did you twist and turn so many times. Why the constant checking behind you?"

The old Essene remained silent, but the corners of his mouth turned up, betraying the smile he concealed. Suddenly the truth of the matter dawned on Eleazor.

"You knew I'd follow you here." He exclaimed, amazed at the old man's cunning. "All of that stealth - turning and doubling back - only served to attract my attention. You knew I'd never lose your trail."

"I suspected." Nathaniel admitted. His voice was calm and his expression impassive.

"Where's the scroll?"

The old man shrugged. "I don't know. I sent it away to be handed to another. My responsibilities have ended. Kill me if you must. This was my last act to defend it."

"Who have you entrusted it to?"

Nathaniel hesitated. "Four men go to Jerusalem. They know not what they carry, but there they will find Barabbas. He'll know what to do with it."

At first Eleazor was stunned. Barabbas - a protector! *What had he done?* Pilate would squeeze the truth from him like juice from a pomegranate. He had to intercept the party before they reached the Holy City.

Then he thought of Barabbas' stubbornness and laughed. "Barabbas is dead, you fool. I handed him over to Rome myself. By now he'll be so much rotting flesh on a Roman cross outside Jerusalem." He chuckled again. "I'll go to Jerusalem and I'll find your men. Then I'll take your precious scroll for myself. You've lost, old man. May you die with the shame of that knowledge."

He struck Nathaniel with his sword. The blade caught the elderly man on the hairline of his cranium and crimson blood spattered as he fell to the earth.

He looked down at the scribe with contempt. "May the jackals feed on your rotting innards."

He kicked the old man's inert body before turning north to seek out the four unwitting men who carried the scroll. Near *Qumran*, he found his horse where he had left it, tethered to a tree. He mounted it, pleased by the extra speed it afforded him and spurred it on northwards, hoping to overtake the Essene party before they reached their destination.

✝ ✝ ✝ ✝ ✝

At the commune in *Khirbet Qumran*, Mattithyahu prepared for his journey to Jerusalem. He was to travel with three companions - men from the community. They were all under the impression that they were headed to the Holy City to buy food and supplies, and to trade some goods that the community produced such as pottery and salt.

Mattithyahu knew that such stories were a mere pretext to get him to Jerusalem. Once there, he'd been instructed to find Barabbas, Simeon and Levi, his co-protectors of the scroll and tell them the news of Eleazor. The prostitute, Deborah would be able to tell him where they were. Although Nathaniel had been unable to tell him exactly where her house was, he knew it lay somewhere in the *Kainopolis*. It wouldn't be difficult to find.

If they were dead - but they had to be alive. He didn't have the energy to convince a man who had long since rejected his responsibilities that he was now the scroll's only hope. Besides, how would he find him? None of the protectors had had any contact with him since he'd left the zealots. The man was dead to them.

"The sun's already high, Mattithyahu."

The voice outside his room startled him. He looked up to see Amos peering around the doorway.

"Patience, brother." Mattithyahu suppressed a smile. Amos was young and always impatient, especially when there was a party headed for Jerusalem.

In his heart, Amos was an Essene, but the bustling city of Jerusalem held infinite temptations that appealed to his youthfulness. He always volunteered when a trip to Jerusalem was required and the community saw no harm in it, as long as he had older, more sober-minded men to guide his steps through a city fraught with sin. Even the so-called righteous Pharisees had compromised their faith to the point of heresy, as far as the Essenes were concerned. As for the hypocritical Sadducees, the Essenes considered them to be little more than Gentiles, followers of the wicked priest, who would corrupt Israel as surely as leprosy corrupted the flesh of men.

"The third hour approaches, Mattithyahu." Amos pressed him.

"Wait for me outside. I'll join you shortly."

Amos sighed in exasperation. Mattithyahu waited, quietly checking that he had everything he needed for the journey. *Do not leave until two full hours have passed.* That had been Nathaniel's instruction. The old man had wanted to be sure that he was well away from the commune before Mattithyahu embarked on his journey. Mattithyahu checked everything again. Finally he joined Amos and the others for the journey to Jerusalem.

They left as per Nathaniel's instructions - exactly two hours after dawn. Four men straddling donkeys, with extra pack animals to carry goods and provisions for the journey there and back. Amos led the group, as if anxious to get there as soon as he could.

Behind him, Mattithyahu rode with their two remaining travelling companions, Eli and Reuben. They were both older men with thick, greying beards. Eli had a particularly dark complexion while Reuben, a father figure in the community, wore a permanent, stern frown on his weathered face. He seldom spoke but was well respected, even feared, by his brothers in the commune.

He was a powerful man and a pillar of righteousness in the Essene community. A perfect choice to watch over the group of men headed for a decadent city. Where others might falter in the face of temptation, Reuben would remain pious and see to it that those with him behaved likewise.

Before they had gone many miles, Mattithyahu called them to a halt.

"What now?" Amos was irritable. "We're already late and the city gates close at sundown."

"I have stomach cramps." Mattithyahu dismounted and ran for the bushes, bent over and wincing with pain. As soon as he was out of sight, he changed direction, climbing a gully. He gazed at a small hill, not far ahead. From his thick, woollen belt, he removed the heavy object and carefully wrapped it in leather parchment. He secured it so that it could not fall open. It took several minutes of searching before he found the spot he was looking for - a cave near the dome of the mountain. It had been many years since he'd last been there and it was a tight squeeze getting through the narrow entrance. He placed the leather bag under a flat stone, to protect it from the elements as well as inquisitive eyes that might visit the cave.

He said a quick prayer and then exited the grotto. He raced back down the gully and emerged from the scrub where his friends had last seen him.

"We're never going to make it before dark." Amos complained, glancing at the sun.

"Sorry." Mattithyahu mumbled.

Eli looked concerned. "Are you feeling alright? We can still turn back to *Qumran.*"

"What!" Amos shouted in alarm. "The community needs these supplies. We can't return without them."

Mattithyahu waved a hand in protest. "No, no. I'll be fine. I think we should continue to Jerusalem. What do you say, Amos?" He grinned at the younger man.

"If we push the mules, we can still get there before dark." Amos said hopefully.

"Right. To go back now would waste time."

Eli considered Mattithyahu's words. Finally he nodded. "Alright, we'll continue. I only hope you feel strong enough for the journey."

Mattithyahu nodded, relieved by the decision. He needed to get to Jerusalem as quickly as possible. Later, he would wonder whether things might have turned out differently, had he not been so anxious to reach the protectors in the Holy City. It was a lifetime later and one filled with regret.

The men continued on their way. The only intrusions on their tranquillity came from Amos, who was too young to have learned the value of silence. He spoke incessantly of the weather, the scenery and where they intended to stay when they arrived in Jerusalem. The rest of the men travelled quietly, keeping their thoughts company, occasionally grunting in reply to one of Amos' conversational gambits.

In truth, Mattithyahu was too worried to be in the mood for conversation. He kept wondering about the men he was to meet in Jerusalem. It seemed impossible that they could still be alive, and yet they had to be. For generations, the priests had guarded the scroll, but now the warriors were called for. The scroll had never needed its protectors more than it did at this moment.

As the mules picked their way up the treacherous slopes of the Great Rift Valley, he considered the decisions that lay before him. Nathaniel had undertaken a perilous journey that he refused to talk about. Mattithyahu had no idea whether he would return at all. The old man had merely told him what he should do and wished him well. That left him with the full burden of the secret. It was a weight too great to bear alone.

Distressing thoughts engulfed him like a mist, obscuring the danger that lay in wait. Later, he blamed himself for the events that occurred. Events that were beyond his control.

9

HAVING PRONOUNCED sentence on the prisoners, Pilate strode from the *Gabbatha*. Surrounded by legionaries, he returned to his palace. Barabbas was released but remained in the open air court. The three remaining prisoners were led across to the flogging poles. The crowd had become strangely silent as they watched the soldiers shove the men roughly towards the vile instruments.

Above the city, the ominous, black and dust-yellow clouds of the approaching *Khamsin* swirled like steam in a warlock's cauldron, casting down their oppressive heat and twisted shadows on the population of the Holy City. They showered the hushed crowd with their ashes of desert sand, turning the mob into a procession of mourners as they shuffled across the silent stones of the *Gabbatha*.

The condemned men were taken to a line of bloodstained wooden posts, where they were stripped naked in the semi-darkness and tied securely to restrict their movement. Three soldiers entered the pavement area. One was a large, heavy-set legionary with a creased face and dark, thick eyebrows. He eyed the crowd sullenly as he headed towards the prisoners. The second was smaller, but that was all Barabbas noted about him.

His gaze was drawn to the third legionary. It was Publius, the chubby torturer with the friendly smile. The sight of the man filled him with rage and he had to suppress the urge to charge and snatch the whip from his hand. It was a *flagrum* with a thick, wooden handle and multiple, leather thongs of varying length. Woven into the brutal thongs were tiny barbs, sharp bits of bone and lead, designed to bruise and tear the flesh of their victims.

Cruel though it was, the flagrum was, in fact, an instrument of mercy. It would drain the life and strength from its victims, thus shortening the far greater agony that was to come. The crowd seemed to suddenly revive. Pressing forward, it began to roar its bloodthirsty approval.

The heavy-set soldier approached the rabbi from Galilee, while the shorter legionary headed for Yoseph. It was obvious that Pilate had instructed that Simeon be left to Publius, thus compounding Barabbas' agony with memories of Joshua's torture.

The mass of bodies rushed forward and Barabbas found himself pushed to the front of the mob.

"One!" The heavy-set legionary in the middle counted the first blow. The thongs snapped and coiled like enraged vipers, hissing at their helpless prey. They whistled in frenzy and then swooped down with an angry crack. Barabbas felt sick with revulsion.

The first thin beads of crimson sprang forth from the tiny cuts the whips had inflicted. The crowd bellowed in murderous applause.

"Two." The counter's cry echoed above the roar. By the fifth blow, Yoseph was horribly bruised by the lead balls that had been woven into the leather.

Simeon's bruises had already begun to crack in countless places, cut open by the cruel barbs of bone. He was bleeding profusely. The whips cut deeper and deeper into the subcutaneous tissue of their victims. The thongs sliced through the capillaries of the skin with vicious determination. Blood oozed from a mat of wounds on the prisoners' backs.

Barabbas felt more nauseated with each new blow. He screamed, trying to drown out the angry roar of the crowd, desperate for the suffering to end. The whips shrieked their bloody intent again and again and the oozing gave way to spurting, arterial flow as the thongs cut through the muscles beneath the skin. Torn ribbons of flesh hung from the backs of the groaning prisoners, forming a woven tapestry of pain.

"Stop." Barabbas whispered in mute horror. He turned his face from the suffering of the people he loved.

Finally, mercifully, the flogging came to an end. The condemned men's backs were little more than a mass of torn and bleeding tissue, mutilated beyond recognition. Nausea engulfed Barabbas as he saw what had become of his brother and Yoseph. The flesh had been stripped from their backs with such brutality that even some of their internal organs lay partially exposed.

Breathing came hard for Barabbas as the bedraggled figures were untied. They were so weak that they needed soldiers to support their arms. Six soldiers entered, pushing their way through the crowd. Between them, they carried three rough, wooden bars. When they pressed the bars onto mutilated backs, the helpless prisoners collapsed under the weight and the fresh pain.

Barabbas was filled with a growing loathing for the soldiers who carried out their wicked orders. They were enjoying their job and he hated them for it.

"Get up!" they cried, kicking the bleeding bodies and dragging the men to their feet.

The three prisoners staggered under the weight of their crucifix crossbars. They didn't get far before they stumbled again, smearing the dirty streets crimson as their flesh wiped the stones like sodden rags. Again, they were forced to their feet. They staggered a few more paces. The wooden bars jarred against their backs, pressing sharp splinters into exposed and damaged flesh.

Barabbas was caught in the current of the crowd. Once again, he found himself at the front of the mob, with the ghastly scene right before his eyes. Simeon and the man from Nazareth stumbled again, falling to their knees. The soldiers began kicking and beating them, forcing them to continue up the hill. Help came from an unexpected quarter. Gaius marched from the crowd and barked an order at the legionaries. Barabbas couldn't hear what he said above the din of the people around him, but the soldiers ceased their violent activities.

The centurion then searched among the spectators. He pointed out two men and ordered them to take the bars from the bleeding prisoners. The men stepped forward obediently. A Roman centurion's orders were never questioned.

With a sudden rush, Barabbas dived forward, placing a strong hand on the arm of the man who bent down to take Simeon's crossbar. The man turned and looked at him. Barabbas shoved him aside and bent down, gently lifting the bar from Simeon's back. Simeon stared for a moment with haunted eyes into Barabbas' own. He couldn't be sure, but Barabbas thought he saw a moment of recognition, before the eyes glazed over once again, seeing, yet not seeing.

He choked back a sob as he felt his brother's hot, heaving breath against his face for an instant. Then Simeon turned away, staring in a daze at his surroundings. He swayed, as if unsure of which direction to head. The soldiers prodded him forward along the path that led to Calvary, the hill where his crucifix lay.

The blood on the bar was warm and it seeped through Barabbas' tunic, staining it a rich crimson colour. He heaved the bar into a more comfortable position on his shoulder and trudged up the path towards the summit. The crowd still roared in his ears. People stampeded, hoping to find a good position from which to view the proceedings at the top.

When he arrived at the summit, Barabbas laid down the heavy chunk of wood.

"Not there," yelled a legionary. Barabbas turned to see the man beckoning. "Over here," the soldier barked and pointed at the tall, upright bar that lay on the ground. The bar had a second piece of wood attached to it, called the mercy seat. Its name was misleading because, although it gave the victim a small measure of relief, it made the ordeal last far longer than it ordinarily would.

Barabbas picked up the crossbar, wincing as the splinters of the rough wood jabbed painfully at his shoulder. He carried it to the upright bar the legionary was pointing at. The soldiers took the bar and quickly attached it to the upright, creating the cruellest instrument of torture ever devised by man.

They brought Simeon, torn and bleeding and placed him on the cross. The man from Nazareth was brought next, followed by Yoseph on the other side. Each of the men was placed on his own crucifix, bleeding and gasping for breath.

Barabbas felt as if he was losing his already tenuous grasp on sanity. It was his helplessness that hurt him the most. All he could do was watch as the soldiers took the seven inch spikes and drove them into the wrists of their victims. The screams died in choking coughs as the men gasped at the agony of severed nerves. Next, their legs were crossed at the ankles and a large spike was driven through, tearing ligaments and sinew as it bored its passage with each fresh blow into the wood beyond. Barabbas heard one of the men wail in pain, until finally the wail died away into a weak sob. How can men do this! He threw back his head and screamed silently at the sky.

The crosses were raised, carrying their victims high into the air, above the heads of the crowd and then the ordeal began.

Hopeless and dejected, Barabbas felt he had to stay with his brother to the end. Simeon's face contorted with agony as his arms weakened and great waves of cramp swept through his muscles, knotting them in a deep and infinite, throbbing pain.

Unable to pull himself up, he slowly began to suffocate. The crucifix allowed its subject to breathe in, but made it impossible to breathe out. Suffering increased with each moment as carbon dioxide built up in the lifeless blood stream. This caused the cramping to abate somewhat until the subject was finally able to pull himself up and exhale.

Gratefully, he swallowed the life-giving oxygen into his lungs. The cross demanded a price for this precious gift, however, and along with the oxygen the cramps returned with a vengeance. They paralysed their subject with pain and, as he succumbed, so he began to suffocate once more, repeating the process over and over again.

To his left, Barabbas saw the soldiers taunting the rabbi who had gone to the crucifix in his place. The man hung where Barabbas knew he himself belonged. Above the man's head, Barabbas read the sign. *"Jesus of Nazareth, King of the Jews."* He shook his head as he watched the man experience the same suffering as his brother and Yoseph.

Barabbas turned back to face his brother, staring into the terrified eyes. Simeon gazed down, but did not see him, blinded by the pain.

† † † † †

"Deborah!" The yelling was frantic. "Deborah, come quickly."

She opened the door, aghast, and stared into the face of the young street urchin – the son of a widow - who lived two blocks east against the city wall. "What is it, Absalom?"

"Come quickly. My mother says it's urgent."

"Why, what's happened?"

"Simeon." The boy panted. "Simeon and Yoseph —"

"What about them?" She asked the question, but feared she already knew.

The boy was gasping for breath. He still panted from his race through the city streets.

"They're being crucified."

Deborah gasped. She had known it must happen, but so soon! The Feast of Unleavened Bread was upon them and the Sabbath started at sundown. "Barabbas?" She was terrified to ask, but she had to know.

"He's there."

"At Calvary?" Her heart sank, expecting the worst.

"Pilate released him. Another man was crucified in his place. The prefect said he could find no guilt in him."

"In Barabbas?" She frowned in confusion.

"No, the man from Nazareth. Pilate said he was innocent, but they crucified him anyway."

"And Barabbas is free." She laughed with relief. "Where is he now?"

"He's with Simeon."

"Is he alright, did you speak to him?"

"My mother wouldn't let me. She said he needed to be alone. Then she sent me to call you."

"We must go." She turned to fetch her key.

She closed the door behind her and locked it, sliding the bolt into position. Outside the courtyard, she pulled her veil up to shield her face against the hot wind that gusted between the buildings. The *Khamsin* had filled the city with an eerie dimness, hiding the sun from view behind pus-filled yellow and black clouds. The result was a depressing twilight scene.

Deborah glanced up at the dull, white disk in the sky. It seemed as if a shadow had spread across part of its surface. The city grew rapidly darker as the sun seemed to slowly hide its face behind a creeping shadow. Filled with fear, she hurried towards the hill called *The Skull.* The sun continued to disappear behind the frightening shadow until, in a final flash, its face was gone and the city was plunged into blackness. Confusion erupted in the streets. Children wailed and parents shouted their alarm.

"What's happening, Deborah?" Absalom asked nervously.

"I don't know, child. Powerful forces are at work in Jerusalem today. Come, now. Barabbas needs us. We must go to him."

✝ ✝ ✝ ✝ ✝

Barabbas sat entranced at the foot of his brother's cross, listening to the condemned men as they spoke. Soldiers stood around, jeering at the man from Nazareth.

"You healed others, but you cannot save yourself." One of the legionaries guffawed. To Barabbas it sounded distant, as if he'd had too much good wine to drink.

"Come down, son of God." Another soldier cried amidst the raucous laughter.

Yoseph began to laugh hysterically on the cross, choking as he gasped for a tiny breath of air. "Do you hear their jesting?" He panted and turned his head towards the quiet man.

Still, the man made no reply.

"Did the Roman whip tear out your tongue?" Yoseph yelled. "Answer me. Why don't you save yourself and us as well, you performer of miracles?"

Simeon pushed himself up to snatch a breath of air. "Leave him alone, Yoseph."

"Why?" Yoseph chuckled. Pain had overcome his sanity. "Is he above a joke? Has he no sense of humour?" His chuckle ended abruptly in a choking splutter.

"Quiet, I said." Simeon's voice was sharp. "You and I deserve to be up here. We've lived all our lives in disregard for the law, but this man has done nothing wrong."

He gasped as a fresh wave of agony washed over him, but he kept himself raised, so that he could speak. Shuddering, he pushed himself up with his legs. He winced as the cruel nails tore at his flesh and damaged nerves. Barabbas watched, stunned, as his brother turned his head towards the man from Nazareth.

Simeon looked with pleading eyes at the man on the cross beside him. "Teacher," he begged. "Will you remember me in paradise?"

The man turned slowly and looked at Simeon. Even in his state of weakness, his charisma was undeniable. Barabbas swallowed. If only he were a zealot soldier. That man could have led the nation of Israel to freedom. If he had called them to overthrow Rome, thousands would have followed him, even to their graves.

The rabbi from Nazareth opened his mouth to speak. "I tell you the truth." Each word came as a painful gasp as the man battled for a breath of air. "This day, you will be with me in paradise."

Barabbas looked back at his brother. Simeon seemed to relax, allowing his body to fall back down, filling his lungs with air. Another wave of cramps engulfed his contorted muscles. In the midst of his suffering, there was peace on Simeon's face. The pain no longer seemed to matter and he gave himself up to the torture and the inevitable call of the grave.

Barabbas gazed at the rabbi, his heart filled with gratitude. The man had eased Simeon's suffering with a few well-chosen words. As long as he lived, he would never forget that act of kindness.

Looking about him, Barabbas noticed for the first time how dark it had become. The sun seemed to have suddenly vanished and lonely wails emerged from the crowd as people stared nervously about them. The mass of humanity had become strangely mute. All eyes rested on the man from Galilee, as if the whole world had halted, waiting for him to breathe his final breath.

At the foot of his brother's cross, Barabbas knelt, staring across at the man who claimed to be the king of the Jews.

"My God, my God, why have you forsaken me?" the man cried. A flow of blood trickled from his heel, making its way down the wood's rough grain. The trickle fell into a crimson pool, staining the earth at the base of the cruel instrument of torture.

"Barabbas." He turned at the sound of the woman's voice.

Deborah stood wide-eyed and beautiful. Her expression was a melting pot of conflicting emotions. There was relief and joy, but also deep sorrow that empathised with his loss and mental torment.

Barabbas was unable to speak. He merely reached out his hand and she came to him, flinging her arms around his neck and burying her face in his shoulder.

"I'm so sorry," she whispered.

He held her tightly, but never uttered a word. He was consumed with guilt for his brother's tortured death. He wanted to tell her how he felt - how it should have been him on the cross, but could not express the pain that gripped his heart.

One of the prisoners was mumbling. He turned back to locate the source. It was Yoseph, muttering incoherent words as he bled on his cross. Simeon was nearly dead. His breath sounded like the intermittent sawing of an unskilled carpenter.

Watching his brother's final battle for survival took what was left of Barabbas' fortitude. He sank quietly to his knees, slamming his head against the ground, and moaned through clenched teeth. For the thousandth time, Simeon's body convulsed with pain. He shivered and strained every muscle, clawing his way a few inches higher for the life-giving breath that would not come.

The man next to him did the same. He looked like an old man, trying to rise from a chair. He gasped for air and raised his head heavenward.

"It is finished." He cried and fell back down on the mercy seat. Once again, he struggled, lifting himself a few inches higher. "Father," he cried, "into your hands, I commit my spirit." With another cry, he fell forward. His head slumped to one side and his body relaxed.

Barabbas had seen too many lives end, not to recognise death when he saw it. The crowd was hushed. Many people had died at Calvary - crucified mercilessly - undergoing hours of agony, but no death had been as moving as that of the innocent man from Galilee. The soldiers all stared mystified at the torn figure on the middle cross. None uttered a word.

Gaius had a look of awe about him. "He truly was the son of God," he murmured.

Barabbas turned back to his brother, focusing on his own pain. Simeon and Yoseph were still alive, albeit barely. After a while, the sun emerged from behind its shadow, returning to its rightful place in the world. The light was still dim amidst the abating, desert storm, but the dust had settled and the dry wind had become more tolerable.

After about an hour a Roman soldier broke away from the group. He carried a large club in his hand and strode across to the men on the crosses. First he inspected Yoseph, who was still breathing. Muttering inanities, he clung on to life with a tenuous grasp.

The soldier leaned back and swung the club in a mercifully vicious blow, breaking Yoseph's leg in the middle of the shin. The second blow smashed the other shin, rendering the condemned man helpless and unable to push himself up for the life-giving breaths that sustained him. Death by suffocation would follow in minutes.

The soldier proceeded to the man from Galilee, but didn't use his club. The state of the man was obvious. There was no need to inspect the body. The legionary glanced at the man briefly, and then reached for his spear. He drove it with a vicious thrust into the body, between the third and fourth ribs.

Barabbas shook his head at the man's childish antics. Did Rome have so little respect for human dignity that it treated a corpse as a toy for its amusement? He was too overcome with grief to feel truly angry. The rage would come later and when it did, it would blaze with the fury of the sun, consuming all it touched, destroying everything in its path.

The soldier proceeded to Simeon's cross and, once again, brought the club to bear. His brother's legs shattered under the vicious weight of the blows. Barabbas winced, but he also felt relieved. The torment had finally come to an end.

He turned and looked back at Deborah. She stood behind him, clinging tightly to his waist. She pressed her face against his shoulder, sharing his loss. Barabbas felt strangely detached as he accepted his brother's death. There was no deep sorrow. Only emptiness and relief that the agony had ended.

With a guilty start, he realized that he was already contemplating the freedom of his remaining comrades who were still being held in the dungeons of the praetorium. He remained with Simeon for the last minutes of his life and, when it was finally over, he turned away.

"We must bury them," he said simply. The words were dull, without inflexion. He'd pushed his pain down into deep recesses, where it would join the memory of his father and foster his hate for Rome.

"I sent Absalom to find Hephzibah. She's on her way with the grave clothes.

They will be buried according to the traditions of our fathers." Deborah spoke quietly.

"Where?"

"There are many supporters of the zealot cause. Hephzibah will make the arrangements." She looked into his face through strained eyes and reached out to touch him. "I only thank the Lord that you're alive."

He nodded with a wry smile. "I don't deserve to be."

Deborah shook her head. "No, Barabbas, you belong here, with me."

Hephzibah arrived, interrupting their conversation. Her face was taut and pale, and tears streaked cheeks.

Barabbas merely nodded. He didn't feel like speaking. The crowd had dispersed to a large extent, leaving only close friends and families of the victims. The people milled about in small groups. They cried and consoled one another, waiting for the Roman soldiers to confirm death so that the bodies could be handed to them for burial.

Many who stayed were supporters and friends of the zealots. One man, a well-known businessman who sold some of the finest linen in Jerusalem, approached Barabbas.

"I'm sorry for your loss." He said, clasping Barabbas' shoulder. "Your brother was a good man. I remember all the evenings we spent, dining together and singing. The harp in my home will never sound the same again."

"Thank you, Ephraim." Barabbas nodded.

"I don't know what arrangements you've made for the burial of Simeon and Yoseph, but I would consider it an honour to give you my tomb for their bodies. It's not far from here, just north of the city."

"Thank you, again. I appreciate the offer. It was a concern."

"Good. It's settled." The man smiled. "I'll have my servants show you to the tomb and assist you with anything you need for the preparations. Where are you staying, now that you're free?"

"He's staying with me," Deborah cut in before Barabbas had a chance to reply.

He didn't protest. It was where he usually stayed when he was in Jerusalem.

"Very well," Ephraim replied. "If I can do anything, just let me know."

"Thank you, Ephraim, you've been most generous."

"It was the least I could do for men who have fought so bravely and given their lives for Israel's freedom."

Barabbas nodded again and Ephraim said goodbye, wishing them peace. Others gathered about Barabbas, offering him their condolences and assistance. He stayed for a few minutes and then excused himself. He was beginning to feel claustrophobic and he longed for some solitude and peace. On the other side of the rise, he found a spot where he could sit quietly and be alone. Thoughts of loss and loved ones consumed his mind.

He closed his eyes and saw the whip tearing the flesh from his brother's bones. He heard Simeon's anguished cries and smelt the sodden earth, stained thick with blood. In the vision, his brother turned, but it was not his face. It was the gaunt face of their father, bloodied and beaten, with deep gashes that would never heal into scars.

The legionaries' laughter sounded like the echoes in a tomb. Barabbas wept for his family's pain. Beyond the suffering and soldiers were blackness and the windswept sands of a barren desert.

He found that he was hyperventilating and struggled to gain control of his breathing. He panted like a marathon runner. It was suddenly cold. Barabbas realised that he was drenched with sweat. Slowly, agonisingly, he controlled his breathing, clenching his fists so that his nails tore at the skin of his calloused palms.

Once he gained control of his emotions, his gaze became cold, gripped with fury and hatred for Rome. He wanted to run, to kill, to tear down the fabric of the empire, but he controlled his emotion, allowing the flame to burn white with heat.

He would strike when the time was right. Controlled anger was infinitely more dangerous than hot blooded emotional reaction. For now he would content himself with planning and waiting. When the moment arrived, he would strike and Rome would rue the day it had touched his family.

The sound of weeping brought him back to his immediate surroundings. He cocked his head and listened. The sound emanated from somewhere to his right, around the summit. He walked the short distance to investigate.

It was a woman. He saw her just beyond the rise, seated on a bare rock that rose defiantly from the earth about it. She was wealthy. He could tell from her clothes and jewellery. Her dark hair hung in waves, almost to her waist. She hadn't heard his approach and he inspected her in a leisurely fashion.

He finally spoke. "How is it that such sweet beauty knows sorrow so bitter?"

The woman whipped around. She was surprised, but not afraid. Her eyes were wide with curiosity and she wiped her tear-stained cheeks. "I didn't hear you approach."

Barabbas shrugged and smiled apologetically. "It's a bad habit of mine. Sneaking up on people comes naturally to me."

"Not appropriate behaviour for a poet."

"Do I look like a poet?"

"Your introduction has all the traits and spirit of Homer."

An educated woman. Unusual. She was obviously widely travelled. Probably the daughter of a merchant - or wife. "My father believed education brought freedom to her possessor. I was influenced as much by Greek thought as I was by the Wisdom of Solomon."

"Yet you chose to seek your freedom through violence."

He was thrown by the fact that she knew who he was. The attack was unexpected. He gazed out over the hills of Jerusalem. "What makes you weep so bitterly?"

"The man who took your place on the crucifix."

Barabbas nodded in understanding. "Was he a family member - a brother, perhaps?"

She shook her head. "He was a great teacher. We believed he was the *Messiah*, of whom the prophets spoke."

"He was too passive to be the *Messiah*. Rome is a violent nation and our freedom will be only brought about by a violent leader." He regretted the words the moment they were uttered, but it was too late.

Her eyes flashed with anger. "The freedom you speak of is merely another form of tyranny. You may have sought it all your life, but you still have no understanding of the word."

The fiery dart struck its mark, but Barabbas maintained his cool. He smiled and replied. "A woman who is as opinionated as she is beautiful. I respect that. It's refreshing to see one who is not downtrodden by the men of her society. What's your name?"

"Leila." She self consciously pulled the veil across her face.

Barabbas was mildly disappointed. "Our last meeting was so brief, we didn't get the chance to introduce ourselves."

It was the woman's turn to be surprised. "You remember me?"

"It's not every day I fall headlong into the arms of a woman so beautiful. I should be stoned for that act alone."

She smiled for the first time. "I'm sorry I ruined your escape."

"You should be. I was up half the night trying to break those fetters."

He lounged against an ancient olive tree, relaxing on the lee side of the hill. The woman opposite him spoke quietly. The mere sound of her voice soothed his soul. Nearly two hours passed as he and Leila discussed their loss, their pain and even their childhood and aspirations.

Though she opposed his every belief, Barabbas felt he could never get too much of her company.

"But why do you find Rome so reprehensible?" she argued. "Our roads are safe, we have water piped to our cities and trade is blossoming under their rule."

"Is all that worth the price of our freedom? We pay all our hard-earned wages to an emperor who breaks our backs with taxes, while Roman soldiers practically enslave us to do their bidding."

Leila smiled. "When last were you forced to carry a Roman's pack for a mile?"

"I would kill a man, or die in the attempt, before I carried so much as a Roman helmet."

The smile became a scowl. "Don't you think that's a little extreme?"

"Not in the face of what they've done to us," Barabbas replied with an idle glance at the angle of the sun on the horizon. He was surprised to see how far it had drawn across the sky. "I must go," he said simply. "My brother must be buried before the Sabbath."

She looked disappointed. "Would you like to join us at my uncle's home for dinner tonight? He loves guests and a good argument. He's also opposed to the zealots' extreme beliefs."

"Thank you, but no. The women will have prepared food for me at my lodgings."

"Where are you staying?"

"In the *Kainopolis*. You?"

"The west end, near Herod's praetorium."

He nodded. "That explains his friendly attitude toward Rome."

Her face flushed. "What's that supposed to mean?"

Barabbas shrugged. "The wealthy never feel oppression as much as the poor. They prefer the status quo."

The anger flashed in her eyes again. "My family believes in Israel's freedom as much as any Jew. Don't you dare judge us for seeking it through methods that differ from your own."

Barabbas grinned. "I'm sorry. You're entitled to your beliefs, misguided though they are."

She smiled. "Goodbye, Barabbas. I hope we finish this debate some day."

"Goodbye," he said and jogged slowly down the path that led to Jerusalem.

† † † † †

Mattithyahu's brow furrowed. He considered his options and the weight of the knowledge he carried. At this moment he was the only surviving protector who knew where the scroll was hidden. He had to get to Jerusalem and find another. It was not good for only one man to know.

An arrow whistled across his line of sight, mere inches from his face. It ripped him from his pensive reverie. His mule jerked in shock and Mattithyahu heard a gasp to his right. He looked across to see Eli clutching wild-eyed at the shaft protruding from his bleeding neck.

Mattithyahu spun back to face the source of danger. As he did so, the rocks about him erupted with figures that rose like ghouls from the landscape. They rushed forward, yelling as they did so, brandishing a hideous assortment of swords, knives and clubs.

Eli fell from his mount, gasping for breath, his eyes wide with terror and shock. Mattithyahu spurred his mount forward to escape the attack. The others were too slow. Reuben, pillar of the community, was dragged from his mule and butchered just behind him.

At first it seemed that Amos might escape. He was a short way ahead of the group. The young man spurred his mule into an ungainly canter. The animal snorted and stumbled over the rocky pathway. He managed to break free of the bandits and beat a path up the steep slope beyond.

Then the murderous archer emerged from his lair and aimed after the escaping Amos. The man had wild locks of once dark hair that hung, like frayed cords of grey, down past his shoulders. Amos bounced wildly in his seat, leaning first one way and then the other, bending low and catching his mule around the neck as he clung desperately to his mount. His erratic movements were born more out of the rough terrain and poor riding than calculated intent.

Mattithyahu's mule panicked and left the path, bolting across the rough ground lower down the slope. To his left, he saw Amos arch backwards and fall from his mount. The archer turned and reached for another barb to rout his last victim.

Mattithyahu bounced wildly in his seat. The mule's spine pounded him like a smith's hammer. He clung to the animal's neck, trying to keep his balance amidst its awkward gait.

He felt a sudden, red hot burning sensation, just below the left shoulder blade. He forced his body forward, ignoring the agony. The mule bolted panic-stricken over the deadly terrain. *Just don't let go.*

He felt himself slipping and his head dropped down next to the mule's shoulder. The blurred rocks seemed to reach up for him with wicked intent. Mattithyahu gasped, choking on the dry sand thrown up by the beast's sharp, flailing hoofs.

In a desperate attempt to save himself from the savage rocks, he gripped a handful of the mule's short mane near the base of its neck. His fingers closed like a vice on their tiny hope. Mattithyahu dashed his head against a large boulder. He blinked away the blinding flash of pain. The beast plunged down another ravine and Mattithyahu bounced up high and then dropped again. He felt his right arm snap as he brought his full weight to bear on it in the downward swing. Razor-like hoofs swiped at his face with every step the animal took. Two more searing hot sensations. A second and then a third arrow embedded themselves deep in his lower back.

His mount continued its perilous journey into oblivion. He felt as though he was being flung about like a torn rag in a gale. His whole being existed in the vice-like grip on the mule's mane. Darkness began to cloud his vision, but he refused to yield to it. To fall from his mount now meant death and the secret of the scroll would die with him. He clung like a lion to its prey and did battle with the blackness until it began to recede.

After a while, the mule's gait slowed to a trot and then a walk. He used his last vestiges of strength to pull himself up onto his mount with his left hand. The deep, cavernous panting of the animal rang in his ears. Mattithyahu tried to push himself upright, but his back would not bend. It had all the stiffness of a Grecian pillar. He tried to open his eyes. With a sudden surge of panic, he realized that he was blind. His efforts revealed nothing but blackness.

The joints in his body ached with the pain of a thousand lifetimes. His right arm hung limp down the beast's withers. It announced its presence with intermittent, bursts of agony whenever it was struck by the animal's front leg.

He tried to move, still clinging to the beast's neck, but it was impossible. Each attempt brought with it waves of agony that dwarfed the pain in his arm by comparison.

The mule stopped. It reached down with its neck and began to forage for meagre scraps of food in the barren terrain.

"No," he croaked, feeling blindly for the reins. He located the bit and followed the reins from there, pulling them back and shortening their reach with his left hand.

It took him a long time, working by feel and using only one good hand, but he finally managed to get both reins in his grasp. He used his teeth as a second pair of hands on more than one occasion and the musty taste of leather, mingled with beast of burden, clung to his palate.

The sun beat mercilessly on his bruised and blood-clotted back, draining him of all moisture. Once again, he felt the mule reach down for a morsel of food in the desolate landscape. He jerked the reins hard, pulling the animal's head up from the ground.

"No, you brute," he moaned weakly. His dust-dry tongue stuck to the roof of his mouth. The sun sapped the little strength left in his broken body, but he hung on to the reins with grim determination.

"You want food? Then go home. Find a way home." He mumbled deliriously.

The mule fought stubbornly to get at the tasty morsel, but Mattithyahu refused to let go. Reluctantly, the animal continued on its way. He had no idea which direction it carried him.

He could only hope. They were not far from *Qumran*. Eight miles at the most. If the beast became hungry enough it would return there. *It must return there.* The alternatives were too terrifying to contemplate.

Hours passed and Mattithyahu drifted in and out of consciousness. He was still blind, but dared not release his grip on the reins for fear of falling from his mount. In his condition, he would die where he lay. With a gargantuan display of willpower, he forced back the numbing tranquillity of unconsciousness and applied what little strength he had left to the reins. He couldn't remember when or how he had knotted them, but the knot had shortened them considerably, making his task easier.

He jerked them again, just to remind the mule that he was still aware, lest it be considering the pursuit of another blade of vegetation in the barren land. The animal jerked its head slightly against the bit and continued its aimless plodding. It seemed to Mattithyahu that the beast was wandering without purpose. It never seemed to follow one course, always meandering first one way and then another.

The pain in his back had become a dull throb that burned with searing heat every time he tried to move. It forced him to remain riveted in an uncomfortable position on the mule's back, but the discomfort was preferable to the agony caused by movement.

If only he could see. He tried yet again to edge his way forward to feel his eyes, in the hope that they were merely caked with blood, but it was impossible. The pain in his back became unbearable. It felt like a thousand fires that burned with all the fury of Hades. He collapsed once again, accepting the pain, hoping only to survive until he could get word of the scroll's whereabouts to someone.

His breath rasped in his ears as he rolled with the trundling gait of the beast beneath him. He felt like a cinder under the scorching rays of the sun and his parched throat cried out for life-giving fluid. He needed water soon, or all would be lost.

10

JOSES, THE pale-eyed bandit and terror of southern Judea, surveyed the carnage he had wrought. The inert bodies of the Essene party lay like scattered laundry over the terrain. His men, ten in all, were already rifling through their belts, collecting the spoils of their raid.

Joses stretched his arms, pulling back the long, grey locks of hair that had fallen across his face. He felt little pity or remorse for his victims. He waited patiently while his men gathered what few valuables they could find on the dead. Off to the left he saw Ben-Ammi, his second-in-command, approaching. The man wore a permanent scowl on his face and his dark brows resembled an approaching thunderstorm.

"Any luck?" Joses asked quietly.

Ben-Ammi shook his head. His reply was morose. "Just a few coins and some personal belongings. Nothing of any real value."

Joses' features creased into a languid smile. "Some we win, some we lose." He said philosophically.

Ben-Ammi snorted with disgust. "It wasn't even worth the sweat we lost in the attack."

Joses rolled to his feet with the easy, fluid motion of an agile athlete. "With that attitude, you'll never be a wealthy man, my friend. Perhaps the pack mules will carry greater reward."

"If we find them. I sent two men to track the beasts after they bolted into the valley."

"And the last man?"

"I sent Cornelius after him."

Joses scowled, remaining silent for a moment. "I've never trusted him fully, you know that."

"He's still the best warrior we've got, next to you."

"If he could turn against his own nation and desert the Roman army, he could betray us too one day when it serves his purposes."

"He was running for his life. He murdered his superior in the army. If he'd stayed and faced trial they'd have had him executed."

Joses smiled at his subordinate. "You brought him to us, Ben-Ammi, so naturally you feel the need to defend him. I'm just saying he should be watched. And in future don't send him alone to retrieve valuables or treasures. I wouldn't put it past him to hide them somewhere and then return to tell us he couldn't find the man."

"He'll find him." Ben-Ammi replied. "You put at least three arrows in that man's back. I'm amazed he managed to hang on at all. The mule may disappear, but he'll certainly have fallen off before he's travelled a mile."

"We'll see." Joses looked up. Two men returned, leading three of the pack mules. He rubbed his beard thoughtfully. "Those animals should fetch a fair price in Masada, and who knows what troves they carry." He jumped down from his vantage point, landing with cat-like lightness on the hard, dusty soil.

"You men clear up this mess and bury those bodies. I don't want any trace left to alert future travellers. Then take up your positions and keep your eyes open for any approach. We'll use the usual signals."

Ben-Ammi took over and Joses went to examine the contents of the mules' packs. He'd barely begun to open the first pack when a shrill whistle alerted him to the approach of someone from the south. A second call told him that the traveller was alone and approaching fast.

"Must be on horseback." He muttered to the thugs with the mules. "Right, get these beasts out of here and take up positions. A horseman must be a military man of some sort, and probably wealthy. We'll strike gold this time, for sure."

He turned and clambered up to his position on the rocky knoll. Although he couldn't see the rider approaching, he could hear the animal's hoofs beating a hasty path up the mountain trail. Joses listened intently. The man was obviously in a hurry. What was so urgent that the man would risk such speed on so dangerous a trail?

The horse slowed its pace somewhat as it negotiated a tricky part of the trail. Then the sound stopped abruptly. Joses strained his ears but could no longer hear any hint of the animal's passage. Just the infinite silence of the desert. Someone coughed, and a sword scraped carelessly against a rock. He scowled. He would have the culprit flogged before the day was out.

Still no sign of the horseman. Joses risked a call. He pursed his lips and gave the familiar shrill call of the masked Shrike, a common species of bird in the area. Beyond the ridge, his man would hear it and answer. No sound came. That meant the approaching horseman was no longer visible. How could they lose sight of him at such close range? It was impossible for a man to vanish like that. He waited. Once again, he pursed his lips, whistling the mournful call of the desert bird. He listened. Nothing.

It was as if the man had never been there. He decided to move. He rose quietly to his feet and peered over the rock behind which he was hidden. His gaze was drawn to the horse. It foraged just off the path below. The rider was nowhere in sight.

He frowned in confusion and stepped forward, around the rock. A cold, hard blade pressed malevolently against his throat.

"Not a word." The man whispered in Joses' ear. "You'll be dead before the sound escapes your lips."

He knew when a man was stating a plain fact. This man could kill him and melt back into the desert before his comrades even reached his body.

"Who are you?" he whispered.

"My name's not important and your life is less so. You're coming with me to a safe, open area. Then you're going to tell your men to fetch me my horse."

Joses moved quietly with the man down the far end of the rocky outcrop. He was impressed with the direction the man had chosen. He was obviously acquainted with the position of his adversaries.

"How is it that you know the desert so well?" he asked conversationally.

He was answered by a short flick of the knife and he felt the warm fluid begin to trickle from the thin cut on his neck. The man didn't answer and he dared not speak again. They moved in silence, descending the slope. Their path was erratic. The horseman used the sparse scrub and rock that was available for cover. Joses was amazed at the stranger's ability to hide in such seemingly open terrain. There was precious little plant life and yet his men seemed unable to locate them, even though they must be scouring the area frantically for any sign of the traveller. Presently the man stopped and relaxed his grip.

"Alright, call your men. Tell them to send one man only, with my horse. If I see more than one man, I'll kill you and I'll be gone before your body hits the ground. They'll never have the chance to avenge your death."

"How did you know we were there?" Joses chanced the question. He reasoned that the man would not kill him, now that he felt safe. The knife curved menacingly up against his throat.

"Didn't I tell you to be silent?"

"Not if you want your horse back." Joses replied casually.

"It would be an inconvenience to lose it," the stranger admitted.

"You haven't answered my question."

There was a moment's hesitation. Then he relaxed and replied. "You should tell your men not to wear reflective earrings in the sunlight like that. I was nearly a mile away when I saw the first glint. How long were you waiting there?"

Joses was evasive. "Not long, why do you ask?"

"I was wondering whether you'd come across a small group of Essenes on their way to Jerusalem."

"Not while we were here," Joses lied. "If we'd seen them we would have attacked their party. Why are you looking for them?"

"That's not your concern." The man pushed him roughly onto the path. "Now call your men, and you'd better tell them to cooperate. I don't want to dirty my knife."

Joses sighed and then called his men. They appeared in small pockets from among the rocks with stupefied frowns. Ben-Ammi rose from behind a rock with a stunned look of incomprehension. This quickly turned to a cold glare full of loathing when he saw the knife at Joses' throat.

"Wait, Ben-Ammi." Joses cautioned. "Don't do anything rash. This man has threatened to take my life and, believe me, he's extremely capable."

Ben-Ammi held up a hand, cautioning the men who had already begun to advance on the pair.

Joses spotted three of his men advancing behind the rocks to his right. He called frantically. "Tell those fools behind the rock to stop advancing on our flank! Even I can see them. Then fetch the horse."

The men began to retreat. He felt the knife relax slightly against his throat. Ben-Ammi barked some orders and two men disappeared around the bend in the path.

They returned a few minutes later with the horse.

"Right," yelled Joses. "Now send one man with the animal. Bring it to us and make sure he leaves his sword behind."

Ben-Ammi nodded, removing his sword.

"Not him." The man with the knife spoke quietly.

"What?"

"I can spot a dangerous man and I make a habit of avoiding conflict with them. It's one of the reasons I've lived so long."

"Who, then?"

"The big one with the earrings."

Joses called to his second in command. "Not you, Ben-Ammi." His second-in-command stared at him with a questioning look. "Send Abimelech, and make sure he's unarmed."

Abimelech removed his sword. The stranger eased the blade's pressure on Joses' throat. "Good."

Joses spoke quietly while Abimelech fetched the horse. "Assuming you don't kill me now, if ever you're in need of a friend, you're welcome in my tent. I could use a man like you in my band."

"What makes you think I'd join you?"

Joses shrugged. "Circumstances change. Who knows what the future holds?"

"If I were in your shoes, I'd bear a grudge."

"Our purposes crossed and you were the victor. No harm done. If I'd won, you'd be dead already. I can't blame a man for defending his life."

The traveller watched suspiciously as the large man with the earrings led the horse down the path towards them. Once again, he scanned his flank to make sure that Joses' men did not try to launch another attack. The giant, Abimelech, plodded slowly toward them, hateful eyes glaring at the knife.

"Stop there!" the stranger instructed when Abimelech was no more than ten paces away. The giant hesitated, looking at Joses for orders.

"Do as he says, Abimelech. It'll be alright."

Abimelech did as he was told. "Good. Now leave the horse and go back to your friends."

Abimelech's features contorted into a blood chilling scowl. "First let him go."

"You must think I'm as stupid as you look. Now do as I say, or your friend won't see the sun go down." He pressed the knife against Joses' throat in a menacing gesture.

"Do as he says." Joses spluttered. Beads of sweat ran down his face like ice-cold trickles of fear.

Once again the mammoth was overcome with confusion. He looked back at the men waiting patiently at the ambush scene and then back at Joses.

"Abimelech, listen to me well." Joses spat the words like venom from a cobra's mouth. "If you don't go back right now, I'll kill you myself when this is over. Go!"

The man's features slid to and fro like the mechanism on a door lock as he slowly processed these instructions. After an agonising period of silence, he nodded and let go of the reins. Then he turned and plodded back to join the rest of his comrades at the foot of the outcrop.

Joses heaved a sigh of relief and relaxed. The pressure of the knife against his throat no longer held the fear it had while Abimelech was there. He watched in silence as the man retreated. Then he felt the grip on the knife change. The man grabbed his long locks of hair and arched his neck back, quickly shifting the knife to a position behind him, jabbing the point against the skin between his ribs.

"Don't think you're safe now that the knife is away from your throat. I could easily puncture your lung. It takes longer, but the end is the same."

Joses nodded submissively. His head jerked against the taut locks of hair in the man's clenched fist.

"Now move towards the horse."

The two men approached the beast. It ambled between tufts of vegetation, sniffing hopefully. The man jerked Joses to a halt.

"Lie down on the path. Spread your arms and legs wide apart."

Joses did as he was told. The man still gripped his hair, lowering him to the ground. Joses felt his hair being released, and turned to speak. He was amazed at his captor's alacrity. The man was already on his horse.

"Remember my offer, friend," Joses called after him. "I need men like you. No grudges."

"I'll bear it in mind." The man smiled and spurred his horse to a canter, heading for Jerusalem.

Joses jumped to his feet. He dusted his tunic and gingerly rubbed his injured throat. He gazed in awe after the solitary horseman who had outwitted his entire band of thugs. How he wished he had ten men like that. Shaking his head, he turned to rejoin his men.

† † † † †

Mattithyahu lay like a corpse on the mule's back, far more dead than alive. Where he had once felt pain, he now felt only the cold, numb sting of death. Each breath came with intense effort and only prolonged his agony.

He heard a distant cry of alarm. Then voices chattered excitedly and strong hands lifted him gently from his mount. It seemed strange. The voices were so far away. Someone administered small mouthfuls of water. It brought relief, quenching his parched throat. More cold water was brought and his body was sponged. The water was icy against his skin. Mattithyahu clenched his teeth in pain.

Someone wiped his forehead and eyes. He blinked and realised he was able to see. The images were blurred, but he could see shapes. He tried to speak, but was unable to acknowledge the people who had saved him. Darkness began to cloud his newfound vision and then he found himself in another world. It was filled with angels and beautiful music. Sometimes he heard Nathaniel's voice, but he could not see him.

He searched for him among the angels and the trees that were so much greener than any he had known on earth. He tried to call for him but he could not speak, struck dumb by the beauty of the music and scenery.

The music grew fainter and then, with a sudden shiver, his body became a blazing furnace. The air was so cold that it stung his skin. He convulsed with agony. He pressed his arms against his sides, trying to shield himself from the stabbing icicles that scathed his fever-ridden body. The shivering was uncontrollable and his eyes were wide with terror and pain. How he longed to go back to that other world.

Nathaniel's gentle eyes stared down at him. "It's alright, my son. You've been badly wounded, but you're safe now."

Mattithyahu tried to speak, but he found it impossible. His voice was a faint croak in his ears. Somehow Nathaniel seemed to understand him.

"Yes I'm alive," the old man said. "What happened, did Eleazor find you?"

Mattithyahu shook his head vaguely. The clouds began to encroach on his vision once more. He concentrated, trying to force them back. He had to tell Nathaniel where to find the scroll. He fought in vain, however. The vapours closed relentlessly about him. Then his whole world became dark again.

After a few moments, the music began to play and he opened his eyes once more. The trees were green and the air was warm on his skin. He felt strong, too. Running without pain, he breathed in the beauty of this angelic world.

✝ ✝ ✝ ✝ ✝

Leila's eyes followed Barabbas as he headed back to the city. She felt confused by the emotions this man engendered in her. Watching him leave filled her with a sense of emptiness and loss.

She abhorred violence and bloodshed, yet she felt strangely drawn to Barabbas - even thrilled at the danger he represented. The dusk wind clutched at her. She pulled her shawl over her head to ward off the chill. It was as well that he hadn't accepted her invitation to dinner. The less she had to do with such men, the better.

In her heart, however, she knew she would see him again. In the midst of her loss, she felt hope. Apart from the gaping, barren crosses, the hill was deserted. When Barabbas reached the city gates she headed down the hill to join her family for the evening festivities.

At home, she found her father and uncle so deeply engrossed in conversation with Miyka'el that they never heard her enter.

"But how in Hades can you bring goods through Jericho at that price?" Her uncle asked.

"I assure you I can. You have to trust me." Miyka'el replied.

"You keep saying that, but the desert is a hostile place." Zebedee spoke earnestly. "You only die of thirst if the *Bedouin* don't get you first. Surely it would be safer to travel around the Fertile Crescent, like all the other merchant caravans."

"It takes two months longer following that route. By cutting across the desert, we halve our time and thus double our profit."

"But it's so dangerous. If it was as easy as you say, why don't all the merchants follow that route?"

"They don't know the people I know."

Zebedee smiled quizzically at his brother. "And because he knows people, that makes the desert safe."

Miyka'el smiled. "Look, my father cut covenant with men all over the desert lands. I grew up with their sons, like brothers. When we came of age, we cut covenant with one another."

Both Timothy and Zebedee were astounded. "You cut covenant with Gentiles?"

"I would give my life for those men and I know they would give theirs for me. I assure you, I can travel from India to Jericho without losing so much as a night's sleep."

Leila announced her presence with a polite cough. The men looked up, startled.

"The sun has returned to our home," her uncle exclaimed.

Zebedee turned to his daughter with a friendly smile. "Where have you been, Leila? You've not been running amok with that rabble outside, polluting the city with their barbarous yelling, I hope."

"I've been at Calvary. They've —"

"What's happened?"

"They crucified Jesus of Nazareth."

Zebedee was unable to speak for the shock. He stared at her with his mouth agape, stunned by his daughter's words.

Her uncle spoke first. "Why! What crime did he commit?"

Leila merely shook her head and shrugged. She took a deep breath and looked up. "I'm going to prepare dinner now. I'll be with the other women in the kitchen."

"Why they should kill a good and decent man, I can't fathom." Zebedee lamented. "And of all the days, to do it at the Feast of Unleavened Bread."

Miyka'el appeared unmoved by her news. "On a lighter note, I can get goods from the east to Jericho at half the price of our competitors."

Leila scowled and headed for the kitchen. *How could he steer the conversation back to trade so quickly? Hadn't he heard what she said?*

Her father's reply carried all the way into the passage. "Not now, Miyka'el. I don't feel like talking business any more."

"If you can get them to Greece and Rome, where the money is, we'll corner the market on eastern goods. All we need to do is finalise the merger."

Leila froze. Was her father honestly considering doing business with this man? There was a long pause before Zebedee spoke. "As I told you, Miyka'el, I will not pressurise my daughter into something she doesn't want. I will talk to her, however. But not today. I'm too upset now, and so is she. We'll talk again tomorrow." He sighed and stood up. "I'm going to see Joseph of Arimathea. He's followed the career of this man for two years now. It's best he hears the news from a friend."

Leila shook her head in disgust and headed for the kitchen. She would never marry a man as heartless as Miyka'el.

✝ ✝ ✝ ✝ ✝

Pilate lounged in his seat at the head of his table. He glared at Gaius Claudius. Gaius chose to ignore the prefect and reached for another handful of grapes.

"The gods hate me, centurion. And they've sent you to torment me."

Gaius remained silent. He spat the pips into his hand and tossed them onto the floor under the table. He hated the pips. Chewing them felt like biting into sand. They grated against his teeth, turning his tongue to dust.

Pilate continued. "Only two men can tell us where to find the copper scroll. I had to watch while one walked right out of the *Gabbatha*. Forced to give him his freedom because of some accursed tradition, started by my predecessors. And you let the other one get away."

"He was given a letter of pardon, signed by your hand as I recall."

"Your insubordination is tiresome to the point of anguish, Gaius."

"I was merely saying that —"

"Be silent!" Pilate hissed through clenched teeth. He sighed, rubbing his temples as if to alleviate a throbbing pain. "Do you know how valuable that scroll is?"

Gaius considered his superior's words. "I assume its value reaches beyond mere monetary wealth."

Pilate shook his head. "It's far more than that. When we get back to Caesarea, I'll show you what Coponius wrote about it. Then you'll understand. And you let the one man that was willing to talk of the treasure escape."

"Eleazor doesn't know where the treasure is. Barabbas is the man you want."

"You forget Barabbas is no longer in our grasp."

"We'll arrest him again." Gaius was unencumbered by Pilate's pessimism.

"On what charge? He's a free man."

Gaius chuckled. "Barabbas will never be free. He's a slave to his own hatred. It won't be long before he strikes out at Rome again, and when he does, we'll be ready."

"So we arrest him. To what end? He'll never reveal the secret."

Gaius raised his eyebrows. "Not even with your great powers of persuasion?"

"Your sarcasm leads you into dangerous territory, centurion. I could have you sent to Rome to stand trial on any number of charges. As to your question, torture won't work. He watched his own brother - as far as we know, his only living relative - die on a crucifix. Do you think he'd crumble under his own torture?"

Gaius shrugged. "Probably not."

"I think our best chance of finding the scroll lies with the other man. What have you done about finding him?"

"I did as you requested. I despatched another group of soldiers to *Qumran*. They'll begin their search at the Essene community and then work their way south to Masada. If anyone has seen him we'll hear about it. A man like that can't have many friends."

Pilate regarded the centurion thoughtfully. "I want that scroll, centurion. See that you get it for me." A knock on the door interrupted them.

The prefect scowled. "Who's bothering me at this hour?"

Quintus entered the room, almost tripping in his haste to apologise. "Sorry, prefect, but I was unable to stop him. He just barged up here demanding to see you. I did all I could."

Gaius glanced beyond the babbling assistant, searching for the source of his discomfort. Marcus strode into the room. His face was haggard from lack of sleep.

With each step, his uniform spouted clouds of dust that fell to the pristine floor.

Pilate's tone was quiet, but menacing. "What makes you think you can walk into my private chambers uninvited, soldier?"

Gaius rose to Marcus' defence. "I told him to come here."

His gaze shifted to Gaius. "You've overstepped your bounds this time."

"I thought you'd want to hear immediately that the soldiers returned with news of Eleazor."

The anger in Pilate's glare evaporated and was instantly replaced with a keen look of anticipation. Marcus shuffled uncomfortably under the prefect's intense gaze. He glanced at Gaius.

"I don't have him yet, prefect, but I know where he is."

"Where!" Pilate demanded. His lips were moist and his eyes shone with greed.

"He's in Jerusalem."

"How do you know this?"

"We spoke to an old man in the Essene community at *Khirbet Qumran*. He was vague, but he told us the man we wanted was headed here."

"How can you be sure he wasn't lying? He could be a sympathiser, throwing you off the trail."

"I don't think he was lying, prefect. He referred to him as the betrayer and claimed he sought someone here in Jerusalem."

"Not exactly a wealth of information, was he?"

"He was sure of this much. Eleazor expects to find what he seeks in Jerusalem. He's here - somewhere."

"Right. I want him found and brought to me."

"On what charge?" Gaius asked.

"Did I say anything about an arrest? We're merely questioning him about a treasure that rightfully belongs to the emperor. When the gates close, I want an all-out search of the city. Mobilise every soldier if you have to and apprehend any man fitting his description."

Gaius added. "Also dispatch men to patrol outside the city walls. We don't want someone lowering him through a window."

Pilate glanced at the centurion and nodded. "Search every house until you find him."

"Yes, prefect." Marcus replied. Gaius glowed with pride. The man must have been crestfallen at the idea of working through the night yet again, but no sign of it showed in his expression.

"If he's in the city, we'll find him."

"You'd better. Who's going to take charge of the search?"

"I'll see to it myself, prefect." Gaius trusted his men, but if they had to work all night, he felt obligated to work alongside them."

"Good. I want that man in front of me - in chains — when I have my breakfast tomorrow."

It crossed Gaius' mind to mention that chains implied an arrest, but he thought better of it.

† † † † †

Barabbas picked his way up the rocky path toward the tomb. The cave lay in an olive grove, about a mile north of Jerusalem. It was a peaceful setting to lay his brother's and friend's bodies to rest.

There were no more than a handful of people at the tomb, mostly women, who had come to help dress the bodies in their grave clothes. They busied themselves with the ceremonial bandages, clothing Yoseph and Simeon.

Two large water jars stood against the wall. Steam still rose from the warm liquid that had been used to cleanse the bodies of the departed. The bodies lay on a large, stone table in the centre of the burial chamber.

Deborah and Hephzibah applied copious volumes of ointments and spices before deftly wrapping the spotless, white grave clothes around the bodies. The fragrance hung like thick honey in the still air of the tomb. He watched in reverent silence.

"Pass the aloes." Deborah's voice was demure. She reached for the pottery jar in Hephzibah's hands.

The aloes were a fine dust, pounded from a fragrant wood. They were mixed with myrrh, a sticky, redolent substance produced from yellow teardrops formed by the gum from the southern Arabian plants.

She mixed the spices and applied them liberally before wrapping the cloth tightly around Simeon's inert body. Both women worked in sombre silence, careful to avoid knotting or entangling the grave clothes in any way. This was in keeping with Jewish custom, signifying the soul's continuity through eternity.

The process was laborious. The grave clothes were wrapped until the bodies were encased up to their armpits. The women then placed the men's arms against their sides and began with the second of the three garments, wrapping them up to their necks.

When they had finished wrapping the second grave cloth, the women began with the third and final garment. They carefully embalmed the heads of the dead men in the fine, white linen until their bodies were completely covered.

Once they had completed their task, the bodies were moved to the burial chambers and gently placed in recesses in the walls. After paying their last respects, the small group left the tomb and rolled a large, round rock into place, sealing it for eternity.

The funeral was a silent one. Barabbas detested loud, pretentious mourning. He tore his clothes in the custom of mourners and placed the proffered ashes on his head. The few who had stayed to mourn with Barabbas gathered about him to give their condolences, staying for a while to comfort him in his grief. After a few hours, the first people excused themselves and left. Soon, only Hephzibah and Deborah remained with him. Deborah cradled Barabbas' head in her arms.

"I'm going home to prepare dinner for you. Do you want to be alone for a while?"

Barabbas nodded. "I'll join you soon," he said quietly.

She caressed his cheek. "You know it's good to weep sometimes - to share your hurt. You don't have to withdraw into a shell when your emotions torment you."

Barabbas took her hand and squeezed. "It's just how I am, Deborah. Don't worry about me. I'll be fine."

She smiled in understanding and squeezed his hand. "I'll see you at home," she said as she rose to leave.

Hephzibah rose too, hugging him before she joined Deborah. Barabbas sat alone in the olive grove among the dark, green leaves and gnarled bark of the thick stemmed trees until the sun's crescent disappeared beyond the western horizon.

He was not one who could mourn for long and his thoughts quickly turned to his comrades in prison - and vengeance. Rome would pay dearly for what she had cost him today.

He thought of all the others still awaiting trial or torture, and of all the soldiers who had had a hand in the deaths of his brother and friends.

"An eye for an eye," he whispered. Blood had been taken and that blood would be avenged. He thought for a long time about what needed to be accomplished, considering all the possibilities and pitfalls. What he intended was risky, but it had to be done.

Finally he rose and returned to the city. He looked forward to the warmth of a home and the comfort of a woman's arms. Deborah was always there for him. She had been a friend for many years and a lover in times of need. Yet the memory of the woman on the hill plagued him. Thoughts of her beauty clouded his mind, filling him with a mixture of joy, coupled with the agony of longing.

If only he had accepted her invitation. At the very least he could have found out where she lived. But that would have been too forward. They came from different worlds. The best thing he could do was forget her.

His thoughts returned to his friends in the dungeons of Herod's praetorium. There was still a chance that they could be saved. Barabbas puzzled over the problem of how to secure their freedom. It wouldn't be easy and would require help, but Jerusalem was a city filled with zealot sympathisers. The network would be easy to contact. The outline of a strategy began to form.

The shadow moved in lethal silence and the blow was as swift as it was unexpected. Barabbas sensed, more than saw, his ghostly attacker. He dropped to the ground, rolling under the blow. In one fluid motion, he was on his feet and facing his attacker with his sword drawn.

"Eleazor, I hoped we'd meet again." His thin smile burned with hatred.

Eleazor faced him with a similar smile. "How did you know it was me and not some street thug looking for his daily wage?"

"I can smell the stench of your cowardly form. It wasn't difficult." Barabbas waited for the man to react to the insult.

Eleazor grinned. "How's your brother?"

Barabbas fought to control his rage. Don't strike when he expects it. Wait and fight on your own terms. "You can ask him yourself when I'm done with you. I'm amazed you came back."

Eleazor's expression sobered. "It does seem an unnecessary risk, but you have something I badly want."

"That's breaking the tenth commandment. You'll burn in Hades for that."

"This is no joke, Barabbas. It seems my deception has become a reality. Nathaniel told me he sent it to you."

"Sent what?" Barabbas was genuinely confused.

"I want the copper scroll."

Barabbas smiled like a man who has seen the sunrise for the first time. "Ah, the copper scroll. There seems to be a lot of recent interest in that mythical document. I'll tell you what I told Pilate. I've never heard of the copper scroll, and I certainly don't know where to find it."

The man circled Barabbas, brandishing his sword. "Now it's you who flagrantly breaks the Law of Moses. Nathaniel told me he was sending it to you, just before I struck him down with my sword."

Barabbas was afraid for the first time, but had to let his bluff play out. "You killed Nathaniel? Did it ever occur to you that a man, knowing he was about to die, might deliberately misinform you to avenge his own death? He sent you to me for a purpose and I'm going to fulfil it."

He lunged at Eleazor. There was the hiss of steel against steel and they separated.

"I knew it would come to this one day, Barabbas. You were always too confident, too sure of your own abilities. The first time I saw you fight, I knew we would cross swords one day. Give me the scroll and at least I'll let you live."

The clatter of hobnail boots interrupted their joust. Eleazor backed away and sheathed his sword. Barabbas did the same. He was surprised when one of the soldiers yelled, alerting his comrades.

"There he is! That could be him. You, don't move. The prefect wants to see you."

Barabbas glanced about for a way of escape. Seeing none, he put his hand on his sword. Eleazor fled. He hurtled through the approaching soldiers, bowling one over in his rush to escape.

The legionaries regrouped and gave chase, baying as they went. Barabbas was left alone and puzzled in a quiet street, with his hand still on the hilt of his sword. Inquisitive residents emerged from their homes to see what the ruckus was about. He avoided their questioning gaze and proceeded to Deborah's courtyard.

At least he knew Eleazor was in Jerusalem. With that knowledge, locating him would be easy. Then he could carry out his revenge, but first there were more pressing matters. Once inside Deborah's home, he announced his intention to free the remaining men in the dungeons of Herod's praetorium.

† † † † †

The atmosphere had become tense in Deborah's home. She disapproved of his intentions. Not because she felt they were morally questionable, but because they put him in danger. Deborah feared for his life. That was why she opposed him so vehemently.

He ignored her pleading eyes. "I'm going to see Zechariah tomorrow."

Deborah faced Barabbas with her arms folded. There was a tremor in her voice as she spoke. "Will you listen to reason for once in your life? Your brother's body isn't even cold yet!"

Barabbas raised his voice. "What would you have me do, Deborah? Should I just abandon my friends and leave them to Rome so they can join him? Besides, Simeon would have wanted me to avenge his death."

"Getting yourself killed is not vengeance. It's insanity." Tears welled in Deborah's eyes. Barabbas scowled and shook his head. She knelt at his feet and took his hand in hers. "If there was any hope of saving them, I'd agree with you." She paused, gazing into his eyes. "It's impossible, can't you see that?"

Barabbas leaned back and glared at the ceiling. "I won't leave them to die."

Deborah tried a new tack. "You're a free man now, pardoned by Pontius Pilate himself. You can finally start a new life for yourself."

Barabbas sighed. "Levi and —"

"No, no, Barabbas." She held his face, forcing him to look at her. "Simeon, Levi, so many others. They're all gone. Only you escaped. This is your chance! You're free now. You can start over, with a clean record. Why don't you put this war with Rome to rest and pursue other dreams? What about a stud farm? You always said you could breed the finest horses in the empire, if you put your mind to it."

"That costs money, Deborah - money I don't have."

"You could borrow money from your uncle. He's made the offer before."

"That was a long time ago. I doubt whether it still stands."

"You could at least ask him," she persisted.

"I'm not going to go crawling back to him like a disobedient slave, begging forgiveness and charity. I chose my course years ago and I'll live with the consequences, no regrets."

"What consequences, Barabbas? You're free."

"I'm not free!" Barabbas shouted. He pushed her away from him. "Don't you understand? None of us are. As long as Rome rules Judea, we're nothing but slaves to her emperor."

"I'm not a slave. Only you are, Barabbas - a slave to your own pride and hatred."

"Do you have any idea what it was like?" he whispered through clenched teeth. "I watched them beat my father until his life hung by a thread. Today I watched them do the same thing to my brother. My whole life, I've seen a foreign nation rape our land and mock our God. Do you think I'm going to forget all that and breed horses because one man was forced to grant me a pardon in the face of a screaming crowd?"

In despair, she flung up her arms. Then she turned to fetch the food from Hephzibah who stood with her back to them, stoking the fire with an over-zealous arm.

She brought a steaming leg of roasted lamb and placed it in front of Barabbas. As she turned to fetch the unleavened bread from the shelf, he caught her wrist. She turned, staring at him through bloodshot eyes.

"Don't worry about me." He smiled. "I always survive, you know that."

"Just promise me you'll be careful," she replied quietly. "There may not be another man to take your place next time."

"I promise," he murmured. She nodded and turned again, but Barabbas did not release her wrist. "Your face bears the burden of too many sorrows, Deborah."

She returned his gaze with a doleful smile. "You are the source of all of them, Barabbas."

He squeezed her wrist lightly, and winked at her with a mischievous grin. "My plan is foolproof, so the Romans haven't got a chance. All I have to do now is talk to Zechariah and make the arrangements."

11

THE FOLLOWING morning Barabbas entered the immense temple of the Holy City, the bastion of the Jewish faith. The huge building towered skywards, pointing to the very majesty of God on high.

Inside the court of Israel he scanned the crowd, singling out those with priestly garments, as he searched for the elderly zealot sympathiser. He spotted the rotund figure washing his hands in an ornate bowl, a ritual cleansing for priests. Barabbas moved into his line of sight and waited for the man to acknowledge him. The priest glanced in Barabbas' direction and then continued with his cleansing. He washed his arms up to the elbows in the holy water, making sure that no trace of uncleanness remained.

Presently the chubby priest completed his task and headed toward the far end of the court. Barabbas followed quietly. The man had seen him and was headed for a private place, where they could talk. He was puzzled when Zechariah headed up some stairs and into the court for priests. Was he trying to hide? Barabbas could not follow him inside.

Dark thoughts clouded his mind. What if the priest refused to come out? To take his mind off his worries, he examined his surroundings. The temple building was relatively simple in its design, built with large, cream coloured stones. Against the door was an ornate, golden vine hung with golden bunches of grapes and vine leaves, gifts from devout Jews who had brought their ornaments from the furthest reaches of the empire.

Barabbas was busy doing a rough calculation of the value of the gold on the wall when the priest emerged.

"Are you trying to hide from me, Zechariah?"

The man smiled. "No, my friend. I had to be certain that nobody would overhear our conversation. You've become rather infamous these past few days."

"So, the Sanhedrin still doesn't look too favourably on zealot activities, I take it."

Zechariah shook his head sadly. "I'm afraid you bring too much insecurity to an already flimsy political structure."

"I will never understand why godly men would condone the activities of Rome and refuse to support our cause."

"We're not all like that." The priest replied, stroking the greying hair on his temples.

"Too many are."

"It's a complex world, Barabbas. You've got to understand that people like you make them nervous. The high priest is appointed by Rome. Where does that leave him if the Jewish nationalists overthrow her and usurp power? At best, he would lose all his possessions as well as his standing in the community. Anyway, enough of such depressing talk. You came to discuss more important matters than politics in religion."

Barabbas explained what he intended to do. The older man listened quietly. When Barabbas had finished, he took a deep breath and raised a hand to his chin. He spent several seconds in deep thought, choosing his words carefully before replying.

"My son, Deborah is right. What you plan is nothing short of suicide."

"I'm not asking you to convince anyone. Just talk to the men. They can make their own choices."

"You'd be leading them to their deaths, Barabbas."

"Why does everybody keep saying that? The strategy is sound. Did it ever occur to you that it might actually work?"

Zechariah seemed to come to a decision and shook his head. "This plan is the work of a madman. You've been under extreme stress, Barabbas. It's never easy losing a loved one."

"Will you just talk to them?"

"No."

"I'm not forcing anyone to help me."

"If I tell them you devised this, they'll follow you and you know that. These men have a blind trust in your abilities."

"Their faith is not blind, Zechariah. My plans work. Now who is available in Jerusalem at the moment?"

The priest sighed. "Well there's Jacob of Bethany, Gilead, Eleazor —"

"You know where Eleazor is?" Barabbas interrupted.

"Of course. He's here. I gave him refuge from the Romans. I don't mind telling you I risked my career to —"

"Where is he?" Barabbas was gripped with fury.

"Why, what's happened?"

"He's a traitor. He betrayed us to Rome and he's responsible for the deaths of my brother and Yoseph."

The old priest was incredulous. "Are you sure about this?"

"The Romans knew our hideout as well as we do. Their information could only have come from a zealot and he was the only one in their custody who could have given them the information."

"Barabbas, I am truly sorry. I had no idea."

"Take me to him."

"What are you going to do?" Zechariah asked nervously.

"What do you think? He's going to pay for his treachery."

"No, Barabbas." The priest was suddenly firm. "I will not let you profane the temple. This is holy ground."

"Well then it's being defiled by his presence. I'd be doing the Lord a favour by ridding the temple of such filth."

"Barabbas, think. The temple guard is here. You'd never get away with it. Rome is looking for Eleazor. I can notify them and hand him over to the military. Let justice take its course."

"No, he'll die by my hand. Now take me to him."

One of the temple guards approached across the court. Zechariah glanced nervously in his direction. "Get a hold of yourself. The temple guard is already beginning to notice your antics."

"Take me!"

"No." The old man was defiant.

"Then you will die." Barabbas' voice was a deep rumble. He slipped a long, curved blade from beneath his belt.

"Put that thing away. Do you want to get arrested again? I can't believe you'd threaten me after all the years we've been friends."

"If you were a true friend you'd take me to the man who killed my brother and betrayed me to Rome."

"Everything alright here, Rabbi?" The voice of the uniformed officer startled Barabbas. He slipped the knife back beneath his cloak.

Zechariah nodded. "Er, yes. Yes, thank you, captain. Our brother here is - a little upset, that's all."

The man looked Barabbas up and down. At length, he said. "Alright, if you need any help, I'll be right over there." He pointed vaguely at the foot of the steps.

Barabbas faced Zechariah with a blank stare. The old man smiled.

"I know your pain, my son. I've watched you carry it since you were a boy. But this is not the way. God will avenge you in good time, you'll see. I'll talk to the men, but I warn you up front, I'm going to discourage them from getting involved. Come and see me in three days. I'll have news for you then."

Barabbas groaned. "Three days. They could be dead by then."

"Nobody will be executed during the feast. You still have time."

"And what of Eleazor?"

The priest nodded and called the guard at the foot of the steps.

The man approached, eying Barabbas with suspicion.

Zechariah instructed. "Will you go to the Antonia and tell the centurion, Gaius Claudius, that the man he seeks is hiding in the temple. Tell him to send a Roman guard to the court of the Gentiles. We'll bring the man to him. Before you go, call the temple guard together to arrest the man, and please escort my friend here to the street outside."

"Where is the man, Rabbi?" The guard asked.

Zechariah glanced at Barabbas. "I'll show the guards where he is. Just see that you assist our brother here out of the temple courts."

The guard nodded, motioning for Barabbas to follow him. Barabbas acquiesced, deep in thought. He allowed the temple guard to escort him to the exit and into the court of the Gentiles. From there he moved quickly, heading for the golden gate which led directly out of Jerusalem from the temple.

The wood store was situated against the wall at one end of the women's court. In the dark room, Eleazor skulked sullenly among the large bundles of rough, chopped wood, trying to find a comfortable spot among the knots and splinters that seemed able to locate the more tender parts of his anatomy with uncanny accuracy.

Yet another splinter spiked his palm. He cursed quietly in the darkness and began pulling at it. The tiny barb was impossible to reach and merely burrowed its way deeper beneath the skin with each new attempt to extract it.

With a sigh, he leaned back against a wood pile that stretched to the roof of the tightly packed chamber. It was then that he heard the approach of the temple guard.

"In here." A hand began to rattle the latch on the door outside.

Suddenly alarmed, he dodged between the piles of wood, doubling back and scrambling up a pile near the door. Logs clattered to the floor behind him.

"I can hear him inside." A second voice spoke in the court outside.

"Never mind, he can't go anywhere."

He gritted his teeth until he reached the top of the pile. Then he flattened his body against it, obscuring himself from view on the floor.

The door opened and sunlight streamed into the room. Eleazor closed his eyes against the brightness. When he opened them again, he saw five men of the temple guard just inside the doorway. He let them pass by. Their heads were mere inches below his position on top of the wood pile. As they worked their way to the back of the chamber, he launched himself from his position and bolted for the door. He found his way blocked by two burly guards. The men moved to grab him but Eleazor dove to the floor, rolling head over heels under their slab-like arms. He rose to his feet inside their defence, using his momentum to smash them off balance. They lunged at him but he swung back towards the wood shed, slamming the door and locking the rest of the men inside before turning to flee from the area.

He emerged from the women's court and into the court of the Gentiles. To his consternation the golden gate was blocked by a Roman patrol. He didn't bother to check the other gates. They would be guarded too.

Instead, he raced south towards Solomon's colonnade, dashing between the traders and moneychangers' tables. He upturned them and broke cages as he ran in the hope of slowing his pursuers down.

Eleazor jumped onto a table and launched himself upward onto one of the pillars of the colonnade, finding handholds in the ornate masonry. Desperation and skill produced the impossible. He slithered with serpentine alacrity up the pillar to the top of the colonnade, pulling himself over the edge where he could run unimpeded toward the east wall of the city.

From there he climbed over the top and began a daring descent of the three storey wall. Slowly, carefully, he worked his way down the sheer wall of the city, finding tiny hand and toeholds in the cracks between the large stones. It would not be long before the soldiers emerged from the city gates to intercept his escape.

Beneath him, the Kidron valley yawned, falling away from the city wall. One slip and he would be swallowed by its gaping jaws.

He was halfway down the outside wall when shouting soldiers emerged from the city gate to his right. In panic, he quickened his pace.

The soldiers loomed into his view, drawing ever closer. Eleazor forced them from his mind and concentrated on the task at hand. Finally he judged himself to be low enough. The soldiers were approaching rapidly and would soon be upon him. He decided to risk it and launched himself from the wall. He struck the ground with a force that drove the air from his lungs. His feet and ankles protested against the jarring pain that ran like shock waves up his legs. There was no time to massage the injured joints. He forced himself to run, heading down the steep sides of the valley for the Mount of Olives beyond. As he ran, the pain began to recede. He forced himself onwards, putting more distance between himself and his pursuers.

In the valley bed he turned south, following the course of the seasonal river that ran toward the Great Rift Valley. Friends were becoming scarce in Judea. He had to find Barabbas soon and get the scroll before all was lost and he was forced to flee the country.

Glancing back, he noticed that the soldiers were making slow progress over the rough terrain. Soon he would be out of their line of sight. As he rounded the bend, he spotted a form plunging into the valley from the mountains and rocks above. The figure moved swiftly in a controlled free fall with his tunic billowing about him.

Barabbas! Eleazor felt a wrench in his gut. Now was not the time. Barabbas slid down the steeper parts of the valley wall in an avalanche of dirt and rubble. He found his footing on the sturdier rocks and ledges in a frantic race to intercept Eleazor.

Eleazor raced toward the point of interception, hell bent on reaching the mark first. As he got closer, it became apparent that Barabbas would win. Tumbling and sliding, using the foliage and rocks to keep his balance, Barabbas drew his sword and raced toward his approaching foe. Eleazor drew his own sword in a swift, easy motion, never slowing his pace or losing his footing.

They came together in a titanic clash of swords and fury. Their bodies crushed up against one another, each testing the power and speed of the other in a frenzy of swordplay. With a final push, they lurched apart. Eleazor's lungs burned as if starved of oxygen under furious water. He gulped air and stared into Barabbas' eyes.

Adrenalin coursed though his veins. "How did you find me?"

"I guessed the temple guard would be no match for you. The east wall was the logical escape route. You fooled me by turning south through the valley, though."

"I don't have time to fight you now, Barabbas."

"This won't take long."

"Roman soldiers approach as we speak. If they catch us fighting, we'll both be arrested."

Barabbas cocked his head, listening for the approaching legionaries. With a look of disappointment, he lowered his sword. "You're right. I can hear them coming."

Eleazor smiled, circling Barabbas and backing away. "I look forward to our next meeting."

Finally, he turned and fled down the valley.

Barabbas watched in frustration as his betrayer disappeared around the bend in the riverbed. When Eleazor was gone, he turned and headed back toward Jerusalem. The soldiers approached from the north. At their rate of progress they had no hope of catching Eleazor.

Gaius, the loathsome centurion, led the group, urging the soldiers on as they raced over the uneven ground. He slowed his pace as he approached Barabbas, stopping as he neared him.

He narrowed his eyes. "What are you doing here, Barabbas?"

The soldier's breathing was deep and even. He was in good shape.

"Taking care of unfinished business." Barabbas replied casually.

"What business?"

"It regards my brother's funeral and it's none of yours."

Gaius let the remark pass. "Did you see Eleazor pass this way?"

Barabbas chuckled. "You know I did. You won't catch him. Your men crawl through the desert with all the speed of creeping sand dunes."

"So you thought you'd take care of Eleazor yourself."

"I don't remember saying that."

"If I catch you waging your personal vendettas, I'll have just the excuse I need to throw you in prison again. Pilate would love to have you back in his clutches and he wants Eleazor alive, so stay away from him."

"Who's going to catch him, you? Even when you weren't standing around bantering like women at the well you couldn't keep up."

"Keep insulting me, Barabbas. Get angry, strike me. I'm itching to throw you back in jail. You escaped me once, but next time there won't be a Jewish Messiah to take your place on the crucifix."

"My Messiah would have carried a sword and he would have struck you and Pilate down in the *Gabbatha*."

Gaius shook his head in amazement. "A free man and still you return like a dog to its vomit. Next time, I'll be waiting for you. Make your move and we'll end it. Just you and me."

Barabbas smiled and nodded toward the south. "Your prisoner will be getting away, centurion."

Gaius gazed at Barabbas, his cold eyes penetrating like the sharp steel of the sword on his side. He waited for Barabbas to break the challenge and look away, but Barabbas merely gazed back with a lopsided smile. Finally, Gaius nodded slowly and turned back to his men.

"Let's go. We've got work to do," he growled.

The soldiers moved on, following Eleazor's trail to the south. The mere sight of Gaius' back fanned the flames of Barabbas' hatred. Once they had gone, he continued back to Jerusalem. His frustration was eased by the anticipation of his next meeting with Zechariah.

As he walked, he thought of Eleazor's words the previous evening. Why would Nathaniel tell him he'd sent the scroll to Jerusalem? Was it possible that the old man had been telling the truth? What if he truly *had* done that and the scroll had never arrived?

No, Nathaniel would never endanger the scroll by sending it unprotected on such a journey. Besides, even if he did so, he would have brought it himself. No protector would entrust the scroll to men who had no understanding of its importance.

Still, Eleazor's words troubled him. The scroll danced in his mind, filling him with a sense of dread. He needed to talk to Levi. The man had spent a lifetime protecting the secret. He would know what to do.

There was nothing he could do now, but wait. Three days, Zechariah had said. For the time being, he would have to occupy his mind with other matters. He entered the city gate and headed for the eastern district, where he could study the comings and goings of soldiers outside Herod's praetorium.

Moving quickly through the city, he soon found himself in the wealthier part of Jerusalem. As he passed by, Barabbas glanced at the costly homes that lined the wide streets. Most of the houses were double storey affairs, large with plain but tasteful exteriors that spoke of abundant luxuries inside.

While he walked, he considered his approach. He needed a vantage point from which to watch the praetorium, unobserved. He thought he knew of a spot near the gates of the palace and headed in that direction. After turning another corner, he found himself at the *Gabbatha*, the dreaded site of his brother's sentencing. He skirted it and moved toward the palace.

He was not far from the praetorium when he saw a couple emerge from one of the large, stately homes. The woman's robe was predominantly green, with a scarlet and blue pattern woven into the cloth. It was made of the finest linen money could buy. The man with her was large and his complexion was as dark as the rich soil of Galilee. He too was elegantly dressed and his robe spoke of great wealth.

The woman glanced in his direction. Her eyes suddenly grew wide. "Barabbas!" she exclaimed.

"*Shalom*, Leila," he greeted her.

The man next to her frowned.

"What brings you to this part of the city? Looking for me?" Her eyes reflected the seductive smile hidden beneath her veil.

Barabbas' lips curled into a languid grin. "In truth, no, which makes me a stupid, stupid man."

Her enigmatic smile charged him with such desire that he could actually feel his pulse begin to race. She turned to introduce the man next to her.

"This is my father, Zebedee."

"*Shalom*." Barabbas nodded in greeting.

"*Shalom*, Barabbas. It's nice to meet the man who has caused such a stir in Jerusalem these past few days." The words were friendly, but the smile was guarded.

"The fame is a burden I can live without." Barabbas replied modestly. "In my world, one survives better in anonymity."

Zebedee nodded gravely. "The zealots' world is a harsh and unforgiving one. Have you not considered putting it behind you, now that you're a free man?"

"Perhaps some day."

"The one who gave his life for your freedom was a man of peace. You could do worse than honour his death in your newfound life."

Barabbas glanced at Leila She raised her arm, brushing the hair from her face. Zebedee scowled.

"What do you think, Barabbas? Time to make a fresh start?"

Barabbas shrugged. "I wish I could, but I have things to take care of. I need to set some things in order before I can pursue a life of freedom."

Zebedee nodded. "I see. Well then, we mustn't keep you. I can see you're a busy man." Barabbas nodded uncomfortably. Then he turned to Leila. "Goodbye, Leila. Perhaps I'll see you again sometime, if God smiles on me."

"Goodbye, Barabbas."

† † † † †

Leila and her father watched Barabbas until he was out of sight.

"Miyka'el will make a good husband for you, if you would give him the chance," Zebedee said quietly.

"What!" Leila laughed. "Where did that come from?"

"I'm just saying you should consider what he offers you. He may not be as strong or passionate as some, but strength wanes and passions die."

"Why this sudden intense interest in Miyka'el?"

"He has stability, loyalty, kindness. Above all, he loves you. There is nothing he would deny you and, with his wealth, there's nothing he could not give you."

Leila frowned. "This is not like you, father. You've always let me find my own way before."

"Leila, you know I love you. I would never tell you what to do, but surely a father is entitled to express his opinion. And a wise daughter would, at least, consider his counsel if not heed it."

She forced a smile. "Yes, father. I will consider it." *But I know I could never love him. He lacks that – I don't know. Something is missing. I could never love him.*

† † † † †

After watching people come and go via the gates of Herod's praetorium for several hours, Barabbas felt he had all the information he needed. He'd left his vantage point on one occasion only, to take care of some business that warranted immediate attention. His errand had taken him up an alley that ran between the praetorium and the barracks where the soldiers resided.

The task was completed in no more than a few minutes after which he had returned to his post. Other than that one time, his eyes had remained riveted to the gates.

He now knew the procedures of the guards and the times that shifts changed. He had seen the strengths, as well as the weaknesses, in the system and knew when and where the best time for attack lay. He would strike when the guard was at its weakest - when the legionaries least expected a rescue attempt.

It was on his way home that he had met Absalom in the market, north of the barracks. His heart had been gripped with panic by the news that the boy had brought. Absalom had heard the news less than an hour before, via the zealot spy network in the city, and had been searching for Barabbas ever since. Barabbas had left immediately and run all the way to the temple.

Now he headed up the steps that led into the court of Israel. Sweat streamed down his face and body, stinging his eyes and making his garments feel clammy. A great many people stared at him, as he was not wearing a prayer shawl. Indeed, he had none of the customary garments or accessories traditionally worn into the temple.

Zechariah was already on his way over, filled with concern. Barabbas' worry must have been apparent to him.

"Barabbas, what's wrong?"

"We must stop them." Barabbas panted. "Pilate means to kill the remaining prisoners tomorrow. Levi, everybody."

"He wouldn't dare." The priest exclaimed.

"Well he has. I need those men immediately. We have to move now."

"Barabbas, I haven't even been able to contact them yet. I told you it's going to take three days."

Barabbas blurted. "We don't have three days. I need them now."

"I can probably get you two men at most."

"Two is no good. I need at least nine."

"It's impossible. You know how it is. There are procedures to follow. If I go rushing in, demanding to see them, they'll melt like the winter snow."

"Then we have to stall them."

"Stall who?"

"The Romans! We need to stall them for two days."

"And how do you propose to tell the prefect when and how he should execute his prisoners? He's difficult. He won't listen to reason."

"Talk to the Sanhedrin. Surely they can do something."

Zechariah shook his head. "You know they won't. They speak to the people of freedom and salvation, but when all is done, their allegiance rests with Rome. They won't upset the political structure."

"Surely there must be someone you can talk to. Please, Zechariah, I'm not just trying to free some friends. One of those men has information that's vital to the zealot cause. He may be the only one left who can help me. If he dies, all is lost."

"What information?"

"I can't tell you, so don't ask. It has the power to change the course of Israel's history, however. Please talk to the council. I only need two days."

After what seemed like an eternity, the priest nodded. "Very well, I'll try. There's Gamaliel. He's reasonable and respected by the council. Maybe he can motivate them to use their influence in the matter."

"Thank you, Zechariah. You're a good man."

The priest smiled. "It's kind of you to say that. I'm a coward who loves worldly comforts too much to live out my convictions. I speak of freedom with my lips, but my heart longs for the comfort and stature of the priesthood. I could never give my life for the cause as you and others like your brother have done."

Barabbas grinned. "You're braver than you think, Zechariah. You're about to go and face the Sanhedrin."

The older man laughed. "Go home, Barabbas. I'll do what I can. Meet me at my home tonight and I'll give you the news."

"Let's pray it's good news."

"We live in hope, my son."

Barabbas nodded and left the temple. It was odd. His father had been a devout man but, since his death, this was the most Barabbas had seen of the temple in any given year. The only time he entered a holy place these days was to meet a conduit, or to give instructions to a messenger for the zealot movement. It was ironic that so many zealots still believed they were fighting for a holy cause, when so few were found at synagogue on the Sabbath.

He trudged back toward the *Kainopolis*, head down and deep in thought. Periodically he shook the chest of his tunic, allowing the rush of air to cool his drenched body. Now he had no choice but to wait. When darkness fell, he would head for Zechariah's home and accept whatever news the man brought. He hoped fervently that the news would be favourable.

✝ ✝ ✝ ✝ ✝

Gaius passed by the two goliath sentries outside Herod's praetorium. They respectfully stepped aside and nodded in greeting. He ignored them. Pressing matters weighed on his mind.

Despite all his abilities, he was becoming increasingly frustrated by the men he now confronted. It was as if a curse had hung over his life since that fateful day when Barabbas had launched his one-man offensive against the barracks in Jerusalem.

Gaius frowned. His new antagonists, Barabbas and Eleazor, seemed to confound him at every turn. They taunted him, defeating him in each new contest with an apparent ease that drove him to despair. He was not used to losing and his current state of defeat was teaching him to hate. He loathed Eleazor and Barabbas as he had seldom loathed anyone in his life.

Seething with anger, he marched through the corridors of the palace. He arrived at Pilate's private chambers and knocked on the door, steeling himself for the meeting that was about to take place. A slave answered the door. Gaius took a deep breath and marched through the doorway with his helmet in the crook of his elbow.

The prefect glowered as he digested the news that Gaius brought.

"So he's gone." Pilate's voice carried the ominous calm of a serpent uncoiling.

"Yes, prefect."

"I presume you've dispatched soldiers to search for him in the surrounding towns."

"It's already been done, but I don't really expect any positive results. Once outside the city, these people generally vanish."

"Dare I ask why you didn't fetch him from the temple yourself?"

"He was inside the Jewish courts. We can't just march in there and drag an Israelite from the temple."

"Do you think I care at all about Jewish customs?"

"It's not mere tradition, prefect, you know that." Gaius retorted. "If Roman soldiers marched into the temple and started arresting Jewish citizens, it could precipitate a war. All Israel would rise up against Rome in their indignation. Even the Sanhedrin, which seems so friendly at the moment. They could never let the insult pass. We had no choice but to wait for the temple guard to bring him out. Every conceivable exit was guarded. What would you have had us do?"

"Every exit guarded and yet he got away. How do you explain that?"

"As I said he went over the wall. Nobody could have expected that."

"Your incompetence knows no bounds, centurion. I shall include this in my next report to Rome, whereupon I shall request your dismissal from the military. I will also recommend a trial before Caesar for gross negligence in your duties. You're not fit to command men and your career is over. Hand your staff and uniform to the officer on duty and remain confined to barracks pending news from Rome. Now get out." Pilate turned and stared out into the gardens.

"No."

When Pilate looked back, his face was flushed with fury. "You defy me?" He spat.

"I will not resign my post and nor will you write that letter."

"You're under arrest for insubordination."

"Go ahead, arrest me, but know this. It might come out in the trial that my failed duties included arresting a man who had already been granted his freedom for services rendered to Rome. There was a letter signed by you and I have witnesses to the effect. It might come out in the trial that I was given charge of prisoners who were tortured and killed without trial and that you participated in questioning these men."

Pilate stared for a long while at Gaius, considering the centurion's threat. Finally he smiled. "You're more devious than I gave you credit for. Where does that leave us?"

"Back where we started, I suppose. I've let these men slip from my grasp, I admit it. They've bested me time and again, but I assure you I have not been negligent."

"What do you want, centurion?"

"An opportunity, prefect. It's only a matter of time before they give us a reason to arrest them again. All I want is the chance to vindicate myself and punish them for the embarrassment they've caused me, as well as Rome."

"What if you can't do it? Your track record to date does not inspire confidence."

"If I can't do it then nobody can. Look at my official record, prefect. I'm the best centurion you have under your command. The Roman army is not incompetent. These men are exceptional. Their cunning and strength speak for themselves. It will take an expert to bring them to justice."

"And you consider yourself to be that man."

"I believe I can rise to the challenge."

Pilate spoke at length. "Well, centurion, it seems for the time being that I don't have a choice. I don't intend to ruin my political career over some small irregularities in prisoner detention. We'll forget your recent spate of failures for now. Just understand me. I don't like you. Do your job and bring me those men. Once I have the scroll in my possession I may feel more lenient and forgive your past offences. Good day, centurion."

Gaius hesitated. "There's something else."

Pilate sighed and rubbed his temples. "I'm afraid to ask. What is it?"

"One of our soldiers was killed in an alley between the palace and the barracks."

"Anyone I know?"

"Publius, the torturer. It was definitely a revenge killing. He died hard."

Pilate sighed again as he considered the centurion's words. "Of course, it's possible that some good can come of this. The suspect is obvious."

"It's the excuse we've been looking for. I can search for Barabbas and have him arrested."

"And what about the other matter?"

"There's no guarantee we'll find him, so it might be our only chance of catching him. I suggest we let it play out."

"Right. At least we can arrest him legitimately. Keep me informed of any new developments. I wouldn't be surprised if more dead legionaries turn up in the next few days. Look behind you as you walk, centurion."

"I always do, prefect." *And not just for Barabbas.* Gaius held the prefect's hawk-like gaze. His adversaries were not merely among the Jewish nationals.

Gaius left the praetorium and headed for the Antonia to write a letter to Publius' family. When he got there, he learned of two more letters he would have to write. He didn't know the men, but suspected that he would find they had been soldiers involved in the crucifixions of the previous day.

† † † † †

As darkness fell upon the city, Barabbas headed for the home of Zechariah. He arrived at the luxurious mansion with a deep feeling of trepidation. A servant ushered him to the main reception room. It was beautifully decorated with strong Hellenistic influences.

Zechariah was alone in the lounge, reclining on a sofa. "Good evening, my friend." He smiled and rose to greet his guest. "And how was the rest of your day?"

"Pleasant enough. I had to settle a few debts which kept my mind occupied."

"Please, sit down." Zechariah motioned toward the sofa and called for the servant who had answered the door. "A cup of our finest wine for my guest here."

Barabbas waited for the servant to leave before speaking. "Do we have something to celebrate?" he asked carefully.

"Forgive me, my son. I forget you must be anxious to hear of your friends' fate. Let me tell you. I had a long meeting with Gamaliel, do you know him?"

"Yes, what happened?"

"Well I told him what you had told me, with some details omitted, of course. He listened carefully to all I had to say. It took a little persuasion on my part, but not much. He agreed. Men should not be executed during the Feast of Unleavened Bread."

"Are they safe, that's all I want to know?"

"Well, Gamaliel agreed to talk to the council. He was before them for a long time, nearly an hour, stating his case. He's a brilliant orator."

"Zechariah!" Barabbas became exasperated.

"Sorry." The old man took a deep breath. "They're safe, until after the feast, at any rate."

"Thank you. Now I know you're itching to tell me how you achieved it."

The priest beamed and then continued. "Gamaliel told the Sanhedrin the grave news. He put it to them that Jews should not be executed on such a holy occasion, not even criminals – sorry. He appealed to their sense of justice to speak to Pilate about the matter."

"Which they obviously did."

"They were not easily convinced. They said that by defending the rebels, they might be considered sympathisers. One can't be too careful in the arena of Roman politics. Gamaliel finally appealed to their piety. He put it to them that it was an offence, not against men, but against God, that men be killed in such a manner during the feast.

They eventually agreed. Caiaphas himself went before Pilate. He told him that the Sanhedrin was concerned by Rome's apparent lack of reverence for God and asked him to delay the execution of the prisoners."

"I'm sure Pilate loved him for that."

Zechariah shrugged. "The prefect is always difficult, but Caiaphas and Annas have dealt with him over a long period of time. They know how to handle him. He eventually agreed to their demands, albeit unwillingly."

"If my plan works, he's going to want the Sanhedrin's blood. He'll probably accuse them of collaborating with zealots."

"He'll probably blame them, but what proof has he got? They can claim complete innocence. They have no knowledge of what's planned."

"They may come after you, Zechariah. Tread lightly about the temple."

"You let me worry about that. The priesthood is as political as it is holy, perhaps more so. You don't get where I have without learning to cover your tracks."

"As I said, you're braver than you think, Zechariah."

"How about that wine?" Zechariah smiled at the compliment.

The two men drank and chatted of politics, religion and Israel's bondage under Rome. The wine flowed and their animated discussion lasted late into the night. Finally, Barabbas excused himself and rose to leave.

After rising to embrace him Zechariah said. "I've sent word to the zealots. In a couple of days I'll have an answer from them and you can put your plan in motion. Until then, may God watch over you and all in your house."

"Thank you, Rabbi. I won't forget this. Look after yourself. It may become dangerous for you in the days to come."

✝ ✝ ✝ ✝ ✝

Eleazor pulled his shawl up around his ears as a barrier against the stellar chill. At night the desert became as cold as it was hot during the day.

He reached out to stoke the fire, blowing on the powdery off-white ashes to ignite the glowing embers beneath. He added some wood to the fire and took some leftover meat from his dinner.

Although the sky still shone with a myriad of stars, it was early morning. Dawn was no more than two hours away. The cold sands blew past on both sides of his jagged shelter in the lee of a small outcrop.

He gnawed hungrily on the tough, sinewy chunks of meat that he had roasted the evening before. His trophy had been an unwitting goat that had strayed too far from its herd. He had taken a joint and left the carcass for the jackals and other scavengers to dispose of.

In the early morning gloom, he considered his predicament. He would be foolish to approach the zealots now. News of his treachery was travelling quickly. He would have to confront Barabbas again if he wanted the scroll, however.

Eleazor coughed, shifting his position slightly to avoid the thin threads of smoke from the fresh firewood. He was mildly annoyed by the way the smoke seemed to track his movements around the fire, always finding its way to his face, no matter where he sat. He sniffed, pulling his cloak about him like a shield to ward off the cold.

At the moment it was impossible to return to Jerusalem. Pilate would stop at nothing to see him in chains. He would have to disappear for a while until the matter was forgotten, or at least pushed aside in lieu of more pressing ones.

He could return to Jerusalem in a month or so and pick up Barabbas' trail again. He wouldn't be difficult to find.

Eleazor munched morosely on his breakfast, glancing at the shimmering horizon as it ushered in the morning sun. He would go east, into the desert, he decided. It was a vast and desolate place, hostile to creatures foreign to its nature.

Where Roman soldiers would debilitate and die, he would find it welcoming and hospitable. He would be able to move, find food and shelter, as well as the all-important water to sustain life. He knew the desert's moods. Her wild storms and stifling heat held no fear for him.

To zealots the desert was a place of refuge, a welcome protection beyond the reach of Roman power. Munching silently, he waited for dawn.

When first light shone brightly on the horizon, giving shadows shape, Eleazor rose, killing the fire, and headed east in the direction of Moab. There, he would find refuge, a place where he could live comfortably until he felt ready to return to Jerusalem and his quest for the copper scroll.

As dawn broke, Gaius strode once again through the gates of Herod's praetorium.

He was puzzled by the early summons. It was unusual to be called to a meeting with the prefect before dawn. As Roman governor, he was theoretically available for public duty at sunrise, but he didn't usually have his personnel summoned at first light.

Gaius was ushered through to the public chambers where Pilate held council with the citizens of Judea. He was led through the hall where various citizens already sat awaiting their audience with the prefect. The group comprised mostly wealthy businessmen looking for political favours and tax collectors bringing their tribute to Rome.

Some were messengers with news from abroad. Gaius nodded at one of the official military messengers that he recognised. He couldn't remember from where.

A sentry ushered him past all of the hopeful citizens and took him straight into the official chamber. Pilate was seated on a high-backed chair with velvet cushions. He seemed to be in a good mood for a change.

"Good morning, centurion. I thought I'd give you the news as early as possible."

"Yes, prefect?" Gaius knew that Pilate detested inane chatter and pleasantries.

"It seems your prediction was right. The zealots were appalled by news of the early execution of their friends in prison."

"What happened?" Gaius tried to conceal his excitement, but his stomach trembled in anticipation.

"I had a visit from that fat high priest and his father-in-law, Annas. They begged, actually insisted, that I delay the execution until after the Feast of Unleavened Bread. Why do you think they'd do that?"

Gaius frowned. "From what I know of Jewish religion, it seems plausible that the Sanhedrin would make such a request, but I'm more interested in how they got the information in the first place. We specifically leaked the news to known zealot informants."

"Only zealots and Barabbas in particular would have an interest in feeding them the information."

"It shows inventiveness on his part - to mobilise the Sanhedrin to speak on his behalf. Once again, I've underestimated my opponent."

"You're going to have to learn to stop doing that, centurion." Pilate chided him. "Why do you think they want the execution delayed?"

"It gives them a chance to mobilise their rescue. Obviously they're not ready yet."

"As I thought." Pilate's narrow eyes darted to and fro as he considered the implications. "They'll probably attack outside the city gates. It gives them their best opportunity for escape."

"Which is why I don't think they'll do that. It's too obvious. They'll attack when we least expect it."

"And when do you think that would be?"

"Almost certainly inside the city. The soldiers will be on their guard when they collect the prisoners, and once they leave the city gates. It's inside the city walls that they'll be lulled into a sense of security."

"What about inside the palace itself?"

"Just the type of thing Barabbas would love to do. I think he'd find it extremely difficult to escape, but I will prepare for that eventuality. I'll have the guard alerted from the hour that we release the prisoners from their cell. Any time from that moment on, we can expect the zealots to act."

"How do you intend to spread the net to catch them?"

"I'll have men posted at every phase of the prisoners' journey from their cell to Golgotha. I'll have them check every building and corner where the zealots might hide. We have an additional advantage, now that we don't have to wait for Barabbas to act. He's already incriminated himself by killing the soldiers who had a hand in his brother's death."

"What about the city wall?"

"I think they've proved adequately that a guard on the city wall is useless. They can ferret their way through holes and tunnels we don't even know about. This time I will place men on every known route that leads east or south from Jerusalem. They'll almost certainly flee in one of those directions."

"What makes you so sure? What if they decide to head in another direction?"

"Unfortunately I don't have the manpower available to cover all possibilities. I will, of course, post soldiers on the more likely routes in those directions, but I want to cover the other routes thoroughly. I reasoned that the desert is where they feel most comfortable. It's also where our soldiers are weakest, so even if they slip through the northern or western cordon, we are at least forcing them to fight on our terms."

"The strategy is sound. I only hope you succeed. That Jew is my only hope now that the other one has escaped."

"I must warn you, prefect. Even if we catch him, he may not tell you anything."

"I don't intend to ask him about the scroll. That would be futile. I'm sure he'd be willing to assist us in our search for the other man, though. From what I hear they don't like each other very much."

"He might have some insight into the other's whereabouts."

"We'll see. What do we do in the meantime?"

"We wait. They can't act until the prisoners are brought for execution and we can't execute until after the feast. For now, I'll begin to brief the troops."

Gaius left, satisfied in the knowledge that the bait had been taken. Now all I have to do is close the trap, Barabbas. Then you're mine.

12

EIGHT DAYS had passed and the Feast of Unleavened Bread had ended. The sunrise over Jerusalem found Gaius and Pilate hidden in the Phasael tower, just north of Herod's praetorium on the external wall of the city.

Preparations for the trap had been extensive and each soldier had been thoroughly drilled by Gaius in preparation for the moment Barabbas showed himself.

"This is good. We can see everything from here." Pilate stared, through the narrow slits that were his eyes, at the gate below.

"It won't be long now. The legionaries have been instructed to fetch the prisoners as soon as the escort arrives."

They waited a while longer, filled with mixed feelings of anxiety and anticipation. The sun rose, a bright orange crescent beaming over a pastel horizon, casting its first rays on the city streets. Gaius carefully scanned the city below. He examined each position where soldiers lay in wait for their prey and was pleased to see the groups of drunkards and street-side hawkers all blending in quietly with their surroundings. Nothing was amiss and Barabbas wouldn't suspect a thing. If only the escort would arrive! They were already late and Gaius voiced his concern.

"You worry too quickly, centurion." Pilate was in a fine mood.

The atmosphere in the tower became tense as time passed and still the escort did not arrive. Gaius became more anxious with each passing moment. He sighed audibly as the legionaries finally marched into view, approaching the main gate of the praetorium. Everything was running according to plan. The legionaries moved across the cobbled stones, coming to a halt at the gates. His gaze remained riveted on the proceedings as two legionaries raced away to fetch the prisoners for the escort.

"Are the soldiers all in place?" Pilate asked nervously as he watched the legionaries below, quietly adjusting their belts and helmet straps while they waited for the prisoners to be brought out.

"They're there. The fact that you don't recognise them is proof that the trap is effective." Gaius assured him. He pointed to one of the groups down in the street; five men quietly playing a game of chance with a pair of small, wooden dice, exchanging monies as each round was won or lost. Short, Roman swords were carefully concealed beneath billowing *abeyahs*. The soldiers were ready to act the moment the enemy showed himself.

The prefect nodded in approval. "It seems you've done your job properly, for once."

"I'll feel better once he's safely inside the dungeons of the Antonia." Gaius never took his eyes off the street below, raking the area as he searched for any sign of the elusive Jew.

"He'll show himself any minute now, and when he does —" Pilate chuckled quietly, rubbing his hands together to rid them of the morning chill.

A tense silence fell over the pair in the tower as they waited for the prisoners to be brought out. From their vantage point, they watched the proceedings with a keen interest as the escort waited patiently in the courtyard. One of the soldiers adjusted his belt, while another quietly stroked his chin.

Gaius scanned the street again, but could find no sign of Barabbas or any rescue party. The tension gnawed at his stomach, causing it to ache and reminding him that he hadn't eaten that morning. He stared down at the scene, willing Barabbas to show himself.

Below, the soldiers chatted quietly among themselves. Some pulled at the straps of their helmets, scratching the irritated skin where the straps had chaffed them. Finally the prisoners were brought out. They were emaciated and filthy and their tunics were sodden with muck. They staggered, shielding their eyes from the morning sun.

"Well, if it's going to happen, now's the time." Pilate murmured.

† † † † †

Down in the courtyard, the prisoners were dragged across to the waiting legionaries. As they drew close, Lazarus looked up and gasped. "Wha —" He was cut short as the legionary in charge swung a vicious blow across his cheek.

"You'll speak when spoken to, Jew." The man snarled, leaving the prisoner to mop the blood that flowed from his injured lip.

The man turned and gazed at Levi, who stood staring intently at the ground. "I'll take this one," he said, offering his hand to the guards holding Levi. The soldiers locked his wrist securely to the chain. Presently, each of the prisoners was chained between two guards and ready to be escorted from the praetorium.

"Let's go." The guard in charge called and marched off, jerking Levi roughly by his collar.

"Jerk me like that one more time and it will go the worse for you." Levi spoke quietly, staring at his feet.

"Shut up." The guard glowered and jerked the collar again.

† † † † †

Up in the tower, Pilate scanned the streets, peering carefully at each corner as they passed. "They're down there somewhere."

"They should have struck already." Gaius murmured as the prisoners and their escort circumvented the *Gabbatha.* "They'll never strike outside the city. It's too obvious."

"I think maybe you double-guessed yourself, centurion."

They watched the patrol approach the city gate, below the tower. The soldier bringing up the rear adjusted his helmet's strap again and Gaius felt a chill run through his body as he realized what was bothering him.

With a sudden lurch, he spun and headed for the steps. As he ran, he yelled behind him. "Stop them. The men in that patrol are Jews!"

Pilate gazed after him in confusion for a moment. This quickly turned to consternation as the truth of the centurion's words dawned on him. He leaned from the tower and began yelling orders at the soldiers below.

Gaius smashed his centurion's staff against the wall, shattering the dry vinewood into splinters as he raced down the stairs. His heart was filled with fury. How could he have been so stupid! They'd been fidgeting with their uniforms since the moment they'd arrived in the palace court. Only new recruits did that, or people who were not used to the constrictions of the uniform.

As he raced down the spiral steps of the tower, he only hoped he wasn't too late.

† † † † †

As they emerged from the city gate, Barabbas looked back at the prefect, waving like an angry flag from the tower. "How fit are you?" he asked Levi. "We may have to run for it."

"Loosen these chains. I don't want you slowing me down."

"Are you fit enough to run, Lazarus?"

"I'll make it." Lazarus was still gingerly massaging the bleeding lip where Barabbas had struck him.

Just then, Gaius emerged from the city gate, barking orders at the guards who manned the exit. Barabbas couldn't hear what the centurion was saying, but he didn't waste time guessing.

"Time to go," he urged, breaking into a run.

The group surged forward, turned right and followed the road that led to Calvary. They hadn't gone far when they suddenly turned and dashed in among the trees that lined the path. As soon as they were hidden from view, they began to fragment, using classic zealot tactics. Within minutes, Barabbas' comrades were lost from view. Each small group was now responsible for its own safety.

As they ran, Barabbas reached for the clamps, unlocking the chains that fettered him to Levi. Once loose, he came around and released Levi from the man on his other side.

"You remember Zebulon, I hope. He fought with us when we raided the tax collector's carriage en route to Caesarea two years ago."

"A pleasure." Levi nodded. "Let's hope we have a chance to catch up later."

"This way." Barabbas urged his two companions. He and Zebulon tried to help Levi who was struggling bravely in his weakened state. Barabbas knew it must be taking every bit of strength left in his friend just to stay on his feet, but Levi never complained.

The three of them raced through the cultivated orchards, using the thick foliage for cover. They avoided roads, skirting around Jerusalem, heading north. Their route followed a continuous curve to throw their pursuers off track.

As he ran, he saw shapes and movement ahead of him. The colours reflected between the trees signified Roman uniforms. Alarmed, he altered his course yet again. Fortunately the legionaries hadn't seen him. He held up his hand, cautioning his companions and pointed in the direction of the figures.

"Fellow zealots." Zebulon whispered. "I can't see who they are, but look at the way they're weaving and changing direction. They're not searching systematically as soldiers would."

Barabbas felt relieved, but kept an eye on the figures ahead of him in the grove. Presently he lost sight of them again.

"This way." Barabbas started making his way up the hill, heading for high ground.

Levi and Zebulon followed. They moved up the hill cautiously, slowing their pace in favour of stealth.

"It's a logical lookout. There may be Romans guarding it."

"Did you see how many were down there today? It was as if they were waiting for us."

"They were." Barabbas answered. "They were hiding in every conceivable alley and doorway."

"Protecting prisoners, perhaps." Levi panted.

"No." Barabbas replied. "They weren't positioned to protect you. I led everyone into a trap."

"If they were so well positioned, then why didn't they catch us?" Levi's voice rasped as he gulped huge breaths of air. He winced, leaning his hands on his knees.

"That's just it. Properly positioned, they would have recognised us, but they weren't interested in the prisoners. You were just the bait. Their eyes were elsewhere."

"Another thing." Zebulon said thoughtfully. "Why would they protect the city so well and have so few soldiers outside the city walls?"

"We'll know that when we reach the lookout. I want to see their positioning."

The men moved silently. When they arrived near the top of the hill, they found no Roman soldiers there at all. Barabbas was still careful. He turned aside and began to move quietly through the undergrowth, circling the hilltop. Halfway around, Zebulon froze and pointed. Barabbas followed his line of sight and finally saw what had caught his friend's attention.

Hidden among the undergrowth, near the summit, were two soldiers. Barabbas would have missed them had it not been for his comrade's sharp eyes. He gave a signal and the trio moved forward in effortless silence. Knives were unsheathed and the legionaries never even uttered a cry of surprise. They left the two corpses resting in wide-eyed horror under the bushes where they had hidden.

The zealots continued around the summit. Two more groups were found hidden around the lookout point and were dispatched with an equally silent and ruthless efficiency. Once sure that the way was clear, Barabbas moved out onto the summit. Still taking no chances, he moved alone, leaving Zebulon and Levi in hiding to guard his rear.

It was an unnecessary precaution, however, as no soldiers remained. From his vantage point, Barabbas surveyed the surrounding area. From what he could see, the Roman army had formed a loose cordon around the west wall, guarding the most likely routes that would be taken. They were visible from where he was, but would not be from the ground. Hills like this one were obviously similarly guarded. Barabbas returned to his comrades.

"What does it look like?" Zebulon asked.

"It doesn't make sense. They have guards hidden in various strategic positions, but we can easily slip through. Gaius has only used a fraction of the men available to him. Also, there are almost no search parties out there. That's why we've been able to move so easily."

"What about the soldiers inside the city?"

"They're out there, beating about the bushes, but it's only a show. There's no real urgency. It's as if they want us to escape."

"No it isn't." Levi was thoughtful.

"How so?"

"Think about it. Gaius has limited manpower for such an operation. He'll want to waste as few men as possible. Even the men he has placed here are a waste. We never run north. That would be like running into the lion's gaping jaws. We head for the desert. I'll wager my life, that's where Gaius has placed his men."

Barabbas thought about Levi's theory. "Do you think we can break through?"

"I doubt it. You saw the soldiers below us. What you describe is a fraction of the Roman force in Jerusalem. The rest will be hidden on every conceivable route east and south of us. We'd be foolish to try."

"We have to."

"Why?"

Barabbas hesitated, glancing at Zebulon. "Nathaniel may be dead."

Levi's eyes narrowed. "How?"

"Eleazor killed him, or so he claims."

"He may have been lying."

Barabbas shrugged. "We don't know that. Either way, we have to find out."

Levi nodded and glanced at Zebulon, who listened to the conversation with concerned interest. It was obvious he had no idea of the true implications.

"We'll talk again later. First we need to get away from here and find a bath. I feel like rat droppings."

"Lord knows you smell like them."

"I say we head north, at least until we're clear of the cordon. The Romans can't stay out there for ever."

Barabbas nodded in agreement and the three men turned north, following the contour of the city wall on their right as they headed for the Judean hills beyond.

A few hours later, the group found themselves in the hills of Jerusalem, not far from the town of Gibeon. They headed for a cave which served as a traditional zealot resting place. Hidden in the grotto were rations and various stockpiles of weaponry.

They flopped down in the cave and Zebulon went to look for some food hidden in the dark recesses. He returned with some dried dates and a few hard cakes of crusty bread. He also brought some bandages and assorted ointments to dress Levi's wounds. These were new items and the men were grateful for their predecessors' thoughtfulness.

They tucked in to the food with voracity. Levi finished first and rose. "There's a pool of water outside. I'm going to wash this stench off me."

"See that you do a good job, or you'll be sleeping outside tonight." Barabbas called after him.

Later that evening the men relaxed in the relative comfort of the cave around a fire - made of dry wood to keep smoke to a minimum - feeding off its warmth as they massaged their aching muscles.

They fell asleep early, curled under shawls they had found stashed in the cave. The shawls were dusty and full of holes, but they kept the men warm, warding off the worst of the nocturnal chill. The three men took turns standing watch through the night, looking out for the ever present danger of the Roman army.

The following morning they rose with the sun, stoking the fire as they breakfasted on more dry cakes of bread and discussed their plans for the future.

"I think I'll stay with my cousin in Gibeon for a few weeks. Just until my beard grows back out." Zebulon said.

"Wise." Barabbas agreed. "We can't move about looking like this. We'll stand out like oases in the desert sands."

"What about you?" Zebulon asked between mouthfuls of crusty bread.

"I don't know. We'll give it a few days and then try to head south again. We have to find out about a friend of ours."

"The man who Eleazor killed?"

Barabbas nodded and quickly changed the subject. "Thanks for your help, Zebulon. We couldn't have done this without you."

"It was an honour, Barabbas. I hope to have such an opportunity again some day."

"Speed the day when such struggle is no longer necessary, my friend. When Israel can govern her own people and bow to nobody but the God of Abraham."

Zebulon nodded gravely as he finished chewing on his meal. "Goodbye, Levi." He embraced him and turned to Barabbas. "*Shalom*, my friend. Go in peace."

"Peace, Zebulon." Barabbas embraced their friend and comrade.

The two men watched as Zebulon headed north for Gibeon. Soon he was lost from sight, having melted away in the undergrowth.

"He's a good man." Barabbas murmured.

"They're all good men. I hope they made it out."

"If they found their way blocked, I imagine they would merely head north and slip through the Roman guard there."

"Speaking of which, what is this of our friend in the south?"

"Eleazor found me in Jerusalem. He told me he'd struck Nathaniel down with his sword."

"So Nathaniel is dead."

"There's more. Eleazor knows I'm a protector now. He said Nathaniel told him he'd sent the scroll to me in Jerusalem. Eleazor was convinced I had it, but I never received it."

Levi threw his head back and laughed.

"What's so funny?"

"Nathaniel would never do that. If he moved the scroll, it would only be because it was about to be discovered, and then it would be no more than a mile, two at the most."

Eleazor said four men were bringing it to me in Jerusalem."

"If Nathaniel wasn't coming to Jerusalem, then neither was the scroll. He probably told Eleazor that in the hopes that he would find us and get himself killed.

Barabbas was relieved. "That's what I told him, but I was bluffing. I didn't know what to believe."

The scroll is safe, I assure you. We still have to go to *Khirbet Qumran*, though. If Nathaniel is dead, it means we have a new priest. I must find Mattithyahu and make contact with him. There's information he will need."

"What sort of information?"

"The true value of the scroll is not monetary. It is prophetic and political."

"In what way?" Barabbas demanded.

"As Nathaniel said, some things are better left untold. When I die, you will be the only remaining warrior. Then the priest will tell you."

"Do you want me to come with you?"

"No, it's just a formality. With Nathaniel gone, Mattithyahu has to assume more responsibility. That responsibility requires knowledge, which I must impart. You have family matters to attend to. I can meet you in Sepphoris when I'm done."

Barabbas nodded sadly. He had driven the knowledge of what he had to do from his mind for too long already. He had a mother in Sepphoris and she had a right to know what had happened to her son.

The two men set the cave in order, readying it for the next visitors, and then bade one another farewell. Barabbas headed for Galilee while Levi turned east, hoping to circumvent the Roman soldiers who desperately scoured the eastern and southern parts of Judea for the zealots who had taken part in the raid.

✝ ✝ ✝ ✝ ✝

Nathaniel was troubled by Mattithyahu's continued fever and semi-comatose condition. Hours had dragged into agonising days as he tried to communicate with his dying protégé. He looked at the doctor who had just finished dressing the wounds on Mattithyahu's back, with a questioning gaze.

The doctor shook his head sadly and turned to leave the room. The putrid stench of decaying flesh still hung in the air. Mattithyahu hadn't even groaned as the bandages were removed. The gangrenous wounds had been washed without protest. Now he lay with fresh bandages, oblivious to his surroundings.

Nathaniel caught the doctor at the door. "How much time do you think he's got?" He whispered.

"Not much more. The sooner the better, I think. He's suffering now."

"Yes, you're right." Nathaniel patted the elderly man's shoulder. *But he's needed here.*

He waited for the man to leave before turning back to the inert form on the floor. "Wake up, my son." he whispered, gently shaking the body. "You have to wake up."

He looked down at the jaundiced face and noticed the eyes flutter slightly. It was only there for a moment and then it was gone. He shook Mattithyahu gently again. "Please, my son. I need you to be brave now. Don't allow yourself to fail so close to the end."

Mattithyahu's breathing became uneven and his body turned rigid. Then the convulsions began and finally, he opened his eyes. He shivered violently and gazed at Nathaniel. "I thought you were dead," he said weakly.

Nathaniel's heart exulted. "No, my son. We don't have time; you must tell me where you put the scroll."

Already, Nathaniel could see Mattithyahu slipping away. The man's eyes became glazed and he was becoming incoherent.

"Bandits, bandits, ban —" he muttered. "Everyone - dead."

Once again, he lapsed into unconsciousness.

"The scroll!" Nathaniel pressed him, but it was useless. Mattithyahu continued muttering, but none of the words made any sense. Most of it was so garbled that Nathaniel couldn't make out the words at all.

It was several hours before Mattithyahu became responsive once again. He rolled and suddenly shrieked at the pain. His eyes became wide and he stared fearfully into Nathaniel's face, gripping his arm with the tenacity of a predator on its prey.

"*Dov Harim*, Bear Mountain!" he whispered with hoarse urgency. "*Dov Harim!* Scroll - the scroll. *Dov Harim.*"

"I don't understand, my son. Please try. I need to know before you leave this world."

With an effort that all but drained him of every last flicker of life, Mattithyahu pulled himself up amidst convulsions and gasped the whispered message into Nathaniel's ear. The old man frowned, but patted Mattithyahu's shoulder. The young man fell back and lost consciousness once again. Thirty minutes later, Mattithyahu breathed his last and the community went into mourning for their friend. He was buried in the communal graveyard and the Essene commune mourned for three days.

It was during this time that Nathaniel decided upon his course of action. It was with an old and weary heart that he took up the burden of the scroll once more. He had to find Levi and Barabbas and tell them the tragic news.

Mattithyahu had tried his best, but in the end, death had won. Nathaniel had lived in *Qumran* for nearly fifty years. He had travelled the road to Jerusalem and back over a thousand times, following every conceivable route or trail. Few men in Judea could claim to know the area as well as Nathaniel and he had never heard of *Dov Harim*.

The scroll had vanished. Everything that he and his friends had worked and died for was lost. How many times had he wanted to read it? He recalled the countless times he had held it in his hand and forbidden himself from gazing upon its words. Some things are better left unknown. It's safer this way. The scroll is burden enough.

He cursed his discipline and tears of frustration ran down his wrinkled cheeks. A numbness came over him as he was struck by another thought. Barabbas, Levi and Simeon might even be dead by now. Their lives would have been given in vain for a scroll that had been lost through his carelessness. No, they must still be alive. There must still be hope. He would go to Jerusalem and tell them what had happened. Then, together, they could search for the scroll. He began to make preparations for his journey.

✝ ✝ ✝ ✝ ✝

Barabbas headed north for the road that led to Galilee. He felt more comfortable in the traditional Jewish clothes he had donned back in the cave than in the restrictive Roman uniform he had worn during the raid.

Although he was still careful, he found the road relatively free of Roman soldiers and was able to move freely for the most part. He had not travelled far when he saw a coach party approaching from behind him.

They were catching up quickly and, with a caution born of habit, he rounded a bend and slipped off the road into the tree line. As they drew closer, he examined the party. It was a Jewish party headed for Galilee and he relaxed, emerging back onto the road in the hopes of getting a lift. It would be far faster and more comfortable.

He waved as the carriage drew near and was surprised to see Zebedee's head appear out of the window.

Zebedee smiled. "May I offer you the hospitality of my carriage? You're obviously headed for Galilee and it's a long way yet."

It was apparent that he hadn't recognised Barabbas without his beard.

"Thank you. You're most generous." Barabbas swung himself onto the carriage and opened the door. His sleeve slipped back as he clambered aboard, revealing the fresh cut that would later become the mark of his covenant with the protectors of the copper scroll. Covering the mark quickly, he sat down and beamed at the occupants of the carriage.

Inside the carriage, he found Leila opposite her father, looking demure, and another man he didn't recognise. "It's good to see you again, Zebedee - and your lovely daughter."

"Barabbas?" Leila was stunned.

"I didn't expect to see you again so soon." Zebedee frowned slightly.

Leila asked. "What happened to your beard?"

"I needed to lose some weight." Barabbas replied with a sly smile.

"Were you involved in that uproar outside the praetorium yesterday?" Zebedee asked sternly.

"Uproar?" Barabbas feigned ignorance.

"You can't tell me you know nothing about it. There were soldiers all over the place."

"If you must know, it was a trap and, yes, it was set for me."

"But were you involved?" Zebedee pressed him.

Barabbas evaded the question. "Do you think I'd be so stupid as to walk into a Roman trap?"

Leila tried to break the tension between the two men. "Barabbas, I don't believe you've met my father's friend."

"I don't think so." Barabbas was grateful for the change in subject.

"Miyka'el." The man's smile was hostile.

"*Shalom*, Miyka'el." Barabbas sized the man up. He was tall and well built, but there was a softness around the mouth and eyes that spoke of an easy life.

The man had curly, brown hair and a neatly trimmed beard. Barabbas guessed they were about the same age.

Zebedee spoke again. "So, Barabbas, what takes you to Galilee?"

"I have family there. I'm going to see my mother and uncle in Sepphoris."

"Sepphoris!" Leila exclaimed. "That's where we live."

Zebedee scowled again then asked. "Who is your uncle? Perhaps I know him."

"His name is Ehud."

"Ehud." Zebedee thought briefly. "A wealthy farmer. Owns vast lands all around the city."

Barabbas smiled. "Then the years have been good. He only used to own vast lands around half the city."

Zebedee chuckled. "He's a good man. I'm surprised you're not involved with him on his lands."

"It's a complicated relationship." Barabbas replied quietly.

Miyka'el finally decided to join in the conversation. "I know you only by reputation, Barabbas. What do you do when you're not fighting the loathsome Roman Empire?"

He wore a slightly amused, almost mocking expression, but his eyes bored into Barabbas like a carpenter's drill. It annoyed Barabbas instantly.

"I fight with collaborating Jews who have forgotten their nation's heritage and sold out to Rome for their own profit. Know anyone like that?" He smiled back at Miyka'el's discomfort. "What do you do, Miyka'el?"

"I'm a merchant. I transport goods from the east to Jerusalem and places north. I may merge my interests with Zebedee in his business. If we can negotiate a suitable agreement." He glanced across at Leila as he spoke the last sentence.

Barabbas looked across at her and noticed her discomfort. "Slave trade?" He enquired coldly.

Miyka'el shrugged. "Sometimes, when there's a demand." Either he had missed Barabbas' insinuation, or he ignored it.

"The thing about slaves is they never serve their masters properly. They're forced to serve out of fear, not love."

"Some have learned to love their masters in time." Miyka'el scowled.

"The next one I see will be the first." Barabbas growled and looked out of the window. He wasn't sure why Miyka'el disliked him, but he knew the feeling was mutual.

Leila turned to Barabbas and smiled. "How long will you be staying in Sepphoris?"

Barabbas shrugged. "I don't know. Perhaps I'll settle there. I could take your father's advice and work for my uncle."

She smiled again and Barabbas wasn't sure whether she was happier at the news or the discomfort it seemed to cause Miyka'el. The coach lapsed into an uncomfortable silence, during which Barabbas gazed across at Leila out of the corner of his eye. How he longed to see the face behind the veil again. Just to look at her made his heart ache with a painful longing he had seldom experienced, if ever.

✝ ✝ ✝ ✝ ✝

Levi was becoming frustrated. He had moved east, avoiding main roads and following small, winding trails, used more often by the local fauna than by people. He'd been careful to make sure he was not seen, finding the sparsely inhabited areas and steering clear of the larger settlements.

This had slowed his pace considerably, but he had consoled himself in the fact that he would at least be able to slip through the Roman blockade with these tactics. It was not to be, however, as he found the back roads even more heavily guarded than the main routes.

Twice now, he'd nearly been spotted and he was still caked with mud from the pool where he had remained hidden for almost half an hour while legionaries scoured the area around him. His mood had become dark as he retreated miserably before the Roman soldiers. He would have to get clear of them and try again in a few days.

He scraped the dried crusts of mud from his arms. They made him look like a cracked and badly hewn statue. The mud clung to him, drying his skin and scratching his body. He had to find water and get the filth off him.

He jumped, startled by a sharp crack to his right. It was the sound of a twig snapping underfoot. Levi dove for cover, finding refuge in the plant life beside the trail. As he entered the undergrowth, he rolled to his left, changing direction.

The Roman spear missed by inches, thudding into the soil next to him. Levi rolled frantically away from it, finding shelter behind a low mound of rocks. He was forced to crawl on his belly. Any higher and he would be exposed.

"I could have sworn I heard him go this way," the soldier said.

Levi snaked slowly around the far end of the rocks and then risked a glance. He counted four soldiers on the narrow trail, peering intently into the foliage. They were no more than a few paces away, but searching almost ninety degrees off course. He ducked below the rock again as one of them turned to look in his direction.

"He must be here somewhere. Spread out and look for him."

The soldiers entered the bush and began their search. Levi rose silently and stole across the pathway into the bushes on the other side. Behind him the legionaries thrashed about the brush on the opposite side of the path. Grinning quietly, he continued on his way.

† † † † †

The atmosphere in the coach had become charged with tension. Most of the conversation was between Barabbas and Leila. Zebedee had fallen into a gruff silence and Miyka'el had been completely excluded.

He sat sullenly, peering out of the window. Suddenly he narrowed his eyes and craned his neck. "Roman horsemen coming up behind us. They look like they're in a hurry."

"Which side!" Barabbas was suddenly alarmed.

"They'll pass on this side."

Barabbas leaned across the coach to look. He didn't stick his head outside the carriage but hung back, leaning over Miyka'el to get the angle. When he gazed back, he saw the horsemen racing up behind the coach. There were five of them in all.

Moving back to his side of the carriage, Barabbas moved around Leila so that he was opposite Miyka'el. He listened carefully to the beat of the hoofs on the road behind them. As they approached the carriage, the Roman horsemen began to slow.

"Halt, there. Stop your carriage." A soldier called.

Slipping to the floor, he pressed himself up against the side and unsheathed a knife from his belt. The coach rolled to a halt and the soldier trotted his steed up to the window.

"We're searching for a party of armed men. They're a party of zealots that was involved in a prison break yesterday. Some of them are clean shaven; they impersonated Roman legionaries. Have you seen any men fitting the description?"

Miyka'el, Barabbas and Leila all stared at Zebedee. He hesitated and then looked directly at the soldier.

"No," he replied. "The road has been quite clear today. Not many people."

The soldier stared intently into the carriage for a moment, looking around. His horse swung about skittishly as he examined the passengers. "Very well." He nodded. "If you do come across them, report it at the next military post."

"We'll keep our eyes open."

"Thank you," said the soldier. "Have a good journey."

"Goodbye." Zebedee smiled and nodded

As the soldiers sped north, Zebedee leaned forward and watched them disappear around the next bend. When he turned back, his face burned with anger.

"You come in here and abuse my hospitality. You put my family's life in danger and you force me to play a role in your violence that I did not ask or care for."

Barabbas rose from the floor. "I'm sorry, Zebedee, truly. I never meant to involve you this way. I think, under the circumstances, it would be best if I travelled alone."

Leila pleaded. "But Barabbas, you –"

"Enough, Leila," Zebedee was quiet, but firm. He looked back at Barabbas. "Don't you dare ever put me in that position again."

"Thank you for your hospitality and, again, I am sorry for the trouble I've caused. Goodbye, Leila," Barabbas nodded as he exited the coach.

"See you in Sepphoris," she smiled.

"Maybe." Barabbas smiled awkwardly as he hung on the door of the carriage. He hopped lightly to the ground and continued along the road on foot. The carriage was quickly gone from sight.

† † † † †

With the time of mourning over, Nathaniel came before the elders of the *Qumran* community. He found them taking in the sun at the entrance to the commune. They stopped their discussion at his approach.

"*Shalom*, Nathaniel. I see the Lord makes his sun shine upon you."

"*Shalom*, Merari," Nathaniel greeted the elderly man.

"You've come to discuss a matter of importance. I see it in your eyes." The man to Merari's right spoke quietly. His voice wheezed with the effort, but his eyes shone brightly from the wrinkled face that always made Nathaniel think of ancient parchment.

"You have the wisdom of Solomon," Nathaniel answered the old man. He was taking his time, coming to the point, but that was the way of the community and especially the elders. It would not do to rush the conversation.

"It's the wisdom of many years," answered the man. His name was Zelophehad and he was the oldest member of the community. "Even when you were young, I was an old man."

"Old in years, but not in spirit."

"What have you come to tell us, brother?" the third man spoke for the first time. He was younger than the other two, but still older than Nathaniel.

"It grieves me to say this, Gershon, but I have come to tell you that I must leave *Khirbet Qumran*."

The men nodded sagely, digesting the news at their own pace. Nathaniel waited patiently for their reply. Finally, Merari spoke.

"How long will you be gone for?"

"Some time, I fear. At my age, who knows? I may never return."

Once again the men considered his words, as if seeking the answer to a great riddle. After nearly a minute of silence, Zelophehad spoke. "Where is it you would go, Nathaniel?"

"I wish I knew the answer to that. I'm searching for a man, or men. They have often taken refuge with our community."

"Zealots. Levi is among their number, is he not?"

"Actually, he's the one I seek."

"Why? Can you not just wait until the next time he visits?"

Nathaniel shuffled uneasily. "There have been a lot of complications in Israel these past weeks. I don't know if he'll be returning here either. I must find out what happened to him. If he's alive, I need to get a message to him."

"Is there any way we can assist you in this?"

Nathaniel shook his head. "It was a secret entrusted to me long before I came to the community. Now I must honour my oath and find Levi, if it's not already too late."

Once again they slowly digested the information, each content with his own thoughts. After an interminable pause, Zelophehad finally spoke. "An oath should be honoured," he wheezed. "You must go to Jerusalem and find this man. We will pray for your safe return." He looked at the other elders who nodded in agreement with his wise words.

"As I said before, that may not happen."

"Then we will pray God's blessing as you go. You've been a good brother and an upstanding member of the community."

"Thank you. May God fill your days with peace and joy. You've become my family and *Qumran* has become my home. I'll keep you always in my prayers."

Nathaniel quickly bade his farewells and packed his belongings for the journey. When he had walked no more than a mile, he turned and looked back at the buildings that had been his home for so many years. He trembled slightly at the thought of what lay ahead and a tear trickled down his cheek in the knowledge that he was looking at the community for the last time. He would never return.

13

BARABBAS COULD see the city of Sepphoris from a long way off. It was a sprawling metropolis, by far the largest city in Galilee. Tall buildings jutted above the skyline and cultivated lands spread out around the city in every direction.

How much of that land belonged to his uncle? Barabbas wondered. Probably all the bits that didn't belong to Herod, the Idumean king, he thought cynically.

The land had changed form and colour drastically. The hills of lower Galilee were littered with tall, evergreen forests and the bountiful rainfall made it the farming capital of all Palestine.

As Barabbas approached the city, he saw a group of men at work in one of the fields next to the road. One of the men looked up and squinted in puzzlement as Barabbas drew closer. At first he did nothing, merely breaking away from the rest of the group. Then he turned back and said something to the men, but Barabbas couldn't hear him.

From their demeanour, though, Barabbas guessed that they'd been given some sort of instruction. He watched as the group turned back to their labour. The man who seemed to be in charge moved slowly between the young vines that grew to his waist and waited for Barabbas to approach. As he drew near the man nodded and, still not sure of himself, ventured to speak.

"Barabbas?" he asked cautiously.

"Yes?" Barabbas was curious as to how the stranger knew him.

He examined the man. Young, Barabbas thought, and wealthy by the look of his clothes. Yet the hands were calloused and his body was lean from years of hard, physical labour.

The young man smiled. "Do you mean to tell me you don't recognise your own cousin?"

Barabbas frowned and then, as if in a dream, the features seemed to shift imperceptibly, melting into a recognisable face.

"Jashan!" Barabbas laughed and embraced his cousin in a giant bear hug. "The boy has become a man now, I see. You've grown a beard since I last saw you."

"And you seem to have lost yours," Jashan smiled.

"One of the drawbacks of my occupation." Barabbas joked.

"What were you doing; masquerading as a woman at a well?"

Barabbas laughed. "Nothing that dangerous. Just a routine jail break, that's all."

"You must tell me all about it. There's no excitement in our home when you're not there."

"Come with me some time. Then you can experience it for yourself."

Jashan shrugged. "You know what it's like. Always another crop to harvest."

"It's not all that bad, I'm sure. The farmer's life seems to have treated you well."

"It's a living."

"And a good one by the look of you."

Jashan chuckled and called across to the men in the field. "Finish up here. I'm going back in to Sepphoris with my cousin. I'll be back later."

The men nodded and waved as Jashan joined Barabbas and the two of them headed for the town."

"Where's Simeon? Didn't he come with you?"

Barabbas looked away for a moment. "That's what I came to Sepphoris about."

Jashan looked at Barabbas fearfully, but said nothing. Barabbas remained silent for nearly a minute.

"He's dead, Jashan."

Jashan's expression became impassive. "How?" he asked softly.

Barabbas looked down, not wanting to meet his cousin's gaze. "They crucified him at Calvary, just before the Feast of Unleavened Bread."

"I'm sorry, Barabbas. After your father - I can't begin to understand what you're going through."

"I don't look forward to telling my mother."

"Or my father," Jashan murmured

Barabbas sighed. "How is he these days?"

"Same as always. You know what he's like."

"Still not a good word to say about his nephews."

Jashan smiled. "You know he means well."

"I know that, but he and I will never agree when it comes to Israel's freedom."

"He sees too much of your father in you. I think that's what frightens him. He loved Cephas like few brothers do. When he was taken and killed, my father mourned for months, so my brothers tell me."

"He grieved in his way and I in mine."

"I see you still grieve," Jashan said quietly.

"Is there a wine tavern in Sepphoris? I'm as parched as the sands of Moab."

"You'd better come straight home, Barabbas," Jashan chuckled. "I've drunk the poison those taverns sell in the name of wine. It tastes like viper's spittle."

"Very well, as long as you promise to break open a jar of your finest as soon as we get there."

He fell silent, becoming more anxious with each step that brought him closer to his uncle's home. As they walked through the streets of Sepphoris, Barabbas marvelled at its beauty. The city had changed somewhat since he'd last seen it. Vegetation was lush and green and the bustling hordes that thronged in the street spoke of the city's prosperity.

"This is our home," Jashan indicated as he ushered Barabbas to the front door.

"The years have made the family prosperous, I see."

"Times have changed, Barabbas. Come in. The family will be eager to know you're here."

Barabbas entered the plush residence designed along Roman architectural trends.

He was surprised to see the garden adorned with lush vegetation and several water features of varying shape and size.

Jashan led Barabbas through to the large living room. The furniture was expensive and thick rugs covered the floor. Ehud, Barabbas' uncle, was laughing as he chatted animatedly with two servants about an incident at the market.

"Father," Jashan called. "We have a guest here to see you."

Ehud stopped laughing and stood, stunned as he gazed at Barabbas standing in the doorway.

"*Shalom*, Ehud." Barabbas greeted his uncle.

"Barabbas." The greeting was stiff and formal. "Welcome to our home."

"Thank you, uncle."

"I presume you will be staying with us?" Ehud posed the question carefully.

"If I'm welcome, I'd be most grateful. Of course if it's an inconvenience, I can easily find a place to —"

"No, no." Ehud forced a smile. "You're most welcome here. What's mine is yours. We're just surprised to see you back after such a long time." Ehud was suddenly brisk. "Call Carmi." He instructed one of the servants. "We have a guest in our home."

The servants ran off to call the slave to wash Barabbas' feet after the long journey.

"Also, bring our finest wine," Jashan yelled after them, as he went and sat down.

A short while later Barabbas sighed in satisfaction after a long draft of wine that seemed like the first he'd had in years. He relaxed, enjoying the feel of the warm water as Carmi expertly massaged his feet. A spicy aroma filled the air as one of Ehud's servants brought through a steaming pot of lamb stew. He placed it on the table and went to fetch some bowls, returning just as the slave completed the ritual of washing Barabbas' feet. The servant placed a basket filled with fresh bread on the table next to the bottle of olive oil.

"Please, allow me." Ehud leaned forward and broke off a large chunk of bread. He smeared it with healthy dollops of olive oil and offered it to Barabbas.

"Thank you, Ehud. I've been away so long I'd forgotten what wonderful meals you have here."

Ehud smiled and watched as the servant filled a large bowl of the mouth-watering stew for Barabbas. Presently, all three men were reclined, chatting and catching up on the past few years. Both Ehud and Barabbas were careful to steer clear of any conversation concerning the zealots or Rome. The conversation remained pleasant and light-hearted. When they had finished, Jashan rose.

"You'll have to excuse me. I must go back and see how the farmhands are doing. You can't turn your back too long, or the vineyard becomes a desolate wasteland. I'm sure you and my father have a lot to talk about." He looked pointedly at Barabbas.

"I'll see you when you return this evening." Barabbas chuckled but his throat was dry, despite the excellent wine. He watched Jashan leave and then smiled at Ehud. He felt sick inside.

"He's grown into a fine man. You must be proud." Barabbas tried to avoid the issue he desperately needed to discuss.

"He has and I am." Ehud smiled reminiscently. Then he became serious. "What's really brought you here, Barabbas?"

"You mean other than to see my family?"

"You've always sent letters in the past. Your mother keeps them all under the bed in her room. She reads them constantly. Why now, after all these years?"

Barabbas' expression was grave. "Is she here?"

"She's weaving with the other women, why?"

"I'd rather tell you all together."

Ehud sighed. "Very well." He called for the slave who came through from the kitchen. He was stained with coal and the smell of smoke hung on his clothes.

"Yes, my lord?"

"Call the women into the house. Tell them Barabbas is here."

The man left an uncomfortable silence behind him as he ran to call the women from outside.

"Have some more wine," Ehud said, trying to ease the tension.

"Thank you," said Barabbas, offering his cup.

The two men sat in silence, sipping wine as they waited for the women to arrive. It seemed much longer, but after about fifteen minutes they heard the urgent patter of feet.

Five women raced into the room at once, all out of breath from running, and one of them flung herself into Barabbas' arms. He lifted her off her feet, embracing and kissing her, surprised to feel her slim figure under the dress.

"Mother, do you never put on weight?"

"She eats so little." His beaming aunt stepped forward to embrace him. "It's from all the worry you cause her."

She was a rotund woman with plump cheeks and huge, bear-like arms that squeezed the breath out of Barabbas. She kissed him on the cheek. "It's good to have you back. I hope your stay is a long one."

"I haven't decided yet." He turned to the three younger women who waited shyly behind his aunt and mother.

"And who are these women who adorn your home? If I'd known of such beauty, I would have returned sooner. Hello, Nanette, Eden." He nodded at the two older cousins. "Jacqueline?" His eyes twinkled as he gazed upon the youngest girl.

"Hello, Barabbas." She beamed.

She was shorter than her two sisters, but her features were far more striking. Dark hair framed her beauty and the *stola* she wore clung to her curves, making her look like the work of a master sculptor.

"I hope your father never lets you leave the house unattended." Barabbas grinned.

His mother asked. "How is Simeon, Barabbas. Why did he not come with you?" Her smile wrenched his heart in two.

"Please sit down, mother. That's what I came to tell you about."

"What is it?" She brought her hand to her mouth as she allowed Barabbas to seat her on one of the sofas around the table. The hand trembled slightly.

He took a deep breath. "Simeon is dead."

His mother seemed to pale visibly in front of him. Staring in wide-eyed horror, she covered her mouth with a trembling hand. Everyone in the room gaped in disbelief at the news.

"What happened?" His aunt's voice was a mere squeak as she tried to speak in her shock.

Barabbas turned to her and opened his mouth, but choked on the words. He merely shook his head and gazed up at his aunt's pale face. Then he turned back to his mother.

No sound came, but she began to shake violently. Barabbas went to her and held her, trying to calm the convulsions. He turned back to face his aunt who had begun to weep openly. Tears streamed in wide sheets down her oval face as she moved forward and flung her arms like cushions around Barabbas and his mother.

"Nooo!" the first anguished cry escaped his mother's lips.

"It's alright," he tried to console her.

"No!" she shrieked and shook herself free of his grasp. She jumped up and ran from the room.

"Lydia." Ehud called after her.

Barabbas rose to go after her, but his aunt held his arm firmly. "She needs to be alone for a moment. You can go to her in a few minutes." She summoned her daughters. "Come girls, let's get some drinks for everyone. The two older girls went with to assist their mother, but Jacqueline stayed with Barabbas and her father in the living room. She sat down next to Barabbas and put an arm around his waist.

"What happened, Barabbas?" Ehud asked earnestly.

He hesitated for a moment. "He - he was crucified."

"Crucified!" Ehud exclaimed in anger. "For what? Crimes against Rome?"

Barabbas nodded quietly.

Ehud ranted. "I always knew it would come to this. How many times didn't I warn the two of you? When will you stop this madness? Can't you see what it's cost your family - your mother?"

"Father, please," Jacqueline begged.

"No!" Ehud shouted. "I see it every day. Your mother wastes away. She spends half her life fondling letters sent by you and now her worst fear has been realized."

"Father!" Jacqueline raised her voice.

"I don't have to listen to this." Barabbas hissed, rising from the chair.

"You will listen to it. Do you ever think of anyone but yourself?"

"I have given my life for my people and their freedom and you dare accuse me of selfishness?" Barabbas was shouting now, but could not control his anger.

"Don't play the martyr, Barabbas. Your antics have torn your family apart. Do you have any idea how much pain you've caused? No, because you're never around, but I am. I see it every single day while you run around waging war with the demons of your past."

"All my life, it's always been the same. You sit here and judge me while I fight for the very freedom you yearn for. I don't have to take this from you."

He turned to leave, but Jacqueline blocked his way. "No, Barabbas. Please stay.

Your mother needs you now. We're your family. You should be with your family at a time like this. Don't you agree, father?"

Barabbas glared across the table at his uncle. Ehud glanced at his daughter and then nodded, withering under her gaze. When he spoke, his tone was somewhat subdued. "Yes. Barabbas, please sit down. Stay a while. Your mother needs you now."

"I'm going to see how she's doing." Barabbas burned an angry track across the floor. It was only when he was half-way down the passage that he realized he didn't know where his mother's room was. Jacqueline was right behind him, however. She merely took his hand and led him through the house.

When he reached his mother, he found her sitting on the floor at the foot of her bed, quietly reading the letters that he and Simeon had sent over the years. It was a surprisingly small pile of paper, he thought, for the amount of time that they had been away.

† † † †

Dinner that evening was a subdued affair. The weight of Barabbas' news hung heavy on the hearts of the family as they reclined around the table. He glanced across at his mother as he took a sip of wine from his cup. She was pale and drawn. Her hair was tied back and the veins stood out on her long, slender neck.

"Please, mother, you must eat something." Barabbas said as he watched her toy with the food on her plate.

"I'm afraid I'm not very hungry this evening," she replied with a taut smile.

"Leave her be, Barabbas. Your mother will eat when she is ready," his aunt intervened gently.

"She might find her appetite if she had less to worry about," Ehud murmured quietly.

"What was that?" Barabbas asked sharply.

"Father, you promised," Jacqueline pleaded.

"I'm just saying." Ehud replied innocently. "Nothing meant by it." He bit into another juicy chunk of lamb loin.

Jashan tried to diffuse the tension. "How was your journey from Jerusalem, Barabbas?"

"Fairly uneventful. I travelled with a family from Sepphoris. The man says he knows you."

"Oh?" Ehud looked up from his dinner. "Who is he?"

"Zebedee, the merchant."

"Yes. He buys much of my produce."

"He said he'd only dealt with you on a few occasions."

"Well, that's the way of business. I can't be involved with every transaction and neither can he. We've negotiated a couple of times. The rest is handled between our servants."

"I'm sure Barabbas would be more interested to hear about his daughter." Jashan jibed.

"Shame on you, Jashan," Barabbas' aunt chided.

"I've met her." Barabbas replied.

"And?"

Barabbas shrugged. "We spoke. She's extremely opinionated on many subjects."

"I can tell you where she lives if you're interested." Jashan grinned.

"Oh, where's that?" Barabbas tried to feign disinterest as he reached for a large chunk of bread.

Jashan leaned back. "Who would have thought it?" he chuckled. "The terror of Judea has lost his heart to a sweet flower of Galilee."

Jashan's sisters giggled and even Ehud relaxed enough to smile. Barabbas grinned over his cup and his eyes twinkled as he spoke.

"Any more of that and you'll find yourself in the sheep well again, cousin."

When dinner was over, the women cleared the table while the three men remained in idle chatter. Eventually, Ehud heaved an exasperated sigh.

"I can't do this any more, Barabbas. I must know what happened. How was he caught?"

"We were all caught - betrayed by a fellow zealot - God curse his soul."

"All of you? How many?"

"There were ten of us. Only three survived."

"What were you doing?"

Barabbas sighed, steeling himself for another argument. "A strike on one of the Roman barracks in Jerusalem. We had hoped to burn it to the ground while they slept."

Ehud shook his head. "What made you think you could succeed in such foolishness? This is the mightiest army that's ever lived."

"We almost succeeded."

"Almost! And then you were caught."

"No, we escaped. Only two were caught. The betrayer was captured in the rescue attempt."

"So where were the rest of you taken?"

"At our hideout. The Romans knew everything. Even the rear exit was guarded. They ambushed us as we emerged."

"Was Levi among your number?"

"Yes, he's one of the men who survived."

"Tell me." Ehud asked gravely. "How is it that you came to be free while the others were left to their fate?"

Barabbas couldn't decide whether Ehud's look was one of accusation or not. "It was the Feast of Unleavened Bread. One prisoner was to be released. It's tradition."

"So the people called for your release. They could think of no other man?"

"There was another. Pilate offered them his freedom, but the people called for me."

Ehud raised his eyebrows. "He must have been an evil man indeed that the people would call for a murderer and insurgent to be freed instead."

"Father, that's not fair." Jashan protested but he was too late.

Barabbas was on the edge of his seat and his eyes blazed with rage. "Don't you ever say that again."

"Easy, Barabbas." Jashan leaned forward, placing a hand on his cousin's shoulder.

Barabbas didn't even notice him. His eyes shone with an intensity that bordered on insanity as he pointed a finger at his uncle's face. "He was a man of peace. He never did anyone harm in his whole life."

Barabbas was surprised by his own words, but they had been blurted out before he'd had time to think. Ehud was unmoved by his nephew's outburst.

"Who was he?"

Barabbas glowered at his uncle, slowly bringing his emotion under control. "His name was Jesus of Nazareth."

"What!" Ehud could not hide his shock. "Why?"

"I don't know, I wasn't there. The sign above him read something about his being the King of the Jews."

"That's impossible. Who would want to kill such a man?"

"The Sanhedrin for one," Jashan replied. "Did you see how many men followed his teaching?"

"That's not the end of it." Barabbas continued. "Some of his followers have begun telling anyone who'll listen that he's alive. They say he rose from the grave."

"Did you go and look?" Jashan leaned forward in excitement.

"No, but I spoke to a priest in the temple. He said the grave is empty. His guess is somebody stole the body."

"A logical explanation." Ehud shrugged.

"Not when there was a Roman guard of sixteen men outside the tomb's entrance."

Ehud was puzzled. "Why would they put a guard there?"

"For that very reason. They expected someone to come and steal the body."

"Sounds like Jerusalem is in an uproar."

"The temple in particular."

"What do the priests believe happened?"

"They're convinced the body was stolen - only they can't come up with an explanation that fits the facts." Barabbas took another sip from his cup. "I must say you still make the finest wine in Palestine."

"They must have some explanation." Ehud disregarded the compliment. He was too engrossed in the topic.

"Absolutely. It's quite simple for them. A group of unarmed, untrained, passive men who have devoted their lives to the teachings of a passive man, disarmed and beat a Roman guard of sixteen men senseless. They then rolled the stone and opened a sealed tomb. After that they removed the grave clothes and stole away the body, leaving only the white bandages and no other trace of their passing. Would that I could find such men to fight alongside the zealots."

"Perhaps the guard fell asleep." Jashan ventured.

Barabbas snorted. "I've devoted my life to dealing with Roman guards. The next one I find asleep at his post will be the first."

"Isn't it possible that someone merely went to the wrong tomb? Those hills around Jerusalem are littered with caves."

"I suppose it's possible that such a dim-witted man exists. I never cease to be amazed at man's capacity for stupidity. But it wasn't just one person. It was several followers of this man, not to mention the entire Roman guard and the priests, who went to verify their claims. They couldn't all be that stupid."

Ehud and Jashan thought about this, while Barabbas continued.

"Anyway, even if they did all go to the wrong tomb, it was still empty, the grave clothes still left inside. To my knowledge, corpses aren't in the habit of grabbing a change of clothes and nipping out for a quick drink. Something strange happened in that tomb and make no mistake."

"You seem to have given this a lot of thought." Ehud regarded Barabbas with a look of interest.

"I've had time to think about it. It's all the people of Jerusalem talk about at the moment."

"What do you believe happened there?"

Barabbas shrugged. "I don't know what to believe. What I know is that the body is gone. Nobody disputes that. Not even the Sanhedrin."

✝ ✝ ✝ ✝ ✝

Nearly a week had passed and Levi, fitter and stronger since his escape, found that the Roman soldiers were heading back toward Jerusalem. It had been an uncomfortable time for the local population as legionaries had searched homes and questioned travelling parties incessantly, scouring the countryside for the offenders.

Levi had come across several of the zealots who had assisted in the escape. They were also moving surreptitiously, living in hiding as the giant net of soldiers had closed in toward Jerusalem. Now, as the soldiers gave up all hope of finding the culprits, Levi had found it easier to break through the cordon and head for *Qumran*.

As he moved down the rocky slope toward the commune, he basked in the sunlight, looking at the sky and enjoying the feeling of freedom the vast blue expanse engendered. He approached the gate of the community to find the three elders sunning themselves there as they so often did. They eyed him with a quiet air of peace as he approached.

"*Shalom*, men of Israel."

"*Shalom*," they greeted in unison.

Levi sat down and went through the usual pleasantries and small talk. At his earliest opportunity and without seeming rude, he steered the conversation to the matter on his mind.

"I've come to see your holy brother, Nathaniel. Is he here?"

The men nodded, each searching their deepest thoughts as they contemplated their answers.

"Nathaniel is not here," Zelophehad wheezed. "He left the community in search of you."

Levi was shocked. "When did he leave?"

"Some days back." Gershon replied quietly as he toyed in the sand with his walking stick.

"Was it before or after the Feast of Unleavened Bread?"

"It was after," Gershon replied at length.

Levi exulted. *Thank the Lord for that.* It meant that he had not been killed by Eleazor. Nathaniel was still alive. "May I speak with Mattithyahu, then?"

A shadow of sadness seemed to pass over the elderly faces. Eventually, Zelophehad spoke. "Our brother Mattithyahu is dead. He was killed by bandits on the road to Jerusalem, along with three others."

Four men travel to Jerusalem. They know not what they carry. Levi felt ill. Could it be that the scroll had truly been lost?

"Did Nathaniel say where he was going?"

Gershon looked up from his patterns in the sand. "He only said he would not be returning. When he left, he headed north along the main road to Jerusalem."

"Thank you. I will find him there."

Levi bade his farewells and raced north, heading for the holy city. He knew it was dangerous to approach it at the moment, but he had no choice. The priests had left *Qumran* and that meant the scroll was no longer there. There was nothing in *Qumran* for him now. He had to find Nathaniel and learn where the scroll had been moved.

His soul was consumed with a deep feeling of dread as he raced toward the city of death. He could no longer think of it in any other way. Worry gnawed at his mind constantly and, though he tried, he could not take his thoughts off the scroll.

† † † † †

Pilate paced back and forth in his private chambers like a caged beast. "I cannot believe that after a week of searching we can find no clue as to the whereabouts of these rebels."

"I told you they were good, prefect, but don't worry. We'll find them."

"I can't stay in Jerusalem much longer," Pilate lamented. "I have to return to my duties in Caesarea. I want that scroll found."

"It's going to take time, prefect. Months perhaps. May I suggest that you return to Caesarea and leave me here to deal with the problem?"

"I don't want someone to deal with the problem, centurion, I want results," Pilate bawled. His face was flushed and his eyes seemed to bulge through their slits.

"Results will come, prefect, but they'll take time," Gaius replied patiently.

"I have to go," Pilate agreed. "But I want the city searched again. Arrest everyone that could possibly have anything to do with these zealots. I don't care who they are. Priests, businessmen, it doesn't matter."

"I wouldn't recommend that, prefect. From the little we know of the scroll, it's a well kept secret. Only a handful even knows of its existence. To do as you suggest is not only risky, it's futile."

The hostility of Pilate's gaze would have crushed a weaker man, but Gaius held his gaze and continued. "To arrest priests without solid evidence. There would be an outcry."

"I don't care. I'll take full responsibility, but I want that scroll."

"I'll need those orders in writing before I arrest so much as a street urchin." Gaius said carefully.

Pilate stopped pacing and subjected Gaius to a cynical smile. "Always the cautious one aren't you, centurion."

"Wouldn't you be?" Gaius knew he had outmanoeuvred his superior. By writing such a letter he would incriminate himself. What Pilate was suggesting bordered on illegal and he knew it.

"I'll write the order." Pilate snarled. "You can return to your office, centurion. I'll have the instructions sent down to you and I expect them to be carried out to the letter, do you understand?"

"Yes, prefect." Gaius was relieved. For all Pilate's bravado, he would have to modify the order if it was put in writing.

"Good, you may go."

As Gaius left, he heard Pilate bellow for his aide, Quintus.

Gaius returned to his office at the Antonia. He busied himself with his duties and was interrupted shortly after lunch by a messenger who brought an official document that bore Pilate's seal. He sat down and read through it.

When he had finished, he read it a second time. This time he had to steady a shaking hand. In disbelief, he read it a third time, filled with revulsion for the words written on the page.

He rose and called for his aide, Marcus. A feeling of numbness slowly crept over Gaius. When Marcus arrived, Gaius coughed, clearing his throat as he handed him the document. "Will you read that?"

Marcus frowned as he took the parchment and read through it. His mouth fell open in horror and disbelief and when he was finished he had turned pale.

"We can't do this." He shook his head.

"We have no choice." Gaius sighed and slumped down on his seat.

"But it's unthinkable," Marcus pleaded.

Gaius merely shrugged and sighed in defeat. "I believe the prefect is losing his sanity, but we have to follow his orders."

"Surely something can be done."

"What, pray tell, and I'll do it. A letter to Rome would take months and the reply months more. By then it will all be over and our heads with it. There's nobody else to appeal to. The prefect is Rome's highest authority in Judea."

"Have you tried to reason with him?"

"I refused to carry out his orders. I told him I wanted them in writing. At the time I thought nobody would be stupid enough to do that. Even then, I never envisaged anything like this." Gaius stared blankly at the letter Marcus had replaced on his desk.

"This," Marcus said with complete conviction, "is the act of a madman."

"Should we go to the prefect and tell him we refuse to carry out the order?" Gaius was serious.

Marcus thought about it for a moment and then shook his head. "It's too cleverly worded. The order is extreme, but it can be justified."

Gaius nodded. "We would be executed for disobeying orders and the operation would go ahead anyway."

"So we have no choice," Marcus said sadly.

Gaius sighed again. "Call the centurions together. They have to read the orders."

The following morning the madness began.

† † † † †

Nathaniel moved about Jerusalem carefully, enquiring discreetly in the grubby market places and less reputable inns whether anyone knew where he might find the home of Deborah, the prostitute. He had long since grown weary of the knowing looks and sly winks of the people he questioned.

Nobody seemed to know her or, if they did, they weren't telling him where she was. One fact brought him comfort, however. It seemed Barabbas and Levi were at least alive. Barabbas' miraculous release was still the talk of Jerusalem and, if the rumours were true, Levi had escaped in a prison break en route to his crucifixion at Calvary.

Nathaniel exited another market, emerging from the dim light of the stone alleyway as he stepped around the produce that littered the floor. He was beginning to despair when a beggar called for his attention.

"Yes?" Nathaniel looked at the man. A tattered tunic peeped from beneath the man's moth-eaten and badly soiled cloak.

The man staggered over with a knowing grin. Several teeth were missing, Nathaniel noted.

"You seek Deborah, the prostitute?"

Nathaniel recoiled at the smell of cheap, stale wine on the beggar's breath. "Do you know her?" he asked cautiously.

"You could say that." He winked in a manner that Nathaniel had become grudgingly accustomed to over the past few days.

"Where does she stay?" He tried to sound polite.

"Ah." The beggar wagged a bony finger in the air, breathing alcoholic fumes from a grimy, toothless smile.

"Will you tell me where I can find her?"

"It's a scorching day, my lord. Perhaps you could buy a poor man a drink?" The beggar staggered drunkenly and Nathaniel stared at him with disdain.

"You don't look that parched," he replied primly.

"I've drunk my last drop, my lord. I don't have a single coin left to buy another jar."

"Then you've probably had enough."

"Tell you what." The man lurched toward Nathaniel, trying to get close enough to whisper into his ear. "For the price of a drink, I'll show you right to Deborah's door."

Nathaniel considered his options. He abhorred everything about the grimy man, but it was the first positive result he'd had since his arrival in Jerusalem. Reluctantly he agreed. "Very well. This is half of it." He took a coin from his belt. "I'll give you the other half when we get there."

The man snatched the coin with gleaming eyes and beckoned Nathaniel. "This way," he said, trying to throw a friendly arm about Nathaniel's shoulder. Nathaniel ducked under it and kept his distance.

He followed the beggar through the crowded streets and markets, past the temple and into the *Kainopolis*. The man shuffled quickly through the narrow streets and alleyways, finding his way like a rat through a sewer. Nathaniel began to fear that the man was planning to rob him as he glanced nervously at the unsavoury shops and people loitering about the wine taverns and derelict buildings.

Presently the beggar emerged into a wider street that ran from east to west near the northern wall of the city.

"Nearly there," the beggar panted and subjected Nathaniel to another toothless smile and sly wink.

Nathaniel noticed a number of shorter streets that ran between blocks of houses and ended at the city wall. The beggar chose one such street and lurched up it. He beckoned to Nathaniel who followed his foul smell up the steps which led into a communal courtyard. Nathaniel was surprised to find the houses deserted, but the beggar seemed not to have noticed that anything was amiss.

"Here it is," he said. "Second door on the right."

"There's nobody here," Nathaniel said doubtfully.

"She'll be along shortly." The beggar nodded confidently, holding out a hopeful hand.

Nathaniel was reluctant to give him the money. "Are you sure this is where she lives?"

"Absolutely, my lord. I speak the truth." The man looked around desperately as he began to realize that he might not be compensated for his work.

"What does she look like?" Nathaniel asked him suspiciously.

"You know." The man waved his arms vaguely.

"Of course I know." Nathaniel lied. "I want to be sure you know."

"Well er - she's - very beautiful. You know, tall. And - she has red hair."

"Dark or light?" Nathaniel asked sharply.

"Dark. Long, dark red hair, almost brown."

Nathaniel noted the desperation in the beggar's expression and made his decision. "Alright." He reached into his belt for another coin.

The man couldn't have made all that up, he reasoned. The laws of chance were stacked in his favour.

"Thank you, my lord. Thank you." The beggar took his hand and shook vigorously. He had a surprisingly strong grip and held Nathaniel's hand for a long time.

He backed away and then shuffled up the stairs. Nathaniel glanced about the courtyard. It was small and dusty, with a communal clay oven that had steps leading down into its interior, and a stone olive press for making oil.

Nathaniel seated himself on the edge of the olive press. By sundown, still nobody had returned. Time had filled Nathaniel's imagination with a host of terrifying prospects, but he had nowhere else to go. He used his cloak as a blanket and curled up against the external wall of the oven for warmth. He slept on the hard, dusty paving.

At first light, he awoke from a fitful sleep. His joints were stiff and painful, punished by his stony bed. He sniffed and sat up, pulling his cloak about him and waited for the first rays of the sun to warm his old and frail frame.

He listened to the early morning sounds of a stirring city. The angry clatter of carts rang on the cobbled stones and sheep bleated outside the city walls. He heard the call of voices as people began to leave their homes, heading out to workplaces.

Soon all of the noises blended into the dull drone that was the city of Jerusalem. No sound distinguished itself from any other. Instead, all the sounds formed a whole that was the bustle of the city by day.

The courtyard, however, remained strangely untouched by the noise outside. It had an eerie silence about it that filled Nathaniel with a growing sense of dread. The sun rose in a steady arc, first warming, then baking his leathery skin, but he never moved from the courtyard, not even leaving for meals. Having devoted a lifetime to regular prayer and fasting, he was well able to live without a meal or two.

Instead, he prayed until sunset for Deborah's speedy return, but still she did not come. If he had only known what had truly happened to Deborah, he might have acted differently. The truth became apparent too late, however. Too late for Barabbas and Levi, too late for the scroll and far too late for Nathaniel.

14

AT DAWN the soldiers came. The military swept through the city like an apocalyptic horseman, unleashing indescribable horrors on the people of Jerusalem. Many soldiers used the blitz as an opportunity to satisfy carnal lusts, stepping way beyond the bounds of their authority.

The innocent were arrested along with the guilty, sometimes on a whim, other times with more evil intent. The racks in the dungeons began to creak like an assembly line as hundreds of prisoners screamed their innocence, while thousands more were detained without trial, awaiting questioning with no food and very little water.

Many died on the rack before soldiers accepted their pleas of innocence and many watched as loved ones were tortured and killed, never knowing why, as they were unable to furnish their interrogators with the information they wanted.

Priests were dragged from their beds, their houses looted for any evidence of collaboration with the zealots. More often than not, items of value were blatantly stolen from their homes. The fearful men dared not protest lest even greater danger befall them or their families. They considered themselves lucky if only their possessions were touched.

All the residents along the north wall were arrested, as this was a preferred escape route of the zealots. When men could not be found at home, women and children were held with the threat of death unless the men turned themselves in.

Families huddled fearfully together, mothers covering their children with their cloaks in an effort to shield them from the madness. Deborah crouched in the corner of a cell which she shared with nearly thirty other women, many of whom had one or more children with them.

Down the hall, she could hear the screams of those on the rack or in the other interrogation rooms. At the end of each hour, some were returned to the cell, badly abused and beaten. They wept bitterly as they staggered, doubled in pain and pulling what was left of their *stolas* about them to cover their injuries and nakedness. Many never returned at all and no explanation was given for their disappearance.

The door of the dungeon opened and a legionary entered. He gazed about the cell and his eyes fell on Deborah, who cowered in the back corner. He smiled and headed towards her. The cell was emptier now, as many of the prisoners had been questioned already. Only a few had been returned and held for further questioning.

She was taken to a small room with stone walls and a wooden post in the centre. A fire burned in one corner, with a long, metal rod sticking out of it. The rod had a dirty rag wrapped around its end that served as a handle. She was stripped by three soldiers and tied to the wooden post. The legionaries chuckled among themselves and one approached her, shrugging off his belt and gently caressing her neck as he reached under his tunic.

Just then the door opened and a centurion walked in. "Enough of that," he said curtly and turned to face her. She remembered him as the centurion who had questioned her in the courtyard on the night Barabbas had burned the Roman barracks.

"Hello," he said softly. "My name is Gaius. We'd like to ask you a few questions about the zealot movement and about two men in particular. Do you know of Barabbas and Eleazor at all?"

She gazed back with nervous innocence. "I know of Barabbas by reputation. He was released by the prefect during the Feast of Unleavened Bread. Of this other man I know nothing."

"Have you ever been involved with the zealots or do you know anyone who has had any dealings with them in the past two years?"

"Not to my knowledge, my lord." Behind her fearful front, Deborah studied the centurion intently.

"Surely you must know something of the movement."

"Only that it is a secretive one." She swallowed.

Gaius shook his head sadly. "Please, if you know anything, tell me now. I cannot prevent what will follow if you don't."

"Please, my lord. If I knew anything I would tell you. You must believe me." Her lip quivered slightly and Gaius held up his hand, cautioning the guard who stepped forward, tapping a staff menacingly against his palm.

"I saw you in the courtyard where the zealots escaped Jerusalem on the night they burned down the barracks. Coincidence?"

He stared into the almond pools as tears ran gently down her cheeks. Weeping openly, she shook her head. The centurion clenched his teeth and turned away, shaking his head.

The blow came from the side without warning. It smashed into her stomach, winding her and she collapsed, hanging by the ropes that fettered her arms as she sucked in giant gulps of air that never seemed to reach her burning lungs.

Gaius turned back, drawing close as he whispered in her ear. "Tell me something. Anything. I'm under orders. I can't stop this."

She thought of Barabbas, but could not bring herself to betray him. Once again, she shook her head and stared at him through horror-stricken eyes and tear-stained cheeks. The second blow was more savage than the first. This time she felt a rib crack under the weight of the blow.

"She knows something, I'm sure of it." Gaius murmured. Then his voice turned harsh. "Tell me about Barabbas."

More blows followed, bruising her flesh and damaging her bones. Then came the iron, glowing from the coals and searing her torso. Her groans turned to shrieks of pain and the room began to spin about her. Her surroundings became surreal and blurred as waves of agony were interspersed with echoing questions from faceless men who seemed to dance about her, meting out their cruelty on her torn and defenceless flesh.

† † † † †

Outside, Marcus closed his eyes, trying to shut out the screams that came in intermittent bursts of fiery pain. The interrogation lasted for nearly an hour and when the door finally opened, he wanted to weep at the sight of the body that the soldiers dragged from the room.

"Gaius, how could you do this to a creature so beautiful?"

"The wounds are superficial. They will heal."

"You mean she's —"

"She's alive, just unconscious. Here, help me with her." He took Deborah from the legionaries, noting their disappointment as Marcus slipped an arm under her knees, lifting her from their grasp.

They took her to Gaius' office and placed her on the thick rug that lay on the floor. Gaius threw her *stola* over her to cover her nakedness.

He turned to the legionaries who had followed him and said. "The first man who tries to enter this office for any reason will end up working the tin mines in Gaul. We're an army, not a barbaric horde."

Once the legionaries had left, Marcus shook his head. "I can't believe you allowed this, Gaius."

"This one knows something," he replied quietly. "She fooled me the last time I met her, but she knows Barabbas. I'm sure of it."

Marcus shivered and looked at Gaius. "So what now?"

"I can't put her through that again. She won't talk anyway. She's motivated by love. No amount of pain will break that."

Marcus smiled. "It seems I misjudged you, centurion. I apologise."

Gaius answered with a weary nod. "I'm going back down to the cells. You can stay here. When she wakes up, tell her she's free to go."

† † † † †

Inside the office, Deborah shut her eyes tightly against the pain, waiting for it to subside. She had sensed from the first that the centurion had fallen under the spell of her beauty. The ordeal might have been painful, but she had never feared the worst.

She had controlled him from the very beginning. Still, the knowledge of that fact brought little comfort. Her tortured mind was a fragmented mass of terror from her ordeal. It would still be shattered long after her bones had healed.

Some hours later, Deborah limped up the stairs that led to her home. Her torn dress hung like a used rag about her, barely covering her modesty and the wounds that ravaged her torso. She sobbed as she gingerly touched the burns caused by the searing rod. They had formed large red welts now, and watery blisters embalmed the agonising wounds.

As she entered the courtyard, she was startled by a movement near the oven off to her left. She whipped round, recoiling from the intruder.

"Who are you?" she sobbed, glaring at the man like a wounded lioness.

"I am Nathaniel, an Essene from *Khirbet Qumran*," he replied quietly.

"What do you want from me?" Her voice trembled with fear.

"I seek some men, mutual acquaintances. They have spoken often of you, and fondly."

"Stay away from me!" Deborah crouched against the door, trying to disguise her terror.

The stranger backed away slightly and continued patiently. "I'm looking for Levi and Barabbas. Can you tell me where I might find them?"

"You're a spy, sent by Rome," she yelled. "Leave me alone. I told you I don't know anything!"

"Please." Nathaniel stepped forward, but she lunged at him.

"Stay back," she hissed, then recoiled again, clutching at her wounds.

"What has happened, my child?" Nathaniel asked.

She made no reply, but inched her way to the door handle, never breaking her terrified gaze. Once she managed to get the door, she flung it open and fled inside, slamming the door in his face.

He knocked, but she refused to reply. During the night he tried a few more times. Deborah curled up in the corner of her tiny home, staring in terror at the door.

✝ ✝ ✝ ✝ ✝

Nathaniel spent the night against the now cold oven. In the morning, his joints were stiff, but he rose and tried again. It was useless. The woman refused to answer her door. It was about midday when other residents began to arrive. All were badly beaten and uncommunicative. They gruffly pushed him aside and some even turned aggressive when he tried to get their attention. During one such incident with a stocky, middle aged man, Deborah suddenly emerged from her home. "Get rid of him. He's a Roman spy, sent to torment us further," she yelled.

Several residents emerged from their homes at that point, fixing him with a collective glare. Although none of them moved to assist her, Nathaniel could tell from their mood that he was in serious danger. He dared not remain in the courtyard much longer.

He nodded kindly and smiled at the residents. Then he turned to leave and shuffled sadly up the steps to the street outside. As he made his way down the narrow street, he thought uncertainly about his next step. To wait in Jerusalem would be foolish. The zealots would long since have fled the city.

He was beginning to realize that to pursue Deborah was futile. He had no idea what had precipitated her fear, but one thing was glaringly apparent. She would not assist him in his search for his friends.

There was no choice, he thought sadly. He would have to go to the source and trace the families from there. Levi and Cephas, Barabbas' father, were from Gamala.

That was where he would begin.

It would take some time, as he needed money and food for the journey. He would head north, he decided, and find work as a teacher or scribe as he moved towards Galilee. Someone in Gamala would surely know something about the family's whereabouts.

✝ ✝ ✝ ✝ ✝

As Nathaniel headed north, along the road to Galilee, Levi raced towards the city of Jerusalem. When he arrived, he found a city of carnage. Although the buildings were intact, the people were cowed with terror. The entire network of zealot contacts and communication had been destroyed. Families had fled the city, while many more were in prison or had died under torture in the dungeons of the Antonia and the barracks. Even friends who had never been involved with the movement had been arrested.

In shock, Levi raced to Deborah's home. He was frantic when he arrived, desperate to find any sign of her.

Deborah!" he yelled, knocking loudly at the door. "Open up. It's me, Levi."

At first there was no answer. He banged on the door again, calling desperately.

"Levi?" he heard the woman's quiet, fearful answer.

"It's me. Open up here."

There was shuffling and a cry of pain and the door opened. Levi stared in shock at the mutilated body of the formerly beautiful woman.

"Deborah, what happened?" he asked in disbelief as she pulled a shawl around her.

"You have to go, Levi. It's not safe," she whispered. Her terrified eyes darted about the courtyard.

"Tell me what happened," he insisted.

The woman quickly reached out and pulled him inside, slamming the door behind them. "They're everywhere. Everyone's been taken, even the innocent ones. Nobody's safe here. You have to leave Jerusalem. Take Barabbas with you."

"He's not here."

"Where is he?"

"He's with his family in Sepphoris. Listen, this is important. I'm looking for an old man. An Essene. He knows you are our contact in Jerusalem, so he may try to locate you here. If you see him, tell him he can find Barabbas at the home of Ehud in Sepphoris." Levi hesitated. The woman's expression was most peculiar. Was it fear he saw in her eyes? "What is it?"

"It's nothing," she averted her gaze.

"Deborah, this man holds the most important link to our cause and our nation's future. If you've seen him, I have to know."

"I had no idea, Levi. I'd never seen him before. I feared for my life."

"You sent him away!" Levi's voice bordered on hysteria.

"I didn't know," she pleaded.

Levi clenched his jaw and sighed, trying desperately to conceal his anger. It wasn't her fault. She'd never met Nathaniel. In fact, almost none of the zealots knew about him. They couldn't be trusted with the secret.

"Alright, don't worry. He's probably returned to *Qumran*. I'll head there first. Then I'll go to Sepphoris and tell Barabbas what's happened."

"Levi, I'm sorry. If I'd known —"

"You didn't." He held her shoulders gently. "Don't worry. I'll find him. Just let me have something to eat and I'll be on my way."

An hour later, Levi bade Deborah farewell.

"Take care, Levi." The woman held him lightly.

"You too," he said. "If you need anything, send word to Barabbas in Sepphoris. It's a lengthy route, but until we get our network back in place, we'll have to relay messages through him."

"He's not going to like it."

"He has no choice. Jerusalem's become too dangerous and we don't have any safe-houses left. We'll wage our war again when we're strong enough."

A short while later, Levi was on his way back to *Qumran*. He wouldn't stay there for long. He had to get word to Barabbas at Sepphoris and, since all the zealot messengers had either been arrested or fled, he would have to do it himself.

† † † † †

Barabbas woke with a start. He reached for the sword at his side and listened intently for the sound that had awoken him.

Time passed and nothing happened, but Barabbas remained awake, long after any normal person would be expected to drift back to sleep. He heard it again.

It was a deliberate scraping of feet on the ground. He relaxed. It was a standard zealot greeting, announcing an unexpected arrival. It had saved the life of many a brother in the past, as zealots awoken by stealthy footsteps in the dead of night tended to be extremely jumpy and quick with their blades.

Barabbas rose quietly and slipped from his room. He stole through the house and let himself out the front door, glancing up at the clouds that hung like dark, torn ribbons of cloth in the inky black sky, blotting out the stars as they cast their mournful shadows on the earth below.

He moved along the south wall and peered around the corner at the shadowy figure near the window. The man moved once again, grinding his sandals in the dirt.

"Levi." Barabbas called softly from the corner.

Levi quickly turned and slunk across the yard towards him. The two men embraced briefly and then headed away from the house where they could talk more freely.

"I can see from your mood, you bring grave news," Barabbas said carefully.

Levi nodded quietly before he spoke. "The Romans launched an offensive against the zealots in Jerusalem. They stormed through the city, arresting thousands, most of whom weren't even involved. They even tortured women and children to learn about our activities."

Barabbas was stunned as Levi continued.

"They've taken out our entire communications network. Those who haven't been arrested or killed have fled to the hills."

"But how could they know who was involved?" Barabbas demanded.

"I don't think they did. They arrested more innocent people than guilty. According to Deborah, they killed aimlessly, arresting and even torturing whole families in order to extract information. Now they're busy moving out to cities all over Judea."

"Deborah?"

Levi hesitated. "She's alive."

"What happened to her?"

Levi sighed and shuffled uncomfortably. "They tortured her, Barabbas."

Barabbas' eyes blazed with fury. "Who was it?"

"Gaius Claudius was among the men who interrogated her."

"He's dead!"

"In time, Barabbas. It doesn't help to strike from a position of weakness. That's what they're hoping we'll do. It will flush us out into the open."

"We can't just sit here and do nothing." Barabbas raised his voice in exasperation.

"That's precisely what we're going to do." Levi also raised his voice. "I didn't survive the deserts of Judea and the arena in Rome by being rash. Besides, there's more important business to attend to."

"More important than our zealot comrades and our nation's honour?"

"The attack on the zealots was merely a smokescreen. In truth, they seek only two men - you and Eleazor."

"The scroll." Barabbas suddenly became subdued. He thought about it for a moment. "We have to go to *Qumran*. It's only a matter of time before their enquiries lead them to Mattithyahu."

"I've already been to *Qumran*. Nathaniel survived Eleazor's sword. He left the community some time after the feast and headed for Jerusalem. He sought us at Deborah's house, but she sent him away."

"Why?"

"She was scared, Barabbas, and not thinking clearly. You'd understand if you saw what they did to her."

"And now?"

Levi shrugged. "He didn't return to *Qumran*. I've no idea where he is."

Barabbas remained silent for a long time, too afraid to ask the question. Eventually he sighed. "What about the scroll?"

"I asked about Mattithyahu. He's dead. Killed by bandits en route to Jerusalem. They say he was on his way to the Holy City with three others to buy supplies."

"Four men travel to Jerusalem —" Barabbas' thoughts trailed off and blood in his veins turned to ice. "By all that's holy, Levi, what if Eleazor was telling the truth?"

"I won't believe that. That would mean the scroll has fallen into the hands of thieves."

"Do you think Nathaniel took it with him?"

"I don't know. Maybe. The only thing I'm sure of is that we need to find Nathaniel quickly. He's the only person left who can tell us where to find it."

The two men sat in silence, sharing their pain. Their loved ones had been tortured and murdered. The zealots had been all but destroyed and now Nathaniel, their only link to the scroll, had vanished leaving no trace of his whereabouts.

"I fear for him, Barabbas. He's not acting rationally. I've never known him to act so irresponsibly before. A man of his age should not have to bear such responsibility."

"Do you think we can find him again? Palestine is a big place."

"We have to try, at least."

"I'll help. Let me come with you."

"No, Barabbas. You have to stay here. You're the only link to what's left of our people in Jerusalem. Deborah can reach you here and so can I. That way we have a contact if Nathaniel returns."

"You want to reduce me to a messenger?" Barabbas was incredulous.

"Neither of us is safe in Jerusalem, especially not you. Besides, I left word at *Qumran* that if Nathaniel returned he could contact you here."

"That's risky. The Romans are bound to reach *Qumran* soon. They could find out where we are."

"It's a risk I had to take. That scroll represents everything I've worked for my whole life."

"Alright," Barabbas nodded in agreement. "You concentrate on finding Nathaniel. I'll stay here and busy myself rebuilding the network in Judea."

Levi placed a large hand on Barabbas' shoulder. "Take courage, brother. We're not defeated yet. I'll send word to you as soon as I glean any information."

"Just find him and bring that scroll. Then I'll go after the men that did this to us."

"I'll be right by your side. May God curse their worthless lives and may we live to see every evil come upon them."

Levi turned and then he was gone, melting into the darkness as if he had never been there. Barabbas returned to his bed, but he could not sleep. His mind was plagued by a thousand fears. He worried about Deborah, the zealots and the hundreds of innocent families who had been tortured for things they knew nothing about.

Most of all he worried about Nathaniel and the scroll. What if they could not find him, or worse, what if Pilate found him first? He was still awake when the first light crept through his tiny window and the household began to stir, rising to begin their day.

For Barabbas it was the beginning of a nightmare.

15

BARABBAS HEAVED under the weight of the young heifer on his shoulders.

"Push!" Jashan yelled above him. "I almost had her."

"If you'd done your job properly the first time, we'd be drinking from that water skin under a tree right now." Barabbas grumbled. The heifer weighed more than he did and his muscles ached with the strain.

He cursed the animal for falling into the ravine. In his next heave, he cursed the fact that it hadn't broken a limb in the process. If it had done so, they would merely have slaughtered the beast and then dragged out the carcass any way they pleased. As things stood, he was jammed under the moaning animal, trying to duck the flailing limbs as the men above tried to get ropes around her torso.

"Should I send someone down there to help?" Jashan called down.

"No good. It's too narrow. Just get those ropes around her and take this fat lump off my shoulders."

There was a short pause as the men above got back into position. "Alright, we're ready. Now heave!"

Once again, Barabbas shoved upwards, ducking the animal's ungrateful hooves. He felt the rope slapping against his face as it had done countless times before, with the rough fibres scratching his cheek and neck. Groping hands reached under the cow's belly in search of the elusive cord that would finally end his misery.

"I've got it." Jashan exclaimed.

"Well pull her up then." Barabbas groaned.

"Don't you think I should rather tie a knot first?" Jashan smiled, peering down into the gully.

"Just do it." Barabbas gritted his teeth. His eyes bulged and he felt the animal beginning to slip. He heaved again, trying to hold her, but it was futile. The weight of the heifer had shifted in her struggles and he could feel the soft fur of her underbelly slipping relentlessly from the centre of balance.

"She's falling." Barabbas uttered a panicked yell and suddenly, the weight was gone.

He panted as the young heifer swung up and over the lip of the narrow ravine. The men strained above him on the other end of the taut rope and the animal bawled its terror to the world.

A few moments later, the beaming face of Jashan appeared over the edge of the ravine.

"Is she alright?" Barabbas called breathlessly.

"She's fine. Can I send the rope down for you now?"

Barabbas grinned gratefully. "I thought you'd forgotten me down here."

Jashan laughed as the rope was thrown down. Barabbas looped it under his arms and called. "Hurry up. It's cold down here. Do you expect me to sit in the damp while you take your lunch?"

The rope drew taut and the men lifted Barabbas from the dark crack in the earth. When he emerged, Jashan came over and patted him on the shoulder.

"You know, Barabbas. You work with the strength of ten men but, as the Lord lives, you moan with the voice of a thousand as you do it."

Barabbas laughed heartily as he took Jashan by the arm and said. "Come, let's get that drink."

He headed for the cool shade of a large oak that stood near the edge of the field and flopped down under its broad boughs, soaking up the shadows that fell like refreshing rain about him.

Jashan sat down next to him and reached for the faded wineskin filled with water. He took a long swig from it and then passed the container to Barabbas.

"You drink like a camel after a trip through the Negev," Barabbas griped as he took the skin from his cousin.

"Your incessant grumbling gives me an insight into the suffering of Job. How long must I endure it?" Jashan asked in mock martyrdom.

"Until God decrees that your time of trial has come to an end," Barabbas grinned.

Two Passover feasts had come and gone since Barabbas had first returned to his family in Sepphoris and he and his cousin had become firm friends.

The feasts had become different as, it seemed, so many things had since that fateful Passover when Barabbas had been released from prison.

At the most recent Passover, even his own family had broken with the traditions of their forefathers and drunk of the Passover cup in remembrance of Jesus of Nazareth, rather than in remembrance of Israel's escape from Pharaoh and the Egyptian tyranny.

The man's teachings seemed to have inflamed the hearts of thousands and Barabbas was of the opinion that this man alone had done more damage to the zealot cause in the two seasons since his death than the Roman army had accomplished in a generation of war.

Their numbers had dwindled as disillusioned rebels, fleeing the harsh command of the prefect and the massacre in Jerusalem, had sought solace in a new belief that promised to bring redemption of a different kind that Rome could never touch.

It had been a difficult time during which Barabbas, Levi and Deborah had tried to rebuild the all but obliterated zealot network. During most of that time, he had been forced to remain in Sepphoris as the order for his arrest stood in Jerusalem and Gaius was driven by a demonic obsession to bring Barabbas to justice.

His stay in Sepphoris had not been a hardship, Barabbas reflected, as he noticed a small group of women returning from the well with heavy alabasters of water held high on their shoulders.

Jashan nudged his cousin in the ribs. "It seems one of those flowers is trying to attract your attention."

Barabbas smiled and waved back at Leila, waiting for the group to draw closer before rising to meet her.

Jashan glanced at Barabbas with a knowing smile. "So when do you plan to betrothe yourself to her? It's been over two years now."

Barabbas shrugged with a glum expression. "You know how it is. Sometimes here, other times in Jerusalem. I'm always disappearing on some task while we try to rebuild the network. If something happened to me - it wouldn't be fair to her."

Jashan considered his words carefully. "Maybe it's not for me to say, but are you being fair to her now? For two years, all others have been put off. She refuses to even answer the door when a suitor knocks. I see that merchant, what's his name?"

"Miyka'el?"

Jashan nodded. "He still visits regularly, but she won't have him, despite her father's urging."

"Miyka'el is a fool!" Barabbas spat. "He could never give her what she needs."

"At least he's shown himself willing."

Barabbas rose, tossing the wineskin across to his cousin. "I'm going to talk to her. You may not believe this, but I do care for her and I will take her for my wife. There are some things I must take care of first."

"I only hope for both your sakes that you don't lose her between now and then."

"To whom! Miyka'el?" Barabbas laughed as he started towards the road.

His argument with Jashan had inflamed his pride and bolstered his courage. He'd been challenged by his cousin to confront his fears. Jashan had even dared suggest that Miyka'el was a braver man than he.

You'll see, Barabbas thought. He shook as he approached Leila who smiled at him from the road. There was little in this world that caused Barabbas to fear. He'd stared into the face of death a thousand times and faced the might of the Roman army. Neither held much trepidation for him, but rejection from the woman he loved...

The women who walked with Leila separated from her and headed for the city. They giggled as they walked and shot sneaking glances back at him as Leila waited for him at the edge of the field. Barabbas struggled to gain control of his breathing.

She greeted him with a mocking grin. "*Shalom*, mighty man of Israel. How many Romans have you slain today?"

Barabbas smiled. He would not be goaded into a debate today. Leila was diametrically opposed to his entire belief system. Her disapproval of the zealots and all that they stood for had caused numerous, heated arguments between the two, which was what made his task so much more daunting.

He would not argue today, however. He'd not wasted the last two years working for his uncle between raids on the growing Roman forces in Israel. The money earned had been carefully saved and the purchase not taken lightly. He felt the comforting weight in his belt as he approached.

"*Shalom*, Leila. It's good to see you again. I've missed you these past weeks."

"Perhaps if you'd spent more time in Sepphoris instead of running amok all over the countryside." The smile was still there, however. "I heard a shipment of Roman taxes was taken on the road to Caesarea just over a week ago."

"Is that so?" Barabbas feigned disinterest.

"Apparently they cornered the perpetrators in a pass just above the coastal plain. The men put up a defence for nearly half a day before vanishing into thin air."

"Who's to say they entered the pass to begin with?"

"Somebody hauled the wagon up into the pass, and somebody finally set it on fire before running it down into the Roman cohort at the foot of the hill. Five legionaries died in that fire." The smile had vanished and she had become serious.

At another time, Barabbas might have shown his lack of remorse over dead soldiers, but today was different.

"And the robbers?"

"As I said - vanished, along with the treasure. By the time the uninjured soldiers reached the top, everything was gone."

"Nobody just vanishes in such a pass."

"Can you explain how they might have disappeared?" Her expression was one of accusation.

Barabbas sighed. "Could it be that they dumped the treasure before they entered the pass - while on the run - and then strapped themselves to the underside of the carriage before setting it alight and running it off the edge of the incline?"

Leila gasped. Barabbas could see that, as so often happened, she was torn between her respect for the ingenuity of the plan and her abhorrence for the violence of the act.

She stepped closer and her concern was no longer for the Roman soldiers. "Were you hurt?"

Barabbas shrugged and tensed himself as Leila touched his tunic, gently pulling aside the collar to reveal the blisters on his chest.

"Burns!" She exclaimed. "Barabbas have you had these seen to?"

"They'll heal, given time."

"Come with me." She snatched his arm and dragged him away with her.

Barabbas didn't resist until he saw that they were headed for her home. "Your father wouldn't approve, I'm sure. He doesn't like me very much."

"He's not home right now, besides he doesn't hate you. He merely thinks you're arrogant, egotistical and far too militant for your own good. Sometimes I tend to agree."

She took him inside and made him sit in a large reception room while she fetched some water and ointments to dress the wounds. A servant was summoned to help and, between the two of them, they dressed and bandaged the raw wounds on Barabbas' chest.

When they had finished, the servant left them alone for a moment and Barabbas took Leila's hand.

"I've got something for you which I hope you'll accept." He reached into his belt and withdrew the beautiful sapphire necklace. It hung from his hand as heavy as his spirits when he'd first approached her at the road.

He held up the sparkling stones so that she could see them glitter in the light.

"Barabbas," she whispered. "Where did you get this?"

"I bought it at a market in Jericho - with money from my earnings on the farm," he added hastily.

"I've never seen anything like it." Her tone was subdued as she searched for the words.

"I'd like you to consider it a gift of betrothal. We see the world through very different eyes, but no man could doubt my love for you. Will you accept it?"

"My father —"

"I'll talk to your father. No man could resist me if I know that you share my love."

She took his hand and squeezed, but still no words came. After an interminable silence, Barabbas risked the question. "Does this mean you accept?"

"Did you have any doubt?" she asked quietly as she squeezed his hand again. "Of course I accept. This moment has consumed my waking thoughts for the past two years."

Barabbas relaxed for the first time. He felt as if a yoke had been lifted and he was experiencing freedom for the first time.

Leila looked at him. "Come for dinner tonight, as my father's guest."

"I don't know if that's the best way." Barabbas shook his head.

"Contrary to what you believe, he enjoys your company."

Barabbas raised his eyebrows. "He does?"

"Of course. He loves a good debate and, since my mother died, he hardly ever finds people willing to disagree with him."

"Alright," Barabbas relented. "I suppose the sooner we broach this the better. I'll just go home and change, then I'll come back and speak to him."

As they chatted, a man appeared, ushered into the room by the servant who had helped tend his wounds. Barabbas recognised him as one of the new messengers from the city of Capernaum. He rose to meet the man who stepped forward, wide-eyed and out of breath.

Barabbas rose from his seat. "Tobiah. How did you know where to find me?"

"Your cousin told me I'd find you here," the man gasped. He didn't even look at Leila and dispensed with all formalities and greetings. "I bring an urgent message from Levi. He says the Essene has been taken by the Romans."

"Taken!" Barabbas exclaimed. "Where?"

"In Capernaum."

"Why would they arrest him?"

"He was in the city asking after you. A tax collector recognised your name and gave him up to the Romans, knowing you were a wanted man."

Barabbas frowned. "Where is this tax collector now?"

"Levi gave us some instructions when he heard the news. The zealots in Capernaum have seen to it that he never enjoys the fruits of his reward from Rome."

"And the Essene?"

"The Romans have taken him to Caesarea. Apparently Pilate wants to interrogate the man himself."

Barabbas nodded. He was pleased at how far the zealots had come in the past two years. They had done far more than merely rebuild their network of informants. They had access to more information than ever before. The zealot army had doubled in strength and cunning, if not in numbers, since that fateful day when Rome had swept through Jerusalem and destroyed their force.

"Where will I find Levi?"

"He told me he'd be staying at the inn on the waterfront of Caesarea's harbour. You can find him there."

"Thank you, Tobiah, you've done well. Would you spend the night in my home? I have an appointment this evening, but it's too late to travel back to Capernaum now."

"That's good of you. My feet are caked with dirt and I feel as if I haven't eaten in three days."

Barabbas bade Leila farewell, promising his return that evening, and went with Tobiah to find Jashan. His cousin would gladly cover for him for a couple of days, as he had done so many times over the past two years. Jashan was an important ally and, more often than not the family never even knew that Barabbas was gone.

† † † † †

That night, Barabbas reclined at the table with Leila's father, brooding over his impending journey. He thought of Nathaniel in Pilate's hands and what might happen if the prefect discovered the old man's involvement with the protectors of the scroll.

He'd been faithful to his duties, but he was frail and Barabbas had seen what Pilate was capable of. There was every chance that Nathaniel would break under torture and reveal the scroll's whereabouts. His only hope lay in the fact that Pilate had no knowledge of Nathaniel's involvement.

However, he was an Essene - that was plain to see - and Pilate was many things, but he wasn't stupid. If he knew about the *Qumran* connection, it would only be a matter of time before he pieced the puzzle together.

Barabbas knew what had to be done. He had to get to Caesarea and rescue the old man - or kill him if he had to - before Pilate made the connection. Before he could do anything, however, he had to know what had happened to the scroll. He would find Levi in Caesarea and together they could decide on a plan of action.

"What troubles you tonight, Barabbas?" Zebedee enquired.

"I must go to Caesarea tomorrow," Barabbas answered.

"Another mission for your zealot cause?" The disapproval showed in his eyes.

"The zealots know nothing of this matter, but it concerns them more than they could ever know."

"Sounds sinister," the old man smiled.

Barabbas forced a smile and shrugged. "Not really. It's nothing."

"It doesn't look like nothing when I see your furrowed brow."

"My brow always furrows when I think of Rome's tyranny." Barabbas tried to change the subject.

"Why can you not let this war rest? Is Rome so terrible a ruler that she must be destroyed and driven out of Palestine?"

"You will never understand, Zebedee. Rome has destroyed my family. Taken the lives of my father and brother. I have seen the evil that lurks in her heart."

"It's true that Rome has had some evil rulers, but you still see only what you want to see. There is also much good. Her roads are safe to travel by. Trade has blossomed under her rule and men are free to lead happy lives as they raise their families in peace."

"There is no freedom. We are all slaves to godless emperors who have proclaimed themselves gods to all their citizens."

"We have been allowed freedom to worship our own God. All the emperor asks is that we remember him in our prayers as we bow to the God of Israel. Is that not a reasonable request?"

"We've discussed this a thousand times, Zebedee. We should just accept that we will never agree."

"I accepted that a long time ago, Barabbas," Zebedee smiled. "But something else troubles you tonight. What is it?"

"You're a perceptive man, Zebedee."

"I'm a merchant. I can smell a barter long before it approaches."

Barabbas took a deep breath. It was as if the man could read his thoughts and Barabbas was desperate to change the subject. "I want to discuss your daughter."

"Oh." Zebedee frowned and looked down at his cup.

"I know you and I disagree on many matters, but when it comes to wishing her happiness we are in one accord."

"I feared this day would come. I know my daughter wants no other man as her husband, but I am concerned by her lack of judgement."

"You don't believe I would be a good husband to her?"

"What kind of life would you offer her? She is a believer, a follower of the Christ, Israel's redeemer. She believes in peace and yet you make war with Rome constantly. What happened two years ago could happen again. Wives and children were killed for the crimes of their husbands and fathers. Would you put Leila's life in such danger for a cause she doesn't even believe in?"

"I love your daughter, Zebedee. I would never endanger her life."

"And yet you wish to marry her and place her in the path of Rome's wrath. Let's put that aside for a moment. What if something happened to you? Do you want to see her grow old as a widow, raising children by herself because their father was killed for crimes against Rome?"

"So you refuse to give her to me." Barabbas could not hide the disappointment he felt. Regardless of Zebedee's progressive attitude towards marriage, without the man's blessing he had no hope of marrying Leila.

Zebedee shook his head, gazing at the floor. Finally he looked up. "Let me think about it. Go to Caesarea. We'll talk about it again when you return."

The hope reignited in Barabbas' face and his heart pounded with excitement. "Thank you, Zebedee. I don't know what to say."

"I'm not promising anything." The man replied quickly. "Only that we will talk about the matter again."

"At least you've given me hope."

The older man smiled and nodded. His expression seemed positive and Barabbas chose to excuse himself on that note. As he walked home, his heart thrilled at the prospect of marrying Leila. She would be his. He felt it in the core of his being. Zebedee would relent and give Leila to him in marriage.

When he arrived home, he sank down on his bed, staring bright-eyed at the ceiling as he thought about the evening's discussion, amidst the deep, regular sound of Tobiah's slumber on the other side of the room. His mood turned dark again as he thought of his impending trip to Caesarea and what news of the scroll would be revealed. The truth of what he would learn in that journey was more frightening than he could have imagined.

† † † † †

The following morning the two men rose early and parted ways. Tobiah headed back to Capernaum, while Barabbas turned west, heading for the city of Caesarea to meet Levi and finally learn what had become of the elusive scroll.

It was late afternoon when Barabbas entered the city of Caesarea, principal city of Judea. He strolled down the bustling streets, listening to the constant thunder of waves pounding against the shore.

He savoured the salty scent of the air as he passed by the harbour. The water teemed with maritime traffic. Huge military biremes with twin rows of oars protruding from their hulls in symmetric beauty, and a myriad of merchant vessels carrying cargo that varied from silk to slaves, lined the docks. Many more vessels bobbed peacefully on the harbour's glistening water, protected from the sea's fury by the giant breakwaters beyond.

Barabbas glanced across at the antlike figures that carried cargo to and from the many ships docked along the pier. He followed the road up to a large, derelict building just above the docks. The faded sign on the sun-bleached door denoted an inn and Barabbas entered through the narrow doorway.

He was greeted by a surly proprietor who nodded as he entered the dingy lodgings. The innkeeper was large and solid. His face and gnarled fists bore rugged scars that spoke volumes about the establishment's clientèle and the owner's ability to deal with them.

Barabbas strode up to the man who, although only slightly taller, appeared to tower above him through sheer bulk.

"I need a room for the evening." The man's dour glare did not invite a greeting.

"Ten *denarii* a night, to be paid up front and in full," the man snarled.

Barabbas reached into his money pouch, noting the casual way in which the innkeeper craned his neck to see inside it. He slid the money across the counter, keeping his hand on the coins as the proprietor reached out a greedy, slab-like paw.

"A friend of mine is staying here. His name is Levi and he's expecting me. Can you tell me which room he's in?"

"My clients value their privacy." The man avoided the question, glaring at Barabbas over the wooden counter.

"I know how they feel," Barabbas nodded. "See that you extend me the same courtesy, except where this man is concerned. When you see him, tell him his friend from Sepphoris is here."

"Messages cost extra," the man leered in the direction of Barabbas' money pouch.

"You can charge him when you give him the message. Which room am I in?"

"Upstairs, first on your right," the man glowered, taking the coins that Barabbas had left on the counter.

Barabbas proceeded up the steps. The corridor above was dark and the room, when he entered it, unkempt. He threw down his bag and began to tidy the room, clearing up the worst of the filth and throwing it out of the window into the street below.

He smiled at the drunken curses that were yelled up at him and went to fetch another armful. He had barely finished when there was a knock at the door. Barabbas answered and was greeted by Levi's beaming face.

"*Shalom*, brother. It's been far too long."

"It has indeed, Levi," Barabbas smiled, embracing his friend. "What news of Nathaniel?"

Levi looked grim. "It seems he's being held at the praetorium. I can't get any information from the palace though. Some say he's not there. Others say he's been executed already."

"On what charge?"

"Who knows? When last did Pilate concern himself with formalities?"

"Don't worry. He's alive - I can feel it. Let's take a stroll around the praetorium and see what we can find."

"I've already done that, my friend. Believe me, it's impenetrable."

"Did I say we were going to look inside?"

"Alright, I've got time to waste."

The two men chatted about the events of the past few months as they ambled around the harbour towards the praetorium. At the far end, they walked past the main gates and stopped outside the adjacent temple dedicated to Augustus and Rome.

Barabbas chose his position carefully. Anyone passing by would think that the beautiful architecture of the temple merely held a morbid fascination for the two Jewish visitors.

Barabbas however could see the entrance to the praetorium clearly and scrutinised everybody as they went in and out.

"See? Soldiers everywhere. We'd be insane to even try getting in."

"I have no intention of going inside."

"I'm pleased to hear you still have your sanity."

"Watch carefully. I want to see who enters and leaves."

"I see only soldiers."

"Mostly," Barabbas agreed. "But there are some civilians - civil servants and slaves. I'm looking for someone senior, a man who might be close to Pilate."

Levi smiled as understanding dawned. They watched for nearly an hour before they were rewarded for their efforts.

"There's our man," Barabbas murmured as he fixed his eyes on the pompous man who had just exited the palace. He had short, curly hair and walked in a haughty manner that displayed his superiority to the world. Such a man was important, or at least close enough to the prefect to believe he was important.

"Let's go." Barabbas slipped from behind the giant pillar and ambled after the man.

"What makes you so sure he can help us?"

"Nothing, but unless you have a better idea, we might as well see what we can learn from him."

They followed the man who headed towards the docks.

"Our friend seems to have taken a wrong turn," Levi murmured. "He's a little overdressed for this part of town, don't you think?"

"That toga and expensive ring will certainly stand out in the docks. I'm intrigued to know what brings him here."

They followed cautiously and watched as the man entered the harbour and marched down to one of the merchant ships moored at the far end of the pier. He boarded the ship and the two men watched as he was ushered to an aft cabin by a sun-bronzed and wrinkled seaman. It was some time before he emerged. When he did so, he carried a large, leather pouch in his hand. He turned and waved before going ashore and heading back towards Barabbas and Levi.

They lurked in a dark alley, waiting for him to pass by.

Barabbas whispered. "Here's our opportunity. I say we take him. Let's find out what he knows."

The man walked quickly but fearlessly. He hadn't seen them yet. As he drew abreast of the alley, Barabbas dived out, grabbing the unsuspecting man by the throat and cutting off the cry of alarm. He swung him back into the alley and whispered harshly in his ear.

"Not a word. Or I'll kill you faster than you can blink."

The man gasped desperately for air. Barabbas released his throat and swung him around, looking into the man's terrified eyes.

"What is your name?" he asked quietly.

"Quintus," the man clutched his injured larynx as he sucked air back into his lungs.

"And what do you do at the praetorium, Quintus?"

"I'm the prefect's personal assistant and administrator." He quivered fearfully.

"Good." Barabbas smiled and glanced at Levi.

"We want to ask you a few questions about a certain prisoner. I suggest you cooperate and make this as painless as possible. Can you do that for us?"

The man nodded. His face was ash grey and he shook as he gasped for air.

"You have to calm down." Barabbas said casually. "How can you pay attention if you shake like that?"

Quintus swallowed, unable to reply.

"There's a Jew, an Essene from *Qumran*, who was brought to the praetorium from Capernaum. I'm interested to know if he's still there."

Quintus shook his head and stuttered. "No, no. He's not there any more. He's been taken."

"Where, exactly?"

"Dead." The man blurted. "He's dead."

"A moment ago you said he'd been taken." Barabbas watched the man squirm uncertainly under his malevolent gaze. "Are you sure he's dead?"

"Yes." The man nodded. "Yes, I'm positive. He's dead, definitely."

"It's a pity." Barabbas said, grabbing the man's hand. He twisted violently, cutting off the anguished cry with his other hand. "I had hoped you would be more cooperative."

He released Quintus who slid to the ground, blubbering as he cradled his broken wrist.

"Tell me again." Barabbas leaned close to the Roman clerk. "Where was he taken?"

"To the ship," Quintus moaned as the tears streamed down his cheeks.

"Which ship?"

"The slave ship at the end of the docks. I was just there."

"Why?"

"Pilate's instructions. He sells condemned men to Decimus the slaver."

Barabbas snatched the pouch from the ground where Quintus had dropped it. He opened it and examined the contents.

"Gold," he said in breathless awe. "There must be nearly a year's wages in here. When does this ship set sail?"

"It sails with the tide."

Barabbas rubbed his dark beard. "I think I'm going to give Decimus an opportunity to get his money back."

Levi stared across at Barabbas with a puzzled frown, but didn't say a word.

"Hold him here and keep him quiet." Barabbas waved a dismissive hand in Quintus' direction. He took the pouch filled with coins and headed for the ship at the end of the docks. He got to the gangplank and began boarding, only to be stopped by the same seaman who had escorted Quintus aboard earlier.

"What do you want?" the man asked gruffly.

"To see the captain," Barabbas smiled.

"Nobody comes aboard without the captain's prior notice. Get off!"

"I have a proposition for your captain, Decimus, I believe is his name. He'll be extremely interested in my offer, I assure you."

The man was fast. Without warning, he shot down the gangplank and struck a vicious blow at Barabbas' temple. The fist never hit its mark, however. Barabbas caught the sailor's hand and twisted the wrist back painfully, bringing his antagonist to his knees.

"I don't have time to stand and argue with you," he said as the man winced, grovelling desperately in front of him. "Now take me to the captain's cabin before I lose my temper."

He let go of the man's wrist and allowed him to stagger to his feet. With a vicious glare, he turned and led Barabbas to the cabin, rubbing his injured wrist.

Decimus was sitting quietly in his cabin, going over some notes. He had his back to Barabbas, who could only see the long, dark ponytail that hung down between his broad shoulders. He turned around, startled by the interruption.

"A man here to see you, captain. He insisted on coming aboard," said the obnoxious sailor.

As the captain turned, his eyes flitted over the leathery guard who was still rubbing his wrist. He made no comment, but instead turned and appraised Barabbas.

"What can I do for you?" Decimus declined to rise. He was younger than Barabbas would have expected a man of his station to be, and softly spoken. There was, however, an underlying toughness that had obviously gained him the respect of the men under his command.

"I'd like to make a purchase before you leave," Barabbas said, opening his pouch and flashing some coins at the captain who glanced at them with only a passing interest.

"What did you have in mind?"

"An elderly Jew, an Essene, sold to you by the prefect of Judea."

Decimus raised his eyebrows. "May I ask what your interest in this slave is?"

"So he's on board then."

Decimus hesitated, realizing he'd been tricked. "Yes, he's on board, destined for Rome."

"An old man like that would surely be worthless in Rome. I'm prepared to pay you a handsome price for the man right now and save you the trouble of transporting him."

"How much, exactly?"

"I'll pay you three times what you could get for him in Rome."

Decimus shook his head sadly. "It's an attractive offer, I must say, but unfortunately he's not mine to sell."

"You bought him, surely —"

"No, I didn't. I'm merely transporting him to Rome on Pilate's behalf, for a price of course."

"What's to happen to him there?"

"He's to be presented in Rome as a gift to one of Caesar's advisors."

"Who, exactly?"

"I'm beginning to feel like a man accused in a court of law."

"Surely it would be no great tragedy if he never arrived in Rome. Slaves die in transit all the time and nobody misses them. The conditions on these ships are appalling."

"Not possible. Pilate was very insistent that I take good care of this slave. I've been well paid for his passage and I'm not going to risk losing a long-standing supplier over one old man. Slaves are difficult enough to come by these days."

"I have up to one year's wages that I'm prepared to pay for this man."

"That's still not worth losing my primary supplier over. I regret having to turn down your offer, but the prefect's business is too valuable. I'll never find another supplier as competitive and I might even lose my ship."

"Can I at least see the man before you leave, then?"

"What's your interest in the slave?"

"I can't tell you that. I am prepared to pay you for a meeting with him, though."

Decimus considered the request carefully. "I would still be jeopardising his safety. I don't know what your intentions are. I'm sorry. I have to sail with the tide and I must ask you to leave the ship."

"Five minutes is all I ask."

"I don't like throwing people off my ship, but I won't ask you again. You may have been able to damage one of my men, but several would be another matter. Good day." Decimus turned his back on Barabbas to pore over the papers once more.

Barabbas stared in frustration at the captain's back for a moment and then turned to leave. It was a pointless fight. The captain was right. No man could take on the entire crew of a slave ship

"What happened?" Levi asked when he returned to the alley.

"No luck. He wouldn't even let me see him. What happened to Quintus?" Barabbas nodded at the inert form at Levi's feet.

"He wouldn't keep quiet, so I put him to sleep for a while. At least we know Nathaniel's on the ship."

"We also know the ship is headed for Rome."

Levi was amazed. "He told you that?"

"I don't imagine he told me anything I couldn't have found out in a wine tavern on the docks."

"Where do they intend to take him once they arrive in Rome?"

"Pilate intends to present him as a gift to one of Caesar's council members. He wouldn't say which."

"That information will also be common knowledge among the right circles. We'll find out in Rome. What about this?" Levi nodded at the unconscious body.

"We'll have to dispose of him. A dead man in an alley on the docks would merely be put down to robbery."

Levi winced. "Barabbas, he's a worm. Battle is one thing, but he's not even awake, let alone armed."

"I'm not saying I'll enjoy it, but how else do we stop him from telling Pilate we're here and looking for Nathaniel. That would reveal everything."

"I know." Levi looked at the man and shook his head. "It just seems so wrong."

"We can count ourselves lucky that Pilate never suspected Nathaniel's true involvement from the first. Everything would have been lost. Don't worry. I'll take care of it. You can wait for me outside."

Levi sighed, but he knew Barabbas was right. He hesitated, then left the alley and waited in the semi-darkness of the early evening at the alley's entrance.

Barabbas joined him a moment later, wiping his hands on a torn fragment of the clerk's toga. His expression was grim and he didn't speak. He merely nodded and turned back in the direction of the inn.

They walked in silence for a while before Levi spoke. "There's a tavern en route to the inn. We can stop there and find out about any boats that may be headed for Rome."

"There's certainly enough money in that pouch for the passage." Barabbas murmured in reply."

They found the wine tavern with the traditional vine emblem painted in dark red above the door. It lay in the same street as the inn. Entering the grimy establishment, they approached the proprietor. He had the same look about him as the innkeeper.

"Two jars of wine." Barabbas slid some coins across the counter.

The man took the money and fetched the wine wordlessly.

"We're looking for passage to Rome," Barabbas said casually as the man returned with the dark liquid.

"There's a merchant ship from Tyre sailing for Ostia in the morning. Otherwise you'll have to wait at least three days, probably more.

"Where's Ostia?"

Levi answered his question. "Rome lies a few miles inland. Ostia is the closest port."

Barabbas nodded. "Where can we find this ship?"

"The captain is right over there." The proprietor motioned with a nod in the direction of a group of sailors gathered in the far corner of the stuffy tavern. They were casting wooden dice in a game of chance. From the intense looks of concentration, Barabbas guessed that there was a lot of money at stake.

He watched with mild interest as the small wooden dice were cast. There was an outburst of cheers amidst a chorus of groans as a rotund man in the corner leaned forward with a smug grin and raked together a large pile of coins that had been obscured by a hefty sailor on the opposite side of the table.

Barabbas ambled across to the table and greeted the group of sailors who regarded him with quizzical interest.

"I'm looking for the captain of a vessel bound for Ostia. I was told it sails tonight."

"Before these lechers get the opportunity to relieve me of my winnings," the rotund man replied with an amiable grin.

"I was hoping to buy two fares on your vessel. Is there still space available?"

"There's still some space on the deck. No shelter, so you'll have to supply your own covering. We set sail shortly before dawn."

"Where is the ship?"

"I'll show you. It's time I left anyway," the man said, shaking his turgid money pouch and rising from his seat at the table.

The ship looked sluggish, with a bloated hull that lay low in the water. She was made of wood and painted red and gold, with the bronze, sculptured head of a swan arching over her stern.

She was about one hundred and thirty feet long, with two masts. The front mast leaned forward at a forty-five degree angle, reaching well over the bows and huge, square sails lay furled at the cross bars of their masts. There were also two giant paddles aft, which were operated from the vessel's deck and served as rudders. Just in front of them were the cabins for the captain and dignitaries who were headed for the Italian shores.

The superstructure was blue, with arched windows and a door that was a faded red colour. On the stern, just below the sculptured swan, was a painted gold cavalry charging towards some unseen enemy in the ship's wake.

Barabbas and Levi parted with their ill-gotten coins and boarded the ship. The deck was already half-filled with excited travellers who lined the rails waving to loved ones or busied themselves setting up small tent-like structures which would serve as shelters during the night.

Levi found a spot where they could keep to themselves. It was between the anchor wheel and the ship's rail.

"Over here," he called Barabbas.

"The sooner we leave the better." Barabbas sidled over. "Let's hope our friend Quintus isn't discovered too quickly."

The following morning, Barabbas was awakened by a shouting captain and busy seamen as they battled with the ship's rigging. A quick glance across the harbour told him that Decimus' slave ship had already left for Ostia.

It was difficult to make out what the sailors were doing in the dim light, but he could see that the ship had cast off and was sluggishly coming around in the overcrowded harbour.

She slowly made her way between merchant ships and galleys until she eased out of the harbour into the swelling sea beyond the hefty breakwaters. The captain barked orders and the ship's crew heaved under the strained rigging of the heavily laden ship.

Barabbas watched in amazement as the gigantic sails suddenly unfurled with magical ease, like wisps of cloud dancing in the light breeze. Then the wind seized the sails, snapping them taut with a crack and the vessel surged forward like a young colt rejoicing in its freedom. Her bows rose through the huge swells as she rushed for the open sea.

"Well, we've got six weeks of this ahead of us," Levi smiled as he joined Barabbas who leaned against the rail, savouring the fresh, sea air and the rush of the wind against his face.

Barabbas breathed in the fresh ocean air with a deep sigh of contentment. His eyes betrayed his concerns, however. "I only hope we can still find him when we reach Rome."

16

THE TRIP to Ostia lasted rather longer than the two men had anticipated. There were several stops along the way and at least five bad omens that halted the voyage for several days in some instances. Sailors were notorious for their superstitions and would refuse to set sail at the slightest sign of a treacherous journey. On one occasion a persistent magpie held the voyage up for five days with its loud, intermittent squawking as it preened itself in the rigging each morning just before the ship was due to set sail.

It was exactly eight weeks and three days before a weary and frustrated Barabbas got his first glimpse of the approaching landmass that was the heart of the Roman Empire. The gleaming buildings and harbour of Ostia stood out in stark contrast to the green hills that ran off to either side.

Levi joined him at the rail. "Not much longer now."

"It'll feel good to have solid soil under my feet again. At least we're here. Now we can start making some enquiries about Nathaniel's whereabouts."

"That will take some doing. It's unlikely the slave ship had as many stops as we did. Even though they only left a few hours ahead of us, they probably gained nearly a week during the journey."

"We have to find him. The scroll is too important to lose. I won't allow my father's, or my brother's, death to have been in vain."

The harbour at Ostia was far larger than that at Caesarea. The noise was unbearable as ships jostled for position in the murky waters that bore more resemblance to a sewer than seawater. A thousand raised voices mingled with the ever-present clatter of goods against decks and piers as items were moved to and from the gigantic ships that lined the dock.

"This way, Barabbas," Levi called as he joined the rush to leave the ship.

The two men disembarked, passing a mountainous pile of grain bags that practically blocked that section of the dock from passage. It was one of many such colossal mounds that were being moved by a horde of slaves from the ships to the multitude of warehouses that lined the docks.

Barabbas was overcome by the overpowering stench that seemed to constrict his throat. The smell of rotting fish mingled with a myriad of other equally foul scents to produce a stifling odour that burned the nasal passages and choked his breath to the point of asphyxiation.

The air was hot and humid and did little to improve Barabbas' demeanour. He pushed between sweating bodies as he tried to reach Levi, who was already making his way through the crowd that clogged the docks.

Once he caught up to his friend, they made their way past the dockworkers and tax collectors that waited patiently for the passengers to disembark. As soon as the decks were clear of travellers, the tax collectors would move in to establish the value of the cargo and calculate the amount of tax payable.

"Which way now?" Barabbas asked as they squeezed through the last of the mob that clogged the docks and left the harbour area.

"This way. The *via Ostia* runs parallel to the river. It will take us to Rome."

"Let's hope we can find him. He could be anywhere by now."

"Don't worry. It might not be easy, but it's not impossible. You'll see."

† † † † †

Rome was a city of columns and arches. Barabbas gazed in amazement at the splendour of the magnificent buildings that surrounded the Roman forum, the wide open square that was the heart and life of the city.

"I've never seen such magnificence." Barabbas spoke breathlessly.

"Don't be too awe-struck by it," Levi cautioned. "This city is a bastion to idolatry. Every building you see is a temple to a different god. Half of them are temples to Julius and Augustus Caesar."

"How can men spend so much on things so worthless?" Barabbas gazed in wonder and revulsion at the gigantic buildings that lined the forum and skyline on the hill. "What about that one over there?" Barabbas pointed at a small, round building.

It had thin, fluted columns around it and a conical roof. A Doric pillar of smoke billowed from the centre of the dome, weaving its way up into the atmosphere.

"Temple of Vesta," Levi replied. "It's guarded by six virgins whose job it is to keep the fires inside burning at all times. Women dedicate years of their lives to the protection of the sacred flame."

"And up there?" Barabbas pointed at the mammoth building that dominated the Capitol.

It stood high above the buildings around it and seemed to gaze down on the Roman forum from its vantage on the hill. The building was fronted by three rows of beautiful columns, just above the wide flight of steps that led to its entrance. Its sides were lined with two rows of similar columns and its roof was made of gilded bronze tiles that shimmered golden in the sun.

"Temple of Jupiter, chief of all the Roman gods," Levi dismissed the building with a wave of his hand. "The only thing of any interest in there is the mint."

"They mint Roman coins in there?"

"Off to the right, in Juno's section of the temple. If we don't find Nathaniel, we can always find a new treasure with a quick trip up the Capitol," Levi suggested with a wicked grin.

Barabbas smiled. "It's tempting, but we're wasting time. How are we going to find him in this jungle of marble and mortar?"

"Watch and learn, my son." Levi led him from the forum around behind the *Basilica Julia* and the temple of *Castor and Pollux*. Both buildings towered above them, forming cliffs of columns and arches to their right and left, as they strolled through the marble canyon observed by the silent statues that adorned the buildings.

"That's the library of Augustus." Levi pointed at the large building with arched windows that lay beyond the dark, narrow street from which they emerged.

"It's unlikely to list the names and addresses of slaves freshly arrived from abroad."

"Quite right, but I'm not looking for answers from a book. The library is where we'll find the scholars and poets of Rome - people of low social standing, but who rub shoulders with greatness. They're full of every pride and vanity and love to talk freely of the great men whose company they share, or whose children they teach."

Levi stopped outside the tall, arched colonnade, leaning against a pillar in the shade.

"What now?" Barabbas asked impatiently.

"Now we wait. Make conversation, chatter like birds at their roost. It won't be long before we learn what we need to know."

Levi was soon proved correct. Two men draped in togas appeared in the colonnade, loudly discussing an abject point of Plato's philosophy regarding the influence of outside ideas on coastal towns.

"It was still right of the Senate to make the offer to Carthage. It was in their own best interests to make a complete return to the earth," the taller of the two men was saying.

"The agenda was purely political. Carthage posed a threat to Rome and the Senate needed to incite them to war. Even if they had agreed to Rome's demands and moved eight miles inland, it would have changed nothing," his companion replied.

"Plato held that a country's proximity to the sea is a brackish and harmful thing. By introducing trade and traffic, it implants in the soul unstable and uncertain customs."

"Aristotle rejected that theory."

The two men took no notice of Barabbas and Levi as they passed by.

"The traffic and presence of merchants and seafarers in a coastal city leads to Ochlocracy, which all the great philosophers have condemned."

"Yes, but rule by the mob is not directly attributable to a city's proximity to the sea."

"Fools!" A third toga-clad man appeared from under another arch. He glanced across at Barabbas and Levi. "They espouse Plato's ideas, when they can't even quote him correctly."

Levi smiled at the young man. "You disagree with their philosophy?"

"It's not a matter of agreement. It's just that if you believe something, you should at least display a more than rudimentary understanding of your topic. According to Plato, unstable and uncertain customs were a cause of a town's suspicion and unfriendliness towards itself and with regards to other men, not the effect of trade and the presence of merchants."

"A well-studied man, I see," Levi nodded respectfully. "I'm Levi and this is my friend, Barabbas."

"Aelius," the man beamed at the compliment.

"You'd have to be a teacher of philosophy, surely."

"A hobby," Aelius inclined his head in false modesty. "Actually, I'm a poet and teacher of verse."

"A poet!" Levi exclaimed. "You must meet a lot of influential people in your work."

"More than I can count." The man tossed his head with an air of arrogance. "I have dined at every house on the Paletine. There isn't a man in the senate that hasn't sought my company and conversation."

"So, then you're well acquainted with the subtleties of Roman politics in the corridors of power."

"More than any man I know."

"I'd wager you didn't know anything about the provinces, though."

Aelius subjected him to an indulgent smile. "You'd lose your money. The provinces are more often than not the main topic of conversation."

"We're from Judea."

"Ah, the prefect Pilate's domain."

Levi nodded eagerly, encouraging the man. "Would you know anything about the difficulties he's suffered over the past few years?"

Aelius smiled again. "I can tell you he has a tenuous grasp on power, for one thing. Tiberius is none too pleased with him, especially since the execution of Sejanus. He aligned himself with the wrong man and now has no friends left in Rome."

Levi laughed. "That much is common knowledge. It can be learned in any of the wine taverns, or in the public baths of Rome. Pilate is desperately trying to curry favour among Caesar's current advisors, seeking a new patron. Word is he's selected the man already, but only the elite would know who that man was."

Aelius winked and nodded. "You're right, of course. It's only whispered around the most influential dinner tables at the moment, but it's something of a joke."

Levi opened his eyes wide in mock disbelief. "You mean to tell me you know the man on whom Pilate has set his gaze?"

"Vitellius has been plagued by the prefect of Judea. He's even taken to sending slaves as gifts from the province."

"Vitellius!" Levi snorted in disgust. "I'm sure you've never eaten at his table. I've heard he's a boor who can't be bothered with the finer pursuits of men. They say he has no interest in writing or poetry and that his artistic tastes match those of a screaming Thracian in the gladiators' arena."

"You've heard wrong, my friend." Aelius subjected Levi to yet another condescending smile. "That's probably a rumour started by a scholar with more ambition and gall than talent. One who was turned away by Vitellius in favour of a more worthy artist than himself."

"Do you mean to say you know this man!"

"Vitellius? I've spent many fine evenings enjoying the hospitality of his home. He's one of my patrons." It was evident that Aelius was trying very hard to be humble about this.

"Incredible! Where does he stay?"

"His villa is on the Paletine, overlooking the *Circus Maximus.*"

Levi fixed the young man with a cynical smile. "I'm sure the whole senate lives on the Paletine. One could claim any man of means lived there and not be far wrong."

"One wouldn't necessarily know, however, that his villa was the second last one before the Tiber, with the beautiful, three-tiered fountain at its entrance. Nor would one ordinarily know that, though the outside does the villa little justice, the interior is breathtaking and that the dining hall has the most beautiful mosaic floor in all Rome."

"I bow to the more knowledgeable man," Levi nodded in mock awe. "It's been a most enlightening conversation. Unfortunately, though, we have another appointment. Let's hope we meet again sometime."

"If you're looking for me, just ask around the libraries and the baths. There are few who don't know my name."

"We'll do that," Levi called back as he hurried away.

Once they were out of earshot, Barabbas murmured quietly. "A greater buffoon you'd be hard-pressed to find."

"A buffoon who knows where Vitellius lives, though, and that he receives slaves as gifts from the prefect of Judea."

"Well now we know. How do we get there?"

"It's not far. Directly south of here, just the other side of the hill." Levi motioned towards the Paletine which loomed ahead of them.

"Your years in Rome were not wasted," Barabbas smiled as they followed the road south-west, around the hill.

From there they turned left into the *via Aurelia*, the highway that crossed the Tiber River and hugged the coastline all the way to Nicea.

On the other side of the hill, they saw the immense Hippodrome that was the *Circus Maximus.* Its sides rose a breathtaking fourteen stories and the roar of the crowds could be heard for miles around as people chanted and screamed for their favourite colour.

The chariots rode in one of four colours; red, blue, green and white. Barabbas listened to the sound of one hundred and fifty thousand excited voices urging them on.

"This way," Levi called Barabbas, turning up a wide path that ran around both sides of a three-tiered fountain.

"How are we going to get in? I don't think they'll take kindly to two non-citizens knocking at their door and asking to see a slave."

"We're going around the back. Slave quarters must be somewhere there. You'll find the slaves more forthcoming with information."

They found their way around the villa's high stone wall until they were well away from the *villa urbana*, the main house.

Levi glanced over the heavy stones. "Looks easy enough," he said and started to climb.

Soon both men were over the wall and making their way through the beautifully landscaped gardens of the villa. They followed paths that led through dense groves of trees and past every type of fountain, walking through hidden gardens and sanctuaries where household members could find peace and take time to reflect on the day's troubles.

At the far end of the gardens, the path led around a large, rectangular pool with a leaping fountain that shot nearly two storeys into the air. Beyond it the path disappeared behind another high, ivy clad wall.

"This is it, I'm sure." Levi led the way around the gushing fountain. The cool, cascading water splashed their faces lightly as they passed.

They entered a courtyard through a large arch with heavy wooden gates.

"Hello, is anybody here?" Levi called.

He was answered by silence.

"Hello," Barabbas called a little louder.

There was still no answer, but they heard a knock, as if something had been dropped.

"Is somebody in there?"

They listened intently and heard another knock, followed by a rattling sound and then a door creaked. There was a patter of feet on the cold, stone floor and a young woman came to the door. Barabbas couldn't be sure if her expression was one of surprise, or suspicion.

"Can I help you?" she asked politely. The woman was short and her face appeared to be older than her years. Her head was shaved and she wore a dust-coloured tunic that was coarse and rugged in appearance.

"We're looking for a friend." Barabbas greeted her with an uncomfortable smile. "A slave who was sent to Vitellius as a gift."

"The holy man," she whispered.

"What?"

"That's what we called him. He's an old man, a Jew, extremely devout before his God."

"You called him? Does that mean he's no longer here?"

"The master said he had no use for a scribe. As he was old he was of little use at all, so he was sold to the *Circus Maximus* to entertain the people."

"No!" Levi whispered, suddenly flushed with anger. "That man never hurt a soul in his life."

"I'm sorry." The young woman seemed to empathise with Levi's pain. "Rome is a cruel and wicked nation."

"When was he sold?"

"The day after he arrived. The circus officials came to collect him yesterday morning."

"We have to find him."

"Don't try to get into the circus. It's too well guarded. You'd probably find yourself participating in the next day's events."

"Thank you for your help." Levi disregarded her warning. He was too distressed to hear her words.

He took Barabbas by the arm and led him from the courtyard. As soon as they were through the arch, Levi raced for the wall where they had entered the villa. As they shot around a corner, cutting through one of the many hidden gardens on the property, they stumbled upon a large, rotund man, bundled up in a flowing white toga with purple lining.

He was even more surprised than they were. "Who are you!" he demanded. "What are you doing here?"

Levi and Barabbas rushed past him, declining to answer as they headed for the wall.

"Guards!" the man yelled after them. "Intruders. Stop them! Guards!"

They raced away as the obese Roman yelled after them. Men appeared quickly, however, racing down the path towards Vitellius. They saw the two Jews and immediately gave chase.

Levi and Barabbas veered off the path and took a shortcut through the dense foliage, heading for the wall. Their pursuers were close behind. Barabbas could hear them panting as they thrashed about the beautiful plant beds.

"Listen." Barabbas stopped, catching his friend's arm.

Levi tilted his head slightly and turned to Barabbas in alarm. "Dogs! We'll never reach the wall now. There's no way we can outrun them."

"This way," Barabbas hissed, changing direction to race away from the distant baying. Levi followed. Although he was Barabbas' senior in years and knew Rome better than his friend, this was different. Barabbas had not earned his reputation as the finest operations leader in Judea for nothing. He had an instinct and cunning in the field that was so far unmatched. Even Barabbas' father, alongside whom Levi had fought, would have been hard-pressed to match his son's abilities, Levi had often thought.

As they ran, they could hear the animals' vicious snarls drawing ever closer. They rushed out into a clearing, turning down the path towards the edge of the gardens and it suddenly became apparent to Levi what Barabbas had in mind.

"The terraces are that way," Levi panted. "It's nearly a three storey drop."

"Would you rather face those beasts?" Barabbas jerked his head backwards.

They raced across the clearing, past a grove of olive trees and came to a low wall, no more than knee height, with the slavering animals snapping at their heels. Behind the dogs came the men, armed with furious intent.

Barabbas didn't take time to think. Grabbing Levi, he launched himself over the edge, plummeting to the ground three stories below. The hill was steep where they landed and they rolled with the slope as their feet touched the hard soil. Fortunately, the oblique angle broke their fall and they rolled nearly fifty feet before they came to a halt, resting on their bruised and aching backs.

Levi chuckled softly as he gazed at the angry men and canines above them on the terrace wall.

"We'd better get going. It won't be long before they come looking for us."

"Right," Barabbas staggered to his feet. "Next time I suggest such insanity, strike me down before the madness spreads."

"Well it worked. Now let's see about getting into the *Circus Maximus*."

"You worked in the amphitheatres all those years. Is it possible to sneak in or out?"

"If there was a way, believe me I'd have used it in the early days, but the circus is a Hippodrome, not an amphitheatre. It's for chariot races and theatrical performances, not gladiators' contests."

"We have to try. This may be our last chance to find Nathaniel. What do you think they want with him?"

"Sometimes they feed men to wild beasts, or occasionally they kill people in theatrical performances. There's no end to Rome's cruelty. My guess is they're doing a play as a diversion from the chariot races and they need a man for a murder scene. Possibly a crucifixion."

"These people are sick," Barabbas snarled.

The men continued in silence as they approached the monumental stadium, heading for one of the giant archways that was an entrance to the complex.

"What do you want?" A guard suddenly blocked their path.

"We want to get inside to see the races," Levi said politely.

"Since when do Jews take an interest in chariot races?"

Barabbas smiled. "We don't spend all our lives in the synagogue, you know."

"The Hippodrome is full. You should have arrived earlier if you wanted to get in."

"We wouldn't need a seat. We could just —"

"I said it's full." The guard's reply was sullen.

Levi nodded and turned to leave, dragging Barabbas with him. "It's no use arguing. We'd only get ourselves arrested," he said quietly.

"So what now?"

"There are other gates. Maybe one will be less well guarded."

They moved down the road until they were well out of sight and approached a second gate. It, too, was guarded with several Roman soldiers milling about the entrance.

"It's worth a try." Levi shrugged and approached the men. "Excuse me," he called to the guard closest to him. "Is there any way —"

"Levi?" The guard peered in amazement at Barabbas' friend.

"You know me?"

"Of course, don't you remember me?"

"I'm sorry." Levi shook his head, perplexed.

"Patrick. I used to guard your quarters in the gladiators' cells at the training arena."

"Of course," Levi nodded, smiling.

"Calvin!" The guard turned to one of his companions.

Barabbas looked, with raised eyebrows, at Levi who shrugged helplessly, shaking his head. The other legionary came over to see what his friend was so excited about.

"Look who's here. Levi, the greatest gladiator the world has ever seen."

Calvin beamed at the unexpected pleasure of meeting Levi. "I won three years' salary on you in the arena," he said proudly. "What have you been doing all this time? You know, after retiring —"

"Undefeated!" Patrick interrupted.

Levi nodded self-consciously. "I did the usual few years of compulsory training of new gladiators and then was granted my freedom. I returned to Judea and started a new life."

"And now you're back in Rome. Did life in the provinces bore you?"

"Nothing like that. I came to Rome in search of an old friend."

Calvin grinned. "Perhaps one of the many star struck upper-class ladies who offer themselves so readily to the best and most famous gladiators?"

"Believe me, there are women in Judea whose beauty surpasses that of even the most comely sirens in Rome. My friend is an old man who was sold into slavery."

"So you've come to buy him back."

"I fear it's too late for that. He was sold to the *Circus Maximus* yesterday. I understand they're using him in a play today."

"Ah, yes." The soldier's face was grim. "A gripping drama portraying the life of Icarus. You're right. The circus would never sell him now."

"Could I at least talk to him? Say my last farewell?"

"You're not going to try anything foolish are you?"

"There'll be no rescue attempt, if that's what you're worried about. I'm no idiot."

The guard hesitated, looking at Calvin, who shrugged. "I see no harm."

Patrick nodded. "Very well. For the sake of a man who filled my coffers with gold and entertained me countless hours with his prowess in the arena."

"Thank you." Levi sighed in relief.

"You'll have to hurry. The last race is about to commence. When it's over, the play begins."

"We won't take long. Just show us the way."

They followed Patrick through the wet, dingy stone passages, intermittently lit with dull, yellow oil lamps. He led them to the cells under the building where the slaves and condemned men were kept.

"It's alright, they're with me," Patrick assured the guards as they approached.

He guided them to the last cell on the left. "Inside," he said. "I warn you, though. You may not like what you see."

The cell was opened and both men entered. They were repulsed by the sight of the frail man, curled up alone in the corner of the musty chamber. He looked up and his pale eyes brightened when he saw Levi and Barabbas.

"Do my eyes deceive me?" Nathaniel's lip quivered in excitement as he spoke.

Levi stared sadly at the humiliated figure. He wore a light, cotton cloth that covered his loins and a Greek tunic over his frail body. His hair had been dyed dark black and cut in a traditional Greek style and his beard had been shaved from his face.

Thick makeup, normally only worn by harlots or actresses, hid many of the wrinkles in the aged face. Barabbas hugged the man and noted how frail he felt.

"Nathaniel, what have they done to you?" he blurted.

"They have made me young again," the old man replied with a sad smile. "I searched all of Galilee for you."

"You've found us now, old man. What was it you wanted to tell us?"

"The scroll." Tears flooded the old man's cheeks. "The scroll is lost."

Levi was unable to speak at first. He glanced wild-eyed at Barabbas.

"What happened to it?" Barabbas was calm, but his voice was strained.

"Eleazor. He nearly discovered it. I tried to protect it. I had another move it."

"Mattithyahu?"

"He was an honourable man. Like you, he had taken the oath. I thought a younger, stronger man would —" His voice trailed off. He looked exhausted, as if a lifetime of strain had finally taken its toll. "He was attacked by bandits. Although he made it back to *Qumran*, by then it was too late."

"He died."

"He lived for a week, but he was delirious. The madness took his mind long before the heavens took his body."

"Did he say anything at all?" Levi spoke for the first time. His tone was frantic.

"Incoherent ramblings. The words of a madman. He said the scroll was buried on *Dov Harim*."

"*Dov Harim?*"

Nathaniel sighed. "It's a meaningless name. There's no such place."

Levi sagged to the floor. "So it's lost for eternity."

"I'm sorry. All that work!" Nathaniel closed his eyes, trying to stem the flow of tears.

"Don't worry." Barabbas spoke quietly. "I don't believe his ramblings were those of a madman. I've heard of this place. Levi and I will go there and find it."

Hope ignited in the old man's eyes. "You know the mountain he spoke of?"

Barabbas nodded, but before he could reply, there came the sound of steps outside and the door was opened. A reedy Roman in a white toga entered the room. He carried two large, multicoloured wings made of wax and peacock feathers.

"Who are you?" he demanded, glaring at the two strangers.

"We had permission to see the prisoner before the play," Barabbas said quietly.

"Well the play's started. Visit's over. Come old man," he said, turning Nathaniel around and attaching the wings to his shoulders. "Rome awaits the flight of Icarus."

"Come along, my friend." Patrick took Levi's arm and led him from the cell.

"Thank you, Barabbas. I now know why God chose you to be a protector," the old man smiled mournfully.

Barabbas smiled and nodded as he followed Levi from the cell. "Our trip to Rome was not in vain. The scroll is safe. We will find it and protect it with our lives as you did with yours."

They stopped outside in the passage and watched as Nathaniel was led from the cell, waiting until he disappeared from sight around the corner."

"Where is this place?" There was an urgency in Levi's gaze.

"How should I know?" Barabbas shrugged.

"But you said —"

Barabbas heaved a weary sigh. "I couldn't watch him go to his death believing he'd failed his nation and destroyed his life's work."

Levi fixed Barabbas with a blank stare. Finally he smiled. "You're a good liar, Barabbas. You had me fooled."

"You believed me because, in your heart, you needed to believe the scroll was still safe. Nathaniel has that same need. The truth is too much to bear."

"This way." The Roman legionary led Levi and Barabbas back through the passages to the street outside. At the exit, they found the street filled with soldiers.

17

VITELLIUS AND his men had moved swiftly and mobilised the army to hunt down the intruders.

"There they are. Get them," the obese Roman politician yelled as the two men emerged from the Hippodrome.

"Quick, this way." Barabbas grabbed his friend, ducking back inside the giant building.

"What now?" Levi asked as he ran beside Barabbas through the maze of passages under the crowded stands.

"There must be another way out. I saw at least seven entrances on this side. If we can get to the other side of the stadium we can find an exit there."

"It's impossible." Levi cried after him. "Do you have any idea how many people are inside here? The Romans could mount an army before we reached another exit."

"Well then we can melt into the crowd. Use it as a cover until we find a way out."

"Have you looked at the people in the city? They're all citizens. They wear togas and Roman tunics. It would be like trying to hide an idol in the Temple courts of Jerusalem."

"Well in the meantime, can we at least make our way inside and put a few hundred bodies between ourselves and those guards back there with their pilums?"

"This way." Levi took the lead, making his way up some stairs and along another passage.

Light streamed through an arch at the end of the corridor and the tempestuous sound of a hundred and fifty thousand screaming voices could be heard beyond it.

Levi and Barabbas emerged into the sunlight and stood for a moment, awestruck by the colossal size of the stadium. The dust-covered arena was six hundred and fifty yards long and three hundred yards wide. In its centre was a low wall on which stood a concrete forest of monuments and obelisks. It was surrounded by the towering stands with seventy two rows of seats, packed to capacity with the roaring crowds.

There were no horses in the arena, Barabbas noticed. Just a tiny band of actors in multicoloured costumes. Their voices could no longer be heard above the din of the bloodthirsty horde that roared in anticipation of the tragic flight of Icarus.

Suddenly a rope snapped taut as a tall pole was hoisted into position inside the arena. The crowd turned in macabre fascination to see the tiny, colourful figure dangling perilously at the top of the rope, flailing the ornate wings of Icarus in awkward terror. Nathaniel began to slide from the fourteenth storey down the cord. The crowd's call grew louder with each passing moment as the figure gathered more speed.

Levi and Barabbas held their breath as the wings flashed in the sunlight, breaking as they snapped against the rope above, and still the bellowing crowd grew louder as Nathaniel's momentum increased.

When he had covered half the length of the stadium, still at least eight storeys above the ground, a catch was released and Nathaniel plummeted to the earth in a mass of wax and flurrying feathers, smashing into the hard, unyielding earth below. The ground erupted scarlet about him as the snapping bone and cartilage was drowned out by the explosive cheers of the mob.

"God rest your soul, Nathaniel," Levi murmured quietly as attendants rushed to retrieve the body amidst the rapturous applause of the shrieking crowd.

"This way." Barabbas dragged Levi towards the narrow end of the stadium where the stable doors were being opened for the next race.

The two men raced along the narrow walkway, pushing between the congested bodies of men returning to their seats or merely leaning against the railing for a better view of the arena.

"They went this way." Barabbas heard a shout behind him.

"Move!" Levi yelled as the soldiers began to close in.

"Here, use this to stall them." Barabbas handed Levi the money pouch.

Levi grabbed a handful of coins and threw it on the ground behind him. The crowd suddenly lurched with avaricious lust for the coins as they fell to the ground.

"Out of the way!" yelled the frustrated legionary as he tried to push between the grasping hands as people grappled shoulder to shoulder for the glistening coins that lay on the ground.

"Good, they're falling back. Keep throwing the coins, that'll keep them at bay."

"Only for so long. The oval will eventually bring us up behind them, you know."

"You think of everything, don't you?" Barabbas replied with dry sarcasm as he pushed past a drunken peasant roaring inanely for his favourite team, despite the fact that the chariots hadn't even entered the ring yet.

"Here, let's get down into the arena." Barabbas had stopped above the stable gates. He swung himself over the rails in an agile leap, hanging down and then dropping to catch the swinging, wooden beam.

From there, he dropped to the hard, dusty floor of the arena. He watched as Levi shot over the rail and dropped to the stable door. He slipped as the door swung wide and then his feet smashed into the heavy, timber planks. From there, he dropped to the ground below, landing lightly next to Barabbas.

By now the crowd had begun to take an interest in them and they hooted their approval as the soldiers began barking orders and signalling to others in the arena below. Barabbas and Levi slipped from view, entering the stables, and ran down the wide lane between the stalls.

As they rounded a corner, they saw the first chariot, with four horses, waiting for the charioteer. The man was busy adjusting a strap on his sandals when Barabbas took him. He flung the man to the ground, snatching his whip, and launched himself onto the back of the tiny coach. Levi joined him, grabbing the reins from a protesting assistant and flinging him back into the rising charioteer. Barabbas used the whip to drive off the rest of the attendants as Levi slapped the reins, turning the horses away from the arena in search of an exit.

They raced down the wide chariot lane, turning another corner, and came to a heavy wooden gate. It had a large wooden beam that slotted into the wall, locking the gate from the inside.

Barabbas sprang from the chariot and pushed back the beam, unlocking the gate and heaving it open. As he did so, the soldiers burst around the corner in pursuit. He swung the heavy beam and launched it at the approaching legionaries as he dove for the already mobile chariot.

Missing his footing, he caught the back of the vehicle with one hand and was dragged from the stables out into the cobbled street, swinging dangerously close to the whirling spokes as Levi threw the chariot into a turn and began to gather speed.

"Quit fooling about and get in," Levi yelled as he cracked the whip above the horses' backs.

"Perhaps if you knew something about driving a chariot —" Barabbas clenched his teeth as he tried to crawl back on.

Slowly he managed to pull himself up and struggle into the chariot. It was cramped, as it was really only designed for one driver.

"Here, give me the reins. What do you know of horses?" he grumbled, snatching the reins from Levi who cracked the whip over the steeds like an Apocalyptic horseman.

The wheels drummed on the flagstones as the chariot raced through the streets of Rome. The wind swept their hair back behind them and tugged at their clothes as Barabbas gently coaxed the horses on to a speed Levi would never have dreamed of attaining, racing along the banks of the Tiber.

"Turn here." Levi pointed at a street that led back towards the forum.

Barabbas tugged the reins sharply and the chariot careered around the far side of the Paletine hill. People scattered in a flurry of togas and fallen shopping baskets, hurling curses after the retreating chariot.

"What's their problem?"

"We're not supposed to be here. Roman law forbids any horse-drawn vehicles inside the city limits during daylight. Turn right."

"That's taking us straight back to the Hippodrome," Barabbas protested.

"It's the best route. They'll never expect us to go back there." Barabbas swung the chariot sharply, feeling the right wheel lift clear of the road as they went through the turn. He flung himself against Levi in an effort to transfer all their weight to the opposite side of the vehicle.

The chariot continued to teeter as they negotiated the turn and they both leaned in to prevent it from overturning, holding their breath as the horses raced back towards the Hippodrome.

"This will take us down the *via Ostiensis*, the road to Ostia. From there, we can take a boat back to Joppa, or Caesarea."

"Better hope there's one leaving soon. I expect our Roman friends will be finding their own chariots to follow us. Oh, no," Barabbas groaned as he saw the multitude of bodies swarming out of the circus, led by an army of legionaries to block their way down the *via Ostiensis*.

"Turn!" Levi's eyes were wide as he threw his weight to Barabbas' side of the vehicle.

Barabbas swung the racing steeds into a sharp left turn, feeling the wheel lift beneath him. He grunted with the effort as he leaned his body way out over the edge of the toppling chariot struggling to keep its wheel on the ground.

The vehicle creaked its protest as the smoking wheels spun on their axis. Finally, they made the turn and the wheel crashed back onto the paving.

"Which way now?" Barabbas yelled, his eyes streaming from the speed of the wind against his face. Before them, the road split in three different directions.

"Take the middle road. That's the *via Appia*, the Appian highway."

"Will it get us out of Rome?"

"Yes. It's the main highway south. There's a port about fifty miles from here, called Terracina. We can find a boat there. I don't care which way it's headed, as long as we get off this God-forsaken landmass."

They raced through the streets until they exited the giant city.

"What are all these buildings and monuments?" Barabbas gazed at the landscape about him for the first time.

"Tombs. It's forbidden to bury the dead within the city limits, so most of these highways are lined with them. There will be fewer as we get further from Rome."

Barabbas had slowed the horses slightly and glanced back, pleased to see that they were not being followed yet.

"It looks as if they're going to leave us be."

"Don't bet on it. Vitellius is a powerful man and he won't take our intrusion lightly."

"Well Rome seems to be slow in mounting her retaliation."

"Probably battling with crowd control in the city. We've stolen a prize team of horses here, and disrupted the races. The people will demand reparations."

"Well let's hope they hold the army back long enough to give us the lead we need."

"Should do. These are the finest horses in Rome. Even the army doesn't have horses this fast."

"They have other advantages. I saw a stable back there. It was military. The Romans will get fresh horses every six to seven miles. We're stuck with the ones we have."

"Just keep them at a steady pace. We should manage to stay ahead of them."

Barabbas was not convinced but rode on in silence, counting the milestones as their shadows grew longer in the face of the setting sun.

It was almost twilight when he looked back and saw the first of the approaching chariots far behind them on the road.

"Here they come. How many more miles to Terracina?"

Levi glanced back and took a deep breath. "Too many, I fear. I had hoped we would at least reach the Pontine Marshes before our first sighting."

"So we won't make it."

"With fresh horses every six miles we could keep ahead of them, but not this way."

"These are the finest horses in the empire, you said?"

"None better, but after the distance they've covered."

"We'll see." Barabbas reined the horses in, slowing them to an easy lope.

"What are you doing! Are you mad?" Levi demanded. "Those chariots are close enough as it is."

"We can't outrun them either way. We'll have to outsmart them. Trust me. I have a way with these animals. I know what they're capable of."

Levi glanced over his shoulder constantly over the next hour.

"They're gaining. There's four altogether."

"How far back are they?"

"About two miles, coming fast."

"Good. It's another three miles to the next post. I want to bring them in closer before then."

A short while later, Barabbas passed the stables manned by legionaries with an abundant supply of fresh horses. He reined the horses in further, allowing the panting animals a chance to catch their breath.

"Look at them." Barabbas crooned. "My beauties. They can hold this pace all night, if necessary."

"It won't be necessary." Levi grumbled. "Those chariots are barely a mile behind. At this rate they'll catch us before the next post."

"I hope you're right. Keep watching. Let me know if they stop for fresh horses."

Levi watched their rear as the Roman charioteers raced towards them. They approached the post, but showed no sign of stopping.

"Are they slowing?"

"No, they're coming right at us." Levi smiled as he began to realize what his friend was planning. "Wait," he said sharply. "One of them has slowed. He's turning in to the post."

"Curse his leprous flesh. Covering all their options. What of the others?"

"They're still coming. They've passed the station and the stables."

"Good." Barabbas increased their pace slightly. "Keep watching. I want to maintain our distance from them."

He spent the next few miles urging the horses to greater speed. Every time they lost sight of their pursuers around a bend in the road, he would push the animals, slowing down immediately as the Roman chariots came back into view.

"Looking good," Levi called as he glanced back over his shoulder. "I only hope the light is kind. I won't be able to see much longer."

"Just a little while more."

Levi kept watch as the Roman contingent gave chase. "Watch your speed. They're getting closer again."

"That means they've sped up. We can't afford to push our horses any more. The next post can't be far off. We'll have to risk bringing them in closer."

Levi's anxiety grew as the Roman chariots drew ever nearer. They passed the next post with their shadowy hunters no more than a few hundred yards behind them in the twilight chase.

"They're pushing through," Levi announced as the pursuing horsemen passed their second post.

Barabbas nodded and slowed his pace slightly, allowing the men to draw closer still, while leaving his steeds to their easy stride. Levi glanced back at the pursuers who, sensing their victims' fatigue, urged their horses to a breakneck speed.

"They've been pushing their animals hard for the last twelve miles now. Let's see if we can make it eighteen."

The Roman chariots were no more than thirty lengths behind them by the time they saw the next post.

"They're closing fast now, we have to break."

"Not yet. I want to get them well past the next post. Prevent them from turning around." He allowed the chariots to draw ever nearer, until he almost sensed the heaving breath of the chasing steeds on his back as he drove his chariot down the Appian Way. When they were almost upon him, Barabbas made his move. Slowly, without arousing suspicion, he began to increase the pace. The Romans fell back slightly and then closed the gap once again, cracking the whips above their weary animals.

"A little more, my beauties." Barabbas spoke quietly to his horses, increasing the pace almost imperceptibly.

By the time they reached the next post, the chariots were careering over the basalt blocks of stone at a scorching pace. The Romans were almost abreast of them as they passed the post and far too intent on the chase to worry about changing horses.

As he passed the post, Barabbas cracked his whip above the heads of his tired steeds. "Fly, my beauties," he crooned, pulling ahead of the Romans in an attempt to shake them off.

Darkness now enveloped them as the three Roman chariots rocketed down the highway in pursuit of the renegade Jews.

"We're at the swamps." Levi pointed at the dark marshlands that swept by them in the early moonlight. "It's about ten more miles to Terracina."

"They have to blow now. How much more can those beasts have in them? You said they were inferior animals."

"They're not that inferior. The army still owns some of the best animals in the empire."

"If they make the next post, we're finished. These animals can't go on like this."

The two men threw anxious glances back at the pursuing chariots that burned their heels.

"It's about four miles to the next post. It's over." Barabbas felt for the unfortunate beasts that heaved under the strain of their load. "Come, my babies. Just a little longer."

Then it happened. The lead chariot suddenly slowed, falling well behind the other two.

"Yes!" Barabbas exulted, praising his gallant mounts. The horses seemed to sense their victory and stretched their necks forward, increasing their stride.

"That's my beauties. It's almost over now. Show this military dross what you're made of."

"The second chariot has fallen back." Levi laughed with relief. "And the third. You did it. I don't know how, but you outmanoeuvred three Roman chariots."

Barabbas looked back at the soldiers furiously beating their stubborn, exhausted horses that had come to a halt in the road behind them.

"That makes only one more to worry about." Barabbas said, thinking of the last remaining chariot – the one that had stopped for fresh horses. "He can't be far behind us now."

They shot around the next bend and Barabbas slowed the horses immediately, peering intently at the road's edge. About a mile further on, he suddenly reined the horses in and came to a halt.

"Here, help me with this log," Barabbas called, heading for the far side of the road. Levi joined him, lifting the other side of the large tree stem as Barabbas swung it swiftly out of the moist soil in which it lay. The two men dragged the log into the road, leaving it lying lengthways across the eighteen foot width of the highway.

"That should stop him in his tracks." Barabbas listened for the approaching sound of the fourth chariot.

"Hurry," Levi raced back to the waiting horses.

Barabbas peered into the darkness, listening intently to the monotonous drumming of the horses' hoofs and the clatter of the chariot's wheels as it flew over the basalt stones, following the road's inky trail into the gloom.

"Come, Barabbas." Levi's call was urgent.

He turned and ran back to the chariot.

As they started forward, the pursuing chariot came racing around the corner. Barabbas looked back over his shoulder, watching the shadowy horses behind him as he listened to the unsuspecting cries of the charioteer driving his steeds on in the darkness.

They took the log in their stride, not faltering for an instant. The chariot was less fortunate, however, and Barabbas heard the explosive crash as the wheels struck the obstacle in the road. They heard the shrieking of wrenched metal and splintering wood as the wheels crumpled like papyrus under the mighty blow.

The chariot was flung into the air as it jettisoned its occupant from within. The buckled wheels smashed back onto the rigid stone, shattering their spokes and dragging the galloping steeds to a standstill.

The legionary struck the ground with a force that drove the air from his lungs like steam from a furnace amidst the twig-like snapping of bones under the force of the fall.

"Well, that's put him out of the race," Barabbas murmured. "Let's hope we can stay ahead of the others."

"We should be able to now. They were at least three miles from the nearest post and Terracina is less than ten miles away."

"Well let's get moving. I've had my quota of excitement for the evening."

Terracina was quiet when they arrived. Oil lamps burned in the rambling stone houses that shone with light and laughter from narrow windows as families enjoyed their evening meal together in typical Roman style.

"Not a lot of people around." Barabbas commented.

"I'm glad it's quiet. Less chance for our pursuers to find out where we're headed."

"They can still make an educated guess. It's obvious our horses can't carry on much longer, and Terracina is the first port along the *via Appia*."

"If we're lucky, we'll find a ship about to leave. That way we can be gone before they arrive."

They trotted through the quiet streets of the coastal town, finding their way to the small harbour. It was only a shadow of the great port of Ostia, but it still had a fair amount of traffic.

After tethering the horses to a post in a dark street and enquiring at one of the local taverns, the two men found a ship that was to leave within the hour. Barabbas took an immediate dislike to the seedy captain and the few crew members that he met. The deck was void of passengers. This was - as the captain explained - because it was a slave ship. Few passengers would choose to travel on such a ship, given a choice.

The captain was a miserly man with a hook for a nose and cavernous eyes that never held contact for more than an instant.

The price of passage was agreed upon and the two men were permitted to come aboard. They stood at the ship's rail, searching the shadowy docks for any sign of their pursuers.

"There they are." Barabbas' keen eyes picked up the dim movement of chariots on the darkened pier before too much time had passed.

"When do we leave?" Levi asked the captain anxiously, glancing back at the soldiers who were busy making enquiries among the taverns and the handful of people that milled about the pier.

"We're underway," the captain replied. His eyes glanced past Levi, following his gaze, making Levi wonder whether the man had also seen the soldiers moving surreptitiously about the pier.

If he saw the Romans, or made any judgement, he kept his conclusions to himself. They watched as he ambled off, giving quiet orders to his men. The ship began to move quietly though the dark, flat water of the harbour, leaving an ebony ripple in its wake.

"What's the matter?" Levi noticed Barabbas' worried expression.

Barabbas shook his head, but never took his eyes off the captain.

Levi looked back at the man, but also made no comment as the ship inched its way through the harbour. Suddenly, there were shouts and the Roman soldiers began to race, like darting shadows along the pier, trying to intercept the ship at the harbour's entrance.

The two men tensed as the ship reached the harbour's exit. The soldiers yelled to the ship as they raced towards the end of the pier, calling for it to stop and return to the harbour. The captain either didn't hear them, or didn't want to hear. The two men relaxed as they heard the billowing sails unfurl in the light breeze and felt the friendly swell of the open sea under the ship's hull.

"Well, I'm glad that's behind us," Levi smiled as the ship got underway, leaving the furious soldiers dancing madly about the docks as the spray from the breaking waves washed over them.

"Now all we need to do is find a ship to take us from Carthage back to Caesarea, or preferably Joppa."

"That shouldn't be difficult. Carthage is one of the biggest ports on the Great Sea, the Mediterranean. Ships travel all over the empire from there. We'll be home in a few weeks."

"I hope you're right," Barabbas murmured. He thought of Leila waiting for him in Sepphoris and longed for the warmth of her smile.

The chill of the wind caught the back of his neck and he shivered, pulling his cloak about him. He gazed across the deck of the dark, slave ship as she glided like a reptile into the eerie darkness. Then he went and lay down against the aft cabin, trying unsuccessfully to make himself comfortable on the old, weather beaten planks. Much as he tried, sleep eluded him and he was still awake when the first rays of the sun shone their icy shafts of light over the horizon.

"Levi?" Barabbas stirred and looked around.

His friend turned from where he stood against the rail, mesmerised by the swirling waters that swept under the ship's hull. He looked up, breathing deeply as he savoured the crisp ocean air.

"I think I would have enjoyed life as a sailor."

"When do we have breakfast?"

"They'll probably bring it along shortly. Did you sleep well?"

"Not a moment. Every creak the ship made kept me awake, every shuffle of feet."

"You can relax, my friend. We're on the open sea now. I've already had a look behind us. It's still a bit dark, but there don't seem to be any Roman galleys in pursuit. They'll never find us again."

"It's not Rome I'm worried about."

They were interrupted by a gruff sailor who brought each of them an unidentifiable bowl of slop. It was an unappetising off-white shade and accompanied by a crusty chunk of bread.

"Thank you." Levi gratefully accepted the bowls and gave one to Barabbas.

"What is this stuff?" Barabbas was appalled by the repulsive offal.

"Gruel. It's made of grain, it won't kill you."

"I think you make your judgements too quickly," Barabbas replied, toying with the food on his plate. "It has the texture of fresh gum."

Levi took a large mouthful and began chewing happily on the breakfast. Following his example, Barabbas tasted a bit.

"Well, how do you like it?"

Barabbas nodded, chewing suspiciously on the porridge. "Not too bad," he shrugged.

When they had both finished, another sailor appeared and collected their bowls.

"Captain wants to see you in his cabin."

Barabbas regarded the seaman with a suspicious glare. The man's wrinkled skin was deeply tanned and he had an unruly mop of dark hair. He was thin, but his size belied his strength.

"What does he want to see us about?"

The man shrugged and pointed at a derelict, wooden cabin on the foredeck. "That's all I was told. He's in his cabin over there."

"Let's go and see what he wants," Levi shrugged.

Barabbas sighed and joined his friend. When they knocked on the cabin door, there was no reply. With an irritable grunt, Barabbas reached forward and knocked more loudly.

"Come in," the captain called.

They opened the door and entered. The man stood with his back to them.

"You wanted to see us?"

Those were the last words Levi spoke. Barabbas felt the blow on the back of his head and his knees buckled instantly under him. He was unconscious before he hit the deck of the ship.

18

AS CONCIOUSNESS returned, Barabbas became aware of the dull throb at the back of his head. He panicked at the realization that he couldn't feel his hands or move his arms. As he became more aware of his surroundings, he realized that his hands were tightly bound behind his back. The rough ropes had cut off the circulation, causing the numbness.

He heard a grunt and rolled over to see Levi struggling against his own bonds as he lay on the deck next to Barabbas in the darkened cabin. Barabbas looked up and saw the scrawny seaman with the unruly hair leaning against the wall. He watched the struggling prisoners with detached interest.

He moved when he saw that Barabbas had regained consciousness. Strolling over to the cabin door, he yelled for the crew outside. A shaft of light beamed through the open door and gave Barabbas a chance to examine his surroundings.

They had been moved to a different cabin which had been hastily cleared and then strewn with a few empty grain sacks. It was a small room made of dry, rotten planks, and was bare of any furniture or windows.

A little sunlight shone through narrow cracks between the aged, wooden slats of the cabin walls which were held in place by rusty nails.

Presently, the captain appeared in the doorway, greeting his prisoners with a laconic grin.

"I hope the accommodation is acceptable. It's stark but dry and, hopefully, comfortable."

"Why are we tied up like animals? We paid good money for our passage."

The captain shrugged. "Good slaves are hard to come by. I would have put you in the hold with the rest, but it's full so you get to travel in style."

"You're making a serious mistake." Barabbas struggled against his bonds, as if trying to wrench his way to freedom. "People will be expecting us. We'll be missed and you'll have a lot to answer for."

"Two men in such a hurry that they take the first boat out of the harbour? Don't even care where it's headed? Not to mention the Roman soldiers hunting quietly up and down the docks. I doubt it." The captain shook his head sadly. "It's an opportunity I couldn't refuse. You're wanted men and nobody is expecting you at Carthage. You'll merely be marched out with the rest of the slaves and nobody will suspect a thing."

"They will when we tell them we were abducted."

The captain chuckled. "Why should they believe the word of a slave? You'd do better to keep your mouth shut. Lying is a criminal offence and slaves who do so are treated harshly by Rome."

Barabbas nodded quietly. "You'll regret the day you did this to us. As the Lord lives, I will watch you weep for your crimes today."

The man strode across the deck and lashed out with his foot, aiming a vicious kick at Barabbas' stomach.

Barabbas rolled out under the blow and the man's foot passed a few inches above him. In a flash he rolled back, barrelling into the captain's shin, knocking him off his feet. The man fell on his back under the force of Barabbas weight. Helpless to do anything more, Barabbas bit deeply into the seaman's calf, causing the man to shriek in pain. He felt the blows raining down on his back and neck as sailors tried to drag him off the ship's captain, but he clenched his jaws with grim determination until he tasted the warm, salty taste of blood on his tongue.

Finally he was dragged off the captain and the sailors began beating him mercilessly in an attempt to drive the life from his body.

"Stop!" The captain's voice was a harsh croak. "I want him to live. There is more pleasure to be obtained from his sale than from his death." He was seated on the cabin's deck, clutching at the painful wound inflicted by Barabbas.

Reluctantly the men flung Barabbas down on a pile of sacks that had been thrown in an untidy heap in the corner of the room. He landed in a bruised and crumpled heap, turning to see the agony in the captain's expression as he was helped up by a pair of sailors and hobbled from the room. The man's gaze was filled with hate, but also a hint of respect. He would not venture too close to his prisoner again.

The door slammed shut and darkness engulfed the room once more. As his eyes became accustomed to the gloom, Barabbas began examining the walls, hunting for a protruding nail sharp enough to cut through his bonds. He scrambled about the sacks, feeling the planks behind him.

There were no suitable objects, however, and he eventually sagged back onto the sacks, breathing deeply as he considered their options. Levi had moved to another corner and sat there in silence, watching his friend's frustration.

"It's useless, Barabbas. There's nothing we can do until we reach Carthage, so save your strength."

"What do you plan to do when we get there?"

He shrugged. "Something will present itself. For the time being, you might as well relax. Even if you get loose, where will you go?"

"I'll teach our good captain a lesson in customer service for one thing."

Levi shook his head. "It will do you no good. You'd be buried along with him."

Barabbas shook his head and continued his search along the wall. When he found nothing, he turned his attention to the sacks but still failed to find anything useful to loosen his bonds.

Eventually he gave up and lay down on the sacks in the corner. As he leaned back, he felt a sharp pain in his ribs. He cursed and rolled over, moving away from the sacks. Checking his side, he noticed a sharp gash. His tunic was already darkening as blood seeped from the wound.

Turning to the bundle, he hunted for the object that had caused the injury. After a minute spent searching through the crumpled sacks, he gave a satisfied grunt and settled down again, working quietly at his bonds.

"What is it?" Levi asked. He hadn't moved from the corner.

"You'll see in good time," Barabbas smiled.

After several minutes, he had his ropes loose and went across to untie Levi.

Levi stretched and rubbed his aching wrists. "We'll have to put these back on when they bring us our meals. Other than that, we'll have freedom of movement about the cabin, at least."

"Movement inside the cabin doesn't help us. We have to find a way off the ship."

"It's impossible. There's no land nearby that we can swim to."

"What about Sicily?"

"A possibility, but we'd have to be extremely lucky. If we see it, we could attempt an escape, but to cross the deck unnoticed would be no mean feat. They've probably got someone watching the door. Besides, the noise would attract their attention, if nothing else."

"There's still a chance. Just keep a lookout on your side."

"I can see little enough through these cracks as it is. If we pass the island during the night —"

"It's still worth a try, unless you have some other important matter to attend to."

Levi went over and pressed his eye up against one of the larger cracks in the wall. "Nothing, are you happy now?" He turned around.

"Just keep checking every hour or so."

"And what if we don't make it? I'm betting the first time we see land will be at Carthage."

"Then we'll try to escape when we get there. For now, keep a watch and let's not try to arouse their suspicion."

Their days passed in boredom as the ship raced across the cobalt waters of the Mediterranean, carried on the wings of the *Mistro* winds which blew from the northern shores across the Great Sea.

Interminable silence was interrupted by the irregular arrival of gruff sailors bringing unappetising meals of gruel, dry crusts of black bread and water. During these times, the prisoners would pull their bonds back around their wrists and ankles. The sailors took cruel pleasure in throwing the food on the floor and watching them eat like animals, unable to use their hands.

Levi and Barabbas soon took to staring sullenly back at their tormentors until they left to attend to their duties, before throwing off their fetters and swallowing down their meagre sustenance.

The bread was hard and dry and the water had the stale taste of confinement about it that came from the sealed drums in which it was kept. It was during one such meal that Levi peeped through the crack, doing a regular check and exclaimed, "There it is. The island of Sicily."

Barabbas looked up from his bowl of slop. "How long have we got?"

"A good few hours. We won't pass the island until after nightfall."

"Good. Then we should get to work."

As soon as he had finished his meal, Barabbas moved across to the port wall of the cabin and began prying splinters loose around one of the cracks between the planks.

Levi asked. "What are you doing there? Yesterday it was the starboard side and now you're busy at the opposite end."

"A little surprise for our fiendish crew – hopefully," Barabbas replied as he worked away at the crack, widening the small hole that let a bright shaft of light into the dim cabin.

When he had made the hole wide enough, he reached under the pile of sacks that lay in the corner and withdrew the object he had found from its recess.

Carefully, he jammed it between the planks, adjusting the angle to make a snug fit. After several attempts and a bit more picking at the crack, he was satisfied. Fetching one of the sacks, he placed it on the floor so that the light shone in a bright shaft on it. He made a few more adjustments and watched carefully. Nothing happened and he grunted in disappointment.

He removed the object and turned it around. Once again, he began adjusting it, tilting it at various angles until, finally, he achieved the desired result. With a satisfied chuckle, he marked the angle and returned the object to its hiding place.

The men checked at regular intervals, making sure the island was still in view. They decided that the optimum time was dinner time, when the sailors would bring them their food. It would probably be only one man; the men had become lax due to the prisoners' apparent lack of resistance.

By sundown, all was ready. The two men had cast off their fetters and waited patiently for the arrival of their food. Levi lurked behind the door while Barabbas lay in full view of the entrance, obscuring the hole he had picked in the wall where the object now lay in readiness to wreak its havoc after they left the ship.

When the sailor came, Barabbas stirred. The man glanced at him as he entered the room and threw the food down on the floor as usual. His grin froze in shock as Levi's huge hands closed around his throat from behind. Struggle was useless and the man soon succumbed, lapsing into unconsciousness.

Levi released him and let him fall to the floor like an old tunic at the end of a long and tiring day. Quickly, the men took their ropes and left the room. They slunk along the wall of the superstructure, throwing the bonds overboard at the first opportunity. Barabbas didn't want the crew to see the cut bonds and learn the true method of their escape. It was far better that the men think the bonds had been loosened in some other way.

They moved forward, avoiding the stern where sailors were sure to be manning the giant rudders. The coast of Sicily lay no more than a few hundred yards off the starboard bow and Barabbas exulted at the thought of freedom. Checking that they had not been seen, the men shot across the deck and quickly slipped over the side, launching themselves away from the hull. The shock of the icy waters all but drove the breath from Barabbas' lungs as he plunged into the cobalt depths. He found himself far deeper than he'd expected and had to claw his way back to the surface.

As he broke the surface, he looked around and saw Levi already swimming with long, powerful strokes, desperately trying to get away from the ship's wake. Barabbas joined him and soon they were well away from the ship, moving towards the landmass that rose up from the ocean in welcome.

They were already fifty yards away when they heard the call from the ship's deck. A sharp-eyed sailor had spotted them and the crew was already frantically heaving to as they tried to turn the cumbersome ship.

The two escaped prisoners disregarded them and kept swimming for the shore.

"They'll have a tough time turning that thing," Levi murmured. "All we need to do is get close enough to the shore. They can't venture too close for fear of rocks or running aground."

As they swam, the men kept looking back. The ship heaved to starboard, making a surprisingly sharp turn as she began heading back towards the prisoners.

Barabbas looked back again and began to swim that much harder as the ship headed back in their direction. "The wind is against us. They're sailing against it and will have to tack. That will slow them down."

As predicted, the ship tacked and moved away from them, turning after a short while and heading back in. The men swam tirelessly, shedding their tunics to increase speed as the ship alternately gained and lost ground with each new tack.

By the time the men approached the shore, the ship was no more than a few yards behind, bearing down on them, but they had already reached the shallow water. The captain wouldn't dare to risk his ship by running her aground.

Suddenly, the ship heaved to and turned broadside, giving up the chase. Barabbas wanted to laugh out loud as he and Levi swam for the shore, now no more than fifty yards away. Then his world fell apart as the water splashed lightly ahead of him. He was suddenly gripped by an unseen force that hampered his movement, pinning his limbs and dragging him down into the water. Barabbas struggled as the terror clamped about him, tangling him in its web and rendering him helpless in its grasp. Water surged over him, choking his lungs and leaving his limbs to flap uselessly in its grasp. Finally he felt the gentle tug as he was dragged inexorably through the water, back towards the ship.

19

THE TWO men were hauled aboard putting up only a feeble struggle against the net that had been thrown over them. The sailors bustled about the gasping prisoners, trying to untangle them from the net's clutches.

Once they were free, the captain appeared, hobbling between two sailors. One was the thin seaman who had called them to the captain's quarters on the fateful day early in the voyage. The other was a large, solid bulk of flesh and the captain's arm seemed to shrink in his slab-like hands.

"That escapade has cost you a week's food." The captain's leg was badly swollen. It had been bandaged, but the material was discoloured by the septic fluids that seeped from the wound Barabbas had inflicted.

He staggered as the ship rolled slightly, forcing him to put some weight on the limb. The two sailors steadied their captain whose face was contorted with pain. He composed himself and met Barabbas' gaze.

He pointed at his injured leg as he spoke. "You know, but for this, I would probably have left you to swim for shore. It's not worth chasing escaped slaves around the Mediterranean when they cost you nothing in the first place. However, I have a debt to settle. You will make Carthage and your sale will pay the doctor's bill for my wound. Nothing will prevent that now."

The men were thrown back into the cabin and once again their wrists and ankles were bound. The prisoners waited until their captors left. As soon as they were gone, Barabbas reached for the hole in the wall, withdrawing the object that had been placed there and began working on his bonds.

Levi was the first to speak. "That man's wound will not heal."

Barabbas shook his head. "It was little more than a scratch."

"Believe me. It was deep enough to inflict permanent damage. When I was a gladiator in Rome, I watched two men fighting in the arena. The loser was disarmed, but in the deathblow, he bit the victor on the leg, much as you did to the captain."

"What happened?" Barabbas finally cut through his ropes and began undoing the knots about his ankles

"The winner was one of the top gladiators. They brought in the best doctors to clean the wound and change bandages each day, but to no avail. The wound festered and got worse. Within days, it looked much like this man's leg does now. Eventually the doctors told the owners that they would have no choice but to remove the man's leg."

"I can't imagine a one-legged gladiator would be of much use to Rome."

"The owners agreed. They refused to allow it, leaving the wound instead in the hopes that it would heal."

"It never did?"

Levi shook his head. "The rot set in. Eventually it climbed all the way up the man's limb. He finally took his own life to end the pain."

Barabbas grimaced and took a large gulp of water from the clay jar that had been left for them. "May such a fate befall the captain for what he's done to us."

The days passed in morbid boredom as the men awaited their fate in Carthage. Escape had become impossible as a permanent guard had been placed outside their cabin. After several monotonous days, Barabbas saw land through one of the tiny cracks on the port side of their cabin.

"Levi, come look here."

Levi rose and peered through the crack in the wooden wall. "Africa. We're nearly there. We'll probably reach Carthage before sundown."

"Then we must move now." Barabbas began tearing at planks on the floor of the cabin. Levi helped and soon they had a small pile of wood-chips and dry bits of plank. Barabbas scraped together all the splinters he could find and pushed the wood under the pile of sacks that lay on the floor.

Once they had finished, they whiled away the hours, talking about anything, trying to take their minds off their predicament. Periodically, they would stare through the holes in the cabin wall, spying out the harsh, African coastline.

Finally, when the sun had moved far across the sky and was no longer visible from their limited viewpoint, the ship swung southwards, bringing the eastern sky into view with its deep indigo hues and the large yellow, early-rising moon lying low on the skyline.

The sea reflected the last light of the dying sun, taking the form of a stellar landscape as the crests winked at the rising moon.

They gazed from the peepholes they had created as the old slave ship eased her way into the calm bay, sheltered from the rough swells of the sea beyond by a large island that guarded the entrance.

The ship made its way through the narrow channel between the island and mainland and then began to sail across the bay towards the great city of Carthage. The majestic town rose from a peninsula that jutted out from the mainland across the bay, forming a natural harbour.

The ship turned towards a narrow lagoon on the western end of the bay and Barabbas saw Carthage for the first time. The city stood on a small group of hills which rose to various heights on the peninsula. It was surprisingly modern for a metropolis that had its roots in Phoenician history, having been colonised by the great fleets of Tyre some seven to eight hundred years previously.

"It looks like Rome," Barabbas murmured as he gazed upon the magnificent buildings.

"It was destroyed nearly two centuries back. Augustus rebuilt the city about sixty years ago."

"Liked his marble, didn't he?"

The city's buildings were of Roman design, with numerous temples rising up in towers of marble pillars and beautiful arches. They were dedicated to various Roman gods as well as the imperial cults of Julius and Augustus Caesar.

The boat approached the narrow lagoon that ran around the western side of the city, coming close to the shore and affording the reluctant prisoners a close view of the metropolis.

They peered through their peepholes at the congested harbour that rivalled Ostia in magnificence. The large quay teemed with people and goods, even at an hour when most Romans had long since returned home for supper or entered one of the many *Poppinae,* restaurants that littered the city.

"I'd heard that Carthage was second only to Rome in splendour, but I never imagined anything like this," Barabbas breathed in awe.

"It truly is the capital of the Mediterranean," Levi agreed as he gazed from their cell at the bustling wharf.

They continued staring from their limited viewpoint as the setting sun disappeared and the city was quickly shrouded in darkness.

The following morning they were awakened early by the sound of arguing dockworkers and clattering wheels as carts raced to vacate the city before sunrise. A few of the crew members soon arrived to take them to the slave markets of Carthage.

"On your feet," a dour sailor mumbled as he began to retie the ropes that the two men had loosened.

"I see the captain's injury has not improved." Barabbas noted the lack of food.

"Once he sells you into slavery, you'll wish you'd starved to death on this ship."

As they were led from their cabin, Barabbas chanced a glance at the broken piece of glass nestled in the narrow crack that he had so carefully widened and marked for the correct angle. The pile of sacks lay in a carefully crumpled heap beneath the opening in the wall where he had placed it.

All he could do now was hope. Everything was in place. If God smiled on him, the captain and crew would reap their just reward for what they had done to him.

He and Levi were herded in amongst a mass of stinking humanity, men and women who had spent the duration of the voyage in the cramped hold below. They were weak from dehydration and lack of food and their haunted looks spoke volumes about the appalling conditions in the ship's hold.

Their clothes were covered with sodden filth and Barabbas gagged at the stench of human excrement that clung to the desperate bodies and frightened faces. He was pushed in behind a young woman, no more than fifteen, who stared about her fearfully, clutching her filth-laden shawl about her to ward off the chill of the morning air.

Most of the slaves coughed and spluttered, their chains clanking their misery as the sailors pushed them roughly towards the shore.

When they had disembarked and stood in miserable rows on the quay, the captain hobbled from his cabin, leaning on a member of his crew for support. He was no longer able to carry any weight on his inflamed leg.

Barabbas noted the swollen, bandage-laden limb with grim satisfaction. He watched the slave captain as he approached, scouring the group with his eyes. When he saw Barabbas, he hobbled across, stopping at a respectful distance.

"I'm going to see to this injury you've inflicted and then I'm going to return and watch you begin your life of servitude. You're going to regret our meeting, slave."

"Not as much as you," Barabbas replied quietly, holding the man's gaze.

Crew members interrupted them, arriving with buckets of water. They were led by the leathery seaman who had called Barabbas and Levi to the captain's cabin the day they had been locked up.

"Right, you lot," he yelled. "Get yourselves cleaned up, and wash that smell off you. Dirty slaves are worthless, so make sure you look presentable."

Buckets of water were distributed among the grateful group. The first people drank huge gulps of the refreshing liquid, but soon the water was too foul to swallow. The rest of the slaves contented themselves with cleaning the muck off their bodies and clothes as best they could before they were dragged through the bustling streets to the markets where wealthy traders and eager buyers waited in search of an early morning bargain.

As in Rome, the *fora* served as markets as well as venues for public gatherings and political processions. They were surrounded by a myriad of public buildings with arches and a forest of statues that gazed down on the public as they bustled about the open squares in the course of their business.

The slaves were separated into smaller groups and Barabbas found himself, along with Levi and a host of the other better looking slaves, being dragged to the *Saepta*, one of the more fashionable markets where the elite citizens of Carthage shopped. There, they were sold to a chubby merchant who took them to his stand in the forum for resale in the local market. The man's benign smile masked a sharp and unscrupulous business mind.

"Name and nationality?" His tone was brusque and formal.

"Barabbas, Judea."

"Experience?" The man made some notes on a piece of papyrus.

"None. I was kidnapped in Rome. I don't belong in slavery."

The man chuckled. "A likely story. I suggest you keep it to yourself, unless you want your forehead branded to mark you as a liar."

Barabbas glared at the man. "Back in Judea, I'd have killed a man for such an insult."

The man nodded and scribbled on his sheet. "Experienced gladiator, do you know anything about horses?"

"I've worked with them." Barabbas gazed across the square, in the direction of the harbour. The slave-ship floated peacefully at her berth amidst Roman galleys and merchant ships that dotted the water.

"Good." The man scribbled some more notes and then moved on to the next slave in the queue.

Afterwards, the group was taken to a bathing area where they were thoroughly scrubbed, shaved and inspected. Being from abroad, Barabbas and Levi were stripped naked so that they could be properly viewed by the public. A slave came past with a bucket of chalk and whitened one foot of each of the new slaves, who were then marched out to be displayed in the market place. They were placed on a *catasta*, a revolving, wooden stand, where passers by could examine them and read the placards that hung from their necks, describing their abilities and experience as well as good and bad points.

The *catasta* afforded Barabbas a good view of the harbor. Once again, his gaze rested on the ship that he and Levi had arrived on. Then he glanced at the sky. The sun blazed down between intermittent clouds.

"What are you thinking, Barabbas?" Levi spoke quietly. Barabbas noted that his friend's eyes were also riveted on the ship in the harbor.

Barabbas switched to Aramaic. "If God smiles on us, there'll be a diversion in the very near future. It might provide the opportunity we're looking for."

"You're already thinking of escape!" Levi was incredulous.

Barabbas shrugged. "The sooner the better."

"Do you know what they'll do if they catch us? We don't even have any clothes."

"Exactly. They're off their guard now. Nobody will expect us to flee."

"I don't fancy having my forehead branded as a runaway, Barabbas. There'll be other opportunities later."

Barabbas glanced at the slave on his left. He was surprised to see the man was much younger than he had thought him to be. Years of subjection and hardship had broken his spirit and aged him prematurely. The man stared in dejection at the ground, his shoulders bent under the weight of his worthlessness.

"How long before we look like him?" Barabbas spoke quietly in Levi's direction.

Levi shook his head. "That will never happen, Barabbas. Please listen to me —"

Barabbas ignored his friend's pleading. "I'm leaving with or without you. It'll happen very soon, my friend. When it does, just follow my lead."

He watched the people as they passed by, feeling more self-conscious with each passing glance. Some merely admired the merchandise, dreaming wistfully of owning a luxury they could not afford. Others examined the goods more carefully with trained eyes that knew what to look for. Barabbas hung his hands loosely in front of him, trying to cover his nakedness. In that moment, he felt the first twinges of shame and worthlessness. He vowed that he would never become like the man on his left. He would find freedom, or die in the attempt. Anything was better than a life of servitude.

A wealthy-looking farmer began haggling with the brawny merchant who watched over them.

"How much if I take ten?"

The merchant shook his head. "I couldn't possibly consider a discounted price on any sale of less than twenty."

"Twenty slaves! How often do you sell that many in a single transaction? I'm offering a fair price —" and so the negotiations continued.

Once again, Barabbas glanced across at the slave-ship that had brought him to Carthage. It was clear that all the slaves had been unloaded and that most of the crew had gone ashore to squander their wages on the town. Only a few hands remained on deck. Barabbas couldn't see the captain among their number.

He glanced up at the sky which was beginning to cloud over, and he silently cursed the shadowy wisps that intermittently blocked the sun's rays. Levi also noted the clouds and glanced across at Barabbas.

The men spent some time watching the boats being unloaded as the *catasta* spun slowly on its axis. Barabbas kept his eyes riveted on the sun in its relentless rise through the morning sky. His eyes darted between the boat and the sun as he waited impatiently for the trap to spring.

Another cloud cast its shadow over the harbour, robbing the sun's rays of their power. Barabbas scowled, and prayed a silent prayer for the fire of Elijah to fall upon the ship. After an interminable amount of time, the cloud passed and sunlight baked the harbour once more.

On the ship, the glass nestled in its place between the planks in the wall. The shaft of light shone through its convex shape in a concentrated beam that grew ever smaller as it moved across the pile of sacks heaped on top of a small pile of wood-chips and dry timber.

As the sun rose higher, it concentrated the beam into a malevolent shaft that began to blacken the dry, fibrous material of the sack. Wisps of smoke soon began to curl up from the darkened surface, but they were quickly snuffed out as another cloud robbed the rays of their power.

Outside, Barabbas watched the ship with an anxious expression. Levi shrugged and turned his attention to the merchant who was busy negotiating with yet another potential buyer. By now, Barabbas had lost all interest in the merchant's negotiations. His entire being was riveted on the ship and the sun.

The cloud passed by and, yet again, the rays began their work, scorching the material within the ship's cabin. After a minute or so, the wisps of smoke appeared once more, rising off the singed material that began to glow under the intense heat of the concentrated beam.

Finally, the first tiny flames began to flicker on the material, licking at the old, frayed fibres of cloth. From small beginnings, the fire spread as the wood chips began to take, buying precious minutes for the larger timber to begin smouldering. By the time Barabbas saw the smoke seeping through the cracked timber, the room that had been his prison had already become a furnace with flames that licked the roof beams.

All of a sudden, the structure collapsed and the flames leaped from their confinement. As if exulting in its new-found freedom, the fire swept across the ship's deck, quickly engulfing the cabins on the aft deck in flames that reached nearly two storeys in height.

The few sailors left on board sprung into action, reaching for buckets to douse the flames. Their efforts came far too late, however, and proved futile in the face of the inferno that swept across the deck like a blazing tide. The crew was forced back by the wall of heat preceding the volcanic tongues of flame. There was an explosion that sounded like the bark of a dog as the flames leaped up the mast and incinerated the sails in an instant.

Barabbas glanced at the merchant. With a satisfied grin, he noted that the man and all his underlings had already turned their attention to the commotion on the water. Some of the slaves were moving around to get a better view. *Just bide your time. The ship will burn for a while yet.*

The *catasta* halted as the slaves turning it also stopped to watch the spectacle.

Barabbas cursed silently. He'd hoped the *catasta* would keep turning and afford him an opportunity to escape from the rear. Now he found himself at the front, closer to the wharf. No matter. Even the slaves on the *catasta* jostled for position and Barabbas allowed himself to be pushed to the rear of the crowd. Several of their captors joined them on the *catasta* to get a better view.

Barabbas glanced back at the burning ship. People on the shore rushed about the docks with animated yells as they launched boats to assist the helpless sailors who were now jumping overboard to escape the fury of the blaze. By now the entire deck looked like a sacrificial altar, floating in the middle of the harbour.

There was a splintering sound as the mast began to topple. It waved to and fro like a giant flaming torch, until it gave and fell with a cracking wrench of wood and sparks, falling into the water with an explosive sizzle of steam and smoke. Barabbas now found that he and Levi had been jostled to the rear of the crowd.

He noticed a new disturbance on the shore as the captain of the gutted slave ship arrived, carried by two crewmen, having been hastily summoned to wharf. The man had come just in time to see the flames incinerating the last remains of his beloved vessel and source of livelihood. He wailed like a wounded beast, tearing at his long locks of hair as his wild gaze swung from the burnt wreck to the shore. Barabbas nodded quietly as he gazed upon the captain's haunted panic and anguished eyes.

In a remarkably short space of time, the fire consumed the ship, transforming it into a wrecked frame that disintegrated and plunged into the flat, dark waters of the harbour. The ship's belly finally caved, sending up plumes of steam as the ancient timber struck the water in a mass of floating debris. The glowing beams and red-hot metal rivets caused the water to shoot small geysers of steam into the air with a squeaking and hissing sound that had a macabre effect on the listener.

It sounded as if the ship was screaming its final agony as it expired and sank to its watery tomb in the shallow bed of the harbour on the North African coastline. The sizzle of heat on water continued for several minutes as the ripples doused the blackened flotsam that was all that remained of the ship.

The captain threw his crewmen off him in rage as he yelled in vain for someone to save the churning wreck. He collapsed as he tried to put weight on his gangrenous limb, crashing to the ground and clutching the injured leg, wincing, until he looked like a tortured beast, bearing its fangs in fear as he watched the dying embers beginning to sink.

All eyes in the *Saepta* gaped in morbid fascination at the sinking vessel. In that moment, Barabbas made his move. He leaned left and clasped his hand over the mouth of the civilian at his side, pulling the man off the *catasta* after him. He glanced to his right and saw Levi do the same. The man Levi had chosen was a bit small but would have to do.

Barabbas' captive struggled in his grip, his eyes white with fear. His efforts were feeble, however and Barabbas dragged him down a side-alley where a quick blow to the man's jaw, just below his right ear, ended the struggle.

Barabbas nodded at Levi's captive as his friend joined him in the alley. "Move quickly. Let's get their clothes and get out of here."

Levi nodded. He'd already begun to remove the man's sandals. A few minutes later, Barabbas and Levi emerged from the far end of the alley, dressed like local citizens of Carthage.

Barabbas glanced across at his friend and grinned. "That was easy. I told you it would work."

Levi's chuckle dripped with bitterness. "You think we're free? The show you put on at the wharf is ending as we speak, which means that the local Roman garrison will be mobilized within the hour."

Barabbas shrugged. "And?"

Levi shook his head. "You still don't understand, do you? That means letters will be sent in every direction, alerting every city between here and Alexandria that there are two escaped slaves on the loose. We won't be able to enter a single town without alerting the local populace."

Barabbas sighed. "I had no intention of entering a town. I was thinking of traveling by boat."

Levi shook his head. "With what money? If you'd listened to me and allowed us to be sold into slavery we would have had access to our master's cash at some point and could have bought ourselves fare on a ship in Carthage. However, thanks to your impatience, we no longer have that luxury."

"We could get work at —"

"No we can't, Barabbas! They're looking for us now. Every stranger found near the docks or wandering about the local farms, looking for work, will be marked. And that will hold true for every city between here and the Negev. Your pig-headed pride just cost us the best part of two years."

Barabbas glanced up sharply. "That's how long you think it will take us to get back home?"

Levi scowled and shrugged. "Give or take a month."

Barabbas glanced across at a giant pillared temple and sighed. "It never occurred to you to mention this to me before?"

Levi snorted. "Like you ever gave me the chance."

Barabbas shook his head. How could he have been so obtuse? He thought of his beloved Judea. It would have been so easy back home. There, he had safe-houses in which to hide and allies who could smuggle him food and aid with transport. Out here he and Levi had nothing. They would have to live off the land and move under the cover of darkness. Every theft – clothes, food, it didn't matter - would be reported and alert the local Roman garrisons that the runaways they sought might be in the area. Levi was right. It would be a long and arduous journey.

20

LEILA ARRIVED home to see her father anxiously pacing the length and breadth of his garden. The cool trickle of the fountain in his luxurious, three-tiered water feature appeared to have no calming effect on him. He glanced up as she stepped through the gate.

"Where have you been!" Zebedee demanded. "I've been searching all day for you. You left before I was awake without telling anyone where you were going and you return at this hour. What have you been doing all this time?"

Leila stared silently for a moment before replying. "I went to see Jashan, the son of Ehud."

His voice softened. "Barabbas' cousin. Did he have any news?"

She shook her head. Zebedee took a deep breath. Leila tried to hide the tears that welled in her dark eyes.

Her father placed his hands on her shoulders. "Something must have happened. For all Barabbas' problems, I know he loved you. He would never abandon you like this unless something had happened to him."

"What could have happened that he would not return for nine months?"

"Has Jashan's family had no word since he left?"

"Jashan has given me a name. A zealot contact who lives in Jerusalem. They may know something of his whereabouts."

Zebedee frowned. "Leila, I think you should prepare yourself for the possibility. He may never return."

Anger welled up inside her. "Don't speak like that, father. He will return."

"It's been nearly a year. Surely he would have returned by now, or at least he would have sent word to you."

She shook her head and looked away. "I know in my heart he's alive. He will return."

"Leila, don't do this to yourself. I've watched you over these past months. Your days are filled with sorrow. You don't eat as you should. Do you think this is what Barabbas would have wanted for you?"

"Stop talking as if he's dead. He isn't!"

She stared into her father's face, searching his dark eyes. "There's something else. What is it?"

Zebedee's shoulders sagged in a heavy sigh. He looked away, gazing towards the home's entrance.

"Miyka'el's coming. He arrives tonight, tomorrow latest. I've invited him as our guest."

Leila glared at her father for a moment. "Must you insist on inviting him to our home every time he comes to Sepphoris?"

"He's a friend, Leila. How can I refuse him?"

"I'm the only reason for his friendship. Give me to Barabbas and you'll never see Miyka'el again."

He hesitated a moment and then replied softly. "Barabbas is not here, Leila."

"He will be - soon. And that will be the end of your great friendship with Miyka'el."

"All I ask is that you show him some hospitality. Is his love so evil that you cannot live in the same house with him for a few days?"

"It's not evil, father. It's futile. I love another."

"Who is —"

"Who will return, and I am growing weary of this constant pressure you place on me to consider Miyka'el as a husband."

"I've never done that. Years ago, I decided to allow you a choice in the matter. I even promised to consider Barabbas' request, despite my disapproval of his lifestyle. Now I've been proved right. His chosen profession has taken its toll and you are the one left alone, mourning like a widow without any children. Even if Barabbas returns, I don't know that I would give you to him as a wife. You can't be sure that this wouldn't happen again. Every time he left the house, you would wonder whether he'd return. This is the very thing I wanted to spare you from, Leila."

"So you choose to spare me the pain of losing him by denying me the joy of having him forever," she replied softly.

Zebedee faced her with an exasperated stare, unable to reply. After a moment, she turned and headed back into the house.

Leila went to her bedroom where she threw herself down on the bed and wept bitterly.

Times grow dark, Barabbas. Please return quickly before the darkness engulfs us. It was late in the evening when she finally rose and washed her face. She prepared for bed, afraid to leave her room lest Miyka'el had arrived unnoticed while she had been there. At breakfast the following morning, she found that Miyka'el had, indeed, arrived the previous evening.

"Good morning, Leila," he smiled as she entered the *peristylium*.

"*Shalom*," she replied, taking a fig from a large, ornate silver bowl and turning to leave.

"I missed you last night when I arrived. You had already retired for the night."

"I wasn't feeling very well. I'm afraid I'm still not."

"Leila, come eat with us." Her father's tone was far too jovial for Leila's liking. He lounged on a garden bench around the outdoor dining table.

"I think I should go lie down again, father."

"Nonsense," Zebedee smiled. "The fresh air will do you good."

With a deep sigh, Leila sat down on one of the long, couch-like benches and dipped the fig in a small pot of honey that stood on the table.

"Miyka'el's brought us a thousand spices from the orient, along with many delicacies. You should see them, Leila. I've bought far more than I intended to." He laughed.

Miyka'el smiled. "Never mind. You'll make all your money back when you sell your goods in Caesarea. These items are rare. You can ask any price you like and men will pay it with a smile."

"You're a good merchant, Miyka'el. Maybe too good for me. What do you say, Leila? Is Miyka'el not the finest merchant in Judea?"

"I'm afraid I've not met enough of them to make a judgement," she replied sweetly. The smile was thin and her face strained.

Miyka'el was concerned. "What troubles you, Leila? You look tired. Did you not sleep well during the night?"

"Don't trouble yourself over me, Miyka'el. I'll be fine. In a few days, my troubles will all be gone."

A shadow passed across her father's face, but Miyka'el appeared to have missed the implication.

"I'm glad to hear that. I wouldn't want anything to happen to you."

Leila shrugged noncommittally and forced a smile. She finished her meal in silence while the two men discussed the benefits and disadvantages of various trade routes between Caesarea and Rome.

"What about going north and then through Macedonia?" Miyka'el suggested.

Zebedee shook his head. "Too expensive."

"It's cheaper than shipping costs."

"Yes, but the taxes are horrendous. The journey to Rome would take sixteen months and every city demands tax from the merchants who pass through."

"Do harbours not demand tax?"

"Of course they do, but I would rather pay the harbour tax on an eight or sixteen week voyage than all of that city tax over a sixteen month period. You also see your money that much sooner when you sell the goods in Ostia."

"But what about the dangers of sea travel? There are very few safe months to travel by sea. The others vary from perilous to suicidal. Would you risk your entire cargo for the few sesterces you save on the imperial taxes?"

"It's not as dangerous as you think. As long as a ship hugs the coastline and runs for safety every time a storm brews, she can remain out of harms way."

"And every time a ship finds safety, the harbours extract more tax."

Leila rose from the table. "Will you excuse me, please? I have things to do."

"I'm sorry Leila. We should have been more considerate. We didn't mean to bore you with our conversation." Miyka'el's tone was condescending.

"It wasn't the conversation that bored me. You forget I was raised in a merchant's house. While your argument of travelling by land through Macedonia has merit in that it is safer, you forget the amount of time saved by sea travel. The ocean route, although more expensive, can carry ten times the amount of goods in the same amount of time. If you lost an entire cargo, or even two cargoes a year, you would still come out with five or ten percent more profit at the end of a sixteen month period. Not to mention the fact that the chances of losing two cargoes a year are so negligible as not to warrant consideration. I believe the term is acceptable risk."

She turned and strode back into the house before either man had a chance to reply.

Miyka'el remained in their home for nearly a week and Leila found more reasons each day to leave the house on some errand or another, often returning after dark and heading straight to her room. It was down at the market the day after Miyka'el left that Leila made her announcement. "I'm going to Jerusalem, father."

Zebedee frowned. "Why, Leila? What good would it do?"

"Jashan has given me a name, a contact in the city. This person may know where Barabbas is. I could stay with Uncle Nathaniel."

Zebedee became angry. "Leila, I think this has gone on long enough. Barabbas isn't coming back, and I'm not going to allow you to wander all over the countryside searching for what isn't there. These zealots are dangerous people. They're suspicious of intruders, and I'm not sending you into the lion's jaws in the vain hope that Barabbas is still alive."

"I'm going, father. At least if I go with your blessing you can send a servant along to see to it that I'm kept safe."

"You're not going anywhere; you're going home and you will stay there until this lunacy passes."

† † † † †

That night left Zebedee brooding over the day's discussion as he climbed into bed. It had practically become a routine, with the arguments becoming more heated by the day as Leila insisted on pursuing the whereabouts of this man she had such strong feelings for.

He lay down and stared at the low ceiling, thinking about his daughter's words and how adamant she had sounded. It didn't help trying to reason with her. She only became angrier.

We used to be so close. Zebedee suddenly realized how long it had been since he and Leila had shared a truly meaningful conversation. *It's not that I haven't tried, but she just keeps pushing me away.*

Leila had gone to bed early with no explanation. She had merely excused herself and left. Zebedee failed to understand her. She had been mourning for Barabbas for months now and remained convinced that he would return.

Zebedee had known all along that Barabbas would meet some untimely end and was secretly glad that it had occurred before he had married Leila. Even though he disapproved of Barabbas, Zebedee knew he was too weak to refuse his daughter's wishes. There was no doubt in his mind that he would have allowed her to marry Barabbas, against his better judgement.

That will all change this night, he promised himself. Tomorrow I will take charge of this household and put an end to Leila's suffering. Although she may not see it that way, in the end she will realize that it was for the best.

But no matter how he tried, sleep eluded him.

It's for her own good, he kept telling himself. Finally, dawn broke and Zebedee rose to face his daughter. She didn't arrive for breakfast, however, and finally

Zebedee went to her room.

The bed was neatly made and the room was empty. He rushed through to the kitchen to check whether any of the servants had seen her, but nobody had. Immediately Zebedee called the household servants together.

"Go out along the road to Jerusalem. She must have left early this morning. When you find her bring her home immediately."

The servants hunted the miles of road that ran from Sepphoris to Jerusalem. A full three days passed and it was late in the evening before the last of the servants returned. None had been able to find any clue as to her whereabouts. Leila had vanished.

† † † † †

The barn was filled with grain, newly harvested from the surrounding farms. It had just been packed and Leila had known the morning she left that it would be at least a week before her father's servants arrived to collect the grain and ship it out to the markets. She uncurled in the early dimness of first light, stretching as she rose from her makeshift bed on a pile of sacks in the far corner of the barn.

It was the logical place to hide. Her father would almost certainly have sent servants along every road to Jerusalem in search of her. There was no way she could outrun them and a woman alone would find it difficult to hide among the many travellers between Sepphoris and Jerusalem.

Nearly a week had passed since she had left. This morning would be a good time to leave for Jerusalem. She pondered her journey as she munched on the last of the dry bread she had packed to sustain her while she lay in hiding. She took a sip of water from a hastily filled wineskin that was worn with age and then counted her money. There was enough to get her to Jerusalem. From there, she could go to her uncle who, she knew, would send her home. But only after she had accomplished what she had set out to do.

By sunrise, Leila was well away from Sepphoris, hoping fervently that all of her father's servants had given up their search and returned to the city. The further she got from Sepphoris, the more her spirits lifted and she was even able to appreciate the lush vegetation and farm lands in the valley of Jezreel and the beautiful hills of Samaria that lay beyond as the sun rose in its giant arc over the eastern horizon.

She chose the shortest route and spent the night at a small inn along the way. The building was made of stone and only had room for about ten guests, but the food was good and the innkeeper went out of his way to make her stay a pleasant one.

She was mildly amused by his wife's reaction as the man rushed about catering for Leila's every want.

"It's our duty to look after our guests, my dear," the man had defended himself from his wife's sharp tongue.

"Would that you took care of those who are not so young and beautiful as well as you do this one," the woman replied with a sour expression.

When Leila arrived in Jerusalem, she immediately headed for the local markets where she began to enquire about the zealot contact Jashan had told her about, taking heed of her father's warning and being careful not to mention anything related to the zealot cause.

People were less forthcoming with information than she had hoped and it was a full two days before she found her way to the cramped courtyard against the city's northern wall. She passed a small group of beggars who littered the alley outside, stepping over two of them as she headed up the stairs that led from the street.

One of the men made a remark that bordered on a drunken proposal, which Leila chose to ignore as she headed down the stairs into the courtyard beyond.

The door was answered by a woman whose beauty was marred only slightly by a harshness of expression that had obviously built up over a lifetime of emotional abuse.

"Are you Deborah?" Leila asked politely.

The woman eyed Leila suspiciously. "You took longer to get here than I expected. I heard you've been searching for me since the day before yesterday."

"Your informants have done you proud," Leila nodded, but immediately realized she'd said the wrong thing.

The woman was suddenly hostile, stepping back into the shadows of her tiny home. "One wrong move and you'll never leave this courtyard. The drunks you saw in the alley outside - they're there for my protection and far more sober than they look. We know you weren't followed. That's the only reason you're still alive."

Leila quickly tried to set the woman's mind at ease. "I assure you, I 'm not here to hurt you in any way."

"What do you want!"

"I'm from Sepphoris. A man there gave me your name and told me you might be able to help me."

"Sepphoris?" The hostility suddenly vanished.

"I'm looking for someone. I'm told you're the only person who might know where he is."

Leila couldn't be sure, but it was as if a hope had flickered for a moment in the woman's face and then suddenly vanished.

"The man's name is Barabbas. He disappeared nearly a year ago and nobody has seen him since. Do you know where he might be?"

"Are you a family member?"

"No, I'm - yes."

The almond coloured eyes seemed to reach into the depths of Leila's soul. Once again, she could see the mistrust in the woman's expression. It was different this time, though. In some ways, less sinister and yet even more vindictive. Leila had seen that expression in women's eyes before, even in those of her closest friends.

The woman nodded slowly and the expression softened as she seemed to gain control of her emotion. "So, you're the reason Barabbas was so insistent on staying in Sepphoris."

"He was away more than he was there."

"I haven't seen him since he left Galilee."

"Do you have any idea where he might have gone?"

Deborah shrugged. "If he wouldn't tell you, what makes you think I will?"

"Please. I must know what happened to him."

The woman sighed and closed her eyes, as if blocking out her own pain. "He went to Caesarea. I sent some among our number there when he didn't return. They lost his trail in the harbour area. Nobody has heard from him since."

"Surely he sent some word."

Deborah chuckled bitterly. "It happens in his line of work, dearie. Men go out and sometimes don't return. You should learn to accept it. Barabbas isn't coming back."

Leila stared into the woman's eyes. The words had been intended to hurt. She realized that, even if this woman knew where Barabbas was, she would never tell her. Jealousy was the cruellest of all emotions. It was something Leila had learned at an early age. Even her sisters had treated her as a leper at times when men had glanced past them to view the younger, more attractive sibling.

Without saying anything more, she turned to leave. At the foot of the steps, she glanced back and saw the penetrating eyes that glowered at her departure. It was only when she reached the top of the steps that the woman called after her.

"When Jericho fell, only Rahab was spared. Tell them that. They'll never let you pass otherwise."

Leila glanced back again and nodded. She continued down the steps on the other side of the wall, repeating the message to the group of men sprawled in the alley below. None of them acknowledged her remark and she began to wonder whether the woman had made it all up.

She only became convinced of how real the danger had been when she approached her uncle's home on the western side of the city. Glancing over her shoulder, she noticed the man following her for the first time. He was one of the drunks from the alley, she was sure of it. Only he wasn't drunk. He feigned interest in the huge castle that was Herod's praetorium, glancing at her out of the corner of his eye.

Leila wondered how long the woman in the courtyard had planned to wait before giving her the code that would save her life, or whether she had perhaps planned not to give it at all and then changed her mind at the last moment. Deborah was a woman to be feared, Leila decided as she knocked at the door of her uncle's home.

She was suddenly despondent at the thought of returning home. Her journey had proved fruitless. She was no closer to finding Barabbas and she had angered her father in the process.

A servant answered the door and Leila sighed as she heard her father's voice emanating from the living room inside. She should have expected him to be there, but hadn't given the matter a thought. He was in earnest conversation with her uncle - something about her whereabouts from what she could hear. With a heavy heart, she entered the home and went to face her father's wrath.

The following day Leila headed home, accompanied by her father and two servants of his household. An uncomfortable silence hung in the carriage as it rocked gently from side to side on its way back to Sepphoris. There was no need for conversation; everything had been said back in Jerusalem. Accusations had been made and voices raised. Even with Leila's uncle present, the argument had run out of all control.

Apologies were owed - both Leila and her father knew that - but none were forthcoming. Instead, a chasm was growing between the two of them. Leila could still see her father's flushed face as he had thrashed about her uncle's living room like an enraged behemoth, cursing like a godless drunkard. He was quiet now, however, and Leila realized that, though they might find harmony again in the future, something had changed in Jerusalem. The bond between father and daughter had been irrevocably severed and their relationship would never be the same again.

Her thoughts turned to Barabbas. How long had it been? A quick calculation showed that it was in fact one Sabbath short of ten months since he'd left for Caesarea. She was surprised at the amount of time that had passed. It had somehow become distorted since he had left. Her days had become such tormented agonies of worry and wondering that she had learned to merely exist, never giving in to emotion or considering the reality of the situation. It was easier to deaden the pain if you didn't think.

Where are you, my love? What could have kept you from me for so long? She was plagued by thoughts of what might have happened to him.

✝ ✝ ✝ ✝ ✝

The sun was already high in the sky, clawing its way to midday, as Zebedee sat brooding over his decision. Leila smiled at him as she entered the living room from the garden outside. Time had healed the wounds that had caused the rift between them, but the scars remained and Zebedee felt as far from his daughter as he had on the road back to Sepphoris.

It was the reason he had put off the conversation for so many months. As an astute businessman, he knew when a negotiation was futile and had decided to bide his time until the moment was more promising, if not right.

Leila glanced across at her father. "The last time I saw you this morose was when Tiberius raised the port taxes."

Zebedee tried to smile, but failed dismally in the attempt. Leila was suddenly concerned.

"What's the matter, father? You look like a professional mourner."

"Please sit, Leila. There's something I need to discuss with you."

She sat down and waited expectantly. It was a while before he spoke.

"This isn't easy for me, but I've given it a lot of thought," he began with a heavy sigh.

Leila remained silent, waiting for him to come to the point. At length, he continued. "I've - watched you over the past year. You mourn for a man who was, in my opinion, never worthy of you. One who placed his beliefs and misguided principles above your happiness."

"That's why I love him. He has passions and beliefs that transcend the ordinary."

"I've watched you await his return, knowing in my heart that day would never come."

"You're wrong about him, father. I know that he's alive and that he will find his way back to me."

"I had hoped for your sake that you were right but, if that were so, he would have returned by now. Surely you must see that, Leila." Zebedee found himself pleading with his daughter.

"I grow weary of this conversation, father. Its interest is dulled by repetition."

"I so desperately wanted you to get past this. To move on with your life, but I realize that this, too, will never happen. You can no more shake the memory of Barabbas than I can bring about his return."

"What was it you wanted to say?" She had become sullen.

"As I said, I've given it a lot of thought." He paused again, staving off the inevitable. *It's no use. You have to tell her.* "Miyka'el has made me an offer. It's a good offer and —"

"And?" Her tone was icy and her face had turned to stone.

Zebedee sighed. "And – I've accepted his offer. I would like you to drink the cup of betrothal with him."

"You want me to do what?" Leila had risen from her seat and stood before her father, shaking with rage and, though she would not admit it, a little fear.

"You heard correctly. I wish for you to marry Miyka'el."

"Never!" The word raged like the *Khamsin* between them.

"He is a good man, Leila. He loves you and will take good care of you."

"I do not love him. Where is the good in that?"

"You will learn to love him in time."

"Eternity would not be long enough! I love another. My heart holds no room for a man like Miyka'el."

Zebedee rose from his seat. "Leila, I'm not asking you to do this. I have made a decision. You will be given in marriage to Miyka'el before a year has passed. You may consider yourself betrothed."

"You would give me in marriage to cement a business deal? That's all this is to you, isn't it? Treating me like a mere bargaining chip."

"It's not like that, Leila."

"It's exactly like that." She spun around and left the room like a receding storm.

"I'm doing this for your own good," Zebedee called after her. "You'll see. In time you will thank me."

His words bounced off the cold, stone walls of his residence and fell unacknowledged on the marble tiles of the empty floor. She was already gone.

This changes nothing, he thought purposefully. *I have made up my mind and nothing will change it.* Reaching for the letter that he had already written, he glanced over its contents. With a nod, he rolled it into a scroll and sealed it.

He handed it to a servant who had been hovering outside the room for the duration of the argument. "Have this sent to Miyka'el, the merchant in Jericho. See that he gets it as soon as possible."

"I'll have it sent immediately, my lord. He should receive it before the coming Sabbath."

After the servant left, Zebedee mulled over Leila's words. It's the right decision, he told himself for the hundredth time. It's for her own good.

21

MIYKA'EL ARRIVED at their home within a month. Leila tried her best to avoid him but it was impossible. She flat refused to drink of the betrothal cup with him but her father remained unmoved. The marriage would happen, he insisted, with or without her consent.

Miyka'el seemed equally unperturbed by her lack of cooperation. He remained in their home for over six weeks. Evening meals were the worst, as it was impossible to avoid him then. She refused to eat with him but, as the lady of the house, it was her duty to serve guests at her father's table. Leila sighed and entered the dining hall, having dismissed the servants for the night.

"It's late and I see no reason why you should suffer while those boors indulge themselves," she had told the staff, who gratefully headed home.

The table was raucous with the mirth of an enjoyable evening and a few too many cups of good wine. Leila returned the good humoured greetings with hostility. She had little time for the men around the table.

"Leila, my dear. It's good of you to help with the clearing." Zebedee grinned good naturedly.

You wouldn't think so if you knew why the servants had left.

To say that their relationship had become strained was an understatement. Since her father had announced her betrothal to Miyka'el, Leila had shut him out completely. Their diminishing conversations had been reduced to emotionless dialogues that merely conveyed information without any feeling or compassion.

Whenever her father had tried to bring up the subject of her engagement, Leila had shut down completely, not even deigning to reply and leaving the room at the earliest opportunity. He had tried on numerous occasions to draw her out of her shell with false bravado and weak attempts at humour, but that had only served to antagonise her further. Instead of getting angry and raising her voice in reply, she had merely withdrawn until he had learned to avoid the subject altogether.

Zebedee had made it plain, however. The wedding would go ahead regardless of her antics and, try as she might, she had been unable to change her father's mind.

She glanced across at the other two men around the table, making sure her gaze merely brushed over Miyka'el without acknowledging his smile or his attempt to make eye contact. The other man was Matthias, Miyka'el's younger brother.

He was a chubby man with a mop of unruly dark hair and short stubby fingers, bedecked with rings. He lifted his nose out of his plate for a moment and wiped the back of his hand across a greasy chin. "We're honoured by the presence of one so beautiful at our table."

"You have food on your face," she replied, looking down as she gathered the empty dishes and turned to leave.

Matthias nudged his brother playfully. "She's a spirited one, brother. She'll make you a good wife."

Leila winced at the words, but didn't turn around. She left the men to their idle chatter and hurriedly returned to the kitchen. All she could do now was wait. Leila busied herself cleaning pots and serving bowls, listening intently for the sound of voices in the dining room.

When there was a lull she returned, hoping to find the men retired for the evening. She was disappointed, however, to find them poring over a document that seemed to be the source of an animated debate.

"I'm telling you, Zebedee, it's authentic. This document came to me via the house of a zealot. He claimed his great-grandfather had inherited the parchment and had been called a protector."

Zebedee threw his head back and laughed. "Did this man also tell you he could show you the river with golden sands where Midas bathed himself?"

"The copper scroll exists. The only question is where to find it and how vast the treasure truly is."

"And you think this document will point you in the right direction."

Miyka'el shrugged. "I admit it's a small beginning, but at least it proves the treasure exists."

With a chuckle, Zebedee continued. "I must remember to write several such documents before my next trip to Jericho. I had no idea it was so easy to get wealthy merchants to part with their wages."

Miyka'el smiled. "It's been a hobby of mine since I was a boy. That's when I heard about the treasure for the first time. I vowed that when I was a wealthy man, I would use my wealth to obtain the scroll."

"The copper scroll is a myth, Miyka'el. A three hundred year old legend, perpetuated by the priesthood in order to explain the mysteries of missing treasures that were pilfered away by wicked men who hid their sin behind their Levitical cloaks." Zebedee grinned.

"Well, if you want no part of the bounty, then don't help us. But I'm telling you, Matthias and I intend to find it. And when we do, the world will reel at the riches in our possession."

Zebedee patted the younger man on his shoulder. "I too was a dreamer when I was your age. It's a good thing you're a wealthy man already because this vast treasure you speak of is like a mirage in the Negev. Young men would spend a lifetime chasing it, only to discover that their greatest assets - their wisdom and the sweat of their brow - have lain wasted their whole lives and left them to die as paupers."

"My riches are nothing compared to the riches I'll have once I find the scroll."

Leila contented herself with clearing what was left of the dishes and returning to the kitchen while the men argued over the mythical document. She continued her work, pacing herself so as not to finish too quickly.

Zebedee stuck his head through the door, interrupting her. "Still busy, daughter?"

"Nearly done. I just thought I'd finish here first."

"Well the rest of us are going to sleep. Don't work too hard. The servants can do that in the morning."

"I won't be much longer."

She continued her work for a while, peering out into the passageway to make sure that nobody was around before she left the kitchen. Once sure nobody was about, she raced quietly through to the atrium where the heavy, iron safe stood against the south wall.

Carefully, Leila extracted a hidden parchment from behind it. She had known it would be secure there as the servants were forbidden to even touch the safe, let alone move it. She peered at the document in the darkness, examining it closely before glancing about one more time. Then she slipped it under her shawl and slunk from the house into the darkened streets of Sepphoris, hoping fervently that she wouldn't have to use it.

Five minutes later, she arrived at the town's local synagogue. Instead of approaching the entrance, she slipped down an alley that ran along the side of the building, hiding in the welcome shadows it provided. Then she waited.

Not many minutes passed before she heard the slow, measured steps as her appointment approached. She couldn't make out the form in the darkness, but knew who the person was. Still, she had to make sure. She remained hidden as the form drew closer.

She stood motionless, waiting for the shadow to pass by. The man stopped for a moment, breathing deeply as he listened intently for any signs of movement. Once again, he walked a few paces and stopped. Still she didn't move, holding her breath so as not to give herself away.

The figure moved forward once again and this time a shaft of moonlight caught his face, illuminating his features until he passed into the next shadow, moving only inches from her recess.

"Jashan," she whispered quietly.

"Bah!" the young man shot back with a startled yell.

"Shhh!" she whispered, glancing nervously about.

"You scared me," he complained.

"Sorry. I had to be sure it was you."

"Who else would be out here at this time of night, and why all the secrecy?"

"I need to ask you a favour, and I daren't let my father, or his friends know what I'm doing."

"*I* don't even know what you're doing."

"It's so brazen it makes me blush, but I'm so desperate I don't know what else to do."

Jashan smiled kindly. "What is it you need from me?"

"As you know, your cousin and I were to be married."

"He spoke of it before he went missing."

"He will return, Jashan. I know it more surely than I know my own name."

"May God hasten the day. My father still blames me for Barabbas' disappearance.

I covered for him when he left."

"My father believes Barabbas is dead."

"So does mine. In fact my whole family does. You still haven't told me what it is you want."

"I've been promised to another man. We are to be married before a year has passed."

"And you don't want to marry this man."

"It's impossible. I would be miserable for the rest of my life."

"How can I help?"

She glanced around furtively before replying. "My father believes he's doing this for my own good. If you were to go to him and ask him for my hand in marriage - it's just possible he might consider your proposal."

"You want me to marry you?" Jashan was incredulous.

"A betrothal. Just until Barabbas returns."

"And if he doesn't?"

"He will, Jashan. Don't tell me you've given up hope as well."

"It'll never work."

"How will we know if we don't try?"

Jashan took her shoulders gently and held her pleading gaze. "Look, your father will see this for what it is. It's common knowledge that I've drunk of the betrothal cup with the daughter of Hirah, the Levite. I'm to be married as soon as I've finished the extension on my father's house. Nobody would believe us if we did this now."

Leila took a deep breath before she replied. "I'm sorry. I didn't know."

"Then you're the only one in Sepphoris."

She hesitated a moment before she continued. "I'd hoped it wouldn't come to this, but I have no choice. The servants are loyal to my father. I can't let anyone in his household know what I'm doing."

She reached under her shawl and extracted the roll of parchment that had been hidden behind the safe. "This is a letter I've written to a friend in Bethany. She's the wife of Ahiezer, the glassblower."

Jashan smiled as he peered at the document in the moonlight. "There can't be too many of those in Bethany. You want me to get this to your friend?"

"Please be careful. If anyone in my father's household found out –"

"I'll send one of my most trusted servants. He won't tell anyone. How will she send her reply?"

"The instructions are in the letter. She must send her reply back with the same man. He can bring it to you."

"And how will I get the message to you?"

"Obviously we can't be seen together. Otherwise everybody will blame you when it happens."

"I know. We'll use the field on the way to the well. You fetch water there, so you pass by it every day. When I receive her reply, I'll tether a donkey to the large oak near the edge."

"An easy signal. I'll sneak out the same night and we can meet here again."

"Same time," Jashan agreed. "We'd better get back before your household notices you're gone."

"It's alright. My father has gone to bed and I sent the servants home early, so nobody was there to see me slip away."

"Just be careful. We'll talk again in a few weeks."

When Leila stole back into the house, she noticed that the safe had shifted slightly from its position against the wall. Must have bumped it, she thought, relieved that she'd noticed it before anyone else had. She quickly leaned against the studded iron box and shifted it back against the wall. The safe was heavy, but she managed to slide it back into position.

Exhausted from her exertion and nervous energy, it wasn't until much later that she realized the implausibility of her conclusion. The safe was far too heavy to have been moved by mistake and to think she had bumped it by accident and shifted it was foolishness that bordered on criminal.

The weeks that followed were an unbearable agony. Each day, she headed for the well gazing in vain hope at the oak tree in the empty field. Nearly three weeks passed before she spotted the young colt tethered to the tree. Her heart leaped and she began to dream of her meeting with Jashan that evening.

Leila returned from the well, carrying a large jar of water as she had done every day since her early teens. She was accompanied by two friends that she usually met with at the well, to catch up on news.

The daily trip was not a chore, but rather a social event that could last for hours as the town's women gathered to ogle over each other's new garments and jewellery, or to hear about the latest engagements and births as well as the triumphs and scandals that formed the vibrance of life in Sepphoris.

She was in no mood for chatting today, however. Ever since she had seen Jashan's donkey tethered to the ancient oak tree, her mind had been in a world far away from the well and the scandals of Sepphoris.

She didn't care about Hilkiah, the butcher who had been brought before the leading Pharisees of the local synagogues for selling camel meat to the unsuspecting population, making himself and everyone who bought it unclean. Some said the accusation was unfair, started by a rabbi in a local synagogue no less, who owned shares in a rival butchery. Hilkiah would probably have to close his shop because of the incident as nobody would ever risk buying meat from him again.

None of this mattered to Leila, however. All she could think about was her impending meeting with Jashan and the news from Bethany.

"Don't you agree, Leila?"

"What?" she turned to her friend Carmen with a guilty start.

"I said Hilkiah will probably be forced to leave Galilee altogether. Maybe even move to a city south of Jerusalem."

Elissa, a tall angular woman spoke. "I think Leila's mind is elsewhere today."

Leila smiled. "Is it that obvious?"

"What are you thinking about?" Elissa was slightly older than the other two and the only married woman among them."

"I was thinking about a place east of Jerusalem," she replied secretively.

"Would your thoughts have anything to do with a certain handsome merchant in

Jericho?" Elissa smiled knowingly.

"Actually, they do," Leila replied. *But not in the way you think.*

Carmen was eager not to change the subject. "Hilkiah has family east of Jerusalem, but I don't think it's in Jericho. It's one of the smaller towns, like Bethphage, or some such place."

Leila was no longer paying attention. They were approaching the oak tree and her eyes were riveted on the spot where the ass was still tethered. Jashan was nowhere in sight and the field was still bare and desolate. The ancient tree had shed its leaves in the face of the approaching winter and now stood bare and lifeless - a withering beacon of hope in a bleak field of dry and vapid soil.

The cold breeze caused Leila to pull her shawl about her. She shivered slightly and then went on her way. Tonight, I will hear what arrangements have been made, she thought. Then I can make my decisions and take control of my own destiny.

That night, Leila rose from her bed long after the household had retired. She hadn't bothered to undress and quickly donned a pair of sandals.

Quietly, and with extreme caution, she slunk through the large family home. She froze when she heard a movement at the far end of the house, near the guest rooms where Miyka'el and his brother were staying. When no further sounds were forthcoming, she continued on her way, fleeing the dark trappings of her home as she raced to her meeting with Jashan.

It wasn't until she had walked about six blocks that she realized she was being followed. She had turned to cross the street and then glanced furtively over her shoulder, just in time to see a shadow dodge into a door recess At any other time she might have thought nothing of it, but guilt, combined with a keen sense of self-preservation, made her turn the next corner, heading away from the clandestine rendezvous.

Her mind raced as she quickened her pace, considering her options as well as the identity of her pursuer. Whoever it was must have followed her from the house, she felt sure. Probably Miyka'el or Matthias, since the noise had come from their rooms.

Leila felt her world changing as she began to experience emotions and instincts she had never felt before. They were frightening and exhilarating at the same time. Is this the life Barabbas experienced, she wondered.

What would he do in this situation, she pondered as her breathing became deeper and her pulse quickened. She turned another corner, running blind as she fleetingly considered her position and what she needed to do.

Do the unexpected. Barabbas' words came to her mind. When your enemy thinks you're in one place, be somewhere else. Leila thought of the lengthy debates they had shared. Many times, the arguments had even become heated and she could still recall her loved one's mocking grin as she battled with fiery eyes and a scorching tongue.

Leila was grateful for those conversations now. As she turned the next corner, she bent down and picked up a loose stone that lay on the street. Then she continued for two blocks before freezing and listening intently for the sounds behind her.

She was rewarded with a scrape as her pursuer, suddenly caught off guard, ground to a halt. Leila stepped forward again, heading towards a narrow alley that led to the vegetable market. It was an area she knew better than any man ever could and the ideal choice for the arena of battle.

In a sudden, lithe movement, she shot to her right and raced ten paces up the alley. The intersection was so dark that she nearly missed it, but she knew it was there. As quickly as she had started to run, she stopped and slipped silently into the narrow alley that led off to her left.

Within moments the panting figure came into view, racing to keep his quarry in sight. He didn't notice the intersection at first and ran right past it. From her darkened recess, Leila recognised Miyka'el's features as he stopped, confused and hunting for a sign of his vanished prey.

Quietly raising her hand, she hurled the stone away from her, down the dark, narrow street opposite. There was no way for Miyka'el to see the stone in the darkness. He could only hear it as it bounced along the darkened alleyway.

Quickly, he whirled around and raced off in the direction of the sound. As he did so, Leila turned and disappeared noiselessly down the alley that had been her refuge.

Fifteen minutes later, having made sure that she was no longer being followed, she approached the darkened street that ran alongside the synagogue.

"Where have you been!" Jashan demanded. "I was about to leave already."

Leila's diaphragm still trembled with the excitement of her escape. "I'm sorry, Jashan. I was followed. I had to be sure nobody could overhear us. What news of Minette in Bethany?"

"Here," Jashan handed her the scrolled letter.

"Did she say anything?"

"Don't you want to read it?"

"In this light! Just tell me what she said."

Jashan grinned. "She's made arrangements for you to stay with her sister-in-law. She awaits your arrival with great anticipation."

"Thank you." She flung herself into Jashan's arms

"Calm down. Now tell me, who was following you?"

"Miyka'el - the man I'm supposed to marry."

"Did he hear you sneak out?"

"I don't think so. I was quiet and he was at the other end of the house."

"So he had somebody alert him to the fact that you were leaving."

Leila blinked, considering the theory for the first time. "I hadn't thought of it like that. Why would he do that though? He had no reason to suspect anything."

"Then you must have given him one. Think back. Did you do or say anything that could have tipped him off?"

"I can't think of anything."

"Try! It's important." Jashan pressed her.

"There was the safe - no, it couldn't have been."

"What about the safe?"

"It – it was moved slightly away from the wall. I must have bumped it when I extracted the letter.

"Nobody bumps a safe hard enough to move it without noticing. Did you push it back?"

"Yes, I did. You're right. It wasn't easy."

"So Miyka'el saw you and went to inspect. When he didn't find anything and saw you'd left the house, he posted a servant near your door at night to keep an eye on your movements. Your fiancé doesn't trust you very well."

"He's not my fiancé." Leila could almost taste the bitterness of her words.

"You can't go back there." Jashan spoke quietly.

"What?"

"They've found out you're up to something and they'll want to know what. You were lucky to escape once. You'll never make it twice."

"But my things. I had money saved."

"If you don't flee Sepphoris tonight, you may not get another chance."

Leila closed her eyes, shaking her head as she considered the possibilities. This was not the way she had planned things.

Jashan shrugged. "Do you want to go back to Miyka'el?"

When she didn't reply, he nodded. "Come. I'll introduce you to the man that carried your message to Bethany. He'll take you to your friend. If you need anything, tell him. I'll arrange it for you, but you must leave Sepphoris tonight."

Leila stopped and looked into Jashan's eyes. "You're a good man, Jashan. I don't know why you're doing this for me."

"I love Barabbas as a brother. He and Simeon always had the courage that I never did. Courage to stand up to Rome – my father. You're the only one left who believes in Barabbas. You give me hope that he will return."

The servant's name was Shamgar, Leila learned, when Jashan had introduced them. The man impressed her immediately with his loyalty. He had not complained when Jashan had woken him in the small hours, but had dutifully fetched some belongings and joined Jashan and Leila at the barn where he had fitted a carriage for the journey to Bethany.

Now, some hours later, Leila sat chatting to the man who had sworn to get her to Bethany in safety and complete secrecy.

"Promise me something, Shamgar," Leila said.

"Anything," Shamgar replied. He was a softly spoken man, Leila had learned on the journey, and one not given to idle chatter.

"When Barabbas returns to Sepphoris, I want you to bring him to me in Bethany, so you can attend our wedding."

The man smiled. "It would be an honour."

Their conversation fell silent as the carriage trundled south towards the city of Jerusalem from whence it would turn east along the road to Bethany. Although Shamgar was not a great conversationalist, he was good company and, above all, she knew her secret would be safe with him.

After an uneventful journey, Leila's reunion with Minette in Bethany was charged with excitement. Minette's animation was a drastic change from Shamgar's quiet nature and seemed to dance with excitement as she rushed to greet her friend.

"Please, you must stay with me for a few days before you move across to my husband's sister. She's no more than a half hour's journey from here, but we have so much to catch up on."

"What have you told her about me?" Leila asked nervously.

Minette smiled. "The truth, of course. That your family turned against you and made it impossible for you to remain there. She's very excited about your arrival. I think the two of you will have a lot in common."

"What makes you say that?"

"She's also one who believed in Jesus of Nazareth from the first, long before that fateful Passover. She meets with the church at the house of Lazarus and can't wait to take you there. He knew Jesus of Nazareth extremely well. You know, the rabbi often stayed with Lazarus before he was put to death."

"I'm sure he knows him still," Leila replied softly. "Have you never thought of embracing his teachings?"

Minette laughed in protest. "My dear friend! I get enough of this from my sister-in-law. It's not his teachings I reject, but his claims. Come, we have so much to catch up on. You must tell me everything that's been happening. I couldn't believe your letter. You and your father have always been so close."

† † † † †

Back in Sepphoris, Zebedee's household was frantic. Servants and friends rushed through his home like the Jordan River in flood, as Zebedee waited for any news of his daughter. All the reports came back equally disappointing. Leila had disappeared without a trace.

Her friends were summoned, as well as people like Carmen and Elissa that she met at the well, but she had given them no indication of where she might be headed. They were as surprised as her father.

"I only hope she's alright." His voice sounded like a mournful wind. "Anything could have happened to her."

Miyka'el consoled him. "I'm sure she's fine. Wherever she is, I'm certain of this much. She arranged her own disappearance."

"Tell me everything again. There must be some clue as to where she might be."

"The first time it happened, you had already gone to bed. I forgot my documents in the dining hall and returned to fetch them. That was when I heard her at your safe in the atrium."

"But what would she want there? She can't open it. I have the only key."

"She took something from behind it – I couldn't see what it was – and then slipped from the house."

"Did you follow her?"

"I was already undressed. By the time I had pulled on a tunic and sandals, she was gone. I checked behind the safe, but couldn't find anything."

"And the second time?"

"That was last night. I had left my attendant to guard her door every night – as her fiancé, you can understand my concern – with instructions to call me if she rose and left her room. This time she didn't go near the safe. She headed north towards the market, but she must have known I was following her."

"Did she hear you leave the house?"

Miyka'el shook his head. "She was acting strangely, turning this way and that. When she finally fled, I had no idea which way she'd gone. The last I heard was when her foot caught a stone as she fled up an alley near the fruit market."

"So you never saw her again."

"I followed the sound and checked all the other offshoots from the alley, but she'd vanished."

"Perhaps she was trying to reach one of her sisters, or a friend maybe."

Miyka'el sighed. "I'm afraid your daughter is too shrewd for that. Wherever she's gone, she would have chosen an unlikely ally. It would be somebody you barely know, if at all."

"So what do you suggest?"

"A reward. Put the word out that you'll pay a sum of money to anyone bringing information concerning her whereabouts. I'll match whatever offer you make. That will double the incentive and, perhaps, swing loyalties our way."

✝ ✝ ✝ ✝ ✝

The large converted barn buzzed like a beehive in poppy season. Dozens of women spun and sewed industriously. Leila gazed about the giant room with a troubled look as she quietly reached up and touched her bare neck. She'd noticed for the first time early that morning that the necklace was gone. Her first assumption was that it had fallen off somewhere in the factory while she was working, but she'd spoken to all the women there and none of them had seen the beautiful jewel.

None of them would have stolen it, she felt sure. Everybody knew how much the necklace meant to her. It must be at home, Leila thought. She longed to return there and look for it, but Minette was out, having escorted one of the staff home. Jessica had been pregnant when she started working for them some seven months earlier and had insisted on working right into her final month. When she had fallen ill earlier in the day, Minette had insisted she leave immediately and only return once the child was weaned.

It was all Leila and Minette could do to stop the woman lifting heavy bundles of garments even so far into her term and they had both agreed that it would be best for Jessica to stop work for a while.

What's taking so long? Leila was becoming desperate. The necklace was the only memory that she had left to cling to. If it was gone! She shivered at the thought of losing it.

Nearly a year had passed since her arrival and she had found Bethany a welcome haven. Minette's family had taken her in as one of their own and the bond had strengthened between her and her childhood friend.

Leila had been unable to sit idle for long after reaching Bethany and the thought of mundane work around the house had revolted her. She had suggested to Minette that they start making garments of clothing and selling them in Jerusalem.

Now, after only nine months, they employed eight other women and their garments fetched the highest prices of any in the markets of the Holy City.

As soon as she returns, Leila thought, I'll go home and find it. It has to be there. She was suddenly flooded with relief as Minette stepped through the door. There was a woman by her side who looked vaguely familiar. At first Leila couldn't place the woman, but then she remembered their earlier meeting.

Minette grinned. "You remember Naomi?"

"You introduced us last week," Leila nodded as she replaced a finely woven fabric, fresh from the spindle.

The woman nodded in greeting, but her eyes never left Leila's. Her stare made Leila uncomfortable and she turned to speak to Minette instead.

"Minette, I need to go home quickly. Can you look after the factory while I'm gone?"

"With pleasure," her friend beamed. "Are we on target for our next delivery?"

"We'll probably have a hundred garments ready for transport to Jerusalem by the end of the week."

"Wonderful!" Minette exclaimed. "Our greatest number yet."

"And growing each week." Leila endured the conversation, but she ached to leave.

"We still can't keep up with the demand," Minette complained. "Even if we doubled our production, they would still be yelling for more."

Leila grinned and shook her head. "One step at a time, my friend. First we need to train more staff. We daren't increase production at the cost of quality."

"That's why I've brought Naomi to see you. She's just recently arrived in Bethany and her workmanship is exquisite. Look at this seam."

Leila's eyes were drawn from the cloth back to Naomi's face. The woman hadn't averted her eyes for a moment and Leila could feel them following her every tiny gesture.

She forced a smile as she examined the seam of the woman's robe. "This is good quality."

"Thank you." The woman's tone was so subdued that Leila wondered whether she was capable of raising it. She didn't smile and her eyes still bored into Leila with a sort of morbid fascination.

"When did you arrive in Bethany?"

"About three weeks ago, with my husband."

"And where did you come from?"

"Up north, near Galilee." The woman averted her eyes for the first time and Leila could have sworn she saw the woman's lips twitch as she answered.

"I see." Leila gazed back at the cloth thoughtfully. "It's a long way from Galilee."

The ensuing silence was intended to make the woman uncomfortable, almost forcing a response, and it achieved its goal.

"He came to help his cousin with his business. We've been thinking of moving here for some time."

"His name?" Leila's voice was casual as she continued to study the fabric.

"What?"

Leila looked up sharply. "What's your husband's name!"

The woman stuttered nervously. "His - his name's - er"

"Hilkiah." Minette interrupted. "I told you about him, don't you remember?"

"No I don't." Leila swallowed. She suddenly felt dizzy, as if the world had begun to spin about her. "Will you excuse me? I need to fetch something at home."

She turned and fled from the room, leaving Minette wide-eyed and confused.

† † † † †

"I'm sorry, Naomi. She's not normally like this. I'll just go and see what the matter is." Minette rushed after her but when she reached the street outside, Leila had disappeared.

"Did you see where she went?" Minette asked a servant who was busy unpacking large bundles of scarlet cloth from a wagon outside.

"I think she was headed home," the man replied. "She didn't say anything, but she was running like a gazelle that had taken fright."

When Minette reached Leila's home, she found her friend frantically searching through her belongings, some of which had been hastily thrown into a palm-fronded bag.

"Leila, what's going on with you? You're not normally like this."

"I'm looking for my necklace!"

"Why did you run out like that?"

"She knows - she knows who I am." Leila called as she hunted frantically through a cupboard for the jewelled chain.

"What are you talking about!"

"Sepphoris!" Leila snapped as she continued her search. "Hilkiah is from Sepphoris. He was a butcher there."

"They never said they were from Sepphoris. They could come from anywhere in Galilee."

"I'm telling you, they know me. I have to leave."

Minette laughed to ease the tension. "You're jumping to conclusions, my friend."

Leila left the cupboard open and began searching under the bed. "I can see it in her eyes, Minette. I'll be alright if I leave now - where is my necklace!" she cried in desperation.

"The one with the blue stones?"

Leila nodded. "I couldn't find it this morning."

"It's at my house. You were outside somewhere and Jessica brought it to me just before I took her home. It must have fallen off while you were working in the sewing room."

"Thank the Lord!" Leila almost sobbed with relief. "I have to leave now."

"But where will you go?"

"Jerusalem. I'll take a room at an inn there until I make up my mind where to go."

"Aren't you overreacting? Hilkiah and Naomi have no reason to betray you even if they recognise you, which I doubt."

"I can't deduce their motives, Minette, but I'm sure they've sent word to my father."

Minette shook her head, but there was no arguing with Leila when she was in this sort of mood. "How can I help?"

"We need to fetch my necklace. Barabbas gave it to me. I won't leave without it. Then just don't tell anyone where I've gone. I'll send word to you later to have my things sent on."

Having packed her bag, Leila fled through the large empty home. Minette raced after her, bumping into her friend as Leila came to an abrupt halt. The front door stood slightly ajar and Leila stared in horror at the sight in the street beyond. A group of men had just arrived outside the home, some of whom she recognised as Miyka'el's employees. At the head of the group was Matthias, Miyka'el's younger brother.

Minette was stunned. "You were right. How could they have got here so quickly!"

"Miyka'el lives in Jericho. Quick! We must use another exit." She spun on her heels and headed to the far end of the house with Minette in tow. Leila managed to squeeze through a tiny window on the second floor of the home just as they heard the banging on the front door.

"Go and answer it." Leila instructed her friend. "If anyone can stall them, you can. Just give me as long a start as you can."

Minette squeezed her friend's hand and then rushed to the door to intercept the servants while Leila slipped from the window and groped her way along the ledge outside with her legs dangling below her, looking for a purchase on the wall that ran from just below the window away from the home.

† † † † †

In the early morning sun, Eleazor lay in wait, hiding amongst the rocks in the barren Judean desert. The sun drummed on his sweating back as he lay quietly awaiting his signal. Across from him, Joses, the gang's leader waited patiently for the call. The group of unsuspecting travellers was on its way to Jericho, unaware of the impending danger.

As he waited, Eleazor reflected on the events that had brought him here. After fleeing Jerusalem he had found refuge among the *Fellahin*, the farmers who lived in the arid wilderness east of Jerusalem, eking out a living in the barren desert soil. The Romans had been more persistent in their search than he had expected and he had been driven even further east where he had joined a band of *Bedouin*, wandering desert dwellers who lived far beyond the reach of the Roman Empire in the harsh desert land. This lifestyle had not suited him, however, and he had begun to enquire about the highwayman, Joses. He had learned that the group usually found their way to Masada where they bought supplies, trading their stolen goods for cash.

Risking discovery, he had headed to the mountain-fortress where careful enquiry had led him to a market that the band frequented. There he had spotted Abimelech, the large man who had brought him his horse the day he had met Joses on the road between Jerusalem and *Qumran*.

Instead of approaching him directly which, he knew, would only draw aggression, he had followed the man discreetly back into the desert to Joses' hideout. There, he had waited until he could approach Joses alone. He got his chance late in the afternoon when the bandit leader went to relieve himself outside the camp.

"You should be more careful, walking alone in the desert like this." Eleazor announced his presence.

Joses had whirled around in shock, drawing his sword as he did so. He smiled, sheathing his weapon when he saw Eleazor. "The stranger who moves with the stealth of desert sands. How did you find us?"

"It took some time, but I heard you bought supplies in Masada. I waited and followed your Goliath with the earrings. I see his skills have not improved since last we met."

"I'll have to have another word with him," Joses replied with a wry smile. "Am I to assume you've come to offer your services?"

"Jerusalem has become an undesirable place to live. I had hoped you could find a use for my skills."

"As it happens, I have a vacancy. Ben Ammi, my second-in-command was killed in a raid some months back. I can't put you in charge of the men immediately but, with your talents and abilities, I'm sure they will accept you as a leader in a very short space of time."

That had been nearly two years ago. Since then, Eleazor had become a trusted member of the band of outlaws. He had proved himself a capable warrior and a strong leader. The men had learned skills that they had not believed possible and had become one of the stealthiest and most lethal groups of highway robbers in the Judean desert. Even Abimelech had learned to move like a desert cat and could sneak up on the most alert of travellers undetected.

Now Eleazor lay in wait, listening for the signal to attack. It came in the form of a shrill whistle that sounded like the cry of the masked shrike, small birds with hooked bills that abounded in the area. The victims of the attack were a group of armed civilians who well knew the dangers that lurked on desert highways. They were well prepared for such dangers but even so, they were hopelessly outclassed. The battle was short and one-sided. It ended with an aftermath of bodies strewn about the area while, among the outlaw gang's number, only Abimelech had sustained any injury. The battle left him nursing a deep cut that ran across his bulging shoulder and down into the upper part of his bicep.

"Quickly," Joses called from his vantage point. "Clear all these bodies away and round up the mules. Make sure you remove any valuables from the bodies before you dispose of them. And somebody attend to Abimelech's injury. I don't want blood all over the stones, giving away our presence to the next group of travellers that pass this way."

He strolled across to Eleazor. "The take should be good today. This was a wealthy party."

"Those mules will fetch a handsome price, too," Eleazor agreed.

"We might as well pack up now and head back to the camp. The sun grows high and it's getting too hot to work."

"I think we've earned a rest. This should amount to a week's take once it's all tallied up."

Later that evening, the men relaxed around a campfire. Eleazor joined Joses who basked in the warmth of the flames.

He nodded towards the leather pouch that hung from Joses' wrist. It was a holy artefact containing extracts of scripture usually worn to the temple or at prayer time. "I never thought of you as a religious man."

Joses smiled. "I'm not. I took this off the body of an Essene I murdered. Sometimes I feel bad for killing a holy man. I don't know why I kept this really. Perhaps it was to remind me that there is still good in some parts of the world."

"Why did you kill him?"

Joses shrugged. "The usual reason. I wanted his money. There were four of them, headed for Jerusalem."

Eleazor looked up sharply. "A group of four? When was this?"

Joses frowned, trying to remember. Suddenly he laughed. "Ironically, it was the same day I met you. You were a few hours behind them."

"I asked you about them that day. You said you hadn't seen them."

The bandit shrugged again. "It's possible. I can't remember what I said. You did, however, have a knife to my throat. I probably lied to you on general principle. Why were you so interested in them? They had nothing of value."

"They had information I needed. It's not important, although it was at the time." Eleazor hoped the half-truth would allay any suspicions.

"What was so important that you had to learn from them?"

"They knew the whereabouts of a man I was looking for. Have you heard of Barabbas?"

"The zealot? I know him by reputation. They say he's possibly the greatest leader the zealots ever had."

Eleazor snorted. "The only thing great about him is his opinion of himself. He's an arrogant fool who put the lives of his men in constant danger, although he never risked himself."

"You didn't like him then."

"We have an ongoing vendetta. The day will come when I will kill him. That's what I'd hoped to do in Jerusalem the day you tried to rob me."

"Since the Essenes were killed, I assume you never found him."

"No. I found him. We met twice in Jerusalem, but they were turbulent times. Both incidents were interrupted by Roman soldiers and we had to flee the city. I haven't seen him since, but I will."

"Well, I'm going to sleep." Joses rose from his place near the fire. "I'll talk to you in the morning. It's time we headed for Masada again to sell our takings."

Eleazor nodded but made no effort to rise. His mind was racing and his heart pulsed with excitement. Could it be that he had found the scroll? One thing he knew for sure. Joses hadn't found it on the Essenes after the attack. If he had, he would have long since retrieved the treasure and retired on the money.

It had to lie somewhere between *Qumran* and the place where Joses had attacked the Essenes. Only a few miles. How hard can it be to find?

He quickly began to formulate a search plan.

22

BARABBAS GRINNED as he made his cautious way down the slope. His path led to the city gates, which were lined with lush grass that grew as high as a man's knees and a forest of date palms. With a contented sigh, he finally approached the city of Jericho.

His arduous journey had led him through the Numidian deserts, via Egypt and the fertile Nile delta which stretched for miles like an emerald blade through the stark and barren lands of Northern Africa. His travels had taken him through the dazzling city of Alexandria, founded by Alexander the Great. It had flourished through the centuries and become one of the largest and most powerful centres of trade and learning in the Roman world.

He had gazed in awe at the gigantic lighthouse that towered above the city with the flaming torch at its pinnacle. It was the only time that Barabbas had relented in his journey eastwards, but he had insisted that they wait until sunset to see the mammoth structure lighting up the darkness.

From there, he and Levi had continued through the lush delta, taking boats across the famous river of the ancient world and pushing on into the Sinai desert beyond. They had traded their total accumulated savings for camels. The trip through the harsh land had lasted over a month as they sought constant refuge from the sun and the inevitable *Khamsin* which blew from the east.

Sinai had given way to the Negev as they moved further east and, for the first time, Barabbas had felt he had arrived home. Finally he had come upon Masada, the giant fortress built by Herod, which stood on its natural rock mound. It was the homecoming Barabbas had dreamed of across all the arduous miles in his journey from Carthage.

The camels had been sold and the two weary travellers had taken the opportunity to enjoy the many luxuries that the fortress had to offer. Hot baths had washed the caked dust from their bodies and clothes, while new sandals and delicious food from his native land were purchased in the market place that thronged with people.

Barabbas had spent the night there before leaving Levi and heading north for Jericho. Levi had decided to remain in Masada to try and make contact with the zealot faction once more.

Although the faces and codes may have changed over the previous two years, some things would never change. The zealots would definitely still be found at Masada. On the surface, the fortress community may have looked peaceful, but there was an undercurrent of rebellion there that would never rest until the emperor was overthrown and his forces driven permanently from Palestine.

Now hope rose within Barabbas as he descended the last stretch, moving through the desert towards the glittering oasis that stood out in stark contrast to the barren rock around it. Jericho was a city of palms and abundant vegetation that flourished amidst the copious supply of water from Elisha's spring in the midst of the Judean wilderness.

It was a strategic outpost that received the trade route from the east and its economy had blossomed as much as its vegetation. The wealthiest men in Israel either lived in Jericho permanently or resided there during the winter months, in luxurious homes that many religious sects had condemned as so decadent that they bordered on sinful. Indeed, Jericho was a city that was synonymous with sin in the minds of the people, but nobody could deny its beauty or the quality of the dates and many other crops that abounded in its fertile soil.

For Barabbas, it was also the city where he would find Leila, as Zebedee's winter home was in the oasis. It was a mansion of palatial size that dripped with wealth and comfort. Barabbas increased his pace as his yearning became more urgent, longing to hold her in his arms and breathe the perfumed scent of her hair.

Once he'd entered the city, it didn't take long to locate Zebedee's house. After being ushered in by a bald servant with skin that had the lustre of polished ebony, Barabbas waited impatiently in the atrium of Zebedee's home.

"Whom shall I say is calling?" The servant was obviously new. Barabbas had never seen him before.

"Just tell him it's an old friend."

He turned at Zebedee's approach and the older man froze as he recognised his guest. His shock was complete and he trembled as if the ground beneath him was about to give way.

"What's the matter, Zebedee? Don't you greet your future son-in-law?"

"Barabbas!" Leila's father choked out the word.

Barabbas smiled. "It's good to see you again."

"We thought you were dead." The words were uttered in a hoarse whisper.

"So did I, for a while," Barabbas replied, lost in thought as he considered the many nights spent without food or shelter. Months spent hiding from Roman soldiers as he tried to eke out a living or scrounge a few coins to help pay for the next leg of his relentless journey eastward to the land of his birth. "I've got so much to tell you, but first, where's Leila?"

"Come, you must first eat something, and let's have your feet washed. I can tell you've had an arduous journey."

He led Barabbas through to an intimate dining hall where Barabbas related the story of his capture while a slave came and washed his feet. Zebedee launched a barrage of questions which carried on until well after the food had arrived.

Barabbas eventually waved a hand to forestall any more curiosity. "That's all behind me now. Please, you must fetch Leila for me. I want to marry her as soon as possible."

The old man was evasive. "If you remember, I never promised her to you. I merely said I would think about it."

"Come on, Zebedee. Enough of these silly games. I love your daughter and I'll be a good husband. Besides, these past years have changed me. I have no interest in fighting a pointless battle any more. Where is she?"

Zebedee sighed and hung his head. "She's not here. I did a foolish thing. She told me you'd return, but I'd given up hope. When I tried to force her to marry Miyka'el, she fled to Bethany."

"You did what!"

The old man looked up at Barabbas, his expression consumed with pain.

"She disappeared, leaving no trail to follow. I didn't even know she'd gone to Bethany until a butcher from Sepphoris told me he'd seen her there."

"What happened then?" There was a knife-edge menace in Barabbas' voice.

"We sent servants along with Miyka'el's brother to fetch her. She was about to flee again when they found her."

"And where is she now?"

"It's no use, Barabbas."

"Where!"

The anguish showed in the old man's eyes. "They were married three weeks ago. God have mercy on me, what have I done!"

But for the fact that the man was Leila's father, Barabbas could have killed him where he lay across the table. He was silent for a long time, trying to gain control of his emotion before he replied. When he spoke, the words were quiet with no inflection.

"Tell me where Miyka'el's house is."

"Barabbas, she's married to another now. No good can come from your going there."

Barabbas sat up and leaned across the table. "I'm not leaving here until you tell me."

"May God strike me down if I tell you. I won't assist you in this folly."

With a growl, Barabbas reached across the table and plucked the old man from his seat. He dragged Zebedee across the table, upsetting bowls of fruit and food with such a racket that the servants rushed to see what was going on

Zebedee recoiled from Barabbas' onslaught, tearing the sleeve of his tunic as he defended himself. Barabbas suddenly froze in shock as Zebedee flung his bare arm up to protect his face. The gesture was futile, but the jagged scar on the man's forearm left Barabbas stunned.

In a daze, he let Zebedee slip from his grasp. The man was shaken and quickly waved the servants away as he slipped back into his seat.

With a glare, Barabbas pointed an accusing finger Zebedee. "So, you're the coward who forsook his oath in pursuit of worldly riches."

Zebedee frowned as he straightened his tunic. "I never forsook my oath. The secret still rests in my heart. I've never breathed it to a living soul."

"Did you know I was involved?"

Zebedee nodded. "From the start. Your scar was still fresh on the road to Sepphoris. It's why I discouraged your interest in my daughter. I know what price the scroll demands. It's no life for Leila."

"So instead you gave her to another."

The old man's eyes brimmed with tears as he shook his head in despair. "Barabbas, if you'd only come back. Did you find it?"

"What do you care? You relinquished your responsibilities." Then he glanced up sharply. "How did you know it was gone?"

"I'm a merchant. It's my business to read people. Only when you know a man's hidden thoughts can you deal with him properly and persuade him to part with his wages. Your veiled secrecy before you left was as obvious as was the depth of your fear. The combination could mean only one thing. The scroll was in jeopardy. Where is it?"

Barabbas shrugged and shook his head. "It was nearly discovered. Nathaniel and one other determined to move it. The young man who moved it was killed before he could tell any of the remaining protectors where he'd hidden it."

"He lost it! Did this man leave no clue to its whereabouts?"

"He spoke of *Dov Harim* near the *Qumran* valley. He was delirious. There's no such place."

The old man gazed at the table, deep in thought. "You have to find it, Barabbas. Have you considered that he might have been more lucid than you'd believed?"

"I'm assured that's not the case."

"You say he was young. Did he grow up in *Qumran?*" There was an urgency in Zebedee's voice.

Barabbas' weary nod conveyed his disinterest in the conversation. His mind was on Leila and the whereabouts of Miyka'el's home. It was only much later that he would begin to grasp what the old man was getting at.

Zebedee continued. "So it's safe to assume that he played in the hills as a child. If you're ever to find the scroll, you have to see the *wadi* through a child's eyes, Barabbas."

"I don't care about the scroll. I want to see Leila!"

Zebedee gazed hard at Barabbas, nodding slowly as he weighed him up. "Now you finally understand why I forsook my duties and left the movement."

Barabbas looked up. "For the love of a woman?"

Zebedee nodded. "She gave me three wonderful daughters. It ripped my heart apart when she died."

"Then you know how I feel, Zebedee. You have to tell me where Leila is."

"To what end? Would you make an adulteress of her? She'll never consent to that."

"I can find Miyka'el's home. There must be hundreds in the city who would tell me where he lives."

"You're right, of course. But not in this household."

"Then we have no further business." Barabbas rose and nodded a hostile goodbye.

As he was leaving, Zebedee called after him. "Remember, Barabbas. Unless you become like a little child, you cannot hope to ever see the scroll again. God will show you the way."

Dusk found Barabbas espying Miyka'el's palatial home near the edge of the city. The house was impressive, even by Jericho's standards. The huge structure followed Idumean lines, copying the architecture of Herod the Great with its large stones and strong Hellenic influence.

He remained hidden from view in the lengthening shadows of the twilight sky as he observed the wide entrance to the grounds. The gate was well guarded and would be shut come nightfall. Turning around, he gazed back at the sinking sun. The clouds on the horizon blazed orange and yellow like fiery chariots racing across a distant plain.

He had to get inside before the gates closed. To simply walk up and ask to see Leila was as foolish as it was futile. Nobody in the household would allow a strange man to go in and see the master's wife.

For what felt like the hundredth time, Barabbas examined the towering walls. They had the appearance of smooth marble cliffs. The thought of scaling those walls under a blanket of darkness held no appeal. He would have to bluff his way in.

Once again, his eyes fell on the guards at the gate. There were two of them, leaning casually against the heavy gateposts. They were not warriors but brawny henchmen, obviously hired to keep away overzealous salesmen trying to peddle their wares. A man like Miyka'el would probably have hundreds of unwanted merchants and charlatans attempting to gain access every week, each offering a new way for him to part with his fortune.

The guards were infinitely capable of dealing with the rabble that collected outside the gates. They were large, stocky and looked as if they would be free and fast with their fists if the need arose.

To bluff his way in would not be easy. These were men who dealt with glib tongues every day. If only Levi were with him. One extra pair of hands was all he would need. Barabbas thought about it for a moment and then rose and left, heading for the synagogue.

† † † † †

In the serene gardens of Miyka'el's home, Leila rested near a fountain that gurgled in the large round pool. From her vantage point, she could see the wide gates that led onto the property.

The two mammoth guards lounged against the gateposts as they had done every day since she had arrived after her wedding. Today they were distracted, however, as two drunks had started a brawl in the street outside. Although she was too far away to make out the words, the angry voices reached her ears as the tension mounted. Leila watched with an amused smile as the two drunks became more aggressive. The guards exchanged knowing grins as the antagonists became more heated.

Suddenly, a third bystander joined the argument. That was when matters took a turn for the worse. Aggression suddenly erupted in violence and more people quickly joined the melee. Leila watched in amazement as the quiet street was instantly transformed into a surging storm of bodies. One was flung from the group and lurched into one of the gate guards.

By then the stocky guard had had enough. He steadied the man and stepped forward to break up the remaining antagonists. His good intentions were badly received as three of the brawlers rounded on him, pummelling his torso with such vigour that the second guard had to come to his comrade's rescue. Between them, the two guards managed to pry apart the lunging and clawing bodies and within seconds, the brawl had dissipated.

Soon, men began to scatter as they heard the approaching sound of hobnail sandals. By the time the Roman guard arrived, no trace of the brawl remained. It was as if it had been carefully orchestrated.

In the fury of the battle, nobody had noticed the skulking figure slip from the shadows and into the grounds of the wealthy estate. Even from her vantage point, Leila's attention had been so transfixed on the surprising battle that she had missed the fleeting figure as it slipped through the gates.

Barabbas had not missed her, however. He had caught sight of her while he sat in the shadows across from the gates to the mansion and then waited patiently for his zealot friends to create the diversion.

Leila was about to rise and go inside when Barabbas slipped from the undergrowth, gently grasping her shoulders as he inhaled the wondrous scent of her hair.

She spun to face her assailant. "What do you think you're doing?"

"Hello, Leila," Barabbas smiled in greeting.

"Barabbas." Leila froze as she stared into the face she'd dreamed of seeing for so many months. Her voice sounded hostile, she thought, as she gazed upon her lost love. It was only with a conscious effort that she prevented herself from leaping into his arms.

Leila's mind was a thundering torrent of conflicting thoughts and emotions. Relief, joy, anger and love heaved like a turbulent sea at the sight of him.

Barabbas spoke with a nervous grin. "Is that any way to greet the man you were betrothed to?"

"Where have you been?" her voice was still a husky monotone.

"Carthage. I was kidnapped and sold into slavery."

Leila forced a smile. "I'm glad to see you're safe."

"Only glad?" Barabbas reached for her, but Leila stopped him.

"No, Barabbas. You're too late."

"You no longer want me?" Barabbas was puzzled.

She looked down, fearful that he would melt her resolve. "I belong to another now."

"Do you feel anything for him?"

"What I feel is irrelevant. I took a vow before God."

"Leila, stop this foolishness. What is Miyka'el to you? Come away with me. We can forget this place and build a life together."

Leila closed her eyes and shook her head. "I thought you knew me better than that, Barabbas, and I had hoped that some of my convictions would rub off on you."

She could see that for the first time, Barabbas was beginning to understand. He was also becoming angry.

"Leila, what are you telling me? For two years I was held against my will and I have travelled across the length of the Roman world just to be with you. The only thing that kept my sanity was the thought of seeing you again and this is the reception I get!"

"I waited for you, Barabbas!" Leila's raised voice was filled with anger and grief. She knew her words were a punishment, but she couldn't prevent her anger. "For nearly two years I stalled my father's decision. When he finally betrothed me to Miyka'el I fled, but still you never came. You were too busy to think of me."

"I thought of you every day that I was in slavery. I risked torture and death to come to you sooner. Would you deny our love because of circumstance?"

"I'm a married woman, Barabbas."

Barabbas nodded and when he spoke, it was with all the malevolence of Hades. "Then I will find your husband and release you from your vows."

"You wouldn't!"

"Why not? I already carry the blood of hundreds on my hands. What is one more?"

"As the Lord lives, Barabbas, if you do this, I will remain a widow for the rest of my days. I would never marry a man who had killed another to take me as his wife."

For a long moment, Barabbas held her gaze. Finally he shrugged. "So it's over. I should just as well have remained a slave and died in Carthage."

"Please leave, Barabbas. If Miyka'el finds you here, he'll kill you."

"He'll try." Barabbas replied with a bitter smile as he turned to go.

He'd gone no more than a few paces when Leila called after him. "Barabbas, what will you do now?"

"What I've always done. My home is with the zealots. They're my family. They'll receive me and I can count on their loyalty. For a while, I thought I could put that behind me, but I see that notion was foolish. The zealots are my future."

"You still seek your freedom in circumstance. When will you realize that true freedom can only be found within?"

Barabbas disregarded her words. "Send my regards to your husband."

Leila watched as he walked away. Bitter tears moistened her cheeks as she watched him stroll through the gates, leaving the puzzled guards to wonder where he had come from. Once he was out of sight, she sank to the ground and sobbed, hiding her grief-stricken face in her arms.

The fountain gurgled in sympathy as its tranquillity enveloped her sorrow. Some time later, she rose and went into the house. Its opulent candle stands and decor had suddenly become a prison cell from which there was no escape.

† † † † †

Barabbas raced into the desert with Jericho silhouetted on the horizon behind him. The stark wilderness embraced his solitary form as he turned south, heading for *Qumran*.

There were no dark thoughts of self-pity, for Barabbas loathed weakness of any form. Instead, he buried his sorrow in anger that burned as hatred. He directed his hatred at his amorous feelings which, on reflection, were a weakness. He would never permit himself such weakness again. Not for any woman.

Leila's rejection had been a lesson. She had been a diversion, distracting him from his true purpose. In the cold fury of her rejection, Barabbas knew what that purpose was. He would rejoin the zealots in their nationalist cause and wreak destruction on Rome, but above all else, he would find the scroll and unleash its secret to bring about Rome's final undoing.

He would bury himself in his cause and thus forget Leila forever. Soon he would be so busy that thoughts of her would begin to fade, until she became nothing more than a distant mist in an ocean of memories.

The first step was *Qumran*. Levi was the only other surviving protector of the scroll. It was fitting that they should find it together. Slowly, his thoughts turned to the matter of the scroll's disappearance. Mattithyahu had been a true protector. He would not have been so irresponsible as to lose it. Wherever the scroll was, it was well hidden and Mattithyahu had tried to tell Nathaniel where it was.

He found Levi in the *wadi Qumran*, already training young zealots in the art of swordsmanship. The man had wasted no time in finding the zealots and resuming his duties, Barabbas thought. The eager young men hooted and yelled as Levi defended himself against four aggressors simultaneously.

A cheer rose from the small crowd of onlookers as Levi casually disarmed the last of his opponents and levelled his sword at the young man's throat.

"You are as fast with a sword as you are strong, Amos. But remember, technique and expertise will always outweigh strength and stamina. You didn't protect your inside and you paid the price. In battle, you would have paid dearly."

Barabbas taunted his friend while he was still a way off. "The jackal defends himself easily against pups that still suckle mothers' milk, but how does he fare against a true warrior?"

"Barabbas!" Levi laughed as he turned to greet his friend.

There was a hushed awe among the young zealots as they laid eyes on Barabbas for the first time. Until now, they had known him only by reputation. In his absence, the stories of his exploits had grown to legendary proportions. Barabbas had become a hero and martyr of the Jewish nationalists as well as a symbol of freedom for all revolutionaries in Palestine. News of his death had fuelled his legend and made him immortal in the minds of those who carried on his legacy.

"I need to talk. It's urgent" Barabbas was suddenly serious.

"Carry on, gentlemen. I'll be back shortly." Levi followed Barabbas until they were out of earshot.

"Where's Leila?" Levi ventured cautiously.

"Forget about her. I'm here about the scroll. Did you know her father was the prodigal protector?"

"What!" Levi was shocked.

"I saw the scar on his arm and he as much as admitted it. Why did you never mention it?"

"I didn't know. He walked away before your father recruited me. They would never talk of him by name. He was dead to them. How did you find out about this?"

Barabbas shrugged. "It's not important. I've decided to go after the scroll. I want you to help me find it."

"Barabbas, it's vanished. Are you proposing we walk the entire length of the wilderness, upturning every rock we find?"

"There is a trace of it. I don't believe Mattithyahu lost it. The fault was not his, but Nathaniel's in misunderstanding him and mistaking his words for delirious ramblings."

"I'm not following you."

"Zebedee asked about the scroll and I told him what had happened."

"You walk a fine line with your oath, Barabbas," Levi cautioned him.

"It wasn't as if he'd never heard of it. He's still a protector."

"Who broke the loop!"

Barabbas ignored him. "He said the strangest thing. He suggested that Mattithyahu would have played in the hills around *Qumran* as a child and that to find the scroll, we had to look through the eyes of a child."

"Sounds as if he's just as delirious as Mattithyahu was."

"I think I have an idea of what he meant."

"We don't even know where to start looking."

"We have Mattithyahu's words."

Levi shook his head. "Delirious words of a dying man."

"He was delirious, but I'll wager that man had a strength none of us gave him credit for. I believe that through his delirium, sanity prevailed and a dying man passed a message to those left behind in the only way he could."

The hope that ignited in Levi's eyes was slim, but at least it was there, Barabbas thought.

"Where do you believe the scroll lies?" Levi asked.

"My guess is it's not far from here. Mattithyahu knew the road was treacherous. He would have carried the scroll just far enough from *Qumran* to remove it from danger. Then he would have hidden it in an appropriate place."

Levi nodded slowly. "So we begin our search near *Qumran* and work our way north."

"We know he was headed for Jerusalem with three others. They weren't protectors, so he would have had to separate himself from them first. At the same time, he couldn't stray too far from the road, or they would have begun to wonder what had happened to him."

"It could still be in a myriad of different places. The scroll is a tiny item in a vast wilderness."

"We're not looking for a tiny scroll. We're looking for *Dov Harim*. Once we find that, it will narrow our search considerably."

"Nathaniel spent most of his life in *Qumran* and so have I. Believe me, there's no such place."

Barabbas smiled. "But through the eyes of a child —"

Levi sighed. "When do you want to start?"

"I don't have any pressing engagements."

The irony of the pun was not lost on Levi who nodded. "I'll get my coat for the journey."

† † † †

The valley was stark and bare and glared white against their eyes as it reflected the searing rays of the sun. The two men followed the winding riverbed that hadn't seen a drop of water for at least nine months, picking their way over the sun-baked boulders and pebbles that lay scattered about the valley floor. The endless stone landscape was marred only by the chalk white bones of a long dead mule that lay about a hundred paces from the end of the valley on the northern bank near the edge of the winding river bed.

The bones were hollow and cracked and had obviously lain there for a number of years. They told the story of an animal that had strayed and possibly broken a limb. It had finally succumbed in the unforgiving climate, having found no water or food to sustain it. There wasn't a scrap of vegetation either in the valley or on the steep walls that rose like blinding white mirrors on either side. Levi stopped briefly and wiped the sweat from his eyes with the back of his tunic's sleeve.

He squinted as he gazed up the final stretch of the valley that ended at a steep cliff that would become a raging waterfall for no more than a few weeks in the rainy season.

"See anything likely?" he asked Barabbas who was a few paces ahead of him.

Barabbas turned back, shaking his head as he did so. "We might as well try the next *wadi*. There's nothing here."

Instead of hunting under every rock and in every cavern the men had rather opted for a broad search of the area. As Barabbas maintained, they were not looking for the scroll directly. Their objective was to find a landmass that might fit the description they had been given. When he found that, they would begin a more intensive search.

They stopped briefly, resting in the shade of a giant boulder as they opened their bags and extracted large chunks of unleavened bread, dipping pieces in healthy dollops of olive oil. Their spirits were still high. Neither of them had expected to find anything on their first try.

Once they had finished their meal, Barabbas and Levi turned around, heading back to the main trail that ran between *Qumran* and Jerusalem. They moved north until they found the next *wadi* which they entered and followed to its source, about two and a half miles further along.

Their second attempt proved no more successful than their first. By then the sun was sinking fast, having long since disappeared beyond the towering cliffs that marked the western edge of the Great Rift Valley. Lengthening shadows soon began to lose their shape as darkness filled the cracks, melting their edges, and the chilled winds of the desert night began to blow, bringing tiny granules of sand that stung like icicles as they assaulted exposed skin.

The men made a camp in the wilderness that night and resumed their search the following day. A week had passed before they had finished scouring the first three miles between *Qumran* and Jerusalem and still no sign of the elusive scroll had been found.

By then Levi was becoming disillusioned. "It's impossible, Barabbas. We don't even know what we're looking for. Do you have any idea how many hiding places there are between here and Jerusalem?"

Barabbas was not to be dissuaded. "Less than you think. Hurry up. I want to get to the next valley before sundown."

They had trudged another mile before they reached the next valley. This was a much larger *wadi* than any of the previous ones they had come across. It was about five hundred paces across and offered several likely hills and slopes on both sides where the scroll might be hidden.

Barabbas spent a lot of time climbing the various hills that seemed to appear with each new bend in the river. His hopes soared on several occasions, only to be dashed as the hills proved to be barren of any hiding places.

The wadi wound for two and a half miles before it ended abruptly against a giant rock-face. With so much ground to cover, it took the two men nearly a week to complete their search of it. Two more valleys left them equally empty handed and even Barabbas began to feel despondent. By then, they had been searching for over a month and seemed no closer to finding the scroll than when they had first started.

As they finally reached the end of the fifth *wadi* and stared up at the familiar, towering cliffs, Barabbas stopped to catch his breath. The cliff formed a broad ledge that would become a group of at least three torrential waterfalls when the rains struck. The edge was wide and flat, with several broad overhangs that would separate the water's flow into three distinct streams of water. Gigantic flat rocks, resting like huge lids that reached out into space, hung suspended above the deep basin that had formed at the cliff's base.

The base had been hollowed out by eons of floods and formed a series of caves just beyond the hollowed-out basin. The caverns yawned their invitation, beckoning the two men to enter. Levi's pulse quickened as he rushed towards the smallest cavern, second from left of the five gaping holes.

"There's something in here," he called from the dark cavern. "It looks as if the cave has seen some human activity."

"Let's hope it's not the cave where Mattithyahu hid the scroll, then." Barabbas replied as he moved to join his friend.

A cursory search proved fruitless and the two men moved on to the next cave. This one was a large grotto with a double opening. Apart from a few bare rocks, the cave had nothing of interest. Its walls were smooth and there were no other caverns deeper in the cliff's recess. A bundle of dark coals near the entrance spoke of human activity in the not too distant past, but other than that, the cave had little to offer.

Barabbas and Levi turned their attention to the caves at each end of the string of caverns. After an intensive search of the two end caverns, they came up empty. The scroll was nowhere to be found.

"Next valley?" Levi enquired as they emerged from the last cavern and flopped down to grab a brief midday snack.

"We've already come too far north. He would have buried it close to *Qumran*. I was counting on that fact."

Once they had eaten and swigged huge gulps of warm water from a badly scuffed wineskin, the two men headed back for the valley's mouth. It was well past sundown when they finally arrived back at the main road. They quickly found a spot on the leeside of a small cluster of boulders and set up camp, lighting a fire to ward off the dark chill of the desert night.

Levi rummaged through his bag and extracted a flame-grilled quail that they had killed the previous day, tearing the carcass in two and offering half to his friend. "We've done all we can, Barabbas. No man could expect to find an item so small in such a vast hiding place. Why don't we head back to *Qumran*? We can always resume our search later."

"No," Barabbas fumed as he stared into the flames of their campfire. "I'm not giving up. We swore to protect the scroll with our lives and I will honour my oath if it takes me a lifetime to retrieve it."

Levi shook his head but resigned himself to the search. He couldn't leave Barabbas to hunt for the scroll alone. He was worried about his friend. In all the time that they had spent searching for the scroll, Barabbas had never once mentioned Leila's name.

He gazed north along the road to Jerusalem, staring at the mountains that obscured the next valley.

"Funny. It seems we're not the only ones interested in these valleys. There's smoke coming from the lip of that *wadi*."

"Probably a wild fire. It'll die out quickly enough. The vegetation's dry, but there's precious little of it."

Levi shook his head. "This is a single plume. Somebody's camping out there. Surely no traveller would be so stupid."

Barabbas shrugged. "I dare say we'll find out tomorrow. If it's robbers or bandits they'd do well to leave us alone."

He reached for Levi's bag and removed a second carcass of the tasty game fowl, biting huge chunks off the bone and munching the dry stringy meat.

† † † † †

First light found the two friends approaching the sixth valley north of *Qumran*. When they arrived at the valley's mouth, they made a cursory search of the area for any sign of the camp they had seen the previous evening.

All remains had been carefully eradicated, leaving no sign of the stranger's passing.

"Zealots," Levi smiled. "Only our own kind could hide their presence so well."

Barabbas looked as if he had swallowed sour milk. "Still, we'd better be careful. There could be eyes watching from any number of vantage points."

"Fine. Let's get on with it. The sooner I get back to *Qumran* the better."

Once again, they entered a valley with hearts full of hope. Their minds, however, were filled with trepidation and doubt. By midday, their mood had declined drastically.

"Barabbas, we have to stop this madness. If we at least had an idea of what to look for…"

"*Dov Harim*," Barabbas replied, but his voice had lost its confidence.

They had avoided the valley floor, choosing the less treacherous southern slope from which to conduct their search. Being higher, it afforded them a wider view of the area with the added advantage of height from which to defend themselves if they came across the unknown campers that they had espied the previous evening.

Finally they stopped to drink water, resting in a thin strip of shade offered by the steep valley wall. As he gazed across the valley, Barabbas saw a dark shadow moving quickly across the *wadi's* floor. It was visible for just an instant before it disappeared. He peered intently, searching for the figure, but it didn't appear again.

"Someone's down there." He pointed at the dry river bed where he had seen the shadow.

"I saw it too. It could have been an animal of some sort, but I doubt it."

"Our campfire friend still lurks in the valley, it would seem."

"I wouldn't worry. He's not stalking us, that's obvious. Let's finish and get out of here."

They skirted the valley's edge, keeping to the high ground as their eyes scanned the valley and the opposite cliffs. The *wadi* was not long and it was not yet midday when they reached the end of the valley. It had wound a deep path into the mountains and the men panted for breath and water.

Barabbas took a small sip from the nearly empty water skin and offered it to Levi. It was while Levi swilled the water in the back of his throat that Barabbas noticed the dome-shaped hill at the opposite end of the valley. From his vantage point he looked down on the twin outcrops that jutted heavenwards.

He examined it for a minute before the possibilities dawned on him and he turned to Levi with an excited gleam in his eye. "Come! Down in the valley."

Levi glanced at the knoll in confusion and then back at his friend, but Barabbas was already racing down the side of the *wadi* with the speed of a mountain ibex.

"Hurry up!" he hissed as he slid down the steep slope, dislodging an avalanche of loose stones in his wake.

Levi was left with little choice but to follow. When he finally caught up, Barabbas was standing among the smooth stones in the riverbed, grinning amiably as he stared up at the hill opposite.

Following his gaze, Levi saw the hill properly for the first time, through the eyes of a child. From the valley floor, the twin dome-like outcrops looked like the small rounded ears of a bear and the convex shape of the hill changed closer to the foot, becoming concave in the middle and tapering to what looked like a narrow snout

Barabbas rested a hand on his friend's shoulder. "*Dov Harim*! Little wonder it's never been named. Only a child would explore this far up a valley in the middle of nowhere."

"We haven't found the scroll yet," Levi cautioned, but his heart pounded as hope rose from its slumber.

"It's almost in our grasp," Barabbas assured him as he stepped forward towards the mountain.

Now that they had a location to work, their search pattern changed. They began to hunt methodically, examining every overhang and fissure or any other likely hiding place for the scroll.

Barabbas was so intent on his search that he never noticed the dark figure emerge from behind the heavy boulder and long dead scrub that surrounded it. As he hunted through the uneven terrain, upturning every small boulder and sticking his head into each remote gap in the hill, the man stalked him with predatory silence, like a viper that had spied its prey.

Barabbas move ahead of the figure, searching the ground for likely hiding places or any clue as to the scroll's whereabouts. The hunter glided after him, waiting patiently for his opportunity to strike.

23

QUICK REFLEXES and a setting sun saved Barabbas from his opponent's swishing blade. Although he never heard the movement, the lengthening shadow of his attacker flitted across his line of sight. It was only for a moment, but long enough for Barabbas to react.

He rolled to his left, moving in tandem with the shadow and falling beneath the path of the blade. When he rose to his feet, he stared into the hateful eyes of a long-forgotten enemy.

Barabbas grinned as he drew his sword. "Eleazor, is that any way to greet a fellow zealot?"

"Thanks to you, I'm no longer welcome among their number. I've dreamed of driving this blade through your belly, but I thought death had robbed me of that opportunity until I saw you rummaging around these hills this morning."

"It's no coincidence that we both arrived here at the same time. How long have you been searching for it?" Barabbas shuffled around. The uneven ground made it difficult to find a proper foothold.

"Long enough." Eleazor circled carefully, trying to force Barabbas onto the looser rock where his position would be precarious. "I found the place where the Essenes were murdered. It was obvious the scroll was not with them when they were attacked, so they must have hidden it between that point and *Qumran*."

"So you started there and worked your way south."

"I've been searching this valley for over a month."

Barabbas nodded. "We saw your fire last night from our camp."

"We?"

"Levi's with me."

The dark features curled into a smile, but still Eleazor never dropped his guard, circling around as he waited for his opening. "Is that old fool still alive? It's a marvel that you haven't got him killed yet."

There was a movement and the sound of falling rocks behind Eleazor as Levi slipped from the rock he was hiding behind. "On the contrary, Barabbas has saved my life many times."

Eleazor spun away from Levi, backing up against a steep wall of rock where no other assailants could take him by surprise.

For the first time, Barabbas saw fear in his opponent's eyes. He understood why. Eleazor was supremely confident in his abilities, but he could never hope to match two swordsmen of their calibre.

The traitor's eyes blazed as he came to a decision. He lunged unexpectedly at

Barabbas, switching his sword to a left-hand grip and swiping the blade at Barabbas' throat.

Barabbas parried the blow but was unable to retaliate against the unexpected direction of the attack. He was on uneven ground and couldn't find his feet. Before he could bring his sword to bear, Eleazor was past him and beating a path towards the valley bed.

Barabbas raced after him, but the sure-footed coward outdistanced him and disappeared around the first bend in the dry riverbed. By the time Barabbas got there, his quarry had vanished. He was glancing wildly about the slopes of the valley when Levi caught up to him.

"Forget about him," Levi panted. "After a month spent in this valley he'll know every possible path and cave. We'll never catch him."

"Why did you barge in like that? I almost had him." Barabbas rounded on his friend.

"He had you on loose ground, Barabbas. One slip and it would have all been over," Levi growled.

"I knew what I was doing. If you'd left me, I'd have taken him."

"Against a lesser swordsman, maybe, but not Eleazor. I never taught you to take chances like that. Such arrogance would have got you killed, my friend."

"Where did you spring from, anyway? Last time I checked, you were headed for the crest."

"I came back to call you. I found a cave."

"Where?"

"At the base of one of the ears on the dome. The entrance is a narrow shaft, but it opens into a fairly large chamber."

"Let's go." Barabbas raced for the pinnacle, his heart pounding with excitement.

It didn't take them long to reach the summit where the two almost identical domes jutted out like giant granite ears.

"Which one is it?" Barabbas panted.

"Over there." Levi pointed at the right-hand dome.

Barabbas was there in an instant, scanning the base for the opening. The mouth of the cave was small. Large enough for a child to enter easily, but grown men like Barabbas and Levi would have a difficult time squeezing through.

"You went inside this?" Barabbas asked doubtfully.

"Far enough to see what was there."

"Well let's try." Barabbas crouched down on his knees, making ready to slide in on his belly.

Levi let him go. "I'll stand guard here. I wouldn't put it past Eleazor to return and bury us inside with a landslide."

Barabbas made no reply. His entire being was already focused on the narrow shaft. He felt the cold rock scraping against his shoulders, tearing his tunic and grazing his skin as he slid down the cramped passage.

Although narrow, it was only as long as the height of a grown man and soon opened up into a large cavern that he could almost stand upright in. He was surprised to find the chamber lighter than expected. Light filtered through countless tiny holes in the cavern's roof where small rocks that littered the floor had fallen over the years.

As he gazed about the cavern, Barabbas saw numerous signs of human activity but no signs of the scroll's whereabouts.

Levi's muffled call came from outside. "Can you see anything?"

"Not much," Barabbas called back. "No shelves or jars. My guess is it's buried in a recess or under one of these rocks."

He stepped towards a larger boulder near the south wall, disregarding the smaller stones that were obviously nothing more than fallen rubble. Quickly, he reached down and rolled the boulder aside.

There was a spitting sound as a viper struck with blinding speed and venomous fangs from its recess under the rock. Barabbas shot back, smacking his head against the low ceiling. He cursed as a shower of small stones and dust fell about him, obscuring his vision as the snake coiled, emerging from its home. It stared in fury at the intruder.

Barabbas slowly drew his sword and approached the reptile. With one deft swing of the blade, he severed the animal's head from its body and kicked the writhing corpse aside.

The next boulder was approached with a good deal more caution, but apart from a few bugs and ants, it held little of interest. He turned his attention to a large rock on the other side of the cave. It was wide and so flat that it had become almost obscured by the dirt and debris that covered the floor.

Instead of reaching under it with his fingers, Barabbas used his sword to lever it loose. The stone moved easily enough and revealed the hollow that lay beneath. A myriad of insects scattered as the stone was eased aside.

After tapping and poking at the stone, Barabbas was satisfied that no danger lurked beneath its narrow edge. He reached down and lifted the flat rock away to get a better look at the elbow-deep chamber that lay beneath.

He held his breath as he saw an object in the chamber's recess. It was carefully wrapped in a faded garment of clothing that had been eaten through by mice and moths over the years. The cloth had kept its treasure intact however

Barabbas could feel the throbbing pulse in his fingers as he grasped the package. His excitement surged as he quickly unfolded the garment to reveal its contents.

What he saw caused his heart to plunge. The garment fell away to reveal a thick papyrus scroll, yellowed by time and frayed at its edges.

Stunned and disappointed, Barabbas moved it to a light source in the hopes that it might speak of the scroll's whereabouts. The words on the scroll were meaningless, but Barabbas read them anyway.

Who has believed what we have heard and to whom has the arm of the Lord been revealed?

For he grew up before him like a young plant and like a root out of dry ground, he had no form or comeliness that we should look at him and no beauty that we should desire him.

He was despised and rejected by men; a man of sorrows, acquainted with grief.

Barabbas scanned over the words of the prophet. They concerned the Messiah who was to come. He'd heard the words in synagogues *ad nausium* since his youth.

But he was wounded for our transgressions, he was bruised for our iniquities, upon him was the

chastisement that made us whole and with his stripes we were healed.

Barabbas thought of his friend, Yoseph, and his brother, Simeon. He thought of the stripes on their backs that had turned to ribbons of torn flesh as the cruel whip had ripped apart their skin and exposed their innards.

Then his thoughts turned to another. The silent man who had walked with them to Calvary.

He was oppressed and afflicted yet he opened not his mouth; like a lamb that is led to the slaughter and like a sheep before its shearers is dumb, so he opened not his mouth.

Could it be that we have seen the *Messiah*, the Saviour of Israel?

"Barabbas." Levi's muffled call interrupted his thoughts.

"I'm still here," he called back as he hurriedly rolled up the scroll. It glinted for a moment in the bright shaft of light that shone through one of the many holes in the roof of the cave.

"Have you found it yet?"

"Not yet." Barabbas called back as he began his search once more.

After an hour of searching and still no sign of the copper scroll, he finally gave up and emerged into the sunlight once more, still clutching the ancient parchment with the passage from Isaiah.

"What's that?" Levi pointed at the faded cloth fabric that Barabbas carried.

"An old belt. It had this wrapped in it." He handed Levi the scroll.

"What does it say?" Levi enquired as he unrolled it.

"A passage from one of the prophets. It's not important."

Levi examined Barabbas' expression. "Your words and your eyes say two different things. What happened in there?"

"Nothing. It just reminded me of Simeon and Yoseph, that's all."

Levi looked at the scroll again. "A passage from one of the prophets reminded you of your brother?"

"It concerns the Messiah and the manner of his death." Barabbas hesitated. "It suddenly crossed my mind that Israel's redeemer had died to secure my freedom."

Levi laughed. "You think too much, my friend. Come, let's make a camp for the night. We can resume our search in the morning."

Barabbas gazed at the hill about him. It seemed to glitter like bronze in the setting sun. "I know it's here somewhere. I can feel it."

He took the papyrus scroll from Levi and rolled it carefully. On the journey down the steep slope, Barabbas noticed a coin as it glinted in the light of the sunset. He reached down and picked it up. Silver, he thought as he examined the tiny disc. It must have fallen from one of their belts while they chased Eleazor down the incline.

As he stared at the coin, thinking of Eleazor, the papyrus scroll on his belt glinted in the same sunset but Barabbas thought nothing of it. He quickened his pace to catch up with Levi who was already in the riverbed below.

They made their camp in a gully that ran off the valley's edge where they were protected by an overhang and there were only two ways to reach the camp. That gave them a hasty escape route if needed. They were taking no chances with Eleazor still lurking in the hills about them and decided to take turns sleeping so as to maintain a watch throughout the night.

† † † † †

That evening, the two men sat in silence, chewing thoughtfully on dry cakes of unleavened bread dipped in sour wine, mixed with myrrh. They listened to the quiet nocturnal murmur of the Judean wilderness. The cry of a jackal came to their ears amidst the eerie slithering of sands creeping across the barren landscape, carried by their mistress, the sighing desert wind.

Barabbas stared vacantly at the scroll in his hands, not actually reading the words but contemplating their implications. There was something intriguing about the scroll that filled him with a morbid fascination.

The words so accurately described the man who had taken his place on the Roman instrument of death and yet, he couldn't accept that the quiet rabbi was the One of whom the prophets had spoken. To do so meant that he was faced with the reality of the man's life and everything he stood for. It meant that everything he'd believed until now was wrong and it demanded a response that Barabbas was not prepared to make. And yet, the words refused to allow his soul to rest. They continued to torment him long into the night.

The sky was clear and the moon full, bathing the landscape in its milky luminescence. As Barabbas shuffled into a more comfortable position, the scroll glinted momentarily in the moonlight. It reminded Barabbas of something and he frowned as he tried to recall what it was.

The cave, he thought. The scroll had glinted in the sunlight that had shone through the roof of the grotto. Still, the feeling that he had missed something plagued him. He stared thoughtfully at the scroll as he chewed on the dry crust of bread in his hand.

All of a sudden, Barabbas jolted forwards and examined the scroll carefully in his hand. He could feel his temple pulsing as a renewed excitement began to course through his veins.

Levi noticed Barabbas' trembling hand. "What is it?"

"Look here." Barabbas shifted across to show Levi the scroll.

Levi gazed at the document for a long time. "I see nothing."

"Wait!" Barabbas swivelled the scroll about in the moonlight. "There, did you see that?"

Levi shrugged and shook his head.

"It glints in the moonlight," Barabbas said. His hand still trembled with the excitement.

"And?"

"It did the same thing in the cave this morning. I can't believe I was so stupid."

"Do you have no intention of telling me what this is about, or are you deliberately keeping me in suspense?"

"Here, feel this and tell me what you think."

Levi leaned across and rubbed the material lightly between his fingers. "It's parchment," he said simply.

"It didn't feel thicker to you than usual?"

"I'm no expert, but - maybe."

"And it glints in the moonlight. It's so obvious!"

"We should sell it to a mountebank. Thick parchment that glints in the moonlight. Something like that is bound to cure leprosy or some such ailment."

"That's just it. Parchment doesn't shine like a coin, or a sword. Metal does." Barabbas took the scroll in both hands. "Let's try something."

"Before you do anything rash, let's remember that's the word of God you mean to tear in half."

"If I'm right, you'll discover that God meant for this parchment to be torn."

Instead of ripping the material in two, Barabbas carefully took one of the frayed corners and tore at the delicate fabric. It broke easily enough and peeled away to reveal the edge of a stronger, more robust material beneath.

Both men held their breath as Barabbas tore the cloth further.

"Copper," Levi breathed in an awed whisper. Immediately he turned and stared into the darkness, instinctively drawing his sword as if the forces that conspired to steal the scroll would fall upon them any instant. He turned back and stared at the document that slowly appeared under Barabbas' careful probing. "Barabbas, you've found the copper scroll!"

Barabbas dared not reply as he stripped away the cover that had hidden the true contents for so many years.

Levi's voice was hushed. "Nathaniel was a genius. To hide the scroll within a scroll. How many hands have touched it and never known what they truly held, I wonder?"

Barabbas was suddenly filled with purpose. "We have to leave now. It's not safe out here in the open."

"Where would we go?"

"Let's not talk of it now. Eleazor could be listening as we speak. Despite his cowardice, the man moves with the stealth of an owl."

"He may follow us, of course."

"We'll be looking for him. I still yearn for the opportunity to gut him and leave him as jackal fodder."

Levi rose and immediately began gathering his belongings. "You lead. I'll cover our rear."

Barabbas headed for Jerusalem with Levi moving in tow. The two men moved in stealth, continuously circling back to make sure they were not being followed. By sunrise, they were confident that Eleazor had not picked up their trail and they began covering their tracks.

All through the night, Barabbas had considered the scroll and its importance. He now had a document in his possession that legend promised would overthrow Rome and bring about Israel's freedom. It filled him with hope and finally gave him a sense of purpose again.

It was the second hour after sunrise before they stopped to rest. "I think we're safe now. Let's grab a bite of food and take a look at that scroll."

"I'm aching to know what the secret is that we've been guarding for so long."

"You mean you've never read it?" Barabbas was stunned.

"The fewer people who knew, the safer the scroll was."

"Well, now it's our turn." Barabbas slowly unrolled the thin metal document. It was discoloured at its edges, tarnished by age. He scanned the words, reading column by column.

"What does it say?" Levi pressed Barabbas, leaning over his shoulder to see the words on the scroll.

Barabbas shook his head, too intrigued to speak as the words unfolded before him. The scroll was a large inventory with detailed instructions on how to find the treasures that had been concealed for centuries. As he read, Barabbas was filled with awe at the magnitude of the treasure's value. In some instances, the language became vague, lost somewhere in the eons between the time it was written and the time it was read.

It would take some work to decipher and a fair amount of guesswork to locate. Changing landmarks and climates over hundreds of years would compound the difficulties.

"Tell me, Barabbas!" Levi shook his arm.

"There's enough gold here to equip an army," Barabbas whispered.

"Where?"

"I haven't got that far yet." Barabbas read on in silence for a moment. "This is incredible! Do you know who wrote this?"

"Legend says it was written by the five original protectors, just before the destruction of Solomon's temple. Among them were Jeremiah, Haggai and Zachariah. I can't remember the others"

Barabbas shook his head in wonder. "The money is meaningless. The true power of this treasure is in its religious artefacts. These are all items from the temple. In fact, they date back to Simeon's tabernacle. It seems they were taken in haste before the temple fell, to be hidden until it was rebuilt."

"That doesn't make sense. Zachariah and Haggai were still alive when the temple was rebuilt. Surely they would have returned the items then."

"Not according to this. It seems these prophets believed, not in the second dispensation of the temple, but in a third that was still to come, so there was no reason to return the artefacts to a temple that would only be torn down again."

Levi had become very quiet. It was a long time before he spoke again. "What else does it say?"

"It says here that the third dispensation will usher in the coming Messiah's reign and only then can the artefacts be returned."

"Does it list the items?"

Barabbas read on. "Every one. See, here it talks of a silver scroll which is kept underneath the *K'lal*. There's apparently another document that gives instruction on how to institute the temple rituals."

"The *K'lal* it speaks of. What, exactly, is in that container?"

Barabbas read further and then let his hand drop as he turned to Levi in amazement. "The ashes of the red heifer, used for ritual cleansing of the priests in the temple. They've been missing for hundreds of years. Do you have any idea of what this would mean to our nation?"

"Put that scroll away, Barabbas. Now isn't the time to dwell on these things."

"Not the time! If these items were returned to the temple, it would incite our people to new heights of religious fervour. The priests would incite them to rise up against Rome like never before. Caesar couldn't hope to stand against Israel's fury."

"Stop this foolishness. Don't you realize those words were written by a prophet? They have power far beyond our imagination. We have no right to meddle with things like this. You forget, there's also a curse attached to that document."

"The curse is only for those who use the treasures for their own purposes."

"And what do you think the Sanhedrin would do? They have no interests other than the perpetuation of their own power. You could place the entire nation of Israel under the curse of their greed."

"These items belong in the temple, Levi."

Levi shook his head. "Not this way. What you suggest would obliterate Israel from the face of the earth. The emperor would send a tidal wave of legions against our nation and the fervour you speak of would be Israel's own undoing.

"Once those items are in the temple, the men of our nation would gladly perish before they surrender, believing God has raised them up to cast off the shackles of Rome and topple the emperor from his throne."

"And don't you believe that?" The fever of revolution already burned in Barabbas' eyes.

"When the time is right, yes. But we're not qualified to make that decision. We need to find men who understand these things. Only a priest could unravel the mysteries in that scroll and decide when the time has come to retrieve the treasures of the temple."

Barabbas raised his voice in anger. "The priests are dead, Levi. We're the only ones left."

"Then we must find others. Men of God. Not warriors like ourselves."

"Who? The Sanhedrin! You said yourself they're not worthy of the scroll. They can't agree on the colour of cow dung, let alone a document of this importance."

"And you believe you can?"

"I know that this document spells Israel's freedom. Once we release its contents, all our dreams will be realized."

"Exactly. Our dreams. *Our* purposes. God doesn't march to the beat of the zealots' drum. If you release the scroll before its time, you risk placing yourself and all who follow you under its curse. And there's something else besides." Levi glanced away as a chill breeze blew across the desert, causing him to shiver.

"What is it?" Barabbas asked sharply. He was still angry at Levi's apparent lack of zealous fervour.

"Times have changed since that scroll was written. When those prophets penned it, they'd never heard of a Roman Empire. Yet look at your reaction as you read the scroll today. If that document was to fall into Roman hands —" Levi sighed. "It's the most radical form of rebellion I've ever come across. If Caesar were to read it, he'd destroy our nation before we had the chance to mount an army. No Roman could read this document without seeing it as a plot by traitors against the emperor."

"I'm beginning to wonder whether you've come to fear Rome's power."

"Maybe I've seen more of her power than you have. Or perhaps I've had a vision of what this can lead to. As always, Barabbas, you underestimate your opponent. She is more powerful and cruel than you could ever believe. Pilate's strike was mild compared to what an entire military onslaught would achieve.

"I see galleys coming in their hoards, bringing legions from every corner of the empire. We wouldn't just be fighting Romans, but also auxiliary forces from every nation they've conquered. I see soldiers in their thousands, swarming across our beloved country, killing our warriors and butchering our families.

"Blood will flow in the streets of Jerusalem like the Jordan in flood and they won't stop until every stone in Judea lies fallen in a mound of rubble. Is that what you want for your beloved nation and her children?"

"Are you suggesting we bury the scroll for another five hundred years?"

"No. I believe it should be destroyed."

Barabbas' mouth dropped open in shock but no words came. He couldn't believe what he was hearing from his friend. That any Israelite would want to destroy a promise so great was beyond him.

Levi remained silent with his hand resting on his sword and Barabbas realized, for the first time, what frightening thoughts were coursing through his friend's mind. At first he didn't want to believe his instinct. Levi had taught him everything he knew of war and the wilderness.

He'd been a father in the early years after Barabbas and Simeon had left their family to join the zealots in Masada. Fatherhood had turned to friendship as he'd reached manhood, and friendship had become brotherhood when they'd cut covenant, just as Levi had with Barabbas' own father.

What kind of feelings could spawn such thoughts in Levi's mind after all they'd been through together?

Barabbas slowly reached for his own sword, choosing his path should he be forced to defend himself. "Would you really do it, Levi?"

The man hesitated. "You're a brother to me, Barabbas, but I swore an oath to protect the scroll from every danger - even other protectors. I beg you. Don't force my hand in this."

Barabbas sighed. "Alright, I'll listen to you, but to destroy the scroll? That's insanity."

"First, you have to swear to me that you'll forget this business of rebellion against Rome, for now."

Barabbas agonised over the decision. It meant giving up everything he'd hoped for. "I swear it. The secret will remain safe until God chooses to reveal it."

Levi nodded. "The next step is to find another true, wise priest. Someone like Nathaniel who is worthy of the scroll. He must understand the things of God and will need to be in a position to unravel the secret of the scroll."

"Good luck. I was raised in the temple and I've yet to find such a man."

"Then we'll find him outside the temple. There are others. The Essene community in *Qumran*, for one thing."

Barabbas shook his head. "Of all the men in *Qumran*, Nathaniel chose only Mattithyahu. For whatever reasons, he found the other older men unacceptable. We have to trust his judgement."

Levi nodded. "Besides, *Qumran* is compromised. Eleazor knows the connection and it's safe to assume it's only a matter of time before Pilate finds out."

"So, we're looking for another religious sect who understands the things of God, preferably outside the temple and synagogues," Barabbas mused.

"We'll find them. For the time being, we need to find a new resting place for this scroll. I'm beginning to wish we'd never peeled away that outer cover."

"Do you think it's possible Nathaniel's writings were another clue for us to follow?"

"You mean did he unwittingly leave a message that God intended for us to find when we recovered the scroll?"

Barabbas shrugged. "It's just an idea. We're in the dark here. I'm clutching at anything that might point us in the right direction."

"Those words really affected you in that cave." Levi studied his friend. "You said they concerned the Messiah?"

Barabbas nodded. "I'm probably insane to say this, but the disciples of —"

"Disciples of whom?"

"No, it's crazy. Forget I said anything. We'll find the right men. God will reveal them when the time is right."

The two men made up their minds to travel to Jerusalem. Barabbas felt sure he would be welcome in Deborah's home, as he always had been. From there, they could resume their work with the zealots while considering the problem of finding holy men who would know what to do with the scroll.

✝ ✝ ✝ ✝ ✝

It was with exhaustion and relief that Barabbas mounted the stone steps that led to Deborah's courtyard. He saw her as he began his descent into the communal yard.

She was busy turning the heavy olive press and looked even more beautiful than he remembered. Deborah looked up at his approach. Her lips parted slightly and she stared with disbelieving eyes, making no move to greet him.

"Hello, Deborah," Barabbas grinned.

"You're alive." Her voice was almost a whisper and still she remained rooted against the olive press.

He nodded, uncertain of what she was thinking. Suddenly she flung herself across the yard into his arms, holding him tightly and kissing his neck.

"I thought you'd seen death this time for certain."

Barabbas laughed. "Nobody gets rid of me that easily."

Deborah leaned back slightly to look into his eyes. "What brings you to Jerusalem? I thought you'd prefer to settle in Sepphoris."

He glanced away, breaking her gaze. "Too remote. I need to be near the hub of political activity, and that's here in Jerusalem. Can you put me in touch with the local leaders - let them know I'm back?"

"Of course." She took his hand and led him inside. "But first, let me wash this desert grime off you and get you something to eat."

† † † † †

After a gluttonous portion of pigeon stew, Barabbas regaled Deborah with stories of his experiences in Carthage and his journey back home. Deborah told him of all that had happened since he'd left Judea. It felt to Barabbas as if they'd never been apart. He was as relaxed in her company as he'd always been and the moon was already retreating by the time they decided to retire.

Barabbas fetched a woven mat which he rolled out on the roof of the tiny home. He lay there, listening to Deborah tidying up downstairs until she too went to sleep. In the darkness, his thoughts turned to Leila and the man to whom she was now married. He ached at the thought of his loss to the point that even the scroll's recovery became meaningless.

It could never fill the void she had left in his life. At least, in Carthage, he had nurtured the hope of returning to her, but now he was filled with an abiding emptiness. He tried to console himself with the words of the scroll and the freedom they promised, but it was useless. Having achieved his goal, his drive was gone and only a sense of loss remained.

A wave of loathing swept over him as he thought of Miyka'el sharing a bed with the woman he'd been betrothed to. He vowed to make the man pay for the sorrow he'd caused. However, as he lay quietly contemplating Miyka'el's fate, he knew in his heart that he could never take even a fraction of what was taken from him.

Emptiness. Barabbas lay for nearly an hour, but there was no escape from the loneliness he felt. Finally he rose and went downstairs. There was no door to Deborah's room, but he hesitated at the entrance.

"Deborah?" he called softly. There was no answer.

Barabbas entered the room and knelt by her bed. He reached down and gently stroked her hair. The woman stirred and rolled over to look at him. She smiled as she took his hand.

"I hoped you'd come," she murmured, pulling him closer and inviting him under the covers.

A long while later, Barabbas lay quietly on his back, enjoying the feel of the warm naked body next to him. He brooded on thoughts of Miyka'el and how he would somehow make him pay. Finally, he decided on a course of action and, satisfied, fell asleep.

† † † † †

It was nearly six weeks later that Leila felt the first effects of Barabbas' decision. Miyka'el appeared to become more and more morose over a period of days, but steadfastly refused to speak about what bothered him.

Instead, he took his mood out on those around him, yelling at servants for the tiniest error and heaping unreasonable punishments on slaves. Even Leila was not immune to his fits of temper and it was during one of these tirades that she confronted him.

"Miyka'el, what's the matter with you? You've been acting like a tyrant these past two weeks, never satisfied with anything."

"Nothing's the matter. All I want is to be left in peace."

"How is that possible when you rage like a desert storm at the slightest provocation?"

"I don't have to answer to you, woman. Just stay out of my way."

"The Lord only knows how much I wish I could," she blazed fiercely as she spun around to leave the room.

"Leila," Miyka'el called as she reached the door.

She stopped and turned but refused to reply, fixing him with a hateful glare.

"I'm sorry, Leila. I shouldn't have spoken to you that way."

"Will you tell me what's wrong?"

He sighed and rubbed his forehead. "It's only money. At least that's what I keep telling myself."

"How much have you lost?"

"Who told you that?" Miyka'el was shocked.

"You forget I've lived in a merchant's house all my life. The mood is not hard to recognise."

Miyka'el shook his head. "Until now, I've treated losses philosophically. Highwaymen are a continuous hazard, but in the last two weeks I've had more than any man should reasonably expect."

"Highwaymen attacked your caravans?"

"That's just the beginning. They've also raided two of my warehouses and last night one of my stalls in the market burned down.

"I've lost nearly a hundred camels in the last week and some of my best merchants have told me they might have to seek employment elsewhere, as they feel it's no longer safe working for me. Other merchants are not being affected by this sudden burst of activity."

"It sounds as if somebody is out to harm you personally."

Miyka'el shrugged. "It would seem that way, but I don't know who or why."

"One of your competitors, perhaps?"

"I don't think so. The attacks are too organised to be the work of thugs. One of my warehouse managers swears he heard it was the work of zealots."

Leila glanced sharply at him. "What makes him say that?"

"Apparently he has a nephew who is young and impressionable. What's more, he's eager to impress. He's been involved with the zealot faction for some time and, though he's not involved with these raids, he claimed to know those that are."

"Perhaps you could go and see him."

"I tried, but he disappeared into the wilderness. I reported him to the Roman officials, but they say if he's with the zealots there's slim chance of finding him."

"I see." Leila was thoughtful for a moment. "Well, I hope you catch the culprits and put a stop to it."

"Not as much as I do. Much more of this and I'll be ruined. I've already sent some people to Caesarea to appeal to Pilate. I need military protection from this band of ruffians."

Thoughts raced through Leila's mind. "Do you have any idea of how to find them?"

Miyka'el shrugged. "The zealots are notoriously difficult to trace, but we have to try. I've sent word to the prefect that I need his best men to assist me in finding the perpetrators."

"Will he listen to you?"

"He will if he wants me to continue placing undisclosed quantities of cash in his private coffers. Cash placed there without the knowledge of Caesar's tax collectors. Since your father and I merged our interests, the prefect has become our servant as much as we are his."

"At a costly price, of course." Leila's mind was no longer on the conversation. She was thinking of a meeting near the fountain and an argument with a person from her past.

Miyka'el said, "I earn back every shekel I pay to him in tax relief. No tax collector would dare cross me for fear of retribution from the prefect."

"I'm sure you'll sort it out. They can't keep this up forever. Sooner or later, something has to give and you'll have them." Leila was anxious to end the discussion. She suddenly remembered an urgent matter regarding some textiles that had arrived the previous day and excused herself.

As she left her husband, heading for the street outside, her rage boiled at the thought of Barabbas. What did he hope to accomplish by this insanity? She would find him and put an end to this nonsense.

For Miyka'el's sake, she thought. She was doing this for her husband and yet, she couldn't explain the quickening heartbeat and the guilt she felt at the thought of seeing Barabbas again.

No! This was for Miyka'el, but first she needed information. Before she could do anything, she had to locate Barabbas.

† † † † †

The blind man sees more than we can possibly imagine. The gates of the synagogue are a wealth of information for those who care to use it. Leila recalled Barabbas' words from their many conversations.

The synagogue in question was in Jericho and the gates supported several beggars with outstretched arms, hoping for charity from those more fortunate than they were. She selected one who sat alone to one side. A cripple resting quietly on the hard stone steps.

He seemed more distant than the others and less hopeful. Either he didn't need charity, or he had given up hope. Leila decided to find out.

"Good day, old man," she greeted him and immediately felt self-conscious. Her words sounded condescending, even though she tried to make them otherwise. It occurred to her that she had walked this path almost every week since she had arrived in Jericho and this was the first time she had stopped to look at any of these people.

The beggar looked at her appraisingly, and then glanced at his frayed pouch which held a few lonely coins. Leila felt her eyes drawn to it as if by some mystical charm. She shuffled, uncertain of what to do next.

"It's been a quiet day, I see," Leila persisted, trying desperately to hide her discomfort.

The old man stared across the street without looking at her as he spoke. "You seek not to give, but to receive."

Leila tried to hide the relief she felt. "You're a man of infinite wisdom."

"Wisdom is an expensive commodity." The beggar gazed out at some unknown spot far beyond the city limits.

"How expensive?"

"That depends on the information you seek."

"It concerns a man — a friend — I'm trying to locate him."

"Does your friend have a name?"

"Barabbas. I'm led to believe he's involved with the zealots."

"The zealots are good friends, but violent and unforgiving enemies. It would be a foolish man indeed that betrayed them."

"This is not betrayal, I assure you. As I said, he's a close friend of mine."

"But not so close that you know his whereabouts."

Leila knelt down next to the man. "Please, sir. I sent him away and now I need to see him before he does something incredibly stupid."

The old cripple looked at her for the first time, searching for the truth in her pleading eyes. "I've heard of this man you speak of. They say he's extremely capable. You needn't fear for his life."

"It's not his life I fear for, but what he might do to others." She reached into her belt and extracted a large leather pouch of coins.

The ancient eyes gleamed with primal greed at the sight of the gold. Leila offered it to him and he took hold of the pouch with a gnarled hand.

"The man you seek is in Jerusalem, or so they say."

"Jerusalem is a big place, with many people," Leila held the pouch firmly.

The beggar let the pouch go and turned away. "If you were a true friend, you would know the house and the name of the woman he's with. I'll tell you no more. You can keep your money."

Leila had to control her sudden surge of anger. It was unreasonable, she thought. Barabbas was free to live his life any way he pleased. She forced a smile and deposited the leather pouch into the beggar's bag.

"Thank you," she said, rising to leave.

She turned back after a few paces and said. "You've done a good thing today and you need have no fear of the zealots' retribution."

The old man didn't acknowledge her, but stared impassively at a cluster of date palms across the street. Leila glanced down at his bag. The leather pouch was gone and only a few lonely coins lay in the bottom of the frayed container.

Three days passed before Leila was able to get to Jerusalem She had told her husband that she was going there to see about finding new outlets for the clothing that she and Minette were still making.

It was a project that Miyka'el had approved of from the first when he had found her in Bethany and taken her back to Jericho as his wife.

As her carriage rolled towards the Sheep Gate on the north-eastern wall of the city, Leila was suddenly filled with trepidation. The thought of seeing Barabbas again filled her with dread and excitement at the same time.

She had lied to her husband, but surely that didn't matter. After all, she was doing this for him. Why, then, did she feel so guilty?

"This is far enough, Ezra," she called to the driver. He was one of Miyka'el's servants and Leila had taken an instant liking to him when she was first brought to Miyka'el's home.

The silent man pulled the cart to a halt. "Shall I come with you? This is a rough part of the city."

"I'll be alright. You can stay here with the cart. You'll see me before sundown."

"Perhaps Zena and I should find an inn for the night?"

"That would be fine, thank you, but Zena can accompany me into the city." Leila turned and walked towards the city gate, accompanied by her handmaid. Her stomach began to flutter as she made her way past the Antonia, moving north into the *Kainopolis*.

She considered the last time she had met Deborah and remembered the hateful expression in her eyes. What would those eyes reveal this time? An attitude of victory and scorn, no doubt.

Why had Barabbas chosen this woman's house for his abode? Leila sighed bitterly, trying to force back the jealousy that rose in her heart. She was a married woman and Barabbas was free to choose his own path.

The only reason she was here was to put a stop to the vendetta he now waged against her husband. And yet, the mere thought of him living in Deborah's home caused such volcanic emotions that she could not control their course.

She quickly found the north wall and began moving along it, hoping fervently that she would remember where it was. Years had passed since her last meeting with Deborah. After several wrong turns, she found the correct street and ascended the steps leading to the courtyard. The door to Deborah's house lay against the city wall.

24

"**WHAT ARE** you doing here?" The words were cool and hostile.

"I'm here to see Barabbas." Leila tried to look past Deborah to see whether he was inside the house, but the woman blocked her view.

"Why would you even think he's here?"

"May I see him, please?"

"What do you want with him! Why don't you go back to your husband where you belong?"

Leila felt as if she'd been slapped. "He told you I was married?"

"He didn't have to. I know him in a way that you never could."

"Will you let me see him?"

"What for? He has nothing to say to you."

"Maybe, but he will hear me out."

"There's nothing you could possibly have to tell him that is of any consequence."

Leila smiled. "Do you really feel so threatened by me?"

Deborah flushed and glared back at her. The barb had struck a nerve. She turned as a noise emanated from inside the house.

"What's the matter, Deborah?" Barabbas' voice came from inside the house.

"It's not important. You needn't bother —"

Barabbas came to the door despite her objections. When he got there, he froze for a moment, staring indifferently at Leila. "What do you want?"

Deborah stammered. "Barabbas, it's not important. I think —"

He took her gently by the shoulders. "I'll handle this. Wait for me inside."

Once she was gone, he faced Leila. "You're a long way from Jericho. What brings you here?"

"You know what brings me here. The zealots have begun to attack every facet of my husband's business. I've come to ask you to stop."

"Zealots only attack soldiers and Roman collaborators. If your husband is being harmed, it's because he has sold out to a heathen oppressor."

"Barabbas, stop this. Miyka'el is a powerful man and when he finds out who's behind his troubles, he'll destroy you."

Barabbas laughed. "Who'll tell him - you?"

Leila shook her head. "Money buys information - you taught me that. I was able to find you with a bag of gold coins. Nothing can remain hidden from the combined wealth of Miyka'el and my father."

"What does your father have to do with all of this?"

"They're in business together, or had you forgotten what I was traded for?"

Barabbas flushed with anger. "I'll see them fall to their knees with ashes on their heads before I stop."

"Barabbas, listen to me. Miyka'el has already sent word to Pilate, requesting his most competent military officials to oversee the protection of his financial interests. A convoy of soldiers is probably headed to Jericho as we speak."

"Please! Why would Pilate take him seriously?"

"Miyka'el and my father are the most powerful merchants in Palestine, and the prefect never could resist the shimmer of gold."

"Your concern is touching, but I offered you a choice in Jericho."

"You asked me to play the harlot like that tramp inside. I would sooner die than become an adulteress."

"Then might I suggest you return to your husband lest you fall into temptation."

It was an underhand blow and Leila could see Barabbas regretted the words as soon as they were spoken.

Leila was too proud to show her hurt. Tears might come later when he could not see them or be there to console her.

She inclined her head and spoke quietly. "I see you have no need for me here. I've done what I can. Goodbye, Barabbas."

She turned and climbed the cold stone steps that led from the courtyard. At the top, she glanced back. Barabbas leaned against the doorpost watching her leave.

Suddenly, Deborah appeared, draping her arms about him and caressing his neck. Wordlessly, she led him back inside the dark empty house.

Leila returned to Jericho the following day, watching the sky nervously on her return. From early that morning, the clouds had been militant and the wind blew hot against her skin, bringing the grainy sands of the desert on its wings.

It marked the beginning of *Khamsin*, the desert storm in which scorching winds blew out of the east. By noon, the heat of the wind had become unbearable and the sky had become a quagmire of black and yellow, all but blotting out the sun and leaving her with the impression that night had fallen.

The fine yellow grains of sand invaded every fold of clothing, scratching her skin and forcing her to shut her eyes against its relentless advance. The storm brought no rain. Only discomfort, sand and darkness. The miserable trio plodded on in the hope of reaching Jericho before the full force of the gale struck.

After that, there would be no hope of continuing as visibility would be reduced to zero and any attempt at progress would be an invitation to suicide down the treacherous slopes of the Great Rift Valley that led to the city of palms. They achieved the impossible and reached the outskirts of the city ahead of the inferno. The group trudged in mournful silence through the city gates and on to Miyka'el's home.

When Leila disembarked, her mood did not improve. Servants informed her that another warehouse had been attacked in her absence and that Miyka'el's mood had deteriorated to unbearable depths. What's more, the Roman convoy had arrived and their centurion was discussing a plan of action with Miyka'el.

"The master wants to see you the minute you arrive," a fearful servant had told her.

Leila tried to shake the excess dust from her clothes and, especially her hair before heading to the atrium where Miyka'el and the centurion reclined in conference.

The soldier was hard with a sculptured physique. He had an air of competence about him that caused her to fear for Barabbas. He looked up with an appraising smile as she entered. The hazel eyes were not those of a killer, but of one who had killed. They were hard, but not heartless and devoid of life. They showed intelligence and loyalty and, above all, a resolve to do whatever was necessary to get the job done.

This is the man who will kill my love. Leila gazed at the soldier. Her eyes were drawn to the dark mole on his right cheek that marred an otherwise handsome face.

Miyka'el said. "Leila, this is Gaius. He's the centurion sent by Pontius Pilate to subdue all this zealot activity in Jericho."

"*Shalom*, centurion. I hope you can put an end to this madness."

"I'm certain we shall. It seems we already have a likely culprit."

"But surely this is the work of more than a single man."

"Yes, but we think we know who's behind it all. As soon as we bring him to justice, the attacks will stop."

Miyka'el's smile was thin. "It seems an old friend of yours bears a grudge. Do you remember Barabbas?"

Leila swallowed. "You know I do."

"I had a meeting with your father. He told me that Barabbas had returned to Judea and came to see him. He was asking about you and was informed that we were married."

"Have you found him yet?"

"That's what Gaius is here for. I understand he also has some personal reasons for wanting Barabbas brought to justice."

Leila glanced across at Gaius, wondering what her husband meant, but the soldier didn't offer any explanation.

"Well, I only hope you can put an end to these attacks and bring normality back to Jericho."

"I'm sure we will," Gaius replied. "In the meantime, I would appreciate any information you could give me about him. I understand from your husband that you knew this man well."

"That was a long time ago. Barabbas disappeared and was given up for dead."

"A fact that I am all too painfully aware of. I've been searching for him for over two years now. I thought you might know something about his old haunts, people he was in contact with."

"Barabbas and I seldom discussed his zealot activities. It was a subject that caused much contention between us."

Gaius nodded. "Well, if you think of anything, I'll be in Jericho for the next few weeks."

Leila smiled. "I'll bear that in mind. Now, if you'll excuse me, I must go and clean up. The storm outside has all but ruined my clothes and my skin feels like a ploughed field."

She left the two men reclining around their table and headed for the bath house. It was constructed along Roman lines and built with every convenience and luxury available to a man of Miyka'el's means. An army of slaves manned the hot baths, stoking the fires in furnace rooms that heated the water. There were others skilled in the art of massage and attendants to cater for every whim of the bather.

Handmaids attended her, rubbing her skin with perfumes and oils while she relaxed in the steaming water and later dried herself with a scented woollen towel. When she had finished, she found Miyka'el waiting for her in the passage outside.

She smiled sweetly. "Have you missed me that much?"

Miyka'el was not amused. His expression was grim and cold. "Who did you go and see in Jerusalem?"

Leila was taken aback. "You know why I went to the Holy City."

"I know only what you told me. Now who did you go and see!"

Leila blinked, hoping she could conceal her guilt. There was no reason for it, she thought. After all, she had only gone to put an end to her husband's misery.

Miyka'el stepped forward. "You lied to me and you confirmed your deception when you lied to Gaius."

"A bold accusation," Leila replied quietly, gazing at the floor near her husband's feet.

"I spoke to your father after you left. He was the one who told me Barabbas was back in Judea. He also told me that you once met a zealot contact in Jerusalem in the hope of finding out what had happened to him. Why didn't you tell Gaius about that?"

"It was a long time ago. I forgot. Besides, I never met the contact. He was impossible to find."

"Another lie! Why didn't you tell me Barabbas had visited you?"

Leila was jolted by the extent of her husband's information. She thought for a moment. It was useless to deny the meeting. The guards at the gate had seen him and she couldn't begin to guess who else. "You were busy and the meeting was of no consequence."

"No consequence! The man who wanted to marry you came to see you without my knowledge and you think that's of no consequence?"

"There's no need to shout, Miyka'el. He came to see me and I sent him away."

"And then you went to see him in Jerusalem."

"I went to Jerusalem to find buyers for my clothing products. I have remained faithful to you since the day of our wedding. How dare you accuse me of being an adulteress?" she flared.

"You love Barabbas and don't insult my intelligence by denying it."

"You knew that the day you took me as your wife, so don't play the martyr now. I told my father that Barabbas would return to Judea, but what does a mere woman know? You brought this on yourself, Miyka'el. Don't seek a scapegoat for your troubles."

Miyka'el leaped forward and grabbed her shoulders with both hands, sinking vice-like fingers into her arms. "You are my wife and you will remain loyal to me." His mouth twisted in grotesque rage and drops of spittle splattered her cheek. "And if you so much as glance in Barabbas' direction again, I'll have you stoned as an adulteress."

Leila made no reply. For the first time in her life, she truly feared a man. Never before had she seen such violence in her husband's eyes or felt so powerless to resist him.

Her shock and silence seemed to pacify him. He held her huddled form for a long moment as she waited for the blow to come. Then he relaxed and eased his grip on her arms, stroking them gently.

"I hope we have no repeat of this conversation," he said quietly.

Leila inclined her head meekly, but didn't speak.

"Come." He took her by the hand, leading her to his bedroom. "Dinner is not yet served. Lie with me for a while."

That evening, Gaius joined Miyka'el for dinner. The other guests at the table were Leila's father, Zebedee, and Matthias, Miyka'el's brother. Dinner involved long discussions over the fortification of the men's property as well as a variety of plans to lure Barabbas into a trap of some sort. After Gaius and Zebedee had left, Miyka'el reclined at the table, chatting to his younger brother.

"Do you think this man can catch Barabbas?" Matthias enquired casually as he scraped together some leftover scraps of food.

Miyka'el shrugged. "Who knows? He looks capable enough and Pilate said in his letter that Gaius was his most competent centurion."

"On the other hand, he's been chasing Barabbas for years without success."

"You forget, he caught Barabbas once. It was only due to an inopportune political turn of events that Pilate was forced to release him. Otherwise Barabbas would have been removed as a cause of my misfortune forever."

"Have you told the Roman about your wife's recent involvement with this outlaw?"

Miyka'el looked up at his brother sharply. "Do you think that I would admit to a stranger that I was unable to satisfy my wife's passions? I would die before letting him think Barabbas was a better man than I."

Matthias waved a greasy paw. "Barabbas is a fool, steeped in poverty and hopeless dreams. Why even bother with him?"

"You don't see the way she looks at me or the way she dreams of having his arms around her."

Matthias snorted. "Nor would I care. Listen to me. You have one of nature's loveliest creatures in your grasp. Leila belongs to you and there's nothing she, or anyone else, can do about it. She may want Barabbas, but it's your bed she shares."

"That may be enough for you, but it will never be enough for me." Miyka'el stared deep into the flickering flame of the small pottery oil lamp that hung against the wall. "I vow to you, Matthias, I will destroy Barabbas and remove him forever from Leila's reach."

"And you think Gaius can accomplish that for you?"

"I'm sure he can. He seems to loathe Barabbas almost as much as I do. Rest assured, when next he meets Barabbas, there will be one less zealot in the Roman Empire."

"When does Gaius begin instituting his operation?"

"Tomorrow. Then we'll see how determined our zealot friend really is."

† † † † †

It was well past noon the following day and Leila waited impatiently at the fountain in her husband's luxurious villa. Having been forbidden to leave Jericho, she had sent her maidservant, Zena, to call Minette in Bethany.

She had to get word to Barabbas somehow and tell him that Gaius was involved now. The Roman centurion bore a grudge and would not rest until Barabbas bled in agony on a crucifix. Perhaps, if he knew that Gaius was in Jericho, Barabbas would end this foolishness although, in her heart, she knew that he would never back down. Still, at least he would be forewarned.

Leila was unable to go to him in Jerusalem, but Minette could take a message to him, begging him to come and see her. She glanced up in anticipation as two people entered the gates of the villa. With relief, she saw that Zena was accompanied by her childhood friend.

"Leila," Minette called excitedly and rushed to embrace her. "It's so wonderful to see you again. I've missed you these past few weeks."

"How is the work at the factory proceeding?" Leila smiled. Inside, she ached to forget the niceties and unload her deepest anxieties.

"Very well. We'll have to talk to your father and Miyka'el about finding markets further north soon. Jerusalem is saturated." Minette stopped talking and suddenly looked concerned. "What's the matter? I mention your husband's name and you suddenly look like a mourner."

"Minette, I need your help." Leila's voice was slightly hoarse.

"Anything." Her friend embraced her with strong welcoming arms.

"I can't trust anyone, even in my own household. Miyka'el has forbidden me to leave Jericho. I'm virtually a prisoner here at the villa."

"What happened?"

Leila showed her friend the bruises on her arms. "Barabbas returned to Judea. When he found out I was married, he started waging an insane war against Miyka'el, attacking his caravans and warehouses until his business started falling apart."

"It's no more than he deserves after this," Minette replied bitterly, staring at the deep purple and blue bruises.

"Miyka'el is not so easily subdued. He already knows that Barabbas is responsible and sent word to the prefect, asking for Rome's assistance in the matter."

"His power is even greater than I imagined!"

Leila nodded. "Now a Roman centurion has been sent to take up the matter and I fear for Barabbas' life."

"What do you want me to do?"

"Go to Jerusalem and ask Barabbas to come and see me here in Jericho. I can meet him at the fuller's field by the Jordan river."

"Won't Miyka'el be suspicious?"

"We have to bleach our cloth sometime. He won't raise any eyebrows at a trip to the fullers."

"I suppose so. Tell me where Barabbas lives. I'll go tomorrow."

† † † † †

Minette made the journey to Jerusalem with one of her husband's servants the following day. The sun was hot even in the early hours of the day and it was a weary woman that trudged up the steps to Deborah's courtyard.

She found the second door against the wall of the city and rapped on it softly. Deborah got to the door first and subjected Minette to a suspicious glare. It was not often that strange women found their way to her home.

"Hello, I'm here to see Barabbas," Minette felt immediately uneasy in the presence of the dark-haired woman who had answered the door.

"In connection with?"

Minette studied the woman briefly. Her eyes were a deep hazel colour and she exuded a beauty that made Minette instantly jealous. Her lips were powerful sculptured instruments of seduction, but there was a hardness around the mouth that Minette had not noticed at first.

This was a woman who had experienced years of hardship and deserved to be pitied, not loathed. "I bring him a message from Jericho. One of extreme importance."

The woman frowned. "Who sent you?"

"Please," Minette hedged. "I was told to give the message only to Barabbas."

The woman's expression soured. "I'm sorry. I don't know the man you're looking for."

The lie was almost child-like, it was so obvious. Confronting the woman was useless, Minette thought. She considered the woman's predicament.

She was a stranger, unknown to the zealots, and Barabbas was a wanted man. For all this woman knew, she could be a Roman spy.

"Please, I wasn't sent by the zealots. I know them in name only."

"The zealots are outlaws. You would do well not to get involved with them." The door started to close.

Minette quickly stepped forward. "I was sent by Leila of Miyka'el's household in Jericho. It's urgent that I speak with Barabbas."

If the expression had been sour before, it became positively contemptuous at the mention of Leila's name.

"What's the message?"

"I was told to give it to Barabbas."

"Tell that woman to leave Barabbas alone. He's already made it plain he wants nothing to do with her." Once again, the door started to close.

Minette stopped it with her foot. "If you care at all for Barabbas' continued well-being, you'll call him for me. His life is in danger and he needs to hear what I have to say."

For a long moment, the woman held Minette's gaze. Finally, she came to a decision. Leaving the door ajar, she turned and went inside. A moment later, she returned with Barabbas by her side.

"*Shalom*, daughter of Abraham," the man greeted her.

"My lord," Minette inclined her head.

"You wanted to see me?" He raised his eyebrows as the woman with dark reddish hair clung to his arm.

"I bring a message from Leila in Jericho. She has news of infinite importance and asks that you come and see her in the city of palms."

"Why didn't she come here herself?"

"Her husband has forbidden her to leave Jericho."

Barabbas' expression clouded in anger and Minette regretted mentioning Miyka'el. She continued. "Can you come with me to Jericho? Leila awaits my return."

"Tell her to come to Jerusalem."

"My lord, it's impossible. She can't do that."

"Then nor will I go to Jericho."

"But your life —"

"My life is of no consequence to you, or to Leila. Tell her I'll take care of myself."

"How can you say that!" Minette cried. "Do you truly have no concept of how she feels about you?"

"She made her feelings plain in Jericho."

"The time for pride has passed, my lord. Your stubbornness will get you killed."

"If this message is so important, why can't you give it to me?"

"I was told only to call you. She never gave me the information."

"It seems she's complicated things unnecessarily. I can't help but wonder why."

"Can't you guess?"

"She's married and her loyalties lie with her husband. As I said, she made that plain."

Minette smiled scornfully at Barabbas, shaking her head in disbelief. "You blame her for your circumstances and you don't even know why she's married."

She reached into her belt and withdrew a beautiful necklace of blue sapphires. "She would have escaped her father and Miyka'el in Bethany, but she went back home for this. She said it was all she had to remember you by."

Minette threw the necklace at Barabbas' feet. "Take it, and may you never see Leila again. You didn't deserve her anyway."

She turned to leave, but Barabbas stopped her.

"Wait," he said quietly as he bent down to pick up the necklace. "I'll come with you."

The woman on his arm turned in alarm. "No, Barabbas. This is a bad idea. If Jericho is so dangerous, then why does she want you to go there?"

"It's alright, Deborah. I'll be fine."

"Barabbas, listen to me. You don't even know this woman. It could be a trap."

"It's not a trap and I'm going to Jericho. I'll be back soon enough."

"Barabbas, don't go, I'm begging you. If you cared for me at all, you would stay away from Jericho."

Barabbas took her arms gently and looked into her eyes. "I do care for you, but I'm going to Jericho."

Tears welled up in the woman's eyes, but Barabbas was firm.

"Don't weep for me. I'll be back before you know I've left."

He went inside to fetch his cloak for the journey, leaving Deborah to stare hatefully at Minette who waited patiently outside the door.

† † † † †

By the time Barabbas found the fullers' field at the Jordan River, it was deserted, everyone having left for the day. All that remained was the acrid smell of sulphur, alkali and putrid urine which the fullers used to clean and bleach the cloth.

He had to return the following day and found Leila at the north side of the field, near the bank of the flowing waters of the Jordan River.

"*Shalom*, Barabbas," she was reserved - almost nervous. "I thought you might not come."

"I nearly didn't. What's so important that you had to meet me here, and why are you forbidden from going to Jerusalem?"

She shrugged and shook her head. "Miyka'el suspects you're staying there. Barabbas, listen to me. You have to stop this insanity before something dreadful happens."

"Does your husband always send women to plead on his behalf?"

"That has nothing to do with it. If Miyka'el knew I was seeing you, he'd have me put to death. I want you to end this, Barabbas. He's enlisted soldiers from Caesarea to help him and it seems one of them bears a grudge."

Barabbas smiled for the first time. "The centurion, Gaius, I presume."

"This is not a joke, Barabbas. The man is a viper getting ready to strike. What does he have against you?"

"He and I have crossed swords once or twice. Trust me, he's not a problem."

"I think you underestimate him, but you haven't answered my question."

"It's a complex relationship. Suffice it to say that Gaius being here has nothing to do with your husband's business woes."

"Miyka'el is the one who called him here."

"He probably tipped Pilate off to the fact that I was involved. No, Gaius is here for a very different reason."

"Why won't you tell me what it is?"

"Don't worry about Gaius. It was inevitable that he and I would cross paths again. Nothing can stop that now."

"Be careful, Barabbas. He's a dangerous man."

"I'll meet him and then I'll kill him. Thanks for the warning." He left without saying goodbye. Heading south across the fullers field, he disappeared among the small crowd of people thronging the river's bank.

A short while later, Barabbas was headed back to Jerusalem, contemplating Gaius' demise. The Roman had been instrumental in the death of his brother. He looked forward to evening the score.

† † † † †

Leila returned home to find Gaius dining with Miyka'el and his brother. There was another soldier around the table that Leila had not met before.

Miyka'el saw her sweep past the dining hall and called. "Leila, did you get your material from the fullers?"

"Yes, my lord." She forced a smile.

"We were just discussing our plans for Barabbas' final undoing. Gaius believes he can lure the zealot into a foolproof trap. Come and listen."

Leila sighed. Had her husband's obsessive jealousy driven him to such cruelty? Quietly, she did as she was bidden.

Gaius said. "We'll have to do it carefully. It must reach Barabbas via a reliable source."

"How do you propose we do that?" Matthias grinned in anticipation, sitting forward in his chair.

"The information will have to be leaked by you and your brother."

Matthias shook his head. "We don't know any zealots. Besides, it would be far too obvious. It's bound to arouse suspicion. No zealot would ever trust our word."

Gaius chuckled. "They will trust it if it's perceived as an unwitting error."

Miyka'el frowned. "And how do we accomplish that?"

"Go to your local synagogue. Talk freely about the shipment to each other as you enter by the gates - within earshot of the beggars. But be sure not to pay any attention to them. They're far sharper than you give them credit for."

Miyka'el was sceptical. "How will they get word of the shipment to Barabbas?"

"The Roman garrison in Jerusalem has known about the conduit system for some time. It's impossible to prove, so we've never arrested any of them, but we have occasionally used the information to our advantage by misinforming them."

"Incredible. That people would think to use the blind and deaf as their eyes and ears," Miyka'el said in wonder.

Matthias shook his head. "I wonder how many times we've tipped them off through our own carelessness?"

Gaius said, "Never mind that. This time we can use the information to our own advantage. Tomorrow's your Sabbath. You can slip the information to them then."

Leila spoke for the first time. "What makes you think Barabbas will take the bait? He's never been predictable before. Why start now?"

Miyka'el smiled. "The bait, as you call it, will be irresistible to him. He'll take it without question and Gaius will be ready for him."

"Don't be too sure," Gaius cautioned him. "I've dealt with this man before and your wife is right. He's inventive to say the least. Even if he does attack, it will probably be in a way we haven't considered. You must prepare yourself for the fact that, despite the presence of all my legionaries, you may still lose all of your cargo."

Leila spoke again. "Do you really think Barabbas would be foolish enough to attack a caravan guarded by a cohort of soldiers?"

"Well, it's hardly a cohort," Miyka'el answered. "But that's the brilliance of the trap. The bulk of the legionaries will not be visible. He won't even know they're there until it's too late."

Gaius interrupted. "We still need to prepare for the possibility of escape. You said you have reason to believe you know where Barabbas is staying?"

Miyka'el glanced briefly at Leila. "I have sources of my own and I'm persuaded that he's currently living in the city of Jerusalem. Where, I don't know."

"Then that's where I'll be. I've selected a group of men, all of whom can identify him. They'll be posted at every entrance to the city. That's when he'll be at his most vulnerable."

"You mean you won't be with the convoy yourself?"

"No. If Barabbas sees me, he'll know it's a trap. He'll melt into the desert and we'll never even know he was there. Marcus here will run the operation. He's as likely to capture Barabbas as I am."

"You make it sound as if you're already certain that he'll elude your trap."

Gaius shrugged. "Past experience. I think it unlikely, but I must prepare for every eventuality."

† † † † †

Minette arrived in Jericho as quickly as she could after Leila's maidservant called on her in Bethany. After an urgent discussion with Leila she left, heading straight for Jerusalem. *This is crazy,* she thought. She berated herself for being so rash. However, she secretly revelled at the thought of assisting in the Zealot cause, and this spurred her on in her mission.

The information she had been given could not wait until morning. Gaius' plan was already in motion. According to Miyka'el, the zealots had already received news of the shipment and she had no doubt that Barabbas would attempt a strike.

Despite her fear, Leila had marvelled at Gaius' brilliance and begged Minette to do all she could to warn Barabbas in time.

Minette pushed her donkey as fast as she dared, but the animal was still not making very good time over the rocky ascent to Jerusalem. The sun was sinking fast when she crested the final hill and saw the city walls loom over the Kidron valley. Darkness had fallen by the time she reached the Sheep Gate near the Antonia.

She travelled briskly through the streets of the *Kainopolis*, finding her way by the flickering light of a small oil lamp, and arrived hungry and exhausted at Deborah's door. Deborah took one long look at her and smirked.

"He's not here," she said, starting to close the door.

"Deborah, I'm begging you, this is urgent."

"Tell that harlot to go back to her husband and to leave Barabbas alone. How many men will it take to satisfy her?"

"There's no time for this now. Barabbas could be dead before sunset tomorrow."

"I'm not interested in the yarns that you and that woman spin to lure Barabbas to Jericho at every opportunity."

"He doesn't need to come to Jericho. Just give him a message."

"A message from the Jericho adulteress?"

"Does the *Khamsin* look at a light breeze and call it a desert storm? How dare you stand in judgement of her while you carry the seed of a thousand men in your loins?"

"You witch!" Deborah screamed and launched herself at Minette, tearing and scratching at her hair and eyes.

Minette warded off the sharp nails that raked her cheeks, but she fell to the ground with Deborah's writhing body on top of her. Finally she managed to throw her antagonist off and rose quickly to her feet.

"I see you are as lady-like as you are chaste." She dusted herself indignantly.

Deborah knelt wild-eyed on the cobbled stones of her courtyard, breathing heavily as Minette continued.

"Mark my words, woman. Your jealousy will one day cost you this man you desire so deeply. I suggest you hear me out and take this message to Barabbas with the feet of a fleeting gazelle.

"This caravan of Miyka'el's that he intends to strike tomorrow is a trap designed by Gaius. If Barabbas even approaches the group it's unlikely that he'll escape with his life."

Deborah stared up at the woman, barely acknowledging her words. Minette glared in contempt for a moment longer and then left, storming up the steps and out into the darkened street beyond.

✝ ✝ ✝ ✝ ✝

It was a long time before Deborah moved from the spot where she sat, carefully considering the woman's words. Barabbas was still in Jerusalem. He would not leave until the following day. Should she take the warning to him? The woman seemed to have the correct information regarding the planned raid.

On the other hand, perhaps it was just another ploy to get him back to Jericho. Leila would obviously know about the caravan to Caesarea. She could easily use the information to her advantage.

Deborah thought about Leila and the way Barabbas felt about her. Despite his apparent loathing, Deborah recognised those feelings for what they truly were. He may be able to hide the truth from himself, but he could never hide it from her. It would only be a matter of time before Leila lured him back, like a Greek siren luring sailors to her rocky isle of destruction.

Finally, Deborah came to a decision. Barabbas could take care of himself. He always had done so. By giving him the message, she would be playing right into Leila's hands. No good would come of that, she felt sure of it.

Quietly, she rose and went inside.

In the early morning sun, the group of zealots moved eastwards along the road that led to Jericho. Barabbas was quickly bringing Levi up to speed on the information they'd gathered, as he had been in Masada and only joined the group early that morning.

"Slaves!" Barabbas exclaimed. "There will be other goods such as grain and perfumes, but the bulk of the shipment consists of slaves to be shipped to Rome.

"How do you plan to strike the convoy? From what I hear, Miyka'el's caravans are guarded by a garrison of legionaries these days. He'd never chance such a valuable shipment to the elements, especially after the way you've been harassing him recently."

"I intend to separate the guards from the convoy by means of a diversion. Only once we've done that can we mount a successful attack."

The two men went over the plan in detail and arrived at the rendezvous still deep in discussion.

Levi said, "Have you considered the possibility that this is merely a trap? Gaius is no fool and I wouldn't put such an elaborate scheme past him."

"Of course it's a possibility, but the information arrived via a reliable source in Jericho. Still, we should be able to establish whether it's guarded or not. That's why the attack will take the form of three prongs."

"I only see two groups here."

Barabbas grinned. "The third is just outside Jericho, following the caravan as we speak. I expect they'll send a scout ahead to warn us of any unexpected plans that Gaius may have."

It was past midday before the scouts arrived. There were two of them and they looked nervous.

"What news of the convoy, Belshazzar?" Barabbas enquired.

"Not good, Barabbas. Not good. There's a group of twelve soldiers travelling with the convoy."

"Hardly a problem. You act as if a hoard of Philistines is in their midst."

"That's just it. They seemed so vulnerable and when we checked their perimeter we saw why. There are another four concealed groups of sixteen travelling off the road, but watching every step the convoy takes."

Belshazzar was still a few years short of twenty, with a long scar that ran down the length of his left forearm. He was not a spectacular warrior, as the scar confirmed, but his bush craft was unequalled. He was one of the new breed of zealots who idolised men like Barabbas and Levi, feeding off the legends of their prowess.

Barabbas had come to respect Belshazzar's judgement and their friendship had grown quickly.

"A trap then." He nodded thoughtfully. "Did they see you at all?"

"When does the foolish deer see the lion that lies in wait?" Belshazzar answered with a grin.

"Good. The plan goes ahead, with some minor alterations. We'll have to move the ambush to the pass in the mountains about a mile back."

Levi cut in. "You're not still serious about attacking the caravan?"

"Why not? Gaius thinks he has the advantage. This is when he's at his most vulnerable."

"Do you really think Miyka'el would risk a shipment of any great value in such a ploy?"

Barabbas turned to Belshazzar. "How does the shipment look?"

"Mostly slaves. A few camels loaded with grain and oil and probably some spices."

Barabbas looked back at Levi. "It seems Miyka'el is prepared to risk far more than you imagined."

Levi shrugged. "Perhaps, but I still say it's too risky to mount an attack."

"Well then, let's reduce the risk by mounting a dummy raid. We use the first offence to lure away the hidden legionaries and then attack the main convoy when its cover is weakened."

Barabbas discussed the plan of attack and, soon afterwards, the zealot group had moved their ambush to the new position and made ready. It was another three hours before the convoy came into view. Barabbas gazed down at the pathetic figures in the caged wagons, heads shaved and ready for the markets in Rome. They reminded him of his own journey into captivity as they swayed mournfully against the uneven motion of their vehicles.

They were followed by the great lumbering ships of the desert, each carrying large bags of grain and a variety of perfumes and spices. He smiled in grim satisfaction at the thought of the damage he would do to Miyka'el in this raid.

Barabbas tilted his head, listening for any sign of his zealot comrades, but the men moved over the terrain like owls in perfect silent flight. He could hear the approach of the concealed legionaries as they attempted, in vain, to move furtively through the mountain pass.

They sounded like a herd of behemoth, thrashing about the wilderness. Barabbas listened to the shuffling feet, swishing branches and tiny rock falls that they caused. It was ironic to think that the legionaries were of the opinion that they were moving in ghostly silence.

It wasn't that Barabbas had no respect for the legionaries' abilities, but merely that the soldiers were trained to fight a completely different type of battle. On a legitimate battlefield, the zealots would be equally outclassed, but here in the hidden war of the wilderness, Barabbas and his men were unmatched.

It was a style of fighting that had been refined over generations, passed down from the Maccabees who had defeated the Seleucid Empire and retaken the temple of Jerusalem, tearing the city out of the grasp of pagan rule.

Barabbas listened again. It wouldn't be long now and the first group would begin their attack.

† † † † †

From the other side of the ambush area, Levi quietly watched the legionaries' progress. He had divided his men into four groups - one for each of the hidden

Roman convoys. Although outnumbered two to one, he was unconcerned. His objective was not to defeat the concealed men, but merely to lure them away from the main convoy.

When the guards reached his position, Levi first allowed them to pass by below him so that he could strike from behind. His group moved swiftly and three legionaries were slain in the initial encounter.

Levi heard yells from the three other groups as the zealots began their respective attacks. The legionaries quickly regrouped and turned to face their aggressors in battle. Levi and his men put up a token resistance, allowing themselves to be pushed back as they always kept clear of any truly violent encounter.

Within minutes, the first group from the other side of the path appeared, running from the sixteen soldiers that panted like baying hounds at their heels. Levi immediately called for a retreat and joined his comrades in flight. They were quickly joined by groups from two more quarters with Roman legionaries in deadly pursuit.

He swung left, laughing like a madman as a pilum embedded itself in the soft soil two feet to his right. Several more pilums struck the area around the zealots, but none hit their mark.

Levi was pleased to see that the group had not lost a single man. It was not good to waste human lives on mere decoys.

He raced away from the pursuing soldiers, heading for the gully that would lead them to the ridge above. It culminated in a rocky cliff that became a waterfall during the rainy season. The small band of zealots quickly scaled the walls of the cliff as the Roman soldiers congregated at the bottom.

Levi nodded in satisfaction as a thin volley of arrows erupted from above the cliff, forcing the Roman guard on the defensive. The deadly pilums that would certainly have claimed the lives of many of the fleeing band as they hung helpless on the cliff face were now neutralised.

He was one of the last to reach the cliff's top and reached hurriedly for a bow and arrow, racing back towards the mouth of the gully. There, he took up a position to effectively block the Romans' escape from the gully below.

Down in the gully, the Romans quickly formed ranks, using their shields in unison to create the traditional tortoise for which the army had become so well known. The legionaries at the edge of the group held their shields side by side, right up against each other, while those in the middle lifted theirs horizontally, forming a shell-like canopy that warded off the arrows.

The structure was traditionally used when attacking the walls of a besieged city as it protected the army from soldiers high above on the city walls.

Levi let an arrow loose from his vantage point, aiming for one of the tiny cracks in the rigid tortoise shell roof. The arrow missed its mark and ricocheted harmlessly off the wall of shields.

He was satisfied, however, and mentally patted himself on the back. The tortoise shell, although a good offensive structure against a city, was now working against the Roman legionaries. While they were protected from the vicious barbs and spears that rained down, their structure was also rigid and too bulky to move back down through the narrow uneven terrain.

If he wanted to, Levi could now hold them until nightfall. He counted the shields as he watched another volley of arrows hail down on the Romans from the opposite side of the gully. There were sixty-six Romans altogether down below him.

He quickly reached for another arrow as the group below began shuffling about, loosing his shaft at the cracks that formed in the movement. This time his arrow found its mark, slipping between two of the shields. There was a cry of pain and one man fell from the ranks, writhing on the floor as he threw down his shield and clutched at the shaft of the deadly barb.

Levi could see where the arrow was embedded in the base of the man's neck, just near the collar bone. The man's face contorted in pain as he waved the snapped shaft pathetically in his left hand, like a child with a toy sword. His right hand kept grasping at the short, blood-stained end that protruded from his neck.

There were hoots of excitement as more arrows embedded themselves in the helpless legionary.

Sixty-five, Levi thought. He wondered why the soldiers would put themselves at such risk by moving while they were so vulnerable. He wasn't revolted by the man's suffering. It was something he'd been exposed to far too long, both in the war-torn sands of his desert homeland and in the gladiators' arena in the Roman amphitheatre where he'd displayed his murderous talents to thousands of bloodthirsty fans.

He could still hear the roar of approval in his ears as he held his sword to the throat of an injured defenceless man who he had just defeated. Levi had lost count of the times he'd looked up to the emperor's box, pleading for thumbs up, the sign to spare the life of a valiant gladiator, sometimes even a friend. All too often, the sign would be thumbs down, leaving him with a sense of emptiness and futility as he obeyed the emperor's command.

The soldier finally stopped convulsing and lay still. Several spikes protruded at unsightly angles from his inert form. Sixty-five. The number bothered Levi, but he couldn't think why.

A new thought occurred to him as he watched the remaining legionaries still shuffling around down below. He suddenly realized what they intended. The whole squad of men was reorganising itself into a long snake-like structure that would be able to move in safety down the gully and back to the road.

It didn't matter, Levi thought. By the time they arrived back at the main convoy, it would be a scene of carnage. Barabbas will have slain all the members of the party, freed the slaves and burned what he could not carry away.

With only six soldiers left to guard it, the caravan didn't stand a chance. He took another arrow and loosed it absent-mindedly at the shuffling structure. This time, the shaft embedded itself in the leather seam of one of the Roman shields.

Four squads of soldiers moved as one, covering and protecting themselves against the sharp barbs that the zealots continued pelting down from their position of safety on the rocks above. Four squads. Levi became alarmed for the first time since the beginning of the raid. Squads consisted of twelve to sixteen men, which accounted for a maximum of sixty-four. He had killed three himself, which brought the total down to sixty one, discounting any that might have died among the other three squads.

Hurriedly, he turned to the man on his right who was carefully training an arrow on a weak spot in the wall of shields where a crack repeatedly appeared.

"Wait here. I've got to go and check on something."

The man nodded, refusing to take his eye off the spot where the arrow was aimed. Levi rose and raced along the top of the ridge, back towards the convoy where Barabbas lay in readiness to attack.

Where had the extra soldiers come from? The question plagued Levi's mind. The soldiers had followed too easily. It stood to reason that one would keep half the legionaries back in order to defend the convoy against a second onslaught.

Levi ran frantically, hoping to catch his friend in time before the attack, but in his heart he knew he was too late. He arrived at the site of the ambush just in time to witness the most decisive massacre he had ever seen in his military career.

25

BARABBAS WAS surprised when he heard the scouts report that the concealed soldiers had all given chase, leaving none at the convoy. He was even more shocked to see the remaining group of men turn and join their comrades, chasing the zealot decoy back into the hills.

Barabbas frowned. "Does Gaius think I'm an idiot?"

"They're wide open. There are no more soldiers in the area. We've checked thoroughly," Belshazzar whispered, hovering at Barabbas' side like a faithful puppy.

"Well check again - and take Naari with you. We don't attack until he gives us the go ahead."

Naari was a middle-aged veteran and possibly the only man who knew the wilderness better than Belshazzar. Barabbas had learned over a period of time to trust the older man's experience. If there was something Belshazzar had missed, Naari would find it.

The scouts returned with no news of any unforeseen Roman activity, and yet, Barabbas' instincts told him something had been missed.

"How far back did you check?"

Naari shook his head. "We covered all the high ground in the area. Believe me, there's not a Roman in the world that could deceive these eyes in the wilderness. There are none down there."

"They're there," Barabbas growled. "We're just not looking in the right places."

Once again, his eyes scanned the caravan. He gazed down at the bedraggled figures with their shaved heads huddled in their wagons.

Then he began to examine the rest of the caravan. Mostly camels and, perhaps, thirty civilians. The men gazed about the hills, watching for the inevitable attack. Not nervous, merely watchful. Barabbas smiled in grim satisfaction.

"I see them now."

Naari shook his head in disbelief. "Impossible! If they were there, I'd have seen them."

"You were looking in the wrong place. They're in the convoy itself - the one place Gaius did not expect you to look."

"I still don't see them."

"Look at those merchants down there. Not one beard is older than three weeks and the eyes are those of soldiers, watchful and fearless."

Naari peered down at the group for nearly a minute and then looked at Barabbas in wonder. "A new war these Romans fight."

Barabbas nodded. "There's not enough of them, though. Gaius overlooked that."

He drew his sword and signalled for the attack to begin.

"Spread the word and warn the men not to underestimate their foes. These are not Jewish civilians we're fighting."

The zealots flowed out of the hills like torrents of water in a flash flood, spilling out on the convoy. Even though the caravan had been prepared, the attack came unexpectedly.

The soldiers had barely drawn their swords before nearly half their number had fallen dead or wounded in battle. The remaining men fought valiantly but they were encumbered by the unfamiliar dress. Swords glinted as they clashed under a raging desert sun and the odour of blood and sweat mingled in Barabbas' nostrils.

Two of the cumbersome soldiers rushed at him. He spun under the thrust of the first man's blade, slicing at the soldier's knees. His antagonist fell as blood and small chips of bone seeped from the deep wound.

Rising as he completed his arc, Barabbas reached up and blocked his second opponent's attacking arm by placing his left hand in the crook of the soldier's elbow, neutralising the thrust's impetus. As he did so, he drove his own sword up into the man's belly.

There was a choking sound and bright red fluid erupted from the soldier's mouth. The legionary's eyes took on a lifeless shimmer as a vice-like hand clamped itself around Barabbas' wrist where he held his sword.

The battle was over in minutes and as he turned, looking up at the hill behind him, he saw Levi staring down. Barabbas grinned and waved up at his friend, then turned to the task of looting the convoy.

"Naari, get some men to help you take these camels off the road. We can circle back and sell the goods in Masada, but we'll need to put many miles between ourselves and the ambush before nightfall."

"And the slaves?"

"We'll release them. The zealots have found a few allies today. Some of them will be good fighting men."

He turned to the wagons which looked like nothing more than dungeons on wheels, pulled by a group of oxen. Choosing the first, he released the catch.

There was a shuffle of feet and Barabbas noticed the glint of a weapon inside the cart. His reaction was instinctive and he heaved his weight back against the door trying to push the latch back in place.

As he struggled with the latch, he felt the heaving door against his shoulder. In desperation, Barabbas lunged against the wooden bar which slid reluctantly back into place. Then he shouted a warning to his comrades.

Barabbas' warning came too late, however, and he watched in horror as soldiers streamed from the remaining prison carts. Swords appeared from beneath rough woollen tunics and the prisoners attacked with all the fury of men who had been forced to stand as spectators and watch their fellow legionaries being butchered in battle.

Barabbas ran to assist his comrades, experiencing the bitter taste of defeat as five of his men fell under the vicious thrust of the Roman counter-attack. Naari was the first to fall, cut down by a Roman legionary while he still struggled to untangle himself from several camels' nooses. The old desert fox never had a chance to reach for his sword.

The Romans turned and rushed at the remaining zealots like a pack of angry wolves tearing at their prey. Barabbas raced in towards them, moving with cat-like agility between the flailing blades that cut like ploughs through their pasture of flesh.

He shot between the soldiers, taking a second sword from the hands of a slain legionary and fighting with both hands. His rage drove him into a trance-like madness that seemed to heighten his senses and caused him to move with inhuman speed as the adrenalin pumped through his veins. He lost all sense of self-preservation and lost count of how many soldiers fell by his hand.

In the midst of the battle, he saw Belshazzar practically torn in two by three legionaries. They drove their swords through his torso, lifting him bodily off the ground as they tore their weapons free of his flesh. The only consolation was that the young man never had a chance to feel the pain.

By the time Barabbas emerged from the melee, he was the only surviving zealot in the battle and realized he had to flee. He raced away as quickly as he could from the throng of ill-clad legionaries, seeking freedom in the path beyond.

Escape was denied, however, as Barabbas heard the sound of approaching hobnail sandals on the dusty road ahead of him. The soldiers, having escaped the gully where they'd been pinned down, were now returning to assist their comrades and block off any escape along the road that led to Jericho.

Barabbas cursed his decision to flee in that direction. His ambush had now backfired, leaving him trapped in the pass between two squads of soldiers. There was no way out, other than through the entrances now clogged with Roman legionaries.

He looked about quickly, searching for somewhere to hide. The dry vegetation offered little refuge, but he had to find a place somehow, for to run now was impossible. He could already hear the footsteps approaching from behind - a scouting party from the convoy going ahead to appraise the soldiers of the situation at the other end of the pass.

Barabbas found a narrow fissure in the rocky cliff face and squeezed himself into it. Once hidden in its shadows, he gazed up, considering the possibility of climbing to freedom. It wasn't an option, however, as the walls had been smoothed by years of flowing water and offered few handholds. Lower down would be easy to climb as he could wedge himself between the two walls, but higher up, the crack widened and he would be forced to climb one wall or the other.

Concealment was his only option. *Blend into your surroundings. Change your form so that though your enemy looks upon you, he does not see you.* He remembered the words of his teachers. It was a lesson that had been taught again today, with catastrophic consequences, he reflected bitterly.

Barabbas froze inside the narrow crack as the soldiers, still clad in slaves' uniforms, passed by him no more than a few paces away. They were not intent on locating him yet, however. That would come later. Their first objective was to seal off the second exit. Then their search would begin in earnest

Quickly, Barabbas removed his tunic, rolling it around in the dust and rubble that lay in the recess. Once it was completely covered in dirt, he replaced it. Then he gazed up at the narrow pipe-like crack and the beckoning light of freedom above it.

† † † † †

When he saw the slave-clad legionaries approaching, Marcus called his group of soldiers to a halt. After a few brief words with the scouts from the convoy, he quickly assigned men to fan out and guard the path. Each legionary was to stand firm and guard four square feet of ground, making it impossible for anyone to pass.

The rest of the men were organised into small groups to search the area. Marcus watched as his legionaries fanned out into the pass, covering every inch of the terrain. He followed a short distance behind the search parties, hunting for any sign of his prey. He studied every move of the search parties in front of him, seeing to it that they didn't miss a single stone or hollow. As an efficient soldier, he was not about to let his prey slip away through carelessness.

Gaius had entrusted him with the task of bringing Barabbas back in chains and he meant to succeed. The rebel Jew had defied Caesar far too long and he would pay for his insolence. The soldier watched as one of his search parties approached a narrow crack that ran all the way up the cliff face.

It was wide enough to permit a man to enter and an obvious hiding place for a cornered man. He stood by as one of the legionaries peered inside. The man reappeared quickly, shaking his head.

"You! Rufus."

The soldier turned with an enquiring look.

Marcus continued. "Check that recess again and do it properly this time. You didn't even give your eyes a chance to become accustomed to the light in there."

There was no argument from the young officer who obeyed the order without question, entering the crevice for a second time. This time he was inside for a full two minutes before he emerged.

"What's in there?" Marcus demanded when the man returned.

"It's very narrow, centurion. There's barely room to turn around in there. It's certainly not big enough for two people."

Marcus nodded and waved the group of men on. As they moved off he approached the crevice, waiting quietly outside for a minute, listening intently for any sign of movement inside. Hearing nothing, he slipped in between the rocky walls of the crevice where he stood waiting for his eyes to adjust to the darkness.

The recess was cool and dusty, but small, as the soldier had said. He poked about in the dark corners of the crevice, but there were no hidden areas where a man could conceal himself.

Marcus looked up to see whether it was possible to climb out, but decided it would be extremely difficult, if not impossible. The walls were too smooth to offer any handholds for a safe ascent.

Apart from that, the path upwards was blocked by a huge rounded boulder that had fallen and wedged itself between the walls where they narrowed near the bottom. He gazed about the crevice once more before turning to leave. Once outside, he quickly caught up with the search parties who were busy examining a small cluster of rocks that offered some likely shelter.

† † † † †

Back inside the crevice the boulder moved slightly as Barabbas uncurled himself, trying to flex his aching muscles. He prayed a silent prayer of thanks for the darkness of the crevice and the bright light that shone from above.

It silhouetted his form but also blinded any onlookers from below, making it impossible to distinguish the fine texture of his cloak. All that was needed was to curl his head and limbs so that they were not visible from below.

Barabbas slipped down in silence and peered from the cave, listening for the sound of Roman feet. Soldiers still scoured the area, hunting for any sign of him, but they had moved beyond the cave entrance.

He considered slipping out behind them and breaking for freedom, but thought better of it. They would almost certainly have guards posted to block any exit from the pass.

Instead, he slunk back into the cave, enjoying the feeling of safety it provided. It would only be a matter of time before the Romans finished their search and turned back for a second, even more intense, run.

† † † † †

Marcus was tired and frustrated by the time the soldiers reached their counterparts in the convoy, still having found no sign of their quarry. He knew that each passing moment was just another opportunity for Barabbas to escape and the man had already eluded him once.

The sun was fleeing westwards and that would make escape still easier for a man who viewed this harsh wilderness as a welcome sanctuary. The centurion gazed about the camp and noticed that the convoy's legionaries were still dressed as slaves.

"Get these men back in uniform," he snapped at Rufus, the junior officer who he had reprimanded outside the cave. The young man's face was deeply freckled, giving it the appearance of alternate light and shadow on a forest floor. "And then get a search party together to join those men over there."

He pointed at the group of weary soldiers that had just completed their search of the pass and hesitated.

"Wait. I've changed my mind. Those men couldn't find him the first time. They'll only make the same mistakes again. Replace them and have them stand guard at this end while the rest change into their uniforms."

The stress of the mission was beginning to take its toll. To appear so indecisive in front of his men would not do. He had to portray an image of one who was in complete control of the situation. He also mentally reprimanded himself for his treatment of Rufus. The young man was a dedicated soldier with a deep commitment to his work. There was no reason to take his mood out on his subordinates. With a deep breath, he made an effort to gain control of his thoughts and emotions.

"Do you want the replacement detail to change first?" Rufus asked.

Marcus shook his head and forcibly tempered his tone. "I want them combing the area in five minutes. Send them to me as soon as they're assembled."

The soldiers were volunteered by Rufus and duly made their run through the pass. Their search was unfruitful, as were the following two searches.

The sun was beginning to set and Marcus became more edgy with each passing minute. His only sign was a hunch that something lurked inside that cave. Something that he had not yet seen. He'd even posted the young soldier, Rufus, outside the cave as a guard, but still no clue as to the whereabouts of their elusive prey had been found.

If they couldn't find Barabbas while it was light, what chance would they have in darkness? He was even beginning to wonder whether Barabbas hadn't somehow already escaped from the pass when the tragic events transpired – events that finally revealed his quarry's whereabouts.

✝ ✝ ✝ ✝ ✝

After the first run, Barabbas remained hidden in the relative safety of the cliff's recess. High above him, he heard the caw of a raven. Its shrill call was a familiar sound in the wilderness and quickly melted into obscurity to the untrained ear.

Barabbas recognised it, however, as it was a common method for zealots to locate one another when in close proximity to the enemy. It was the easiest possible way to guide friends to your position without alerting possible foes.

Unfortunately, to reply from inside the fissure would be nothing short of suicidal. While a call from the cliffs above might go unnoticed, one that echoed from the bowels of the cliff would draw Roman soldiers like moths to the flickering flame of an oil lamp. Discovery would be as swift as it was certain.

Instead, he coated his tunic in dust once more and climbed silently back to his earlier position in the narrow crack above, curling up in preparation for the second run.

Once again, the soldiers entered the cave and once again they passed by. When they were gone, Barabbas remained riveted in his position, focusing his entire being on utter silence as he listened for any telltale sign of someone outside the cave.

He was rewarded after a few minutes by the soft crunch of a sandal on stone. This was followed a moment later by more rustling as the unknown soldier squeezed through the dark narrow crack in the cliff's wall.

The man stood silently below, just as had happened the first time, and Barabbas felt the sweat soaking his tunic as he sensed the soldier's eyes roaming the tiny hovel, staring up at his form silhouetted against the light beyond. Barabbas hoped desperately that the thin beads of perspiration didn't fall to the ground and betray his presence.

This time the soldier – Barabbas felt sure it was the same man as before – stayed in the cave much longer than the first. It was as if he knew instinctively that his prey lurked somewhere in the darkness.

Finally, the man swore quietly and left the cave. Barabbas remained in his position until he felt he'd visibly aged before uncurling from the painful position and relieving some of the agonised muscle cramps that had formed around his strained joints.

Once again, he heard the lonely raven's call. It was closer this time, but still, he dared not respond. The soldiers had not moved too far from the mouth of the cave and were scouring the area like ants frantically collecting food ahead of the approaching winter.

It was only after the third run that Barabbas heard the call directly above the crack that led to the cliff's ridge. He decided to risk discovery and alert his friends above. Instead of calling, however, he took a handful of small stones and tossed them as high as he could. The pebbles struck the walls of the crevice and Barabbas quickly ducked as they fell back like hail about him, pummelling his back and shoulders.

Immediately, he checked to see if the soldiers were reacting to the minor rock fall. On hearing their hasty approach, Barabbas silently took up his usual position, melting into the terrain and becoming part of the landscape once more.

Once again, a soldier squeezed into the narrow chamber and Barabbas listened to the man poking about in the rubble below.

"What is it?" a voice demanded from outside. It was the voice of the hidden man who had followed the legionaries and sworn earlier inside the cave.

"There's nothing here, centurion. Probably just a small rock fall."

"Get out of there and let me have a look."

The first soldier exited the cave and was pushed aside as the centurion entered. Dry soil and loose stones crunched underfoot as the soldier tramped about the tiny recess.

Barabbas nearly choked in shock as a hail of small stones erupted against the wall about him. Some even struck his back and then tumbled back to the ground. After another minute of silent waiting, the centurion finally left the cave.

As before, Barabbas didn't dare move until he was quite sure that the soldiers had left. This time, he waited as long as he felt he had the previous time and then began counting again to double the time spent in his cramped position.

While he was still curled up, a shadow fell across the fissure from above. Barabbas squinted up to see Levi's grinning face. He didn't speak, but his eyes communicated his heartfelt relief and a lifetime of friendship in a common cause.

Wasting no time, Levi disappeared to call the other zealots on the ridge together to organise Barabbas' escape. The soldiers had completed their fourth search before Levi returned. This time he was half-naked, having stripped his tunic and a variety of other apparel, tying it together to form a makeshift rope. Several other men, similarly unclad, peered down, smiling in greeting as the long multi-coloured cord with multiple knots was lowered into the cavern.

Barabbas knew it would be impossible to pull himself out of the cavern from his current position. With the sinewy silence of a serpent untwining, he slowly went through the process of uncurling himself, wincing at the discomfort caused as blood began its reluctant flow once more through cramped limbs.

It was only as he dropped to the ground that he realized a guard had been posted outside the cave's entrance. He was alerted by the shuffle of feet as the guard reacted to the light sound.

Barabbas turned to stone, tensing every muscle in his body in anticipation of being discovered. The soldier moved to the entrance and peered inside, looking for the source of the sound he had heard.

It was then that Barabbas moved, before his opponent's eyes could grow accustomed to the light. His hands reached out like clamps and grasped the soldier's throat, cutting off the inevitable cry which would alert the other legionaries. At the same time, he dragged the soldier into the cave and slipped his forearm under the man's chin, still choking off the air supply.

As he spun the man around, he heaved his forehead against the back of the man's skull, using his forearm as a pivot to snap the soldier's neck.

The crack reverberated inside the cave, filling the air with its echo, and a second voice called from outside. "Rufus? What was that noise? Is somebody in there?"

As the words were spoken, something brushed against Barabbas' cheek. He snatched at it, wild-eyed, before he realized it was only the rope of zealot garments that had finally reached the bottom.

"Rufus!" the voice demanded a second time, closer than before.

"Be quiet! Let me listen," Barabbas reduced his tone to a harsh whisper, hoping it would fool the second soldier outside long enough to facilitate his escape.

When no response came, he quickly fastened the garments around his waist and gave a tug to let the zealots above know he was ready. The rope went taut and he was lifted off the ground. He'd not gone far up the shoot when he heard the alarmed yells from the second guard down below and the sound of soldiers rushing to their comrade's assistance.

✝ ✝ ✝ ✝ ✝

Marcus rushed to the cave's entrance where the legionary had raised the alarm. He was secretly pleased that his instincts had been confirmed. Every time he'd entered the cave, he'd felt convinced that somehow his eyes were deceiving him and that, however small it was, it harboured his prey somewhere in its depths.

His satisfaction was short-lived, however, as he saw the inert body of Rufus being dragged from the narrow entrance. The man's head was bent at an unsightly angle and lifeless eyes stared in stark terror from the freckled youthful face.

Marcus yelled as he raced towards the cave. "Stand back! Let me go in after him."

He drew his sword and entered the cave, glancing wildly about him. It appeared to be as small and unoccupied as before. Then he gazed up and saw the reddish hue of the sunset sky in the cave's mouth high above him.

Only then did the truth of the matter dawn on him and the soldier in Marcus nodded in bitter respect for the man who had fooled him so completely.

"The rock is gone," he murmured quietly, nodding as he gazed at the blazing sky. "The rock is gone."

He felt no hatred or resentment towards Barabbas at that moment. There was only disbelief at his own failure and grudging admiration for the ingenuity of his prey. Then, he was suddenly overwhelmed by anger by the thought of the legionary whose life had been lost through his stupidity. Perhaps, if he'd been more quick-witted, he could have saved Rufus from his fate. He glanced up at the open mouth once more and took a moment to ponder how Barabbas had managed to climb to freedom up the smooth walls of the fissure. Then he shook his head and left the hollow for the last time.

"Pack it in and let's go back to Jericho. It's up to Gaius to catch him now."

† † † † †

Barabbas followed Levi, approaching the city from the east along the Jericho road. When he saw the Holy City with the magnificent temple towering like Babel high above the walls and buildings of Jerusalem, he stopped for a moment to admire its beauty.

Levi read his thoughts. "Takes your breath away every time, doesn't it?"

"There were moments yesterday when I thought I'd never see it again." Barabbas' thoughts turned sombre as he recalled his fallen comrades who had indeed missed the chance to see their beloved Jerusalem again. The Roman swords had been wielded by the very slaves they had intended to free.

There was no time to mourn them, however. It was a luxury he could ill afford. Instead, he would express his sorrow, as always, in revenge. That was the zealot way. Rome would pay for her deception with the lives of legionaries and stolen taxes.

They veered off the road, heading for the Mount of Olives and the Garden of Gethsemane. Their conduit would be waiting for them there, at least, that was what Barabbas hoped. They were a day late as they had decided not to travel by night. Instead, they had waited until morning before heading back to Jerusalem.

Normally the meeting with their conduit was just a formality. The group would exchange news with him which he would carry to the movement's information network. This time it was different, however. The Romans had developed a new tactic and it was essential that all zealots in the field know about it as soon as possible.

Also, their information network had been compromised. Either a street informant in Jericho was to blame or the Romans had learned their methods of gathering intelligence and begun to feed them false information. The network had to be notified.

Barabbas was relieved to find Gahan waiting for them, hidden in the shadow of a natural overhang. There was a large round boulder against the steep slope and an opening which indicated one of the many tombs that littered the mountain's slopes.

Levi waved at the man as they approached. Gahan was a serious man with a non-existent sense of humour that Barabbas always found disconcerting. He didn't smile as they approached.

"You must leave this place immediately," were the first words out of his mouth.

"What's wrong?" Levi asked in surprise.

"Roman legionaries guard every gate to the city. Word from the informants is they're looking for Barabbas. Every legionary has been handpicked to be able to identify you on sight."

"Gaius," Barabbas growled. "How does he know I'm in Jerusalem?"

Gahan shrugged. "No idea, but he knows."

"Who gave us the information?"

"I don't know. Whoever it was spoke to Deborah. She was the one who contacted me."

Barabbas shrugged. "I have no pressing engagements in Jerusalem. There are many cities in Judea and the soldiers can't guard those gates indefinitely."

"One more thing," Gahan stopped him. "Deborah was attacked. She's fine, but badly beaten."

Barabbas' voice was a low snarl. "Where was this?"

"In her home. She said not to tell you, but I thought you should know."

"Do you know who did it?"

"A former zealot – Eleazor. He was looking for you. Deborah said he was completely crazy. He was ranting over some scroll. Then he took some of your things and left."

Barabbas glanced across at Levi. His friend seemed paralysed with fear. Barabbas turned back at Gahan. It was imperative the man should not know their true feelings.

"I have to see her. Now."

"How will we get in?" Levi's words were dull and lifeless, but his expression was tense. It was the first time Barabbas had seen his friend and mentor truly afraid.

"There must be a way."

Gahan was astonished. "You're not seriously considering this!"

"Go and tell Deborah I'll see her before nightfall."

"Barabbas, this is insane. There's nothing you can do for Deborah now."

"And if it happens again?"

"I can arrange for protection day and night until you return."

"That will be in about six hours."

"Does Deborah truly mean that much to you?"

"You think she doesn't?"

Gahan stared at Barabbas a long time before replying. "She must. Either that or there's more to Eleazor's insane ramblings than Deborah realized."

"Don't put too much store by Eleazor's words. He's a fool. Who knows what caused his madness? Tell Deborah I'll see her this evening."

"It'll be through the bars of a dungeon's cell, I'll tell her that."

Barabbas laughed. "Cheer up, old friend. The Romans couldn't find me yesterday. They won't find me in Jerusalem."

He gave Gahan some instructions and arranged to meet the man again in an hour. Then he and Levi waved to the conduit and disappeared, leaving a troubled Gahan dreading for their safety.

They saw their first group of soldiers as they approached the Holy City from the west, near Herod's stately palace. Levi was freshly shaved and dressed in a soldier's uniform that Gahan had reluctantly brought from inside the city.

The small group of legionaries ahead of them moved slowly towards the heavy wooden gates that marked Jerusalem's entrance. It was the opportunity that the two friends had been waiting for.

Levi increased his pace in order to catch up with them as he oversaw Barabbas who laboured under the weight of the legionary's pack and cloak.

It was a burden that the Jewish nation had long since learned to accept, albeit with resentment, that soldiers were entitled to force non-citizens in occupied territories to carry their cloaks for one mile, but no more.

"Ave," Levi hailed the group who turned to greet him, ignoring the poor Jew who laboured under the weight of the stranger's pack.

Levi continued. "Can you tell me where I can find the barracks in this city? I've been sent to bring a message from the prefect."

"Who's the message for?" asked a soldier at the back of the group. The man seemed to be limping but was obviously in charge of the small band of legionaries, although he carried no rank that Levi could see.

"It's for a centurion from Caesarea, a special envoy or something. I was told to give it to anyone at the barracks, however. Apparently they'll get it to the right person."

"It sounds like a message for a centurion called Gaius. You won't find him at the barracks. He's residing at the Antonia on the other side of the city. He may even be in Jericho by now."

"Gets around, does he?" Levi grinned.

The man smiled and shrugged. "He answers directly to the prefect, so nobody really knows what he's doing."

The conversation settled into idle chatter as the group drew up to the city gates. There was a debate as to who the most difficult centurion in Jerusalem was, until the topic swung to the foul food in the barracks and soldiers took turns telling stories of the worst gruel they'd ever been served and where they had been stationed at the time.

Each man competed with the last and Levi laughed along with them as they described disgusting bowls of slop that even dogs had left untouched in some instances.

Barabbas watched carefully as the band of soldiers marched through the city gates. No other soldiers were immediately apparent but he knew they must be there, somewhere in the crowd that thronged in the gates of the city.

It was only once he entered that he saw a group of soldiers gambling with a pair of dice. The legionaries didn't seem overly interested in their game, however, and heads turned every time someone entered through the gates. Narrow eyes carefully examined the faces of those entering and the game never seemed to get going.

Barabbas recognised at least two of the soldiers as men who had guarded him in prison. The gamblers grinned and nodded in greeting as they recognised comrades who shared their barracks and their interest quickly turned to others who were entering via the wide gates.

Nobody took any notice of the Jew who was merely a servant of one of their own. Such a face was not worth scrutiny and was allowed to pass without question.

Once they had successfully passed through the gates, Levi asked. "Where's the Antonia, then?"

"Over by the temple," the legionary with the limp pointed eastwards. "You'd have to be blind not to find it."

"Thanks." He turned and took his pack from Barabbas. "You can go."

Then he turned on an unsuspecting, burly citizen and said. "You! Take this and head towards the Antonia."

Levi waved at the group that had accompanied him into the city and looked around for Barabbas, but his friend had already disappeared among the hordes of people that clogged the city streets.

As soon as he had turned a corner and the soldiers were out of sight, he took back the pack from the heavy-set man. "Here, you don't have to carry this for me," he said in Aramaic.

He left the man confused and resentful, muttering about the shortcomings of the Roman mind.

Barabbas wasted no time getting back to Deborah's home. When he arrived, she flung herself at him, weeping uncontrollably.

"It's alright. I'm here now." Barabbas held her gently, taking care not to damage her already bruised body.

His mind was on the scroll, however, and he ached to see whether it was still safely hidden.

"I was worried, Barabbas. You're a day late."

"It was a trap." Barabbas' mind returned to the scene at the pass. He remembered Naari's butchered body, hanging from the camel's nooses that entangled his friend's bleeding corpse. The full impact of what had happened was only beginning to dawn on him now. There was no inflexion in his voice and he spoke as if in a daze.

"They were all killed. I led those men to their death. What happened here?"

Barabbas looked around the small apartment for the first time. It was neat and tidy, but he noticed that there were no longer any pottery jars in the room. Bowls also seemed to have vanished and one lonely metal plate rested on an otherwise empty shelf against the wall. Even that plate had a dent on its edge.

"Eleazor." Deborah shuddered as she spoke the name. "He's a madman, Barabbas. He kept ranting about a scroll that you have. The one Gaius seeks, he said."

"What did he take?" Barabbas immediately regretted the question. His concern was too apparent.

"I don't know. He went through your things. I tried to stop him, but - what scroll did he want, Barabbas?"

"You must rest," Barabbas led her through to her room.

He sat with her, waiting patiently until she fell asleep. While he waited, he heard Levi arrive. His friend came in briefly and forced a smile, but left Barabbas alone with Deborah. Barabbas shared his friend's anxiety, but nothing could be done until Deborah was asleep.

Finally, Barabbas heard the deep rhythmic sound of her slumber. He rose quietly and stepped into the living room where he found Levi seated on a mat in the corner. His friend rocked back and forth like a horse straining against its chariot before the commencement of a race.

Levi roused himself when Barabbas entered the room.

"Where is it?" His voice had the tautness of a badly strung harp.

"I haven't looked for it yet." Barabbas strode across the room and knelt down by the flat stone against the wall. Digging his hand into the crack, he quickly prized away the stone with Levi peering anxiously over his shoulder. It came away with a dusty scrape and revealed its contents.

"Thank the Lord it's still here," Barabbas whispered.

Levi slumped to the floor. "We have to move it now. It's no longer safe here."

"I'll keep it on my person until we find a place."

"You're sure you don't want me to keep it?"

"What good would it do? Eleazor could find me; he'll find you."

"Well where, then? We can't just bury it somewhere. We must be able to keep an eye over it."

"We'll have to give it to someone else. We're marked now. Until we remove Eleazor, the scroll is still in danger."

Levi swallowed to relieve his parched throat. "Who would we give it to? Not the zealots. If they had this information, they would destroy us all."

Barabbas was deep in thought. It was as if he'd not heard Levi's words. "The Essenes at _Qumran_ would be ideal, except that their connection must be common knowledge by now."

Levi shook his head. "As we discussed before, it's the first place Pilate would look and Eleazor is bound to return there at some point. It has to be someone far removed from us but who will never say a word."

"What about this new sect, the followers of the Nazarene rabbi?"

Levi chuckled. "You want to mend fences with Simon, the convert?"

"I wasn't thinking of him. There are others that hold to his teachings. My family for one thing. Jashan would be good. He's assisted us before."

"Still too close. It wouldn't surprise me to learn that Eleazor has already poked around Sepphoris to find out whether you've been there in the recent past."

"There are others." Barabbas was still distracted as thoughts rushed about in his mind.

Barabbas watched Levi's expression. He could see that his friend was coming around to the idea. He never uttered a word, though. Levi had to agree without any urging, but Barabbas already knew who would receive the scroll. Someone close, yet so far away from their world as to be above suspicion.

He would have to lay an old grudge to rest, he decided, as the conversation drew to its conclusion. Levi finally nodded and Barabbas grinned. All that remained was to remove the scroll to safety.

Neither of them noticed the figure that watched them from the darkened doorway. She had been roused when Barabbas had risen to leave and watched them now as they discussed the scroll. How long had Barabbas been with her? And never a word about something that was so important to him. Deborah was confused and hurt by his lack of trust.

Her whole body trembled. In the entire conversation, her name had not come up once. Why wouldn't he tell her the secret of the scroll? Silently, she turned away and slipped back into her room.

26

LEILA NEVER left the grounds, but spent her day tramping the villa's gardens like a lioness pacing back and forth in a cage. She refused all meals to the point that her stomach burned as if it had been pierced by a glowing hot needle.

Where was Barabbas? Had he got the message in time? Her mind was plagued by questions that had no answers.

You shouldn't be thinking like this, she told herself. What concern is it of yours what happens to Barabbas? He doesn't belong to you. The words of her rabbinic Lord echoed in her ears. *"If a man even looks at a woman with lust, he has already committed adultery with her in his heart."*

She thought of the times she had dreamed of Barabbas while sharing her husband's bed, longed for him while she belonged to another. Had she committed adultery? In her heart, she knew the answer.

If only she could know what had happened to him! He'd been warned early enough. And yet, if he had got the message in time, why had the soldiers not returned? She had been watching the villa's gate since their departure early that morning and still none had returned. Gaius had given his word to Miyka'el that he would keep him informed, whether they caught Barabbas or not.

The waiting had left her tired and haggard. She dipped her hand into the cool waters of the stream that ran through the garden and then continued her pacing.

The sun had long since set when she finally ended her vigil. Still no soldiers had returned. No word had been sent from the centurion. After a second day spent waiting, she could stand it no longer. That evening she made her decision. It was a course of action that she knew would loose the wrath of her husband, but she had to know what had happened.

She called Zena, her maidservant, and left her under instructions to maintain the strictest secrecy. The two women met the following day long before dawn and set out for Jerusalem. They arrived in the Holy City late that afternoon and headed immediately for Deborah's home. When Leila knocked on the door, Barabbas answered.

He glanced over his shoulder like a guilty child. "Leila, what brings you to Jerusalem?"

"Praise the Lord in heaven you're alright," Leila cried with relief.

"Why wouldn't I be?"

"You got my message in time."

"Leila, you're not making sense. What message?"

Leila was suddenly confused. "About the trap. If you're here, you must have avoided it."

"You knew about that!"

"I sent Minette to warn you. She told me –"

"When did you send word?" Barabbas glanced back inside the house again. This time his eyes blazed with anger.

"The night before the convoy left Jericho. Minette told me she arrived just as darkness was falling, but you had already left."

"We met to discuss the raid. What was the message?"

Leila closed her eyes and bit her lip. Her voice choked as she spoke. "How many did you lose?"

"Every one," Barabbas spoke through clenched teeth. "That woman's jealousy has cost me some of my closest friends."

"Is it possible she tried to get the message to you?"

Barabbas shook his head. "I came back here afterwards and spent the night with Deborah. She never said a word."

Barabbas' confession stung like a wet leather thong. Leila blinked, hoping he hadn't divined her true feelings, and chided herself for the jealousy she felt. She was suddenly uncomfortable like a child before a stranger.

There were so many things she desperately wanted to say to him, but none of them could be permitted. She had to deny her feelings and somehow forget the hurts that had passed between them.

She inclined her eyes and shuffled. "Well, I - I just wanted to be sure you were alright."

She started to speak again, but hesitated. Then she looked up and forced a smile. "Well, I'd better be on my way. People in Jericho will be wondering what's happened to me."

As she turned to leave, Barabbas stopped her. "Leila, wait – please."

Leila turned, smouldering embers of hope suddenly igniting in her. She had no idea what she was hoping for, but she hoped nonetheless. Barabbas chanced another furtive glance back into the house and then said. "Let me walk you to the city gate."

After they left the courtyard they walked in silence for a while, neither of them sure how to breach the chasm that had grown between them.

Finally, Barabbas spoke. "I need your help with something. A matter of even greater importance to me than the zealot cause."

"Is there such a thing?" Leila asked carefully.

Barabbas held her gaze and, for the first time, Leila saw the great pain in his eyes. "There were once two such things."

She quickly glanced away, gazing across at the pool of Bethesda with its huddled group of ailing occupants. "What do you need from me?"

He reached into his tunic and removed the scroll, tarnished by age. "This document is possibly the most important item in all of Judea. It's in danger of discovery and there's nobody else I can give it to for safekeeping."

"What is it?"

"You have to give me your word that you'll never try to read it, or show it to anyone. Nobody can know of its existence."

"What's written there, Barabbas?"

"Your word, Leila!"

She hesitated for a moment and then nodded. "As you wish. I give you my word."

"Thank you. If this scroll falls into the wrong hands, it could precipitate a war that would destroy our nation. In the right hands, at the right time, those words will bring the Roman Empire to its knees and free Israel forever from bondage to a godless master."

"So it is a zealot cause."

"No, the zealots can never know of its existence. They would use it for their own ends and bring its curse upon the whole of Israel."

"What secret is so great, Barabbas?"

Barabbas shook his head. "I took an oath to protect this document and, right now, I'm endangering it. Those who seek it would never expect me to give it to you. Please, never try to read it. Just take it to Jericho and give it to your father."

"My father!"

Barabbas nodded. "Please, don't ask questions. Just promise me you'll do it."

Leila nodded. "He's in Sepphoris at the moment. I'll keep it with me until he gets back. He'll have it ready for you when you return for it."

Her heart pounded with excitement, not merely because of the scroll but also because of Barabbas. He had entrusted his greatest secret to her, one that he would give to no other person, including the woman he lived with. It meant that he trusted her and, above all, it meant he would see her again.

Barabbas led her to an inn just south of the *Kainopolis* where they found Levi. He agreed to accompany Leila back to Jericho. The scroll's safety was essential and they wouldn't risk losing it to bandits along the road.

As they headed towards the city's exit, Leila held the scroll close to her chest as if it was an only child that had to be protected from harm. Barabbas stopped about five hundred paces inside the city gate.

"I can't go any further. Soldiers are still looking for me. Go with God. May He bless and keep you on your journey back to Jericho."

"Goodbye, Barabbas." Leila had to fight the urge she felt to hold him close to her but she had resolved that, no matter what happened, she would remain faithful to her husband. It was what she had vowed before God and what was required of her by law.

He nodded and smiled. Then he squeezed her hand and was gone. Leila turned her face towards Jericho, thinking about her explanation later, when Miyka'el questioned her about her whereabouts.

† † † † †

Barabbas hastened home to Deborah. She had been inside when he left. Hopefully she had not seen him leave. Their arguments over Leila had become more heated as time had passed.

There would be another one, he knew, but this time he would not be on the receiving end. Deborah had put her own petty jealousy ahead of the zealot cause and cost the movement an entire unit of men. She was responsible for their deaths and he would have his say.

He couldn't begin to understand what had motivated her to keep the information from him, but he intended to extract an explanation. After that, he would decide what to do. He wasn't sure, but to stay with a woman who could be that treacherous – perhaps he should simply walk away.

By the time he arrived back at the apartment, he had worked himself up into a rage. Her name sounded like an angry snarl in his ears when he called her, but she didn't answer. He stormed through to her room, thinking she must be asleep, but she wasn't there.

After checking the roof, he returned to the living room and sat down to wait for her. He was still waiting when the sun rose the following morning. Deborah had left no word as to her whereabouts.

In desperation, Barabbas sent word to sympathisers in the city. They, in turn, sent word to the movement's eyes and ears on the streets - the beggars and street urchins - who spread the word like a silent plague. Deborah was missing and Barabbas was looking for her. If they could locate her, rewards would be forthcoming.

It was late that afternoon when a young zealot appeared at Barabbas' door. His hair was dishevelled and his clothes covered in dust, but he brought news that would later lead Barabbas to the blood-chilling conclusion that would drive him back to Jericho.

"*Shalom*, Barabbas." The man was one of the more promising youngsters Barabbas had met in the wilderness near *Qumran* after he had returned from Carthage.

"Amos," Barabbas nodded in greeting. "Any news on Deborah's whereabouts?"

"News, yes, but it doesn't make any sense."

Barabbas frowned. "Well where is she?"

"One of the beggars saw her near the temple late yesterday afternoon. He said she went into the Antonia."

"The Antonia? Why would she go into the Roman fortress?"

The young man shrugged. "Like I said, it doesn't make any sense."

"Was she alone, or accompanied by soldiers?"

"We questioned the man at length. He was adamant. She went in alone and of her own accord."

"Do you think she's still there?"

Amos shrugged. "Who knows? He didn't see her come out but he left the area at sundown. She may have exited after dark."

"And no word from her since." Barabbas was deep in thought, trying to fathom her reasons for going there.

Amos shuffled as if unsure of what to do. Barabbas suddenly noticed the young man was anxious to go.

"Alright, thank you, Amos. You'll keep me informed if we hear any more news?"

The young man nodded and left quickly. Barabbas closed the door, puzzling over

Deborah and her whereabouts. It was about an hour later that the truth of the matter struck him. Only one thing could have precipitated her behaviour.

A vice gripped his heart and the panic began to pound at his temple as he realized what was about to happen. Without even stopping to grab his coat, Barabbas bolted from the house. He was halfway up the steps of the courtyard before logic began to fight its way through the chaotic thoughts that raced about in his mind.

Soldiers were still looking for him - men who could identify him. He would have to find another way out of the city. That wasn't difficult. He lived in a home that specialised in alternative routes out of Jerusalem.

Twenty minutes later, he had lowered himself down a stout rope that hung from the window on Deborah's roof. Soldiers might find it there later, but that was no concern of his. This was the second time the woman had betrayed him. He had no intention of returning there.

Barabbas quickly circumvented the city and set off on the road towards Jericho. He panted as he ran, hoping desperately that he wasn't already too late.

27

DEBORAH HAD been resting in her room, enjoying the cool dark shadows that kept the scorching Judean heat at bay. She had heard the knock at the door and risen to answer it, more out of habit than anything else.

Barabbas had got there first and Deborah had frozen in fear when she had heard him utter the name. Why could that adulteress not leave him alone! She listened carefully, hoping desperately that Barabbas would send the woman away.

Would her own deception be revealed, she wondered. The woman was bound to mention her warning. Anything to endear herself to Barabbas!

It was a minor difficulty. She could merely claim Minette had never arrived. And if it was her word against Minette's, Barabbas would believe her. *Please, Barabbas, send her away.*

The conversation was subdued and Deborah couldn't hear clearly what was being said. Finally, the woman left.

Then Deborah's world crumbled about her as she heard Barabbas call the woman back. Deborah slumped to the floor, holding her breath as she bit back the waves of rage that surged through her body. She could hear the inflexion in his voice, the gentle way in which he spoke.

I knew it! The words echoed over and over in her mind. *Even after all this time, he cannot forget about her.* The tendons in her neck tensed at the taste of bitterness that filled her mouth. She peered around the corner again. He was gone.

Quickly, she rose and left the house to follow him. When she reached the street outside, she saw the man she loved disappearing around the corner alongside the woman she despised.

It was while she followed them that she made her decision. She would stop at nothing to keep Barabbas. The other woman had to go.

As the two headed towards the Antonia, Deborah followed discreetly. Barabbas suddenly stopped and reached into his tunic. Deborah watched in disbelief as he removed the small copper scroll from his belt and handed it to the harlot.

She could almost taste the bitterness she felt at the thought of the bruises she still carried for that document and, when pressed, Barabbas had implied that the scroll didn't even exist. He would pay for his betrayal too.

She moved sideways out of the main street and into a dark corner to think. She could not hear or see them any longer. Her breathing was heavy, as if she'd run a Greek marathon, and it came in sobs of hatred.

She peered outside again from her recess and saw the two of them head south towards the temple. They bypassed it and headed for the inn where Levi stayed.

Eventually, the three emerged and set out towards the city gates. Deborah followed them at a distance until Barabbas stopped, as if ready to turn back. She quickly slipped into another alley and watched from the darkness.

Finally, Barabbas returned, alone this time, and passed by no more than ten paces from her place of hiding. Obviously the harlot had been sent back to her husband in Jericho. Deborah let Barabbas pass by while she formulated a plan of action. She now had information she could use. All that remained was to make sure it was used to her best advantage.

Deborah remembered Eleazor's words. Gaius also sought the scroll. Although she had no idea why, she knew one thing for certain. He would destroy anyone who kept it from him. A small nudge in the right direction and she would be rid of Leila forever.

It was a sure bet that Leila would protect the scroll from discovery and Gaius dealt harshly with those who stood in his way. Deborah gently caressed one of her scars as she remembered her dealings with him.

If, on the other hand, Leila relinquished the scroll, well - it was extremely important to Barabbas. If she lost the scroll, she would probably lose Barabbas' love along with it. Either way, Leila would no longer be a feature in his life.

Deborah quietly straightened her garment and hair. Then, drying the tear stains on her cheeks, she headed for the Antonia.

† † † † †

Gaius prowled the walls of the City, stopping every now and then to question guards who had been posted as lookouts. All reports were negative. Barabbas hadn't been seen.

Numerous men fitting his description had been arrested, only to be released the following day with no explanation or apology. Unless they were Roman citizens, they had no rights and were not protected by Roman laws.

The centurion was growing anxious. Two days had passed since the raid on the caravan and the trap had been a decisive, but incomplete, success. Although the zealots had been taught a lesson, the instigator was still at large.

He had received yet another message that morning from Pilate. The prefect's obsession with the scroll had grown to such proportions that Gaius was beginning to fear for the man's sanity.

Since the death of Sejanus, Pilate's patron, the prefect's political stature in Rome had become shaky, to say the least. It didn't help that Sejanus had been implicated in a plot to kill Caesar. He had been found guilty and executed and all those who were close to him had been deemed guilty by association.

Tiberius was obsessed with treason and trusted nobody, not even his closest advisors. The only reason Pilate had survived the emperor's wrath was because of his distance from Rome and all the events that had culminated in Sejanus' execution.

Staying in Judea presented problems of its own for the prefect, however. Herod Antipas, king of Judea, was an upstart who had all the political savvy and treachery of his father with the added advantage of having grown up in Rome amongst

Tiberius and the current members of the senate.

He was in constant opposition to Pilate and forever sending word to the emperor to undermine the prefect's authority in Judea. Herod's network of informants had grown so large over the past few years that the prefect had become hard-pressed to get any information to Rome ahead of him and that had also discredited him in many instances.

The Sanhedrin was the other thorn in Pilate's already tormented flesh. They had the approval of the people of Judea and could incite them to revolt at any time. A revolt at this point would be sure to wrench power from Pilate's all too flimsy grasp. That meant that the prefect was forced to give in to their every demand, which in turn provided more ammunition for Herod.

Pilate needed an angle - something to prove his loyalty to Tiberius - and, perhaps, something to win the loyalty of the Sanhedrin. The copper scroll provided for both of those possibilities. The quantities of gold and silver that the Jew had implied existed would make a worthy gift, even for a man as wealthy as Caesar, while the religious value of the document could be used as a bargaining chip against the Sanhedrin.

Gaius imagined that, with the copper scroll in his possession, Pilate could secure any promise from them and solidify his political position in Judea. After reaching a suitable agreement with the Jewish religious authorities who despised Herod anyway, problems with the Judean King would take care of themselves.

If he didn't lose his sanity first, which Gaius believed was becoming more likely with each passing day. His thoughts were interrupted by the arrival of the messenger.

He was one of the legionaries that worked in the Antonia - a small reedy man that Gaius could never picture on any battlefield he'd ever fought on. Others had obviously concurred with Gaius' judgement of the man and assigned the legionary as a clerk to manage administrative duties in the fortress.

"Centurion, sorry to bother you, but you're needed urgently at the Antonia."

"What is it?" Gaius had been introduced to the man, but the name escaped him.

"There's a woman at the Antonia who wants to see you. She says she has information that may be of value to you."

"What information could she possibly have that would interest me?"

"She wouldn't say, even when we pressed her for it. She's been thrown in the dungeon to await your return."

"And you have no idea what this is about?"

The man shrugged and shook his head. "She says she needs to talk to you."

"Very well. Hold her there until I come. First I'm going to finish my rounds on the city wall. The men are becoming less alert as time passes. By dawn Barabbas could parade through the gates on a camel and they wouldn't notice him."

Gaius nodded, dismissing the man, and continued his journey around the city wall. It was well past midnight when he arrived back at the Antonia and he first went through to the mess hall and found something to eat before proceeding to the dungeons to collect the woman. He was surprised to find her bruised and dishevelled, shivering in the dark hovel.

"Did my soldiers do this to you?" he demanded.

"No, my lord. It was an outlaw that broke into my home."

He responded with a curt nod, wondering where he had seen the woman before. He couldn't remember, but felt certain that he had dealt with her in the past.

"What's this information you have for me?"

She hesitated before answering. "It concerns a scroll that I believe you're looking for."

Gaius was stunned. He could hardly believe that any Jew would know why he was truly there. "Who told you I was looking for it!"

"We have eyes and ears all over the city." She held his smouldering gaze.

"Zealots." Gaius murmured. Her admission surprised him. He could have her killed for the words she'd just spoken. He was almost afraid to hope for too much from this woman, but she seemed too confident to be bluffing. "Do you know which scroll I seek?"

"I have no idea what it contains, but I know the material it's made of."

His heart pounded like the drum of a racing warship. The material - she had to know!

"Where I can find it?"

"I suspect it's hidden in Jericho, my lord."

"How could you know this?"

"I watched someone collect it here in Jerusalem. Someone from the household of a merchant in that city."

"Which house!" he urged her.

"I believe it was the house of the merchant, Miyka'el."

Gaius swallowed, trying to conceal his shock. The man had brought him here to find Barabbas. Was it possible that he had an interest in the scroll as well? The more Gaius thought about it, the more it began to make sense.

Every time he'd pressed Miyka'el about Barabbas' motive for his attacks, the man had been evasive or changed the subject. Perhaps the vendetta Miyka'el and Barabbas waged concerned the copper scroll.

Gaius needed more information before he could make his decision. "I don't believe you. I know the man you speak of. He's an upstanding citizen and friendly towards Rome."

Deborah shrugged. "Very well, my lord. I've told you what I know. May I go now?"

The woman was not fooled by his bluff. That in itself told Gaius something. He smiled at her intuition. "No you may not. Why did you bring me this information - what do you hope to gain?"

"Nothing, my lord. I merely —"

"Don't lie to me, woman!" He grasped her wrist and twisted it painfully. "I could keep you locked up here indefinitely. Now tell me - why!"

Deborah cowed under the heat of his outburst. Her mind was racing. To tell him the truth was to lead him to Barabbas. Even the mention of Leila's name might lead him to the truth. No! The harlot must reveal her guilt alone.

Pain erupted as Gaius twisted her wrist again. "Answer me, woman."

"I want him dead," she cried in agony.

"Who, Miyka'el?"

"Eleazor." She winced as she rubbed her sprained wrist. Her eyes watered from the pain.

"What does he have to do with all this?"

"He was the one who gave the scroll to the member of Miyka'el's household."

"Where did you see this?"

"At the Sheep Gate - yesterday. By now the scroll must be in Jericho."

Gaius considered her words. They made sense. If Miyka'el and Eleazor had managed to steal the scroll from Barabbas, the rebel Jew would certainly have had more than enough reason to strike out at the merchant.

There was no more powerful motivation that Gaius could think of to cause Barabbas to attack with such harshness. Only one thing still bothered him.

"Why do you want Eleazor to die?"

"Look at me, my lord. Can you not see the reason?"

Gaius' eyes narrowed as he reached out and touched a kaleidoscope bruise on her cheek, examining it carefully in the dim light.

"He did this to you?"

Deborah nodded as Gaius thought carefully about the action he would take.

"Very well." Gaius said. "I'll go to Jericho. You will stay here under guard, however, until I get back. If I return with the scroll you can go but if not," he paused, "I'll want a further explanation."

✝ ✝ ✝ ✝ ✝

After he'd left, Deborah leaned back against the damp dungeon wall and smiled to herself. She silently blessed the chauvinistic male mind that was so easily manipulated because it could not grasp the idea of an intelligent woman with an agenda of her own.

By sunset the adulteress would be dead. A fitting payment for her crimes. Barabbas would have lost his precious scroll. That would be his payment for betraying the woman who cared for him so deeply.

She would be forgiving, however, and in his sorrow he would find comfort in her arms. Then they could forget their tortured past and look towards their future together. She smiled blissfully, cradling herself in her arms as she dreamed of a life with Barabbas in a world without Leila or the scroll.

It would be a world without secrets, except one. Barabbas would never learn who had handed the harlot over to the Roman wolves - sons of a she-wolf - and given the scroll into their hands.

The flickering yellow light of the oil lamp caused demonic shadows to dance about frantically on the walls as Deborah caressed her own neck, imagining that it was Barabbas' fingers that were entwined in her long sun-bronzed hair.

The shadows seemed to grow larger as the tiny flame flickered in eerie silence, consuming the darkened wick until, finally, the lamp was snuffed out, engulfing the dungeon in darkness and setting the shadows free.

Darkness had settled in Jericho when Leila's carriage rolled through the gates of Miyka'el's home. Levi had hopped off several streets before she arrived home and followed discreetly on foot until the carriage had reached the safety of the villa.

She exited quickly and raced through the gardens, heading for her room. Careful not to let anyone see her, she entered the house via a kitchen door and stole down the passage. With any luck, Miyka'el would have been at work all day and might not have noticed her absence.

The passage was deserted and she moved quickly towards her bedroom. She would hide the scroll there – in a place that was close by where nobody else would look.

All hopes of avoiding discovery were dashed as she entered her room and met Matthias' round greasy form lounging on her bed. He grinned broadly as she entered.

"Hello, beautiful flower of Sepphoris. May I ask where you've been all day?"

Leila flushed in anger. "How dare you come into my room. When Miyka'el finds out about this, he'll have you stoned."

Matthias' voice cut like an icy blade. "You can dispense with the Greek theatrics, although I admit you have all the makings of a fine actress."

The insult cut deeply; actresses were considered to be lower than prostitutes. It was not uncommon for them to strip naked, or even copulate on stage, in an effort to enthral their audience. Their morals were such that men of higher standing were forbidden to marry them under Roman law, even though they were freeborn citizens.

"Wait until my husband hears of this." She turned to leave, feeling humiliated under his lustful gaze.

Matthias grinned again. "What a good idea. He's waiting to see you anyway. In fact, he sent me to fetch you when you arrived."

The man stood up and motioned with mock politeness for her to lead the way. It was with trepidation that Leila entered the atrium where Miyka'el reclined on a sofa. He scowled as she entered the room, making her feel even more nervous.

Matthias shoved her forward with a devilish smile as Miyka'el rose from his seat. Leila waited quietly for her husband to speak, but he remained ominously silent. The tension mounted as silence escalated into a chilling war, each side waiting for the other to speak first.

Leila composed herself as fear turned to defiance and resentment for a man who was too weak to utter his thoughts. Miyka'el continued pacing before finally turning to face her.

"You defied me."

"I am your wife, not a prisoner in your household."

He nodded quietly, but a possessive madness burned in his eyes. Instead of speaking, he lashed out and struck her across the cheek with the back of his hand.

Leila jolted, trying to evade the blow, but Matthias was ready and shoved her forward, back into the path of the striking hand. Enraged by her predicament and helplessness, Leila rounded on the slug-like form behind her.

The move was so unexpected that neither of the men had time to react. Matthias bellowed like a wounded behemoth as a savage finger dug into his eye, clawing deep into the protective recess of the skull. He clutched at the bloodied sightless organ in agonised fury as he shoved Leila to the floor. Miyka'el was upon her as Matthias reeled away, shrieking threats from a private world of pain.

"You'll die for this, Leila," Miyka'el rasped. "I'll have you stoned as an adulteress and then your body – what's this?" He suddenly clutched at the hard object under her tunic.

"No!" Leila shrieked, trying to push him away.

She was powerless, however, and Miyka'el pinned her down as he ripped away her garment to reveal the copper scroll. Leila wept in despair as she tried to wrench the scroll from his grasp, but he pushed her down again.

"You'll be confined to your quarters under guard until I decide your fate." He glanced at the scroll as he turned to place it on the sofa.

† † † † †

Miyka'el called for guards to take her to her room and ordered someone to send for a doctor. Matthias was taken to have his eye attended to, while Miyka'el sat down to read the scroll he had taken from his wife.

The words on the document burned his eyes, etching themselves on his mind. Their revolutionary sentiment pointed directly to Barabbas. Miyka'el glowered. He would see her dead for this.

Then all thoughts of Leila's fate vanished as the scroll revealed the secret it held. Its reflection gleamed golden in his eyes and he re-read the hurriedly carved words. Could it be that this was the legend he'd heard of?

The scroll unveiled the story of its massive fortune, buried for centuries in an effort to protect it from heathen nations and foreign gods. Turbulent times had led desperate men to take action and remove valuables from the temple, hiding them from the marauding armies that invaded Israel's borders. Although the words were vague and even cryptic at times, they pointed to the pool of Bethesda as the place where the treasure was buried.

Miyka'el realized the very real danger he placed himself in by even keeping the scroll in his possession. Rome was a superstitious nation ruled by omens and this document, although written some few hundred years ago, implied that the empire would one day fall.

The emperor would not treat the words, or the man who possessed them, lightly. It occurred to Miyka'el that the best course of action might be to hand the scroll over to Gaius and say it had come into his possession via a zealot informant.

He didn't consider this for long, however. Such a course of action would mean giving up the treasure, which Miyka'el was loath to do. He'd dreamed of finding this document since childhood, when he had first heard of the legend. Now it had come into his possession and he was not about to give it up. The artefacts listed in the scroll were of such immeasurable value that no man could resist the temptation to keep them for himself. With such a treasure in his possession, he could restore all the losses Barabbas had caused him and have fortunes to spare.

He carefully rolled up the scroll and placed it in the large metal safe. Then he went to bed, trying to fathom a way of getting at the treasure undetected. People thronged the pools day and night in the hopes of finding their healing. It seemed impossible, but Miyka'el vowed to find a way. He finally had the information in his grasp. Soon the treasure would be his.

✝ ✝ ✝ ✝ ✝

The early morning sun gently cascaded over the forest of date palms and palatial buildings in the oasis, warming the city from the cold desert night. This morning, however, forces gathered around Jericho.

Men converged on the city, all gathering for a single purpose; a secret, hidden for generations, but one which, when unleashed, had the power to destroy a nation. The forces converged on Miyka'el's home. Its inhabitant was unaware of the interest or violence that the document in his safe invoked.

Gaius arrived early that morning, along with Marcus and several legionaries, having travelled through the night. He was covered in dust from his journey and unshaven when he entered the merchant's home. It was the first time that Miyka'el had seen the centurion less than perfectly dressed, but Gaius didn't seem to care.

After the ritual greetings, Miyka'el asked. "Any sign of our militant adversary?"

"I'd have thought his capture no longer concerned you," Gaius replied.

Miyka'el was puzzled. "Why wouldn't it? I want to see him hanging on a Roman crucifix just as much as you do."

"Did you know he was involved with a certain copper scroll?" Gaius flopped down on a couch, uninvited and uncaring of the layer of dust that settled on the expensive fabric.

"No I didn't. What is this about, Gaius?" Miyka'el was becoming annoyed with the centurion's abrasive manner.

"You never told me why Barabbas was attacking your caravans and warehouses."

Miyka'el shook his head. "Why do zealots do anything?"

"For all their faults, they attack with purpose. They attack Roman invaders and Roman sympathisers – tax collectors and the like. You're neither. Why does Barabbas chase you like a baying hound?"

"It's what I was hoping you would be able to find out when you caught him, which you have yet to do." Miyka'el reached nonchalantly for a bunch of grapes on the atrium's table.

"Tell me about the scroll."

"What scroll?" It seemed the centurion wasn't going to be swayed that easily.

"The one you seek to take from Barabbas."

Miyka'el popped one of the small sweet morsels into his mouth, gathering his thoughts. It was obvious that the Roman somehow knew about the scroll, but how much could he know? It had only just come into his possession.

It was one thing to take it voluntarily to Rome, but if discovered now, he would have some explaining to do. It would look as if he was somehow involved and the revolutionary words still scorched his mind when he thought about them.

There was also the matter of the money. He needed that. It was the easiest way to restore his losses. Admission of knowledge would never do. It could only lead to trouble. He had to play out the bluff.

"There's no such thing. I asked you to come because Barabbas was destroying my business interests – costing me money. That's all."

Gaius nodded. There was a vicious gleam in his gaze. "Tell me, Miyka'el, where do you keep your valuables?"

Miyka'el shrugged. "I have many possessions. They're kept in many places."

"I was referring to business contracts – cash – that sort of thing. You work from here, don't you? Where do you keep those belongings?"

"Why do you ask?"

The centurion rose from the chair. The former mock exuberance was gone and his voice was a deathly purr. "It's a simple enough question, Miyka'el. I won't ask it again. Now take me to your office, or wherever you keep your valuables in this house."

The merchant sighed and shrugged. He stood up and headed for his private office. When they got there, Gaius glanced about the room. His eyes rested on the stout metal safe in the corner.

"The key," he held out his hand.

Miyka'el went to a corner and retrieved a leather thong with several keys from a pottery jar that rested on an expensive oiled shelf. He selected the correct key and handed it to the centurion.

Gaius opened the safe and hunted briefly through its contents.

"Nothing," he muttered and turned back to study the merchant again. There was nothing Miyka'el could do. All he could hope for was that the centurion would be satisfied with an empty safe and leave it at that.

Gaius glanced at Marcus and then down at the other keys in his hand. "What are these for?"

Miyka'el tried to swallow, but his throat suddenly felt as dry as the sands of the Negev. He was quickly becoming aware of the fact that he had never experienced true fear before. This was the first time in his life that he'd looked into the eyes of a man who was prepared to kill him.

"I have time, Miyka'el. Take me to your other safes."

Miyka'el suddenly felt numb all over, but moved in a mesmerised stupor out of his office. The centurion followed him, along with the other soldiers, back to the atrium where Miyka'el ushered him into a side room hidden behind a heavy scarlet curtain with a white candle stand embroidered on its face. There was another safe in the dark corner of the room.

Miyka'el felt as if his skin would blister under the centurion's gaze. Gaius quickly searched the safe, sifting through the multitude of documents that spewed from its gaping mouth onto the cold stone floor. Once again, there was nothing of interest inside.

Gaius glanced at the leather thong, grasping the two keys he had used in his palm. Jiggling the remaining three keys, he raised his eyebrows and nodded. "Lead the way."

The centurion didn't deign to replace the items or close the safe. Instead, he allowed Miyka'el to lead him to the remaining safes in the house. Two of the keys were for private chambers where many of Miyka'el's larger valuables were kept. Gaius carefully searched each room, making sure to palm the respective keys so that he didn't miss one out by mistake.

When he turned to face the merchant with the final key, Miyka'el suddenly sagged to the floor, retching violently as the bitter yellow bile rose up in his throat. Gaius shook his head and called a servant.

"Take me to your master's bedroom," he instructed.

The servant hesitated, but buckled under the centurion's commanding gaze.

✝ ✝ ✝ ✝ ✝

Gaius found a third safe in the bedroom and, using the last key on the thong, opened the safe easily. He plunged his hand into the recess and the copper scroll was the first item that emerged.

He sat down on the merchant's bed and quickly scanned the document. The words on the scroll erupted like a volcano in Gaius' mind. As he read, column by column, he realized that, in Jewish hands, this document would incite an uprising that would never be abated until either Israel or Rome was destroyed. He was confused by the fact that Barabbas had, for some reason, kept it a secret for so long.

In Pilate's hands, the scroll was unlikely to be any less volatile. He would have to reason with the prefect and convince him to bury the scroll somewhere, or better yet, destroy it.

He knew in his heart, however, that Pontius Pilate would never agree to that. It even occurred to Gaius to destroy the document himself, but his long ingrained sense of duty prevented him from doing that. He had promised Pilate that he would produce the scroll. It was the only way to clear his record.

He spent the next hour poring over the document, considering the possibilities and trying to decipher the cryptic wording. Once he was sure he had the gist of it, he returned to Miyka'el who was busy wiping his mouth in the atrium under the watchful eyes of Marcus and the three other legionaries.

"It seems you've been less than honest with me."

Miyka'el's lip quivered slightly and his face was deathly pale. "You have to give me a chance to explain."

"I gave you a chance and you lied to me. Why would I believe you now?"

"Listen to me, Gaius. Greed kept me from telling you the truth. I had no idea how important this scroll was to you. It only came into my possession last night. I found it among my wife's belongings."

Gaius' smile was thin. "First you lie, and then you hide behind the garments of a woman, pushing her into the face of the storm. I'll hear no more of this."

He turned to the legionaries who guarded Miyka'el. "Put him in fetters and if he continues his pathetic bleating, gag him. Then prepare for a journey to Caesarea. We leave within the hour."

He rose to leave the room, then stopped. "One more thing. Send a messenger to Jerusalem. I want him to tell the centurion of the watch that I want a guard posted around the pools of Bethesda. Nobody enters or leaves until the prefect arrives. Also, when he gets there, he must go to the dungeons and have the Jewish woman released."

Having issued his orders, Gaius left the atrium, heading for the household's baths where he could clean himself and shave. He took the scroll with him as he did not intend to let it out of his sight until he presented it to Pilate in Caesarea.

True to his word, he and his detail left Jericho within the hour. The scroll hung on Gaius' belt and Miyka'el was in fetters between two soldiers, heading to Caesarea to stand trial for his involvement with the document. The merchant needed a good scare, Gaius decided. He'd become too familiar with his Roman masters and too bold by far. Nothing that a suitably intimidating trial wouldn't take care of, but the lesson had to be taught.

† † † † †

It was a race against the sun to reach Jericho, but Barabbas made it to the city gates before nightfall. His head ached from dehydration and he was out of breath. While his body felt as though it could take no more punishment, he forced himself on anyway.

Quickly, he traced his way through the twilight streets lined with palms, heading directly for Miyka'el's home. By the time he reached the gates of the villa, he was beyond caring and didn't even offer the guards an explanation.

"I'm here to see Leila," he growled and walked through.

When they tried to stop him, he pushed one roughly aside while violently twisting the wrist of the other. "Call the guard if you want, but you'll find I have every right to be here."

The two men swayed in confusion, not sure whether to believe him or not. Barabbas could not know that the master of the house was no longer there. He was merely grateful that the guards no longer tried to stop him.

Once inside, he quickly found a servant and asked where he could find Zena. Only a fool would ask for directions to Leila's quarters. The maidservant was found among the women at the servants' quarters. When she noticed him, she glanced about nervously, rising to meet Barabbas before he got too close to the group and quickly took him away where the other slaves wouldn't hear her. The news she gave Barabbas filled him with rage.

"Take me to her," he snarled.

Zena escorted him through the myriad of buildings and passages that made up Miyka'el's palatial villa, until they arrived at Leila's room.

It wasn't until he arrived there that Barabbas encountered any serious conflict. The door was guarded by a surly slave that seemed to fill the doorway. This, Barabbas decided, could be one of nature's immovable objects.

"Nobody enters or leaves. Master's orders."

Barabbas didn't waste time arguing. He reached forward slowly so as not to arouse suspicion and grabbed the slave's thumb, twisting counter-clockwise. The man pivoted instinctively to prevent the joint from snapping and Barabbas used the man's own weight to complete the throw, twisting the wrist violently while heaving the man's body in the same direction.

The slave flew through the air, landing a few feet away. Barabbas quickly slammed his foot into his antagonist's neck, just below the ear. The man lost consciousness before he could raise his head from the floor.

There was no key so Barabbas kicked the door open, smashing the makeshift lock that had been hurriedly attached. Inside, he found Leila, glowering on her bed as she examined the bruise on her cheek in the dull handheld mirror made of polished metal.

He rushed to her and held her head in his hands, gently caressing the bruise. "Did Miyka'el do this to you?"

She nodded, taking his wrist in an attempt to push it away. It was a pitiful attempt, however, and ended with her merely holding his wrist.

"He's a dead man," Barabbas growled.

"No, Barabbas." She reached for his face to make him look into her eyes.

"This is nothing to do with you and me, Leila."

"Barabbas, listen to me. Miyka'el's not here. Gaius has taken him to Caesarea." She suddenly closed her eyes, unable to look at him. "I don't know how to tell you. It's too terrible."

Barabbas took a deep breath. The dreaded news was confirmed in her broken gaze. "How did he find it?"

Leila shook her head. "It happened while he was beating me. He felt it under my tunic - I hadn't had a chance to hide it - and took it from me. Then he locked me in here."

"When did he give it to Gaius?"

"He didn't. The slaves who brought me my meals said he tried to hide it. Somehow the centurion knew it was here."

Barabbas suddenly leaned back with a bitter chuckle.

Leila looked up. "This is funny to you, Barabbas?"

"They destroyed one another with their own jealousy."

Leila's look of incomprehension demanded an explanation.

Barabbas said. "It was Deborah who told Gaius about the scroll. She must have followed us and seen me give it to you. If Gaius had found the scroll in your quarters, you would be the one headed for Caesarea, but it seems Miyka'el, for reasons of his own, wouldn't tell Gaius the scroll was yours."

"Never mind that, Barabbas. What about the scroll?"

He shrugged. "What's done is done. I've been looking forward to a good war my whole life, but we still have time. It's the treasure they're after. Everyone sees the gold and forgets the scroll's true significance. Pilate will be no different."

"Treasure?"

Barabbas nodded. "The scroll reveals the whereabouts of an ancient treasure."

"So you're going after it."

"The difficulty is getting to it. People are constantly coming and going through the area."

"Why, where's it hidden?"

Barabbas hesitated. "I can't be sure, but every clue points to the pools of Bethesda."

"Of course!" Zena spoke for the first time.

Barabbas regarded her with a puzzled frown.

Zena explained. "None of us could understand why but, before he left, the centurion sent one of his legionaries to Jerusalem with instructions to post a guard around the pool of Bethesda. Nobody is allowed to enter or leave until the prefect arrives."

Barabbas narrowed his eyes, considering the situation. "I've given it a lot of thought over these past months, and I think we can find a way in. We'll have to act quickly. Pilate will waste no time getting to Jerusalem."

"And Miyka'el?" Leila asked.

"Forget about him. His fate is not important."

"He's still my husband, Barabbas."

He saw the pain in her eyes and his heart softened. "I know, but there's nothing you can do for him now. Only time will reveal his fate. Right now, I'd better get back to Jerusalem. I'll need Levi to help me get at that treasure."

"Can I help?"

Barabbas shook his head. "I can take care of it."

"No, Barabbas. I want to. What can I do?"

"I don't want you involved. I've placed you in too much danger as it is. I cringe at the thought of what might have happened to you had Gaius found that scroll in your possession."

Leila smiled. "I'm not suggesting you let me plunge into Bethesda's swirling waters. I have access to items you might need. Carriages, donkeys. How were you planning to carry such a vast treasure out of Jerusalem?"

"I suppose we do need some form of transport," Barabbas sighed. He was secretly glad of the excuse to take her with him.

They took a large ox-drawn cart and several donkeys as pack animals. As they left the villa, Barabbas fixed the guards with a defiant glare, daring them to make a move to stop him, or Leila, from leaving.

The sentries remained at their post, however. These were confusing times with the master having been taken away in chains. There was a void of authority. For all they knew, the master's wife was heading for Caesarea to sort it all out.

Soon, the travellers had left the city gates and were trundling up the steep pass that led towards the Holy City. Barabbas never bothered to enter the city gates. Soldiers still searched for him and it would have been foolish to risk his life unnecessarily. Instead, he sent Leila to call for Levi, who met him on the Mount of Olives.

The rendezvous was near an ancient olive tree, stooped with age and gnarled by centuries of exposure to the sun and rain. There, Barabbas told them how he intended to retrieve the treasure.

Levi was suitably impressed by his friend's initiative. "We'd better hurry then. Although we can't move it until tonight, we can make our preparations in the meantime."

About an hour later, they reached a suitable point along the Herodian aqueduct that fed the city with water from the north. The two men worked like oxen round a mill under the hot Judean sun, smashing their way through one of the heavy concrete slabs that formed the roof of the water pipe. While they did this, Leila and Zena kept watch for any intruders.

Their work was completed without incident, however, and soon they were able to dip their hands inside and splash the cool water on their heads and necks. They then packed several items that would be needed to retrieve the treasure. Sacks, oil lamps to light their way through the tunnel, spades and bars to lever any slabs that might have to be removed. That done, they rested, waiting until nightfall when they could enter the city undetected.

As the sun began to vanish behind the clouds on the western horizon, leaving a gilded sky and charcoal-coloured mountains in its wake, the two men took their equipment and entered the gentle current of the aqueduct, allowing the running water to wash them towards the city.

The lamps were held high as there was no more than a few inches of musty air at the roof of the watery tunnel.

Barabbas soon lost all sense of time in the dark current as the water began to chill his bones. His head bumped constantly against the roof of the aqueduct, but he was too tense to become truly annoyed. His mind was fixed on one thing only; the treasure that lay in the chamber by the pools.

They travelled for what seemed like miles through the darkened void until, with a jolt, Barabbas struck the obstacle.

"What is it?" Levi grunted as he came up short behind Barabbas.

Barabbas' heart sank. "Bars blocking the entrance to the city. Why didn't I think of it!"

"So it's over. A curse on Herod for his thoroughness." Levi's disappointment was like a heavy load, forcing them under the water, drowning all hopes for Israel's future.

Barabbas didn't reply. Instead, he felt around the base of the bars and then asked Levi for the heavy bar they had brought with.

"Forget it, Barabbas. We're wasting our time here."

"You give up too easily, old man." Barabbas sounded almost cheerful.

"Those bars were built to withstand the onslaught of an entire army," Levi protested.

"Yes, but generations of water and air have done what an army couldn't hope to accomplish. These bars are practically rusted through."

Barabbas heaved against the grid, levering his metal rod against the bars in the tunnel. The bar slipped and splashed as Barabbas slammed against the grid. He cursed as he withdrew to check for any injuries in the dim light of the oil lamp.

Satisfied that there were no cuts, he approached the bars a second time. Repositioning the bar in such a way that it wouldn't slip again, Barabbas threw his weight against the grid.

This time Levi joined him in the narrow tunnel, adding his weight to Barabbas' efforts. There was a creaking sound as the rod scraped against the bars, but Herod's defences held firm. The two men retreated, panting from their efforts in the cramped tunnel.

"What now?" Levi wondered.

"We keep trying. Those bars are bound to break eventually."

After a third attempt, Barabbas checked the bars and found that, although slightly bent, they remained intact. He decided to try another pair of bars to see if they would have more luck.

This time the bars bent easily and, after a second attempt, there was a crack as the weaker bar gave way. A second bar snapped shortly after that and the two men, spurred on by their success, heaved their all into the original bar that had remained so stubbornly rigid. It took time, but they eventually broke it in two and made enough room to pass.

Barabbas flashed a grin over his shoulder. "Looks like Herod didn't think of everything."

Not long afterwards, the two men washed into the quiet pools of Bethesda. Barabbas peered up at the portico, filled with sleeping figures all waiting for the waters to stir. He didn't need the scroll to find the treasure chamber as the words were so etched in his mind that he could rewrite the scroll from memory.

As quietly as he could, and taking care not to splash, Barabbas swam across the pool and began scraping at the third slab from the left edge of the pool. He'd been busy for nearly twenty minutes when he felt Levi's hand clamp over his wrist, preventing further work.

Barabbas froze, pressing himself against the wall of the pool as a Roman guard crossed the portico, gazing about as if in search of the noise Barabbas had been making. They waited many minutes before continuing.

Soon, Barabbas had scraped away the mortar from between the slabs and was about to begin levering the block away when the soldier returned, this time actively hunting for the source of the noise. The two men ducked quietly beneath the surface of the dark waters as the soldier approached the edge of the pool.

Barabbas remained below until his lungs flamed like a smelting furnace, screaming for oxygen. He cautiously clawed his way to the surface, floating up like a long-dead waterlogged bough finally released from its muddy prison, rising without a sound. He forced himself to exhale quietly and then took a silent breath of fresh air, feeling the relief it brought. His heart was pounding and he had to fight the urge to pant for the air his lungs craved.

Peering quietly over the edge of the pool, he saw the soldier heading back towards the portico, still gazing about the area as he went. Barabbas heard the quiet trickle as Levi rose to the surface with the caution of a Nile crocodile seeking its prey.

They waited again with infinite patience, facing one another with tense expressions as they listened for any sign of movement outside the pool.

Finally, Barabbas took the bar and levered it between the slabs once again, trying to pull the block back from its position against the pool's edge. The heavy stone slab refused to budge and Barabbas cursed the watery pool that offered no foothold, reducing his weight and power to that of someone half his size.

Levi helped, but the two men found it impossible. The stone remained stubbornly in place.

They struggled through the night and, twice more, had to stop work as soldiers patrolled the portico or came to the edge of the pool. Eventually, overcome by fatigue and frustration, Barabbas gave up. He looked up at the sky, noting the glimmer of first light on the eastern horizon.

"Time we were gone from here," Levi echoed his thoughts.

Barabbas nodded and the two men slipped silently back across the pool. They found the aqueduct's outlet and entered the cool current. Barabbas felt as though he was entering the mouth of a giant serpent as he ducked under the water.

When they reached the bars, they secured the equipment there. No need to carry it all the way back, only to return with it the following night. Then followed an arduous trek back through the narrow tunnel of water, this time without light, as the oil lamps had long since become sodden and useless.

Although there was no equipment to carry, Barabbas felt like Atlas under the weight of his failure. All the way back, he did the maths in his head, calculating how much time they still had before Pilate would arrive.

It would take Gaius two days to reach Caesarea and it was certain that Pilate would leave immediately, probably at first light on the third day. The trip back would be made by carriage, which meant that Gaius and Pilate would be at the edge of the pool by sundown of day three.

Would they start digging immediately? Or would they wait until the following morning before beginning their hunt? These were the questions that plagued Barabbas in the darkness of the tunnel.

Once again, he lost all sense of time as he pushed his way back towards freedom. Eventually, he saw the shimmer up ahead of him. It was a flash of light that told him escape from the deathly tunnel was near.

It gave him a sense of unreality. It had been dark when he'd left the pools and he'd missed dawn while down in the tunnel. The light was bright when he emerged and the sun already well above the horizon.

Barabbas emerged into the blinding light of the sun, hearing a concerned voice as he felt his way out. He closed his eyes against the painful rays.

"Are you alright, Barabbas?" Leila asked.

Barabbas nodded, reaching out for a steadying hand. Levi emerged behind him and was helped by Zena, who brought thick coats of sheepskin to dry the men off. Once more or less dry, they headed to the wagon, reaching for the dry cakes of bread that the women had packed for the expedition. Leila made no mention of the treasure until the two men had rested and eaten.

Barabbas finally told the women what they were aching to know. "We couldn't get to it. The stone was as stubborn as Balaam's mule."

"Never mind. We'll try again tomorrow." Levi bit into his bread, scattering crumbs as he did so.

They slept during the day and entered the aqueduct again at nightfall. Barabbas had forced himself to doze, but sleep came in short feverish bursts. A new fear had now entered his mind. What if the women were discovered before he found the treasure?

Legionaries patrolled the aqueducts on a regular basis, checking that they were maintained. If one of those patrols came upon the broken slab with the women camping nearby, his quest would be over.

He forced himself not to think about it as he entered the dark flowing water, heading back to Jerusalem and the pools of Bethesda. The following morning they returned empty-handed. Barabbas refused to speak of the matter and spent the day in morose silence, brooding over the treasure.

By his reckoning, they had one more night, if they were lucky. After that, all was lost. Pilate would probably be in Jerusalem by this evening. If God spared them, the prefect would sleep off the journey and return the following morning to begin his search.

Barabbas thought it unlikely. After the way the prefect had been pursuing the scroll, he would almost certainly begin digging the moment he arrived in Jerusalem. And he wouldn't be digging with a couple of bars and an oil lamp, Barabbas thought bitterly. The prefect would have the benefit of hundreds of legionaries, as well as all the equipment of the Roman army at his disposal.

If the prefect arrived tonight, all was lost. The legionaries would descend like locusts and clear the pools of every scrap of treasure, every temple artefact. Everything he and Levi and Nathaniel and all the other protectors had spent a lifetime defending would be lost.

He couldn't let that happen, he decided, as he entered the tunnel for what he knew would be the third and final time. He would either return with the treasure, or not return at all.

As he entered the icy water, Barabbas stopped and looked back at Leila. "If we're not back by dawn tomorrow, climb on the wagon and run. Don't go back to Jericho. The legionaries will be coming from the south."

"No, Barabbas," Leila shook her head. There was a deep pain in her eyes.

"Dawn tomorrow. Run. I want you as far away from here as possible. There's nothing you can do for me after that."

Gaius pushed his men as hard as he could and made it to Caesarea by sundown on the second day. He headed straight for the palace where he was ushered into Pilate's private quarters just as the prefect was about to start having dinner.

Pontius Pilate rose from his seat and excused himself from the table, leaving his guests to start the meal without their host. When he entered his study, his expression was sour.

"You've interrupted my meal. The news had better be good."

"Barabbas is still at large, whereabouts unknown."

"I had to leave my guests at the table to hear that?" Pilate raised his eyebrows in question.

Gaius slowly brought his hand forward, revealing the scroll that he held behind his back. "Barabbas will seek us out now."

"Give me that!" Pilate leaped forward, snatching the scroll from the centurion's hand. He raced across to the lamp with feverish excitement and carefully began to digest the scroll's contents. He read it a second time before acknowledging Gaius.

When he did, it was with rapt admiration. "You've done it. By all the gods, you've done it."

"Barabbas must still be found."

"You'll manage that too. I never doubted your abilities."

"The sooner we find him the better. As long as he's out there, the treasure remains at risk."

"You read this?" Pilate became petulant.

"Do you think I'd have risked bringing you the wrong document?"

Pilate thought a moment, then nodded. "So where do you think the treasure lies?"

"It's not totally clear, but it points to the pools of Bethesda in Jerusalem. They certainly fit the description. It's the first place I'd start looking."

"And Barabbas knows this?"

"It stands to reason he's read the scroll."

"What you should have done was place a guard around the pools of Bethesda."

"That was done before I left Jericho."

Pilate beamed. "For once, it seems you've done your job properly. How did you find it?"

"It was in the home of none other than the merchant who tipped us off to Barabbas' presence in Jericho in the first place. I suspect he was using us to locate the scroll."

"Does everyone know about it? What's his interest in the document?"

Gaius shrugged. "My guess is it was purely mercenary. He's no real threat."

"Have you read these words? This could be a personal attack on Rome. I assume you arrested him."

Gaius nodded. "I brought him with me to Caesarea. I thought the trip would shake him up enough to put him in his place."

"Good. Execute him." Pilate didn't even look up from the scroll as he gave the order.

Gaius was shocked. "But surely he must stand trial first. Roman law –"

"Do you presume to tell me how to do my job, centurion?"

"Prefect, we have laws," Gaius protested.

"You've redeemed yourself. Don't throw it all away by challenging my authority now. He knows about the scroll and is therefore a danger to Rome. I'll sign the order, but he will be executed before we leave tomorrow. We don't have time to waste with mere formalities."

Gaius nodded submissively, but his mind was racing as he tried to think of a way to save the man. He felt responsible for Miyka'el's fate. After all, he was the one who had brought him here.

The merchant had lied to him, deceived him perhaps, but he hadn't committed any crimes that warranted death. If anything, what the prefect was doing was illegal. Going after a treasure that had nothing to do with Rome could only cause an uprising in the province.

Finally he knew what he had to do. It might cost him his military career, but he owed the merchant a chance at life, at least.

† † † † †

The two men reached the pool and carefully gazed about before approaching the far side. There seemed to be no sign of the prefect yet, Barabbas noted with relief. Carefully they crossed the water and took up positions to insert the lever. This time, Barabbas shoved it underneath the slab, however. Levi frowned as he glanced at his friend.

Barabbas said. "We've been idiots. This will give us far more leverage."

They began heaving against the stubborn stone, but had trouble finding a purchase as the groove underneath wasn't deep enough. Barabbas eventually put down the lever and began scraping again at the bottom seam.

All the while he kept glancing up, half expecting the prefect to enter the pools and discover them. Eventually Levi had had enough.

"By all that's holy, Barabbas, if you spent half as much time scraping as you do looking about, we'd be inside by now!" he exclaimed in a harsh whisper.

Once he had a deep enough groove cut, Barabbas inserted the bar again. It took nearly an hour of hard labour before they finally felt the mortar give. They stopped work for a moment, staring at one another with gleaming eyes. Then they jumped to with renewed energy. Slowly, the stone began to inch its way out of the wall, making each subsequent attempt a little more successful. It took another hour, but finally, the slab came free.

There was a sudden gurgling sound as water rushed to fill the cavern beyond. The pool swirled as the current swept into the cavern like a mini tidal wave. Soldiers rushed into the portico, seemingly from every quarter.

The two men gazed at one another in horror. There would be no escaping this inspection. The pools would be searched thoroughly and discovery was certain.

28

THE MORNING after his arrival, Gaius rode in Pilate's carriage. They left at dawn as the prefect was eager to get to Jerusalem before sundown.

As they left Caesarea, Gaius noticed several crucifixes already in place beyond the city wall. The legionaries had been busy with the condemned men since before first light and the bodies were already nothing more than contorted bundles of shattered nerves. Gaius looked at the face of the man nearest to them. The body was mutilated beyond all recognition but his face was strangely untouched. It wasn't the merchant, however. Gaius wondered where the man was. Had his surreptitious orders already been executed, or had he failed?

He looked at the man on the second crucifix. Gaius could see the agonised expression as the outlaw strained against the ropes that held him, gasping for every breath of air.

Pilate gazed callously at the forlorn figure. "He won't see the third hour. May his life be a lesson to those who would challenge my authority in this province. Was the merchant from Jericho among the men crucified this morning?"

Gaius nodded. "I did as you instructed."

He neglected to mention the additional instructions that had been left with the soldiers. Miyka'el's name would appear on the list of outlaws crucified that day. There was no way he could have avoided that. Pilate was bound to check that Miyka'el's name appeared on the register.

He looked out again at the group of men on the cruel wooden posts, but most were unrecognisable. Then they were past the crosses and he could no longer see without raising suspicion. His thoughts turned to the treasure lying in Jerusalem. If he could only keep the prefect's mind occupied with that, he might pull off his deception.

They rode quickly, leaving Caesarea behind them and heading inland, via Antipatris, towards Jerusalem. By the time they arrived, the sun had already set and Pilate was exhausted from the journey, but he insisted on going past the pools of Bethesda first.

After checking the guard and wandering about, he was satisfied and left the pools for the comfort of the palace. They could start digging in the morning.

"Be sure you remain vigilant tonight. Barabbas could come through any of these entrances and he seems to move with the silence of a viper," Gaius left his legionaries with a parting warning.

Pilate rose early and joined Gaius outside the pools of Bethesda before first light.

He was anxious not to waste any more time and wanted the soldiers digging by the time the sun broke on the horizon. He was in a buoyant mood.

"Well then, let's get on with it. We've got a treasure to find."

"Wait, prefect. First we have to get all the people out of the pools."

"What are they still doing in there?"

"I thought it best if nobody was permitted to enter or leave until you arrived. That minimises the chance of anyone smuggling treasure out of the area."

He also cherished the secret hope that he might catch Barabbas inside and pin him there, but he kept his thoughts to himself. To mention it would only draw further attack from the prefect if Barabbas was not in the pool area.

Gaius watched carefully as each person was marched past him and searched. He didn't bother with the search, leaving that to other soldiers. His main concern lay in catching the Jewish renegade. He was mildly disappointed when the last person had passed and Barabbas had still not been found.

Pilate stood by anxiously clutching the copper scroll, trying to read it every now and then in the darkness by the flickering flame of an oil lamp. He pushed his way through as soon as the last person had hobbled past.

"Now, show me where this treasure lies."

Gaius motioned for several soldiers to follow as Pilate led the way up to the portico. "It says here that the treasure is located on the south side of the pool."

Gaius scanned the document again, trying to find his bearing in the portico area.

He then strode confidently across to the pool's edge. "My guess is that it should be right about here."

The soldiers and Pilate came to the edge and stared in disbelief at the gaping hole in the wall of the pool.

"What's this?" The prefect's voice was cool and an uneasy feeling began to rise up in Gaius.

He gazed down at the hole. It was not immediately apparent. He had to lean over to see the gap in the wall.

Pilate grabbed one of the legionaries and, with a vicious jerk, flung him into the pool. "Well don't just stand there. Look inside."

The legionary fell with a colossal splash into the water and began wading quickly to the edge.

"What's in there?" Pilate demanded as the legionary peered about inside the cavern, disappearing up to his waist.

"Nothing, prefect," the man's voice echoed from inside the watery cavern.

"What is the meaning of this?" Pilate was white with rage and shaking as he glared across at Gaius.

"Barabbas." Gaius' voice was a violent whisper that would have melted desert sand.

"Find him," Pilate's voice quavered through clenched teeth. "Find him and kill him slowly. I want him to experience such agony as no man has ever known since the inception of time."

"I'll get a search party together," Gaius turned to go, racing towards the Antonia.

As he ran, such hatred burned in his heart that he had not felt for any human being before in his life. Never before had anyone bettered him as consistently as this man. He despised Barabbas with a passion he had not thought possible before today.

As he ran, all the memories of his encounters with this loathsome Jew were dredged up in his mind. From the first day outside the flaming barracks, right up to the moment he'd looked down at the empty cavern. Each memory inflamed his hatred more. He knew he would never rest until the Jew had perished. And he would perish by the hand of Gaius.

Arriving at the Antonia, he strode purposefully across the bridge over the *Struthian* pool, waving aside officials as he entered the imposing fortress. Inside, he found the centurion in charge and issued his orders.

"Have letters written to every garrison in Judea. I want a detailed description of Barabbas and his cargo - it's a vast treasure of silver and gold - sent to every guard or sentry in the province. If anyone finds him, he's to be arrested and held."

"How soon do you want the letters sent?"

"What are you wasting time talking to me for? Send it out with the mail horsemen. I want these letters in Tyre before sundown."

"The mail's about ready to go out. I'll hold the horsemen while you draft the letters."

"Good man. Now get me every scribe in the building, anyone who can write, in fact. I want to give them the man's description."

The centurion rushed away, leaving Gaius pacing the room, impatiently waiting for the scribes to arrive.

† † † † †

Barabbas and Levi panicked when they heard the loud slurping sound of water rushing into the chamber. Then came the crash as the stone fell away. Air exploded from the recess and water flooded in to fill the void.

The soldiers would arrive in a matter of seconds, but before any legionary had a chance to react, a cry rose from the portico and hundreds of lame, crippled, or otherwise feeble individuals started a hobbling stampede towards the whirling waters of the pool.

By the time the Romans entered the portico area, the waters were already swamped with bodies as people splashed about in the hopes of finding their healing. There were cries of anguish as well as hopeful, premature joy from members of the crowd as people barged against one another, first trying to get in, then out of, the dark, icy water.

All but two emerged, slowly limping or crawling back to their places as they began to wring the excess water from their clothes. The Romans did a cursory check but nothing appeared to be out of the ordinary.

The waters stirred every so often and people rushed towards the pool. It was a well known phenomenon, not strictly a Jewish custom. Such pools existed all over the empire.

Within minutes the riot had subsided and things returned to normal. After nearly an hour, two figures emerged quietly from the cavern, straining under the weight of the first chest.

They lugged the bulky item through the waters as quietly as possible, grateful for the slight buoyancy that the water provided. At the other end, they carried it into the tunnel and up as far as the rusted grid that had once guarded the holy city against her enemies.

After that they returned for a second, then a third. The night was half gone before they had removed all the chests from the vault. It was a tight squeeze, but the two men managed to drag themselves over the boxes and finally began to haul the first one through the eternal blackness and up to the entrance where the women were waiting.

It was well beyond dawn when they returned for the final chest and began the tiring hike back through the cramped tunnel. Barabbas' back felt like an ancient rusted door that moaned every time it opened and shut. His muscles ached with a thousand cramps and his neck felt as if it had fossilised into one position from which it refused to budge.

It took them another hour to get the chests out of the tunnel and onto the cart. All the while Barabbas expected a Roman patrol to arrive. Finally, their task completed, the two men collapsed on the cart, exhausted by their night's toil.

"Where to now?" Barabbas murmured, panting for breath as he screwed his eyes closed against the glare of the sun.

"I recommend Sebaste."

"But that's Samaritan country," Barabbas protested. No self-respecting Jew would venture into Samaria. In fact, many would rather add days to their journey in order to circumvent it.

"Exactly. It's the last place Romans would think to look."

Barabbas pondered the logic. "Makes sense, but where do you intend to keep it?"

"There's a man there who owes me a favour. Years ago your father and I saved him from a band of robbers on the road that led to Galilee. He'll help us if we ask him to."

"What makes you think he's still there?"

"Where else could a Samaritan go?"

The women joined them as they began their journey towards Sebaste in Samaria. Once he had rested for a few minutes, Barabbas began hammering at one of the chests. The lid was quite waterlogged and almost riveted in place by age. Finally, with Levi's help, he managed to open it and was awestruck by the amount of gold it held. Several other chests contained various artefacts as well as silver and gold coins enough to establish a kingdom.

"You could buy all of Judea with this money," Barabbas whispered as he began heaving at yet another chest.

This chest opened almost immediately and Barabbas fell back, stunned as he stared at the mountain of holy temple artefacts. Levi was equally fearful.

"Put that lid back, Barabbas, and don't open it again."

Barabbas nodded nervously, half expecting his hands to shrivel as he did so. They quickly turned their attention to the remaining chests.

The carriage had to backtrack slightly, passing Jerusalem in order to join the road that led to Samaria. There were tense moments as the group passed by the city, as if afraid that Roman legionaries would come storming out of the city to ransack their cart.

Finally the carriage turned a corner and left the city wall behind it. Barabbas began to relax. It was the first time in his life that he felt glad that he'd left Jerusalem behind him. It was about an hour later that they saw the lone horseman approaching. He was a Roman legionary - an Equite - and he pressed his horse at a quick canter.

Both Barabbas and Levi were immediately on edge. Daylight would certainly have revealed their crimes and the alarm would have been raised.

Leila noticed their tense expressions. "It's just the mail. The man has no interest in us."

"That doesn't mean we're not in danger," Barabbas reached for the whip that was used to drive the oxen.

"Barabbas, what are you doing?" Leila was suddenly fearful.

"There could be a warning to look out for us. We can't risk allowing a letter to get to a garrison ahead of us."

"But what if there's no such letter?"

"What if there is?"

Levi nodded in agreement. "Barabbas is right. If anyone's looking for us and that mail arrives at a garrison ahead of us, none of us would leave the next town alive."

"But you can't take a man's life just because he might prove a threat."

"We've lived this way all our lives, Leila." Barabbas replied, turning in a casual way as the soldier approached from behind.

As the man drew abreast of them, Barabbas swung the whip without warning. The vicious leather thong sang as it whipped through the air and entwined itself around the legionary's neck.

There was a cry of surprise as the soldier arched back like a dying swan. His helmet jerked loose as the man's impetus ripped the whip from Barabbas' hand. The legionary sailed through the air in a macabre backward somersault, trailing the whip like a wayward scarf until his head struck the hard stone road.

The huge bag he carried landed, scattering scrolls and sealed parchments in every direction as it rolled and bounced to a standstill. Barabbas dived from the cart and immediately checked the soldier for life signs. He hadn't really expected any and was not surprised to find none.

He removed the whip and began rummaging through the letters, opening them to check their contents. Levi did the same and it was he who found the first letter giving their description and detailing their crimes.

"I've got it. Gaius and Pilate wasted no time."

"Good. Leave some of the open letters so it looks like an accident. It won't be long before the next mail post comes looking for him. We'd best be long gone from here by the time they arrive."

Leila was silent when the men returned to the cart, refusing to speak or even acknowledge them. Barabbas disregarded it. He'd never tried to justify his actions before and was not about to start today.

Although the letter was proof of his justification, Barabbas couldn't help but feel the guilt of what he had done every time he looked across at Leila. She merely stared down, chewing thoughtfully on her lower lip. Her silence carried more accusation that any words she could have spoken.

It was a sullen group that trundled into the city of Sebaste late that evening. They spent the night at an inn and began their search for Zechariah's home the following day. It didn't take long before somebody pointed them in the right direction and they headed for his home.

The door was answered by a servant who, after ushering them in, went to call the master of the house. He returned with a thin dark-haired man whose beard and temples were laced with grey. He had deep brown eyes that had an out of place sparkle in the furrowed face.

"What can I do for you?" He wore a puzzled expression as he addressed Levi who had stepped forward.

"How quickly we forget. Do you not remember the man who saved your life on the road to Capernaum?"

Puzzlement gave way to shock as memories returned. "Young Levi! I see the young man has matured. Come in, come in."

He hustled them through to a living room, calling for servants to come and wash their feet while others were instructed to get some food. "What of your friend, the one who was with you?"

"Cephas."

"Of Gamala, that's right. Is he well?"

"He passed away in the Galilean uprising." Even after so many years, Levi's tone betrayed his sadness at losing so close a friend.

The old man sighed. "Such turbulent times. He was a great man."

"This is Barabbas, his son."

Zechariah examined Barabbas properly for the first time. Then he smiled and the eyes twinkled as he spoke. "I see the father lives on in the son. You have his eyes and, I suspect, his heart."

"And he's twice as fast and dextrous with a sword," Levi chuckled.

Zechariah seated them around a table where they were joined by five men who, judging from their dusty clothes, had been working in the fields outside.

"These are my sons," Zechariah announced proudly. "Medan, Jokshan, Bethuel, Ishbak and Shuan."

He turned to his sons and said. "This is one of the men I told you about who saved my life on the way to Capernaum, and this is the son of the other."

After going through the formalities of greeting, the men sat down at the table to eat. The family quickly endeared themselves to Barabbas as they were quick-witted and friendly, making the meal a festive occasion.

They begged Barabbas and Levi to regale them with stories of their exploits and listened with rapt admiration to stories of Rome and the circus, as well as the city of Carthage where the two friends had fought their way to freedom from slavery. Lunch extended to supper and it was late that evening when the men finally retired.

Zechariah said goodnight to each of his sons in turn, kissing them on the cheek and waited until all of them had left the room before broaching the subject. "Tell me what brings two Jews to Sebaste, the heart of Samaritan country."

It was the first time he'd hinted at the enmity that existed between their respective races. The smile on his face told them that it was a feeling he did not share with the rest of his people, however.

"I've come to ask a favour," Levi replied.

"It is not a favour I owe you, but a debt. I would be more than happy to help in any way I can."

"There are some items that are dear to us. We need somewhere to keep them, but forces too great to number work against us in Judea. I'm afraid there are few we can entrust our secret to. We need to find a place far removed from our walk of life and someone we can trust."

The old man smiled. "So you came to Sebaste. These items - you wish me to keep them for you?"

"Not directly, no. There's too much traffic through any home. We were hoping you could show us some quiet place where we could put them."

Zechariah was thoughtful for a moment. "I have a tomb that I bought some years back for my burial. It's rather unkempt and overgrown at the moment as nobody ever goes there. It should suit your purposes."

"It sounds perfect. Can you take us there?"

"Now?" the old man raised his eyebrows in surprise.

"It's something best done at night."

Zechariah nodded. "I understand. I'll just get my coat."

The tomb was about a mile outside the city. It was a tiny unkempt cave where shrubs had grown so thickly around the entrance that it would have been almost impossible to see, even in the light.

Zechariah pointed out the opening and then wandered off, back towards the main road. "Join me when you've finished and we can head back to town."

The two men examined the heavy circular stone that lay three quarters across the overgrown entrance. It had a wedge under it which held it in place and prevented it from rolling closed. Once closed, it would take a team of oxen to reopen. First they had to clear a path, removing shrubs before they could get the heavy chests through the opening.

Once the chests were safely inside, Barabbas removed the wedge that held the stone in place and the rock rolled across the entrance, closing the gaping hole with a heavy thud.

They quickly covered their tracks and rejoined Zechariah who rested patiently under a large sycamore tree near the main road.

"You've done what you need to do?" the old man asked quietly.

"Yes, thank you," Levi replied, equally quietly.

Zechariah nodded silently and then changed the subject. It was plain that this man would never break their trust or even look inside the tomb to know the nature of the treasure. Levi had chosen their ally wisely.

They left Zechariah's home the following evening, heading north towards Galilee. After enjoying the Samaritan's hospitality for the entire day, they travelled by night, hoping to avoid the search that would surely take place. They had stalled the post, but news of the treasure's disappearance would be impossible to stop.

Although the route north seemed an unnecessary detour, Barabbas felt it would be safer than moving directly east or south where they would be sure to run into Gaius' troops.

By morning, they had left Samaria and found shelter in the home of a zealot sympathiser, a wheat farmer just north of the Samaritan town of Ginae, who spat on the ground every time he mentioned Rome or Caesar, which was often and with contempt.

"Now we head east via Scythopolis and then north to the Sea of Galilee." Barabbas looked at Leila.

She smiled and gazed out at the hills in the distance. Barabbas was starting to worry about her. She had been fairly unresponsive since they had left Sebaste. He was beginning to wonder whether she still bore a grudge for what he'd done to the Roman soldier on the road, but when pressed about it, she had merely withdrawn more.

From Galilee they travelled quickly with the assistance of the numerous zealot factions in the area, until they reached the Sea of Galilee. They arrived just as the sun began creeping over the eastern horizon. There was a sole fisherman with a pristine white net wading knee-deep in the gilded water near the edge of the lake.

He was surrounded by glistening reeds and an odd looking shrub that jutted from the winking copper-coloured water as it reflected the morning sun. Off to the right lay a small fishing boat, large enough to hold about eight people. It stood unattended no more than twenty paces from the fisherman.

It was the sign they had been told to look for. If there had been soldiers about, the fisherman would have sailed the boat out onto the water and they would have known to remain concealed.

The man disregarded them as they approached the boat and put out from the shore. The breeze was light and the water calm and both Barabbas and Levi took oars and rowed for the opposite shore.

The trip across the lake was fraught with silence. The friction became so intense that Barabbas even began to wish for one of the many storms for which Galilee was so well known. At least that might ease the tension in the boat.

Levi had noticed it too and had tried to compensate with bravado, talking non-stop to Zena who was obviously also relieved to have someone break the silence. As a result, the lake crossing consisted mainly of small talk between Levi and Zena, while Barabbas and Leila sat in sullen silence at opposite ends of the boat.

On the eastern shore of the lake they found another fisherman who similarly disregarded them as they rowed for shore and secured the boat at the water's edge.

He appeared to be too busy gathering his net to notice them, but when they crested the rise they noticed that the man had bundled himself and some comrades into the small craft and the group was paddling back to the western shore, now no more than a misty hue against the horizon.

From there the group made their way towards the King's Highway, a wide but treacherous road that formed the main artery from north to south at the eastern end of Palestine.

It was there that Leila finally voiced her wish. "I want to go home, Barabbas."

He was shocked at her statement. "Why, Leila? After everything that's happened there. How could you want to return?"

"My mind is made up. It's where I belong."

Barabbas looked to Zena for help, but the girl had found an item of interest in the dust around her feet and was engrossed in the examination thereof.

"Is this because of the Roman soldier on the road to Sebaste?"

Leila blinked and shook her head. "You did what you had to do and now I must do the same."

"Leila, I was saving our necks, don't you realize that! Am I to be punished for what fate threw my way?"

"I tell you, it's nothing to do with that, Barabbas. I have to know what happened to Miyka'el."

Barabbas looked at Levi in disbelief, but his friend had dropped to his knees to secure a thong on his sandal that had come loose.

Barabbas looked back at Leila. "Miyka'el is dead, believe me. There is no way that Pilate would have let him live."

"I have to know for certain. How can I go on with my life, never being sure if I am legally married or not?"

Silence returned, but Barabbas knew it was useless to argue. She had made up her mind and would not be swayed. He silently cursed her sense of honour and fidelity.

Finally he shrugged and sighed. "Will you at least allow us to accompany you back to Jericho?"

"Thank you," she looked up, smiling for the first time.

In truth, she dreaded the journey and what the end might hold more than Barabbas could imagine. However, nothing could have prepared her for the reality of what awaited her at her villa.

† † † † †

The trip to Jericho was an agonising three week journey. Barabbas' relationship with Leila became more strained with every passing step towards her home.

Why go there at all? Miyka'el was surely dead and no good could come of returning to the villa. On the other hand, what if he was still alive? Leila would then truly be lost to him forever.

His torment grew in the realization that he could not prevent her from returning. Until she knew for certain that she was a widow, she would never consider sharing her life with him. All he could do was wait - and hope.

As they approached the city, heavy gusts of wind carried the sands like a tide over the barren landscape. The travellers pulled their shawls up to cover their faces against the stinging grains of fine yellow sand. The gusts marked the coming of another *Khamsin* and the air became hot and oppressive as the sky began to darken, slowly changing into a molten yellow sludge.

Leila had become completely uncommunicative over the last few miles, fixing her eyes on the road ahead. Finally they saw the first palm trees breasting the horizon. The oasis looked like a lonely pool of green about to be engulfed by the ravaging winds and the yellow sand.

As they drew closer, they could see the frayed leaves, scorched by wind and sun, on the palms near the edge of the oasis.

The weary group reached the city gates and trudged through the streets of Jericho, heading for Leila's villa. When they reached the entrance, Leila pulled the shawl down slightly and greeted the guard.

"Hello, Hazor."

"Leila!" he exclaimed in surprise and then scowled at her companions. "The household has been looking everywhere for you."

"Is the master here?" she had to know.

The guard's face turned sour. "He's here, but he's not who you would expect."

"Miyka'el?"

Hazor shook his head. "Word was sent from Caesarea. Your husband was executed for crimes against the emperor. The master I speak of is Matthias. He's sent messengers all over Judea looking for you."

"What happened to Miyka'el?"

The guard grimaced. "Crucified. It seems someone tried to save him. The soldiers were left with instructions to take him down as soon as the prefect left Caesarea. It didn't help though. Even after so short a time, he never recovered. His body was brought back to Jericho for burial. Matthias really wants to see you. Something about your inheritance."

"Well, I'm here now. Can I go in?" Leila didn't know what to feel. Elation and sorrow were at war, tearing her heart in two. Although she knew she should be in mourning, all she really felt was a sense of freedom.

Hazor nodded. "He'll be anxious to hear from you. He's in his quarters."

"These people will accompany me," she motioned at Barabbas and Levi.

Inside the lodgings they were ushered into the atrium where Matthias soon appeared. His expression was surly as he stared at the group.

Leila's chest went tight as she noticed the patch covering his right eye. It was the eye she had damaged at their last meeting. She swallowed, feeling the guilt rise up in her.

"Matthias, I'm so sorry."

He held up a hand. "Spare me. You'll have years to make up for what you've done. Who are these people?"

"This is - Barabbas and his friend Levi." So this was how it was going to be. Leila steeled herself for an unpleasant meeting.

Her brother-in-law fixed the two men with a thin smile. "The infamous outlaw under my roof. The prefect has a standing order for your capture and execution. Did you know that?"

Leila interrupted him. "You wanted to talk to me about my inheritance."

He swung and smashed a bowl of fruit from the table. "Inheritance! Your husband is dead - killed by your deceit - and you ask me about that?"

"It's what you wanted to see me about."

"Oh, you'll get your inheritance alright. As I said, you'll have years to make up for what you've done."

"How exactly?"

His rage abated as quickly as it had been inflamed and he smiled. "You will bear your husband a son. Our laws are clear. If a man dies and his widow has no children, she will be given to the brother. It's my duty to raise up children on Miyka'el's behalf."

Leila was horrified. During all the events of the past few weeks she had never considered the implications of her husband's death. Waves of nausea washed over her as she was faced with the prospect of spending her life with this man. The short-lived freedom she had felt came crashing down around her as she was suddenly engulfed by the horror that awaited her.

Barabbas stepped forward and Leila heard the same quiet menace in his voice that she had heard when he had spotted the soldier on the road to Sebaste.

"I'll see you dead before you have this woman."

Matthias was scornful. "You have no weapons. You were searched at the door."

Barabbas smiled, shaking off Levi's restraining hand on his shoulder. "You think I need a weapon to kill you? I could end your life right now so painfully that you would beg me to fetch a knife just to stop the agony."

Leila glanced across at Barabbas to see if he was bluffing, but there was no deception in his eyes. Only white, burning fury.

"No, Barabbas." She choked out the words, but he didn't seem to hear. She tried again, more forcefully. "I warned you before, Barabbas."

This time he replied, but he never took his eyes off Matthias. "It's no good, Leila. You're lost to me anyway. If I let him live you become his wife. If I must spend a life without you, at least let it be with the satisfaction of knowing I saved you from this."

Matthias had suddenly become nervous. This was an unexpected turn of events and the situation was rapidly becoming beyond his control.

Leila caught Barabbas' tunic. "Listen to me, Barabbas. I would rather spend my life in this man's clutches than see you commit murder for my freedom."

In one quick movement, Barabbas shook her hand off him and lunged. He caught the merchant by his chubby arm, spinning him around as he ripped the belt from his waist. There was a choking sound as Barabbas brought the belt up around Matthias' neck and began to tighten his grip. The merchant's eyes bulged and his face turned a bright red as he gasped for breath that would not come.

Now the eyes were filled with terror. It was a terror that knew any yell for help would be his last. Leila knew there was only one way to prevent the tragedy.

"Matthias, look at me." There was an urgency in her voice.

His jowls wobbled as he gazed wild-eyed at her.

Leila spoke gently. "Let me go with him. In return I will relinquish all claims on Miyka'el's estate. You can have it all if only you let me go." Barabbas loosened the belt slightly.

The terror in the merchant's eyes began to recede as Matthias considered her offer. "My alternative?"

Barabbas growled in his ear. "Your alternative is plain."

Matthias breathed the relief of one who had glimpsed the far side of the grave and then been given a reprieve. The view had not been pleasant.

He gazed wistfully at the beauty that could so nearly have been his. Leila spotted the slight tightening of the belt around his neck once more.

"Very well," he gasped. "We'll sign an agreement. There's a stylus and some parchment in the study."

Barabbas released the man and accompanied him to the study. Matthias quickly drew up a document and gave it to Leila to read.

Only when they'd left the villa did Leila speak to Barabbas again. Staring nervously into his eyes, she asked, "Would you really have killed him?"

There was a twinkle in Barabbas' eye as he answered with a roguish grin, "I knew you'd think of a way to prevent me from doing so."

Leila smiled for the first time that day and leaned a little closer to him. Barabbas reached for her hand and said, "I promised once that I'd come back for you and I have something for you if you'll still wear it."

She was puzzled as he reached into his belt and withdrew an object. It glinted in the dull light as he offered it to her.

"My necklace!" She exclaimed, snatching at it. "Where did you find it?"

"Minette gave it to me. She said it was the only reason Miyka'el managed to find you."

"I can't believe you had it all this time," she beamed as she placed it around her neck.

"Next time, leave the cursed thing and look after yourself. I can always get another necklace."

The marriage was a quiet affair. Barabbas scraped together his last coins, found a willing rabbi, and purchased a room at an inn on the outskirts of Bethany for the night, where he took Leila as his wife. The following morning the exultant couple were joined by Zena and Levi.

They discussed their future over a light breakfast of dates, unleavened bread and honey.

"The treasure is safe for now. We're the ones in danger," Levi was saying.

Barabbas nodded. "The best thing we can do is disappear for the time being. I suggest the wilderness beyond the Jordan."

"The wilderness! But how will we survive out there?" Leila protested.

"The desert is our friend, Leila," Barabbas smiled. "Many live in it quite comfortably. The trick is to know her moods and flow with her cycle. Only those who resist her perish."

They crossed the Jordan River later that day, fleeing into the barren desert beyond where Rome could not follow. After journeying for nearly a fortnight, they found shelter among a *fellahin* family that subsisted by eking out a living from the barren unyielding earth. The farmer, whose name was Enos, was grateful for their help as he had a large family but only two sons, both of whom were far too young to help work the land. Enos had inherited this small patch from his father who, he claimed, had passed on the curse of spawning mainly daughters.

Enos himself had been an only son and had been left to provide for a family of widows and wives. His sons had arrived only after a succession of daughters, all of whom needed to be provided for, but who didn't have the strength that the merciless land demanded.

Barabbas and Levi settled there, helping him in the fields as the *fellahin* were crop farmers who tended to settle in one place, unlike their nomadic *Bedouin* cousins who bred livestock, wandering from place to place in search of grazing.

They remained with Enos and his family for over a year. In that time they formed a bond with the family and even began producing enough food to begin trading with passing *Bedouin* caravans.

Leila proved a major asset to the small community, with her knowledge of cloth and material manufacture, making garments which she traded with the desert nomads while teaching the rest of the women in the household her craft.

Her only fault was that of her overzealous religious beliefs. She had set out to convert the entire family to her belief in the *Messiah* who had taken Barabbas' place on the cross so many years ago and secured his release from prison, giving him another chance at life.

This was pointed out to him on a regular basis as his wife begged him to live a life worthy of such a sacrifice, but he would have none of it. The rest of the family were not so immune to her witness, however, and all the women came to gladly embrace the teachings of the man they had heard so much about. It seemed Levi was Barabbas' only ally in the household.

Even Enos had placed his faith in the man from Nazareth and yet another Passover was celebrated in remembrance of Jesus of Nazareth, rather than of Moses and Israel's exodus from Egypt. Barabbas tolerated Leila's continuous urging, however, and their love blossomed despite their conflicting beliefs.

Barabbas and Levi's hunting skills proved extremely useful and the family enjoyed fresh meat on a regular basis. This meant that they not only saved money by not having to maintain livestock, but were also able to sell their excess products to neighbouring farmers.

The small farm soon became a well-known port of call among the desert people as a place where goods and crops could be purchased in return for meat and spices from places east. Even merchants from Judea began to hear about the farm and they would arrive to buy goods that the family was able to acquire from the *Bedouin*.

Barabbas was able to purchase a fine stallion and a couple of brood mares from among the *Bedouin* tribes and began breeding and trading horses with the nomads. It wasn't a thriving business, he admitted, but it was a start. He had finally found happiness and a degree of freedom in this harsh climate.

Their life was filled with bliss, Barabbas thought. He was quite content to live out the rest of his days in a place like this, but at the back of his mind, he knew that his responsibilities to the treasure and the secret of the scroll would not permit it. He was not completely surprised when the utopia ended, although he was far from prepared for the loss that it brought.

Eleazor was in a wine tavern on the eastern end of Jerusalem when he heard the news. He'd spent the days since the attack on Deborah's house mulling over how to locate Barabbas and get the scroll from him.

Now he sat in a dark corner of the tavern, drinking from a large decanter of wine. He had no company as he did not find it easy to make friends, even in the social atmosphere of the tavern. He was too morose and intense, making people tend to steer clear of him.

In truth he preferred it that way. He loathed inane chatter of any sort, rather keeping to himself and listening to the conversations around him, observing but not partaking.

Three soldiers approached and took a table near to him. They disregarded the group that was already there, not even acknowledging the men who were forced to vacate their table.

Eleazor leaned forward in his seat when he heard the mention of treasure in their conversation. Sipping nonchalantly at his wine, he tried not to make his eavesdropping obvious.

The information he learned made his nerves tingle. The scroll had been discovered in the home of a merchant from Jericho and Pilate had come to Jerusalem. He recognised some of the names. Gaius the centurion and Barabbas were both mentioned. Apparently an urgent message had gone out, but the mail north of the city had never arrived. He nodded quietly to himself when he heard about the dead horseman. *Barabbas*. It was obvious that he'd taken the treasure north, but where?

He became irritable at the din in the room. It was impossible to follow the conversation properly. Straining his ears, he gleaned what information he could. Eventually he managed to piece together enough to work out that everything had happened at the pools of Bethesda and decided to go there and see for himself.

He was cautious in his approach, but needn't have been. Rome's interest in the pools had long since waned. It was now merely a pool where diseased men gathered to wait for the waters to churn and perhaps find healing.

After a quick search he found the empty chamber, just as the soldier had said. The next few days were spent searching northwards. He found the spot where the Roman soldier had been killed. The bloodstains were still relatively fresh.

However, a few more weeks of searching still left him no closer to the truth of where the treasure had been taken and he decided to head for Jericho. Perhaps if he could find the merchant's family, they might be able to tell him where Barabbas was hiding.

In the city of palms, he found a beggar near the gates of the synagogue. It didn't take long to learn that it was a merchant called Miyka'el who had been taken to Caesarea and executed. For a nominal sum, the beggar told him where to find the villa.

Eleazor approached the gate, but was stopped by a guard.

"Nobody goes in without an invitation from the master."

Eleazor replied. "I'm sure the master would want to see me. I have something of interest to him."

The guard's smile dripped irony. "Fifty traders pass by here every day, even on the Sabbath sometimes. They all claim to have a great idea, but seldom do. The master is not interested in your wares or schemes."

"This has nothing to do with money."

"Then I'm sure he'd be even less interested." The guard was well drilled in the handling of unwanted guests.

"I have information for him."

"What sort of information?"

"It's personal."

"Well write it down and seal it. I'm sure he'll get the message."

"I have to see him in person," Eleazor insisted.

The guard grinned and shook his head. "That's not going to happen. Now run along before you make me angry."

Eleazor's hand itched to run a sword through this self-important buffoon. He decided to try one last gambit. "Tell him it's to do with a man called Barabbas."

The guard's eyes narrowed as he subjected Eleazor to a long, thoughtful glare. Finally he nodded. "Alright. I'll tell him you're here, but don't expect to be ushered in. He doesn't take kindly to uninvited callers."

There was a long wait before a servant returned from the main lodging. He spoke quietly to the guard as the two glanced repeatedly in Eleazor's direction.

Eventually the guard turned and said, "the master will see you. This man will show you where to go."

Eleazor followed the servant up to the main lodging where he was invited to recline on a couch in one of the most opulent rooms he'd ever seen. When I find that treasure I'll have a home just like this, he smiled to himself.

After another interminable wait a large, well rounded man with several chins and an eye patch entered the room.

"I am Matthias," his introduction was curt. "What can I do for you?"

There was a hostility in the man that surprised Eleazor. He had expected the family to welcome him as a friend of Barabbas.

"I was looking for a man called Barabbas and heard that your family might know where to locate him," Eleazor replied cautiously.

"Where did you hear that?"

"I understand your brother was arrested for possession of the copper scroll."

Matthias glowered. "It was that harlot he married that should have been sent to Caesarea. She was the one who brought it here."

Finally Eleazor smiled in understanding. This was no friend of Barabbas. Now he knew how to handle the interview.

"I've been looking for Barabbas for some time. He has something of mine and I want it back."

Matthias frowned. "Owes you money?"

Eleazor inclined his head. "You could say that."

"And you intend to see that he honours the debt."

"In every way," Eleazor nodded secretively.

Matthias smiled. "He owes me something as well. The woman he's with is the wife of my late brother. She has refused her obligations to him in bearing him a son. I would pay a handsome price if you were to return her to me."

"Do you know where they are?" Eleazor rose from the chair.

Matthias shook his head. "I wish I did, but you know your way around their world. I imagine you could find them with the right information."

"Barabbas is good at covering his tracks. The information would have to be very specific."

"They left the day before yesterday. I feel sure they would have married not far from here. Jericho or Bethany would be my guess. Certainly no further than Jerusalem."

"With Pilate's decree for Barabbas' arrest he would never venture into Jerusalem. We can eliminate the Holy City."

"So it's Jericho or Bethany."

Eleazor nodded. "I can start with the inns. There are several that are frequented by zealots in the area."

Eleazor started in Jericho, stopping by at several inns, but nobody had seen the party he described. The following day he went on to Bethany where he found his first piece of useful information. After some persuasion, the innkeeper told him that the party had planned to cross the Jordan and disappear into the wilderness beyond.

That was a blow. The wilderness was vast and they could be anywhere. It would be difficult to find them even if they hadn't covered their tracks, which he felt sure they had.

Still, it was worth a try. He headed east through Jericho and crossed the Jordan River. From there, he searched through the smaller settlements and farming communities that littered the desert, but there the trail ran dry. Nobody had seen the party or men fitting the descriptions he gave.

It was too much to have hoped that Barabbas would be careless. He contented himself with offering a reward for any information and settled in a small nameless farming community some fifteen miles east of the Jordan River. He was also wanted by Roman authorities and the wilderness was as good a place as any if one sought anonymity.

Work was easy to come by and his income was supplemented by the occasional nocturnal foray into the wilderness to raid a caravan or travellers who were too stupid to travel the more populated routes.

It was over a year before information began to filter through to him about the small but thriving *fellahin* community about two days' journey east of his settlement. At first he didn't give the stories any consideration, but as bits of information were pieced together over a period of months, a picture began to form.

The family had lived in the area for generations. It was only since the arrival of the strangers from Judea some fourteen months previously that the farm had begun to do so well.

Nobody knew who these people were, but it appeared it was two families that had arrived with no children. They never gave their reasons for leaving Jerusalem, but that wasn't unusual as people seldom did in the wilderness. It was the horses that finally tipped the balance and eventually pushed Eleazor to go and have a look.

Barabbas never could resist those creatures.

He approached the farm from the north where there was more cover thanks to the uneven terrain. From what he could tell, the farm was occupied mostly by women. Barabbas was nowhere to be seen and after an entire morning spent watching the homestead, he was about to give it up as a fruitless venture.

It was then that the men returned from the fields. There were two of them. The first he didn't recognise, but the second he remembered well. It was Levi, the old desert fox who had taught them all their craft of violence and stealth.

His pulse began to race. If Levi was here, Barabbas would not be far away. Eleazor knew he would have to act quickly. Alone, he could handle either Levi or Barabbas, but together they would destroy him. While he still had surprise on his side, he moved.

He scuttled down the path that led to the tents like a weasel approaching a chicken coop. Unseen, he moved around the makeshift shelters, using them for cover until he came up behind a large stone oil press.

As the two men approached the house, Eleazor could hear their conversation. He smiled in the realization that they would walk right by his hiding place. As they came abreast of him, he sprang from concealment, lunging with his sword.

Levi had no warning but reacted with the speed of a thunderbolt. What should have been a fatal blow merely grazed his ribs, tearing his tunic and exposing the white bone beneath the flesh.

He spun to his right, drawing his sword and striking in one smooth movement. The blade passed harmlessly by as his attacker moved out of range and Levi looked at his adversary for the first time.

"Eleazor," he smiled as he pushed the other man back. "Leave it, Enos. This man won't hurt you unless you get in his way."

Eleazor watched as the farmer sheathed his own sword and backed away. "A wise course of action," he nodded. "Where's Barabbas?"

"Hunting. He could be back tonight or in a week."

"He can wait. You have the information I need."

Levi grinned, his eyes beginning to shine with the battle madness. "If you're looking for the scroll, Pilate has it."

"The scroll is worthless now. Where did you move the treasure?"

"I don't know what you're —" Levi lunged in mid-sentence, catching his opponent off guard.

There was a metallic clash as Eleazor parried the thrust and countered, swinging low and aiming at his opponent's knee.

Levi leaped above the path of the sword and lashed out with his foot. The flying kick caught Eleazor's shoulder, knocking him off balance. He landed on his back and had to roll from under the vicious blade that embedded itself in the dry soil where his throat had been.

He rolled to his feet as Levi extracted his blade from the ground. With a sudden lurch, Eleazor came at his opponent. Swords flashed in the heat of the sun and blades crackled with the intensity of an electric storm. The family rushed from their tents to witness the two foes locked in titanic battle. Finally, Eleazor saw the opening and thrust.

Levi parried the blow, but his defence came too late. Eleazor struck with a ruthless speed that made any defence impossible, driving his blade through his opponent's guard deep into his flesh.

There was a gasp and an expulsion of air as Levi sank to his knees. Eleazor held the sword in him, propping him up as he savoured the moment.

"It's over, old man. The student has outgrown his teacher. Now tell me where you hid the treasure and I promise to end it quickly."

Levi gazed up at Eleazor and chuckled. There was madness in his eyes and blood trickled from the corner of his mouth, making the picture grotesque. Then he did the impossible.

With a gasp, he lunged upward with his sword. Eleazor was stunned by the speed and strength of the injured man. He was forced to let go of his sword as he leaped back, shying away from the deadly blade.

Then Levi rose to his feet, the sword still embedded in his torso, and came at Eleazor with savage heat. Eleazor was forced to flee the torrent of blows. He drew a knife from his belt, but that was no match for the reach of his opponent's sword.

After a full five minutes, Levi's strength began to ebb. As he slowed, Eleazor shot inside the sword's swing, grabbing the crook of his opponent's elbow and neutralising the weapon.

He took no chances this time and the knife's thrust was swift and clean. Levi fell to the ground jerking convulsively and died with a crazed grin on his battle worn face.

Eleazor turned to face the small crowd that gazed at the scene in muted horror.

"Which one of you is Leila?" he addressed the women.

Enos stepped forward and drew his sword. His face was flushed and his eye twitched with nervous outrage as the adrenalin pumped through his veins.

Eleazor raised his sword in warning. "Put that sword away, friend. The man lying there was one of the greatest warriors our nation has ever seen. I doubt you're in his league. Where's Leila?"

A woman with dark hair stepped forward. "What do you want with me?"

"I want Barabbas. He'll come after you."

29

BARABBAS HAD been fortunate in his hunting expedition and returned early with the carcass of a gazelle. He was pleased with his catch as the beast had run with a speed and grace that would have presented an impossible target to a lesser hunter. He had used a bow and brought it down in mid stride, at the peak of its arching leap. The shot had been clean and the animal was dead before it hit the ground.

The tents seemed unusually quiet, with nobody moving about and Barabbas became puzzled. When he reached the yard and still no signs of life emanated from the household, he dropped his prey and drew his sword, more out of habit than anything else.

It was then that he saw the blood and tell-tale signs of a battle. Immediately, he rushed inside the first tent, brandishing his sword, but there was nobody there. Once again, Barabbas returned to the yard. He could see signs of the scuffle, but as he examined more closely, he noticed that only two people had been fighting. He quickly searched the yard and saw several footprints that led into the rocky terrain north of the property.

Please, God, no! It was obvious that one of the people, Enos, judging the size of the indentations, had been carrying something heavy. Barabbas panicked as he followed the tracks towards the family tomb.

He didn't bother with the tracks, but raced towards the small cave in the rocky hills. When he arrived, he found the family in sackcloth and ashes.

"What happened?" he demanded, fearing the worst.

Enos turned and Barabbas could see where the tears stained his cheeks. "I'm sorry, Barabbas. I should have done something."

Barabbas pushed past him and into the cave. There he saw Levi's inert form lying on a stone bench that had been carved out of the wall. He could see the gaping wound that had caused his friend's death, as well as the spices and bandages to prepare the body.

The scene left him strangely unmoved. Yes, he would miss his friend, but he was not consumed with grief. The only thing that concerned him now was revenge. It was a calm man that emerged from the cave.

Barabbas gazed over the small group of women wailing off to the side, a short distance beyond the cave's entrance. It was then that the true reality of what had happened dawned. His chest went into a vicious knot as he asked. "Where's Leila?"

"He took her with him after he killed Levi." Enos replied.

"Did he say who he was?" Barabbas clenched his teeth as he desperately tried to control his breathing. The question was unnecessary. He already knew the answer.

"He said you would know who he was. Told us to give you a message. You are to meet him at a place called Killer's Pass."

† † † † †

Leila sat alone in the dark recess of a strange cave. She was bound but not gagged. Her captor had told her that screaming was useless. They were miles from anywhere and only the desert sands would hear her calls for help.

She had shifted herself into a relatively comfortable position, but her wrists and ankles were numb from lack of circulation. As she lay quietly in the corner, she wondered at the fact that Eleazor had not asked her about the treasure. He'd obviously not considered the possibility that she might know where it was buried.

Shuffling again, she rolled onto her other side and tried to get more comfortable, but the ropes continued to constrict her limbs and caused a painful sensation of sharp needles stabbing at her hands and feet.

† † † † †

Eleazor had ensured that Leila was safely trussed up in the cave before leaving to guard the entrance to the pass. Barabbas was no fool and it would be just like him to reach the rendezvous at night to catch his opponent off guard the following morning.

He gazed up at the clear starlit sky and silently blessed the milky luminescence it brought. The desert shimmered under the nocturnal haze, giving him a clear view for miles around. He trained his eyes on a gazelle that moved soundlessly across the landscape. It was the only movement out on the plain.

The pass was a well known, if old, zealot haunt. Its main advantage was that it could only be approached from the pass below, giving those at the rendezvous complete control and the full advantage over their foes.

It had been the ideal place for ambushes on unwary soldiers and rich merchants who had grown fat off their Roman masters. The pass had fallen into disuse some years previously as people now tended to avoid it altogether, knowing the dangers that lurked there.

The only signs left of past zealot activity were old landslides, set up but never used. Most had already fallen into the pass below, where they now lay in piles of rubble, but one or two still lay in position, pressing against the rotting wedges that held them in place. It was only a matter of time before those wedges gave way and the booby traps would tumble into the pass below.

He gazed out over the desert, looking for any sign of Barabbas, but found none. His keen eyes picked up the gazelle in the darkness. It was the same one he'd been observing since sunset. The animal trotted skittishly towards the pass, moving quickly across the desert.

Probably trying to avoid a predator, Eleazor thought. Suddenly it occurred to him that perhaps Barabbas was moving in and had frightened the animal. He trained his eyes on the area but, from his vantage point, saw no sign of his enemy. The gazelle moved off to one side and found shelter amongst the rocks near the foot of the slope. After a while it moved on, but he still saw it intermittently as it sought grazing in the frugal soil.

Eleazor continued his vigil until dawn when he left to fetch Leila. After one more glance around the area, he felt satisfied that nobody was approaching. The ambush would remain safe until he returned.

The cave was only a short way away and Eleazor found Leila sitting up, leaning against the back wall.

"Get up," he said gruffly. "Time to go."

He untied the ropes around her ankles and pulled her to her feet. The woman's wrists were rubbed raw and the ropes around her wrists were frayed where she had been trying to cut them against the stone wall of the cave.

"Clever," he said with a grim smile. "Try that again and it will go the worse for you." He cuffed her on the back of the head and turned to fetch more rope.

Her wrists were quickly retied and the two of them proceeded to the rendezvous.

The sun rose higher in the sky, but Barabbas never arrived. Eleazor gave her water at lunchtime, but no food. They waited again, but by sunset there was still no sign of Barabbas.

Eventually Eleazor decided to take Leila back to the cave.

"It seems your husband cares less for your well being than I had hoped," he said, trying to hide his disappointment. "We'll try again tomorrow. If he doesn't come then, there's a certain man in Jericho who has offered me a handsome price for your services as a slave girl. He's eager, it seems, to do his brother a service and sire a son on his behalf."

Leila didn't answer. She was exhausted from lack of sleep and food and beyond caring about her fate. She followed Eleazor back to the cave.

† † † † †

The news of Leila's capture pressed in about Barabbas like a heavy blanket of fear quietly suffocating him, as it tightened its grip on his chest. That, added to the death of his friend, all but broke his spirit. Thoughts of revenge were suddenly overwhelmed by rage and sorrow. Desperately needing to break free, he turned in a daze. Leaving the family at the tomb, he first walked, then ran frantically into the desert.

Dark emotions clouded his mind, making it difficult to think clearly, and he ran until his lungs burned like the fires of *Gehenna*. Finally, he came to a halt, panting for breath as he tried to ease the agony in his flaming chest.

Slowly, as he rested his hands on his knees, gasping for breath, his pulse stopped its racing and the burning in his lungs began to abate. The physical exertion had cleared his mind somewhat and he gazed about him for the first time. There was no vegetation and the tents of the little *fellahin* community could no longer be seen, having disappeared behind an endless bank of sand dunes. All that surrounded him were the infinite golden sands and the engulfing silence that seemed to blanket the landscape in eternity, forever muting everything it touched. He found a small dune, climbing to its pinnacle where he sat down to consider his options.

In the wilderness, he found peace, feeding off its vastness and silence. It gave him the chance to consider his predicament more clearly. Levi was gone. Nothing more could be done for him. Leila might still be alive. At least he could try to save her.

His thoughts turned to the treasure. It was what Eleazor had come for. Would he be prepared to break his oath and reveal its whereabouts in return for his wife's safety? In his heart, Barabbas knew the answer to that question.

After a while, he began thinking about the rendezvous. It had been carefully chosen, with much deliberation and forethought. By arriving there first, his enemy had the complete advantage and could dominate the situation. Barabbas had to find a way in without being seen.

He had some ideas, but whether they would work was doubtful at best. The only way to reach Eleazor was by the road that led through the pass and that would leave him in full view of his foe.

What he needed was a miracle, he thought. For the first time in his life, Barabbas did not feel capable of handling the situation on his own. To get help from the zealots was impossible. They might be able to take the pass, but Leila would be dead long before they reached Eleazor. Barabbas had no desire to avenge his wife's death. He wanted her back.

His help would have to come from an unseen source. With difficulty, Barabbas fell to his knees and began to pray. The worst of it was that he felt he didn't even know the God he was praying to. If his father could see what he'd become - he was suddenly consumed with guilt.

On an impulse, he prayed in the name of Jesus of Nazareth as he had so often heard his wife do. He needed a redeemer and she had spoken of her *Messiah* as such. He prayed the only way he knew how, making a deal with God.

Nearly two hours passed before he finished. It was as if something inside him had taken over and words had flowed like a river that would not be swayed from its course. He felt strengthened, however, and ready to face his fears.

The deal was made and, somehow, Barabbas felt confident that God would honour his part. All he needed now was a sure-fire way to enter the pass without being detected. That had been part of the prayer. The first thing he had requested of the Almighty was a plan that would work. He sat down and waited for some sort of revelation. The form it took left him stunned, however, and a little afraid.

It was while he sat on the solitary dune, waiting for inspiration, that the thought flashed through his mind. The idea was so daring that Barabbas was loath to try it, but the more thought he gave it, the more plausible the idea became. It was almost impossible, he told himself – but only almost. There was the smallest chance that, with the cover of darkness, it could work.

Barabbas returned home and skinned the gazelle, keeping the head attached to the pelt. The limbs were also left in place and, after cleaning it, he headed for the rendezvous. Before the rocky knoll appeared above the horizon, he stopped and waited for sunset when darkness would blanket the landscape.

Once it was sufficiently dark, Barabbas pulled the skin over himself like a shawl, strapping the limbs to his wrists and ankles. He bent over double and began a meandering journey towards the pass. Moving at inconsistent speeds, he drew ever nearer, first standing still and then skittishly trotting a few paces closer. He varied his direction as well, but always drifting more or less in the direction of the pass in the indigo light.

The journey took half the night, but once he reached the rocks, he slipped between them and shed the skin, now using the terrain for cover. Taking the most difficult route, he headed for the high ground, seeking a vantage point where he might find Eleazor. Barabbas moved with ghostly silence, fleeting between two boulders, keeping low and making sure he never presented a silhouette against the skyline.

He found Eleazor seated on a flat boulder, using the shadow of the rock face behind him for cover. The man gazed with the patience of a night owl over the landscape hunting for his quarry.

As he watched the bundle of greed that was Eleazor, Barabbas yearned to drop from his vantage point and run a sword through his spine. That was impossible, however, as then he might never find his wife.

Instead, he settled down and waited for dawn. When the sun crested the horizon, Eleazor stirred. Barabbas watched as the man moved off, glancing back continuously as if confused.

He smiled to himself. The idiot had expected him to make his move earlier and arrive under the cover of darkness. Eleazor's conceit was such that he never expected Barabbas to think his enemy would be watching for him.

Barabbas moved as little as possible, not wanting to betray his presence to Eleazor. He moved just enough to keep his enemy in sight, even losing sight of him on a couple of occasions. Eventually, Eleazor disappeared inside a small cave and was lost from sight. Barabbas searched about until he found a suitable vantage point from which to launch his attack. It was around the corner, out of sight from the cave entrance but along the route back to Eleazor's vantage point.

There he waited, but was disappointed when Eleazor did not return. After several minutes, he was just about to poke his head up when he heard a scrape behind him.

He turned and saw Eleazor with Leila. Cursing, he flung himself flat against the rock in order to remain hidden. His stupidity had nearly cost him everything. It had never occurred to him that Eleazor would return via a different route. Once again, he realized he had underestimated his opponent. This time, he had not merely put his own life at risk, but also that of his wife.

Now he was out of position and unable to commence his assault. He followed the pair back to the flat rock where Eleazor took up his vigil once more. Barabbas dared not approach as close as he had the previous evening. The sunlight would cast shadows which were bound to give him away.

He would have to wait for dusk before launching his attack. It was the longest day of his life as he watched the sun's slothful journey across the sky. His foe was no more than thirty paces away, but he might have been in Rome for all the good it was to Barabbas.

Finally as dusk came, Barabbas moved quietly away, heading back for the vantage point from which he could launch his counterattack. With two paths to choose from, there was a fifty percent chance of selecting the correct one. He decided to gamble with the idea that Eleazor would not use the same one twice in a row and chose to remain on the path he'd chosen that morning.

Sunset finally proved his guess correct as he heard the approaching footsteps. Eleazor and Leila would pass directly beneath him. He readied himself as quietly as he could. There was only one chance to take his enemy by surprise. If nothing else, Barabbas knew he had to separate Eleazor from Leila in that first encounter. It was his only possibility of success.

Eleazor led the way, followed by Leila who was still trussed up, stumbling behind him. Barabbas allowed his enemy to pass beneath him and then launched himself like a plummeting raptor, falling on his prey.

Eleazor saw the shadow, but had no time to react. Barabbas knocked him to the ground and then spun to his feet, brandishing his sword. The sheer shock in his opponent's eyes told him how complete the surprise had been, but Barabbas gave no quarter. He lunged like a demon at the shaken form on the floor.

The wiry man rolled, drawing his own weapon from its sheath. He tried to move around Barabbas in an attempt to get near the woman again, but Barabbas blocked his path, shielding her from the assailant. The defensive move gave Eleazor the time he needed, however, and the two swords clashed as the smaller man countered with an underhand strike that raked up at Barabbas' lower torso. His sword swung in a vicious arc, but Barabbas deflected it easily and lunged forward, thrusting at his opponent's stomach just below the breast bone. Eleazor spun to the side, striking at the same time, but Barabbas sidestepped and swung again.

It didn't take Eleazor long to spot the weakness in Barabbas' defence. With Leila behind him, he dared not allow his enemy to circle around and reach her. Eleazor was quick to use this to his advantage, continuously circling right onto Barabbas' weaker side and forcing his opponent to engage in combat before he could reach the woman.

Barabbas found himself constantly forced to attack from a defensive position and paid dearly as Eleazor countered with blinding speed and faultless swordsmanship. He felt the searing pain as Eleazor's blade raked his flesh, causing his tunic to erupt in scarlet as he drove the man off yet again. Eleazor, sensing his advantage, circled right once more, waiting for Barabbas to strike and open himself again.

Barabbas waited until the last possible instant and then struck. Eleazor was ready and immediately parried, countering in one swift movement. He was fooled, however, as Barabbas' initial strike proved to be a dummy. Instead of finishing the thrust, he withdrew and shot to his left, parrying Eleazor's strike and countering with a speed and power that shook the ground in his wake.

Eleazor was thrown back on the defensive and his sword rang like a metal smith's anvil as he defended himself against Barabbas' barrage of crushing blows. He was forced to shrink back, fleeing the sweeping blade that seemed to strike from several angles at once.

The fight raged and blood was drawn on both sides, but it was apparent that Barabbas was the better of the two. Eleazor emerged from the mêlée with several wounds where Barabbas' sword had grazed his flesh, while Barabbas carried only two injuries

Barabbas pressed his advantage as he saw his opponent glancing around, looking for an avenue of escape. He forced him back, cutting off the route to the road below and Eleazor became desperate. Once again, Barabbas' sword struck flesh, grazing his opponent's rib cage. The blow was not fatal, but it was clear that Eleazor was weakening and it was only a matter of time before Barabbas' sword would find its mark.

Eleazor lunged in wild-eyed desperation at Barabbas who deflected the sword and lashed out with his foot, kicking his opponent's exposed kidney. As Eleazor arched back in pain, Barabbas thrust forward with his blade, striking his opponent's wrist. The cut was deep and Eleazor was forced to drop his sword. Barabbas advanced on the disarmed man who backed away fearfully until he bumped against the rocky face behind him.

"You killed my best friend - a man who was like a father to me," Barabbas growled as he held the point of his sword against Eleazor's throat.

The man clutched his injured hand, staring in blank terror at his enemy. He was unable to speak.

Barabbas continued. "When I send you to your grave, may God show you the mercy you showed Levi." He pulled back in order to lunge, but Leila stopped him.

"No, Barabbas!" she yelled as she rushed forward.

In the moment that Barabbas was distracted, Eleazor shot beneath his arm. Barabbas lunged at his foe, but missed the fleeting figure.

Eleazor slipped past him and snatched at Leila, pulling her towards him. He let her go for an instant as he slipped a knife from his belt, holding it in his left hand, and placed it at her throat, using her as a shield.

"Drop the sword," he instructed. Barabbas hesitated and Eleazor twitched the knife against Leila's neck. "Quickly!"

Barabbas had no choice. He threw it down a few paces in front of him where he could easily pick it up again if the opportunity presented itself.

Eleazor laughed with relief. "Now you will tell me what you came here to tell me."

Again, Barabbas hesitated. He had known it could come to this and had already made up his mind in the desert. The treasure meant nothing to him any longer. It had cost him his brother and his best friend, not to mention his father. He had already lost the woman he loved over it once and now stood to lose her a second time.

He sighed, rubbing the sweat from his eyes. "It's in a tomb outside Sebaste on the south road that leads to Jerusalem. The tomb is overgrown so it's difficult to find, but it's exactly one mile from the city gate. There's a sycamore tree on the side of the road - the tomb is a short way off the road to the west."

He had become too weary to lie any longer. The treasure, as far as he was concerned, had become a curse over his life. The sooner he was rid of it the better.

Leila was shocked. "Barabbas!"

"Quiet, woman." Eleazor shook her roughly, and then smiled. "I can see the truth in your eyes for once. Wouldn't it have been easier to just confide in me years ago? Then things would never have come to this."

"Go and take it, Eleazor, and may its curse fall upon you as it did me. I pray it destroys you."

"I will get the treasure, but I think I'll keep your wife for the time being. Once I find the treasure, I'll release her. Not before. If you're lying, there's a willing buyer in Jericho who will pay a handsome price for her. Consider it repayment for all the trouble you've caused me."

Barabbas stepped forward in rage, reaching for his sword, but Eleazor gently fondled Leila's neck with his blade.

"Would you rather she died here?" he asked sharply.

Barabbas wanted to scream but there was nothing left for him to do. He stood by in bitter resentment and cursing God in his heart as Eleazor backed away, heading into the pass below.

He heard the first creak as the two figures began their descent towards the road. It sounded like the quiet moan of a door opening in the dead of night. Barabbas was unable to place the source of the sound, but it had an eerie ring to it that caused him to shudder.

He listened again, but the desert was filled with a strange silence as Barabbas watched his enemy descend the slope with his wife in tow. Down in the pass, Eleazor looked up and made a mock bow, daring Barabbas to try something. Barabbas merely scowled as Eleazor turned towards the road that ran through the pass.

The second creak occurred just as they reached the road. It was louder this time and was accompanied by a cracking sound, as well as the sound of falling rubble. Barabbas glanced across in the direction of the noise and, in an instant, realization dawned. He was suddenly filled with horror at the thought of what was about to happen.

Gazing in mute terror, he stared at the shifting sand and giant boulders as they pressed against the ancient wooden wedge that held them in place. The wedge had dried and weakened over a period of decades since the pass had fallen into disuse and it creaked again, splintering as the weight of the avalanche pressed against it.

He rushed towards the deadly danger in an attempt to halt the inevitable, but he was too far away and unable to prevent the impending tragedy. It occurred while Barabbas was still several paces away, just as Eleazor was about to leave the pass. The final crack sounded and the wedge that held the ancient zealot trap in place gave way. The cliff suddenly erupted, sending an avalanche of stones pelting down on the two figures below.

In a panic, Barabbas raced down after them, yelling his wife's name as he ran. He reached the foot of the hill just as the last of the stones from the trap rolled to rest in the midst of a cloud of dust that filled the pass.

"Leila!" he screamed, choking on the dust-filled air.

He searched for several minutes before he found the first inert figure covered by rocks. Heavy stones were flung aside to reveal Eleazor's broken body lying amidst the rubble. The man had a deep gash on the back of his skull and blood soaked through the dark matted hair.

His arm was twisted at an impossible angle and two ribs had broken the skin, protruding like ugly fish hooks from his chest. Barabbas rolled him aside and looked at Leila who lay beneath him. Her breathing was shallow but, apart from some bruises, she seemed to be remarkably unhurt.

"Are you alright?" he rasped through the dust cloud.

Leila nodded and then winced as she tried to rise. "Help me. My foot's stuck."

Relief flooded through Barabbas' veins like a welcome breath of cool air in the midst of the scorching summer heat. He quickly removed some more stones and Leila was able to rise. Her ankle had already begun to swell like a melon, giving her a painful limp, but she appeared otherwise unhurt. It was ironic that her own kidnapper had shielded her from the rock fall.

"What happened, Barabbas?"

"A miracle," he replied with a smile. "Those zealot traps have been known to spring themselves, but the timing of this one stretches coincidence a little too far.

Leila stared at him in confusion.

Barabbas didn't bother to explain. "Let's go to Jerusalem. It's time I rekindled an old relationship."

"With whom?"

"You'll see. I made a deal with God in the wilderness and now I must honour my part."

"And what about him?" she pointed at Eleazor.

Barabbas glanced at the still unconscious, bleeding figure. "I would dearly love to run a sword through him, but I no longer have that luxury. The Almighty can decide his fate. My days of killing have come to an end."

He put his arm around her and headed east towards Jericho.

† † † † †

Simon, the zealot - or convert as Barabbas referred to him - proved more difficult to find than expected. Although believers were frequently to be found in the temple and reports of their activities filled Jerusalem, they were shy men. More often than not, they spent their time hiding from the wrath of the Sanhedrin and they were frequently forced to flee the city.

When Barabbas finally located him, Simon was overjoyed to be reunited with his old friend. Barabbas was ushered into his friend's home where a delicious meal of roast beef was prepared while the two men lounged around a table, drinking wine by the dull glow of an oil lamp in the early evening. Their initial meeting went on long into the night as the two men discussed the events that had transpired over the years since their parting.

It was as if Simon had been waiting all this time for his lost friend to find forgiveness in his heart and if there was any bitterness or resentment for the way

Barabbas had treated their friendship in the past, Simon never showed it.

They reminisced, talking of the old days when they had fought alongside one another and even chuckled at the rift that had developed between them when Simon had left the cause to follow the man from Nazareth.

The events surrounding the tragic Passover, when Barabbas had lost his brother, also came up in their conversation and Simon felt relieved to finally be able to give Barabbas his condolences.

"I went several times to Simeon's tomb the night after the crucifixion to pay my respects," Simon said quietly. It was the first time the smile left his face.

"I never saw you there." Barabbas smiled

Simon shrugged. "I didn't think you'd want me there after the way we parted."

Barabbas nodded. "You were probably right. The stupid things we do."

The conversation progressed naturally from there to the events that had led to Barabbas' freedom and the crucifixion of the Nazarene. Simon smiled as he listened to Barabbas' story and perspective from the dungeon, but never pressed Barabbas to convert as Leila so often had.

When Barabbas finally told him about his experience in the desert and the deal he had struck with the Almighty, Simon simply smiled and nodded.

"I'm glad you've come around to his teachings. Is this what you came to tell me?"

"I came because I need to be baptised. I've embraced a belief I know nothing about, but I must honour my agreement. God has done his part."

Simon nodded. "We'll do it tomorrow, but first you must have questions. I'll try to answer them as best I can."

Barabbas agreed. His mind was filled with questions about the man's teachings and the reports of an empty tomb. He wanted to know what it meant to them now that the *Messiah* they'd been waiting for had come and how this affected the zealots and the Kingdom of Israel.

He was so engrossed in his conversation and so eager to learn that he never noticed Leila and the two other women who appeared at the door, sitting down to listen to the two men speak. When he finally retired for the night, he joined Leila and found her weeping on their bed. He'd never thought he would see such joy in her eyes.

Barabbas was baptised in the Jordan and, in the weeks that passed, learned a freedom that he had never experienced before. It was the freedom of forgiveness and it filled him with joy and a peace he had believed he would never experience.

There was pain and suffering too, however, as many among their number were constantly being thrown into prison, beaten, or worse. Days were often spent in hiding and many times, believers were afraid to answer their doors.

A new champion of Judaism had risen from among the masses in Jerusalem and he carried out a campaign of terror against the church, killing believers in their droves as he waged his vendetta with the followers of the *Messiah*.

His name was Saul of Tarsus and he struck a chord of fear in many, but somehow never deterred them from their belief. Barabbas watched men go gladly to their graves or return from a flogging, joyful for the privilege of suffering for the name of their *Messiah*. Every time he witnessed such an incident, he became more convinced that this man truly was who he had claimed to be.

In moments of reflection, Barabbas remembered the words spoken to his brother on the cross. *Today, you will be with me in Paradise.* He smiled and sent up a silent prayer.

"Tell him I've become a convert too, Lord. Set his mind at rest."

Barabbas looked up as Simon entered his room. The man was tall and sunburned with a large round face that rested like a boulder on his thick neck and heavy-set shoulders.

His face shone with a vibrance that could only emanate from the Divine. "What's on your mind, friend?" he asked, seeing Barabbas' pensive expression.

"An oath I took a long time ago."

"You wish to share the burden." It was not a question. Simon sat down to listen.

Barabbas sighed. "A gift was entrusted to me several years back. My father was a protector of the gift and I inherited the responsibility. It's part of the reason Simeon was killed."

"What was it?"

"It's a treasure of such importance that no amount of money could purchase it. The prophecy was written on a copper scroll when the treasure was buried. I see now in retrospect that it was talking of the time *Messiah* came. We've been protecting the treasure for generations, but I'm beginning to realize that none of us understood the true significance of the words on the scroll."

Simon shook his head in bewilderment. "Copper scroll? Who is *we?*"

"The copper scroll was the document that listed the treasure and gave instructions for its retrieval. By *we* I mean the protectors of the scroll. I'm the only one left. The last one was killed by Eleazor."

"And where is this scroll now?"

"It's no longer important. The treasure was moved after Pilate got his hands on the scroll. I need to take you to it."

Simon shook his head. "I don't want responsibility for such a thing."

"You would if you understood the nature of the treasure. It requires holy men who will use it wisely to establish God's Kingdom here on earth."

"A holy treasure?"

"More than you can imagine," Barabbas told him. "The treasure comprises a multitude of artefacts from the Temple, including the *K'lal* with the heifer's ashes."

"The atonement of Israel - the coming of *Messiah*," Simon whispered.

Barabbas nodded. "For generations we've believed these ashes would usher in the coming of the *Messiah* who would make atonement for Israel's sin."

"Now the *Messiah* has come and the temple artefacts are being brought to his followers." Simon was in a daze. "I must talk with the other eleven."

"Don't talk too long. Eleazor knows where the treasure is buried. He may be dead, but then again —"

Simon rose in haste. "It must be moved to safety."

He disappeared to find the other eleven apostles whom Jesus of Nazareth had chosen to lead his church.

To say the twelve were excited by Barabbas' news was an understatement. They pressed him for information at every point of his story, asking all sorts of questions as they sought clarification. When he finally finished, they decided to leave immediately for Sebaste.

Fifteen men were chosen and sent with Barabbas and his wife to the city to retrieve the treasure. They made the journey in a large cart that one of the believers had loaned them to bring the treasure to Jerusalem. The trip to Sebaste took two days and, when they reached their destination, the men jumped eagerly from the carriage, heading for the tomb just a short way off the road.

They finally arrived at the clearing and Barabbas went cold as he gazed at the site before them. The area was littered with tools and the door stood slightly ajar. Someone had arrived there before them and the seal on the tomb was broken.

30

IN THE dark chill of the desert night, Eleazor stirred. He had lost count of the number of times he had regained and then lost consciousness. At one point, he remembered having to fight off a pair of crows that had taken an interest in him. Then darkness had blanketed his mind once more.

He lay still, terrified that the waves of blackness that assailed his vision would once again envelop him. Breathing was painful and his hand recoiled at the shock of touching the sharp chipped bone that protruded from his rib cage, breaking the skin.

Still he made no movement, allowing consciousness to push back the black haze lurking at the edge of his vision. Slowly the darkness receded, only to be replaced by waves of nausea and a fever that tormented his body with painful convulsive shaking.

Once he felt strong enough, he tried to roll over. Although he managed it, the darkness returned and it was some time before he dared move again. Willpower forced him on, however.

He now knew where the treasure lay and that knowledge drove him to his feet. He would survive. Afterwards, he couldn't remember how he had reached his donkey tethered out of sight on the far side of the knoll, or how he had managed to mount it. The beast got him to Jericho, however, and once there he kept mumbling Matthias' name until someone helped lead the animal to the villa.

Having survived the journey, Eleazor collapsed and didn't wake up for two whole days. When he finally came to, he found himself bandaged and attended by a local physician. Food and water were administered and, once he assured the doctor that he was feeling better, Matthias was summoned.

When he entered, he brushed the doctor aside. "Thank you, you can go." Turning, to Eleazor, he grinned. "I sometimes wonder if they don't do more harm than good. How are you feeling?"

"Better, thank you," Eleazor replied weakly.

"I assume from the condition you're in that you found Barabbas."

Eleazor winced and nodded as he tried to sit up.

Matthias asked bluntly, "Is he dead?"

"No. There was a rock fall. He escaped."

"I hope that you got what you wanted from him."

When Eleazor nodded again, Matthias continued, "And the girl? Is she still alive?"

"I don't know. The rock slide got her too. She may still be buried out there in the wilderness."

"Pity, pity," Matthias murmured absent-mindedly. His gaze rested a long way off.

"Well, can't be helped. You tried. Feel free to rest here until you're recovered. You may find her yet, and my offer still stands."

It took several weeks for Eleazor to recover. It was a frustrating time waiting for his body to mend before he could finally embark for Sebaste. His recovery, followed by the journey, felt like an eternity, but finally, Eleazor arrived at the city. He wasted no time seeking out the tomb, but it was dusk before he laid eyes on the burial site for the first time.

✝ ✝ ✝ ✝ ✝

Eleazor found the entrance to the cave blocked by the traditional large round stone. It was heavy, but could be moved with enough leverage. First, he returned to the town where he purchased the necessary equipment.

After spending the night at an inn, he began work the following morning. By midday, Eleazor had dug the beginnings of a trench around the far side of the stone where he intended to roll it away. The trench ran away at a steep angle, cutting into the rise in order to make moving the stone possible.

It was no easy task as the terrain held several boulders which had to be shattered before being cut out of the ground. Although healed, Eleazor's body no longer responded as willingly since the beating it had taken in the rockfall at Killer's Pass. Sunset was long gone before he finally gave up. After thumping his hand for the last time, he threw down his tools in a temper and crawled up against a fallen tree trunk to sleep for the night.

He began his work again at first light. Once the trench was completed, he began making preparations to get a long enough lever under the stone so that he could roll the heavy door away.

He was so busy with his preparations that didn't hear the approaching soldiers on the road below. Eleazor also didn't realize how much noise he was making. What had started out as careful preparations that morning had become heavy thuds and scrapes as he shifted the heavy rocks and foliage about.

The two legionaries that arrived to investigate took him completely off guard as they leaped at him, pinning him to the ground. Struggle was futile and a few minutes later, he stood under the sycamore tree on the road before a short centurion with tightly curled hair.

"Do you know the penalty for disturbing a tomb under Roman law?" The man had a pompous air about him.

Eleazor stared at the man in sullen silence.

"Augustus commanded that grave robbers be put to death." He spoke as if informing a child. He waited for Eleazor to say something, but the captive merely stared at his shoes.

The soldier continued, "By happy coincidence we're on our way to Caesarea. I'll hand you over to the proper authorities there."

It was the first time Eleazor appeared fearful. Caesarea meant trial before Pilate. The prefect would not be forgiving and Eleazor had no doubt that he would be recognized.

✝ ✝ ✝ ✝ ✝

"Now tell me where the treasure is buried!" Pilate demanded.

"Do you guarantee my freedom if I do?"

"I guarantee nothing. You're a grave robber, wanted for numerous crimes against the emperor, including treason. Cooperation will only make the end bearable for you."

True to his expectations, Eleazor had been recognized. Of all the cursed luck, the very first soldier he'd been handed to happened to be one of the men who had escorted him to Barabbas' lair all those years ago. The man had a keen memory and took great pleasure in making him squirm before going off to tell the centurion on duty. Curse his luck!

He was taken to Pilate and Eleazor realized that now only one thing could save him from his fate. He shook his head as he thought of how close he had come. The treasure had been within his grasp, no more than a few feet away. How could he lose it now!

For some reason, the prefect believed that he had given the scroll to the merchant in Jericho and therefore knew the location of the treasure. Absurd, but it might just save him, he thought.

"If you have mercy on me, I'll show you where the treasure is buried."

"You'll tell me now."

Eleazor refused. He knew that if he told the prefect, he would never leave the courts alive. "It's impossible. I have to take you there myself."

"Only to escape before you produce the goods like you did last time? You will tell me now or face the most arduous session on the rack that any man has ever known."

Trembling, Eleazor shook his head. He knew what would follow, but he had to try. To give up now would only seal his fate.

The torture rack was an instrument of unspeakable agony. Eleazor broke after only ten minutes and told the prefect all he wanted to know.

"It's in a tomb outside Sebaste. The same tomb where I was caught. You'll never find it, though. Let me take you there."

"You're not leaving this cell," Pilate growled. "Give me accurate directions and if I don't find it, we can – chat – some more."

Eleazor groaned at the agony and hopelessness of his situation. "What do I get in return?"

"Only my promise that once I have the treasure, you will die quickly."

Pilate smirked as he left the centurion in the cell to get the directions from Eleazor. Shortly afterwards, Gaius was summoned and a group of soldiers was assembled to head for Sebaste, led by Pontius Pilate himself.

The group of believers was shocked when they found that the tomb had been tampered with.

"Don't worry," Barabbas assured them, ignoring the sick feeling that churned in his gut. "It doesn't look as if anyone's been inside."

Four men helped Barabbas lever away the stone. It took all their weight, even after all the effort that had already been expended to open it, but the large grey rock finally rolled back like a giant wheel, running down into the groove that Eleazor had dug. It came to rest four feet back, leaving enough space to slip through the opening.

Barabbas entered and the group outside became unnaturally silent as they waited for a word from him.

"It's all here," he yelled from inside the cave.

The men outside breathed their relief and chuckled as Barabbas stuck his head out of the entrance.

"Someone going to help me here?" he enquired cheerfully.

The chests were taken and loaded onto the cart. Then the men turned to thank Barabbas.

"What will you do now?" Simon asked him as they bade one another farewell.

Barabbas shrugged. "Maybe I'll head north and settle there. I've got a good stud of horses out in the wilderness. If I was to move to Tyre, I think I could make a good living."

Simon frowned. "You realize that you'd be selling mostly to Roman Equites."

"I think my days of violence have reached an end. The world is different now."

His friend smiled and gave him a giant bear hug. "Go with God, my friend. And remember, if you ever need anything, you have brothers in Jerusalem."

"I think that my new family is growing. It wouldn't surprise me if I found I had brothers in Tyre as well."

"Just preach the good news wherever you go." Simon and the men with him waved as they headed back to Jerusalem.

Barabbas and Leila remained under the sycamore and watched the cart trundle southwards until it was out of sight, bumping around the first bend in the road.

"Where do we go now?" Leila turned to Barabbas, taking his hand.

"I think we should head for Tyre. If we find a place to settle there, I can always return to Enos for the horses. It's a good stud. The offspring will fetch a fine price up north."

They turned east, heading for the coast, and were nearly ten miles away from Sebaste when they saw the convoy approaching from Caesarea.

$$ † \; † \; † \; † \; † $$

Pilate's convoy was moving fast. His carriage was horse-drawn and only horsemen accompanied him.

"We don't want foot soldiers slowing us down," he'd told Gaius before they left Caesarea.

Gaius was out front, making sure all other traffic was cleared from the road before Pilate's entourage arrived. He noticed the two travellers heading towards Caesarea. Something about them struck him as familiar. He watched them as they passed by, heads down, counting the steps to their destination. Caesarea was still a long way away, he thought as he rode by.

Minutes later, Pilate's carriage raced by. Barabbas turned and watched the chariot race on towards Sebaste.

"Was that the prefect, do you think?" Leila wondered.

"Probably. Did you see the centurion, Gaius, out front?"

Leila nodded. "I don't think he recognized us."

"Why should he? Gaius wouldn't expect to see us here."

All sorts of thoughts plagued Barabbas' mind. Why was the prefect headed to Sebaste? Did he know about the treasure?

All needless worry, he felt sure. There was no way that Pilate could know the treasure had been there. On the other hand, the tomb had been tampered with, if not entered. Someone had been there.

"Never mind Gaius," he said to his wife. "The treasure is safely on its way to Jerusalem and we are free of our responsibility."

Despite his words of assurance, Barabbas found himself constantly looking over his shoulder as they made their way slowly towards the coast. Thirty minutes later, he and Leila were caught in a deathly chase, running for their very lives ahead of Roman fury.

A quick search revealed the cave exactly where Eleazor had said it would be. Pilate exited his carriage and gazed about at the myriad of fresh footprints, as well as the ditch and apparatus that had been used to open the tomb.

He entered the cave in silence and emerged a moment later. "It seems our Jewish friend is in for another session on the rack. He won't find me as pleasant as last time."

Gaius could see that the prefect's complexion was pale with rage and his hands trembled slightly.

"Who owns this tomb, I wonder?" Gaius murmured.

"Find him and bring him here," Pilate growled and then turned away, closing himself in his carriage.

Gaius took several soldiers into the city with him. It didn't take long to learn the name of the owner and where he lived. They found Zechariah at home and asked him to accompany them to his tomb. It was a nervous man that appeared before Pilate.

Gaius whispered, "I suggest you cooperate in every way with the prefect. It's the only way your life will be spared."

Pilate emerged from the carriage. He looked more composed now, but Gaius could see the knuckles of the prefect's clenched fists were white and he thought he noticed a twitch at the corner of the man's mouth.

"Your name," Pilate asked curtly.

"Zechariah, my lord."

"And you're the owner of this tomb?"

Gaius glanced at Zechariah. The man trembled as he answered. "That's right, my lord."

"I assume then that you know what the contents were and where they are."

"No, my lord."

The twitch returned. "Don't toy with me. I could end your life on a whim. Now tell me about the treasure."

"Treasure?" Zechariah was confused for a moment. "The treasure in the tomb," he added hastily.

"Where is it?"

"I honestly didn't know that the tomb had been opened. Nobody ever showed me the contents."

"You allowed strangers to use your tomb for a purpose they never explained to you? I find that hard to believe."

"I owed the man a debt - he saved my life once," the man stammered.

"And what was this man's name?"

"Levi of Gamala, prefect."

"Did he have any accomplices?"

"One, a man called Barabbas."

Pilate glanced sharply at Gaius, but the centurion's mind was some ten miles back along the road to Caesarea.

"Gaius! Did you hear me?"

"He was here. I saw him on the road to Caesarea." Gaius spoke as if in a daze.

"Barabbas?" Pilate was stunned.

"There were two of them. I thought I recognized them from somewhere, but couldn't be sure. He never looked up."

"Well go after them, man!" Pilate yelled, but Gaius was already racing for his horse.

As he ran, Gaius screamed for several soldiers to follow him. Within minutes, ten horsemen were racing back along the road to Caesarea.

✝ ✝ ✝ ✝ ✝

Zechariah waited in trepidation for the prefect's verdict, Pilate having retired to his carriage to think. At one point, he had called a soldier and given him an instruction which Zechariah could not hear. The soldier had taken several other men with him and headed back to Sebaste.

All Zechariah could do was wait. After another hour, Pilate emerged from the carriage and approached him.

"I've decided to await Gaius' return. If you're lucky, he'll bring Barabbas with him. If not, I hope for your sake that you have the answers I'm looking for."

Zechariah was broken. He knew that he would never be able to answer the prefect's questions. Pilate left him with the guards and returned to his carriage.

It was only half an hour later when the soldiers returned from Sebaste that the true horror of the situation dawned on Zechariah. He fell to his knees and a loud mournful cry began to rise up in his throat. It echoed in the tomb, filling the air with his sorrow. No tears touched his cheeks, but the echo reverberated throughout the camp and the soldiers were unable to keep him quiet.

✝ ✝ ✝ ✝ ✝

Barabbas looked over his shoulder for the hundredth time and suddenly, his worst fears were confirmed.

"It seems Gaius was more observant than we gave him credit for." He tried to speak calmly, but adrenalin was already beginning to churn through his veins.

Leila turned and looked back. From the rise where they stood, she could see the horses behind them in the distance.

"Maybe they're returning for some other reason."

Barabbas shook his head glumly. "I'm not so lucky. Let's go."

"Do you think they've seen us?"

"Almost certainly, but we'll be out of sight in the next ten paces."

They proceeded down the rise and as soon as they disappeared from sight, Barabbas took Leila's hand and turned right, heading for the hill country to the north.

"It's impossible, Barabbas. We can't outrun horsemen."

"There are a lot of bends in the road ahead. As long as we remain out of sight, they'll probably assume we're still on the road."

"We won't fool them for long."

"With any luck, we'll fool them long enough to reach those hills to the north. Once there, the horses will be useless," Barabbas reassured her as he raced across the field, heading for the cover of a small clump of cedars.

"They'll still chase us on foot. There are ten of them, Barabbas." Leila was not naturally given to panic, but this was a different world for her.

"All we have to do is elude them until nightfall. After that, they'll never see us again. The hills are our haven. Roads are theirs."

Barabbas led Leila quickly to the tree line which he used for cover. When the soldiers came into view, he held her close to him, hiding behind the small group of saplings. Glancing from the shadows, he watched the soldiers race by along the road, constantly glancing over the terrain on both sides of them.

As soon as they had passed by, Barabbas bolted along the tree line, being sure to keep the small clump of trees between him and the soldiers as he turned north towards the hills. Despite his confident manner, Barabbas was worried. The hills lay several miles away and there was precious little cover ahead of them.

He shot across an open stretch of ground, reaching a small gully which ran north-west where he fell flat on his belly to hide himself. He kept a constant eye out for the soldiers who he expected to return at any moment. Safely in the gully, they rushed up it, always moving towards the distant hills.

Barabbas gazed back at Leila in rapt admiration. She crawled on her belly, following him without a word of complaint. He risked glancing over the edge of the gully and saw the soldiers returning. This time they rode more slowly, their search more intent.

"We have to reach that clump of boulders over there," Barabbas pointed at the large group of rocks to their right. "Wait for my signal. We'll be as conspicuous as a purple stain on a white robe."

He watched carefully, allowing the soldiers to pass by a second time. As soon as he judged them to be beyond the horsemen's line of sight, he climbed from the ditch, pulling Leila up with him. They rushed across yet another open stretch of ground and fell behind the rocks. The rocky knoll was about eight feet high and no wider than several carts measured from end to end. It was the only cover for hundreds of yards around them.

Too many open stretches. The hills were still too far away. Barabbas carefully raised his head between two dome-shaped boulders and watched the soldiers begin their turn. This time they left the road and began moving northwards into the open field.

"We've got a few miles on them and they're moving more slowly now. There's a chance as long as we can remain hidden."

Leila said nothing, but her gaze over the open expanse of ground with no cover spoke volumes.

Barabbas winked at her. "Trust me. I've eluded these people all my life. I don't intend to get caught now."

He moved in a wide arc, heading for some low land about a mile to the north, with constant glances behind him. Barabbas noted Leila's growing amazement as he somehow managed to keep the tiny clump of rocks between him and the soldiers until they reached the dip and the legionaries disappeared behind the rise.

"An old zealot trick," he grinned. "Their search patterns are predictable. If the land lies correctly, you can travel for miles across open country using only the tiniest obstruction as cover. The closer they get to the obstruction, the more their vision is obscured until their own search is working against them. If they'd remained on the road, they'd have seen us the minute we left the rocks."

Barabbas followed the lowland back east until he found a small riverbed that ran from the north. He followed the river's course, using the trees along the bank for cover. The rocks were slippery and both of them stumbled on several occasions, grazing knees and ankles. Fortunately there were no serious injuries.

As the ground became steeper, the water course grew more violent. Barabbas left the stream and checked the ground beyond. A moment later he returned and checked the ground on the other side.

"What's the matter?" Leila asked nervously.

"Just checking to see which side our Roman friends are searching. They're over there." He nodded towards the eastern side of the river.

"Where to now?" She shivered.

"The water's getting too rough here. We can still follow the river's course on the west side, using the trees for cover."

"Won't they follow it on the other side?"

"Of course they will, but the closer we get to the hills the less likely they'll be to find a place for the horses to cross.

Leila smiled. "So they'll be reduced to following on foot."

Barabbas nodded. "That should even things slightly."

They walked north for another mile and the hills drew closer. They could hear the horses gaining as they raced up the other side of the river. Barabbas constantly checked the water course and was pleased to see that as the ground grew steeper, the river cut a deeper canyon in its course.

"Another mile and this river will be impossible to cross." He grinned as they made their way quietly along the water course.

"The soldiers are getting closer. They'll still be able to cross."

Barabbas agreed. His concern was that, by leaving the river's edge too soon, the Roman horsemen might still find a safe crossing. With the hills still so far away, they could never hope to outrun the steeds. On the other hand, the foliage was thinning, making them easier to spot.

If they weren't a healthy distance from the river by the time they were spotted, the soldiers would catch them, even on foot. After another mile, Barabbas decided to risk breaking cover and running for the hills which still lay a mile or so to his left. With no cover, he knew they would be spotted, but it was a chance they had to take. The horses were getting closer by the minute.

As he began ascending the steep ground, he heard cries from the far side of the river. Turning back, he saw the soldiers racing up the river bank, pointing in his direction. Two others were further east, but they quickly cut across, heading for the riverbank.

"We'll be alright." Barabbas puffed as he glanced back at the river's course. "That canyon must be nearly ten feet deep with sheer walls on either side. There's no way a horse can cross that river."

Leila ran alongside him, but didn't reply. Her eyes were fixed on the hills beyond.

Barabbas looked back again, laughing with relief as he saw the horsemen come to a halt on the east side of the river. The men glanced up and down the banks, looking for a place to cross.

"They could still go back and cross further downstream," Leila ventured nervously, through panting breaths.

"That's almost certainly what they'll do, but it won't help them. By the time they get back here, we'll have reached the hills."

The rising landmass beckoned like a welcome haven ahead of them. The hills were their safety. Only time stood in their way. They carried on towards the refuge that the hills offered.

It was when Barabbas turned and saw the two remaining horsemen heading for the river's edge that disaster struck. He watched the pair racing hell-bent for the river while the remaining legionaries dismounted and moved up and down the bank, looking for a likely place to cross.

The leader of the two rushed like a madman, forcing his horse to greater speed. As he drew near to the river's edge, Barabbas recognized the centurion's face.

"He'll never do it," Barabbas whispered, stopping as he gazed in numb disbelief at the scene below.

Soldiers trotted up and down the river, gauging their chances as they looked for a suitable place to cross the narrow gorge. Then Gaius was among them, driving his steed in a frenzy of speed as he fixed his eyes on his prey halfway up towards the hills.

Barabbas heard Leila gasp as the animal leaped across the expanse of the gorge. Horse and rider sailed across what seemed like endless space and landed without even breaking stride. The other soldiers gazed at the spectacle in horror, followed by disbelief as Gaius spurred his horse on up the rise.

"That was the finest riding I've ever seen," Barabbas whispered like an awestruck child.

Leila tugged frantically at his tunic. "Come, Barabbas, we have to go."

Coming to his senses, he turned and ran but, in his heart, he knew that they would never reach the hills in time. The horse's gait thundered in their ears as they ran, growing ever closer until Barabbas was forced to turn and fight.

✝ ✝ ✝ ✝

Gaius was not so foolish as to rush in and dive from his horse. Such an action was liable to leave him skewered on Barabbas' sword by the time he hit the ground. He came to a halt and dismounted several paces away.

"So, Jew, we finally get to finish the battle you started at the barracks in Jerusalem."

"That was a long time ago, Gaius. All I want now is to go in peace and raise a family."

Gaius chuckled bitterly. "You should have thought of that before you set the Roman quarters on fire. Pilate wants the treasure that you took from the pool of Bethesda. Where is it?"

"That treasure belongs to the Jewish nation. It's our heritage and has nothing to do with Rome."

Gaius advanced with drawn sword. "We'll let the emperor decide that."

"I have no wish to kill you, Gaius. I'm a changed man."

The centurion ignored his plea and thrust with his sword. Barabbas drew and parried in one smooth motion, countering, but his opponent eluded the blade. From his first encounter with Gaius, all those years ago at the burning garrison, he already knew that this man was probably the most dangerous foe he would ever face.

Once again, the Roman centurion came at him, forcing him to retreat under the relentless heat of the blade. Barabbas blocked a strike and saw an opening, lunging with his foot at the centurion's torso, but Gaius sidestepped and thrust with his sword once again.

There was a tear and Barabbas felt the sharp edge of the steel as it sliced his upper arm. The drawn blood released a fury in Barabbas, who countered with a flurry, forcing Gaius back on the defensive. For all his ability, however, his sword was unable to find its mark and Gaius emerged from the skirmish unscathed.

He came back at Barabbas with a vengeance, but this time Barabbas was able to evade the sword. He managed to nick Gaius' ear and saw the thin trickle of blood that ran like a crack down the soldier's neck.

The centurion spun, falling to his knees, and Barabbas felt a shaft of pain. Glancing down, he saw the gaping wound where his opponent had struck his leg. He groaned as the centurion extracted the sword from his left thigh and staggered back, still stunned by the speed of the blow. He hadn't even seen where the sword had come from.

Gaius came at him again as he hobbled about in agony. All he could do was deflect the blows that rained on him like stinging silver shards. In a desperate attempt to gain the upper hand, Barabbas ducked under Gaius' blade, striking the soldier's solar plexus like a bull with his head.

The wind was knocked out of the stunned centurion, who could hardly believe that a man could still move like that with such a wound. He tried to force a break to regain his composure, but Barabbas was upon him, thrashing his sword about like an injured shark churning in the water.

Seeing his advantage, Barabbas pressed home, striking high, aiming at the centurion's neck. When Gaius raised his sword to defend the blow, Barabbas struck, using his injured leg. He caught his opponent on the joint behind the knee, buckling Gaius' limb.

Shafts of agony shot through Barabbas' thigh, but the Roman centurion went down. Barabbas took his sword in both hands and struck at Gaius' wrist, severing the centurion's thumb and knocking the sword from his hands. The weapon swung in a wide arc, embedding itself in the soft ground some six paces away.

Barabbas approached Gaius who struggled helplessly to his knees while clutching his injured hand. The Roman was unarmed and Barabbas put his sword to the centurion's throat.

"I told you, but you refused to listen."

"What are you waiting for? Kill me now while you have the chance," the centurion snarled.

"I can't do that," Barabbas replied. "Sorry about your hand."

He raised his hand and struck Gaius just below his bleeding ear with the handle of his sword. The centurion slumped to the ground and Barabbas turned to Leila who gazed at the soldier in concern.

"Did you —"

"He'll be alright," Barabbas grinned. "Although I don't envy him the headache he'll have when he comes to."

He looked east and saw the remaining soldiers who had found a place to cross the river and were headed his way. They were a long way downstream, but approaching quickly. Barabbas glanced at the horsemen approaching from below and then back at the hills behind him. Too far, he thought. Gaius had slowed them down just long enough to get the others across the river.

"We'll never reach the hills now," Leila wailed as they watched the approaching horsemen.

Barabbas glanced about and his gaze suddenly became determined. "Oh yes we will. Let's see if they can outrun this."

He limped across to Gaius' steed and took the animal by the bit. Using his arms, he pulled himself up onto the mount and painfully swung his leg over. Then he trotted across to Leila and lifted her on behind him.

Digging his heels into the animal's ribs, he shot forward, heading for the towering mounds and safety. Every time he looked back, the soldiers were closer and it seemed to Barabbas that they'd never reach the hills in time. Then suddenly they were there and the horse could go no further. Barabbas tried to ignore the agony in his leg as he dismounted and began the painful climb into the mountainous area, abandoning the animal at the foot of the rocky terrain.

Below them, the legionaries dismounted and began to climb up after the hobbling couple.

✝ ✝ ✝ ✝ ✝

When Gaius came to he found himself alone. The sun had long since set and darkness had settled like a blanket over the land. He felt the warm muzzle of his horse sniffing at his damaged ear and struggled to his feet.

Once he'd shaken the grogginess from his mind, he decided that searching for Barabbas in the dark was pointless. He mounted the animal and headed back to Pilate's camp. His hand was in such pain that he nearly fainted when the leather rein brushed against the wound, but he pushed on, finding the road and turning east towards Sebaste. When he arrived at the camp, he was immediately summoned to Pilate's carriage.

"Where are the rest of the men?" the prefect demanded.

"I don't know. Maybe they cornered him in the hills. He was badly injured. I don't think he could get very far."

Pilate thought about this for a moment. "Well," he said at length, "since you haven't captured Barabbas, we might as well start the interrogation. Bandage that hand and then join me outside."

Gaius did as he was told. When he rejoined Pilate, he was horrified at what he saw. Not only Zechariah but his entire family was lined up before Pilate. Five sons with all their wives and a multitude of children were fettered and held by the guards.

The stark terror in the old man's eyes revolted Gaius and he felt outraged at what the prefect intended to do. There were thirty-seven people in all, men, women and children, pale with fear and helpless to do anything about their fate.

"Please, prefect. I know nothing about the treasure you speak of. I've never even seen it." Zechariah wept as he spoke. His guards had to hold him upright before Pilate as his legs had lost their strength.

"I think a lesson needs to be taught." Pilate turned to Gaius. "Centurion, fetch me that man over there."

Gaius gazed at the strong young man with fine features who stepped forward, trying desperately not to show his fear.

"What is your name, friend?" Gaius asked gently.

"Medan," the man replied. There was a quiver in his voice.

Pilate interrupted, shoving the butt of a knife into Gaius' injured hand. "Show Zechariah what happens to people who don't cooperate with me."

"Please, prefect," Gaius protested. "These people haven't broken any laws. Look at this man's eyes. If he knew anything, don't you think he would tell us?"

Pilate's gaze was cold. "We'll find out what he knows soon enough. Now do as you're told."

Gaius fixed the prefect with a defiant glare. He thought carefully as he realized he was dealing with a madman. Finally he replied in subdued tones. "I won't do it."

Pilate's lip twitched for a moment as he digested the news. When he finally spoke, it was in a hushed purr. "You defy me, centurion?"

Gaius held his gaze, but remained silent.

Pilate's voice had the menace of a sword's edge. "You have failed me too many times to risk challenging my authority. Now take the knife and do as you're told."

"This is not the law we practise. These people are innocent. They haven't even stood trial."

"If you don't obey me, centurion, I will have you arrested and sent back to Rome on charges of insubordination. Take the knife!" The last sentence was a shrill screech.

Gaius folded his arms and stared into Pilate's eyes with baleful contempt.

"So be it." Pilate said. "Guard. Arrest the centurion and put him in shackles. See to it that he's made suitably uncomfortable."

The soldier that Pilate addressed hesitated and Pilate scowled. "Do it! Unless you want to end up in shackles with him."

With a pleading look at Gaius, the soldier stepped forward and took him by the arm. "This way, centurion," he said, unable to look Gaius in the eye.

Gaius followed the legionary without resisting. They shackled him behind the carriage where four soldiers stood guard around him to prevent escape.

He spent the night in chains, forced to listen to the blood-curdling howls and agonized weeping that emanated from the other side of the carriage. His legionaries did the unspeakable, committing the most heinous acts of torture and abuse ever devised.

He felt sick to his stomach every time he heard the cry of a woman or child. Each time, the cycle would be the same. The cries would become screams and the screams would grow more horrific until the voice finally gave up. Then the moans would come until, finally, only sobbing remained, and then the silence.

It was dawn before the whimpering finally died down and the camp was blanketed in silence. After a while, two legionaries arrived and mounted Gaius on a horse. The chariot pulled away, revealing the carnage that had been left behind. It was a scene of such horror that he was unable to control his heaving stomach and yellow bile spewed from his mouth, dripping down his mount's withers.

The bodies had all been stripped naked and were caked with dirt, mingled with blood. Zechariah had been left till last. His face was a contorted mulch, crushed by repeated blows, and not a bone in his body remained intact.

Worst of all, Gaius would never forget the stench of death in the air. It hung like a decaying carcass, nauseating him and making it impossible to close his eyes to the tragic scene.

He retched again, leaning over to avoid the vile fluid that flowed from the depths of his stomach.

"This way, centurion," one of his guards spoke, thankfully turned his attention away from the carnage.

It was no good, however. Gaius knew he could never forget the scene. Many years from now, he would still awaken in the terror of darkness, hearing the screams outside the tomb at Sebaste. He would never forgive Pilate for the horror he had wrought.

He returned to Caesarea in chains, imprisoned by men he had once commanded. There, he waited, kept in the stinking dungeons where he had thrown so many men in the past. While he was incarcerated, some of the more loyal legionaries smuggled information to him. Pilate had returned to Caesarea in mental turmoil. The prefect had locked himself in his chambers and refused to come out, even to hold court.

It seemed the remaining soldiers who had accompanied him on his final hunt for Barabbas had returned empty-handed. The Jew had disappeared and no reports of his whereabouts had come in. Gaius wondered whether they would ever hear any news of Barabbas again.

When he was finally taken from the dungeons, he was put on a galley bound for Rome. The captain was given a letter with instructions from the prefect of Judea, outlining the crimes Gaius had committed as well as his gross negligence over a period of years that had led to the consistent escape of one Barabbas, the most wanted outlaw in Judea.

There was no mention of the treasure, or the copper scroll, which were destined to remain a myth, as far as Gaius could see, until the end of time.

† † † † †

"Look at me, Daddy," the small boy called across the yard. "I'm riding by myself."

The father straightened up from under the bay mare he was tending. He gazed across the yard at the proud youngster who held the reins of his giant mount.

Riding already and he'd barely been walking for more than two years, the man thought. He wasn't worried, as the mare was placid and had a way with children. Besides, one of the servants was right there, ready to grab the reins if needed.

"You'd better be careful you don't fall, Yusef. It's a long way down from there."

"I never fall," the youngster crowed. His legs barely straddled the mare's broad back.

The man chuckled. "You'd better get back into the house to your mother. She's been calling you for over half an hour already."

"Are you coming too?"

He shook his head. "In a few minutes. First, I've got a meeting with the centurion from Caesarea."

A voice suddenly spoke from the shadows behind him. "Is Cornelius coming today? I thought you said tomorrow."

Barabbas turned in surprise to see Leila skulking near the entrance to the stable yard and nodded. "He's bringing the new Legate to see our stud."

She smiled briefly. "Raising eyebrows in high places, I see. Really, Barnabas, I wish you wouldn't let Yusef ride the horses like that. He's too young."

Barabbas grinned. It still caught him by surprise sometimes when she called him by that name. Four years had passed since they'd arrived in Tyre and everybody in the city knew him as Barnabas, the horse breeder from the wilderness beyond Judea. It was said that he had been born on the back of a horse and that he had learned all he knew among the *Bedouin*, the nomads of the wilderness.

It was also common knowledge that his stud was the finest in the district. It had grown as much in numbers as it had in stature and Barnabas now had two of the finest stallions in Palestine and fifty-seven brood mares. His fillies and yearlings were the best trained and fetched the highest prices of any in the province and his was always the first stop for anyone looking to purchase a horse in Tyre.

"Don't worry about Yusef. He's doing just fine."

The look he got could have withered an entire wheat field in Galilee, but his wife chose to change the subject. "I'd better hurry. I promised to send a parcel of garments through to Caesarea with Cornelius when next he came and they're not even packed yet."

It was a good arrangement. Leila was still manufacturing her garments, but relied on contacts in Caesarea to market them for her. She found it easiest to send a new batch of garments through to Caesarea with Cornelius whenever he came through to Tyre, which was rather more often than was truly necessary.

Cornelius and Barnabas had become firm friends since the centurion had first arrived in Caesarea. They shared a mutual interest in horses and also had their faith in common, since Cornelius had met with Cephas, the apostle, and been baptized along with his household several months before they had first met.

He was a promising young soldier who had been assigned as assistant to the new Legate, commander of all Roman forces in Judea, when he had arrived a month previously. At their last meeting, Cornelius had told Barnabas that, although the new Legate was an imposing figure, he felt he'd made an impression on the man. He had been efficient and professional and shown the Legate that he knew and understood the local people and their customs thoroughly.

When asked where the legion got their horses, he had told the Legate the only place to buy the animals was in Tyre. The best breeder in all Palestine was there and, although his stud was small, his horses were of the finest quality anywhere in the empire.

Barabbas smiled as Leila crossed the yard and removed a protesting Yusef from the back of the heavy-set mare. Then he turned his attention back to the bay whose foot he had been scraping, while his son was taken inside.

Cornelius arrived a few minutes later, a little after the seventh hour. "Barnabas," he called as he crossed the yard with the Legate in tow. "I'd like you to meet the new Legate from Rome."

Barabbas quickly finished working on the mare's hoof and then turned to greet his guests. He froze as he stared at the Legate through pale golden eyes.

Cornelius seemed not to have noticed the tension. "Barnabas, I'd like you to meet Gaius, the new Legate in Judea."

Gaius stepped forward and smiled. "Pleased to meet you, er - Barnabas was it?"

"That's right," Barabbas replied warily and greeted the Roman soldier, noting the missing thumb on the man's right hand.

The Legate turned to Cornelius who had introduced them. "Thank you, centurion. I'd like this man to show me the stud himself. I'll meet you back at the carriage."

He waited for Cornelius to leave before he faced the horse breeder again. "Easy, Barabbas. That hammer you're staring at is eight cubits away and I've become quite dexterous with my left hand."

Barabbas gave up any hope of finding a weapon with which to defend himself. "How did you find me?" he asked carefully.

"Pure chance really. I was interested in purchasing some horses and Cornelius told me you have the finest stud in Tyre. I see your leg's healed nicely."

"I still limp when the weather changes."

Gaius nodded as he quietly examined the mare. "I'm curious. How did you escape nine legionaries with a woman in tow and a damaged leg?"

"Once we reached the mountains it was easy. I left a bloody trail for them to follow and then doubled back. They ran right under the tree I was hiding in. Are you going to arrest me now?"

The man appeared not to have heard the question. "Why didn't you kill me when you had the chance?"

Barabbas sighed. "I told you, I'm a changed man. I'd become a follower of Jesus of Nazareth. There was no way I could have killed you in good conscience, when you were unarmed. Not that I expect you to understand."

Gaius turned and faced Barabbas. He held his gaze for nearly a minute without speaking. "So," he finally said, "you and I are brothers."

Barabbas glanced up sharply. "You too!"

"After my trial I was sent to Corinth. I met some men there who preached the good news. When they spoke, I remembered the man on that crucifix all those years ago."

Barabbas smiled at the irony. "Brothers! After a lifetime of war, it comes to this. What happened at your trial? I heard reports you'd been sent to Rome."

"I was proved innocent. Pilate was recalled to Rome because of my testimony." Gaius moved around to the front of the mare, patting the dark brown neck as he stroked her muzzle.

"So where did he end up, the Senate?"

Gaius smiled slightly. "He took his own life on the boat across, rather than face Tiberius. The irony is that Tiberius died before the boat ever arrived in Rome. He might never have had to stand trial. Do you have any horses available for sale?"

Barabbas brightened. "This way. I have some yearlings you might be interested in. None that could leap across a canyon, mind you, but I think you'll find them more than acceptable."

Gaius grinned as he remembered. "I'm told the soldiers spoke for months afterwards about that jump. It was the most terrifying moment of my life."

"I said it then and I'll say it now. That was some of the finest riding I've ever seen. I went back there a year ago, just to see if I could do it, but —" Barabbas shook his head.

The memory seemed to ease the tension between the two men. Having faced their past, they felt somehow able to deal better with the present. Gaius remained for dinner as a guest in Barbbas' house where he met Leila and their two sons. He purchased four fillies with the promise of a further contract next season.

"You and I have no quarrel any longer, Barnabas," he replied in parting. "As long as you abide by Roman laws, the secret of your past is safe with me. Only be careful. There are others who could still recognize you. If they do, there's nothing I can do to prevent your arrest. You're still wanted by Rome."

"Thank you, Gaius. Go with God and may He bless you in all your ways."

Leila joined her husband as he waved to the Legate who was headed back to Caesarea with Cornelius.

"Do we need to move in a hurry again?"

"I don't think so," he smiled as he held her close to him. "I really don't think so."

ABOUT THE AUTHOR

SEAN YOUNG started writing in the late 1990's. After spending the best part of a decade as a lead singer in a rock band, he found himself frustrated after the group split in 1997. For over a year, Sean's need for a creative outlet burned within him. The out came through his idea for a novel.

He threw his all into the project. Working in his spare time and over weekends he compiled his first draft and, three years later, Violent Sands was born.

Sean is a software developer by profession. He lives in Johannesburg, South Africa, with his wife, Carolyn, and daughter, Danielle. He has no lions, tigers or any other dangerous Wildlife in his garden - apart from a vicious sparrow that fights with the mirrors on his wife's Volkswagen. He loves the African bush and spends his holidays and weekends visiting the many wildlife and nature reserves his country has to offer.

He can be reached at: sean_young@dreamcoatpublishing.com

ALSO FROM
BREAKNECK BOOKS

Available September 2006.

"...a rollicking Arctic adventure that explores the origins of the human species." -- James Rollins, bestselling author of Black Order and Map of Bones

www.breakneckbooks.com/rtp.html

Available November 2006.

"...an intense, action packed sci-fi story with a heart." -- Jeremy Robinson, author of Raising the Past and The Didymus Contingency.

www.breakneckbooks.com/soone.html

THE
CHRONICLES
OF
SOONE
HEIR TO THE KING

BREAKNECK BOOKS
PUBLISHING COMPANY

Printed in the United States
144722LV00003B/1/A

9 780978 655136